ROSE MORTIMER

OR

THE BALLET-GIRL'S REVENGE

BEING THE ROMANCE AND REALITY

OF A PRETTY ACTRESS'S LIFE BEHIND THE SCENES

AND BEFORE THE CURTAIN

BY

A COMEDIAN OF THE T. R. DRURY LANE

LONDON

Published for the London Romance Company by the

NEWS-AGENTS' PUBLISHING COMPANY LIMITED

147, FLEET STREET

CONTENTS.

ILLUSTRATIONS.

ROSE MORTIMER;

OR,

THE BALLET-GIRL'S REVENGE.

[ABEL BOOTH SEIZES ROSE MORTIMER.]

CHAPTER I.

THE NIGHT SHRIEK—A ROSE IN THE MIRE—
THE RUFFIAN AND HIS VICTIM—THE RESCUE
—THE RECOGNITION—THE THREAT.

"HELP, HELP, HELP!"

It was a wild and piercing shriek, which sounded
through the stilly night.

A cry drawn forth by pain and terror.

The earnestly beseeching cry of one in dire distress
—an almost despairing appeal for succour.

The hour was late, and the streets were nearly
deserted save by the homeless wanderers and outcasts
of society. A cold wet night with a biting wind—a
pitiless blast that seemed to mock the thinly-clad
wanderers whom want deprived of warmth and shelter.

It was a night on which few from choice would have

ventured abroad — a night on which the utterly miserable crouched shivering on dreary flag-stones, praying God to take away from them the life which was so bitterly hard to bear.

In the stony-hearted streets there was no kind sympathising soul to hear that piteous cry for help — no strong arm to come to the rescue of a fair and fragile girl, struggling frantically with her brutal assailant.

Scarcely eighteen summers had she seen, though her lovely face, pale and delicate, showed the not-easily-mistaken record of sorrow and want. Poor thing ! her troubles had in truth commenced early.

She was miserably clad, though her few fluttering garments were arranged with care and neatness, and seemed to show a striving at a better position in life.

It was difficult to guess at the occupation of this young creature, but it was plain that, young as she was, her life had been a hard struggle with want and sorrow. One glance into that sweet gentle face and those clear open eyes of heavenly blue proved that hers had been a sinless life, and that she, though reared perchance in some vile hot-bed of poverty and crime, had yet remained undefiled by her hideous surroundings.

From the recess of a low frowning archway leading into a dark narrow alley in Lambeth a man had sprung upon her as she passed and seized her by the wrist.

"Help, help, help !"

But no one was there to deliver her from his vice-like grasp.

Muttering an oath between his clenched teeth, he bade her hold her peace.

As they emerged from the shadow of the archway, the light of a gas-lamp revealed the features of her worst enemy !

A wolf in sheep's clothing !

Clad entirely in black, with the exception of his necktie, he wore a somewhat respectable appearance ; he was evidently the leader of some highly sanctimonious little flock of true believers ; but no garb could conceal the brutal ruffianism of his countenance, which would have been sufficient to give him six months at the hands of any magistrate.

Holding her tightly by the wrist, he strove with his disengaged hand to cover her mouth.

Again and again she shrieked for assistance, but, though there were lights at some of the windows in the alley, her cries attracted no attention.

The ruffian shifted his hold from her wrist to her waist.

His strong arm encircled her, and, though she struggled and fought with the energy of despair, she grew weaker every minute, and must shortly succumb to her dastardly assailant.

She threw her whole voice into one final appeal.

"Help, help, help !"

Hardly, however, had the cry ceased to ring through the deserted street when a strong hand was thrust in the ruffian's neckerchief, a strong arm wrenched it round with strangling violence, and he was flung to the ground.

The girl staggered half fainting to the wall, but, before her champion could render further assistance, the other man had picked himself up, and came rushing at him head-first like a bull.

His antagonist, stepping coolly on one side, let out his left with steam-engine velocity and power, and again the ruffian fell headlong to the pavement, but this time bleeding and senseless.

"I think you've had enough of it, my fine fellow," said the poor girl's deliverer in a mocking tone ; "if you differ from me, don't hesitate to say so."

He walked up to his prostrate foe and bent over him, but the parson lay motionless as a log.

"I hope I havn't settled him altogether," said he ;

"those blows under the ear are not very highly recommended by the faculty."

Then, turning to the still trembling girl, who was standing with a face white as death, and with her little hand pressed to her beating heart, he addressed her for the first time.

"Can I be of any further service to you ?" he asked in soft winning tones, which contrasted strangely with the muscular power he had just shown.

"No, no, I thank you, sir," she answered, timidly lowering her eyes as she spoke ; "I am deeply grateful to you for what you have already done, but—"

"But—"

"I am close home, sir, and I need trouble you no further."

"I beg your pardon," said the stanger, who was a tall handsome man of about five or six and twenty, with a profusion of light brown curly hair, laughing eyes, and a huge beard and moustache, rather ragged and uncared for—"I beg your pardon, but, if I am not mistaken, I have the pleasure of speaking to the young lady who was waiting to-night at the stage door of the theatre in Hardress Street ?"

The girl, blushing crimson, looked at him with surprise, and stammered an inaudible reply.

"Miss Rose Mortimer, is it not ?"

"Yes, sir, that is my name. I was at the theatre to-night, waiting to see Mr. Flathers, the manager."

"I thought I was not mistaken. I heard your name given to him, and I could not help noticing you ; you were so different from—"

She looked at him inquiringly.

"So different from the majority of those who come on similar errands."

The girl blushed again, but made no reply.

"I am engaged at the theatre myself," continued her communicative preserver. "My name is Jack Halliday, and I am a scene-painter there."

"Indeed."

"It is very late for you to be out alone, Miss Mortimer ; may I have the pleasure of escorting you to your door ?"

"Thank you," said the girl uneasily, "I am close to my home and will not trouble you any further, though do not think me ungrateful for the service you have rendered me."

"Psha ! dont mention that. It was a real pleasure to knock the blackguard over. Hullo ! What do you want now ?"

The latter portion of his speech was addressed to his late antagonist, who had struggled to his feet, and was swaying to and fro unsteadily.

The light from the lamp at the entrance to the court fell full upon his face, ugly at all times, but now doubly hideous, smeared with mud and blood.

"Nothing now," he growled, rubbing the hair from his eyes ; "nothing now, but I won't forget you."

"Nor I you, my friend."

"I never forgot nor forgave in my life. Did I, Miss Mortimer ?"

The diabolical sneer with which he uttered these words made the scene-painter double his fist involuntarily.

"There's a long score to wipe out," continued the ruffian, "a very long score ; but I never forget !"

"I shall give you something more to remind you of me," said Jack Halliday, "unless you make yourself scarce pretty quickly."

But the young girl eagerly caught his arm, and drew him back, with a cry of horror.

"No ! no !" she said, "do not touch him."

"Why not ?"

"Do not ask me."

"But I must ask you, for unless you have some powerful motive I certainly cannot resist the pleasure of—"

"No! no!" she exclaimed wildly; "do not strike him again, I implore you."

"Well, if you don't wish it, I won't," said the scene-painter reluctantly; "but it *does* seem a pity."

"For Heaven's sake!—unless you would be my ruin—"

The painter looked at her with the greatest surprise.

He was well used to mystery and adventure on the stage, but he had never met before with it in real life.

He looked down at the poor girl, who clung imploringly on his arm.

She was deadly pale, and quivering like an aspen leaf.

"At any rate, Miss Mortimer, allow me to see you home."

She made no reply, but her little white hand rested trustingly on his arm, and she walked by his side, though with weak and uncertain steps.

Her brutal assailant stared after them, his evil eyes lighted up with a glare of savage hatred.

"Curses upon her!" he muttered, shaking his fist at their retreating forms; "why was I fool enough to risk so much when I could have had her still more securely in my power? There are hundreds prettier than she, who would open their arms to me willingly, but I must needs long after her baby face; long for it? ay, that I do! and by all the powers of heaven and hell I swear she shall yet be mine!"

CHAPTER II.

A WRETCHED HOME—A POOR GIRL'S TRIALS—THE MIDNIGHT ASSIGNATION — MYSTERY!—THE ATTEMPTED MURDER—THE CRUEL TERMS — DIAMOND CUT DIAMOND — THE NOBLE FORGER — THE FATAL MEETING — THE RAKE MARKS HIS VICTIM.

"COME in, can't you? Now don't stand letting in all that cold. Confound it, this infernal hole is bad enough without that!"

So spoke in a peevish complaining tone a man huddled together over a handful of fire, and seated in a room as miserable as can be imagined.

A room in which stood two rickety cane chairs, and a deal table which seemed to be only deliberating as to which of its remaining legs should give way in order to bring a cracked plate and a stale loaf to the level of the carpetless floor.

"Oh, it's you, Rose," said the man, slightly turning his head; "what a time you've been!"

She made no reply, but busied herself in taking a few small articles of food from her pockets, and arranging them round the loaf.

"Can't you speak, eh? You go out and leave your father the whole evening, and haven't a word to say when you come in. Where have you been?"

"To the theatre, father."

"Well, what success?"

"None."

Poor Rose, unable to restrain her feelings any longer, burst into tears.

"Curse it! I'm hanged if your whimpering isn't enough to drive a man mad. Cry, cry, cry; you're always turning on the water as if your father had been a turncock instead of a gentleman."

"I can't help it, father—indeed I can't, I—I—"

"Speak out, can't you?"

"I have been frightened, and—and—"

"Frightened? Psha! Did you see a ghost in the alley?"

"No; but as I passed along a man seized me by the wrist and held me fast."

"Ha! ha! ha! A pretty thing to frighten you! Who was it?"

Rose made no answer.

"Did you know him?"

"Yes."

She replied so faintly, though, that her father scarcely heard the word.

"Well?"

"Oh, father! you *must* guess who it was. There is but one man we have cause to dread."

"You don't mean to tell me it was—"

"Yes, yes, father. It was Abel Booth."

"Well, you're a strange girl. What did you say to him?"

"I don't know what would have happened but that a gentleman kindly rescued me, and—"

"Rescued? Confound his meddling impudence! What do you mean? You can't stand there and tell me you refused to listen to him?"

"Father! father!" said the trembling girl, in tones of piteous supplication; "what would you have had me do?"

"Do? I like that! That's a nice selfish speech! Do you know he can send me to prison to-morrow? Do you know he can ruin me with a word? Do you know he is as spiteful and revengeful as Old Harry himself? A pretty business you've made of it!—but you never had an atom of feeling in your nature."

Again poor Rose broke down, and sobbed aloud.

"There, leave off whining and make yourself scarce; I expect a visitor."

"A visitor, father? and at this hour of the night?"

"What the devil do you mean by talking so to me? Am I bound to get your permission before I ask a friend to call upon me?"

Poor Rose only sighed! she was too well accustomed to hard words to be surprised at them.

From her earliest infancy, curses and threats and abuse had sounded in her ears.

She had some faint recollection of a happier time, when she saw finely-dressed ladies and gentlemen about her; but it was a dim hazy remembrance as of a dream, and she hardly knew whether it had any other origin than her own imagination.

Slowly and sorrowfully at her father's command she gathered together the scanty out-door clothing she had discarded on entering the room; but ere she quitted the cold dreary chamber a peculiar knock sounded at the door.

It was followed almost instantaneously by the lifting of the latch, and with quick strides a stranger entered the room.

"Hullo! what's the meaning of this?" he asked angrily as his eyes lighted on Rose; "couldn't you take care we were alone?"

"Leave the room," said the other man, with a threatening gesture; "leave the room, or I'll not leave a whole bone in your body.—It's only my daughter, sir," he added, turning to his visitor, and addressing him in an apologetic cringing tone, which contrasted strongly with that which he had used to his daughter the moment before.

Rose retired without a word, though not until she had closely observed the features of her father's visitor.

He was considerably above the middle height, and possessed an appearance which seemed to stamp him as belonging to the upper class of society, despite his being attired in a shabby coat wrapped round with a well-worn plaid.

His face was strikingly handsome, but in his eyes, which were dark and deeply set, there was a cold glitter, which at times imparted to his face an almost diabolical look.

A jet black moustache carefully tended showed off his white shining teeth, which at times seemed to snarl beneath the hair ; but, in spite of these disagreeable attributes, when perfectly calm his form and features were those with which painters and sculptors of old embodied the heathen gods.

"Now," cried the stranger, as Rose closed the door behind her, "are they finished ?"

"Yes, count, yes," muttered the elder man, at the same time fidgetting somewhat uneasily in his seat.

"Well, out with them, then ; I've no time to waste."

The other rubbed his hands together, but made no movement.

"Do you hear ?"

"Yes ; I hear."

"By Jove, then, you had better obey."

"Yes, count, I hear, and will obey, but—"

"Speak, man, can't you ?"

"I have been considering, noble count, that the risk I run is very great, and—"

"And, therefore, you are entitled to a greater recompense than that we agreed to originally ?"

"Precisely."

"You also think, I suppose, that I am in urgent want of those bits of paper ?"

"I suppose so," smirked the other.

"And that, consequently, I shall be quite prepared to pay a large sum to obtain them ?"

Rose's father seemed to be somewhat taken aback by the supreme coolness of his visitor, and his face lost something of his look of cunning pleasure, but he answered in the affirmative, though faintly.

"Precisely. Now, from your own lips I learn you to be an extortionate rogue, but yet I am willing to deal fairly with you."

The countenance of Hugh Mortimer brightened up considerably, and he mechanically stretched forth his hand.

"Not so fast, my good fellow. Do you see this purse ?"

He not only saw it, but almost devoured it with his eyes, as the man he addressed as count held up a knitted purse, through the meshes of which the quick sight of Rose's father detected the glistening gold, at the same time that his ears drank in the sound of the chinking of the precious metal.

"Good. It contains the exact amount we agreed beforehand was to be the price paid. Give me the paper and take it."

Hugh Mortimer shook his head.

"You refuse ?"

"Yes."

"How much more do you want ?"

"Double."

The count put his hand into his pocket, and Hugh Mortimer's eyes brightened as he fancied another glittering purse would be produced.

But he was wrong.

He had reckoned without his host.

Something glittering came from the pocket, but it was not a purse !

With two rapid strides the stranger reached him, and ere he could utter a word or cry had twisted his fingers tightly in his neckcloth, and had hurled him to the floor.

Half strangled, and totally incapable of uttering a sound, he lay prostrate, his visitor kneeling on his chest, holding the shining something, which was the barrel of a revolver, within a few inches of his forehead.

"Now, Hugh Mortimer, we are upon a more equal footing. Who now is to dictate the terms ?"

The prostrate man strove to call for help, but a tighter wrench at his neckerchief showed him the folly of the attempt.

"It is useless to struggle," said the count. "Listen to me. I wish to converse with you, but I do not wish any witnesses called in ; so remember, though I loose my hold at your throat, I still keep a loaded revolver in my hand, and, if you utter one single word in a louder tone than that in which we were just now speaking, that word shall be your death-warrant. Remember too that, though I have no wish to commit murder, still to me my life is of greater value than yours. Get up."

He relaxed his hold, and Hugh Mortimer rose slowly and staggered to his feet.

The first thing he saw was the barrel of the revolver pointed straight at his head.

"Now, Hugh Mortimer, bring me the paper."

"And—and—the money ?" stammered the frightened man.

"You have forfeited all right to mention terms to me. Bring me the paper."

Slowly and reluctantly Mortimer took from a cupboard a roll of thin tissue paper, upon which several words had been engraved.

The pieces of paper were not large, but at the top of each was engraved in Old English letters, ornamented with many flourishes, "Bank of England."

"Good," said the count, examining them ; "you were not taught engraving for nothing, I see."

So saying, he pocketed the roll and looked with a sardonic smile full into the face of the man who had handed them to him.

"Here," said he, with a short laugh ; "here is half of the sum agreed upon. You have forfeited the other half by asking double ; take it and be thankful. It isn't everyone who would have given you that much."

"Stay," said Hugh Mortimer, his face white with passion. "Listen to me ; I can denounce you as an adventurer, a swindler, a——"

"Yes, my good fellow you can, but who will believe you ? while, on the contrary, if I denounce you as a forger—transportation for life remember !"

With a pleasant smile upon his face the count turned and left the miserable room, totally heedless of the look of baffled cunning and hate with which his tool regarded him.

Just before he quitted the house he came again face to face with Rose, and now for the first time observed her personal appearance.

For a moment they stood regarding each other in the passage, his face expressing admiration of her beauty, and hers astonishment at the presence of one so handsome and evidently patrician in this house of squalid poverty.

She shrank back abashed by his lawless gaze, and he smiled at her alarm.

It was a first meeting, and destined to result in misery : bitter, bitter misery to the poor unhappy girl !

CHAPTER III.

THE POOR GIRL'S PRAYER—THE REPULSE—THE MYSTERIES BEHIND THE CURTAIN—THE COUNT AGAIN—A DEMON'S SMILE—TREACHERY—THE SPY—AN AWFUL NIGHT—A DEED OF BLOOD—THE STRUGGLE—A RUN FOR LIFE.

WHEN Jack Halliday's muscular arm had been called into requisition to protect Rose Mortimer from the insults of the ruffian who had dared to lay his hand upon her, she was returning to the dismal dreary house she called home, after having spent many hours waiting in vain to see Mr. Flathers, the well-known manager, in the hope of obtaining an engagement in the ballet for the forthcoming pantomime.

Again and again had she been to that dark grimy

stage-door, hoping and longing for the good fortune of seeing the great man and urging her suit.

Upon the afternoon of the day following her meeting with Jack Halliday she set forth yet once more to the theatre in Hardress Street.

A faint hope still buoyed her up, though repeated repulses had done much to crush her sanguine nature.

She found it hard to believe that one willing and able to work might starve in the streets of such a city as London.

Weary and faint (for her last night's excitement had had a considerable effect upon her), she arrived at that gloomy door, through which so many passed thinly and slatternly clad to emerge upon the stage in all the glories of muslin and spangles.

"Can I see Mr. Flathers?" she asked timidly of the stern doorkeeper.

"I'm very sorry, my dear," he commenced, grinning from ear to ear as he spoke; "I'm very sorry, but——"

"Miss Mortimer!" exclaimed some one behind her in a tone of surprise.

She turned and confronted the bearded artist Jack Halliday, who had come to her rescue so opportunely on the previous evening.

Tremblingly she held out her hand to him, and a deep blush spread over her beautiful face as she remembered how greatly she was indebted to him, and how utterly incapable she was of repaying him for his kindness to her.

"Do you wish to see Mr. Flathers?" he asked kindly.

"Yes, sir, I do indeed; oh, if you could only persuade him to give me an engagement!"

"I fear I cannot undertake that, but I can take you to him, and I am sure he would pay more attention to a request from your lips than mine."

"Oh, thank you, thank you very much."

"Follow me, then; take care how you go. You see, Miss Mortimer, I am in a very humble position here myself, but anything I *can* do for you—take care of the steps; now then, straight on."

So saying, he piloted Rose through all the intricacies of the mysterious region spoken of as "behind the scenes," and conducted her safely to the manager's room.

"Mr. Flathers is particularly engaged," said a man who was lounging about, with a paper cap on his head and a pewter pot in his hand.

Jack Halliday turned to Rose.

"I am sorry, Miss Mortimer, that you will have to wait, and still more so that I cannot keep you company, but I am late as it is, and we are very busy now preparing for the pantomime."

"Oh, thank you very much for what you have done; I cannot tell you how much I am obliged to you."

Then, turning to the man, Jack Halliday whispered a few words to him, at the same time slipping something into his hand.

"This man, Miss Mortimer, will show you into Mr. Flather's room as soon as he is disengaged, and believe me I wish you success with all my heart."

So saying, with a polite bow he turned away and soon disappeared in the gloom.

For nearly half an hour Rose remained standing looking at her dismal surroundings of black beams, complicated machinery, and coarsely-painted scenery, and wondering how it was possible that what she saw could ever look so bewitching from the other side of "the float."

She was aroused from her meditations by a hoarse voice, which proceeded from the gentleman with the paper cap.

"Miss! I say, miss!"

"Yes," said Rose, turning round, supposing it to be herself who was thus addressed.

"Mr. Flathers 'll see you now, I think. There's a gent with him, but I don't think he'll mind."

With a fast-beating heart Rose followed her hoarse guide into a little close hot room, where, seated carelessly on a table, with a bottle of wine and a couple of glasses by his side, she beheld the theatrical king, Mr. Flathers.

There was another gentleman in the room when Rose entered, but his back was towards the door, and she could not see his face.

"Hullo! how did you come here?"

This was the young girl's greeting, spoken in a harsh rough voice, and with unnecessary sharpness.

"I came, sir, hoping that you would give me an engagement at the theatre."

"Oh, this sort of thing won't do; they shouldn't have let you in. I can't be bothered by every woman who thinks she has a dramatic genius."

Poor Rose shrank abashed before the words of the manager, and could not summon up courage to answer him.

Mr. Flathers looked at her, and could not fail to notice her extraordinary beauty.

"Well, what is it?" he asked in a somewhat softer tone; "do you want to be a tragedy queen?"

"No, sir, I—I thought, perhaps, in the ballet in the pantomime you might—"

"All the vacancies were filled up six weeks ago."

"Or anything, sir; I would do my best, indeed I would."

"Very likely," said the manager, drily.

"Oh, sir, can't you find me some employment?"

"No."

Rose hid her face in her hands.

"Come, my good girl, we can't have any whimpering here; you must clear out, and the sooner the better."

As she raised her head the other occupant of the room, who had hitherto remained silent and with his back towards her, turned round.

In an instant Rose recognised him.

He was her father's mysterious visitor of the previous night!

There could be no doubt of the matter. There was the same handsome face, the same distinguished manner, the same luxuriant moustache.

He started slightly when his eyes rested on her, but otherwise gave no token of recognition.

"What are you doing, Flathers?" he said, as Rose made her way to the door; "that girl's face is worth a dozen of those frights you had last year."

"Can't be helped, count, the number's made up."

"Well, what of that? Give one of them the sack."

"Nonsense! you know I can't."

Though this conversation was carried on in a low tone, it reached Rose's ears, and she paused irresolutely.

"I know you can if you like; if you *won't* do it—"

"My dear count."

"Take her on, then, to oblige me, Flathers."

"It's very awkward."

"Not at all; it can easily be arranged. So Miss—Miss—I beg your pardon, but your name is——"

"Rose Mortimer, sir."

"Well then, Miss Mortimer, you come to rehearsal to-morrow, and I'm sure my friend Flathers will be delighted to see you."

"Oh, thank you, sir; thank you very much," stammered Rose in her delight at this unexpected good fortune.

The count smiled grimly.

"You are going home now, I suppose, to tell your mother of your good fortune?"

"I have no mother, sir," said Rose, and the tears rose in her eyes.

"Are you an orphan?"

"I have a father."

"And his name?"

"Hugh, sir; Hugh Mortimer."

A demoniacal smile again passed over the count's face, but he asked no further questions, but sat caressing his moustache while Rose again returned her thanks.

When the young girl left the manager's room she found Jack Halliday waiting for her outside.

There was no need for him to question her.

The bright smile which lit up her face was proof sufficient that she had been successful, and the good-hearted scene-painter took her little fingers in his big hand and congratulated her warmly.

Willingly, in reply to his questions, she told him all that had happened at the interview.

When she mentioned the count, however, his face darkened and he clenched his fist.

"Beware of that man," he said.

"Beware of him? In what way?"

"He is a—he is a villain."

"Why, what has he done?" and Rose opened her beautiful eyes very wide.

"I cannot tell you, for I only suspect and mistrust him."

"Surely you are unjust; he appeared to be very kind."

Jack Halliday made no reply, but conducted her back to the stage-door.

It was late in the afternoon when Rose reached her home. As she was about to enter the house the door opened silently, sufficiently wide to admit of a man's egress.

It was a tall sanctimonious-looking person who came forth.

His clothes were black and of a clerical cut, his white tie was dirty and tumbled, and his face was bound up on one side with a coloured cotton handkerchief.

With a half-suppressed cry Rose started aside, for in him she recognised the scoundrel who had assaulted her the night before.

Shuddering, she shrank away as from a reptile.

He did not see her, but pursued his way, a grin of satisfaction making his face appear still uglier than usual.

No sooner had he passed than Rose entered the house and hurried up the stairs.

"Father, father," she cried, as she entered the room "what brought him here?"

"Who do you mean?" asked Hugh Mortimer with an oath.

"Abel Booth!"

He turned ghastly pale.

"What do you mean, girl? Speak!"

"I saw him quit the house not a minute ago."

Hugh Mortimer grasped the edge of the rickety table and stared vacantly before him. Then, suddenly rousing himself, he sprang to his feet.

"Curse him! a thousand curses on his prying sneaking eyes! If he has seen—"

"Seen what, father?"

"Nothing, nothing," he said, letting his head fall into his hands, and groaning.

"Rose," he added presently, "I have seen no one since you left the house this morning. Are you *positive* of the man?"

"I am."

"And that it was from *our* door he took his departure?"

"I could not be mistaken."

"Then we shall hear of his visit in another way before many days have elapsed. Something must be done—something must be done."

"But father, dear father, explain to me what is the cause of your fear."

In vain, however, did she appeal to him. He waved her fiercely off when she would have clung to him and encircled his neck with her soft white arms.

Mumbling unintelligibly to himself, he paced to and fro in the little room, ever and anon wandering to the window, and, peering down into the silent and deserted street, with a scared white face and bloodshot eyes.

The girl, crouching in a corner, dared not speak or move, lest she should again rouse his displeasure; and thus the weary hours passed, and night crept down upon the city and filled the room with its shadows.

It was not till it was quite dark that she rose to her feet, and was stealing away as noiselessly as possible, when her father called out, in a loud terrified voice, "Who's there? Who's there?"

"'Tis I, father," replied the trembling girl.

"You? Curses light on you! What do you want, stealing about like a thief? Are you in league with them? Are you playing the spy upon me? By Heaven! if I thought so—"

As he spoke he clutched her by the arm, his face distorted by passion, his whole frame trembling with his rage.

"Father! father!" she cried in terror, and raising her hands to ward off a threatened blow.

"A blight upon your pale face and smooth tongue!" exclaimed the desperado; "it is your fault that it has all happened—it is your namby-pamby modesty that has brought this evil upon me."

His fingers tightened their hold upon her arm till the pain almost made her shriek.

"Father! you hurt my arm," she cried.

With a savage oath, he shook her violently; then, with all his strength, he hurled her from him.

With a low sobbing moan she staggered and fell, and, covering her face with her hands, cried aloud in the anguish of her heart.

It was not the blow, though that was bad enough; it was the cruelty which prompted it.

This was all that she had ever known of home—this the only parent she had had to cling to through many long years of penury and privation, and whom, brute though he was to her, she yet dearly loved; ay, loved, as suffering woman will love till the world's end, in spite of cruelty and neglect.

Leaving her unheeded, Hugh Mortimer returned to his post by the window and stared down into the street. The flickering of the uncertain light upon his face half led her to think that she saw tears in his eyes.

Was he sorry for his harshness towards her? Should she creep back to his side?

Suddenly, while Rose stood yet irresolute, he uttered a wild cry, and, with outstretched arm pointing to some object in the street, screamed to her to come and look also.

Rose, hesitating no longer, sprang to his side and asked in terrified accents what had happened.

He stood as if transfixed.

His eyes glared wildly.

His limbs trembled.

He regarded her not, but still remained with outstretched hand, staring in one direction.

Rose looked towards the place to which he pointed.

Standing beneath a gas-lamp on the other side of the way were the figures of three men, though, in the rapidly increasing darkness, Rose failed to recognise in them any cause for alarm.

Presently the lamp was lit, and a glare was thrown full upon the upturned face of one of the trio.

Rose turned ghastly pale.

"Abel Booth!" she exclaimed.

"Yes," cried her father fiercely; "Abel Booth. But this night's work shall be his last: he has signed his own death-warrant!"

"Father, do not talk so wildly!" said Rose.

"Ah! are you there? Get to your room. Do you hear?"

"Oh, what does this mean, father?"

"Listen to me, girl," he said suddenly, in an unusually gentle tone: "go to your own room, and remember, whatever you may hear during the night, remain there."

"What dreadful thing is this? Oh, do not look at me in that way!"

"It means that this very night, in this very room, Abel Booth and I will play a game, and the stake we play for will be *life!*"

Rose lifted up her hands imploringly.

Hugh Mortimer took no notice of her gesture.

Carefully he removed a plank from the flooring of the room and took from a place of concealment a large old-fashioned pistol.

"To your room, girl," he cried fiercely, pointing the muzzle towards her. "If you stir outside the door till broad daylight to-morrow morning, your blood be upon your own head."

Slowly and sadly she turned and quitted the room.

In the excited state in which her father was she knew that words would only aggravate him.

She knew but too well the savage fits of frenzy to which he at times gave way.

Tremblingly she left the room and sought her own apartment, which was immediately overhead.

Silent and motionless she remained in the cold, listening eagerly to the faintest sounds which reached her from below.

That some terrible calamity was hanging over her father she gathered from his words.

That some dreadful scene would be enacted in the room below her she had little doubt.

What was this terrible influence which Abel Booth exerted over her father?

She herself dreaded and disliked him, but it was evident that some stronger feelings moved Hugh Mortimer.

It was quite dark.

Even the faint glimmer of the street lamps was shrouded in thick fog.

It was bitterly cold, and Rose could hardly keep her teeth from chattering.

To go to bed with such a presentiment of evil was an impossibility.

Rose took all the warm things she could find, and wrapped herself in them, and sat down to watch and wait.

The chimes from a neighbouring church steeple smote every quarter of an hour upon her listening ear, but as yet no unusual sound had startled her.

She heard her father's step every now and then below.

She heard sounds as if he were dragging about the scanty furniture.

Then there was a long silence.

A strong smell of burning arose after a while, and thin wreaths of smoke came curling up through the flooring.

Had he set the house on fire?

A thrill of terror passed through her frame as this thought occurred to her.

She was high up at the top of the house.

There was no trap-door!

To fly down stairs, with the lower portion of the house in flames, was an impossibility.

To cast herself from the window was certain death.

So alarmed did she become as this thought momentarily took a stronger hold upon her mind that, heedless of her father's warnings, she rushed to the door, fully determined to descend the stairs at all hazards.

She turned the handle, but the door did not open.

She shook it with all her strength.

She pushed against it with all her energy.

It remained quite immoveable.

It was locked on the outside!

Large beads of perspiration stood upon her forehead at the thought of the dreadful fate that she believed awaited her.

So terrified was she that it was some time before she noticed that the smell of burning had gone, and that the smoke no longer came up between the chinks of the boards.

He had not set the house on fire after all.

What could he have been doing?

Why was she made prisoner?

Who had locked the door?

Was it possible, she asked herself, that her father had been destroying papers, in the expectation that the house might be searched?

It was all a riddle to her, only to be cleared up by time.

Again she settled herself to wait patiently and listen for sounds from the room beneath.

The chimes from the church steeple sounded again and again, but, although it was past midnight, nothing out of the common had occurred.

Wearied with waiting, and exhausted with fatigue and excitement, she sank into an uneasy doze, from which she was suddenly awakened by the sound of voices.

She started to her feet and listened intently.

The voices came from the street.

She ran to the window, opened it, and looked out.

The fog had partially cleared away, and she could just distinguish the forms of three men standing together at the door of the house.

"Open," said one—"open the door there."

There was no reply.

Hugh Mortimer was silent, and Rose did not dare speak.

"Open, or it will be the worse for you, I say."

Still there was no reply.

Then Rose heard a low whispered conversation between the three.

Then a crowbar was produced and Rose heard the crazy door give way in a moment.

The three men entered the house one after the other.

Rose hardly dared breathe, for she knew the crisis was at hand.

A dreadful longing to know the worst took possession of her.

She lay down upon the floor, so that her ear might catch the slightest sound.

There was a slight movement in the room beneath, which told her that her father was on the alert.

The few minutes she lay in this attitude seemed hours to her.

There was a sound of more whispering.

Then a fierce oath from her father.

The report of a pistol.

A shriek of pain and terror.

A cry of some poor creature in the agonies of death, hurried without a moment's warning into the presence of his Maker.

Rose shuddered.

Who was it that had met with this dreadful fate?

Who was it that had uttered that death-shriek in the stilly night?

Was her father the victim, or was he the murderer?

After a silence of only a few minutes' duration there was the sound of a heavy fall, and then the noise of scuffling and fighting.

Eagerly Rose listened, to learn from the sounds, if possible, who was the victor.

She fancied she heard her father's voice in a tone of pitiful supplication.

She rose and ran to the door of her room, for she felt she could stand this horrid uncertainty no longer.

She must go and aid her father—her poor aged father—who was struggling against such fearful odds.

Poor girl! She did not remember that the door of her room had been fastened on the outside.

She threw herself violently against it, as if her fragile form was sufficient to break it down.

She strove to smash the lock with the poker, but without success.

What could she do?

As a prisoner she stood in her own room while the sounds of the struggle beneath her grew louder and louder.

She felt sure that in the tumult she could distinguish her father's voice.

Then came a low deep gasping moan, and a heavy fall.

After that, silence!

The solemn stillness was even more awful to bear than the noise of the scuffle.

Suddenly an idea occurred to Rose.

Seizing the fire-irons she forced up a part of the old and rotten floor, but her heart beat so violently at the thought of the horrors which might meet her eyes when she saw into the lower room that for some minutes she could not go on with her task.

Presently recovering herself, she set to work, and carefully scraped away sufficient plaster to enable her to peer into the chamber of mystery.

She could see nothing.

She listened intently, but there was no sound to tell of any living creature being there.

In her eagerness to see more of that dreadful room she leaned forward, forgetting that the lath and plaster were far too weak to support her.

She felt them bulge with her weight.

They yielded more and more.

She struggled to reach the beam which had supported the flooring, but with a loud crash the ceiling gave way beneath her, and she fell into the room beneath.

For some little time she lay stunned and insensible, but after a few minutes she revived.

Bruised and hurt, but happily without any serious injury, she rose to her feet and gazed fearfully around.

The scanty furniture of the room had been all piled up before the door to make a barricade.

It was covered with blood!

Great pools lay on the floor, while in three places a hand literally soaking with blood had been pressed against the white plaster of the walls.

A sickening horror came over Rose.

The room appeared to be turning round with her.

All colour deserted her cheeks.

Her limbs trembled so that she could hardly move.

Just then were borne towards her the chimes from the church steeple.

It was three o'clock in the morning.

No one living or dead was to be seen.

The room was deserted, and, save for the tell-tale blood, Rose would have been inclined to believe the whole of the struggle but a fever-wrought phantom of the brain.

"Could it be fancy?"

As her eyes roamed about the chamber of crime, she thought she heard a low chuckling laugh.

She paused and listened.

"Ha! ha! ha! ha!"

It was not a good cheery wholesome laugh, but a low, quiet, demoniacal chuckle.

Whence did it proceed?

There was no one near her.

Suddenly raising her eyes she saw, peering through the hole, the hole which she had made in the ceiling, the hated face of her assailant on the previous night, when Jack Halliday had so bravely come to her rescue.

"Abel Booth!"

Her cheek blanched and her lips quivered as she spoke the name.

"At your service, my dear," said the man, laughing. "Did you think to escape me?"

Rose was too frightened to reply.

"Isn't it nice, my pretty one," said the ruffian; "we've got the house all to ourselves, and no nasty scene-painter can come here to spoil our love-making. Ah! my beauty, you will have to listen to me, whether you like it or not."

Rose shrank as far away as she could.

Abel Booth noticed the movement and laughed.

"Don't be frightened, my dear; people always like me when they know me well enough."

"What have you done with my father?" asked the poor girl, her anxiety getting the better of her alarm.

"What will you give me if I tell you?"

"I have nothing to give."

"Oh! yes, you have. A kiss from those pretty lips would be a reward for a king."

Rose shuddered.

"I tell you what, Miss Rose, if I am at your side, I can talk to you a deal better than up here, peeping at you like a bird in a cage, so I shall just come down. Did you come through this hole? Lord! how nice you must have looked a-coming through! I wish I'd been there to see you."

As he spoke Rose saw that he was about to put his threat into execution, and swing himself down into the room where she was.

With a cry of terror she darted to the barricade which still blocked up the doorway.

Hastily she scrambled to the top, just as Abel Booth dropped into the room.

The young girl darted through the doorway, and the ruffian sprang after her, with an explanation of baffled rage.

She had but a short start, but

"Fear to her feet lent wings,"

and she ran on, knowing that her only chance of safety lay in flight.

In wild alarm she flew down the stairs, dragged open the street door, and rushed into the street.

She heard her pursuer's footsteps close behind her, and every moment she expected to feel his hand upon her shoulder.

Half fainting with fatigue and fear, she still ran on, and paused not until, her strength utterly failing her, she was fain to cling to a doorpost to save herself from falling.

As she did so, the surrounding objects seemed to dance confusedly before her, a dark cloud fell over her eyes, and she sank down in a death-like swoon.

CHAPTER IV.

GLITTERING VICE—THE SWINDLER AT HOME— PREPARING FOR CONQUEST—THE BLACKLEG— THE DUEL—A COWARD'S ACT—RETRIBUTION— HORSEWHIPPED — DISCOVERY — DISGRACE — THE PROFLIGATE'S VOW.

THE Count Lerno had been a resident in England for more than two years.

When he first appeared in the fashionable world no

[ROSE CARRIED OFF BY COUNT LERNO.]

one knew whence he came, nor, in fact, anything respecting him.

He appeared suddenly, and shone brilliantly, like a comet, and speedily obtained admission into the best society.

He was handsome and well-bred, besides which he had at his command an apparently inexhaustible supply of money.

But a dark mystery hung over his earlier years.

He had travelled a great deal, and was supposed to be a foreigner by birth, though what land owned him none but himself knew.

On this subject he was ever silent.

Now and then he gave charming little bachelor parties at his chambers in Piccadilly, and invitations to them were eagerly sought by those who admired the man that had the best wine and rode the best horses in London.

There were not wanting those who declared that the count made a good profit out of those little parties, and that after a night at cards he invariably rose a winner to a large amount.

Be that as it may, he had many friends, and those of unquestionable character, who were prepared on every occasion to defend him against the attacks of enemies.

It was nearly ten o'clock, one cold wet foggy December evening, when the count sat alone in his luxuriously furnished apartments.

He was in evening dress, and in the front of his embroidered shirt he wore diamond studs which must alone have been worth a small fortune.

His face was as handsome as ever, and bore not a trace of care or anxiety; yet he must have desired much not to be intruded upon, for before he had taken his seat he had carefully locked the door, and then even taken the trouble to hang a cloth over the lock, so that no spying eye at the keyhole could note his movements.

A silver urn, from which the steam spurted and hissed, stood near where he sat, and beneath it a spirit-lamp burned to keep the water constantly boiling.

Over the steam he held an unopened pack of cards till the gum which held the covering gave way, and the pack lay open before him.

Carefully he selected certain cards, and with a small needle made some microscopic scratches on the backs of those he had chosen.

This done he returned the cards to their proper covering, and refastened it so that no one, even with the closest observation, could tell that it had been opened.

Having served several packs in a similar way, he put them carefully aside, unlocked the door, and by a bell summoned his servant to the room.

"François," said he in French, which language he spoke to perfection,—"François, clear away these things, and let me know directly any of my guests arrive."

The valet bowed, and silently set to work, the count withdrawing into an inner chamber.

The reception-room was a beautifully furnished and admirably well-arranged apartment.

Everything was in perfect taste.

In each of the small recesses stood a lovely white marble statuette, relieved by a dark crimson curtain, and each statuette was lighted by a small globe-shaped lamp suspended before it.

A few choice paintings hung round round the room, while one end was devoted entirely to a collection of arms, arranged in fanciful devices against the wall.

There were swords and pistols of every age and every nation.

There were Indian bows and arrows; there were formidable tomahawks, and, low down, within easy reach, a brace of handsome revolvers, the stocks curiously inlaid with silver, and the barrels beautifully wrought.

When the count returned from the inner room he found the first of his guests intently regarding his small armoury.

He was a short thickset man, and rejoiced in the name of Captain Roper.

He was well known on the turf, through not particularly favourably; indeed, there had been a strong suspicion of foul play respecting a horse of his which had *not* won a race, but, as nothing could be proved, and he was a well-known fire-eater, he was still welcomed in such society as he had previously admission to.

"Well, captain," said the count gaily; "glad to see you here again. What's the latest news from Melton?"

The captain grasped his host's outstretched hand warmly.

"I've been studying your collection of arms; you have some curious ones here."

"Mere trifles. My hobby lies rather that way."

"Those revolvers are handsome weapons."

"Ah, yes; they are the only arms I keep for use; the others are only for show, but they—"

"Well?"

"Oh, one never knows what may happen. I

always keep them loaded and ready for any emergency."

"That's a strange fancy. I should think you—"

"Sir Harold King," said François, throwing open the door and announcing another guest.

The count stepped forward and welcomed him, and his conversation with Captain Roper ceased.

Sir Harold King was a young cheery light-hearted baronet who had just succeeded to the title, and a large estate, which latter he was doing his best to squander in dissipation.

The remainder of the guests came in quick succession.

They were mostly men of sporting propensities.

Ireton the owner of the Derby favourite, the Marquis of Brighton, Admiral Grouse, and other turf celebrities, were soon assembled, and in and out amongst them went the count with congratulations for one, and compliments for another, and a cordial greeting for all.

Choice wines were brought up and placed upon a side table, cigars were lighted, and two whist tables were speedily formed.

Two or three rubbers were played quietly enough, the count and his partner losing considerably; but at the end of that time the guests cried aloud for something more exciting, and *rouge et noir* was proposed and agreed to unanimously.

The count threw aside the cards with which they had been playing whist, and sport commenced in earnest.

Gold stood in heaps upon the table.

The wine circulated freely.

Bank notes changed hands with marvellous rapidity.

Captain Roper and Sir Harold King were the chief losers.

Luck seemed to be dead against them.

Every stake they made was a loss.

"I tell you what, Sir Harold," said the captain; "my purse can't stand this any longer; suppose you and I withdraw, and have a quiet little game at *écarté* at the other table?"

"By all means; I'm so deuced unfortunate tonight, it's no good backing ill-luck."

Almost without notice from the others they were suffered to leave the larger table, and take their seats at a smaller one.

There was no dearth of cards, and these two men were soon immersed in their game.

Yet, though the avowed object in leaving the other table was to avoid high play, the stakes for which they played were considerable.

The gold at Captain Roper's side was steadily increasing.

He won every game!

All the good cards were in his hand at every deal.

In spite of his opponent's entreaties, Sir Harold ceased to drink, and bent his energies to the cards.

Yet as he played his eyes were ever fixed upon the captain's hands.

Did he suspect foul play?

There was an ominous contraction of his brow now and then when his opponent with a smile laid down the winning card, but yet he said nothing.

He spoke not a word, but watched.

The captain's luck was so extraordinary as to be almost incomprehensible.

Yet he associated with good and honourable men, and it was hard to suspect him of unfair play.

Meanwhile at the other table the play was high and exciting.

The majority of those who were gathered round it were seasoned players, who could bear their losses with calmness and receive their winnings with apparent unconcern.

The count, as was usual with him, was a large winner.

Still, everything was to all outward appearance so fair, and above-board with him, his conversation so pleasant and amusing, and his manner so well-bred, that no one questioned the fairness of his play.

"He has the devil's own luck."

That was the general opinion openly expressed.

The count showed his white teeth beneath his jetty moustache, and appeared to consider it as a compliment.

He played on—and won.

While the more eager of the gamblers were waiting with outward calmness, but with inward anxiety, to see the fate of a larger stake than usual, a cry arose from the side table.

"D—— you, sir, leave go! How dare you seize my hand?"

The words were spoken in a fierce angry tone.

The speaker was Captain Roper.

So loud and ferocious was the tone that every one turned on the instant.

The pile of gold on the *rouge et noir* table was left, and the players all flocked to the further side of the room.

A small table was overturned on the floor.

Cards, sovereigns, and broken champagne glasses lay scattered about.

Captain Roper was held firmly in his chair by Sir Harold King, his face crimson with passion.

The baronet's grasp was on his collar, while his other hand clutched tightly the wrist of his opponent.

"What is the meaning of this, Sir Harold?" asked the count, his clear ringing voice sounding above the tumult.

"The meaning is this, count—we have amongst us a swindler and a rogue."

Sir Harold spoke with perfect calmness, and showed no unwonted excitement.

It was plain to all that he was acting from conviction.

The captain, as he heard these words, struggled vainly to free himself from his opponent's grasp.

"It is a grave charge you bring, Sir Harold," said the count; "and one which you must prove, or take the consequences."

"Listen to me, gentlemen," said Sir Harold; "I have been playing *écarté* with this man; I suspected him, and watched. At last I caught him in the act of concealing a card in the hand which I now grasp. If in that hand you do not find a card hidden, I can only say I regret my violence."

"Regret your violence? Do you think that will suffice? I will have full revenge for this insult. Unhand me! and I will convince you all of my innocence."

"Watch, gentlemen, for a proof of his roguery."

As he spoke the young baronet loosed his hold.

The captain turned an *empty palm* to them all!

There was no card concealed!

Sir Harold King staggered back aghast.

He was positive he had not been mistaken, and could only attribute the failure of the proof to some jugglery on the part of his opponent.

"Sir Harold," said the count gravely, "there appears to be no foundation for your accusation; you must answer for this strange disturbance."

"Answer! by Heaven he *shall* answer!" cried Captain Roper, starting to his feet; "ay, and on the spot!"

With a hasty hand he snatched a couple of rapiers from the collection of small arms hanging against the wall.

With a curse, he threw one of them towards the young baronet, and, almost before Sir Harold had picked it up, made a rapid pass at him, which threatened to put an end to his existence.

In an instant swords were crossed, and in a few seconds Captain Roper's weapon was struck from his hand by Sir Harold.

It flew whirling across the room.

The baronet lowered his point.

"Curse it! there can be no deception in these," yelled the infuriated disarmed man.

So saying he seized one of the revolvers about which he had been conversing with the count, and, before any one could guess his intention, aimed and fired at the baronet.

The hammer fell with a faint click.

No report followed.

The pistol had missed fire!

With a groan of disgust, all present rushed upon him.

The count was first.

He seized him roughly, and in so doing tore open his waistcoat.

As he did so a crumpled card fell to the ground.

"The card he concealed!" cried Sir Harold King.

So it was; Captain Roper was but a blackleg and a swindler, and, worse than being either in the eyes of the world, he was *detected*.

He could no longer brazen it out.

He turned ashy pale.

His limbs shook beneath him.

"Mercy, mercy!" he found breath to gasp.

"What is to be done with him?" asked the count.

"Drop him out of the window."

"Horsewhip him within an inch of his life."

"Make him eat a pack of cards."

"Hang him up to the first lamp-post and pop at him with the revolver."

These were some of the suggestions made by the count's visitors.

"Captain Roper," said the count; "you stand here a convicted swindler, blackleg, and rogue. These gentlemen will, I am assured, agree with me when I say, if one of us catches sight of you on any racecourse in England, he will consider it his duty to horsewhip you off it. Now be off, and remember."

The detected swindler, cowed and exposed, cringed before the count.

When he heard the light verdict, and felt his late host's hold removed from his collar, he rose and slunk away to the door like a beaten puppy.

Arrived at the door he turned and cast a look of hate around.

"Curse you all," he cried; "I'll be even with you yet. If I go to the world's end for it, I will have my revenge for this night's work. You, Count Lerno, may recollect what I say one day when *your* tricks are brought to light."

"Scoundrel!" yelled the count, his white teeth showing like those of a savage beast.

With one bound he was upon him.

With one twist of his muscular arm he hurled him back into the room, and, taking a heavy hunting-whip from the wall, administered a very severe beating to the detected one, who by neither sign nor word showed that he felt the pain or the degradation to which he was forced to submit.

Released from the other's hands, however, he crawled away, scowling evilly at the assembled company, turning only once to look back with a deadly white face, quivering lips, and heavy bloodshot eyes full of hellish passion.

As he turned his mouth moved slightly, as though he was breathing curses or muttering threats against his late antagonists, but no word escaped him, and he passed away from the sight of the assembled company in a death-like silence.

For some moments after the swindler's departure the count's guests stood silent and motionless, and then there was a general movement made in the direction of the door.

"Gentlemen, gentlemen," he said with a forced smile; "you will not leave me thus?"

"I don't feel inclined for more play to-night," said Sir Harold, very evidently wishing to avoid meeting his host's eye, and moving away as he spoke.

"Nor I, nor I," muttered the remainder of the company; and now all were on the point of departure, when the count flung himself between them and the door.

"Ere you depart, gentlemen," he said, "you will, I trust, give me an assurance of your belief that I was until now totally ignorant of the character of the man whom I had for a guest."

"Yes, yes; certainly," said one of the gentlemen nearest to him, though in a hesitating tone.

"Your hand upon it, sir."

His guest tendered his hand, and the example was followed by the rest, but then, after an awkward silence, all departed, leaving the count slowly pacing to and fro in his deserted drawing-room.

A fearful sight was it to see his handsome face distorted by passion, as he raised his clenched fists and poured forth a terrible curse upon the head of the luckless swindler captain.

"This night's work," he muttered, "can never be undone. No, the first brick of the house has fallen: the secret of my life is no longer safe. But not yet, I swear before Heaven, not yet, if I have life and strength left to me, will I shrink from the course I have determined upon! No, no! a long and glorious career of profligacy and dissipation is still in store for me! Lovely women will yet be found whom my gold shall purchase—lovely women and ruby wine— what care I for more?"

As he spoke he filled and drained a goblet of sparkling champagne, then laughed a low noiseless laugh which was peculiar to him, and in which his cruel eyes took no part.

"Sweet Rose!" he muttered; "you at least shall not escape me! No; if ruin and disgrace stared me in the face—if instant death threatened me—I would not turn away from the course I have laid down! No, Rose; nothing in heaven or earth can save thee. Thou shalt be mine, thou shalt be mine!"

CHAPTER V.

THE CROWD—THE RESCUE—A NEW HOME—THE BALLET-GIRL'S CAREER—THE FIRST NIGHT— A DEEP-LAID SCHEME—THE FALSE FRIEND— THE ABDUCTION—THE LONELY HOUSE—THE RUFFIAN—FLIGHT—DANGER—THE OLD HAG— IN THE LION'S DEN.

WHEN Rose Mortimer recovered from the swoon into which she had fallen after effecting her escape from her brutal assailant, she found a crowd of strangers round her, and a policeman who was endeavouring to raise her from the ground.

Opening her eyes, she gazed around in terror upon the unknown faces pressing upon her. Then, recollecting the danger which had so lately menaced her, she shrunk back, and faintly murmured a prayer for mercy.

But as she did so a voice, the tones of which seemed familiar to her, bade her not to be alarmed, and, looking up, she saw to her surprise her friend the scene-painter, Jack Halliday.

"Is it you?" she asked with a faint smile; "where am I? Oh, save me from him!"

"Pray do not be agitated, Miss Mortimer; allow me to see you to your home, and you shall tell me what has occurred upon our way thither."

The policeman, at Halliday's suggestion, obtained a cab, and the scene-painter, having placed his fair charge inside the vehicle, as they travelled onwards listened in wonder to the relation of the strange and terrible scene through which she had just passed.

"There seems a fate about our meeting, Miss Mortimer," said Halliday in a voice which, in spite of the effort he made to conceal it, trembled perceptibly; "there is something more than mere chance about it. Would to Heaven, though, I had arrived sooner, so that I might have afforded you more timely assistance!"

They did not expect to find the clerical scoundrel still lurking about Hugh Mortimer's lodgings, and when they got back all was silent and deserted.

The inhabitants of the low and squalid neighbourhood and the poverty-stricken house in which Rose and her father dwelt were too well accustomed to brawls and disturbances at all hours of the night to have been more than temporarily aroused by the noise which Rose had made in her flight from Abel Booth.

The young girl begged her new friend to wait for her at the door, whilst she proceeded tremblingly upstairs to see whether or not her father had returned.

He was nowhere to be seen, and the rooms presented exactly the same appearance as when she last saw them.

What was to be done?

"You must not think of remaining here," said Jack Halliday; "but must allow me to see you to some respectable hotel, where you can stay till the morning, when, perhaps, we may be able to clear up the mystery."

She thankfully took his arm, and they walked along together. Presently he stopped, and said, with a hesitating voice—

"You won't be offended, I trust, with what I am going to say, Miss Mortimer, but, if I might venture to offer the shelter of my mother's roof, she will, I am certain, be only too happy to try her best to make you comfortable until you have time to settle your plans for the future."

Rose would have refused, but a glance at her friend's face convinced her of the purity of his intentions, and, going to his mother's house, she there met with so warm a welcome that from the first moment she felt completely at home and at her ease.

At her ease as far as she herself was concerned, but the dreadful anxiety which she felt with regard to the fate of her father rendered her low-spirited and miserable.

The whole particulars of the fearful scene through which she had passed were communicated to the authorities at Scotland Yard, but, though searching inquiries were immediately made by the most experienced detectives, nothing was discovered either of Rose's father or his supposed murderer.

And thus a week passed, and the mystery was still unravelled.

But the time was soon to come when all would be explained, as the future chapters of this story will shew.

In the meanwhile (strange as it may seem, but necessity has no law) our heroine daily attended her theatrical duties.

Very soon Rose became familiar with ballet life. Mr. Flathers was secretly delighted with the notion of his having secured at a very cheap rate indeed the services of a young creature so exquisitely graceful, and possessing so faultless a form.

Her training under Mr. Totts, the ballet-master, began in earnest the first day she joined the Babylonian company, and, as perhaps some of our young lady readers may feel curious upon the subject, we will briefly describe the sort of life a ballet-girl goes through before she bursts upon your enraptured sight, a lovely vision, as the *première danseuse*.

Some very hard work comes first, and Rose was put through the following course. To begin with, her pretty little feet were placed inside a curious sort of apparatus called a "groove box," and placed heel to heel in a straight line, the knees of course being turned outwards, and the sides of the box being so contracted that the toes could not incline inwards a hair's breadth.

The pain caused by this attitude was at first very severe, but Rose would not own to her sufferings, and, bearing it like a little martyr, she was delighted to find that after six or seven days her supple joints accustomed themselves to the novel position, and her feet fell easily into the required position when she danced.

After she had mastered this difficulty Rose had next to essay another, rather more formidable and fatiguing.

This was to rest her right foot on a bar which she at the same time held in her left hand in a horizontal line, then varying the attitude with the left foot and right hand, by means of which movements the stiffness of the feet was in a great measure destroyed.

Having got thus far, she had now to learn how to walk upon the extreme points of the toes, so that the leg and instep formed a straight line. This done she had to practise what are called "caprioles," in which she was expected to perform four or five steps in the air, a feat productive of the most heartbreaking fatigue.

Then followed all sorts of flings, and cuts, and movements far too numerous to particularise; and then, in the rehearsal of the pantomime, she was compelled to go through a great deal of stage business of so dangerous a nature that every day she risked her life and her limbs, for any bungling upon the part of Mr. Flathers's carpenters, or a more than usual weakness of Mr. Flathers's worn-out machinery, might have dashed her headlong from the "flies" down the traps, to be taken up a bruised and mutilated corpse.

But Rose worked very hard indeed, and Mr. Totts was filled with delight at the improvement his pupil made under his tuition.

"That girl will make a wonderful dancer," he said to Mr. Flathers; "don't lose her, my dear sir, don't lose her. She's a Cerito! She's an Ellsler! She's a Taglioni! She's a Carlotta! Keep her, and she'll make your fortune and her own too."

Mr. Flathers listened with a faint smile.

"I wish I could," said Mr. Flathers with a groan; "I wish I were not in that atrocious villain's power. Poor girl! if she only knew what misery is in store for her!"

Christmas drew near, hourly nearer, and the noise and bustle of the Royal Babylonian Theatre increased daily.

Jack Halliday was scarcely ever able to find time now to come down to speak a few words to Rose after rehearsal, and when he did come he looked far from heroic.

A shabby suit of clothes, splashed with whitewash, and with sundry dabs of various-coloured paints about it, a face smeared in one or two places with Dutch pink, and a beard plentifully besprinkled with gold leaf, could not be said to add much to his personal attractions.

Still, his clear blue eye and his merry ringing laugh were there.

Rose always welcomed him with delight, and he for his part appeared to find a great charm in the pretty ballet-girl.

A constant visitor at the Babylonian Theatre during the getting-up of the Christmas pantomime was the handsome man called the "count."

Whenever the opportunity of addressing a few words to Rose presented itself he did not hesitate to avail himself of it, but, with a smile, would speak to her with a quiet compliment or an amusing joke.

Despite Jack Halliday's warning, she could not but be civil to him, for had he not procured her employment?

Yet she mistrusted him.

The count smiled and showed his teeth. He bided his time.

* * * * * * *

Boxing-night came at last.

The last spangle was sewn on the harlequin's dress, the last touch of paint was given to the Dismal Depths of Desolation, the last piece of gold leaf was laid on the scroll-work of the Palace of King Bobtail, and the early arrivals were hammering at the gallery door, impatient to be let in to secure front seats to witness the first performance of the Fairy of the Dewy Dell, or Harlequin and the Magic Poker.

A dull play to which nobody listened, a merry overture, and then the tinkling of a little bell and the simultaneous rising of the curtain on the Abode of the Demon of the Rocky Gorge, and the burlesque opening of the pantomime commenced.

A clashing of cymbals and a furious belabouring of the drum, and the Rocky Gorge, demon and all, gave way before the stage carpenters to the Dewy Dell of Delight.

Rapturous applause broke from the audience as one of the most beautiful of Cleverly's scenes burst upon them.

The car of the Goddess of Morning descended, and from it stepped one of the most lovely beings that could be conceived, for Rose Mortimer had been selected by Mr. Flathers to personate the goddess.

Deafening applause broke from every part of the house.

All paid tribute to the Queen of Beauty, who, radiant, beaming, and happy, stood before them in the person of our heroine.

Never had a more perfect and genuine success been achieved in the ballet.

Mr. Flathers rubbed his hands and chuckled.

Mr. Totts prophesied great things of his pupil, and, last though not least, Count Lerno, who was behind the scenes that night, showed his white teeth with a grim smile as he followed every movement of the lovely ballet-girl.

"It cannot fail," he muttered to himself; "she cannot suspect."

It was a late hour before the pantomime was over; but at last clown committed his last felony, pantaloon received his last kick, and harlequin made his last leap through a respectable tradesman's window, and the audience turned out into the sloppy streets to make the best of their way home, discussing as they went the merits of the pantomime, but all agreeing in praising to the skies the wonderful grace and beauty of Rose Mortimer.

The frost, which had set in a few days before Christmas, had given way before a southerly wind.

The pavement was slippery and unpleasant.

The lamps burnt dimly, and all without looked miserable and desolate.

The streets were almost deserted.

"Miss Mortimer."

Rose heard her name spoken in a soft tone by some one behind her.

She turned and saw the count.

"Allow me to congratulate you, Miss Mortimer, on your well-deserved success to-night."

"You are very kind," said Rose; "but for your kind aid I should never have been allowed to appear."

She was standing by the O. P. wing as she spoke, and still in her stage costume.

"The pleasure you have given me to-night fully repays me for any slight service I may have been to you," he replied with a graceful bow.

There was a pause.

Rose knew not what reply to make.

In the distance, leaning against one of the scenes, she saw Jack Halliday, and the words of caution he had addressed to her respecting the count came suddenly to her recollection.

"Miss Mortimer," said the count, "it grieves me very much to have to say a word which can in any way lessen your night's enjoyment, but—but—I have a message for you."

"A message! and for me ?"

"Yes, and one which I fear will cause you sorrow."

"Speak! What is it ?"

"Your father—"

"My father ! Oh, do you know anything of him ? He — he disappeared some weeks ago, and I have been unable to learn any tidings of him.'"

"I grieve to be the bearer of evil news, but he is ill, seriously ill."

"Oh, where is he ? Let me go to him."

"You may possibly remember," said the count, "that when I first had the pleasure of meeting you it was in your father's house."

"Yes, yes," said Rose.

"I only mention that to show you that I am to be trusted—that I speak as the friend of Hugh Mortimer."

"Do not keep me in suspense. Tell me where he is, that I may go to him."

"May I not rather have the pleasure of conducting you to him ?"

Rose hesitated.

"Do not allow any false sense of modesty or propriety to hinder you from accepting my offer."

Still she made no reply.

"My carriage is waiting at the stage door, and will take you more rapidly than any public conveyance ; besides, at this hour of the night you should hardly venture out alone and unprotected."

"Thank you, thank you ; I accept your offer."

The count showed his teeth beneath his jetty black moustache.

"Come, then," said he, at the same time offering her his arm.

"I cannot go in this dress," said Rose.

"Remember," replied the count, "every moment is precious. You can wrap my cloak round you, and no one will notice your stage attire. Do not delay, I beseech you."

For a moment she hesitated ; but then, drawing the voluminous folds of the cloak about her, she took his arm.

He led her rapidly towards the stage door.

On their way they met Mr. Flathers, the manager.

"I congratulate you on your success, Miss Mortimer."

He said this with a low bow and a conciliatory manner, but when her back was turned exchanged a sinister smile with her companion.

"Is all well ?" he muttered, almost below his breath. The count nodded significantly, as he led her onwards towards the stage door.

There, in the dark narrow street, a handsome carriage was standing, the door of which a servant in livery opened as they approached.

But some faint suspicion of treachery, flashing across the poor girl's mind at this moment, caused her again to hesitate.

"Come—come," said the count, impatiently, and glancing nervously around as he did so, "we shall be too late."

She knew not what to say—what excuse to urge, and yet her heart misgave her. Timidly drawing back, she had some notion of running up the stairs again towards the stage, but the count caught her by the arm.

At that moment footsteps were heard upon the staircase, and Jack Halliday was dimly discernible in the distance.

Not an instant was to be lost if he was to carry off his prize. The count cast one comprehensive glance around, seized the beautiful girl in his arms, and carried her, in spite of her terrified resistance, to the carriage. Then, springing in with his lovely burden, he bade the coachman drive on, and, the latter lashing his horses, in another moment the vehicle reached the end of the street.

"Forgive me, my dear young lady," said the count, "but every second is of the greatest importance, for your poor father is in a very critical state."

Hastily disengaging herself from his embrace, the terrified girl scarcely knew whether or not to believe that she had been forcibly abducted.

The coachman was already informed as to the road he was to take, for almost before they were seated the brougham started at a rapid pace in a westerly direction.

For some minutes they rode on in silence.

Rose looked from the window, but failed to recognise any of the streets through which they passed.

"Where is it that my father is ?" she asked.

"Do not be frightened ; we shall soon be there."

For a long time she remained without speaking.

They had left the paved and lighted streets, and were going rapidly over a smooth road.

As well as Rose could make out, hedges bounded each side of the way.

They were going out into the country.

"Where are we ?" asked Rose, somewhat uneasily.

"This is the Fulham Road," said her conductor, in reply.

"Have we much farther to go ?"

"No, we shall reach our destination in a few minutes."

Almost as he spoke the carriage came to a standstill.

But it was only for an instant—apparently while some large gates were opened to give the carriage ingress.

The next minute they were driving up a gravelled road, bordered on each side by large trees.

At last the vehicle stopped finally.

The count sprang out and stood to assist the beautiful girl to alight.

"Where are we ?" she asked. "Where have you brought me ? "

"Do not be frightened," he made answer ; "you are quite safe here. Enter."

"My father can never be here ? " she said.

They had stopped before a large old-fashioned house of almost palatial size.

The glimpse which the open door permitted disclosed a handsome hall, and, beyond, a suite of rooms beautifully and tastefully furnished.

Rose, who had ever associated her father with squalid misery and abject poverty, was certainly justified in her doubt.

"Enter ; you have nothing to fear," repeated the count.

She availed herself of his proffered arm, and, descending from the brougham, entered the splendid hall.

Side by side the deceiver and his victim entered the house, within whose walls few so pure as Rose had ever been.

"Where is my father ?" she asked. "Take me to him at once."

"Nay, Miss Mortimer, let me first offer you some refreshment."

"Nothing, nothing!" she cried impatiently.

"You must be fatigued after your evening's exertions. Let me beg of you to rest before you seek your father."

"No, no! Tell me where he is and let me go to him."

"Presently."

"At once!" she cried firmly. "I will not delay."

"To-morrow will be time enough."

"To-morrow?"

"Yes; you will be stronger and more refreshed."

Rose was terribly alarmed.

Jack Halliday's warning seemed to ring in her ears, and she bitterly repented of having left the theatre in the company of the count.

"I insist that you take me to my father—if he be in the house."

"Which he is not," replied the count coolly.

"Then you have deceived me."

"Yes," he answered, smoothing his moustache.

"Where am I, then?" she cried wildly. "Whose house is this?"

"Mine."

With a convulsive sob, which seemed to shake her whole frame, she buried her face in her hands and wept.

"Yes, dearest," said the count, "I am master of this house, and you shall be its lovely mistress."

"Never, never!"

"If I have erred," continued he, heedless of the interruption, "attribute it only to my love; if I have deceived you in bringing you here, still love must plead my excuse. Do not turn your beautiful eyes away from me. Pardon me the trick I have played upon you, and say you will be mine."

"Count Lerno," said Rose, drawing herself up to her full height—"Count Lerno, sooner than agree to your degrading proposals I would kill myself. Do you suppose that there is nothing dearer to a woman than gold and jewels? I scorn and despise you."

"Nay, pretty one, why so angry? Remember you are now completely in my power," and here he showed his white teeth, "and that I have means to compel your compliance."

"Never!"

But the count took her in his arms and, without paying any attention to her struggles or cries for help, bore her easily upstairs to an elegantly furnished apartment.

Here, when he loosened his hold of her, she ran from him terrified, and, tremblingly clinging to the opposite wall, waited with blanched cheek and flashing eyes for a renewal of his violence.

But he only gazed at her for a moment with the same devilish smile, and then, turning upon his heel, left the room, and closed and locked the door behind him.

She stood motionless, listening to his retreating footsteps, and then gazed wildly around her.

A lamp hanging from the ceiling cast a dim subdued light upon the objects which the room contained—heavy old-fashioned furniture, surrounded by oak panellings quaintly carved.

Still as death she stood, her hand pressed upon her heart, her head gently bowed, listening to the sound of his steps until it died away altogether; then, looking about hurriedly to the right and left, with something of the action of a hunted stag when the bay of the hounds is swelling upon the air, she sought for some way of escape.

That there was no time to lose she felt certain, for, whatever motive at the present moment occasioned her jailor's absence, his return would be speedy.

Her only hope of evading him, then, lay in prompt and energetic action.

She must be bold and resolute—dare all or lose all.

With this idea she advanced rapidly towards the window and endeavoured to raise the sash.

It was heavy and swollen with the rain, and stuck fast in its frame; but fear lent her strength, and she struggled desperately to effect her purpose.

At length it was forced upwards, and she gazed, with a fast-beating heart, into the intense darkness below.

She could form no notion of how far she was from the ground, but surely death were preferable to the hideous fate in store for her did she remain longer in the mercy of the miscreant.

Leaving the window, however, for a moment, she cast a despairing glance around, in the hope of seeing something that might assist her, and merciful Heaven directed her attention to a poignard which, among other ornaments, hung by the side of the mantelpiece.

She sprang towards the weapon, drew it from its sheath, and, without a moment's hesitation, busied herself in slashing down the damask window-curtains.

With nervously-twitching but agile fingers, Rose ripped the tough fabric in twain and fashioned it into a rope, which she rapidly but firmly secured to a heavy piece of furniture standing close to the window.

Scarcely had she completed her task before she heard a movement in the house, as though steps were approaching the door.

In speechless terror she paused to listen, and, feeling felt certain that she was not deceived, clambered lightly through the window, clutched the rope, and glided rapidly to the earth.

Trusting to Providence that she might choose the right direction, she rushed from the spot, forcing her way through a dense growth of rank weeds and straggling brushwood, which formed a sort of hedge dividing the garden from a field beyond.

Heedless of the difficulties in her way, she rushed wildly onwards, and paused only when, breathless and half fainting, she reached a fence separating the field from the highroad.

Afar off in the distance she could could see lights flashing fitfully to and fro, and could hear the sound of men's voices calling to one another.

Summoning all the strength that yet remained to her, Rose clambered to the top of the fence, dropped down into the road, and then ran on again.

A wild open country surrounded her on all sides, without a sign of human habitation, for she was at that part of Fulham, lying west of Walham Green, known by the name of "Dead Man's Land."

Ignorant whither her steps were taking her, she ran on and on, down long interminable lanes, until, prostrated by fatigue, she sank in an almost lifeless state upon the ground by the road side.

Fortune, however, did not now befriend her as it had done when she made her escape from her clerical assailant at her father's house, by sending honest Jack Halliday to her aid.

When she again opened her eyes she was shivering with cold and wet to the skin from the heavily falling rain, and the road was still dark and lonely.

Rising to her feet, she staggered onwards as well as her trembling limbs would allow.

Suddenly, in front, she saw a faint glimmering through the window-blind of a mean-looking house.

The sight lent her fresh strength, and she now proceeded at a more rapid pace. As she approached it, however, a strange moaning sound struck upon her ear and caused her to look around in painful suspense.

What had alarmed her, though, she found to be the river running rapidly past the weedy rush-grown bank, where stood the house in question.

Approaching the door, she hesitated a moment, and, summoning up courage, knocked twice.

She fancied, as she drew near that, she could hear the low murmur of voices within, but now there was a death-like silence.

Again she knocked, and then a heavy foot-fall sounded upon the floor, and the door slowly opened.

On the threshold a blear-eyed old hag, with ragged unkempt locks, stood blinking from behind a flaring tallow candle, which she shaded from the wind with one of her long claw-like hands, whilst behind her stood a scowling beetle-browed ruffian who seemed to be clutching a heavy bludgeon in an attitude of defence.

"I—I have lost my way," said Rose, timidly: "would you give me shelter for an hour or two, until light?"

The old hag stood in astonishment at the strange costume which Rose wore, and made no reply, but the man quickly said—

"Yes, yes; come in. Are you alone?"

Rose replied in the affirmative, and crossed the threshold. The door closed heavily behind her, and the old hag, at a sign from her companion, chained and bolted it.

A wretched hovel it was in which Rose found herself, and sinister and threatening were the faces of her host and hostess.

The hour was very late, the spot entirely deserted.

At whose mercy was she now, and what new danger awaited her?

CHAPTER VI.

THE LONELY HOUSE — THE LOFT — SCHEMES OF PLUNDER — THE STRUGGLE IN THE DARK — THE FEARFUL LEAP—TERROR—THE ESCAPE—THE DISGUISE.

As the door closed behind her Rose's heart sank within her.

She had escaped one danger, it is true, but was it only to encounter another?

The interior of the house in which she had taken refuge was mean and shabby in the extreme, and the countenances of its inmates most repulsive. Their rough tongues seemed to find it difficult to frame courteous sentences, and polite phrases sat upon them with bad grace, though both the man and the woman, in a rude uncouth fashion, did their best for her comfort.

Her dress (alas for the poor dress! it was now much torn and mud-bespattered) was taken by the old hag to dry, but on the fair white rounded arm of the poor girl still glistened a bracelet which she had worn at the theatre the night before, and which, if of real stones, would have been worth a small kingdom.

On this the eyes of the beetle-browed ruffian fixed themselves with a covetous glare, but Rose noticed him not as she stood near the dying embers of the fire, sadly thinking over the events of the past few hours.

"Come, old woman," cried the man, in loud harsh tones, "here's this 'ere poor gal a perishing o' cold. Show her to the bedroom, can't yer?"

The old hag stared, and muttered something between her teeth, but, snatching up a flaring tallow candle which, stuck in the neck of an old bottle, served to light the apartment, and signing to Rose to follow her, she led the way to a ladder, which was the only means of communication with the upper story.

Rose shrank back.

She hesitated to ascend a tumble-down ladder, leading she knew not whither.

"Go up, I tell yer," said the hag.

"I'd rather not. No; I will stay down here till daylight."

"*He* says you're to go up," said the hag, "and when *he* says a thing, he means it—*he* do!"

"Now, then, with that light, mother!" cried the man, with an oath.

"Up! up! Quick, or it'll be the worse for you."

Rose ascended the ladder in safety, and saw that she was in a sort of loft.

Her head almost touched the rafters, and the floor was littered with straw.

"Lie down and go to sleep," said the old woman, as she disappeared down the ladder, taking the light with her, and leaving Rose in total darkness.

For some minutes our heroine stood afraid to move a step, but as her eyes became better accustomed to the darkness she grew bolder, and, advancing to the narrow aperture which answered the purpose of a window, she looked out. The wall of the house seemed to go straight down into the water, for beneath her the ripples came sluggishly plashing, and she could just discern the dim outline of a boat moored to a stake driven deep into the mud.

Her present position was fraught with peril.

She could not but mistrust the inhabitants of the hut, though as yet she had no proof of their entertaining any ill-feeling towards her.

Wearily she turned away from the window, and, gathering together an armful of straw, seated herself upon it, determined not to close her eyes; but her efforts were in vain, exhausted nature exercised her sway, and poor Rose soon fell into a deep slumber.

After a while she awoke suddenly.

How long she had been asleep she had no means of ascertaining, but now the faint grey light of early dawn was beginning to make things partly visible in a misty ghost-like manner.

Immediately beneath her she heard the voices of the man and woman in fierce conversation.

"I tell you, yes," said the man, "I saw the jewels a-twinkling on her arm like blazes. They'd set you and me up for life, that's what they'd do."

"How are yer a-going to get 'em?"

"Trust me for that. Give me hold o' that there knife."

Rose instinctively felt that she was the subject of the conversation of these wretches.

She felt that her life was about to be sacrificed for a trumpery theatrical gew-gaw not worth a crown.

What could she do? Would they let her go if she gave them the mock diamonds?

When she next heard the voices the speakers had evidently altered their position.

They had come to the bottom of the ladder leading to the loft in which she lay, pale and trembling.

"Now listen to me, mother," said the man, with an oath: "as soon as I've got up, you pull the ladder away, so that *she* can't escape. Do you hear?"

"Ay, ay; I'm not deaf," grumbled the other.

"Well, you just mind what you're at, that's all."

A moment's pause, and then the sound of heavy footsteps on the creaking ladder.

Rose shrank into the farthest and darkest corner of the loft as the head of the beetle-browed ruffian appeared through the trap.

With the exception of a space of a few feet round the window, where the early rays of light penetrated, the loft was in complete darkness.

With beating heart and bated breath, Rose watched the ruffian, as for a few moments he stood near the window, a long-bladed knife held firmly between his teeth.

[ROSE'S APPEAL TO COUNT LERNO.]

Rose hastily put her hand into the bosom of her dress, and pulled out the poignard which had rendered her such good service when escaping from the count.

It was a tiny weapon, better suited for a toy than for a death-struggle; but on it rested Rose's only hope of life.

With low mumbled curses the ruffian commenced feeling about in every direction.

Rose shrank still further back.

Growling to himself, he stumbled along, but without searching the corner in which our heroine was concealed.

Then he suddenly paused.

"She can't have got away, nohow," he muttered perplexed.

Then, guiding himself by the wall, he commenced making a tour of the loft.

If he only persevered in this plan Rose knew she must be discovered.

Again she saw him cross the light, but it was only a momentary glimpse she obtained of him, and then he plunged again into the shade.

Rose felt he was drawing near her; she heard his low muttered curses and his stealthy footfall, but how near he was she could not tell.

Clutching her dagger tightly in her little hand, she scarcely dared to breathe.

All was silent as the grave.

She knew nothing, heard nothing, of her pursuer's whereabouts till a cold clammy hand rested on her bare shoulders.

With a scream she started from her place of concealment.

With an oath and a yell of triumph, he followed her.

Then, her eyes glaring fiercely, like those of a tiger at bay, she turned and confronted him.

With impetuous force he rushed on her and seized her by the throat.

Her brain whirled round, she almost lost consciousness, and sank to the ground.

With a low laugh he bent over her, and raised on high the arm holding the cruel long-bladed knife.

Then only was it that Rose recovered her presence of mind sufficiently to act.

Striking upward with her tiny dagger, its sharp point entered the cheek of her antagonist as he bent over her, and as he moved started a crimson stream across his scowling face.

With a frightful yell, he put up both his hands, for the blood, raining over his face, blinded him.

To do this he was forced to relinquish his hold of Rose, who, not slow to seize this opportunity of escape, pushed him from her with all her force, and staggered to her feet.

There was not a moment to lose.

How was her escape to be made ?

The ladder was gone !

One chance alone remained—the window.

It was just large enough for her to squeeze through, and, to her great joy, she saw the tide had risen considerably, and that the leap was nothing very terrific for an expert diver.

Without a moment's hesitation she plunged head-first into the muddy river.

As she regained the surface, a few strokes took her to the boat, into which she clambered.

Then, looking up at the window whence she had jumped, she saw the hideous blood-stained features of her would-be murderer glaring furiously at her.

Her nimble fingers speedily unfastened the rope with which the boat was moored, and then, with one vigorous push, she launched the frail bark out into the stream.

She was only just in time, for again that ill-favoured face appeared at the window, and a couple of sharp reports in quick succession from a pistol, and the sprinkling of the shot like hail in the water around her, warned her that she had no time to spare.

With a few rapid strokes of the sculls Rose took the boat still further away from the land, and then, directing its head down the stream, the tide being in her favour, she soon turned a bend in the river, and lost sight of the hateful house.

Now she had time for reflection; so, unshipping her sculls, she allowed the boat to drift with the current while she endeavoured to settle the course which it would be the best for her to pursue.

It was now nearly broad daylight, and in a few minutes she would reach the more crowded part of the river, where she would certainly attract attention, which, however flattering it might be, was not at all what she desired.

While yet she pondered her eye rested upon a bundle lying in the stern of the boat.

Eagerly she seized it, and found that it contained a suit of boy's clothes, which, although somewhat too large for her, would, nevertheless, serve the purposes of disguise and warmth ; for, be it remembered, a ballet-dress, however pretty, is not exactly suited to a river excursion on a frosty December morning.

Again seizing the sculls, she impelled the boat towards the shore at a part where a reed-grown bank seemed to offer her the best concealment, and in a very short time emerged, looking as pretty and fragile a sailor-boy as you can imagine.

"I've got the boat here," she said to herself, "so I may as well float down as far as Westminster."

So saying, she again stepped into the little bark, and in a few minutes was once more floating gaily down in mid-stream towards London.

By and bye the towers of the Houses of Parliament came in sight, and then Rose directed the skiff towards a landing place just on the upper side of the bridge.

It was yet early, and but few people were about, but some half-dozen watermen were lounging at the pier.

"Hullo, little 'un," cried one, "where do you hail from ?"

"Likely-looking lad enough," said another.

"Ugh ! do better in petticoats," growled a third.

It required some little courage on the part of Rose to walk past these men, for the dress she wore was strange to her, and she much feared she might be discovered by her awkwardness.

"Here, you fellows, look after my boat," she said, in as consequential and swaggering a tone as she could assume, and then, putting her hands into her pockets, she strolled past the group of men and walked sharply in the direction of Mrs. Halliday's house, which she had learnt to call "home."

Twenty minutes' brisk walking brought her to the door, which happened to be open.

Rose entered, rapidly ascended the stairs, and knocked at the door of Mrs. Halliday's room.

"Come in," said that worthy old lady.

Rose availed herself of the permission; but when Mrs. Halliday, who had not yet completed her toilet, saw what she believed to be a good-looking sailor boy enter her room she gave a shrill scream, and hastily threw her dress over her shoulders.

"Don't you know me ?—Rose ?" said our heroine.

"Lor me ! and so it is ; and oh ! the state Jack's been in about you ; and where have you been? which the dress, it becomes you well, though fine feathers don't make fine birds, and I hope it's no harm ; none of those masked balls and wickedness, because it's pale you are, my darling, and a little drop of brandy, though it is early in the morning, and such are courses I don't approve, and you havn't told me a bit about it yet."

So ran on the worthy kind-hearted talkative old lady, patting Rose on the cheek as she spoke, and holding her hand in her own.

Rose commenced a narration of her adventures, but before she had half told them her strength gave way, and she burst into a flood of tears.

"Bless you, my dear, don't fret," cried the old lady ; "your troubles are all over now."

Good old soul ! had Rose's troubles even *began*? Oh ! if she had known what fearful fate awaited her ! what dreadful end she was rapidly approaching !

CHAPTER VII.

THE NEW DRESS—THE DARK SUSPICION—THE ABDUCTION—NIGHT—DESPAIR—THE VILLAIN AND HIS COMPANIONS—THE APPEAL.

For many long weary hours Rose lay in a state of dreamy unconsciousness.

Sleep refused to come to her relief, but, as she lay with closed eyes courting repose, the events which had pressed so quickly upon her through the last night once more became realities to her fevered brain.

In her mind's eye she saw again the handsome demoniacal face of the count, the splendour of the courtly house at Fulham, the waterside cottage, and the lazy plashing Thames.

Then the kind motherly face of Mrs. Halliday bending over her recalled her to the present, and she turned with a sigh of relief again to court slumber, but in vain.

"Rose, my dear," said the old lady, "what will you do about the theatre to-night? There is that dress of yours, which from top to bottom is a sight to see, the mud and the rents being such as no Christian needle-woman could mend, let alone a poor widow."

With something like a groan Rose strove to think of the future.

What awaited her?

Must she again brave the dangers of the theatre?

Would not the sight of the count's pale handsome face drive her wild with anger?

Then, on the other hand, if she were to throw up her engagement what could she do?

Her father had disappeared, and there was no one in the wide world to whom she could appeal for help.

Upon her employment at the theatre depended her daily bread, and she must brave all perils or starve.

"I tell you what, dear," continued Mrs. Halliday, "I'll set to work and make you a new skirt. It won't take long, though when poor Halliday was alive it was but seldom I used a needle; but necessity is the soul of business, and I'll do my best."

Rose protested, but in vain.

She offered to assist, but the kind-hearted woman with gentle force compelled her to remain at rest, while with many little interjections and misquoted proverbs she sought her needle and thread, and sent the dingy maid of all work for the muslin.

"Bless my heart!" cried Mrs. Halliday after a while, and so suddenly as to make Rose start from a fitful and uneasy doze into which she had fallen, "bless my heart, its near six o'clock and the dress not half finished, and seven's the latest, and if it is'nt done Mr. Flathers will be in a way, though how a widow with a son christened John but called Jack, who's been gone since morning, can do it in time is more than I know."

Before she had finished her speech Rose had risen, and was busily employed with needle and thread.

There was little time to spare, and when the skirt was at length completed it wanted but a quarter of an hour to the time at which Rose should be at the theatre.

"I tell you what it is, Rose, you'll have to dress here and take a cab down to Hardress-street, though public vehicles are bad, they being always engaged in taking small pox cases to the hospital, and well I remember when poor dear Halliday was alive—"

"Yes, yes," interrupted Rose, knowing how difficult it was to silence the old lady when once she commenced her early reminiscences, "yes, Mrs. Halliday, I will dress for the theatre at once."

With far different feelings from those with which on the previous night she had attired herself for her first appearance Rose again donned the costume of a ballet-girl.

Her heart sank within her, and her limbs trembled beneath her, but the knowledge of the necessity of being at the theatre in proper time gave her strength, and in a wonderfully short time she had arrayed herself as the Fairy of the Dewy Dell.

She looked almost more beautiful than on the preceding night.

The pallor caused by all she had gone through since quitting the stage added a lustre to her beautiful eyes, and as she looked at her own reflection in the glass she saw that she was beautiful, and sighed.

Sighed—for she knew a little of the misery of a pretty girl without a strong protecting arm to fight her battles and to shield her from evil.

She knew something of the perils which she might be called upon to encounter, but could she have foreseen all that cruel Fate had in store for her she would rather have thrown herself from the bridge into the black Thames than have left the shelter of Mrs. Halliday's roof that night.

But there was no friendly voice to warn her of her impending danger, no kind hand to guide her and sustain her faltering footsteps.

Into the cold world, alone and helpless, she was forced to go, to fight and struggle, to sink or swim, as Fate ordained.

Jack Halliday was at the theatre, and to him only, in the whole universe, could she look for advice and assistance.

As Rose put the finishing touches to her toilet Mrs. Halliday knocked at the door.

"For the last two hours and more, my dear, there's been a cab a-loitering in a way the police should not allow up and down the street, but it's turned out lucky, as it happens, and it's now at the door a-waiting, and if you're afraid, say the word, and I'll put put on my bonnet and shawl, and come with you; but the driver looks sober, and a young man, quite the gentleman I assure you, is a-sitting by his side conversing affable and quoting poetry."

"Thank you, dear Mrs. Halliday, I would not trouble you for the world; I shall be quite safe by myself."

The cab was waiting at the door, and the young man got down and assisted Rose, who was wrapped in a long cloak, which quite concealed her ballet dress, to enter.

Hardly waiting to hear the direction she gave, he sprang back to his seat by the driver, and the vehicle drove off at a rapid rate.

Poor Rose! Had she but known, she would sooner have cut off her right arm than have entered that cab.

On, on they drove through the dark streets, over which a thick fog had settled that rendered everything murky and indistinct.

The lamps shed but little light, but still the cab drove on at a great speed, in spite of the shouts and oaths from the drivers of other vehicles with which it nearly came into collision, and the frightened screams of foot passengers who were nearly run over by it.

Rose began to feel frightened.

Was the driver intoxicated?

Was he taking her in the right direction?

Eagerly she peered from the window, but the fog was so dense that she could not make out with any degree of certainty where she was.

"Stop! stop!" she cried, thoroughly frightened.

The speed if anything increased.

She let down the window and put out her head.

"Stop! let me out!" she exclaimed.

There was no answer to her cry.

"Where are you taking me?"

The cab sharply turned a corner, and went jolting down what Rose made out to be a mean-looking street.

Again she shrieked at the top of her voice, but no attention was paid to her cries.

"Help! help!" she cried in despair, trusting some passer-by might come to her rescue.

"Let me out! Help!"

The vehicle stopped so suddenly as to throw Rose forward, and the next moment the man who had been riding with the driver appeared at the door.

"Did you call, miss?"

"Yes, yes. You are taking me in a wrong direction. Let me out."

The man opened the cab door as she spoke.

"I told you to drive me to—"

"Before she could complete her sentence he had sprung into the cab, and firmly placed his hand over her mouth to stifle her cries.

She cabman descended from his box, and the other man with strong arm bore the unfortunate girl from the vehicle.

The door of a house close by was open, and ere Rose could utter a word she was carried into a dark passage, and the door closed upon her.

As it was slammed with an ominous sound the poor girl's heart sank within her.

Again was she the victim of some base plot!

The hand was still pressed tightly over her mouth as she was dragged, rather than led, along the passage.

A sudden push forced her to enter a room opening from the dark passage, which was illuminated by a single ray of light.

The hand was removed from her mouth, and she stumbled forward into the darkness.

As she did so the door behind her was shut, and she heard the key turned in the lock.

The sound sent a cold thrill of horror through her frame.

She was a prisoner!

Whose work was it?

Had she again fallen a victim to the count's evil passions?

What fate had she to expect?

It was so pitchy dark she could see nothing of the room in which she was imprisoned.

She did not even know whether she was alone or not.

For some moments she feared to move, but after a short time she stepped timorously forward.

Frightened and despairing, dreading the worst, she called aloud for help, but the echo of her own voice was the sole response to her appeals.

Her suppliant voice resounded through the house, but reached no pitying ear.

Tired out at last, she threw herself upon the floor, and sobbed as if her poor little heart would break.

What could she do?

She was quite powerless, her cries were unheeded, her strength was exhausted, and she was in the power of some unprincipled ruffian, who had, without doubt, taken every precaution to render her escape an impossibility.

How could she, a poor weak girl, hope to struggle against her adversaries?

The escape she had had the previous night was little short of miraculous. Fortune would not again favour her as it had done before.

It would have moved a hard heart to see the poor suffering one prone upon the ground, her graceful form shaken by the sobs which could not be suppressed, as the knowledge of what might be her fate almost drove her distracted.

It seemed to her that she had been confined for hours in the dark room, when a faint light shone through the cracks of the door, and the sound of whispering struck upon her ears.

Instinctively she rose and gathered the cloak closer about her.

With compressed lips and fixed determination, she waited the entrance of those she heard without.

Her heart beat so that she could scarcely breathe, and her eyes were fixed despairingly upon the door.

Her bosom heaved convulsively, for she knew the time had come.

The key was turned in the lock.

There was another pause, and a short whispered conference, during which she remained perfectly quiet, breathless with expectation and fear, longing, yet dreading to see the form of her abductor.

She half expected that the cold sneering face of Count Lerno would meet her gaze.

She shuddered at the idea of the diabolical expression of triumph which would light up his handsome features on seeing her once again in his power.

She could think of no one but the count who would have carried her forcibly away.

It surely must be his face she thought which would meet her eyes when the door was opened.

But she was wrong.

Slowly the door opened, admitting a stream of light which quite dazzled Rose, who had been so long in the black darkness, and gave admission to a man.

Was it the count?

A moment's glance was sufficient to show her the fears she had entertained of that mysterious man were for the present groundless ; at the same time the light revealed to her the fact that the room was well, even handsomely, furnished.

He who now entered the apartment in which she had been kept a prisoner was a younger man, and his face was unadorned by a moustache.

Another glance showed her that he was no other than the man who had sat by the cabman's side, and who had forcibly carried her into the house.

Behind him, bearing a candle, came a woman of singularly repulsive appearance.

It was not so much her ugliness as a remarkably sinister expression which made her face disagreeable to look upon.

Still the sight of one of her own sex filled poor Rose with delight.

Hope revived in her bosom, and rushing past the man, she threw herself at the feet of his companion, and raised her hands in an attitude of supplication.

"Have pity on me !" she cried, " have pity on me and help me !"

CHAPTER VIII.

EDGAR DEVILLE—THE MYSTERIES OF THE LONELY HOUSE—THE TEMPTATION—THE WARNING—THE DISCOVERY—THE PUNISHMENT OF CURIOSITY.

Among all those with whom Count Lerno was acquainted there was hardly one who knew more of him than that he was rich, handsome, and liberal.

He never courted intimacy with any of his associates.

He would converse with them upon ordinary topics, but any questions respecting himself, his birth, his parentage, or the source of his income invariably remained unanswered ; nay, more, the questioner received some severe rebuke which had the effect of restraining him from again uttering his queries.

It was in his chambers in Piccadilly that the count was in the habit of entertaining his friends, and not at the lonely house at Fulham to which Rose had been taken by him on the night of her first appearance at the theatre.

Respecting that establishment he was ever silent.

Until he made the acquaintance of young Edgar Deville he had never asked one of his male friends to that lonely house, but, for reasons satisfactory to himself, he pressed that young fellow, who was little more than a youth, but who was blessed with a profusion of wealth, and a wonderful capacity for enjoying it, to accompany him to that residence and pass a few days with him.

How their days and evenings were spent in that lonely house it is better not to inquire.

Every luxury, every dissipation, every enjoyment which the human mind could conceive and money purchase was to be had there.

Vicious pleasures and hideous orgies helped to pass

the hours till they seemed to fly, nor was the comparatively innocent excitement of gambling wanting.

Edgar Deville, though the guest of the count, was paying heavily for his amusements.

A week quickly passed by in every kind of pleasure.

At the end of that time the count announced to his young friend that he was compelled to absent himself for a few days upon urgent business.

"I must positively go, my dear fellow," he said, "but I beg you to remain till my return. Treat everything as if it were your own. Do what you like. Go where you like—at least with one exception."

"What is that?" asked young Deville.

"Only a foolish whim of mine; but the further portion of the house—that which is always shut up—do not let your curiosity tempt you thither."

"Why not?" asked the other, laughing.

"Because I am master of the house and I do not choose it," rejoined the count, his brow contracting as he spoke, but in a moment his face brightened and he rattled on in his usual gay and cheerful manner.

Edgar Deville, who was not without a kind of fear of his entertainer, said no more on that subject, and later in the day the count left the house in a close travelling carriage.

A week's incessant dissipation had not been without its effect upon Edgar Deville, for pleasure will pall upon a man, however devoted he may be in his pursuit of it, and he felt but little inclination for the excesses in which he and the count had indulged together.

Listlessly he strolled from the house into the park-like grounds which surrounded it, and lighting a cigar paced slowly up and down upon the lawn.

After a while his eyes rested on that portion of the house which the count had cautioned him not to enter.

It was a projecting wing, older and in a more dilapidated condition than the other portion of the building.

It consisted only of two storeys, the windows of the upper one being closed with shutters, while the lower portion was so out of order and overgrown with ivy as at once to proclaim it uninhabited.

"It's deuced queer," said young Deville. "I can't understand it. Of course, as the count doesn't wish it, I won't go in, but there's no harm in stepping up and looking at the place outside."

He suited the action to the words, but there was nothing to be seen.

The windows of the ground floor came down so low that he could easily see in, but the rooms merely contained heaps of dust-covered lumber, and did not appear to have been entered for years.

As he turned to retrace his steps he became conscious that one of the gardeners was intently watching his movements.

"Hang the fellow!" said Deville pettishly. "Lerno needn't have set spies to watch me. Of course I'm not going in, but I should like to know what he's got locked up there."

The fact was, the young fellow's curiosity was roused, and, in spite of all his host had said, he endeavoured the following day to find out something connected with the mysterious wing, though without transgressing the count's command.

For this purpose he tried to follow a long passage which, from his knowledge of the house, he knew must lead to the forbidden part.

After a while his progress was stayed by a door which blocked up the end of the corridor.

Suddenly as he stood it opened.

He caught one momentary glance, and that showed him, to his surprise, that the seemingly ordinary door was thickly plated with iron on the inner side, and that, moreover, it possessed a complication of fastenings in the way of bolts, bars of steel, and massive chains.

"What do you want here?" asked the man who had come from the mysterious wing, in a gruff surly tone, at the same time putting his hand into his breast.

Edgar Deville fancied as he did so that he saw it grasp the butt end of a pistol.

Faintly he stammered an apology, and the owner of the gruff voice conducted him back along the passage, muttering a caution to him not to wander about the parts of the house he didn't know.

"For fear of accidents," said the man with peculiar emphasis, again putting his hand into his breast, "for fear of accidents, you'd better not come this way again."

Edgar took the hint, and was not sorry to regain the inhabited portion of the house.

Two days passed, and the count had not returned, and his young guest was beginning to feel somewhat dull and tired.

Pleasure was dull and insipid without the count to share it with him, and the mystery of the closed wing still dwelt upon his mind and worried him with a restless curiosity to unravel it.

It was a fine bright night and Edgar Deville had just finished his dinner.

So bright and clear was it that he was tempted forth into the grounds to smoke his digestive cigar.

Wandering about, his steps brought him within sight of the closed wing, when to his surprise he perceived that the shutters of one of the windows were open, and that a bright light from the interior shone through.

It was plain that the building was inhabited.

But who were its occupants?

Young Deville lit a second cigar as he leant against a wall and wondered.

He was idle and curious.

Was there no way in which he could satisfy his curiosity?

Yes.

In looking round, his eyes rested upon a short ladder.

The window from which the light shone was at no great distance from the ground.

Surely he might, without much risk, climb by its aid and peep into that secret upper storey.

He resolved to make the attempt.

Planting the ladder firmly, but noiselessly, he slowly and cautiously ascended till his head was on a level with the window-sill.

Then, scarcely daring to breathe, he peered into the room.

It was a small room into which he looked, and totally devoid of furniture.

The light which streamed through the window came from a powerful lamp placed upon a broad shelf a few feet from the ground.

Upon this shelf were several different-sized packets, and that was all!

The room was untenanted.

Edgar Deville was puzzled, but his curiosity was still further aroused.

What was the meaning of this mystery?

Why was he warned not to enter so very ordinary a room?

It was no dismal ghastly Blue Beard chamber after all.

Still there might be more, if he could but obtain an entrance into the chamber, he thought.

Stealthily he placed his hand upon the window-frame and pushed it upward.

To his surprise it yielded to his touch and opened noiselessly, and in a few moments he was standing in the room.

He was actually in the mysterious wing itself.

The thought of having acted dishonourably to his

host never occurred to him, so full was his mind of unravelling the mystery.

On tiptoe he crossed the floor to where the lamp stood upon the shelf.

Stooping down, he examined the packets which lay about.

Money—money—money !

They all contained money.

Some bank notes, some sovereigns, some half-crowns.

Bright new gold and silver coins, crisp white bank notes.

Deville took up another packet, and dropped it with a cry of horror, for he saw that it contained false coin.

Yes, it was all false.

The bank notes were forgeries.

The sovereigns were of base metal.

The Count Lerno was a coiner !

With white face, he would have turned and retraced his steps, but an iron hand restrained him.

A grip was on his collar !

The cold muzzle of a pistol touched his forehead.

Tremblingly he raised his eyes and met the fierce stern gaze of the count, for it was he who held him.

At the window and at the door were crowded many rough ragged-bearded savage faces, all glaring menacingly at Edgar Deville.

"Spare me !" cried the youth imploringly.

"Not a word !" said the count.   "Come with me."

With the pistol still at his forehead, with the iron grasp still on his neck, he quitted the room, preceded by the gang of coiners, and followed by the count, who never relaxed his hold.

He was about to reap the punishment of his foolish curiosity !

————

CHAPTER IX.

SUPPLICATION—THE HAG'S THREAT—THE FLIGHT
  —THE ESCAPE OVER THE ROOF—THE AGONY OF
  SUSPENSE — THE OATH — THE PERJURED VIL-
  LAIN—AGAIN A PRISONER.

"HAVE pity on me !" cried Rose as she knelt at the woman's feet. "Have pity on me, and help me !"

As she looked up with tearful eyes into that woman's face she saw no pity there.

A cold heartless sneer and a cruel stare met her suppliant looks.

A harsh laugh answered her entreaty.

"Oh ! are you a woman and without compassion for one of your own sex ?" cried Rose passionately. "Can you stand calmly by and see me ill-treated ? No, no. I cannot—will not believe it. You will save me ! You will rescue me !"

In the energy of despair the poor girl clutched at the skirt the woman wore, and held it in her grasp.

Impatiently the other jerked it from her hand and turned aside.

"What have I ever done," continued Rose, "that these indignities should be heaped upon me ? Is it because I am a poor friendless girl ? Is it because of my defenceless position ? Let me go. I pray you let me go. I will bless you for your goodness if you will but let me go."

The woman laughed again, a hard and cruel laugh.

The man turned and gazed upon the figure of the suppliant girl.

"We cannot—dare not suffer you to escape."

"Oh, think what it is for me !" said Rose. "Why am I kept here ? Whose doing is it ? Do you know that my detention here, if it be only a cruel jest, will deprive me of my livelihood ?"

"You'll be well taken care of, my beauty," said the woman in a harsh jeering tone ; "you shan't want for anything."

"How long do you intend to keep me here ?"

"That's as may be. We cage our birds till they are so tame they do not care to fly away."

"I will not stay," cried Rose. "It is a shame. You dare not detain me !"

She rose to her feet and made for the door, which still stood open ; but the woman stretched forth a long bony arm and grasped her shoulder.

"Not so fast, little one. You don't leave us like that."

With a vigorous wrench Rose freed herself from the hand that held her, and then, covering her face, gave way to a burst of hysterical sobs.

"It's an infernal shame," muttered the man.

"What's a shame ?" asked his companion sharply. "What do you mean ?"

"What I say," rejoined the other sullenly. "It's an infernal shame, and that count is a villain."

Rose heard the words and shuddered.

Her worst fears were realised, and the man and woman were but agents of the hateful count.

"Idiot !" said the woman with bitter contempt. "Is this a time for maudlin compassion ? Let the girl escape if you dare !"

"I will have no more to do with the job. It is a blacker one than I like."

"Poor fellow !" rejoined the woman, sneeringly. "How long have you been so conscientious ?"

"You have no feeling."

"Perhaps not."

"I tell you it is an ugly business."

"And I tell you I don't care if it is. What is it to us so long as we get paid for it ?"

"Money ! money ! It is always money with you."

"Of course. Have you come into a fortune, that you can afford to despise the count's gold ?"

"I will have no more to do with the matter."

"Fool ! Suppose I say you *shall* ?"

"You. What can you do if I refuse ?"

"Oh, nothing—nothing. I can only remember."

"Remember what ?"

"Remember when your conscience did not trouble you so much—when one dark night a deed was done in this very room which—"

"Hush ! Hush ! For Heaven's sake be silent."

"Oh, then you remember it ! That is well. Now, at your peril let this pale-faced girl escape. I say at your peril."

Repeating the words menacingly, she left the room, and Rose, who in an agony of fright had listened tremblingly to the conversation, cast an appealing look towards the man.

His back was turned to her.

Rose cast herself on her knees before him.

He turned and confronted her.

He was not a very ferocious looking person. He was not much more than twenty, and had some pretensions towards being a gentleman ; but he was evidently a blackguard.

Evidently he possessed a low and vicious mind, which showed itself in the expression of his face as he carelessly lounged there against the mantel-piece smoking his enormous cigar.

"For pity's sake, hear me !" she cried. "Listen to me, I implore you. You cannot look upon my distress unmoved. Relent and let me go. Think what fate it is to which you would consign me."

"It cannot be," he answered. "I dare not disobey the count."

"The count ! Oh, that hated name ! You know that man, and would let me a second time fall into his clutches. No—no. Sooner death than dishonour. I will never be his prey. You will let me go. You will help me to escape from him."

"No—no," said the man. "I cannot."

"On my knees I beg it. If you have a sister, think of her —"

"Damnation!" cried the man angrily. "I tell you, no! Were you to supplicate for hours, I could not do it."

Hope, which for a few moments had revived in her bosom, sank again.

Her distress and despair could no longer find utterance in words, but she twined her beautiful white arms about the man and looked beseechingly into his face.

For a moment he paused, seemingly irresolute; then, with a savage oath, he pushed her from him with such force that she sank heavily on the floor.

He turned aside ashamed.

When Rose raised her head she saw that his back was towards her. She saw, moreover, that the door was still open.

Possessed of a sudden hope of making her escape, she sprang to her feet, and almost before he had time to turn his head had disappeared through the doorway.

With a savage yell he darted after her.

On quitting the room she, in her confusion, turned to the left instead of the right.

She did not perceive her mistake until too late.

To retrace her steps was but to run into the arms of her pursuer.

Her only chance was to keep on.

A staircase terminated the passage, and up this she ran, the man gaining rapidly upon her.

Up, up she went, knowing not whither it might lead.

On, on came her pursuer, calling to her in vain to stop.

But the stairs could not go on for ever.

She reached the uppermost storey of the house.

What could she do?

She had but a moment for deliberation.

The door of a room stood open, and into it she darted, but what protection could it afford her?

None! it was a bare meagre unfurnished attic.

One chance alone remained—the window!

It stood open, and outside ran a narrow parapet.

Without pausing she stepped upon it, and hurried along the narrow ledge.

Her pursuer entered the room as she did so, and uttered a cry of horror, for he deemed it impossible for her to escape a dreadful death.

He expected she would fall, to be dashed in pieces on the pavement below, and his fear was not without foundation. The ledge was little more than eight inches wide!

Fearing to follow, he leant from the window in terror, for, debased ruffian as he was, he was not wholly bad, and he sincerely pitied the poor girl, though he dared not further her escape.

In him many natures mingled, and had he been left to himself the good might have gained the ascendancy, but, unfortunately, he had not the moral courage to flee from temptation.

The fog which had obscured the streets a few hours before had entirely cleared off when Rose made her escape on to the roof.

The moon, moreover, shone bright and clear over London, and by its light the pursuer saw his victim flitting along the parapet to what seemed certain destruction.

"Stop! stop!" he cried, "you are rushing to a dreadful death! come back!"

Rose answered not a word.

Quickly she passed onward.

The house from which the poor girl was endeavouring to make her escape was one of a long row.

From the other houses in the row, however, it differed materially.

It was a storey higher, and projected a little more into the street; consequently, when Rose arrived at the end of the narrow ledge she saw that she must either return and be made a prisoner by the minions of the profligate count or attempt a gymnastic feat which was difficult in the extreme, and which she could hardly hope to accomplish.

To effect her escape she would have to crawl along for some distance upon the slates, and then drop a considerable distance upon a tiled roof, which was so sloping as to give her but little chance of being able to retain her footing when she reached it.

She did not hesitate for a moment.

Any fate was preferable to the one she might expect should she fall into the clutches of the count.

She knew no mercy was to be expected at his hands.

Her pursuer, who had feared to follow her along the parapet, had stretched himself as far as possible out from the window, expecting every moment to see her fall into the street below, but yet intently watching her movements.

That she would attempt to escape by dropping on to the lower roof never entered his head.

The plan seemed too impracticable.

It was certain death, he thought.

The danger was extreme, but Rose determined to brave it.

Anything rather than the fate for which the count destined her.

When the man saw her commence to crawl slowly and carefully along the slated roof, he uttered a cry of horror.

To call to her, to warn her, was of no use.

She was too far from him to hear him, unless he raised his voice so that it would be audible to any passer-by in the street below.

He watched her till a stack of chimneys hid her from his sight.

For some moments he remained breathless, expecting every instant to hear the shriek of despair announcing her fall.

He waited, but he heard it not.

The suspense became intolerable.

The beauty and innocence of poor Rose had not been without its effect upon him.

Her peril roused the nobler sentiments in his nature.

Snatching up a coil of rope, and hanging it loosely about his neck, he crept through the window.

Then, upon his hands and knees, he crawled along the ledge.

It was a dangerous undertaking.

One moment's loss of confidence, one second's giddiness, and he might be dashed to pieces on the pavement.

Still he persevered.

He had changed his boots for a pair of slippers, when he had entered the house. Now throwing these off, his stockinged feet lent him increased security in his perilous enterprise.

Looking steadily before him, he crawled on and on till he reached the corner.

Then he paused and looked around for the object of his pursuit.

She was nowhere to be seen!

Had she found some other method of making her escape?

Puzzled, he waited, and scanned the roof carefully.

Then, by the bright moonlight, he saw at some distance from him the poor girl in the act of dropping from the higher to the lower roof.

She had gone further up, in order that, should she miss her footing, she might have a better chance of recovering it.

The tiles upon which she was about to drop were at such an acute angle that it seemed all but impossible that she could retain her balance upon them.

As he watched she let go her hold of the edge of the upper, and dropped on to the lower roof.

With breathless interest he rivetted his gaze upon the poor girl.

She alighted on her feet, but was unable to retain her balance for more than a moment.

Her feet slipped from under her, and she glided quickly towards destruction.

He turned ashy pale and gasped for breath.

It was a fearful sight to see this fair young girl hurrying to her death—

To know that no mortal power could save her—

To know, moreover, that he would be indirectly the cause of her fearful death.

As she slipped and glided over the steep roof, now staying her course for a second by clutching at the tiles, only to start again when she could no longer hold them—sometimes almost succeeding in staggering to her feet—then again slipping, falling, and gliding, all the while approaching every moment nearer to the edge, over which she must be carried, to fall down—down—to the level of the street, to be taken up a bruised, mutilated, unrecognisable corpse.

She was already within a few feet of the edge.

She uttered one wild despairing shriek, which rang like a death-knell in the ears of the man who had driven her to attempt the rash act.

Shuddering, he turned away his head.

He could not bear to look upon the sight.

He listened for the dull heavy thud of the fallen body in the street below, but he heard it not.

Then he directed his timorous glance to the roof below him.

Poor Rose had grasped at a leaden waterpipe, and had seized it eagerly.

With the tenacity of one who struggles against death she held it.

It was but a precarious safety.

Any moment the pipe might give way, and then nothing could save her.

She was so near the edge of the roof that her feet rested against the little ridge which terminated it.

This afforded her some little extra support; but already the waterpipe bulged, so that it seemed impossible it could long withhold her from the dreadful fate.

Hope that she might be rescued revived in the bosom of the man whose conduct, though he was but the agent of another, had brought her into her present position.

He crawled further along the higher roof till he was immediately over the spot where Rose hung as it were between life and death.

"Have courage," he said, "and I will save you."

"Never!" answered Rose. "Sooner would I face the most terrible death than return to that hateful house."

"For Heaven's sake do not be so rash."

"Death is preferable to dishonour."

"See; I have a rope here by which I can draw you up to comparative security. Do not sacrifice your life for a fancy."

"I tell you I know the count," said she, "and sooner than fall into his hands I would submit to any fate."

"Your strength cannot hold out much longer," cried the man, eagerly. "It is suicide if you persist in your resolution."

"Better suicide than the lot which awaits me if I fall into your hands."

"No—no! You wrong me. You shall go in peace."

"I cannot trust you."

"I swear it."

"What is an oath to a man like you?"

"Save yourself, I implore you. See; here I make

a running knot at the end of the rope, and throw it to you."

He suited the action to the word.

"Now then, before your strength is exhausted, slip it under your arms—one at a time—that's right—cling to the pipe with the other hand—well managed. Now you are saved."

"You promise me my freedom," cried Rose. "You will not attempt to detain me?"

"Come; come. There is no time to be lost."

Holding the end of the rope between his teeth, he crawled to a place where a stack of chimneys gave him a firmer foothold, and then, by means of the rope, raised Rose to the level of the roof on which he stood.

"Poor girl! By the time she reached it she was completely exhausted.

The man assisted her, almost fainting, to a position of security, though not without considerable risk to himself.

With palpitating heart, heaving bosom, and quivering limbs, she rested.

It was some time before she recovered her composure sufficiently to attempt to crawl back along the narrow ledge.

And no wonder.

All she had gone through would have severely tried the nerves and muscles of a strong man; how much the more, then, those of a poor weak girl!

It took a long time to reach again the window through which she had made her escape, with a heart buoyed up with a hope of deliverance.

Now she returned to it, weakened, bruised, and again in the hands of her persecutors, with nothing but the word of a ruffian that she should be free to depart.

After a while the two once more stood within the walls of the house to which she had been taken in the cab by the myrmidons of the count.

Once again in the room, the man seemed little disposed to fulfil his promise of liberating Rose.

He stood in the doorway, blocking it up, completely preventing the egress of any person.

"Let me go," cried Rose; "remember your promise."

"Ay, ay; we will talk of that presently."

"What do you mean? Oh, say you have not deceived me! Remember the oath you swore."

"All in good time, my pretty one; all in good time; you must need rest and refreshment after all you have gone through."

"I will not rest! I will not touch a morsel in this house!" cried Rose angrily.

"Don't say that, my beauty," answered the man with a laugh; "because I can compel you. However, as you know, I am not hard-hearted. Do you think I am?"

Rose made no answer.

"You're the prettiest girl I have seen for many a long day, and that's a fact, and I'm infernally glad you're safe and sound, though you wouldn't have been but for me. You haven't thanked me yet."

"I have nothing to thank you for," answered Rose, striving to speak calmly, "if you keep me prisoner here."

Then, her voice breaking down, her tone changed to one of wild supplication.

"Oh, let me go, I beg of you! Why should you keep me here? Oh, set me free, set me free!"

"All in good time. You shouldn't be in such a hurry to leave your friends. Besides, those pretty lips must pay a toll first."

He endeavoured as he spoke to put an arm round Rose's slender waist, but she repulsed him indignantly.

"Take care," said he, with an angry gleam in his

[THE HAG AND HER VICTIM.]

eyes; "you seem to forget that I am lord and master just now, and that you are completely in my power."

Rose knew it and trembled.

Should she fail in conciliating him he might refuse to set her at liberty.

"Don't you understand," continued the ruffian, "that I don't mean to take all the risk and trouble of letting you go without my reward?"

"What do you want?" asked Rose, her voice trembling so that she was scarcely intelligible; "what do you mean?"

"Mean that I love you, my pretty one."

Rose was thoroughly frightened.

"Let me go, let me go!" she cried, frantically pushing towards the door.

The man caught her in his arms and held her fast.

"Listen to me," he said. "I not only can liberate you now, but prevent your ever experiencing any annoyance from the count again. I can do this—and will, on one condition."

"And that is—"

"That you remain here with me. We could have a jolly time of it. I know how to get some money out of the count, and—"

Rose pushed him from her and turned a look of scorn upon him.

"How dare you say such words? Keep your oath and let me go in peace. or—"

"Or what?" sneered the man.

"Or it will be the worse for you. I will not stop. You dare not keep me."

"We'll see about that," said the man.

Catching her up in his arms, despite of her struggles, he bore her to another room, and then, setting her down, locked the door and put the key in his pocket.

CHAPTER X.

THE INNER CHAMBER — THE PUNISHMENT OF CURIOSITY—LIFE OR DEATH—THE GANG OF RUFFIANS — THE OATH—THE FIRST CRIME—THE COUNTERFEIT HALF-CROWN—DESPAIR.

THROUGH a narrow passage was Edgar Deville led by the count, the pistol all the while pointed at his head.

A thousand times he cursed himself for his foolish curiosity.

A thousand times he reproached himself for what he had done.

Had he but obeyed his host's command he might have been seated in a sumptuously furnished apartment, with everything which money could purchase to be had for the asking, instead of being surrounded by a gang of ruffians, and in danger of his life.

What were they going to do with him?

There were many ominous whisperings amongst the men.

Would his life be sacrificed?

He looked up appealingly at the count, but his head was turned away from him.

He spoke, and instantly a handkerchief was tied securely over his mouth.

A few moments in the passage, and their further progress was barred by a heavy door.

One of the party unlocked it, and Edgar saw that it was lined with iron and secured in a similar manner to the one which led from the mysterious wing into the inhabited portion of the house.

In silence he was conducted into a large room, which was lighted by a number of oil lamps placed on brackets around it.

The apartment was destitute of furniture, but was filled in a great measure by machinery.

Presses, stamping machines, and others of which he was at a loss to define the use were arranged about, and all apparently in the best working order.

A clear space was left in the centre of the chamber, and thither the count conducted his guest.

At a signal a heavy trap in the floor was lifted so close to Edgar's feet as to make him start back in fear.

It disclosed a black yawning chasm which appeared to be bottomless.

Still a deathlike silence prevailed.

It was not broken till the count spoke.

"Comrades," said he, "we have a law that every spy upon us dies: we play too desperate a game to run the chance of detection."

Edgar shuddered.

He saw the reason the trap had been opened.

Peering into the blackness of that abyss he saw his grave.

He, a young man full of life and hope and energy, felt that in a few short minutes he would be a lifeless mass, a shapeless nameless thing.

No wonder that he shuddered.

No wonder that an icy chill crept through his frame.

There are few men so brave as to remain unmoved when suddenly brought face to face with death.

He strove to beg for mercy, but the bandage about his mouth was too tightly fastened.

An indistinct murmur, and that was all.

"Say," said the count, "what is to be this spy's fate?"

"Death!" answered all the men.

The tone in which they spoke was low, but it was none the less determined for that.

Edgar glanced round appealingly, but not one face did he see with an expression of pity upon it.

He could expect no mercy.

He had been found prying into that with which he had no concern.

He possed a secret which, were he at liberty, would give him a power over all the gang which it was not likely they would suffer him to make use of.

They were judge, jury, and executioners.

His fate was sealed.

Still he could hardly think that Count Lerno—he by whose side he had so recently sat, who had treated him as his honoured guest—would sanction his murder in cold blood.

The count's face was still averted.

He could not speak, but, as a last resource, he threw himself on his knees and raised his hands imploringly.

The count lowered the muzzle of his pistol.

A murmur of disapprobation went through the gang.

"What does that mean?" cried their leader fiercely. "Am I not chief here? By what right do you dispute my will?"

"Our law says ' Death to spies.' Let him die," answered one of the men surlily.

"If I choose to spare this man's life, I am answerable. It is my business."

"And ours also. Our risk is equal with yours, count."

"So be it," said the count.

Again he raised his pistol and pointed it at the head of Edgar Deville.

Edgar firmly believed his last moment had come.

Involuntarily he closed his eyes.

"Wait!" said the count. "I have a plan to propose."

"No—no! Let him die," cried one.

"Why should he be spared ?" said another.

"Death by our laws," muttered a third.

"You speak like fools,' said the count angrily.

To Edgar Deville the agony of suspense was terrible.

He knew not what might be his fate.

The count seemed disposed to spare his life, but the gang of ruffians thirsted for his blood.

Life was dear to him—he never knew how dear till then.

He longed for the power of speech to plead his own cause.

He was prepared to take the most solemn oath never to reveal that which he had seen, but he had not the opportunity to do so.

When next the count spoke, it was in a low calm voice.

"Comrades, I know as well as you do that this spy deserves death at our hands; but, for all that, I propose to spare him."

"No, no!"

"Hear what I have to say."

"Ay, ay, we will hear you, but even you can't talk us out of the rules and laws we have made."

"I don't wish to. The law was made and still holds good. But still there may be occasions in which it is better to depart from it."

"I'm blowed if I can see it."

"In the first place this man was my friend —"

"That's nothing to do with us. It's no business of ours."

"In the second," continued the count, not heeding the interruption, "he has powerful friends and relations, who will move heaven and earth to discover the cause of his disappearance."

"They'll never look *there* for him," said one, with a diabolical grin, pointing down through the gaping trap.

"They will look everywhere," replied the count. "He was known to be staying with me, and how am I to account for his disappearance?"

"There's something in that."

"Suppose we spare his life, what proof have we that he will not betray us?"

Edgar Deville strove to express his determination to reveal nothing of what he had seen and heard.

"I have still more to say," continued the count. "This spy has several high and influential relations, and moves in the best circle of society."

"Well, what then?"

"He may be of great use to us. Should suspicion fall upon us at any time, he might help to divert it. Besides, he could be of the greatest assistance in helping us to dispose of our—our manufactures."

"He wouldn't do it."

"If he refuses he must die."

"What security have we that he will keep faith with us?"

"The best. But let us question him,"

The men murmured, and showed unmistakeable signs of discontent.

The count laid his hand on the handkerchief which bound Edgar Deville's mouth.

At the same time he spoke impressively.

"Remember," said he, "in thus giving you liberty of speech, that a single cry for help, a single attempt at escape, and you die! Remember!"

So saying, he removed the bandage, and Edgar Deville heaved a deep sigh of relief.

"You have heard all that has been said?" asked the count of the young man.

"Yes."

"Are you prepared to take a solemn oath never to reveal to mortal ear what you have seen and heard this night?"

"I am."

"That is well, but it is not all. You must do more than that."

"I will do anything in my power if you will but spare my life," said Edgar.

"Deeds, not words, are what we require. Not only must you swear this, but you must also join us—you must become one of us."

"Become a—a—" stammered Edgar.

"Yes! Become a forger, a coiner, a maker of counterfeit money—whatever you like to call it."

Edgar Deville made no answer.

"No hesitation," said the count sternly, at the same time raising his pistol, "Yes or no! Life or death!"

"Shall I—"

"No questions. Will you join us? Answer, or take the consequences."

"I will join you!"

"That is well."

Turning to the gang standing around, who had not scrupled to show signs of dissatisfaction during this conversation, the count addressed them.

"Now my friends, are you satisfied?"

"No, no!"

"Why not?"

"He will betray us."

"What makes you think so?"

"Because he is forced to join us. He will back out of it as soon as you set him at liberty."

"No!" said Edgar Deville, energetically, "I will never forfeit my word."

"Bravely spoken," said the count approvingly.

"But just to show these gentlemen that you mean what you say, suppose you inspect this pretty little machine."

As the count spoke he rested his hand on a complication of wheels and levers which stood near him.

Almost mechanically Edgar Deville took up his position in the place pointed out by his host of a few hours since.

"You see I have here," said the count, "several medals made of a metal closely resembling silver, but with a perfectly plain surface. I put one into this machine and turn the handle—so. You understand?"

"Yes," said Edgar in a low tone of voice.

"The medal you see falls out here, and has impressed upon one surface a correct image of our most gracious queen, as she appears on the British half-crown. Do you think you could manage to work that machine?"

Edgar made no answer.

"At all events you must try."

Conscious that the least wavering might be his death warrant, Edgar Deville did as he was bid; and, after one or two unsuccessful attempts, succeeded in stamping one of the medals properly.

Then the count bade him insert the base coin into another machine, by which the reverse side was stamped; and then into a third for milling the edges.

All this he did, the gang of coiners gathered round him the while, scowlingly watching every movement he made.

A dozen counterfeit half-crowns were made by Edgar Deville before the count allowed him a minute's rest.

"That will do for the present," said he, as Edgar turned out his twelfth base coin.

Then turning to his gang, he spoke to them.

"This worthy young man you now see is completely one of us. Now if he betrays you he betrays himself, for he has made false coin of his own free will, and is as much a coiner as any one of you. Are you satisfied?"

The answers were divided, some not thinking the test sufficient.

"One thing more you must do," said the count, turning again to Edgar.

"What is that?"

"Those packets you see yonder are all base coin or forged notes, and are about to be sent to our country agents. Yonder is a pen and ink. You must direct them."

The consciousness of being powerless made Edgar Deville do as he was bid.

"In your usual handwriting, if you please," added the count. "If you try to disguise it, it may cost you your life."

At the count's dictation Edgar wrote the directions.

"Now, comrades, you must surely be satisfied. We have his writing as witness against him. What more do you want?"

"Nothing—nothing."

"That is well. Welcome him amongst you as your companion. Take care of him, and instruct him in his work."

So saying, the count quitted the room, leaving Edgar Deville to the mercies of the ruffians who had thirsted for his blood.

It was not till the trap in the centre of the room had been closed and bolted that Edgar felt really safe.

When that was done he heaved a deep sigh of relief at his unexpected escape from the very jaws of death.

But at what a cost had his life been purchased!

Not only had he become a criminal in the eyes of the law, but he had put himself completely in the power of a gang of ruffians, who would not scruple to use any means of quieting him, should he in any way make himself dangerous or disagreeable to them.

For several hours Edgar Deville was kept hard at work.

It was the first time in his life that he had ever exerted himself except for his own amusement.

But now it was real hard work which fell to his lot.

Work from which there was no flinching.

Work which there was no shirking.

As nearly as he could calculate it must have been near daylight when one of the men, whose dress bore some resemblance to that of a methodist parson, and who was called Abel Booth by the others, and appeared to be a sort of foreman or overseer, gave a signal to discontinue work.

In a very few minutes the machine became quiet.

The counterfeit coin was carried away carefully to another room.

Then the gang of coiners passed one by one from the apartment, till at last but one other besides Edgar Deville remained in it.

With a loud clang, the iron plated door was closed and the key turned in the lock.

Edgar and the other one were prisoners.

The man who had been chosen to share Edgar's captivity was past the middle age, and appeared to be of a sullen and morose disposition.

No sooner was the door fastened than he laid himself down upon the floor, and, curling round dormouse-like, closed his eyes as if for sleep.

But Edgar would not allow him to remain unquestioned.

His curiosity, which had led him into his present position, and had nearly cost him his life, was not yet satisfied.

"Are we prisoners ?" he asked.

"It looks like it, don't it ?" rejoined the other surlily. "You may get out if you can."

"How long are we to remain here ?"

"Till we are let out."

"When will that be ?"

"When the count pleases."

"But we shall be starved."

"Not a bit of it. We shall have plenty to eat."

"What are you here for ? To guard me ?"

"Not a bit of it. The bolts and bars will keep you much securer than I could."

"Then you are a prisoner too ?"

"Hang it all. Can't you see that ? What's the good of questioning me ? Here have I been this ever so long beating against those infernal bars—plotting, planning, scheming, but all to no purpose."

"Then you're not one of the gang ?"

"Yes I am."

"Then how is it —"

"Now look here, I'm a-going to sleep, and ain't going to answer any more questions ; so you may just as well shut up."

"But just tell me one thing."

"I won't. I'm blessed if I will."

"This Count Lerno—is he a friend of yours ?"

The question seemed to rouse the man into a perfect frenzy.

"A friend ! A friend of mine ! He's ruined me ; he's shot at me ; I carry a bullet in my leg now fired by his direction ; he has pulled me from my home ; he has insulted my daughter. Curses light upon him ! My *friend* ! Ha, ha !"

"Who are you then ? What is your name ?"

"What does that matter ?"

"What shall I call you ?"

"Call me *Hugh Mortimer !*"

Though Edgar asked other questions, he received no answer to them.

His fellow-prisoner was, or pretended to be, fast asleep.

Edgar Deville strove to follow his example.

He whose limbs had never hitherto pressed aught but the softest linen lay down upon the bare boards, cold, tired, and disheartened, to seek repose.

But slumber would not come to his relief.

He could not obtain a short oblivion of his woes in sleep.

As he lay upon the floor that which he had done came upon him with full force.

He saw nothing but a wretched criminal life before him.

He was so completely mixed up with a gang of ruffians as to be inseparable from them.

His prospects in life were blighted.

He was altogether in the power of a set of unscrupulous men, who could and would force him to the commission of deeds from the bare thought of which he shrank in horror.

He who had ever associated with ladies and gentlemen, and had moved in the best society, was now leagued with a band of low, desperate, illiterate, ruffianly forgers.

How could he ever face the world again ?

Would not the knowledge of what he really was press him down like a dead weight ?

With such thoughts as these crowding through his mind, he fell into a restless and uneasy slumber upon the hard floor of the mysterious chamber.

CHAPTER XI.

THE GHOSTLY CHAMBER—THE APPARITION—THE UPLIFTED DAGGER—ANOTHER CHANCE OF ESCAPE—LIBERTY—TAUNTS AND SNEERS—HOMELESS, PENNILESS, AND FRIENDLESS—AARON HEINE THE JEW—MIRIAM—THE FLOGGING IN THE ATTIC.

When poor Rose found herself once more in her enemy's clutches she felt her heart sink within her.

All life and energy seemed to die out of her frame.

The excitement of her attempted escape had buoyed her up for a while, but when alone in the solitude of the dreary room a reaction took place.

She could not weep.

It was with a hard stony glance she seated herself.

Her eyes fixed, her limbs powerless, she fell into a species of trance.

It was a strange old-fashioned bedroom in which she was.

All in it was dark and dismal.

In one corner stood a large bedstead of carved oak, hung with heavy tapestry, and surmounted by plumes of feathers, which completed its resemblance to a hearse.

Some worn and tattered tapestry hung on one portion of the wall, but the greater part was panelled with the same dark, almost black, wood of which the bed was made.

So much Rose saw by the pale moonlight, but the parts of the room away from the windows were buried in such gloom that her eyes could not pierce it.

All energy had left her.

Even the wish to escape was fainter. Not that she was now reconciled to the terrible fate Count Lerno designed for her, but simply because life and energy had left her.

Worn out, fatigued, tired, and almost heart-broken, she threw herself upon the bed and strove to sleep.

Tired as she was, she could not keep her eyes shut.

A strange fascination compelled her to watch the light thrown upon the chamber by the moon.

From this light her excited imagination formed many gaunt and fanciful designs.

Sometimes to her heated brain it appeared as if a troop of ghosts came sweeping towards her.

It was in vain she told herself it was but fancy.

The illusion had taken such a deep hold of her mind that she could not bear to look in that direction.

For relief she fixed her eyes upon the darkest corner of the room, steadfastly turning her gaze from the window.

Was it still fancy?

Surely in the pitchy blackness, where no ray of moonlight penetrated, she saw something white fluttering to and fro.

Sometimes it seemed nearer to her, sometimes farther off, but still always present.

Intently she watched it.

With a horrid dread she waited to see it take some definite form.

With rivetted gaze, distended eyes, and powerless limbs she saw the white something take the form of a tall woman.

Yet not the form of a woman of flesh and blood, but a horrifying semi-transparent luminous shadow, which noiselessly flitted hither and thither.

Rose uttered a faint cry of terror as this sight met her gaze.

It was too dreadful.

She shuddered and turned away her head.

When next she ventured to look the apparition had drawn nearer to her.

Nearer and nearer it came, with silent gliding motion.

As it crossed the stream of moonlight which came in through the window Rose saw its face.

A hollow cadaverous face, with eyes so deeply sunk as to be wholly in shade.

Twice the figure threw its arms up wildly over its head, uttering a moaning cry.

The second time it did so Rose saw that in one hand it brandished a long dagger.

She had not strength to rise and fly from the approach of the ghostly being.

It drew nearer and nearer.

Every minute brought it closer to the bed.

Rose could not move.

She felt as if paralysed in every limb.

Her tongue clove to the roof of her mouth.

Her heart almost ceased to beat.

Yet she could not move her eyes from that which was approaching her.

On, still on, it glided, till it stood by the bedside!

It stretched forth an arm, and laid an icy hand, a cold, clammy, deathlike hand, on Rose's bare shoulder.

With the other hand it raised on high the glittering dagger, and again uttered the moaning cry,

It was more than Rose in her feeble state could brave.

With a faint cry she fell back fainting upon the pillow.

A stouter heart than hers might have quailed at such an apparition. No wonder that her poor feeble frame gave way beneath the shock.

It was a swoon like unto death into which she fell.

How long she remained unconscious she never knew, but after a time she opened her eyes.

With fear and trembling she looked around, dreading that the dreadful thing might still be at her side.

She saw it not.

Gathering courage, she looked in every direction.

It had gone!

As far as the darkness would permit her to ascertain, she was alone in that haunted chamber.

With faltering steps she walked across the room.

Then she saw a sight which filled her with as much joy as the other had with horror.

The door, which she had seen shut, and had heard locked, now stood open.

Without pausing to think concerning the strangeness of the alteration, she planned an idea of escape.

Could she but find her way to the street door, and open it without noise, she might again be free.

The thought of liberty—of escape from her dreadful fate—gave her fresh courage and strength.

She listened, but not a sound fell on her ear to tell that any one was in the house.

Then, cautiously and timorously, she ventured out into the dark passage.

Dreading the slightest sound, she crept along with fearful steps till she reached the staircase.

Down, down she went, stopping every minute, scarcely daring to breathe, for fear that she might be discovered.

At length she reached a long passage in which a lamp burnt feebly.

In an instant she recognised it.

It was the one through which she had run when attempting the escape which so nearly ended in the loss of her life.

She followed the whole length of the passage, and then to her joy reached the door, now securely bolted, which led into the street.

Her fingers trembled so that she could hardly pull back the fastenings, but after some little time she succeeded in doing so without the least noise.

In another moment she stood in the street—once again at liberty!

It seemed too good to be true.

She could hardly believe fortune had so far favoured her as to let her escape a second time from the clutches of Count Lerno.

Yet so it was.

Undiscovered she had passed through the house, had let herself out, and now stood in the public thoroughfare.

Then for the first time she remembered that she still wore her theatrical costume, and that to walk as she was through the streets was an impossibility.

Keeping as much as possible in the shade, and shrinking away whenever she heard the sound of approaching footsteps, she reached at last a leading thoroughfare.

Hailing the first cab she saw, she entered it without having attracted any attention by the singularity of her dress.

She told the driver to take her to the Babylonian Theatre.

He stared hard at her, and then mounted his box and started for Hardress-street.

When Rose told him to drive to the theatre she had not bestowed a thought upon the lateness of the hour.

The theatres had been long closed, but it happened that at the Royal Babylonian that night there had been an accident to one of the principal scenes, which made it necessary for men to work at it throughout the night, in order that it might be ready for the next representation of the pantomime.

As it happened, Mr. Flathers had stopped to superintend the repairs, and he it was with whom Rose found herself face to face as she entered the stage door in Hardress-street.

"Hullo!" cried Mr. Flathers, who, as may readily be imagined, was not in the best of tempers, "here's a pretty time to turn up, confound you!"

"Indeed, sir, I couldn't help it. I have——"

"There, there—none of your lies for me. Be off with you. Don't let me ever see your face again, that's all."

"Oh, sir, you won't deprive a poor girl of her

living? I really could not help it. If you will only hear me——"

"I won't hear you. Be off, or I'll give you in charge. Gallivanting about the streets in my ballet-dress, hang you. Off with it. Get your own rags, and hook it!"

The tears welled up in Rose's eyes.

"None of your infernal caterwauling. If I find you here in five minutes' time I'll give you something to caterwaul for. Remember *that*, you prowling thieving good-for-nothing baggage."

Speaking these last words in a brutal tone, and muttering still severer and harder names between his teeth, he turned away and left her to seek her proper garments.

Sadly she donned the clothes in which, only two nights before, she had entered the theatre so gay, buoyant, and happy.

Now she was cast adrift.

A waif upon the wide world.

A human being without a friend to help her, for how could she account to Mrs. Halliday for her absence?

Would she believe the story she had to tell?

Again entering the cab, she told the man to drive to Mrs. Halliday's house.

She was evidently not expected there.

There was not a light in any of the windows.

She got out of the cab and knocked.

For a long time no attention was paid to the summons.

At length the door opened as far as the chain would allow, and Mrs. Halliday's head, surmounted by a nightcap, appeared.

"Won't you let me in, Mrs. Halliday," asked Rose.

"No."

She answered her sharply, and with determination.

"Oh! what have I done? Tell me how I have offended you."

"I won't have any such goings on in *my* house," said Mrs. Halliday. "You've brought it all on by your own unrespectable conduct."

This was more than Rose could bear.

This insult, added to all she had gone through that night, made life almost insupportable.

She would have answered the old lady, but the door was violently slammed to, and Rose was standing on the pavement houseless, friendless, penniless.

"P'raps, if you don't want to go no furder, miss, you'll pay me my fare."

"I have no money," said Rose.

"Oh, gammon! Come, none of that game."

"Indeed I have nothing."

"Well, look here: you've got a ring, or a watch, or something."

Rose had in truth a small locket, which she had always guarded with the most jealous care, and ever hid from her father's eyes.

It had been her mother's.

Now there was no help for it.

Money she must have, and in no other way than by the sale of the trinket could she obtain it.

"You'll excuse me, miss, but a highly respectable friend of mine who lives close by would I'm sure give you a good price for anything you wished to sell."

"Take me to him," said Rose.

"His name is Aaron Heine, miss, and he's got a daughter called Miriam, or some such outlandish thing, but he's very respectable," said the cabman.

Though Aaron Heine, the Jew, might have been respectable, it was a queer neighbourhood in which he had chosen to pitch his tent.

It was in one of the narrow muddy waterside lanes near Westminster that Aaron Heine kept what is called a "leaving shop."

Rose shrank from entering the dark close-smelling shop, but the cabman urged her forwards.

She was without money, and until she could satisfy the man's claim she was in his power.

An old man came from the back of the shop as Rose entered, bringing with him a powerful odour of new rum and stale tobacco.

"What can I do for you, my dear?" he asked of poor Rose, eyeing her with a disgusting leer as he spoke.

Tremblingly the poor girl produced the locket.

In faltering accents she offered it for sale.

The locket was of some value, being of gold, set with pearls.

The old Jew scrutinised it earnestly.

"Come in here," said he to Rose, pointing to the back shop, "come in here, while I examine it closer."

She hesitated, but no other course seemed open to her than to obey him.

"Now," said he, closing the door after she had entered, "now you had better confess at once. Whose is this locket?"

"Mine," Rose answered indignantly, for there was that in Aaron Heine's tone she did not like.

"Do you suppose I stole it?"

The Jew chuckled cunningly at her answer.

"I'm sure you did."

Rose staggered back.

Was it not enough that she should be tormented as she had been, without the taunts and insults of Mr. Flathers, Mrs. Halliday, and Aaron Heine?

She held out her hands imploringly and strove to speak, but her tongue refused to utter the words, and she fell forward in a fainting fit, brought on by fatigue, excitement, and want of nourishment.

When she came to her senses she was lying on a mattress in a small low-ceilinged attic.

Watching over her was a girl of about her own age—a beautiful fair Jewess.

She was beautiful in the extreme, but her clothes hung in rags about her, and her face bore the signs of pain and suffering.

"Who are you? Where am I?" cried Rose, starting up.

"I am Miriam Heine. You are in my father, Aaron Heine's, house," said the girl, in sad melancholy tones.

Rose shuddered, for the impression she had of the old Jew was far from favourable.

"Why am I brought here?" asked Rose.

"Heaven knows! If it be for that which I dread, it had been better for you that you had died than lived for such a life."

"Speak! Tell me what you mean?"

"I cannot. They would force a hateful life upon me, and I resist. See," said the Jewess, baring her shoulders.

Rose shuddered, for upon the girl's flesh were long red cuts in every direction, evidently produced by a heavy whip.

"Some hag who possesses an influence over my father does this every day," said Miriam. "Tied to the wall, I am kept powerless, while she flogs me with all her strength."

"Oh, it is horrible—too horrible!" said Rose, shutting her eyes.

The Jewess only sighed.

What new perils was Rose about to encounter?

She hardly dared think of what might be her fate in the hands of her new jailor.

For a few moments the two girls remained perfectly silent, each considering the other's face with deep attention.

Rose was the first to speak.

"I do not know as yet that I am really a prisoner."

"You do not know?" repeated the Jewess, interrogatively.

"No. Is the door locked?"

"The door was locked, but the key was outside. I stole upstairs while father was away, to have a look at you."

"As it is open now, and he away, why should I not escape?"

"Escape?"

"Yes. I have lately suffered so much, passed through so many dangers and perils, that I have become quite brave."

"But—but where would you fly?"

"Where?"

"Yes. Where would you be safe from him?"

"My dear girl, I do not understand you. Of course I should be safe anywhere if I got out of the house."

"Anywhere?"

"Yes. I should only have to appeal to the police."

"Would they protect you?"

"Of course. The law allows no one to be oppressed."

"Does it not?"

"No, nor you among the rest."

"Oh, if I could believe you!" cried the Jewess, clasping her hands, the tears as she spoke welling up into her beautiful blue eyes.

"You can believe me, for I speak the truth."

"And would you, is it possible that you would kindly aid me also?"

"To escape?"

"Yes."

"Willingly."

"When?"

"Why not at once, as your father is out?"

"Why not at once?" repeated the Jewess musing. "Suppose we try? But stay, the old woman is down stairs. I must make sure that she is asleep. She generally takes a nap about this time."

"Go and see, but do not be long. I shall be dying with impatience until you return."

Rose gently squeezed her new friend's hand as they parted, and the beautiful young Jewess stole on tip-toe towards the door.

Noiselessly she opened it and closed it again.

Rose listened intently.

A moment afterwards she heard a suppressed scream.

Then the sound of a scuffle. Then low sobbing and more scuffling.

Then the banging of a door on the same landing.

Holding her breath, and trembling with fear, Rose still listened.

CHAPTER XII.

THE MYSTERIOUS DEPARTURE—THE DEATHLIKE SILENCE—THE DOUBLE DOORS—THE OLD HAG AND HER VICTIM—MIRIAM FLOGGED TO DEATH —THE MURDER—THE GRAVE—A MOMENT OF TERROR.

For a few moments there was a deathlike silence, unbroken by the faintest movement within the house.

Rose, in indescribable alarm, remained in the sitting posture in which the young Jewess had left her, wondering what had happened.

One thing it was easy enough to suppose must have taken place.

She had been discovered coming out of the room by some one in the house.

The question was, Had the conversation that had taken place between her and Miriam been overheard?

If it had, any hope of escape was for the time being gone.

But the silence still continued.

What did it mean?

As minute after minute passed away, and still no sound reached her ears, Rose grew more and more terrified.

The unknown cruelty, if any were being perpetrated upon the young Jewess, seemed by its perpetration in this deathlike silence to become ten times more horrible.

Much more terrible was this dreadful uncertainty than it would have been had the victim's cries been heard—

Had her shrieks of agony rent the air—

Had the heavy thuds of the cruel whip been audible as they fell upon the palpitating flesh.

But the time passed slowly, and yet no sound reached the anxious listener.

At length she could bear this state of suspense no longer.

"Gracious Heaven!" she exclaimed, "what horrors are being perpetrated?"

She felt that, though curiosity should cost her her life, she must know what had happened.

Yes, she would learn the truth, however great might be the danger she would find in her path.

With this intention she prepared to rise.

But she was faint and weak.

With the greatest difficulty she managed to gain her feet.

But her frame reeled and she staggered forward.

Had she not clung to the wall for support she must have fallen headlong to the ground.

To some extent, however, conquering her weakness, and guiding herself by the wall, she slowly and laboriously moved to the door.

She tried the handle. It turned. The door yielded to a gentle pressure.

Without was pitchy darkness.

Rose, however, still guided herself by the wall, and slowly progressed with tottering footsteps.

All was yet silent.

As yet she had made no discovery.

Presently, however, her hand rested upon the handle of a door.

She turned it and the door opened.

But all was dark within.

Dark as a pool.

Closing the door again gently, she continued her journey.

She felt all round the wall.

She reached another wall running at right angles. That was the end of the passage.

She came to another wall again. She was now on the opposite side of the passage.

She still journeyed wearily along, but found no other doors.

While thus engaged, the moon, which hitherto had been obscured, shone brightly forth, and its rays penetrated between the bars of a small grating, serving as a window, and fixed high up against the ceiling.

Its light revealed to her the topography of the place in which she found herself.

There were only two doors.

One led into the attic wherein she had been a prisoner, the other was the one that she had just now opened.

It was this she must have heard slammed to.

There could be no doubt of that. But what was the mystery connected with the darkness within?

Urged on by a devouring curiosity respecting the fate of the beautiful young Jewess, she summoned up all her strength, crossed the passage without support, and approached the door in question.

Again she opened it.

Again she found all pitchy dark within.

But the moon assisting her at the moment, she

found that there was another partition between her and the room—a green baize door.

Advancing, the outer portal closed upon her, and she was, for an instant, as it were, imprisoned as though in a sepulchre.

But feeling cautiously over the surface before her, she presently found a handle and turned it gently.

Scarcely had she opened the door the tenth part of an inch when a piercing shriek met her ear coming from the room within !

It was a shriek of mingled pain and terror.

A shriek, wrung by fiendish cruelty from some suffering victim.

"Oh mercy ! mercy ! ' she heard the young Jewess exclaim. " For Heaven's sake spare me !"

" Spare you, indeed !" cried a hard voice in reply. " I'd cut you all to bits if I had my way."

"Oh mercy ! mercy !"

"I'd cut your lying tongue out, too, that you could'nt tell what I'd done."

"Oh, no, dear Mrs. Starke, you would not be so cruel."

" Don't dear me, you deceitful minx. There's no love lost between us, you know that well enough."

" But what have I done to you ?"

" What have you done ? Well, I like that !"

" I am sure I never meant to harm you."

" Did'nt you ? Well, you harm me by living at all —by ever having been born."

"Oh dear, oh dear, I wish I was dead !"

" Do you ? You should have your wish, too, if it depended on me, young lady."

" But you would not kill me ?"

"There's nothing half bad enough for you in my opinion ; but I don't want to commit murder. No, you're safe enough as far as I am concerned in that respect."

" But you are killing me by these cruel floggings."

" Oh, no, I'm not. At least it's a very slow job. Why don't you die naturally ? That's what I want to know. Why don't you die of cold and want ? Why don't you catch something ? You shall catch a good whipping this time at any rate."

" Oh, no, no ! Do not beat me this once !"

" Yes I shall. You brought it on yourself."

" But I meant no harm."

" You knew you were not to go into the next room."

" You did not tell me."

" You knew you were not to go, without being told."

" Oh, no, indeed !"

" Don't tell me a lie. Take that."

Then followed the sound of a blow.

Then there was a scream and a groan.

Then another blow.

Another scream.

More blows followed with greater rapidity. More screams, still shriller and more piercing.

Unable to bear the suspense any longer, Rose pushed open the door and looked into the room.

A horrible sight met her eyes.

She sickened with terror.

Naked to her waist, the lovely young Jewess was fastened up against the wall.

A hideous old hag was flogging her with savage ferocity.

The unhappy victim's body was covered with the bruises of bygone atrocities.

The blood trickled from fresh wounds.

Twisting and shrinking, she endeavoured to escape from the horrible old wretch's cruel blows.

But she struggled in vain.

Again and again the blows descended.

The poor girl panted for breath.

The colour forsook her cheeks.

Her eyes glazed.

Her bosom rose and fell convulsively. Then she was still as death.

The nerves in her body seemed suddenly to relax.

Her limbs gave way beneath her.

She hung like a corpse, still and motionless.

Only then did the fiend abstain from her cruelty.

She stood still at last, and allowed her hand to fall by her side.

" Have you had enough ?" she asked fiercely.

But the young Jewess made no reply,

" Have you had enough ?" screamed the hag.

Still no answer.

" Will you disobey me again ? Do you hear ? You had better speak."

But it was in vain that she thus questioned her victim.

Her power of speech was gone.

Was she dead ?

This was the question the old woman now asked herself in trembling terror.

The ominous silence alarmed her.

She had gone too far this time.

What was to be done.

She approached the young Jewess and regarded her with nervous trepidation.

In a flutter of fright she then loosened her hands and let her gently down.

She laid her upon the floor, and stood for a moment silently regarding her.

The poor girl, however, moved not a muscle.

" What is the matter with her, I wonder," the old woman muttered. " I—I hope I haven't gone too far."

She stooped down, as she spoke, by the side of her victim, and laid her hand upon the poor girl's heart.

In this attitude she remained for several moments, a grey shadow creeping the while over her evil face.

" I—I've done it," she said at last, with a gasp.

Then rose to her feet with a spring.

" I've killed her !"

The words were uttered in a hoarse whisper which thrilled through the room.

Poor Rose's blood froze in her veins with terror.

She could not, however, have torn herself away from the spot had her life depended upon her so doing.

Something stronger than her will seemed to hold her there.

She was fascinated with horror.

Spell-bound—transfixed.

With greedy eyes Rose watched the movements of the old hag.

She was gazing eagerly around, as though in search of something.

Rising to her feet, she carried a candle in her hand, and by its light made a tour of the room.

She closely inspected the floor, missing scarcely an inch in her scrutiny.

All at once she paused, and uttered a low exclamation.

Then with her hands began scratching at the floor.

Rose looked on eagerly.

The old hag presently got her finger ends down between the boards.

She raised a plank slowly, laid it on one side, and after a slight pause lifted out another.

She now disclosed to Rose's view an aperture about a foot and a half wide and six feet long.

It looked like a grave.

Raising the inanimate form of the beautiful young Jewess in her arms, she carried it to the place.

Then lowered it noiselessly into the chasm.

Rose's heart beat violently.

" She had killed her, then," she thought.

The body of the girl thus disposed of, the old hag very carefully replaced the planks.

["HELP! HELP!" SHRIEKED THE TERRIFIED BALLET-GIRL.]

Fetching a broken piece of iron from the fireplace, she with its aid knocked in the nails again.

The old wretch paused for a moment, and raising the candle above her head, shaded her eyes, and scanned the floor around.

There were the stains of blood upon one of the boards, and these she shuffled out with her feet.

Then she cautiously hid the instrument of torture up the chimney and glanced round again.

There was now nothing in the appearance of the room to lead a casual observer to suppose that so dreadful a deed had been committed in it.

The evidences of her crime had disappeared.

For a time, at least, she was safe.

No. 5.

But for how long?

As she stood now the candle-light fell full upon her evil face, and Rose thought she never yet seen so forbidding a countenance.

Her eyes were bloodshot, and peered out from beneath bushy grey eyebrows, rough and ragged.

Her mouth was like a split in her face, from which protruded two great teeth, more like those of some wild animal than a human being.

Her frame was tall and muscular, and Rose could easily understand that the unhappy Miriam had struggled vainly to resist her murderous attacks.

"And I, too," Rose could not help thinking, "shall I also fall a victim to her brutality?"

As the dreadful idea passed through our heroine's mind the old hag gave one last glance round the room, and approached the door.

For the first time did Rose begin to reflect upon the danger she was running.

How many women since the world began have paid a heavy penalty for their curiosity !

Had her turn come now ?

As the old woman approached the door, Rose felt behind her for the door handle.

She allowed the green baize door to close in front of her, and was now in total darkness.

There was not a moment to lose, and yet, for the life of her, she could not find any fastening upon the inside of the door, which shut her out from the passage.

In scrambling terror she searched for it.

But her search was fruitless.

Great Heaven, what would become of her ?

The old hag's steps approached.

In another moment poor Rose would be discovered.

Wildly she pressed her hands over the surface of the door.

She flung herself against it with all her strength, but it yielded not an inch.

Again and again.

And now the horror of the situation reached its climax.

The door in front of her opened slowly.

She was face to face with the murdress.

Face to face with the fiendish old hag, who glared at her from beneath her beetling brow.

Face to face, though but for one brief moment.

Then the old woman, uttering a dismal howl, flung up her long arms, and fell back senseless upon the floor.

Using all the strength which yet remained to her, Rose dashed herself against the close portal.

It gave way with a crash.

She flew on with lightning speed.

She reached she staircase and bounded down the stairs.

But suddenly a heavy hand was laid upon her shoulder.

She shrieked and struggled to free herself.

But her unseen assailant still held her fast.

Then a deadly faintness crept over her, and the unhappy girl swooned with weakness and terror.

CHAPTER XIII.

MORE MYSTERIES—ROSE'S ADVENTURES IN THE OLD JEW'S HOUSE—THE DEAD BROUGHT BACK TO LIFE.

Upon this dreadful scene there came a long interval of unconsciousness.

A long deathlike sleep, as it seemed to Rose, of the duration of which she could form no idea.

Life was for a time a blank to her.

She awoke at length to find herself lying in bed, in a gloomy but not uncomfortable room, and came to the conclusion, when at length she recovered to some extent her scattered thoughts, that she had been very ill.

At first when she opened her eyes the recollection of the scene of terror through which she had passed when last she was conscious returned to her, and she glanced around in terror, expecting to find herself in the power of the old hag.

With the idea of escape still predominating over all other thoughts she endeavoured to rise.

But she found that this was impossible.

With a deep sigh she sank back on h closed her eyes again.

When she again opened them she found woman standing by the bedside.

She started back with a shudder, for she far first that it was the old hag.

But a second glance convinced her that mistaken.

And yet there certainly was a strong likenes How could it be accounted for ?

Rose asked herself the question in wo astonishment.

There were certainly the features, or features resembling them, but the expression was same.

No, the expression of this woman was eve and gentle.

" Well, my dear," she said in a low soft to That was certainly not the old hag's voice.

" How are you now ?"

" Thank you," replied Rose, " I am much But pray tell me, where am I ?"

" Do not be alarmed on that score, my dear

" No—but—"

" But are you very anxious to know ?"

" Indeed I am. I cannot rest until I le truth."

" Well then, bless your pretty face, so you sl

" Thank you."

" All in good time."

Rose looked rather disappointed.

" Yes, dear, all in good time. In the meantin tell you one thing."

" What is that ?"

" That you are amongst friends."

With this assurance Rose was, for the obliged to remain satisfied.

But it was impossible to rest so long as she re in doubt.

Therefore, when she saw the opportunity, sh endeavoured to draw her companion into conve

" Would you kindly answer me one question asked.

" That all depends, my love, what the questi

" When I fainted away I was in an old Jew's

" Hush, my dear, so you are now."

Rose's heart sank within her.

And yet when she thought the matter o could not believe it possible that this could be of assassins into which she had fallen when end ing to dispose of her locket.

" But—but," she stammered, " where is Mi

" Miriam," replied the woman, " is upstai you shall see her presently."

Rose shut her eyes with a shudder.

Meanwhile the old woman busied herself ab room, noiselessly arranging the furniture.

As Rose looked at her stealthily from time she could not help thinking that she must hav mistaken in her identity. How was it to be acc for ?

The face of the old hag whom she had s brutally ill-treating the lovely young Jewe certainly distorted by passion, but not so as to unrecognisable.

Really it seemed impossible to suppose th could be so changed, and yet there could be no about the fact that she did slightly resemble her

Could she be her sister ?

But this was not the only question which our heroine.

What did the woman mean when she sp Miriam ?

Was not the young Jewess dead ?

Had not Rose with her own eyes seen her fou cruelly butchered ?

She should see her presently the woman said.

Where?

In her grave.

But that would seem as though her hosts intended to murder her, and that was not possible.

No, if that had been their intention they would not be nursing her in this way.

No, they would have let her die, unless they wished to reserve her for some worse fate.

Rose presently summoned up courage to inquire after the old woman.

Her companion seemed not to understand her.

"What old woman?" she asked.

"I—I thought," stammered Rose.

She was going to say what she knew of her, but stopped herself very suddenly.

"You thought what, my dear?"

"I thought—that is, I fancied—"

"Yes. You fancied—"

"At least, I mean Miriam told me—"

"What?"

"That there was an old woman, who—who—"

"Who what?"

"Who lived in her father's house."

Rose's companion had been staring at her fixedly whilst she was thus stammering out a very lame explanation.

When she concluded the old woman's eyes dropped, and Rose could not help fancying that a sinister smile for one moment crossed her face like a shadow and was instantly gone.

The conversation ceased here for a time, and our heroine was left to her thoughts, which were anything but satisfactory.

Indeed, the more she pondered on what little the old woman had told her the less she liked the look of things.

It was altogether very extraordinary and mysterious; but more mysteries were yet to come.

Later in the day the master of the house made his appearance.

Rose started up in bed at sight of him, and her heart throbbed violently.

There was no mistake in his case.

It was the old Jew, Aaron Heine, who had accused her of theft.

But in him, also, there was a great change.

His manner now was mild and gentle.

"How is our patient?" he said, approaching her and smiling blandly.

"A little feverish yet," replied the woman, "but rapidly improving."

"That's right, my dear," said the Jew. "You must get well as soon as ever you can, and we will see if we can't make your fortune."

Make her fortune!

Rose pondered on his strange words uneasily.

But a greater surprise than ever yet awaited her.

The door opened, and Miriam entered.

She was neatly—indeed, prettily dressed.

She was radiant with smiles, and looked the picture of happiness.

She came straight towards the bedside, and, seating herself upon a chair, took Rose's hand in hers.

The eyes of the two girls met in a long earnest gaze, but Rose, in silent astonishment, saw that Miriam showed not the faintest sign of recognition.

Could it be possible that this was the same Miriam whom she had seen so cruelly ill-treated—whom she had seen buried beneath the boards of the attic where the brutal outrage was perpetrated?

As well as she was able to do so without attracting the notice of the other two people in the room, Rose ventured upon some dim allusions to the dreadful scene of which she had been a witness.

But Miriam did not respond—indeed, did not appear to understand what she was talking about.

Wearied and worn out by all this mystery, poor Rose, with a deep sigh, abandoned any further efforts to solve it.

She, therefore, at the woman's suggestion, closed her eyes again and went to sleep.

Next day she was much better, and felt much stronger when she awoke.

She expressed a desire to get up for a short time, and the woman assisted her to rise.

After this she sat in a comfortable armchair by the fireside, and amused herself by reading some novels, of which there were several lying about the room.

The next day passed in much the same fashion, enlivened by conversations with Aaron Heine, the woman (whose name was, as she found out, Mrs. Woodruff), and Miriam, though of the latter she saw but very little.

The next day and the next passed away.

Rose was quite well now, and growing more curious than ever.

Why was she kept there, and thus hospitably treated?

For the life of her, although she puzzled her pretty head a great deal upon the subject, she could find no reasonable solution of the enigma.

Still there was a reason.

Alas! too soon would she learn the dreadful truth! Too soon, and yet too late.

After Rose had been convalescent about a week, she was invited downstairs to a little sitting-room by Mr. Heine, who wanted to speak to her.

She found him seated at a table, about which were littered a quantity of papers.

He was writing as she entered the apartment, and called to her without looking up.

"Well, my dear, and how are you to-day?"

"I am quite well, sir, thank you," answered Rose.

"Quite well, eh? That's right. We must not waste all our youth and roses in a sick room, eh, my dear?"

"No, sir, I hope not."

"Oh, you hope not? You are not without ambition, eh?"

"I should very much like to get on, sir, in the profession I have chosen."

"The theatrical profession, eh? The ballet you tried I think?"

"Yes, sir. I did not wish to be in the ballet at first, but I could not obtain—"

"Another opening, eh? You did well to choose that. You chose what you could excel in."

"Oh, sir," said Rose, blushing, "I am not sure of that. But if I only had a chance—"

"From what little you did, though, I could see very well that you had enormous talent, Miss Rose."

"Did you see me, sir?"

"Of course, I did. You were the—the—what is it?"

Rose named the character she had personified.

"Oh, to be sure—to be sure. I forgot at the moment. Very clever it was too."

"I am delighted to hear you say so, sir. I was a little nervous, as it was my first appearance."

"Your first appearance! Impossible! Bless me. I shouldn't have believed it from any other lips. Ah! you must not be hidden under a bushel any longer, that's certain."

"Do you think then, sir, that there is any chance?"

"I'm sure there is. That's what I've got to say to you. There is a wonderful chance—such a one as does not fall out once in a hundred years."

"Oh! sir."

"What do you say, then?"

"To what, sir?"

"To take an engagement."

"I should be only too delighted, sir, of course."

"Of course, and so you shall. I expect one of the managers here to-day."

"To-day?"

"Yes; in an hour or so. You shall be introduced to him."

"Oh, how can I thank you, sir?"

"Don't do it at all, my dear. There's no occasion."

"How can I ever repay you?"

"I shall take care you never do, Rose, my dear. Good bye for the present. I will call you when I want you."

Rose would have liked very much to make some inquiries, but Mr. Heine did not give her the opportunity.

"I have got some letters to write. Good bye—good bye. Come down when I send for you."

She of course felt extremely curious respecting the promised engagement. How could it be otherwise?

She wanted very much to know what theatre it could be at, and which of the managers it was who was coming to call upon her generous host.

All these particulars, however, she was compelled to wait patiently for.

In about an hour after she had spoken to Aaron Heine the bell rang, and Mrs. Woodruffe told her to go downstairs again.

She found a stranger in the room with the Jew.

Yes, he was a stranger to Rose, although she fancied that she knew most of the London managers by sight, as from her childhood she had been a regular attendant at the theatres, and had often seen them summoned before the curtain, besides having seen several during the last few weeks, whilst making her daily applications for an interview at the various stage doors.

This particular manager, however, was certainly unknown to her, and, moreover, was not at all the sort of person Rose would have fancied likely to occupy such a position.

He was very young.

He could not have been much more than nineteen or twenty, at the utmost.

There were no signs of whiskers on his cheeks. He rejoiced in two or three straggling hairs on his upper lip, but that was all.

He was extremely pale. His hair was straw-coloured. He had no eyelashes at all, and no eyebrows to speak of.

His eyelids were red and swollen, and his eyes weak.

His cheeks were hollow, and he spoke in a faint voice, at times scarcely audible.

He swore fearfully. He was showily dressed, and his clothes was reeking of stale tobacco.

He carried a riding whip, and wore spurs.

"Ah, my dear," said the Jew, looking up, "here he is. Here's my manager."

Rose bowed, and the manager nodded.

"There's the young lady, Tom, that I was talking to you about."

"Proud of the honour," said Tom.

"She'll make your fortune, sir, and her own too; mark my words if she don't."

"I hope so, sir. Ballet you said, didn't you?"

"Yes, to be sure. The ballet. You've got a vacancy you say?"

"Oh, yes; certainly."

"Miss Mortimer will fill it then, sir, with credit."

"I have no doubt she will, sir, if you say so."

"Of course. I have got two forms of engagement written out, and only want your two signatures."

"If I could have seen what the young lady could do," remarked Tom.

"Do!" interrupted Aaron Heine. "Do anything that Carlotta Grisi ever did, only a great deal better. You don't want more than that, do you?"

"Well, no, that will do I think."

"Here, are the forms, then. There need be no more time lost, need there?"

"No, certainly not. I accept the young lady on your recommendation, Mr. Heine."

"That's satisfactory, eh, Miss Rose?"

"Yes, sir," stammered Rose, bewildered and confused. "If you—if I—yes, sir. I think so."

"To be sure. To be sure. Now then, my dear, just write your name to this, or we shall be too late to get it stamped."

As he spoke, the Jew handed her a pen, and spread a large formidable parchment before her, closely filled with crabbed characters.

Aaron placed his finger upon a particular spot, and said—

"Sign here."

She did as she was told, though with some vague suspicion that the proceedings were somewhat irregular.

She wrote her name, taking, as she did so, a hurried glance at the lengthy document.

She could read scarcely half a dozen words, however, because the handwriting was such a curious one it seemed to her.

She made out a few words, though, which were filled in, in another style of caligraphy.

These words were—

"Fifteen guineas a week."

Fifteen guineas a week! What did that mean? Could it be possible that such a salary was going to be hers?

A dreadful suspicion passed through her mind a moment afterwards.

Was her talent worth fifteen guineas? What would she be expected to do? Could she do it?

There was no time to go into any explanation, however. Neither was there any opportunity.

She was on the point of speaking, but, somehow, could not manage to get in a word edgeways.

When she had signed her name Aaron rang a bell standing on the table by his side.

A young man, having the appearance of a lawyer's clerk, entered the room in answer to the summons.

"Jackson," said Mr. Heine. "I want you to witness this signature."

The clerk signed his name on the document.

"Now," said Aaron, "take it at once to the Lord High Chancellor's office, and have his seal manual attached. That will be—let me see—fifty shillings."

He handed the clerk some money as he spoke.

Then, turning to the manager, he continued—

"The stamp money and my fee of two guineas I suppose you and Miss Mortimer will arrange about on the first pay-day. I need not detain you, my dear, any longer. We will have a chat at teatime."

He opened a door for Rose as he spoke, and she passed out without a word.

She was indeed dumbfounded by what had happened.

Surely there never was such a house of mystery as this. Mysteries, indeed—it was chock full of them!

When she reached her own room another surprise was awaiting her.

The old woman was there, and rose as she entered.

"Well, my dear," said Mrs. Woodruffe, "how do you get on? Is it all settled?"

She had not mentioned the subject before, and Rose was surprised.

"Yes," she replied slowly, "it is."

"That's capital. I hope it's as good an engagement as that of Miriam."

"Miriam! Is she engaged also?"

"Yes, she has just gone."

"Gone?" echoed Rose.

"Gone this afternoon. She wanted to say good bye, but could not wait."

"What a hurried affair it seems to have been!"

"Yes; there was not a moment to spare. These opportunities occur so seldom, one must not allow them to slip through one's fingers."

"And so she has gone? You did not say where the theatre was."

"Some distance from here, my dear: it's at Edinburgh."

Rose pondered over what she had just heard. It was all very strange and inexplicable.

What was to be the end?

She had no opportunity of having the promised chat with Mr. Heine respecting her own engagement, and that day and the next passed away without her being able to see him.

Therefore, much to her astonishment, about six o'clock the third day Mrs. Woodruffe said—

"My dear, I ought to have told you. Pray get ready as quick as you can; we have got to go down to the theatre."

"For a rehearsal?" asked Rose.

"I don't know what it is, my dear," said the old woman, "but we haven't a moment to spare."

"What theatre is it?"

"Well, I don't know that either, but we're to meet Mr. Heine at the Bank."

All this was as mysterious as ever.

At the Bank! There were surely no theatres in the East End where a ballet-girl's salary was fifteen guineas a week. Fifteen shillings was much nearer the amount.

As the old woman could give her no information, however, she could do no other than curb her impatience, and wait till time should reveal all.

They started together in a cab at about seven o'clock, and drove westward.

Rose, although she had been born in London, knew very little about its geography, and could form no idea where they were going.

They stopped at length in a dark quiet back street, of a very mean and poverty-stricken aspect, before what seemed to be a stage door.

As she alighted she saw that such was the case, and, turning to her companion, she exclaimed distrustfully—

"I thought you did not know what theatre it was at."

But the old woman made no reply, and the manager, to whom she had been introduced before, appearing at the moment, she accompanied him into the house, in obedience to his desire.

He led her up a long passage, and out upon a large stage, very naked and dingy; then into a small dressing-room, where there was a woman waiting.

"Be quick and dress," said he. "I want you to go on at once."

"Go on!" she repeated. "Why I thought this was a rehearsal."

But at that moment a loud roar of voices and a great thumping of feet convinced her that a large audience was assembled, and that she was expected to go before them. To do what?

CHAPTER XIV.

THE LOW THEATRE—THE TOILET—THE SIGNORA
—A DEAD WOMAN'S CLOTHES—THE DANCE—
THE HOWLS OF THE MOB—THE STRUGGLE—
THE OUTRAGE.

FOR whatever reason she had been brought to the theatre, it was very evident to Rose that its proprietor thought there was no time to lose, for several times during the progress of her toilet he came knocking at the door, anxiously inquiring if she was nearly ready.

She found a ballet-dress ready for her. It was very gaudy, and by no means too clean.

"Am I to wear this?" she asked, with an expression of distaste.

"That's your dress," replied the woman.

"But it is an old one belonging to some one else."

"Yes."

"Well, then, it is not intended for me surely."

"Yes it is."

"Whose was it, pray?"

"The last one's."

"The last one's!" repeated Rose in surprise.

But before she could inquire further the manager came hammering again for the third or fourth time at the door.

"Are you nearly ready?"

"Very nearly, sir."

"Be quick, then, for Heaven's sake, or they'll have the place down!"

He went away again in a rampant state, and Rose ventured once more to question her companion.

"What am I to do?" she asked.

"Do! What do you mean?"

"Am I to appear before the public to-night?"

"Of course you are. What else do you suppose you're wanted for? You can dance, can't you?"

"Yes, I can dance a little."

"You'll have to do your best, or else you'll soon be goosed I can tell you?"

"Goosed?"

"That's hissed. Why, what sort of a theatre did you come from that you don't know the commonest terms?"

Poor Rose was silent. A dreadful misgiving had for some time past taken possession of her mind.

Oh, how she wished herself at home again!

Home! Alas! she had nowhere which she could call by that name.

Utterly homeless and friendless, what fate was reserved for her in the end?

Urged to exert herself to the utmost by the repeated summonses from without, and the flurried orders and suggestions of the woman assisting her, Rose was soon attired.

"Thank goodness you're ready at last!" said the manager, meeting her outside the door.

"Yes, I am ready," replied Rose, still panting from her exertions, "but I—I—"

"Come along, for goodness sake!"

"Am I to go on in—"

"Yes, of course. You've kept the stage waiting ten minutes as it is."

"But—but what am I to do?"

"Go on and dance—anything you like. Something in the *pas-seul* way of course."

"But without any rehearsal?"

"There's been no time for that. Look there!"

"Where?"

"At that picture."

"The poster?"

"Yes, the gal dancing—Signora Selina."

"Yes, sir."

"Well, that's to be you."

"Me?"

"She was billed for to-night, but she can't come, and so we're obliged to shove you on instead."

"But won't they know, sir?"

"Who?"

"The audience."

"No, they'll be none the wiser. She was just about your height, and you're something like her."

"But perhaps she may have circulated a report that she is not performing here."

"Oh no, she hasn't, and she can't now '

"Why ?"

"Because she's dead."

Rose shuddered, and pressed her hand to her heart. She, then, was wearing the dead woman's clothes! She was about to take her place.

By this time they were standing at the wing upon the prompter's side.

"Now then, young lady," said the manager, "keep your pecker up, you know. Go in and win. Keep at it, whatever you can do. Never mind how bad it is. Do something."

Rose looked at him in a bewildered way, scarcely comprehending what he was saying to her.

At the same time casting her eyes around, she now obtained her first fair view of the stage upon which she was to appear.

Anything more dirty and dingy than the appearance of all things round and about her it was difficult to conceive.

The scenes were torn and ragged.

The dresses of one or two actors whom she saw hanging about in a disconsolate way were woefully poverty-stricken and dilapidated.

What theatre could this be ? she asked herself.

How could this be a house affording to give fifteen guineas a week salary ?

There seemed to be no company, no other actress, no green-room that she had as yet seen. It was all a deep mystery.

There was one thing, though, which was not wanting, but which sometimes the first theatres in the world have lacked—an audience.

There was a large concourse of people assembled. So it seemed to Rose, by the deafening thunder of their feet, by their angry shouts, shrill screeches, and piercing cat-calls.

It did not sound very much like an aristocratic audience which she had to face, and her heart beat faster as she listened.

"Drink some of this," said the manager in her ear, and offering her a glass of wine as he spoke.

She drank it willingly, for she felt weak and faint.

In a moment the curtain rose, and a loud crash of music half deafened her.

"Now then! now then!" cried the prompter.

There was a momentary silence, and she bounded on to the stage.

The audience, taking her for the Signora Selina, saluted her with a tremendous round of applause, which was twice repeated.

Although her experience of the terpsychorean art was, as we know, but limited, so great was Rose Mortimer's beauty, so matchless the symmetry of her splendid form, that it was but natural that at her first appearance the audience should be prejudiced in her favour.

Knowing, from what the manager had said, that a great deal was expected of her, she exerted herself to the utmost.

One moment she was floating sylphlike, scarcely touching the ground, the next bounding, whirling, twirling, performing almost incredible gyrations, until, panting for breath, at last she paused, whilst the audience roared forth their approbation.

But with the applause they showered upon her came other and more substantial tokens of their regard, the novelty of which astonished and terrified her.

A handful of halfpence were dashed on to the stage, one of which striking her sharply on the shoulder caused her to start with a half suppressed scream to her feet.

The next moment she turned to fly from the stage.

But her motive being understood, a terrific shout of "Encore, encore," came from all parts of the house.

Then more halfpence came rattling on to the boards.

Turning for an instant to face her patrons, she for the first time was able to form something like a correct conjecture respecting their number and character.

It was certainly a good-sized theatre and densely crowded.

But the audience was composed of the vilest scum inhabiting in the vicinity of Whitechapel and Shadwell.

For the most part it was composed of boys and girls, ragged and dirty, upon the faces of whom were clearly traced the brands of infamy.

Hooting and howling, fighting and brawling, these depraved young wretches were only with the greatest difficulty kept in anything like subjection by certain sturdy ruffians attached to the establishment, who, when occasion called for such a course, laid about them with a thick stick.

This evening the audience was more unruly than usual.

They had been kept waiting so long that they had lost all patience.

Now, therefore, that they had made up their minds that Rose should perform again they would brook no delay.

But they were doomed to disappointment.

The poor girl, scared out of her wits by their discordant cries, fled precipitately from the stage.

She bent her steps towards the room where she had attired herself in the ballet costume, intending to resume her own clothes.

Upon the way thither, however, she met the manager in a state of fury.

"What are you doing ?" he asked, with an oath. "Why don't you go on again ?"

Oh, sir," cried Rose, with tears in her eyes, "how can you ask me ?"

"Ask you! What do you mean ? Don't you hear them calling for you ?"

"Yes, sir. But I'm afraid."

"You must go," said the man, grasping her roughly by the arm.

"No—no. Please—"

"Still you must."

"But, sir !"

"Don't you know that you have signed an agreement ?—that I can punish you if you do not do my bidding?"

"But, sir, they frighten me ! They will hurt me ! Hark how they are screaming and stamping now !"

"You poor pale-faced little fool," growled the man between his clenched teeth. "I have said that you should go on again, and by Heaven you shall !"

There was something in his face which showed that he was determined she should do what he said.

If necessary, he would use violence.

But as Rose saw this, so at the same time she determined that she would not yield to his unreasonable demand.

Wrenching herself from his grip, she ran towards the dressing-room.

He sprang after her, and caught her in his arms.

She uttered a piercing shriek, and struggled desperately to free herself.

He was by no means a strong man, and, her fierce rage lending her strength, she at last broke from him.

Then, with one bound, she cleared what distance still remained between her and the dressing-room door.

Then slammed it to in the face of her pursuer.

He stayed for a moment, striving vainly to force the

lock, and then, with a savage curse, returned to the stage.

The uproar by this time had reached its height.

Upon his making his appearance behind the footlights he was saluted with a torrent of abuse.

"Ladies and gentlemen," said he, appealing to the rabble before him, "it's not my fault. I've paid her her salary, and she won't dance. I can't make her. If you can I wish you would."

Scarcely were the words out of his mouth when half a dozen young ruffians sprang upon the stage.

CHAPTER XV.

THE RABBLE—THE CHASE—UP IN THE "FLIES"—A LAST CHANCE—"FIRE! FIRE!"—THE STRANGERS —THE MYSTERIOUS CONVERSATION—THE FIRST GLIMPSE OF A DARK PLOT.

WITH a savage whoop, which would have done credit to the lungs of Red Indians, they rushed across the stage, flinging the manager upon his back as they dashed passed him.

"Stop! Stop!" he roared. "Police! Police!"

But it was too late now to remedy the mischief.

He ought to have thought what damage this tagrag and bob-tail would do to his theatre before he spoke so imprudently.

Now he might just as well have tried to stem a raging torrent with his hat.

They poured past him howling and shrieking.

They drove the terrified carpenter before them like chaff before a hurricane.

There were two or three ballet-girls whom Rose had not seen, their dressing room being on the other side of the stage.

Into their private apartment the mob burst, howling for our heroine, and sending the girls flying in every direction with shrieks of terror.

One of these damsels, to get rid of her persecutors, informed them where our heroine was to be found, and they instantly turned and rushed in the indicated direction.

Rose seemed to comprehend instinctively their design.

The sound of their hurrying feet coming in her direction, mingled with the shrieks of women and oaths of men, first apprised her of the approaching danger.

The warning was but very short,

Almost the next moment there arose a fiendish yell without the door.

Then came splitting blows upon the panel.

"What are we to do?" asked Rose, in terror, of her companion.

"How am I to say?" retorted the other fiercely. "If they kill you, you will only have yourself to thank."

"What do you say?"

"I say what I mean. Your own stupid squeamishness has brought all this upon you."

"What do they want?"

"They wanted you to dance again, and you wouldn't. You'll be roughly handled, my fine lady, mark my words if you ain't."

"Tell me, without wasting any more time in talk, How can we escape?"

"No way that I know of."

"Yes, there must be a way."

"Well, find it."

"Where does that other door lead to?"

"You'd better go and see, I shan't help you."

The panels of the outer door by this time were splintered beneath the blows of those without.

Had not the door been protected inside by a wooden bar placed across it, it would long since have been broken open.

But the roughs were not to be thus kept at bay by a trifle.

A party of five or six, finding that their separated efforts were useless, formed themselves into a sort of battering-ram.

Altogether they hurled themselves suddenly against the door.

It creaked and trembled.

Another rush.

The doorposts began to tear away from the wall.

The plaster of the ceiling to trickle down upon their heads.

Now came the last effort.

A terrible crash, a dozen strong, and the door was carried, doorposts and all.

But while these vigorous measures were being adopted by the mob Rose was by no means idle.

The other door, about which she questioned the dresser, she found to be locked.

But the lock was not of a very formidable nature.

Fear lent her strength.

She soon mastered this opposition.

Flinging herself against the door, she flung it open with a loud crash.

Then rushed out.

Before her there was a winding staircase, leading to the flies.

Without hesitating a moment she sprang lightly up the steps.

But the mob, breaking in, caught sight of her muslin skirt as she fled before them.

With a ferocious yell they followed in pursuit.

On she fled, caring not where she went, staying not to consider whether there was a safe footing to be found up among the dusty scenery and confused assemblage of ropes amidst which she had taken refuge.

On she ran.

There was a beam before her, scarcely broad enough to stand upon with both feet set together.

She passed across without a moment's hesitation.

The roughs, afraid to follow, howled after her in fury.

Others, taking a hasty glance around, sought out a ladder on the other side of the stage, and scrambled up to cut off her retreat.

With flashing eyes and heaving breast the young and lovely girl turned panting to face her foes.

She cast her eyes around in search of some other outlet.

There was no way of escaping, however, except by the road she had come by or the other staircase, now blocked up by her assailants.

The only chance for her then was to dodge her pursuers about among the flies, across the beams, in and out among the tangled cordage and the lumbering machinery.

A wild and exciting chase it was for both hunters and hunted, but a cruel one to the latter.

From beam to beam she flew with lightning speed, the agile wretches springing after her, utterly reckless as it now seemed of their lives and limbs.

Scarcely a step did she take without the danger of a frightful fall.

More than once the rotten woodwork crumbled beneath her, but she sprang lightly on, now and then tottering and staggering, but recovering herself as though by magic.

The longer, however, the race continued, the more intense became her fear of falling into the hands of the wretches now so intent upon hunting her down.

Their brutal jests and horrible threats scared her out of her wits.

The whole house was now in an uproar, and the audience had scrambled pell-mell on to the stage.

The sound of smashing glass was to be heard every moment, mingled with the shrieks of the women.

Loud cries were raised for the police, and against the barricaded doors the constables without were struggling furiously with the mob inside for admittance.

A more horrible saturnalia than the theatre presented it would scarcely be possible to imagine.

The rabble, dancing and shrieking like so many incarnate fiends, were now for the most part intoxicated, having broken into the refreshment-rooms and helped themselves gratuitously to all the liquors there to be found.

Poor Rose saw that she would be treated roughly indeed did she have the misfortune to fall into their hands.

But how to escape?

Ah! there was one chance which she had not hitherto thought of.

She was now close to the proscenium.

She might descend by one of the curtain ropes, then fly across the stage, and perhaps make her way out by the stage door.

No sooner was this rash project conceived than it was put into execution.

Dropping on her hands and knees, she took a firm hold of the rope below her.

Then swung herself forward.

It was a moment of fearful peril.

Had she loosened her hold (and the strain upon her wrists was enormous) she must have dashed her brains out on the floor below.

But she was safe, and glided down the rope.

Thus, however, did she escape from one danger only to encounter another still more terrible.

In gliding down the rope her muslin garments came in contact with the gas jets by the side.

In a moment she was in a blaze.

Before she reached the ground the flames surrounded her.

"Help! help!" shrieked the terrified ballet-girl, and, with that fatal impulse to which all women in the moment of peril seemed doomed to yield, she rushed wildly about the stage.

The rapid passage through the air fanned the flames into terrific fury above her head and entirely envelopped her lovely form.

She shrieked aloud in an agony of terror.

She flung herself upon the floor and rolled over and over.

She seized her blazing skirts in her hands and tried one moment to crush out the flames, the next to tear her garments from her body.

But, alas! in both efforts she was foiled by her own confusion and fright.

At the moment, though, when her situation seemed to be very precarious a cloak was flung around her.

She had lost all command over herself now, and struggled furiously with her would-be saviour.

But he held her down with a strength against which her efforts were of no avail.

He choked her, half smothered her, but held her prisoner in spite of her struggles.

At length when he removed the cloak she was half fainting.

She was too much frightened by what she had just passed through to remember the pursuit of the ruffians who had been the cause of all.

But opening her eyes now, she found that she was surrounded and hemmed in by a jabbering mob, upon whom her sufferings and dangers had no effect.

She had, however, found a protector.

In his arms she was safely carried through the crowd.

Several rushes were made at her on the way, but his strong right arm kept her antagonists at a respectful distance.

Bearing her as easily as though she had been a child, he carried Rose into the street.

There another man came up to him, exclaiming—

"Poor girl! is she much hurt?"

"No," replied he who had so gallantly rescued her, "I hope I have saved her with scarcely a scar."

"It would indeed have been a misfortune for so lovely a creature to be sacrificed."

Here Rose murmured some words of entreating, though in so low a tone as to be inaudible.

"You are quite safe," said the second man, who was about sixty, with long silvery locks hanging around a mild and pleasant face. "Do not be alarmed."

"Where are you going to take me?" she asked faintly.

"We will take you home, if you will tell us where that is."

Rose looked at him wildly, but made no answer.

Home!

Unhappy girl, where indeed was she to look for one?

"My carriage is waiting here," said the old man. "You had better come into it, and as we drive along you can collect yourself a little and decide where you wish to go."

He spoke so kindly, so gently, that it was almost impossible to believe him to have any sinister motive in making this proposition.

But she had already fallen into such traps, met with such double-faced hypocrites, that it was not to be wondered at if she was somewhat distrustful.

But she felt so ill.

She was so weak and weary.

She had not strength to struggle longer.

Her brain was confused.

She could not reason.

She could not make an effort to save herself from any new danger.

Without a murmur she allowed the old gentleman and his younger companion to assist her into the carriage.

As they drove along she closed her eyes and for some moments lapsed into a half unconscious state.

The two men conversed in a low tone of voice, and she could catch but a faint and confused notion of the subject of their conversation.

"It is most extraordinary," one said.

"I could scarcely have believed it."

"Yet there are some instances of a like character."

"In plays and tales you mean—such as the *Corsican Brothers*, for instance."

"No, I don't. I mean in real life, such as in the case of the courier of Lyons."

"What was that?"

"A respectable man accused of robbery and murder, and sworn to by a roomfull of witnesses."

"Well?"

"Well, after he was executed it turned out that they had got hold of the wrong man."

"But they hanged him?"

"What, the right man! I forget what they did to him, but it doesn't much signify. They hanged the wrong one; that's the great point we've got to look to."

"To be sure. And he was so like the other man, eh?"

"Like! As like as two peas. It was most extraordinary, it would seem. The man wrongfully accused was spoken up for by a score of respectable people, and he proved a very tolerable *alibi*, but they hanged him all the same."

[THE MURDER IN THE GREEN-ROOM.]

"The other—"

"Was a strolling vagabond, escaped convict, or something of that sort. When he was taken the witnesses all swore to him as positively as they had done to the other."

"They were a little bit ashamed of themselves, though, I should fancy?"

"Ah, and said that they never would make such a mistake again."

"They'll make it in our case, though, I'll wager a pound. What say you?"

"I can't see, myself, how they can do otherwise. The likeness is really most extraordinary."

"If she had only happened to be a boy, eh?"

"Ah! there's always some drawback to every good scheme."

"However, the next best thing to her being a boy is being a ballet-girl."

"To be sure ; anything but an actress I should have felt nervous about."

"Oh, a lesson or two will teach her all she will want to know."

"If she does'nt make any objection."

"There's not much chance of that, I should think."

"Goodness knows ; there's no doing anything with some women."

"We'll manage her, though, I think. If she has any nonsense—"

" Hush !"

" Is she listening, do you think ? I fancy she's fainted."

" Let's drop the subject, anyhow, for the present."

They then rode on in silence for a short time.

Presently the wheels crushed upon the gravel in a garden-path.

Then the carriage came to a stand still.   They were in front of a villa, in what appeared to be a suburb.

Rose aroused herself and looked nervously round.

" Where am I ?" she murmured.

" You are quite safe," the old man repeated. " We must get out here."

" What house is this ?"

" A hospital, where you will be well cared for."

" But I am not ill. I am only a little frightened and tired."

She strove to rouse herself as she spoke, and to stand without his assistance.

But the effort was in vain.

She would have fallen, had not the young man caught her in his arms.

Very gently then he carried her up the steps into the house, and laid her down upon a couch in a well-furnished room.

The old man then unlocked a cheffonier, from which he took out a decanter and a wineglass.

Rose drank the wine he offered her, and felt greatly refreshed.

The old man then offered her another, but this she refused.

Presently she began to feel much better, but as she gradually recovered from the effects of her fright she began to be very uneasy.

She wanted to go away from this house into which they had brought her ; but where was she to go to ?

She was not quite in a fit state to go into the streets. Without the cloak which the young man had thrown round her, her dress, owing to the ravages of the flames, was extremely limited.

However, she felt that she could not remain there, and presently, when she was strong enough, rose to her feet.

" I must go now," she said.

" Where to ?" asked the old man blandly.

" To—to—"

But here she paused. Where, indeed ?

" Where do you live ?"

" I—I don't live anywhere, but—"

" But what ?"

" I cannot remain here."

" Indeed !"

" No—I—"

" I think you can. In fact, you *must*."

" Must ?"

" Yes, young lady. Sit down and allow me to speak to you seriously."

He took hold of her wrist as he spoke, and gently but firmly forced her into a seat.

" Now, young lady," said the old man, " you had better understand me at once."

" Ye-es."

" We have brought you here to perform a little part in a comedy in real life, which we are preparing."

" Ye-es."

" You will have to represent the character of a young gentleman. If you act well and we are successfull you will be very handsomely rewarded. If you fail—"

" But if I refuse ?"

" It is no good refusing. We have brought you here on purpose, and you must and shall do what we desire. Besides, you would surely not be a fool to your own interest."

" But do I understand you that I am to act a part in a fraud ?"

" You may understand it that way if you choose, but it is a very innocent fraud, and so I hope you will give us no trouble, because unless you consent—"

Here he took her hand in his and gently caressed it.

" Unless you consent," he repeated in soft low musical tones, " we shall be compelled to do that which we shall sincerely regret."

Rose shudderingly crept back upon the seat.

Although there was a sweet smile playing around his lips, there was a sinister glare in his eyes.

Although his touch was soft as velvet, she felt that it was like the paw of a tiger, and that the claws were but hidden for a while.

" If I do not agree ?" she gasped out involuntarily, eager, though dreading, to hear the worst.

He bent low, so that his lips almost touched her ear, and hissed between his teeth, " *We shall kill you !*"

CHAPTER XVI.

ANOTHER OF COUNT LERNO'S VICTIMS—A STRANGE SCENE IN THE GREEN-ROOM—THE MURDERED BEAUTY.

ABOUT nine o'clock upon the same night that the scene occurred which is described in the preceding chapter a handsome brougham set down its occupants in front of the stage door of the Babylonian Theatre.

One of these occupants was Count Lerno, the successful swindler, blackleg, and forger; the other was a young and beautiful woman.

She was magnificently attired in the most costly silk, which rustled loudly as she entered the narrow passage leading to the Realms of Bliss, and the door-keeper bowed low to her as she passed.

As she ascended the stairs she met Mr. Flathers, who was all smiles and graciousness, and he skipped briskly on one side to allow her to pass.

" The stairs are very dirty," he said. " I must have them looked to."

" It's time they were I am sure," cried the beauty in a gay tone. " It's perfectly unendurable what one has to put up with behind the scenes of a theatre."

" It shall be attended to," said Mr. Flathers.

She swept onwards without another word, and bent her steps towards the dressing-room.

The carpenters touched their caps and shambled out of the way as she approached.

Some of the ballet-girls whom she met crept timidly back, and, murmuring among themselves, looked evilly after her.

Arrived at one of the dressing-rooms, by far the best of all, an elderly female opened the door and bobbed a timid courtsey.

" Now then," exclaimed the beauty, " be quick if you please—that is, if you can. Is my dress ready ? Have you altered it as I directed ?"

" Yes, madam."

" Let me look."

" It is here, madam."

" It's horrible. It must be undone again. Pull it to pieces at once."

" But madam, it is so late, and—"

" Well, leave it. However, you shall do it to-night before you go to bed, and bring it to me the first thing in the morning. Then I can have it altered during the day if you make any more mistakes."

The elderly female humbly bowed her head, and busied herself to the utmost with the beauty's toilet.

When she was attired, and stood looking at herself in the glass, her beauty was so dazzling that even the sewing woman, so accustomed to see her, could not help gazing admiringly, enviously, upon the transcendent loveliness of this fair and imperious woman.

Did it not seem that such as she were made to be queens, while all others were born to be her abject slaves and do her bidding ?

And yet even beauty will fade, and life is uncertain, and death is stealing upon us all—how far off or how near to us who can say ?

Thus death awaited this lovely woman.

A sudden and horrible death.

And as she stood there smiling proudly she was on the very brink of the grave.

She had barely ten minutes more to live.

When she was attired she descended to the greenroom.

As she entered there was but one other person present—a pretty woman, attired like herself for the ballet.

As the beauty closed the door and advanced towards the fire the other started slightly and changed colour.

As she did so her hand wandered to her bosom and seemed to search for something hidden there.

There was a faint flush, too, upon the face of the newcomer as she recognised her companion, and she appeared for a moment to hesitate whether or not she should come into the room.

However, she decided upon doing so, and slowly approached the fireplace, keeping her eyes averted from the other woman's face.

There was a dead silence of several moments.

Then the second woman said in a low and trembling voice, which she vainly endeavoured to render firm—

" Have you thought over what I said to you ?"

" Yes, I have, but this is neither the time nor place to go into the matter."

" Excuse me, but it is the place. As for the time, I have already waited far too long."

" You must wait until it is my pleasure to speak to you, Clara."

" When will that be ?"

" I cannot say."

" But I must know to-night."

" No."

" When, then ?"

" Never. I defy you to do your worst."

" Take care, or by Heaven you will repent your rashness. Will you do what I wish you ? Mind this is the last time that I shall ask."

" No, I will not, Clara."

No other word was spoken.

The beauty drew herself up to her full height and looked scornfully down upon her companion.

The other's face was distorted with passion.

With lightning rapidity she drew from her bosom a tiny pistol.

She presented it at the face of the beauty and fired.

With a scream the victim staggered back and fell dead upon the ground.

At the same moment the manager and a score of other persons came rushing terrified into the room, and found her lying there a blood-stained corpse.

For a moment there was a pause.

A pause and an awful silence, in which, with white terror-stricken faces, Flathers and the count stood gazing in horror upon the blood-smeared face of the murdered woman, while a crowd of frightened men and trembling women blocked up the background.

She whom the victim had called Clara was the first to speak.

In a hoarse whisper she addressed the manager.

" Send them away," she said, " and send for a doctor. Not that it's needed, though," she added to herself.

The manager, half frightened out of his wits, did as she bade him. When the door was closed he asked in a trembling voice—

" What has happened ?"

" Look to the door. Is any one listening ?"

Flathers stepped back and opened it quickly.

No one was near the other side.

" No one can hear us," he repeated, still in a low voice, and still trembling. " What does it all mean ? How did she come by her death ?"

" From my hand !" replied the woman.

The count, who was kneeling by the side of the corpse, started up at these words, and confronted her with flashing eyes.

" Murdress !" he exclaimed.

But she met his gaze with contemptuous indifference.

" You choose to call me so," she replied.

" But — but how did it happen ?" gasped the manager.

" I was sitting here alone. She came in and began to quarrel with me. You know the reason. Gradually she worked herself up into a fury. Then suddenly drew a pistol from her breast and tried to take my life. I snatched the weapon from her. We struggled. She threw me down and endeavoured to strangle me. I pointed the pistol at her face and shot her dead."

There was a deep silence when she thus concluded her narration.

The two men stood as though transfixed, looking open-mouthed and speechless into the cold white face of the speaker.

" Great Heavens ! " cried Flathers at last, finding his tongue. " What will be done ? I shall be disgraced and ruined by the exposure that must follow. You will be tried for murder, and—"

" Why ?"

The men looked at her in amazement.

" What ? Do you suppose that you can commit such a crime with impunity, and escape all consequences ?"

" How will they know that I have committed the crime ?"

" How ? Why, by your own confession."

" What confession ?"

" Haven't you this moment told us that you murdered her ?"

" I know I have told you, but I know that it will go no further."

" But what do you mean ? How can it be kept secret ?"

" Very easily."

" Very easily ! Why the doctor is on his way here now. The police, perhaps, are at the very door !"

" Well, and what then ?"

" The truth will all come out."

" Not at all. What can they discover ?"

" They will find her murdered."

" They will find her dead. They will see that she has been shot through the head. By the side of her they will find lying the weapon with which she did the deed."

" She did the deed ?"

" They will find her own pistol—a pistol which she is known to be in the habit of carrying about with her—which she was seen to have in her possession this very morning."

" Well ?"

" They will then hear my statement with respect to the way in which she committed suicide."

The manager listened in a confused way to all this, evidently too frightened to clearly understand what she was saying.

The count, on the contrary, was deeply attentive.

When she here paused for a short time he said—

" And can you explain as clearly why we should assist you in this scheme of yours ?"

" Yes."

"Why ?"

"Because you dare not oppose me."

As she spoke she drew herself up to her full height, and her eyes seemed to gleam with something of the venomous glitter of those of a serpent.

There was something terrible in the face of this beautiful woman, so calm and yet so cruel.

Very evidently the manager was afraid of her, but she had rather a different person to deal with in the count.

"I hardly see it in the same light," he said. "You think, perhaps, that because our connection enabled you to learn a few trifling secrets of my private life you can trade on them to any extent. But you make a mistake. I, for one, do not fear you."

"You do not fear me?"

"No."

At this moment footsteps were heard approaching. There was a knock at the door.

"We have not a moment to spare now," said Clara. "We must understand one another at once."

"It would be as well."

"You refuse to second my story by your evidence?"

"I do. You have long enough stood in my way. This is a good opportunity of removing you. You have brought it on yourself. Your blood be on your own head."

As he spoke the count moved towards the door. But the woman sprang to his side, and laid her hand upon his wrist.

"Count Lerno," she said in a low voice, which trembled with the pent-up passion that caused her fair bosom to rise and fall like an angry sea, "I tell you you dare not thwart me, nor this man either, for I know too much."

"Yes, yes," gasped the manager in an appealing tone. "For God's sake don't oppose her !"

"What do you know ?" asked the count with a savage frown.

"I know you."

"Indeed !"

"Yes. Not as the man of fashion you pretend to be, but as the thief and forger that you are."

He started violently and clutched her wrist, but with a sudden effort she wrenched herself free.

"More than that I know," she said.

"More than that ?" he asked with a sudden flush, and the manager, creeping towards him, laid his trembling hands upon his arm and whispered, with ashy lips—

"Yes, yes, she knows all ?"

"All what ?"

"She knows all about the past."

"I know this much," said Clara, "that you are escaped convicts, that you worked together in the galleys, that a reward was offered for your capture, and that if I denounced you—"

Again there was a loud knocking at the door.

"Need I say any more ?" she asked.

The count was silent, and Flathers tremblingly advanced to admit the doctor, but as he passed by Lerno's side he cast upon him an appealing glance full of piteous entreaty.

"For God's sake don't oppose her !" he muttered.

CHAPTER XVII.

MORE OF THE COINERS' DEN—DEVILLE MEDITATES ESCAPE—THE MIDNIGHT EXCURSION—THE UNDERGROUND BANQUETING HALL—THE MYSTERIOUS DISAPPEARANCE—A STRANGE VISIT—THE OFFER OF HELP—THE TERMS—THE ROPE LADDER—THE ATTACK—A MOMENT OF DANGER.

MANY weary days passed away, and yet was young Edgar Deville a prisoner in the lonely house at Fulham.

A very dreary life was it which he passed in that strange abode of crime and mystery. All day long he worked very hard under the direction of the foreman or those left in charge during Abel Booth's absence.

When night came he was so wearied that he was glad enough to avail himself of the coarse hard bed provided for him, and sleep off his fatigue.

He had never in his life before done a hard day's work, and he by no means relished the sensations which the hard work of the first of these days left behind it. When the next day had passed as laboriously as the first he went to bed very much disgusted.

Not so much, though, as he was at the end of the next day, or the next after that.

When a week had passed miserably away, and he still found himself a prisoner, still compelled to labour, at the orders of the ruffians around him, a savage rage grew up within his breast, and he swore to himself that he would either escape or die.

The latter alternative was easy enough. He had only to attempt the former and the latter followed as a matter of course.

He did not attempt it. He saw that his every movement was jealously watched. He knew that it would be worse than useless to make a trial yet.

Presently, if he appeared to be active and cheerful, they would, perhaps, relax their vigilance, and then was the time.

With this idea he worked away as hard as he could, laughed and joked with his fellow-labourers, and to all appearance was happy and jovial.

Now and then, though, when he thought himself unobserved, a pained and wearied expression would creep over his face, and none of these signs passed unnoticed.

He fancied, too, that his affectation of contentment deceived them. But he was much mistaken, for they not unreasonably argued that such a frame of mind was most unnatural—indeed impossible.

How could he, a young man of fashion, accustomed to all the gaities of life, settle down contentedly to work like a slave and live like a dog ?

It was impossible that he could do so.

At the same time it very much puzzled Edgar Deville to account for the contentment of the rest.

How was it possible, he asked himself, that they could pass all their lives thus hidden away from the world, working night and day, without any pleasure or enjoyment, without any earthly prospect of amendment ?

Were they all persons whose lives and liberty would be forfeited if they ventured abroad ?

It seemed to him that the tedious misery of the lives they led in this horrible place was scarcely preferable to that of a prison.

With the exception of a tolerable supply of butchers' meat, and a liberal allowance of wine and spirits, Edgar Deville had been able to see nothing in the treatment of his fellow-workmen which at all differed from that of a band of unhappy wretches locked up for life in a dreary prison-house, working their hearts out only to increase the wealth of their cruel taskmaster.

What was done with the produce of their labours ? he wondered.

Every day large quantities of base coin were manufactured.

If these were disposed of for a fourth of the value of the money they were intended to represent an enormous profit must be made.

Who, then, reaped the benefit ?

If it were the Count Lerno alone, it was extraordinary that these men consented to live on as they did, and toil for him without any reward.

The wonderful part of the business was that they did not break out into open revolt.

Certainly they would have done so had they all been as discontented with their lot as he was.

And were they not?

He could not answer for all of them, but he was quite certain of one other besides himself.

Was it possible that each fearing the rest was the cause of them all suffering in silence when all equally desired to free themselves from the hateful thraldom?

He knew very well that there was one other who desired freedom—who was kept there against his will.

This was the man called Hugh Mortimer.

Very soon Edgar found out that he was meditating an escape.

One day he had not been working quite as hard as usual, and when he lay stretched at night upon his hard comfortless couch he found he could not go to sleep.

Wearily he tossed to and fro, and rolled from side to side in restless fatigue, vainly courting sleep.

His companion seemed to be restless also, and appeared annoyed by his frequent movements, for he heard him more than once swearing savagely to himself.

At last Edgar Deville resolutely closed his eyes and determined not to stir again upon any account.

When he had lain silent thus for about ten minutes Mortimer rose in his bed in a sitting posture and coughed.

Deville opened his eyes without shifting his position and stared at him in astonishment.

His companion coughed again, this time louder than before.

Then he softly called to Deville by name.

But the young man made no reply.

It struck him that Mortimer only did so to see whether he was asleep, and he therefore lay perfectly still and silent.

After a few moments' pause Mortimer rose to his feet and began to search under his mattress.

Then he struck a light and lit a dark lantern.

With this he crept on tiptoe towards Deville's bed.

The young man shut his eyes, and the other passed the bull's-eye two or three times across his face.

"All right," Edgar heard him mutter. "He's off at last, curse him."

He then crept away, and presently Edgar heard him fitting a key into the lock of the door.

It turned easily, and he passed out into the passage closing the door after him, but not locking it.

"Hullo!" thought Edgar to himself. "Is my surly friend off for good? If he is, I'll follow suit."

No sooner said than done.

Deville rose hastily, crammed his shoes into his coat pockets, noiselessly unfastened the door, and followed in the wake of his companion.

At the further end of the passage he could just see the reflection of the dark lantern.

In another moment it had disappeared.

Deville worked his way along by the wall very cautiously, for he dreaded to make the least sound.

Reaching the end of the passage, he found a door.

Opening it noiselessly, he peeped in and caught a glimpse of the lantern's rays a good distance beneath him.

Clinging to the doorpost, Edgar groped about nervously until he discovered that a flight of steps lay before him.

Holding by the wall, he descended very cautiously, still keeping the lantern in view.

There was then another passage to be explored, and at the end of it there was a bright light, apparently coming from a window in the floor.

Such, when he got near enough, he found to be the case.

There was a skylight looking upon a large room, and through the glass Hugh Mortimer was now peering eagerly.

"If I could creep round without him seeing me," thought Edgar, "I should very much like to have a peep, too."

It was rather a difficult matter; but, with great care and caution, Deville at length managed to effect his purpose, and, hiding himself in the shade, gazed upon the extraordinary scene below.

Before him he saw a large luxuriously-furnished room, and in it recognised his brother coiners—all, however, handsomely dressed—and as many females, splendidly attired, all young, and the greater part beautiful.

A table in the centre of the room groaned beneath a weight of choice viands, hothouse fruits, and costly wines.

Edgar Deville had already had some experience of the voluptuous orgies indulged in by the count, and could now understand how it was that this band of ruffians consoled themselves for their life-long imprisonment by wild excesses and lawless revelries in the society of these syrens, who were, doubtless, ignorant of their companions' real character and occupation.

He could have spent some time in wondering astonishment at the luxuries unrolled before his eyes, but a movement on the part of his companion caused him to turn his eyes in Hugh Mortimer's direction.

He was wandering on again, and Edgar followed.

But the bright light at which he had been looking dazzled him. He fancied he heard a door close, but was not quite sure from what direction the sound had come.

He began to grope round the walls. He could, however, find no door and no outlet except the passage by which he had came.

What was to be done? He waited and listened.

The murmur of voices below drowned all other sounds. Still he waited, but as the moments flew past he began to feel nervous.

It would not do, he thought, for his friend to retrace his steps to their room and lock him out.

The idea made him feel suddenly hot and cold.

He felt his way back to the passage, and groped his way along as quickly as he could.

He came to the steps, ascended them, opened the door, and felt his way along the other passage on the floor above.

With hardly any trouble he reached his door, found it open, entered the room, and went back to bed.

He had not been there more than five minutes, at the outside, when Hugh Mortimer returned, extinguished his lamp, and also retired to his couch.

Edgar Deville was very much astonished.

"What the deuce made him take that walk?" he asked himself. "It could not have been for the pleasure of peeping down into that room, because he did not stop long enough when he was there. What could he have been about?"

It was difficult to guess, and Hugh Mortimer was not likely to unravel the mystery.

Next night, as soon as he went to bed, Deville pretended to go fast asleep, and Mortimer, after experimenting once or twice to find out whether or not he was awake, rose cautiously, lit his dark lantern, and stole out of the room in the way that he had done upon the previous evening.

When Edgar was about to rise also and follow him he fancied he heard his footsteps returning, and hastily lay down again.

Having waited a while, until all was still, he got out of bed and peeped into the passage.

All was dark and silent. He could see nothing of his fellow-prisoner.

He hurried up the passage as fast as he could, and opened the door at the end, but he was not to be seen.

Then he paused and hesitated. He had been mistaken about the footstep, he thought, and by the delay had given Mortimer an opportunity of getting too far to be easily overtaken.

Under these circumstances, and painful as was the alternative, there was nothing better for him than to retrace his steps.

When he got back to his room he seated himself despondingly upon the side of the bed and pondered.

"Perhaps I shall never get another chance," he thought. "It was very unlucky."

But at this moment his attention was attracted towards the ceiling by a faint scratching noise.

"What's that I wonder?" he said to himself. "It can't be rats surely."

The scratching, however, continued, and then suddenly a faint streak of light appeared.

Could it be Mortimer?

He sat motionless upon the edge of the bed listening and watching.

The streak of light widened. It was a trap-door that was being opened in the ceiling.

Suddenly a bull's-eye flashed into the room and settled with a glare on his face.

Then a soft female voice asked—

"Are you Edgar Deville?"

"Yes," he answered in astonishment.

"And you are a prisoner?"

"Indeed I am."

"And wish to escape?"

"Need you ask?"

"I can help you, then."

"Ah?"

"But only on certain conditions."

"Name them," said Edgar eagerly.

"You will owe me a debt of gratitude if I again restore you to the world?"

"Indeed I shall, and one that I can scarcely ever hope to repay."

"You will serve me, then, in return?"

"However you may dictate."

"Very well. I shall try you at any rate, and hope I may not find you undeserving."

With these words the trap-door was closed again and Deville resumed his seat in silent astonishment. This feeling, however, soon gave place to one of disappointment, as minute after minute passed away without his hearing any more of his new friend.

Perhaps Mortimer would return. What then?

Every moment's delay he felt to be more dangerous than the last, and yet the trap-door remained closed and the silence continued.

At last, when he was beginning to despair, the trap once more was raised, and the same soft woman's voice addressed him.

"Will you come now?" it said.

"Yes."

"You are alone?"

"Yes."

"Take care, then. I will let down a rope ladder. There, have you got it?"

"Yes."

"Can you climb up it without making it fast at your end?"

"Oh yes, easily."

"It is fast above ; so now come quickly."

Edgar waited for no second invitation. He laid tight hold of the ladder and prepared to climb.

But scarcely had he raised his foot when a heavy step behind him caused him to turn his head.

The next moment he received a violent blow in the face which felled him to the floor.

Then Hugh Mortimer sprang past him, rushed up the ladder, and passed through the trap door, pulling the ropes after him.

Half insensible from the violence of the blow, Edgar was still vaguely conscious of the sound of a struggle above and a woman's scream.

And then all was still.

What did it mean? How was it that Mortimer had so suddenly returned? Had he really wrested from his grasp all chance of escape? What had become of the mysterious female who had so strangely offered him her assistance?

He staggered to his feet with an effort, and passed his hand to his head, which was throbbing painfully.

Whilst he stood thus he heard the sound of voices and the tramp of feet approaching.

He looked wildly around, and with the aid of the faint light which struggled in between the bars of a tiny grating high up in the wall, strove vainly to find something which might serve as a weapon of defence.

The voices and the footsteps approached nearer.

They were in the passage. They were at the door.

Edgar Deville turned to face them, and clenched his fists ; but as he did so a deadly sickness stole over him.

He reeled, and, striving in vain to catch at the wall, fell heavily to the ground.

Next moment there was a sudden rush of men into the room, and naked daggers and flashing lights surrounded him.

CHAPTER XVIII.

EDGAR AND THE COINERS—"DOWN WITH HIM!"—THE EXAMINATION—THE TRIAL—THE DOOMED TRAITOR—THE WATER-WHEEL—THE FEARFUL DEATH.

AROUND the prostrate form of Edgar Deville an angry consultation was held by the gang of coiners who had thus rushed in a body into the room.

"Down with him!"

"Stab him at once!"

"No—no ; stay awhile."

"Why should we spare him ?"

"Perhaps he had no share in it. See, he is wounded."

"Mortimer must have done this, then. There has been a struggle between them."

Thus incoherently did the coiners dispute among themselves, whilst their prisoner lay perfectly passive in a deep swoon, caused by the loss of blood from his wound.

Some were in favour of executing him at once, without the benefit of judge or jury. He had never been very popular with the gang, and the greater part of the number were of this way of thinking.

Fortunately for him, however, lawless ruffians though they were, these men were governed by laws of their own, and one and all entertained a great respect for the opinions of their chief, the count.

Therefore, after the first moment's rage was over, they cooled down a little, and began to talk more reasonably.

As it was, they had already got one victim on whom to wreak a bloody vengeance.

Hugh Mortimer had been caught, and was now lying, bound hand and foot, awaiting the judgment to be passed upon him.

The count was absent that night, and was not expected until late on the following evening.

Until then he must wait, suffering agonies of suspense.

They locked him up in a dark cellar, and left him there without food or water or light, his thongs cutting cruelly into his flesh.

All this Edgar learned, when he recovered consciousness, from the conversation of those around him, for he had been removed from his former room, and awoke to find himself lying stretched upon some blankets in front of the workroom fire.

He also learned that the mysterious female had not been discovered, nor her presence suspected.

Throughout the day Egar lay very weak and faint, but he recovered a little of his lost strength as night came on.

He needed it all to be able to bear the horrible sight which was in store for him.

Not until two or three hours after the evening's work was concluded did Count Lerno make his appearance.

The band then all solemnly assembled in the workroom.

The count occupied a raised seat.

"Bring Edgar Deville here," he said, and two of the men helped the prisoner to walk forward; then seated him near to the count.

"What do you know of Mortimer's treachery?" the count asked, sternly.

"Nothing," replied Edgar, in a calm voice.

"Nothing?"

"I was not in his confidence."

"It was from his hand that you received your wound?"

"Yes."

"Had you been struggling together?"

"No."

"How did it occur then?"

"He came upon me from behind and struck me suddenly."

"Ah, to prevent your hindering him from escaping. Was that so?"

Edgar was silent.

He had no intention of betraying the real truth, and left them to come to what conclusions they thought fit.

The count was silent for a time; then continued—

"You were aware that he left the room of a night?"

"Yes."

A murmur arose among the coiners at this reply.

"You were? When did he do so first?"

"I do not know."

"When did you first know of it?"

"Last night."

"Do you know what he did when he left the room?"

"No. I was not in his confidence."

"Do you swear that this robbery and escape was not planned between you?"

"Yes. I swear it was not."

"Were you to have no part of the plunder?"

"No. I never heard that there was any plunder to divide."

Another silence followed.

Then the count and the coiners consulted together, and appeared to come to some conclusion not altogether favourable towards the young prisoner.

When they had talked for a while in a low tone of voice the count resumed his seat and ordered Hugh Mortimer to be brought out.

There was a long delay, which passed in solemn silence.

Edgar Deville's heart throbbed with apprehension—not from any fear upon his own account, but a horrible dread of what was in store for the unhappy traitor.

His fears for him, though, could not have anything like equalled the poor wretch's fears for himself.

He was ghastly white.

His teeth chattered in his head and his knees smote together.

They brought him in, still bound, and stood him opposite to his judge.

When they relinquished their hold of him, however, he rocked to and fro in such a helpless way that it seemed certain he would have fallen on his face had they not caught him by the arms.

"Hugh Mortimer," said the count, in a low but solemn tone, "you have been brought here to be tried by our band. I will ask you a few questions, which you need not answer unless you choose. First of all, have you not been well treated since you have been with us?"

"I never wished to remain here. I have been kept against my will."

"That may or may not be true. You professed to join us of your own free will. We doubted you and kept you for a probationary period as a sort of prisoner. It is a rule that we all observe. In return you plundered us."

"I—I only took a little."

"You robbed us, or attempted to do so. You also attempted to escape. Who assisted you?"

"A woman."

"Do you know who she was?"

"No."

"How was it she assisted you then?"

"I do not know. She held the ladder for me, and told me which way to go."

"When you were taken what became of her?"

"I do not know."

They asked no more, but consulted amongst themselves for some minutes.

When again the count addressed the prisoner, his tone was even more solemn than before.

"You have offended against our laws," he said, "and you must die."

Mortimer gasped as he heard the words.

"Oh, for God's sake don't murder me!" he cried in piteous accents.

And dropping down upon his knees he rocked himself to and fro in terror.

"There is no hope for you," replied the count sternly. "You must die."

"Oh, mercy! mercy!"

"We have no mercy for traitors."

The unhappy wretch worked himself along on his knees until he reached the count's feet, and gazed into his face with an agonised expression.

"You won't let them kill me, count?" he whined. "I am sure you won't let them murder your old friend. We have known one another so long. And my pretty daughter, too. You loved her, count, once, but she was a silly flighty girl, and did not know what honour you conferred on her; but she would listen to me."

The count turned away with an expression of contempt, and made a sign to some of the men.

Obedient to it, they opened a large trap in the floor—the same over which Edgar Deville had stood when they threatened his life upon the first night of his entry into the coiners' abode.

Then some one pulled a cord, and a rumbling plashing noise was heard, which sounded very awful in the deathlike silence.

When it reached the ears of their victim he shrieked and covered his eyes.

"Not that!" he screamed. "Oh! not that! Do not murder me so brutally."

"There is no choice for you. That is the death which we award to all traitors."

"No, no. You cannot mean to do it. You will not do it. I shall be broken to pieces. I shall be torn limb from limb."

The count, however, heeded not his prayers and entreaties.

He waved his hand, and two of the men approached the victim and raised him to his feet.

He, however, would not or could not stand.

His knees gave way under him, and he sank seemingly helpless to the ground.

Then they raised him again and dragged him towards the mouth of the pit.

As he approached its brink his face turned to a livid colour.

Great beads of perspiration burst out upon his forehead.

His teeth chattered horribly, and he moaned dismally like some animal in great pain.

When he had come to the opening, though, and could see down into the black and yawning chasm below, his terror and agony reached their climax.

Summoning all his strength, he sprang to his feet, and wrested himself from the grasp of the men who had been holding him.

But his hands and arms were bound, and he could do nothing to save himself from the fearful fate in store for him.

Very soon again he was in their grasp.

Then they once more dragged him forward.

He plunged, and kicked, and screamed, but they passed a rope around his body and knotted it tightly.

Then they raised him in their arms and poised him over the trap.

By this time he had shrieked himself hoarse. His voice was scarcely louder than a whisper.

But his face was fearful to contemplate, such bitter agony did it express.

He had to deal, though, with men of iron hearts, and they paid no attention to the terrors of the shivering wretch.

Balancing him for a moment, they hurled him suddenly forward.

His body fell with a heavy thud upon a revolving water-wheel below.

An instant afterwards there was a hideous crushing sound, and then another and another, and then the same splashing bumping noise which previously was audible.

"Close the trap," said the count.

He was obeyed.

"Look to the other prisoner."

They crowded round Edgar Deville, who had slipped from his chair and lay in a swoon upon the floor.

They raised him and carried him back to the temporary bed that had been made for him with the aid of a few old ragged blankets, and here he lay white and motionless like a corpse.

*   *   *   *   *

Several hours passed away. The band had betaken themselves to their several orgies in the banqueting room below—all save an old man, who had volunteered to sit by the fire and watch the sick captive.

Edgar slumbered fitfully, and frightful dreams haunted his restless couch. The old man, weary of his long vigil, and sleepy with the hot fire, began to nod in the chimney corner.

A profound silence reigned in the upper part of the house, in the workrooms, and the chambers adjoining, and the distant portion of the apartment in which Edgar lay on his bed was filled with heaped-up shadows, grim and ghastly.

From out the pitchy darkness a form came stealthily—a cloaked figure, creeping, creeping, with noiseless tread, upon the slumbering watch.

Poor wretch, he dreamed not of his danger. He smiled in his sleep and mumbled softly to himself.

The dark figure crept closer still.

Its upraised hand clutched a knife.

The old man in his sleep moved his position and the figure sprang quickly back. Then waited and watched in an awful silence.

Not the faintest sound was to be heard, except the shivering of the cinders as they seemed to shudder upon the hearth.

And now he slept again, and once more the phantom stole upon him.

Once more the knife was raised in the air. This time it fell with deadly purpose.

The old man half rose from his seat, uttering an inarticulate cry, then came down heavily upon his face and lay a corpse upon the hearth.

The figure stooped over him hastily, and laid a hand upon his shoulder.

"Dead!" said a woman's voice, in a low hissing whisper. "Now for the other."

As she spoke she crept towards Edgar Deville, and, kneeling by his side, shook him again and again.

The sick man languidly opened his eyes and stared at her unmeaningly.

"Wake up! Wake up!" she whispered.

"What is it?"

"Escape."

"Escape?"

"Yes. There is not a moment to be lost. If you come now we can get away unobserved."

"Get away?" repeated Edgar. "How? We shall be caught, and then—Ah! the trap. Where have they put him?"

"Don't stay talking here of traps, you fool," said the woman, angrily. "Are you mad? I offer you liberty. Will you accept it?"

"Yes, yes."

He struggled to his feet as he spoke.

He was weak and giddy, and clung to the objects around to steady himself.

"What is the matter?" asked the woman. "Come along."

She did not seem to know he was wounded, or to notice the linen bandage on his head.

"Are you ready?" she asked, presently.

"Yes, yes."

"Come, then. Hold my hand."

He did as she bade him, and, with a tremendous effort, collected something of his lost strength and steadied himself.

Then he followed her.

She led him along through the workroom, down a passage, and another, and another, by a flight of stairs, and out into a courtyard.

He was still giddy and bewildered and like one in a dream.

She led him through a neglected garden and across a shrubbery, through a gap in the hedge, and out into a lane beyond.

There there was a cab waiting.

She told him to get inside and he obeyed mechanically.

Then she followed, and in silence they drove away.

He might have fallen asleep or swooned upon the road.

At any rate he took no notice of the course the vehicle pursued, and only aroused himself at last when the cab stopped in front of a small cottage, standing by a road side, and having a broad open marsh land in its rear.

"We will get out here," said the woman.

Edgar obeyed.

"Now follow me."

She entered the cottage.

"Now you can lie down on that bed for a time and rest yourself. You won't be wanted till the day after to-morrow. Be ready then."

"For what?"

"You will learn when the time comes."

[THE FATAL DUEL IN THE WOOD.]

With these words she left him in charge of a man who appeared to be a cut between a gamer and a poacher.

This person, although of rough manner and appearance, tended him kindly, providing him with medicines and other necessaries. Several times did Edgar endeavour to draw him into conversation, but to each query his wary nurse only replied with an evasive answer.

Thus wearily enough the next day and night passed away, until the time at last arrived which Edgar Deville's mysterious liberator had fixed upon for the performance of the unnamed service she required at his hands.

CHAPTER XIX.

THE FATAL DUEL IN THE WOOD.

UPON this very morning, and almost at the same hour, our heroine, Rose Mortimer, on rising from her couch at the strange house to which she had been taken after making her escape from the theatre, found a disguise waiting for her to put on, in which she was to act an unknown part in some strange comedy, of the plot of which she had no knowledge.

Little dreamt she then that a man destined to play so important a part in the varied drama of her life was also disguising himself under very similar circumstances.

No. 7.

Yet such was the case.

Edgar Deville awoke from his slumbers, and found that during the night his clothes had been removed, and in their place another suit substituted.

The new suit was of very good material, but he by no means relished the idea of putting it on.

It was a servant's livery—the dress of a groom—and consisted of a tight-fitting body coat, leather breeches, boots with dark brown tops, a hat, and a ade.

"Humph!" ejaculated Edgar as he contemplated these preparations. "This is more than I expected, certainly. I wonder whether I shall have a hard lot of it in my new place."

Anything was better than what he had left, though, and this reflection consoled him.

"In for a penny in for a pound," observed Edgar to himself. "I might as well be hanged for an elephant as a hedgehog. It won't hurt me any the more."

He turned the garments over and over, and hesitated about beginning his toilet.

But his jailor quickened his movements by knocking at the door, and calling out to know whether he was not nearly ready.

"In half a minute," responded Edgar.

Then, without further delay, he scrambled into the clothes.

When he was ready the man came and opened the door and told him to follow.

They went together outside the cottage, where a horse was waiting ready saddled.

"You can ride, I suppose?" said the man.

"Yes, I can."

"Get on, then, and trot up to the end of that lane. You'll find your mistress there waiting for you."

Edgar could not refrain from smiling as he put his foot into the stirrup.

This was an adventure with a vengeance.

"I don't suppose a lady ever before engaged a servant in this style," he thought.

Then he turned the horse's head in the direction indicated, and trotted away.

Sure enough, at the end of the lane was a lady on horseback waiting to see him.

Was this the lady he had seen over-night?

Yes, there could be no doubt about her being the same person, although he had not had much opportunity of observing her in the faint and weary state in which he was.

He knew her, though, when she spoke, as the reader does also, for she was the woman called Clara, who had committed the murder, already described, in the green-room of the Babylonian Theatre.

She regarded him attentively as he approached.

"You make a good groom," she remarked, with a smile.

"Thank you," replied Edgar, touching his hat.

"Address me respectfully when you speak," she said in a low but threatening tone. "We shall have an opportunity for a little private conversation perhaps in an hour or two, and then we shall understand each other better. At present remember you are my servant."

Edgar bowed. He would not for the world have offended this imperious beauty, being only too anxious to see a little more of her, and learn something of the mystery surrounding her.

There came a time, though, at no distant period, when he dare not refuse to do her bidding.

But that was when he had learnt the fearful secret of her life, and knew her for the fiend she was.

"Hold this," she said, passing him a box.

Edgar did as she desired.

It was a strange-looking box, and he could not refrain from scrutinising it anxiously.

It was mahogany, and brass-bound. What was it?

Not a dressing case, surely? Not that shape. Not a knife-box? Hardly that either.

Was it a box containing surgical implements? Ah! he was getting nearer the truth now.

"Take care of it," said the lady. "We shall want *them* directly."

"Want *them* !" Ah! he knew now.

It was a case of duelling pistols.

The beautiful and mysterious lady, then, was going to fight a duel.

She rode on at a brisk pace in front of him, and he followed deep in thought.

What part was he to play? After all, perhaps he was the one who was going to fight.

But still that could hardly be, or else why dress him in livery?

"She can't intend to murder me, surely," he thought.

"No. If she had she would not have taken so much trouble to rescue me."

Altogether it was a darkly mysterious business, and grew momentarily more mysterious and dark.

However, very soon he would learn all, and it was no good endeavouring to find out before the proper time, because his mistress did not look like a person to say a word more than she thought fit.

They rode on silently for about half an hour, at the end of which time they reached a low fence, over which the lady leaped her horse.

Edgar followed, and, crossing a large field, they approached a small but thick wood.

Again leaping a fence, they entered the thicket, and made their way onward at as rapid a pace as the growth of the underwood would permit of.

When they had proceeded for about a couple of hundred yards or so they arrived at an open space.

Here two persons were awaiting them.

One was mounted on horseback, like Edgar Deville's beautiful companion; the other was a young groom.

Edgar's lady rode up to the other, and, bowing, said in a cold voice—

"You see, madam, I have come."

"I see."

"But wonder, perhaps. You did not expect me?"

"Scarcely."

"That may, perhaps, account for your own punctuality," said Clara, with a sneering smile.

"Perhaps."

"Since we have met, however, and since we know exactly what we have come for, why waste any more time?"

"I think that quite sufficient has been wasted already. We might have settled our difference a week ago in London."

"No; I think not," said Clara, "as our difference can only be settled by the death of one of us. Had one killed the other in London at the time you first proposed the meeting, the survivor would have had a great deal of trouble in effecting her escape."

"That is true."

"Here, on the contrary, we can arrange matters differently."

"How?"

"We are out of earshot. The sound of our pistols, should they even chance to be heard by any one in the fields, will attract no attention. The servant I have brought with me can be thoroughly trusted. I presume, also, that you have made a judicious selection?"

"Yes, yes. She—he I mean—can be trusted perfectly."

"So much the better. The body of the one who is killed can be left here in the wood. Concealed in a ditch, it may easily lie unobserved for many days, until, indeed, it is no longer recognisable."

The other woman shuddered slightly.

"I myself have taken care that none of the linen I came in should bear any mark by which it might be known. You, too, I suppose have taken care ?"

"Yes."

"Shall we see to the arms, then ?"

"If you please."

The safest and most satisfactory method would be, I think, for each to load her own pistol."

"Yes."

At this point of the conversation Clara beckoned to Edgar Deville, and he bought forward the box containing the arms and ammunition.

It was a strange and marvellous sight to see this woman handling the deadly weapon, carefully and coolly charging it as though it were but a mere plaything.

The other followed her example, but with some slight traces of agitation about her pale and faltering fingers.

"My mistress is very marvellous," thought Edgar. "A plucky one, too, and no mistake. I shall back her as the conqueror. But the other poor girl! It's an awful shame—in fact, I'm not quite certain that it isn't murder."

He had gone through so much lately that he had got to be not over squeamish.

"It is a fair fight," he persuaded himself; "and though duelling has gone out of fashion, and particularly duelling among ladies, still it's all fair enough."

He comforted himself this way as well as he could, and thought no more about the moral side of the matter.

He had plenty to occupy his attention in watching the arrangements.

The other lady's groom, too, somewhat excited his curiosity.

A youthful groom, without any sign of beard or whisker.

A groom whose back hair was rather peculiarly arranged, as though it were so long that he was obliged to turn the ends up and plant his hat securely on his head to keep it straight.

Still more noticeable, a groom with very soft hands! and last of all, and strangest of all, with a plain gold ring on the third finger of his left hand.

Under these circumstances, and taking all these peculiarities into consideration, Edgar Deville began to have some slight doubts whether it was not also this person's first appearance in the character of a groom.

"And what was he in his last place, I wonder ?" thought Edgar. "Hardly anything in the coining way, I should think. What could he have been, unless—unless, to be sure, he was *a lady's maid ?*"

The preparations were by this time completed.

The two ladies dismounted, and gave their horses to their grooms.

Then they chose their ground, took their positions, and presented their pistols at each other, with what seemed to Edgar Deville to be a very careful aim.

"You give the word," said Clara.

Her antagonist nodded.

A moment afterwards she said, "Fire."

At the same instant she discharged her pistol. An instant afterwards Clara fired hers.

Then, with a shrill cry, her antagonist fell to the ground.

At the sight Edgar Deville sprang forward to assist her, but his mistress laid her hand gently but firmly upon his arm.

"Stay."

He looked at her in amazement.

"Am not I—" he stammered.

"No," she answered. "There is no need of your help. She does not require it."

"But—but—"

The female groom, stooping over the lady's prostrate form, at this moment uttered a loud exclamation of terror.

"She is dead," she cried.

"I told you so," observed Clara, with a fiendish smile.

"Now assist me into the saddle."

Edgar did as he was ordered, moving as though he were in a dream.

The other groom, stooping over the body of her mistress, now turned, and, pointing her finger at Clara, said—

"Your secret is safe with me, madam. You may feel certain that justice will not reach you by anything that I shall say of this morning's work, but God's vengeance will follow you sooner or later. That you cannot escape."

Clara laughed and tossed her head, and then, applying her whip, rode slowly away.

Edgar lingered for a moment, and then followed her.

"I beg your pardon, madam," he said, as he approached her, "are we to leave her thus ?"

"What would you do ?"

This, however, Edgar had a difficulty in finding an answer for.

"You are not desirous, I suppose, of getting hanged on her account ?"

They rode on silently after this.

They reached the cottage again in about half an hour, and the poacher-looking man came out to meet them.

"My servant will stay with you, Joe, for a few hours," she said. "You will see that he wants for nothing. Do you hear ? Look after him."

The man nodded, and then Clara, with a smile and a wave of the hand, rode away.

Deville followed the man into the house, wondering what was going to happen next.

He little dreamt, however, what was coming. He felt rather cold, and stooped over the fire to warm his hands.

Suddenly, however, he was clutched round the throat.

He exerted himself and struck out, but could not rid himself of his assailant.

The poacher had " put on the hug."

He hugged so hard that Edgar felt himself suffocating.

The blood rushed into his face. His eyes seemed starting from his head.

At last he became unconscious.

When he recovered he was lying on his back on a very dirty mattress in a damp room, something like a back kitchen.

Trying to raise his hand to his aching head, he was astonished to find that his wrists were in handcuffs.

"What is going to happen to me now ?" he asked himself, and in spite of his sufferings he could not refrain from a faint smile.

CHAPTER XX.

CLARA AND THE COUNT—THE JEWELS—THE "BEAUTIFUL FIEND"—THE SECRET HIDING-PLACE—THE HORRIBLE DOOM.

FOR a time, leaving that question unanswered, we must follow the fortunes of the murdress, for we have some explanations to make before we can return to our heroine, Rose Mortimer, whose part in the strange and exciting plot now hatching it would be difficult to render intelligible to our readers without first unrolling before them something more of the lives of those who are also to play a part in the tragedy.

Accompany us, therefore, to a magnificent drawing-room in a handsome house in Park Lane.

Two persons are present. They are the Count Lerno and Clara St. John.

It is night, and a fortnight after the events which are recorded in the last chapter.

The count was evidently in a rage. The lady, as usual, cold and sarcastic.

She was lolling negligently upon a sofa. He pacing the room with angry strides.

Suddenly he paused before her.

" Clara," he exclaimed fiercely, " I will be obeyed. So come, now, no more nonsense. Those jewels I will and must have."

" Find them and take them," she replied rising. " Give them to you I will not."

" Will not ? Do you think to play with me ? You forget who I am to whom you refuse obedience."

" I know well enough—to Pierre Duval, the forger and escaped convict, the rich man about town, the lucky gambler, the undetected swindler, and my—my husband, alas for me !"

As she answered thus in a bold passionate voice, Clara sat with folded arms looking up into the count's fierce white face.

" Lucky gambler, fool ?" he exclaimed, starting up and clasping her fair white shoulder roughly with his heavy hand. " I tell you, woman, my luck has gone, my skill has failed me, I have lost all I had this very night, and as for the coining, you know that every channel for passing the money has been suddenly closed. I have lost my credit, my honour, my name—nay, my life too for aught I know. They are after me this minute."

The woman laughed a terrible laugh to come from such crimson lips.

" The old story," she sneered, moving away, and going towards the door. " You need not have disturbed me at such an hour to repeat the same old old tale."

" Clara, I swear to you it is true," he shouted.

And rushing after her, he seized her arm and swung her round, dashing her head with such violence that she staggered and almost fell.

" I have lost every farthing I have, I tell you, and have given the Marquis of Brighton my bill for five hundred, which if I cannot take up to-morrow my credit is irretrievably gone. If you care nothing for me, think of your own interest, and do not let a paltry consideration of these few jewels stand between you and thousands perhaps."

" Perhaps," she sneered.

As he spoke the count stooped his ashy white face and tried to look into his wife's eyes.

But there was no tenderness in the act.

Even as he did so his lips quivered with fierce anger.

" Duval," answered the calm beautiful woman, showing nothing of the rage within her, " from the moment that you brought me to your house as your wretched wife you have lied to me. Why should I believe you now ?"

And she looked him full in the face.

" I cannot," she continued, a moment afterwards, turning away with disdain. " No, I cannot believe you. I do not. Your whole life with me has been but one lie, and by your former life I judge you."

" Then you refuse the diamonds ?"

" I do."

" You abandon me to my fate ?"

She shrugged her shoulders mechanically in reply.

For a few moments there was utter stillness in the room.

You might almost have heard the soft heaving of the white bosom under the silken covering as calmly as if jealousy, passion, anger, and revenge were unknown to it.

Clara sat silently regarding the fire.

The count leaned against the mantelpiece, his dark eyes fixed with sullen ferocity on his wife's face.

It was the lull before the storm.

Suddenly the count started up.

Then springing upon the fragile woman, as a tiger on its prey, he put both hands on her shoulders, bending her down under his weight.

" You have hated me and rebelled against me long enough."

He pressed his face close to hers.

" Listen to me, woman. I will search for the diamonds, as you tell me, and if I find them not, look to yourself ; for I swear it shall be the worse for you !"

She made no answer.

" I have lied to you, have I ?" he continued angrily. " This shall be the first example of the truthfulness Pierre Duval gives to you. Beware of it !"

Then he strode from the room, and, as she turned haughtily to look after him, she heard the door locked on the outside.

Even then her calmness did not desert her.

Her fair face became a shade paler, and she pressed her beautiful lips tightly together.

She knew well enough what manner of man Pierre Duval was, but even then her proud heart disdained to fear.

" Search," she muttered, with a scornful smile— " Search, my loving husband, but you'll not find. Your wife's jewels shall never deck the person of her infamous rival. No, no. I have already cleared from my path two women who stood in my way, but not through any jealousy. If, however, it is for her—"

She was silent, and her brow grew threateningly dark.

It was long after midnight.

The fair young face grew very pale as she sat there counting the minutes, and listening for the returning footsteps of her husband.

She was not afraid, but she was very white, and still, and anxious.

Suddenly a stealthy foot crept along the passage outside the door, nearest to her sofa.

A voice muttered softly—

" Madam the countess."

Then the footsteps retreated more quickly than they had come.

Somewhat startled, Clara rose from her seat, and hurriedly picked up a packet, which contained a key and a few words :—

" *For Heaven's sake be on your guard. Give up the jewels without a struggle. The count is desperate, and the ' Beautiful Fiend' is urging him on !*"

The blood rushed to her face as she read.

She looked round on the large handsome room, where not a sound reached her.

What means of defence did it offer ?

There were few servants in the house, and those all females.

Even could she rouse them, would they be able to protect her from danger ?

She placed her hand upon her heart, and, even in her fear, she smiled scornfully to herself to find that it throbbed so.

" Give up the jewels ?" she murmured. " Give them up to that wretch ? Never, never ! come what may."

Again she looked at the paper, and now, for the first time, it struck her that there was something strange in being warned in such a manner.

At first she had fancied it was her lady's maid, but a second glance convinced her that such was not the case.

The writing was not that of a common person.

The letters were sharp and angular.

Who could have learnt her private affairs? her habits? her husband's?

Who had entered the house at such an hour? for it must be a stranger.

"I must go and see," she muttered. "I have never yet feared to face man or woman. Why should I now?"

With a trembling hand, in spite of her daring flashing eye, she lit her small alabaster lamp, and then gathered up her silken skirts to move as noiselessly as possible.

She then unlocked the door and passed silently into the passage.

Not a sound was to be heard.

All the lamps had been extinguished hours ago, and there was something in the dark stillness of the gloomy house which struck with a ghastly chill on the young wife's heart.

Softly and slowly Clara passed through the long passages.

Not a sound disturbed the stillness.

Not a ray of light, but the tiny one shed by her own lamp, broke on the intense darkness.

Upstairs she went, through room after room.

Suddenly she paused.

She had trodden on something.

What was it?

She stooped and picked it up.

It was a woman's glove.

A very small lilac kid glove.

Tiny as Clara's fair hand was, that elegant little kid glove was too small for it.

She flung it down as though it had been some venomous reptile.

More than once had she been insulted by the praises of that Lilliputian hand; and that woman was in her house.

All fear now faded from her heart.

Tumultuous passion, fierce murderous anger, blotted out every softer feeling.

On she went.

A sound caught her ear.

A distant sound, but distinct enough to direct her steps towards her own bedroom.

More quickly now did Clara's noiseless feet pass along the thick carpets.

In a moment more she had reached the door leading to her own apartments.

It stood wide open, and there within she saw a sight which filled her with rage.

The wax tapers standing on the splendid toilet table were all alight, and in the chair in which not two hours ago she herself had sat lounged a woman—a small beautiful woman—with great dark glowing eyes, whose wonderful lustre and equally wonderful wickedness had gained for their possessor the name of the "Beautiful Fiend."

She was bending over the arm of the chair, watching the operations of the count as he knelt on the floor, ransacking the contents of a box, and Clara could see that those dreadful beautiful eyes of hers watched for the appearance of the jewels with an eagerness which was even more intense than her companion's.

"They were for her, then. He told me a lie," Clara murmured fiercely to herself.

"I told you they would not be there," said the Beautiful Fiend, in a voice loud enough to show that she cared little who might be within hearing. "You may be quite sure that they are safer than where mere locks and keys could make them. Count, you are a fool to go on wasting your time about the box."

"What would you have me do?" Lerno replied sharply.

The beautiful woman thrust out her white arm, glittering already with one magnificent bracelet, and pointed over her shoulder.

"You are a man," she said sarcastically, "and can't force a woman to find her tongue."

"You don't know her," sulkily returned the count.

"Introduce me to her, then," laughed the woman, sneeringly. "I'd wager all her diamonds I'd make her say where they are."

"You could not, I tell you," the count returned, angrily. "I tell you Clara would sooner part with her life than those cursed jewels. She has told me so many a time."

"Then take her at her word," hissed the Beautiful Fiend in a low voice, slowly advancing her face towards him.

There was a moment's silence.

"How much longer are you going to delude me with promises, Count Lerno? How much longer am I to wait for the jewels?"

Thus she continued, in the same hissing tone, with her splendid wicked eyes glowing like a demon's.

"How much longer is that woman, that obstinate silly wife of yours, to stand in my way?"

"Madge," the count said, half entreatingly, "trust."

"I won't trust," returned the woman carelessly. "A promise is a promise. You must choose between her and me, and there's an end of it. You've got your answer, Count Lerno."

So saying, she rose from her seat, drew her velvet mantle over her shoulders, and turned haughtily away.

But at the same instant the count's wife came with great stateliness into the room, holding the lamp above her head, and looking with fearless proud eyes at her treacherous husband and her beautiful rival.

For a single moment the latter looked with startling dismay into the face of the wife.

Then, with a shriek of deadly passion, she sprang upon Clara, clasping her throat with her tiny white jewelled hands.

Clara staggered and fell.

Her husband stirred not.

"The jewels!" hissed the Beautiful Fiend in Clara's ear, as she lay gasping and struggling on the floor beneath her. "Give me the jewels, or I will strangle you!"

Those tiny hands grasped with deadly power.

"The jewels!" said Madge, again relaxing her hold. "Will you give them to me?"

Clara moaned.

Her husband, pale as a corpse, crept forward.

"Give them up," he said, in a hoarse voice. "For your life, give them up. She is a fiend. I cannot restrain her."

"Woman," gasped the wife, as the wretch loosed her fingers for a moment, "listen. I will show you where they are. I will not give them to you."

"On your oath?" questioned the other.

Then, getting up, she suffered Clara to rise, saying—

"What has been done once can be done twice if you attempt to play me false."

"Have no fear," replied Clara with a ghastly smile, as she stood up and arranged her dress with fingers still trembling from her late struggle.

"I will tell you no lie. I will show you the place; but to you alone."

"Very well," said the other quickly. "After all, to give them to me is the most direct way. Madam, I am at your service."

With a mocking bow, she pointed to the door, and caught up her velvet robe in readiness to follow.

Clara took the lamp.

"You will await me here?" she said to her husband.

"Yes, yes. Make haste with all this tomfoolery," he said, impatiently.

"Then come."

They went out together, the fair wife and her beautiful rival.

Clara went first, holding the alabaster lamp on high.

Madge followed, her wicked glowing eyes never for a moment losing sight of their leader.

On, on they went, through the silent gloomy house, passing down passages, through suites of rooms, down staircases, till they reached the large marble-floored hall.

A ray of early morning light was creeping through a chink in the closed shutter.

Madge observed it and quickened her steps.

"Lose no time," she said, in authoritative voice. "Where are they?"

Clara turned.

"There is no hurry," she replied, calmly.

Then, with a certain deadly look in her blue eyes, she said—

"Must you have them?"

Madge only answered with a stamp of her tiny foot.

"Your harm be on your own head," muttered Clara.

And, with that deadly look still in her eyes, she held up her lamp and glanced round the hall.

"This way."

She walked to a spot above which was hung a full-length oil painting.

Reaching her hand to the edge of the frame, she leant heavily against it.

Immediately the picture began slowly to ascend, and a large square opening appeared in its place.

Without a word Clara entered this, followed by her companion, and led the way along a narrow passage to a flight of stone steps.

"Are you still determined?" she said, as, descending the steps, they reached a platform, balustraded from what appeared by the feeble light of the lamp to be a deep abyss.

The beautiful rival looked around her, slightly dismayed.

But there was something so mocking in Clara's cold smile that she tossed her head and said, dauntlessly—

"I follow."

Clara turned immediately, and, holding up the light, sought carefully along the brick wall against which the platform was built.

To any other eye that wall was a black mass of rough brick, one part exactly like another, but Clara's practised hand touched without hesitation a certain spot.

Then, almost before she could draw her breath, the whole of that apparently solid brickwork descended.

They now found themselves opposite a large iron-plated door.

Again Clara's magic finger went to its light work of pressing, and the heavy door turned on its hinges.

Then there was disclosed a flight of steps, which seemed to descend into the very bowels of the earth.

"Come," said Clara, sternly. "The diamonds are at hand—close at hand."

Down, down they went.

Down, down till the darkness seemed to close in on them heavily.

Till the damp air seemed to smell of death and the grave.

Till the silence was appalling.

"There," Clara exclaimed, with a faint smile, as they found themselves before an iron door. "The people to whom this house once belonged knew how to secure their valuables. Did they not?"

Madge shivered slightly.

"The jewels," she exclaimed sharply.

Clara took a small key from a velvet ribbon hanging round her neck, and put it in the lock.

The iron door rolled slowly on its hinges, disclosing a square vault, built of strong brick, and impervious to either damp or light.

Two small iron chests stood at the end of the vault.

"There are the jewels," she said, pointing to one of the chests. "Take them."

Madge clutched hold of her dress.

"Come in with me. I will not hurt you."

Clara entered calmly, and stood by while the other opened the chest, and the light at the same moment gleaming into it, disclosed a circlet of magnificent diamonds.

With an exclamation of admiring delight the Beautiful Fiend turned with wild impetuosity towards the jewels.

Utterly absorbed by her greediness to snatch at the wealth she had so long coveted, she forgot her distrust of her companion.

She started forward, almost burying herself in the glittering gems.

Suddenly, though, she raised herself, with a sharp wild cry.

A cry that rang through the silent vault, and woke the echoes of the subterranean passages with its shrill dreadful fear.

She tried to turn from the iron box.

But her two round snowy arms were strained down from within, caught firmly by a concealed spring.

It was an ingenious trap to catch thieves, well known on the continent.

Shriek after shriek.

Surely those agonised crys will reach more pitying ears than those of the white-faced woman who stands beside her, looking on at her agony with a cold triumphant smile.

"For Heaven's sake," she shrieked, "have mercy on me!"

Clara laughed.

"Have mercy, have mercy! Keep your jewels, keep your husband, only release me!"

"I will," Clara answered sternly. "I will grant you the mercy you would have given me. You know what that was."

She took up the lamp and turned away.

The wretched woman uttered another wild scream.

She endeavoured to wrench her strained limbs from that iron grasp.

"You will not leave me here? I shall die! I shall starve! Fiend, devil that you are, do not leave me to die by inches, buried alive. Oh! Pierre, Pierre!"

But those shrieks and cries echoed only under the deep earth.

No human ear but the frozen one of Clara heard them.

She was judge and avenger.

"Listen," she said, flashing the lamp on her victim's agonised face. "Your doom is fixed. There is no mercy for you on earth."

The woman moaned.

"You pray to one whom your conduct has turned into a torturing demon. Your hour has arrived. You have earned my hate, and I will be avenged."

Then stooping, and picking up the diamond circlet at the wretched woman's feet, she flung it scornfully round her beautiful head.

Snatching the glittering jewels from the chest, she threw them on her bare shoulders.

"When he comes to find you," she whispered in her victim's ear, "he will find you a glittering corpse, a gorgeous spectre!"

In vain the lost wretch strained those white arms.

In vain she mangled her little hands.

In vain she turned her great tigerlike eyes towards the door.

In another moment her shrieks rang with a muffled sound, for the avenger had closed the door again.

She was in darkness.

She was left there helpless—left thus manacled to wait for death.

Oh! horrible doom!

Oh! pitiless monster, to go smiling back to her husband, and say that his fair mistress has gone home with her jewels, and sent her love to him!

"What do you mean?" said the count. "What has become of her?"

"What I say."

"And she is gone?"

"Yes."

"Where?"

"Home."

"Home? that is strange."

And he rose and moved to the door.

She saw him go with a smile.

She listened and heard the street door close.

Then she hastily put on a cloak and bonnet, and stealthily left the house.

CHAPTER XXI.

THE MYSTERIES EXPLAINED.

A DARK history was that of the wedded life of the successful swindler calling himself Count Lerno and the ballet-dancer calling herself Clara St. John, but in reality being his wedded wife—the wife of Pierre Duval, the escaped galley-slave.

Through many lands had they travelled together.

Many daring frauds and artful robberies had they committed.

Much gold had they pocketed as the profits of their multitudinous rogueries.

It would be difficult to say which first had helped him on his way through life, his own smooth lying tongue, or his wife's ready wit and pretty face.

He was scoundrel enough to trade with her beauty, and perhaps did.

He sprang up suddenly a fashionable gentleman living in great style in Rome.

He was not Count Lerno then, but enjoyed some other title as euphonious, and to which he had quite as much right.

He came with letters of introduction from the first society at Naples, and he was soon one of the lions of the Holy City.

His wife was one of the reigning beauties.

After a while he suddenly disappeared.

Nothing was said against him.

No scandal was attached to his name.

Some extensive forgeries had been perpetrated successively, and the forgers had baffled all attempts to discover them.

There was not the faintest connection established between their crime and the sudden disappearance of the handsome nobleman.

Very soon after that a fashionable gentleman and his handsome wife made their appearance at St. Petersburg, and soon became extensively popular.

Some unknown persons committed large frauds just about the same time in that city.

It was so again at Strasbourg, at Nice, at Paris, at New York.

Disappearing suddenly from each, there arises almost always immediately after they are gone a great cry, and a great, but unavailing, search.

Awful thefts have been committed.

Daring forgeries, extraordinary burglaries, villanies of all kinds, but the thieves nowhere to be found.

In course of time London is honoured by the presence of a distinguished foreigner, Count Lerno.

He gives choice little parties, as we have seen.

He is said to be a bachelor and a *roue*.

Through his instrumentality a young and lovely lady makes her *début* as *premier danseuse* at the Babylonian Theatre.

She is very beautiful, very graceful, an exquisite dancer.

Lords and commoners fall madly in love with her.

Noblemen lay their hearts and fortunes at her feet.

But she turned away from them in scorn, and they eyed the count with jealous anger, for the beautiful dancer smiled upon him—so the gossips of the greenroom intimated.

The count, however, as has been said, bore the reputation of being a *roue*, a reputation which he certainly did his best to maintain.

Strange was it, then, that the beautiful Clara was not at all jealous.

Whispers went abroad concerning his intrigue with the beautiful Nina Lafleur, who committed suicide by blowing out her brains in the green-room of the Babylonian Theatre.

There are always evil tongues, and there were not wanting among Clara's enemies some who hinted darkly at murder.

The alleged motive was jealousy.

Still it was not believed.

A jury came to a different opinion, and after the orthodox nine days' wonder the affair was forgotten.

About the ninth day, too, there was something else to talk about.

There was another suicide.

This time a rich young lady, the heiress to a great property, committed suicide in a little wood, about twenty miles in a south-westerly direction from London.

She, also, was shot by a pistol.

There was a very great difference between the spheres in which the dead women had moved, and yet they were in some way remotely connected.

The name of the same man was brought into question upon each occasion.

It was a name which, previous to the first nine days' wonder alluded to, had been occupying a good deal of public attention.

It was the name of a young man of fashion, a rather profligate and extravagant young man, very deep in the Jews' books, who had suddenly and mysteriously disappeared.

He was called Edgar Deville, and was a friend of Count Lerno.

Some said he had run away with a certain lady of fashion who at that time happened to be suddenly missing, and it was through jealousy that Nina Lafleur committed suicide.

Others again said he had run away from his creditors.

But when the second lady died he might have come back, for he was the next of kin, and her estates at her death became his.

It was said that Edgar was in love with a balletgirl at the Babylonian, and had offered her marriage, though he was very poor to marry.

But, now he was again a man of property, why did not he return to London?

Whatever his reason might be, he certainly did not come back, or make any sign, although he was advertised for in every London paper, and detective officers were employed to search for him.

At last there was a very general impression that he was dead, and the next of kin began to congratulate himself upon his good fortune.

But he was premature.

All this time, although Edgar could not be produced, preparations were secretly being made in a certain house in the suburbs of London for producing a very fine imitation of that dashing young gentleman's face and figure.

A grey-headed old gentleman, with a sweet smile and cold cruel grey eyes, and a dark-browed young man, his companion, could have told them something of that little scheme.

Fortune had thrown into their path a certain pretty ballet-girl, with whom we are already acquainted.

At the first glance they had been both struck by the extraordinary likeness existing between Rose Mortimer and Edgar Deville, in spite of the difference in their sex.

To coax her to act the character seemed to them by no means a difficult task.

A ballet-girl at such a wretched place as that in which she was then dancing, to an audience composed of the vilest outpourings of the vilest part of London, could surely not be very particular as to right and wrong.

She must be very poor, and could be tempted or threatened, at any rate, into compliance.

Thus far we think we have now explained some matters which before may have appeared to the reader so mysterious as to be almost unexplainable.

One word more, and we can resume the course of our narrative.

Were the murders committed by Clara caused by jealousy?

The first two, decidedly not.

The third to some extent was prompted by the green-eyed monster, but she did not wish to kill the "Beautiful Fiend" because she loved her husband.

No, she was welcome to his love, such as it was, but she should not usurp her influence over him.

Not that she wished any longer to participate in his plots and schemes.

She had done with him—she was determined upon that point.

But she would not quit him without wreaking her vengeance upon him and his mistress.

The revenge upon the woman was sated, but with the count she had yet to deal.

Let us see what she is about to do.

CHAPTER XXII.

THE COUNT GOES A USELESS JOURNEY—TREACHERY—THE FIRE—THE EXPEDITION OF THE POLICE.

WHEN Count Lerno left the house he called a cab, upon arriving in Piccadilly, and told the man to drive as rapidly as possible to Brompton, where Madge's handsome villa was situated.

But when he reached the house in question he was very much astonished to find that it was dark and desolate.

He alighted and rang the bell.

There was no answer, and he rang again louder than before.

A very sleepy-eyed servant-maid came to answer him.

"Is your mistress within?"

"No, sir."

"Ah, she has not got here yet. I will wait for her."

"Certainly, sir. Do you expect her?"

"Yes."

The servant showed him into a handsome drawing-room, lit a lamp, and left him.

He waited an hour, and yet she did not come.

Then he started up, put on his hat, and, without speaking to the servant, left the house.

He was in a frenzy.

"One of the two has played me false," he muttered between his clenched teeth. "Whichever it be, she shall pay dearly for her treachery."

He called to a passing hansom, sprang in, and rolled along towards Park Lane.

When he reached the house he let himself in with his latch key, and ran hastily up stairs.

The servants had not risen yet.

The lights were burning in the drawing-room as they were when he saw them last, but his wife was nowhere to be seen.

He hurried to her bedchamber.

There the lights also burnt brightly. The contents of the boxes and drawers lay scattered about in confusion, as he had left them.

Clara was not to be seen.

He descended once more to the drawing-room.

He strode up and down the length of the floor.

"What does it all mean?" he asked himself. "Where have they gone?"

As he could learn nothing until one of the two returned to tell him, he sat down with what patience he could muster to wait.

"Unless I have those jewels the first thing in the morning they will be of no good to me," he said.

Then he rose and began to pace the room again.

"Where could the cat have hidden them? I wish I had followed and watched. I was a fool not to do so, but I never dreamt that Madge meant to play me false."

Then he swore a fearful oath.

"They were in league together. I see it all now. Why should I wait any longer? And yet—yes, I think I had better wait. Clara could never mean to leave me like this. We have quarrelled often enough before, and she has come round again. Oh, yes, she will come round."

On the table there was a decanter containing some wine.

He approached it, filled a glass, and drank its contents at a draught.

Then resumed his seat.

But he had not been very long in the easy chair before he began to feel singularly drowsy.

He did not intend to go to sleep if he could help it, and, rising, began to walk again.

But he was awfully sleepy.

To keep himself awake he thought he would have one more glass.

Rash act! He could not possibly keep his eyes open any longer.

"It's strange, too," he muttered. "I am not generally this way. I thought I could have sat up any length of time. I have played cards two nights and a day all of a stretch when it has been worth my while, and I was not very tired either, but to-night—"

He yawned and turned in his chair. After all, why should he not take a nap?

Click!

What was that?

He sat up and listened drowsily.

It sounded something like the cocking of a pistol.

Click!

There it was again, but this time at the opposite side.

"What the deuce is it?" he said.

He listened. All was still.

The drowsiness was stealing over him. He struggled with it vainly.

All at once he began to cough, and started to his feet.

The room was full of smoke.

[THE MURDEROUS ATTACK.]

He ran to the door, but found it was locked. This, then, had been the noise that he had heard.

He was locked in.

By whom?

His wife.

Under ordinary circumstances it would have been easy enough to force one of the doors open, but a strange weakness had come over him.

He could not battle with the lethargy which seemed to hold him captive.

The smoke was now rapidly filling the room, coming, as it seemed to him, from under one of the doors.

The house was on fire.

The staircase in a blaze.

Staggering weakly across the room, he approached one of the windows.

It was fastened with the usual bar and catch, easy enough to undo, but his fingers refused to do their office.

Vainly he strove to press the spring, but a baby's hand would have been of as much service.

Again and again he tried, but with the same effect.

Then yelled for help.

He staggered back towards the door.

But now his strength seemed utterly to fail him.

His brain was in a whirl.

No. 8.

With a deep groan, he fell heavily to the ground.

At this moment loud and piercing shrieks rent the air—

"Fire ! Fire !"

The servants were screaming shrilly in their bedrooms above, for the stairs were one raging furnace.

* * * * * *

When Clara left the house she hurried away in a westerly direction, and, hiring a cab, drove as it seemed in pursuit of her husband.

She came in due course to the villa where the count was awaiting Madge's return.

Here, in front of the house, having sent away the vehicle, she waited patiently until he came out again.

Then she followed him to Park Lane.

She saw him go in, and waited once more, with the same patience, for him again to make his appearance.

As he did not come, however, she took from her pocket a small latch key, and quietly entered the house.

Then stole on tiptoe upstairs.

In at most a quarter of an hour she again descended to the street.

Then stole stealthily away.

It was now broad daylight, but the streets were still and deserted.

It was the quietest hour, perhaps, of all the twenty-four.

No one was about, and no one noticed the bright glare within the house, until the piercing shrieks of the servants were heard rending the still morning air.

Caring very little what might be their fate, Clara hurried away.

She this time caused herself to be conveyed in the direction of Scotland Yard.

Before the police station she stopped her cab and alighted.

The inspector taking the night charges raised his eyes as she entered, seemed to recognise her, and bowed.

"I told you," she said, "that I would come unexpectedly."

"Is it time, ma'am ?"

"Yes."

"When will you be ready, ma'am ?"

"This moment. Have you any men here fit for the business ?"

"It will not take very long, ma'am. Not many minutes, although we certainly did expect a longer notice."

"I told you that the notice would be short. It could not be otherwise. I have been anxiously waiting for it myself for the last fortnight."

"And now you can put us on to the gang ?"

"I can take you to the place where you will find them all."

"Are there many ?"

"A dozen."

"Humph. Tough customers, I suppose ?"

"Very."

The inspector looked very grave at this.

"We must use great caution," he said.

"Every caution is necessary."

"And you think that you can put us on to the right scent ?"

"I am sure I can."

"If we could only have reconnoitred the premises previously."

"And ruined the whole business."

"How so ?"

"By letting them know that some treachery was afloat. No. Rely on me, and all will be right. This is the only time when you would have any chance."

"How so ?"

"This is the time when you will find them in their first sleep after their orgies are concluded. At any other time it would required at least three times their number to do anything with them."

The inspector reflected for a few moments

Then he called one of his subordinates and despatched him with a message.

In less than five minutes appeared a party of sixteen policemen, all in private clothes and armed with pistols and cutlasses.

Clara meanwhile had asked to retire to an inner room, and emerged in a few moments wearing a suit of male attire, which became her admirably.

In five cabs the party started for Fulham, Clara leading the way.

CHAPTER XXIII.

THE DANGEROUS EXPEDITION—THE ATTACK ON THE COINERS' DEN — THE STRUGGLE — THE EXPLOSION—THE BURNED TREASURE.

IT was between four and five o'clock when Clara and the police arrived in front of the old house at Fulham.

She was evidently well acquainted with all its details.

She caused the cabs to be stopped at a distance of fifty or sixty yards from the gate, and directed the men to divide and approach in separate parties.

On each side of the house were fields, and through the hedges they made their way noiselessly, under the shadow of the high garden wall, towards that wing of the house where the coining was carried on.

All was dark and silent within the house.

"This is the only time," said Clara, in a low voice, to one who had command of the party, "that we could have hoped to surprise them."

"How shall we now proceed ?"

"You had all better put on your list slippers now. Close to this spot is the entrance to the subterranean passage, and we will all descend together."

"I am afraid that even with all our care we may be overheard. There are so many of us."

"If we are overheard we are lost. The passages through which we are going to pass can be flooded at a moment's notice."

"Flooded ?"

"Yes. Do you see that dyke ? It is a sort of cistern. A ring can be pulled by any of the band. The exits of the passages are instantly closed, and the water pours in through the roof."

"Good heavens ! It is like walking into a trap."

"There is no other way, though."

"It would not be a good plan, do you think, for half the party to remain outside ?"

"What for ?"

"To keep guard."

"Out of danger, eh ?"

"Out of danger ? No. What do you mean ?"

"Would you take command of that part, and shall I go with the other ?"

"I'm not afraid to go, if you mean that. Only I don't want the vagabonds to escape, that's all."

"Ah, to be sure, I did not look at it in that light. However, they won't escape if we mind what we are about."

"I hope not."

"Leave it to me, and I'll take care of you. You see there are twelve of them and only sixteen of you, and they're roughish customers, and won't allow themselves to be collared and pulled along by the ear like a lot of boy pickpockets."

Clara's tone was very insulting, and the inspector was rather jealous of her authority.

He had distinguished himself many times by his sagacity and bravery, and he did not relish being led to glory by a petticoat, even though that petticoat was now disguised in male attire.

There was no help for it, though.

They had been for the last eighteen months vainly endeavouring to obtain some clue to the hiding-place of the gang, but hitherto their efforts had proved unsuccessful.

Even now without Clara's help they would be obliged to abandon the project.

Here they were certainly very close, too, but yet a very long way off.

It would not do to quarrel with the guide just now, at any rate, for they did not yet know the entrance to the cavern.

It was concealed in an artful way by bushes and briars.

Clara pulled these on one side and touched a secret spring.

Obedient to her pressure, a large moss-grown stone revolved slowly.

A flight of stone steps was then disclosed to view, down which, followed by the men, she cautiously descended.

They arrived at the bottom of the steps at the entrance to a passage.

It was long and low, and narrow, and very dark.

At sight of it the inspector made a slight grimace.

" Do you hesitate ?" interrogated Clara.

" No," he replied angrily. " Lead on."

" Hush, for Heaven's sake. A word, and you are lost. We know not now but that we may be walking in our graves."

It was a horrible thought, and the inspector devoutly wished himself safe back again in Scotland Yard.

But he had gone too far now to retreat.

They crept on in silence.

It was pitch dark.

" If we only had a lantern," he said.

" The first glimmer of it would be fatal."

" I hope we're all right," thought the inspector.

Then a little further on he asked—

" Haven't we nearly reached the journey's end ?"

" Very nearly. Now for it !"

As she thus answered, in a low whisper, Clara touched a spring, and a door opened in front of them.

Through the aperture was to be obtained a full view of a large dimly-lighted apartment.

Upon velvet couches around the stalwart forms of the coiners were stretched.

They were apparently unarmed, but close at hand were to be seen pistols and swords ready for use at a moment's notice.

" Now single your men, and make a simultaneous rush."

These were the instructions which Clara gave.

It was a terrible moment.

The heart of more than one of the policemen quaked within him.

But all now depended upon promptitude and energy.

They all prepared themselves.

Each singled out his man.

The inspector gave the signal, and they stole into the room.

When within a yard or two of their men one who was not asleep sprang up with a loud cry.

In an instant the rest were on their feet.

They stood for a moment staring wildly at their enemies, then seized their arms.

A fearful conflict now ensued.

A terrific struggle, in which both police and coiners contended for the mastery with the fury of demons.

While they were thus engaged Clara had stolen back into the passage and closed the door.

Turning in an opposite direction to that in which she had come, she in a few seconds reached the door of the store-room.

Here she knew the wealth of the gang was kept, and to this she intended to help herself.

But at the door she came face to face with an old woman.

She acted as cook, and that night was keeping watch over her master's gold in the absence of its ordinary guard, the old man whom Clara had killed when she rescued Edgar Deville.

She evidently knew the intruder, and doubted the honesty of her purpose.

At the same time Clara seemed to know that she must not waste any time in words.

There was the treasure, and if she must possess it it could only be by laying violent hands upon it.

There must be a struggle.

The sooner over the better.

Without a word she sprang at the other's throat.

She bore her down with a crash to the floor.

The old woman struggled violently, but ineffectually, to free herself.

The other pressed her down, and, wrenching violently at a neckerchief she wore, held her helpless until the black and swollen veins rose up like knotted cords on her forehead.

The first blow is half the victory, and by the suddenness of her attack she had carried the day.

The old woman's struggles grew gradually fainter.

At length she lay perfectly still.

Then Clara rose, and, opening the door, listened.

The sound of the clashing of swords, and the hoarse cries of the combatants met her ears.

She gazed round the room.

"There is plenty of time," she muttered to herself. " While they are fighting I can get clear off."

She approached a small wooden box as she spoke.

It was locked.

On the old woman's neck, however, was a cord, to which a key was attached.

Clara took it off and inserted it in the lock.

It turned easily.

Next moment she was on her knees before the gold, cramming it into her pockets with both hands.

But, while she was so engaged, of a sudden there was a terrific explosion.

A fearful thundering crashing sound.

Then a great smoke, which half choked her, and a violent agitation of all the articles which the room contained.

A rumbling and rolling, and rattling and clattering, in which huge masses of brickwork fell around her like hail.

Huge beams of wood sprang from their places, and flew like chips, and the walls came tumbling down on all sides, like the walls of a house built of cards.

For a few moments she lay crouching before the box in trembling terror, half covered with the ruins, her hands clasped over her eyes, striving as it seemed to shut out from her sight the hideous death which every instant threatened her.

But after a couple of minutes had thus passed she opened her eyes and, raising them, saw that the roof had been blown off by the explosion, and that only the bright blue sky was above her.

Around, all was ruin and desolation.

God, in His great mercy, and for His own inscrutable purpose, had saved the guilty wretch's life.

She rose tottering to her feet, and began to crawl out from the rubbish which surrounded her.

But scarcely had she moved, scarcely had she had time to be quite certain that her life was safe, when her thoughts reverted to the gold.

Could she leave it there?

No.

At the risk of death she must yet stop to fill her pockets with the stolen treasure.

She stooped down again, and busied herself with the box.

But the lid defied all her efforts to raise it.

A falling beam had jammed it down tightly.

She wrenched and tugged at it in vain.

The box was jammed as tightly among the mass of fallen brick and stone surrounding and half covering it as though it formed a portion of a solid rock:

No, she must abandon her prize after all.

Rising, therefore (who can say how reluctantly?), she crawled out of the ruins and crept away, fearful lest she might be seen and questioned respecting what had taken place.

Indeed, she now could hear the voices of the cabmen who had brought down the party to the scene of this terrible tragedy.

They were climbing about among the ruins, searching for the policemen and the coiners.

In vain, alas! for the ruins had crushed all to death.

*　　*　　*　　*　　*　　*

At the stillest hour of the night let us now take the reader to some other ruins, in Park Lane.

Here two ghostly shadows flitting to and fro search for a secret subterranean passage.

One of them is Clara.

The other is Edgar Deville.

This time she is more successful.

With her companion's aid she effects an entrance into the secret passage.

Pursuing the way which Clara and her victim Madge had followed when going upon the fatal journey from which the latter never returned, they came at last to the door of the cell where the hideous crime had been perpetrated.

———

CHAPTER XXIV.

ROSE A CAPTIVE — THE DISGUISE — THE PLOT — THE FRAUD REVEALED — THE ATTEMPTED ESCAPE — AGAIN A PRISONER.

WHEN Rose Mortimer awoke upon the following morning she reflected a while upon the many startling incidents which had concluded the eventful yesterday.

She sprang from her couch in a state of fright, and looked anxiously about her.

The terrible words which the old man and his younger, but no more scrupulous, companion had spoken now began to fill her with renewed alarm.

Upon the preceding day the stirring events which had brought her into contact with them had so completely riveted her attention that she could not give their speeches full importance.

Now she began to ponder over their injunctions, and the threats of terror with which they had been accompanied.

What, then, could be the nature of this real life comedy in which she was destined to play?

Surely something wild and unnatural, or they would not have used such severe measures to prevent all possibility of her escaping.

She looked about her anxiously.

The door, she could see at a glance, was fast closed.

However, some means of escaping from this alarming thraldom must certainly present itself, if she kept continually upon the look-out.

She now became aware of one startling fact.

Her clothes had been removed!

There place, however, had been supplied by a complete suit of male attire.

This, then, was the explanation of some portion of the drama in which she was called upon to play.

She examined the clothes attentively, and found them to be perfectly new, and of elegant material and make.

For an instant she contemplated arraying herself in these garments.

But presently the thought flashed across her mind that she might be unwillingly abetting a foul conspiracy, and she determined to resist this preliminary step.

But how to act?

This was a most difficult question to answer.

However, she was spared much trouble upon this head, for within half an hour she heard footsteps pause by her chamber door.

With one bound she was at the door, grasping the handle with both her hands.

But here she did her detainers a slight injustice.

No violence need have been anticipated for the present.

All that they wished her to do was to put on the male attire with which they had provided her.

There was a rap upon the door.

"Are you waking yet?"

It was the voice of the younger man.

Its striking tones were not to be mistaken.

There was a sweetness about it, which, however, from the associations, struck most unpleasantly upon Rose's ear.

While she was meditating the advisability of replying the young man grew impatient, and repeated his question.

"Rose Mortimer," he called, rather louder than before, "are you awake yet?"

"Yes."

"Are you ready to depart?"

"Where?"

"You answer my question by putting another. Answer me."

"I cannot say if I am ready to depart, unless I am acquainted with the destination."

"That cannot affect you in any way whatever, Rose Mortimer."

"Then I refuse compliance."

"You cannot!"

"Cannot?" repeated Rose, indignantly. "Nay, I do."

"Foolish girl!"

"And I warn you that unless my clothes are immediately restored to me, and I am allowed to depart, I shall at the very earliest opportunity represent my treatment at your hands to the nearest magistrate."

After this desperate speech, which had called for all Rose's courage to utter it, she paused in silence to wait his reply.

None came.   Then her defiance had not been without effect!

Another instant, howeve and this pleasant illusion was most effectually dispelled.

She heard a key placed in the lock!

It was turned, and the sound struck terror to her heart.

"You hear that?" demanded the man from without.

"I do," faltered Rose.   "I pray you—"

"Fear nothing.   No harm is intended you; but I would have you understand how useless it is for you to attempt to resist us."

"By what authority?" began poor Rose, in indignation.

"Pah!" said the man.   "Oblige me by using such despatch as possible.   Time presses."

And then, upon Rose Mortimer still denying his authority, the door was partially opened.

Rose gave a faint shriek.

"You see," said the man, "that we are willing—nay, anxious—to treat you with every consideration and forbearance ; but you must obey us. I think now that you will do as we request."

Rose was humbled.

" What do you wish ?" she demanded in faltering accents.

" Dress yourself."

" But my clothing is gone."

" In the things you have, then."

" At least, let me know the purpose for this strange diguise."

" No—enough for you that you have a mission to fulfil which you must and shall carry out. Don't attempt to thwart us, for you see how you will fail, and the consequences of the attempt must recoil upon you with disastrous effect."

Further resistance was useless.

And now that Rose had no other alternative she hastily arrayed herself in the suit of male clothing.

The alacrity with which she now obeyed the request—or rather command—of the man procured her much more consideration than before, and he waited patiently without, until she announced that she was ready.

Then he entered.

A glance at his costume showed her that he was attired for travelling—a circumstance which she mentally noted, as she wondered if it had anything to do with her own disposal.

For a minute or two he surveyed her attentively, in a way that brought the crimson blood with a rush into her fair face.

She made, in truth, a dashing young man, and her glass had of course assured her of the fact.

The close scrutiny to which she was now subjected, therefore, caused her blushes to rise, for she could not but attribute his glances to admiration.

" It is really marvellous !" he exclaimed. " You will do capitally ; but you must not move about with those mincing little steps now, or you will be discovered at once."

" By whom ?"

" No matter that—by any one who chances to see you—any one that we do not wish should discover you."

" But, at least, tell me the reason I should fear discovery."

" Not a word."

This was all he would utter, and Rose was forced to rest contented.

Arrived below, he led her into an apartment in which a meal of the most sumptuous description was prepared.

Here he handed her to a chair, with a politeness which seemed to come but ill from one who had observed such a singular behaviour towards her before.

" Eat," he said. " Take as much refreshment as you can now, for we are about to start upon a long journey."

Rose did not now even contemplate discussing the authority by which he uttered his commands.

The air of command appeared to be quite natural to him, and after a short time she did not think of gainsaying anything he advanced, even though she was so immediately interested.

While she was partaking of the rich viands before her the old man returned.

He greeted our heroine with a grave inclination of the head, and then turned to the younger man.

" Good morning, Maurice," he said, in the gruff tone which had so startled Rose upon the previous day.

" Good day, sir."

" Are you ready ?"

" Not quite," said the other, glancing at their guest.

Rose caught the look, and at once moved from the table.

" Do not disturb yourself," said the old man. " Maurice will wait for you. You understand ?"

The latter words were addressed to the young man, who bowed in reply.

" Oh, I am quite prepared," said Rose Mortimer.

" Nay, but you had better breakfast well ere we depart," said Maurice. " We shall not make a stage for some time yet."

The old man now motioned to the last speaker to leave the room.

Then he drew a chair for Rose, and placed himself at the table opposite to her.

" Now," said he, " before we leave I have a word or two of caution to impress upon you, to which I beg you will give your best attention."

Rose bowed in silence.

" Your name is henceforth Edgar Deville," he began.

" Edgar Deville ?"

" Ay."

" But—"

" Pardon me," said the old man. " In order to lose no time at present, oblige me by listening with attention to what I have to say, without interruption. I told you yesterday that you had to play a part in a comedy of real life."

" You did, sir."

" Then remember. Explanations for the present are impossible. But bear in mind, as your starting point, that you answer only to the name of Edgar Deville."

" Very well, sir."

" The part we now call upon you to play touches upon a most critical business for myself and Maurice. Follow out our instructions implicitly. Have what confidence in us you may—"

" Confidence ?" interrupted Rose. " Oh ! that is impossible !"

" Perhaps. But no matter. Under any circumstances you must obey us to the letter, and all will be well. You will achieve a brilliant position, be courted and fêted in society, and have incalculable wealth at your command."

Rose was perfectly dumbfounded.

" But surely, sir," she said, " there must be some explanation of this."

" Anon."

" And is it possible for me to play such a part as that to which you allude in utter ignorance of its object ?"

" Perfectly."

" But, sir, I entreat you, if possible, to give me some explanation, and rely upon my discretion."

" Presently, I tell you," replied the old man. " For the present you must be satisfied that whatever you may have to do with us now can only result in your own social advancement. Any other girl would have jumped at such an offer as ours, believe me."

" I do believe you," replied Rose, " and therefore I cannot imagine why you have forced your benefits upon me, who am so unwilling to serve my own advancement."

" Unwilling, ay ? And that's the mystery to me, that you, whom we have rescued from such a precarious mode of existence, should have displayed so much obstinacy."

" Not obstinacy, sir," said Rose. " If I am so well treated by you and Mr. Maurice, as you call the gentleman who has just left us, I can but be grateful for your kindness. I only object to work in the dark."

" Tut, tut !" said the gentleman impatiently. " Let

it suffice for you that this is necessary for us at present."

At this period of the conversation the young man again entered the room.

Rose glanced up, and perceived that he held in his hands a hat and light overcoat.

"The completion of my male disguise," she thought.

Her conjecture proved to be correct.

"Will you put on these, Mr. Deville?" said Maurice.

Rose looked at the old man, but did not offer to move.

"Did you not hear Maurice?" said the latter to Rose.

"I? Oh! yes. Did you address me?"

"Yes," said Maurice. "I addressed Edgar Deville. You are Edgar Deville from this day forth remember."

Rose was so startled by their manner, and so thoroughly overawed, that without a word she took the hat and coat from his hands and put them on.

Both of the men stared at her, as if wonder-stricken at her appearance.

"Is it not wonderful?" exclaimed the old man in a subdued voice, as if he had seen a phantom.

"Marvellous!"

Rose glanced from one face to the other for some explanation of the mysterious words.

But not the faintest notion could she gain of their meaning.

"Come," said the old man. "But before we depart I may as well inform you, in order to avoid any unpleasant embarrassment later, that my name is Wharton. This is my son, Maurice Wharton. And now I think we shall do. Pray be counselled by us and follow our injunctions without question, and, believe me, you shall have no cause to complain of your treatment at our hands."

"Enough, sir," said Rose. "I am prepared to follow you. If it is to harm you would lead me the evil be upon your head."

Neither of them replied to this.

Mr. Wharton took a small travelling bag in his hand, threw a travelling rug over his arm, and led the way downstairs.

Rose followed him, and Maurice Wharton followed her closely.

A coach awaited them at the door, and they handed Rose in.

Mr. Wharton followed, and seated himself opposite her, whilst Maurice Wharton took his seat beside the driver.

Up to the present Rose had really nothing to complain of.

She had been treated by both the gentlemen with the utmost consideration which could be observed towards her under the circumstances.

The only thing of which she had to complain was the strange uneasiness which she experienced in the business.

She felt as if they were conducting her to some fatal spot, from which she would struggle in vain to escape.

Full three hours must have elapsed, and not a word had been spoken, when they paused at a country inn to change horses.

Mr. Wharton, as if arousing from a kind of stupor, looked up, glanced out of the window, and then, as if becoming suddenly aware of Rose Mortimer's presence, addressed himself to her.

"Would you like to descend and rest a while here, Mr. Deville?"

Rose looked about for Mr. Deville before she remembered herself.

She had not yet become quite reconciled to her new appellation.

"I should, indeed, Mr. Wharton," she replied, "if convenient."

"Of course, if you wish it."

"Thank you."

Mr. Wharton tapped at the front window, and his son jumped from the box, and came to the carriage door.

"Did you want me, sir?"

"Mr. Deville wishes to rest until the fresh horses are put to," replied Mr. Wharton.

The young man held his arm for Rose to descend, and then, drawing her arm through his, they strolled into the inn.

"What can I get you, Edgar?" asked the young man.

"Nothing, thank you," replied Rose. "I only wish to rinse my hands before proceeding. The day is so hot, and I am stifling. I think that it would refresh me."

"Very well."

He rang the bell, and a waiter appeared.

"Will you show this gentleman into a room, and provide him with water and towels?"

"Yes, sir."

The waiter led the way, and conducted Rose into a room adjoining.

Here she was provided with the requisites for her hasty toilet, and left to herself.

This was more than she expected.

She did not even dare to hope, from the vigilance previously exercised in her care by her self-elected guardians, that they would leave her for a moment unwatched.

No sooner was she alone than she began to reflect upon her singular position.

Not only to reflect upon it, but to cogitate the chances and the benefits of flight.

Up to the present her acquaintance with Mr. Wharton and his son had only resulted in benefit to herself.

But this should have no weight with her if there were the slightest chance of eluding them.

Something dreadful she anticipated must be the destined sequel of the present luxury.

Therefore she would fly.

But how?

Chance had placed the means at her command.

The apartment in which she now found herself opened by two lattice windows into a little bower or summerhouse.

This led into a kitchen garden.

In an instant she had removed the window fastening and stepped forth.

Violently she trembled now, as if she were about to commit some deed of desperation.

She felt that she was guilty of deceit.

But no, she reasoned that, whatever were their motives in detaining her, her detention had been forcible, and she was perfectly justified in eluding them by any means in her power.

The garden was gained without noise, and Rose trod lightly across the beds, and arrived at a gate.

It was the only opening in the hedge at that part of the ground.

The gate was fastened and the only way to surmount this obstacle to her progress was to climb it.

This was scarcely resolved upon ere it was accomplished.

And now she stood there—free!

The feeling of relief which she now experienced it would be impossible to describe.

She had quitted the house by the back, and nothing remained but to follow straight on the path to which she was bearing.

It was a narrow lane, edged upon either side by a steep embankment.

And now commenced her flight.

But, alas! a cruel disappointment was in store for her.

Before she had proceeded a hundred yards a dark form stepped from an opening in the embankment, and Mr. Wharton stood before her.

"Mercy! mercy!" she faltered.

"So, so!" he said severely, "this is the way you would repay the confidence I repose in you. Henceforth you have made your life less pleasant. Edgar Deville, you may now consider yourself indeed a prisoner."

CHAPTER XXV.

IN THE "BLACK COUNTRY"—FORCED ONWARDS
—ANOTHER STRUGGLE FOR LIBERTY.

POOR Rose Mortimer now allowed herself to be led back to the carriage without a murmur.

Fate was against her.

This she felt must be true.

With this conviction came a feeling of helplessness, which was ruin.

For a while they heaped reproaches upon her head, to which she did not offer the slightest excuse or reply.

And now the journey was once more resumed.

For the remainder of that day they travelled incessantly.

Not a word was exchanged between them.

Night came on, and they put up at an inn till the morning.

Rose did not here venture to repeat her attempt at escape.

Mr. Wharton occupied a chamber adjoining hers, and Maurice Wharton slept below.

At sunrise Mr. Wharton was stirring and at Rose's chamber door.

"Mr. Deville," he called, after tapping at the door, "are you ready?"

"Immediately, sir," said our heroine, awake on the instant.

"Take your own time. We shall wait for you below."

Then she hurriedly prepared herself for another day of adventure, wondering what was to be the next step in her eventful career.

As soon as her toilette was completed she descended, and found Mr. Wharton and his son ready to start.

A light breakfast was pressed upon her and finished with all possible haste.

Then a man came to announce that the horses were put to, and all was ready for departure.

We shall not dwell longer upon this painful journey.

Suffice it to say that the whole day was spent in it, and in the same grim silence as before.

Towards evening they began to pass through a rough country, the inhabitants of which appeared to Rose to be half savages.

Grim weird-looking women, and dark-visaged men, with dirt-begrimed flesh and bristling beards, and with big brawny bare arms, they encountered at every step.

It was here that Mr. Wharton broke a terrible silence which had lasted over two hours.

And much to Rose's relief.

"Where are you taking me to?" asked our heroine in alarm.

"You are alarmed at these people?"

"I am."

"These are the miners and their wives. They all have that wild appearance, from the nature of their employment. They pass three-fourths of their time away from the light of day, and it is no wonder that they should be different from other men."

"They are indeed different."

"But they are perfectly harmless," said Mr. Wharton, observing the look of fear upon Rose's countenance.

"Possibly; but their appearance is enough to frighten one."

"Ah!" said Mr. Wharton. "You will very soon get used to them. I know most of the miners for miles about, and should not fear to encounter any of them alone and unarmed at any hour."

Rose was silent now.

She was brooding over his words—

"You will very soon get used to them."

Did her jailors—for so she mentally designated them—mean to keep her there?

Great as was her curiosity upon this point, she felt that she dared not put the question to either of them.

Less than half an hour's drive through the mining districts brought them to a gentleman's country seat— a handsome dwelling, richly appointed, and situated in the centre of a vast park.

To Rose's surprise the carriage drove up to the principal entrance, and Mr. Wharton dismounted.

"Come, Mr. Deville," said he, handing out our heroine, "this is our destination, reached at last."

Rose descended, and was ushered into the house by a servant in plain clothes, who was humble and obsequious to a degree.

What now puzzled her more and more was that all about her appeared to have anticipated her arrival!

Moreover, all knew her!

The servants, one and all, addressed her as Mr. Deville when they had occasion to mention her name.

At other times it would appear that her sex was quite forgotten, for she was always addressed as "sir."

One of the men, who was rather more loquacious than his fellows, ventured to hope that Mr. Deville was perfectly recovered, adding that, from the latest accounts received of him from Mr. Wharton, they had greatly feared that he (Rose) would not have been able to reappear at the Willows so soon.

Rose saw at once that this was part of the comedy which she was destined to play.

Understanding this, therefore, she very wisely refrained from saying ought in answer which she deemed might compromise her.

At the very earliest moment she determined to seek an explanation from Mr. Wharton, for now she had a fair excuse to offer.

The following day she began to grow more enlightened upon the point, before she had the opportunity of questioning Mr. Wharton as she desired.

The old housekeeper—Mrs. Grundy—came to pay Mr. Edgar Deville a visit of ceremony and offer congratulations.

This proved exceedingly embarrassing for our heroine.

However she endeavoured to fence with the questions put to her, she could scarcely avoid betraying herself.

"I hope that you have perfectly recovered now, sir," began the old dame.

Rose saw that she was supposed to have been unwell, and she replied accordingly.

"Ah, sir!" said the housekeeper, "we had sad accounts of you."

"Indeed?"

"Yes, sir," she continued, "and very much indeed we feared that you were unsettled severely."

She tapped her forehead most mysteriously as she spoke, and at once threw a light upon the subject.

She was supposed to be insane—or, rather, to have recently recovered her senses.

She got over this most unpleasant business as easily as possible, and dismissed the old dame.

She longed to be alone now to commune with her thoughts.

As soon as she accomplished this, and sat herself down to think over all that had occurred, it came to her like a flash of lightning.

She was supposed to be the heir to the property about, who had lost his wits.

But if this was the case, what had become of the actual owner?

This was a question which was not so easily settled.

Had he been removed from the place by fair means or foul?

No matter, she was so far enlightened, and she resolved to communicate her discovery to Mr. Wharton.

That gentleman listened to her without betraying the least surprise.

"You are perfectly correct in your surmise," he said coolly. "And now what do you say?"

Rose could say nothing.

She was so utterly bewildered by the discovery that for some time she could not resolve upon what line of conduct to continue.

She felt an unconquerable repugnance to the duties she was now called upon to fulfil, but she deemed it prudent to disguise this from Mr. Wharton or Maurice, his son.

Did either of them suspect she well knew that a strict watch would be set upon her actions?

She therefore resolved to appear only the better pleased at her remarkable position, and quietly await the moment to make a second attempt to release herself from the painful thraldom which was exercised upon her.

Two days passed, after her conversation with Mr. Wharton, without an opportunity presenting itself.

At length the moment for action arrived.

Maurice Wharton had left the house upon a visit to a friend who resided some few miles distant.

The old man retired early to rest, and all the house followed his example.

Rose determined to take advantage of these circumstances, and therefore very quietly dressed herself, and crept from her chamber.

The fastenings of the doors were very easily removed, for in that rural district no fears of robbers alarmed the peaceable inhabitants.

She was friendless, penniless, it was true; but she was escaping from an act of treachery and baseness which she had unwillingly abetted, and Heaven would lend its protection to the innocent.

With a silent prayer for aid in this hour of trial, Rose Mortimer left the house, and walked boldly out into the night.

CHAPTER XXVI.

FLIGHT INTERRUPTED — A DIFFICULTY — THE SLEEPING CHAMBERMAID—AN ACCIDENT—THE MISSING KEY—ROBBERY—THE ALARM BELL.

ROSE had barely started upon her flight when it occurred to her that it would be an easy task for her two captors to trace her by a description of her apparel.

She drew up short.

Paused and thought it over.

Then retraced her steps to the house.

She must seek a change of dress, and resume if possible the natural costume of her sex, and then her flight could be more easily effected.

Now that she was returned to the house, however, she found it no easy matter to attain her object.

She possessed no feminine garments, and had not the least idea where to procure them.

The servants she knew all slept in remote parts of the building, and were all very difficult of access.

However, it was no use now pausing to consider these obstacles.

A woman's apparel must be obtained at any risk, and she was speedily off in search of it.

In her rambles over the house she had noted the bedchambers of the maids, and had more than once contemplated resorting to one of them for assistance, should it ever become necessary.

Treading lightly over the creaking boards, Rose gained the door of one of their rooms.

The handle was turned almost in silence, and the room was gained.

The occupant of the bedchamber was sleeping heavily, and by her loud breathing assured the fugitive that she had no interruption to fear from that quarter.

Upon a chair beside the bed lay the sleeper's clothes—a whole attire complete!

Rose never paused to consider if the appropriation of these could be regarded in the light of a robbery, but immediately took them.

However, the difficulties were not over, even now that she had found the necessary garments to equip her for her adventure.

She had to effect her toilette.

But where?

She dared not attempt to regain her own apartment, the risk of discovery was too great.

Besides, what mattered it how hastily this was done?

That it *was* done was the main object.

This room, too, was garnished with those endless little aids to the feminine toilet which were lacking in her own masculine apartment.

The thought, the resolve, and its execution were almost simultaneous, and Rose rapidly divested herself of her male attire and donned the petticoats.

Never before had she made so shifty an adornment of her comely person.

However, out of her very expedition sprang a little misadventure, verifying once more the truth of the musty proverb, "The more haste the less speed."

In throwing the dress over her head she did not observe the necessary caution under the peculiar circumstances, and had the misfortune to catch it in the chair from which she had removed it.

Over it went with a loud crash, and up started the sleeping chambermaid, fully awake in an instant.

"Who's there?"

Rose now was in a dilemma!

True, she was in the dark. The only bit of light which the dark moonless night afforded was admitted through a small aperture in the window curtain, and fortunately did not touch her side of the room.

"Any one there?"

The fears of the startled chambermaid were by no means assuaged by the silence, and her voice trembled in a painful way.

But Rose was so occupied with her own perilous position that she could not afford a thought for the troubles of the chambermaid.

"Is there any one in the room?" again said the girl.

And then, upon the painful silence still continuing she slipped from the bed and walked to the door.

"Great Heavens!" mentally ejaculated our heroine, "she is going to alarm the house. Oh! whatever will become of me?"

Happily she was mistaken.

The frightened maiden had no more violent inten-

[THE ARREST.]

tion than to turn the key in the lock to secure herself from intrusion.

However, in her haste, and the trembling grasp she had of the key, she could not withdraw her hold in safety.

Out came the key and fell to the floor.

In an instant the whole force of this mishap flashed upon her.

She was locked in the room, and the key was lost !

But then she watched patiently, listening for the signal of the servantmaid's renewed slumbers.

A long long weary time it was, for the girl had been so throughly startled that she determined to keep awake until morning.

Fortunately for Rose, exhausted nature put in a superior claim to her determination, and the exhausted chambermaid once more slept.

Now began a search upon the floor, which was commenced with very little hopes of success.

The girl herself had spent twenty good minutes in the hunt after the key before she had given it up in despair, determining (she had murmured it aloud, and therefore Rose appreciated the difficulty) to wait until daylight.

Our heroine had a great venture at stake, and was not to be put off with a few embarrassments.

With a patience worthy of emulation she pursued her hopeless search.

No. 9.

At length even Rose's courage was exhausted.

She rose from her reclining position stiffened in the back—and, wonderful chance !—her foot touched the identical object upon the floor which had been the cause of so much patient search and trouble.

Its transition from the floor to the lock was the work of an instant.

The lock was turned,. and she stood in the passage.

Still a little difficulty remained.

She would, if possible, destroy all traces of her flight.

For this purpose she had brought her male attire with her.

Had the girl not been disturbed by that unfortunate accident no other precaution would have perhaps been necessary.

As it was, Rose well judged that she would make known at once the abstraction of her clothing, coupling it with the strange noise which had awakened her so rudely.

Mr. Wharton would at once divine the whole mystery, and pursuit would become an easy matter.

To throw them off the scent, therefore, more completely, the chambermaid must be left in the dark as to the midnight robbery of her garments.

Rose accordingly removed the key, and locked the door upon the exterior.

This accomplished without noise, she pushed the key under the door some little distance.

And now once more to resume her interrupted flight.

The hall door was gained and passed, and she hurried into the grounds.

Barely had she left the door ere a sound caused her to stop short in the utmost consternation.

The alarm bell of the mansion was ringing violently !

CHAPTER XXVII.

FLIGHT — THE POOL—PURSUIT—THE PRESUMED SUICIDE — A COMPACT OF BLOOD — DEVILLE'S DOOM—ROSE ESCAPES — THE LONE HOUSE ON THE MOOR—A MISTAKE—DANGER AHEAD.

FOR an instant Rose Mortimer paused irresolute, holding her breath.

Her heart stood still.

A renewed pealing of the bell, however, more loudly than before, brought her to her senses.

With a start, she hurried on like a frightened deer.

Presently she arrived at a small piece of water, wild and picturesque, but whose beauty had no charm for in her present critical position.

However, it served to jog her memory upon an important point.

The suit of clothes which she yet carried with her had to be disposed of.

Yes. Thus would all traces of her flight be destroyed.

She hastily gathered up some heavy stones and put them in the pockets of the coat and trowsers.

Then, with a handkerchief, she fastened them together, and cast them into the water.

The stones which she put into the hat unfortunately fell out as she threw it from her, and the hat floated !

This was a misfortune not to be remedied she deemed.

Future events, however, will show whether this could really be regarded in such a light.

No time now remained to attend to so trifling an occurrence, and once more she hurried onwards.

The pool was not quite passed when Rose, to her

dismay, caught the sounds of voices at no great distance, shouting apparently to some one following.

It needed no very quick ear to detect the well-remembered tones of Maurice Wharton.

"Come on," he cried, now quite close at hand. "This is the direction I am sure. He could never have got round the road."

Rose was now in sad trouble.

Her pursuers were certainly more fleet of foot than herself.

Added to this, her movements were greatly impeded by the ill-fitting dress which she had abstracted from the bedroom of the chambermaid.

She began to regret that she had paused to change her garments.

Had she hurried on when first she left the house, she would have been safe from all danger of recapture now.

Moreover, the other apparel was far more favourable for her hurried movements.

Time pressed.

In a minute more they would be by the pool, and she would inevitably be discovered.

Fear seemed to paralyse her movements now that she had the greatest need of courage and support.

She could not move.

A bush only screened her from the view of any one at the further side of the pool.

Poor girl! she must certainly be wedded to misfortune and suffering, for her life of late had been but one continued career of unhappiness.

Maurice Wharton now appeared running up in a very excited state.

Then he paused and turned to call impatiently to Mr. Wharton, whose older limbs could not keep pace with the fire and energy of his son.

"Come, come, father," cried Maurice, "she has passed by here—I am sure of it."

"I know it," cried Mr. Wharton, in answer from a short distance in the rear. "I can see traces of her progress yet."

"Yes, yes—and see here are marks—foot-prints upon the bank of the pool."

Rose trembled violently.

"Hurry on, then, boy," cried Mr. Wharton. "Wait not for me. On, on !"

But Maurice Wharton, instead of obeying his father's injunction, only gave a cry of mingled alarm and amazement.

"Great Heavens !"

"What now ?" cried Mr. Wharton, just arriving upon the scene.

"See," cried the young man, pointing to the centre of the pool.

Rose could not see, but she divined what was the object of this speech.

That unfortunate hat !

"I see," said Mr. Wharton, "but what is it ?"

"A hat !"

"Whose ?"

"Hers. Rose's, doubtless."

"Well, then, she has passed here—eh ?"

"Nay, I think not."

"What do you mean ?"

"I mean," said Maurice Wharton, in a still solemn tone of voice, "that Rose Mortimer has been driven to self-destruction !"

The subject of his speech turned all over in a cold perspiration.

The idea of having slain herself was terrible to hear.

"What, do you mean to say that she has committed suicide ?" demanded Mr. Wharton.

"I do."

"How shocking !"

Mr. Wharton said "How shocking !" as if he had

just learnt that his servant had robbed him, or that a favourite dog had been hurt or his hunter lamed.

"Here is the place, too, from which she has jumped doubtless," said Maurice Wharton. "Do you see the foot-prints ?"

"Ah, yes," said his father. "But, dear me, this will be disagreeable."

"It will indeed."

"Yes, the pool will be dragged, and then there will be a *post-mortem* examination."

"No, no, that can be avoided."

"How ?"

"I shall take means to destroy these traces which have told us this much. No one will ever know of this night's work."

"But the hat ?"

"Can easily be sunk or recovered."

"So be it," said Mr. Wharton. "It is a thousand pities, though. This girl served our purpose so well. And she was foolishly blind to her own interests."

"True," rejoined Maurice Wharton. "For a time at least she would have enjoyed all Edgar's magnificence."

"Ay," said his father. "And what matter how soon, or in what manner her existence terminated ?"

Rose trembled so dreadfully at these words that she feared she should betray herself.

They indicated a clear understanding as to her ultimate disposal !

But she had not yet heard all that she was destined to learn of this.

"It is all the more annoying," exclaimed Mr. Wharton pettishly, as if he had lost a shirt button or missed an express train, "that Edgar must now be looked after."

"True."

"Had it been otherwise, he might have been permitted to live on with Clara."

"Possibly," said Maurice Wharton. "But you know that that was always dead against my ideas."

"Yes, yes," said Mr. Wharton. "Young blood is ever too hot we know."

"And old too tardy."

This angry retort appeared for a moment likely to provoke a quarrel between this precious father and son.

However, the guilty tie between them was too strong to allow any matter of personal consideration to stand in their way.

"Yes, yes," muttered Mr. Wharton, rather as a soliloquy than as if addressing his son, "Edgar must be removed. Had that girl stayed until she could have been disposed of in a *legal and medicinal manner* it might have been otherwise. Confound it ! And I am anxious to spare the boy, too. I had always an inclination for him. *I loved his father !* Well, well, I suppose that it is not now to be helped."

And Mr. Wharton walked moodily from the spot, muttering aloud as he went.

"What a fearful man is this !" thought Rose, who was shivering with fright in her hiding-place. "He talks of assassination as an every day-occurrence."

Maurice Wharton remained behind for several minutes, much to Rose's alarm.

He was apparently amusing himself by throwing stones into the water.

A curious pastime, thought our heroine, for such a nature, and to be carried on at such an unearthly hour.

But presently he ceased, and left the spot with an exclamation of satisfaction.

Rose comprehended his amusement now.

He had been tossing stones on to the floating hat until he had succeeded in sinking it.

And now that all danger of immediate pursuit was over Rose Mortimer was in no trifling consternation.

She had become so interwoven in the terrible chain of guilt which these two murderous Whartons were coiling around them that she felt almost as if she had participated in their crimes.

Certain it was that she had become the unwilling instrument of another's undoing.

Edgar Deville, the heir to the vast estate and wealth, and whom she had been impersonating at the commands of the two Whartons, was doomed to a violent death because she had fled !

But she had fled to avoid doing further injustice to the Edgar Deville she was impersonating.

She saw, too, that she had narrowly escaped herself from the remorseless clutches of these terrible men.

Their purpose once achieved she would have fallen a victim to their devices—alone, unaided, and uncared for.

Oh ! could such fearful things be permitted to exist ?

How could such wholesale murderers be allowed to pollute the earth by their poisonous presence ?

With a shudder Rose Mortimer turned from the pool and fled.

Rushed on wildly.

Flew, as if hoping to escape from the agonising meditations she had conjured up.

She had now wandered several hours, and the fatigues of the night were beginning to make themselves apparent.

Up to the present the exciting events which had attended her escape had sustained her.

But now, the immediate danger being over, she began to experience an unpleasant sensation of weariness.

A faintness stole over her, and for an instant she stood in some danger of swooning.

But the dangers to which she was yet exposed sustained her.

On, on she pushed, praying for some dwelling where she could throw herself upon the mercy of the inhabitants.

But many and many a weary step she took without her prayer being granted.

At length she perceived a faint light in the distance.

The sight of this inspired her anew with hope, and she hurried onwards.

Now she was once more in the mining districts, and from time to time she encountered many of those half-clothed slim barbarous-looking men whom she had seen upon arriving in that part of the country.

In truth she was not best pleased with their aspect, but she had wandered so far in the terrible stillness of that eventful night that she was glad to see any human being.

Most passed her without a word, many without a look.

Some few only gave her a gruff good night and passed on.

The light which Rose had observed in the distance she now perceived proceeded from one of the miners' cottages, and up to it she went for shelter for the remainder of the night.

A while she paused before the door irresolute.

Then she gave a low timorous knock, which passed unheeded.

No other result attended a second and a third summons.

And then she rapped louder.

"Hullo ! Who's there ?" exclaimed a voice from within. "Who's there ?"

"A traveller," said Rose faintly.

"What does a traveller want knocking one up at this hour ?"

"I am very sorry," said Rose, "I perceived that a light still burnt, and was not aware that you had retired to rest. I have wandered very far, or I should not have ventured to knock.''

And with this she was about to resume her weary pilgrimage, when the voice demanded—

"Is it a woman?"

"Yes, weary and footsore."

"Hold hard a bit then, I'll let you in."

The next minute the door was unbarred, and a huge miner of ferocious aspect admitted her.

The next instant poor Rose Mortimer repented having taken this step.

She now found herself in a small chamber surrounded by a dozen of the wildest looking men she had ever seen.

As she entered several of them rose and advanced towards her.

One fellow especially attracted the wanderer's attention.

He was of the same build as the man who had admitted her—perhaps still more forbidding in aspect.

"A comely wench," said he, staring insolently at Rose. "Don't be afear'd, my gal. I'll look arter ye. Here Penryth, tell ye what, I'll take her home with me."

Rose was terrified.

Bitterly did she now repent that she had asked for shelter here.

Alone, and at the mercy of this horde of ruffians !

CHAPTER XXVIII.

A NEST OF RUFFIANS—DISPUTED POSSESSION—THE QUARREL—THE BLOW—FLIGHT FROM THE MINER—CAPTURE—THE SWOON—THE STONE—A MURDER—ROSE ACCUSED—"DEATH TO HER !"—PERIL.

As the miner spoke these words Penryth sprang up in a fury.

"What do you mean, Miles Trunnion, by that ?" he demanded.

"That I'll take the gal, Penryth, if she bothers you here," replied the miner.

"Then she don't."

"Then I'll take her, all the same."

The man Penryth, who was, as far as Rose could judge, the owner of the miserable little cabin, dashed his brawny fist upon the table, with a blow which split it across, and overturned a jug of ale.

"No, Miles Trunnion !" he cried, in great wrath. "Curse me if you do that !"

"Gently, gently," said the other, rising also. "Your big words don't frighten me."

"May be."

"Nothing don't. Now, I tell you what, we'll put it to the gal herself. If she likes to stay with you, well and good. If she likes to go with me, so much the better."

"Never !"

"Hullo !"

"Never, I say, by ——"

"Not quite so fast. If the gal wants to go with me, then go she shall."

Several of the miners joined in here.

They were of opinion that Rose should be consulted.

Already they looked upon her as their particular property, but were ready to give her a voice in the matter of her own disposal, in order to avoid an outbreak between the two brawny giants, Penryth and Miles Trunnion.

The former opposed this for some time, observing that, since the gal had chosen his house to come to, there she should stop.

He looked upon it, apparently, as a case of treasure-trove.

However, he was at length forced to yield to the united voices of the whole gang.

"Well, my gal," said Miles Trunnion, "and how do you think now ?"

Rose shrank away from him.

"There, there. You see what she means for her answer," quoth Penryth.

"Devil a bit !" retorted Miles Trunnion. "I only see that the gal is a bit skeared by our roughish ways. But don't ye be afeared, my gal," he continued, turning to Rose, "I'm as tender as a kitten."

"O-ho !"

"You may laugh, Penryth. It's true, though. I've got the bear's velvet paw for a gal. The claws is only out when I'm riled !"

He looked meaningly at Penryth as he uttered these words.

The latter sprang forward, with the uplifted ale jug, and would have administered punishment at once had not their companions interfered.

"I say, Penryth," cried one. "Drop that game, you know. All about a wench, too. Well, I'm dashed if it ain't awful."

"Yes, yes," cried several.

"Look here," resumed the former speaker. "Tell you what. Why don't you *share the gal*."

Poor Rose was in no trifling consternation now.

But she fancied that she yet perceived a loophole for escape.

At any rate it would offer her one more chance to get free from them.

The conversion of our heroine into a joint-stock property of the two miners was at once hailed by all with shouts of approval.

"If I am to be asked," began Rose Mortimer, in a faint voice.

"Oh! Of course. By all means," said Miles Trunnion, who fancied that he perceived in Rose's interruption a favourable omen for himself. "Let the gal decide for herself. I ask nothing better."

"Ay, ay."

And this was carried by the whole mob of ruffians nem. con.

"Then say what you would rather do, my gal," said Miles Trunnion.

"I'd sooner go," said Rose.

"Ha-ha !" cried Trunnion, with a laugh of triumph over Penryth.

"Then curse ye," cried the latter, in a perfect fury. "Why d'ye come here ? No. Hang me if you leave to-night."

To this Miles Trunnion replied, and a violent altercation ensued.

Blows would have very speedily followed had not the companions of the two disputants interfered.

However, the majority sided with Miles Trunnion.

The gal, they said, had a right to make her own choice, and she had decided for him.

Miles Trunnion rose to depart, and beckoned our heroine to follow him, whereupon Penryth sprang forward, and seized the poor girl by the arm in a vice-like grasp.

"Let go," cried Trunnion.

"Never !" said Penryth. "The gal's mine, and I'll stick up for my rights against a dozen of you and your dirty pals."

"D'ye hear that, mates ?" said Trunnion, turning appealingly to the others.

"Yes," said one. "Drop it, Penryth, or else we must interfere."

"Hang you—do you threaten me ?" roared the maddened Penryth.

"Not I, for one," said Miles Trunnion. "I never threaten any man. I act !"

Saying which, he delivered Penryth a violent blow in the face, which brought the blood from his mouth and nostrils, and sent him staggering to the other end of the room.

The door was now thrown open, and Miles Trunnion, with the disputed prize, the poor horror-stricken Rose Mortimer, was hurried out by the remainder of the miners.

As soon as they were outside the cabin Rose darted past the miner and rushed boldly on.

"Hullo, there!" cried Trunnion. "What's that? Come back; d'ye hear?"

Rose, however, only increased her speed.

And now there appeared really great probability that she would get off scot free.

Fortune was once more against her, however, at this critical moment.

Being unacquainted with the country, she made such a round that the miner was enabled to double upon her, saving nearly half the ground.

Leaping a hedge one would scarcely have deemed him capable of, from his big burly figure, he alighted upon the ground just before her.

Then before she could even utter a cry he had clasped her in his arms.

"Help! help!" shrieked Rose.

"What's all this row about?" demanded the miner.

"Mercy, have mercy!"

"Lor' love ye, what's got ye? I don't want to eat you, stoopid."

In vain did the poor girl implore his merciful forbearance.

He pretended to believe that her coyness was assumed.

And in spite of her most frantic struggles, her most earnest entreaties, the huge ruffian took her in his big brawny arms and bore her away.

At length nature could no longer endure the severe trials to which Rose had of late been exposed.

The girl he suddenly found hung a dead weight on his arms.

At first he turned ghastly pale, and trembled with fright.

He deemed that he held a corpse in his arms.

A faint pulsation at the heart, however, very soon convinced him that she was but swooning, and he paused to restore her before bearing her off to his home.

He had a flask of spirits about him, and with some of the liquor he bathed her temples and chafed her hands.

And gradually she revived.

But when she opened her eyes it was only to encounter a new spectacle of horror.

The sight of the brutal miner standing over her was enough to fill her with alarm, but now a third person was added to the scene.

An individual of whose presence Miles Trunnion appeared to be ignorant.

It was Penryth the miner.

He stood there, with his two hands grasping a huge stone, uplifted above the head of Miles Trunnion.

Before Rose could utter a sound, before an eye could wink, the blow came.

Down went the stone upon the head of the unlucky Trunnion, stretching him lifeless upon the ground, without a murmur.

And this was the speedy vengeance of the giant Penryth the miner.

"Ah!" shrieked Rose.

"Curse her! she's seen it," cried the miner, "and she'll sell me for blood money; but never. Dead men tell no tales!"

He darted upon the ensanguined stone and seized it in his hands.

Now it was almost a certainty that Rose would have been sacrificed to his vengeance also, had not the sound of footsteps alarmed the murderer.

He turned and fled.

In an instant there was a rush to the spot, and before Rose Mortimer could gain her feet she was surrounded by a mob of women—old hags, ragged and dirty, and of the most wild and ferocious aspect.

"See, see. This is what she's done," cried one old hag, pointing to the prostrate body of the miner. "And it is Miles Trunnion."

"Miles?" echoed a dozen voices.

"Ay."

"Then down with his murderer—slay her—tear her piecemeal."

"I swear I did not do it," cried Rose, earnestly. "Believe me."

"She lies," interrupted the old hag. "How came she here else?"

"Of course."

"Ay, ay."

"Down with her, then."

Rose shrieked and implored their pardon, but they were inexorable.

Thus had she by the death of the miner but escaped one fate for another scarcely less horrible.

In an instant, and with wild cries and yells, they fell upon her.

———

CHÁPTER XXIX.

THE VISIT TO THE VAULT—CLARA'S VICTIM—THE SHIP ON FIRE—A SCENE OF HORROR—ON THE ROCKS—THE JEWELS—THE MEDITATED MURDER.

AT dead of night Edgar Deville and the woman calling herself Clara St. John stood among the ruins of the house in Park Lane.

They were alone.

Not a soul had seen them approach.

Their movements had been conducted with the utmost caution and secrecy.

Edgar Deville carried a pickaxe and some other tools.

Clara was provided with a dark lantern.

The woman led the way among the ruins, and presently came to a halt at a certain place.

"This is it," she said.

"Is what?" asked her companion.

"Never mind at present. You will learn all in good time. I want your assistance when I ask for it, not without."

Some sort of reply seemed rising to her companion's lips, but he stopped himself in time.

An extraordinary influence did this woman appear to have obtained over him.

He was her abject slave.

He dared not say his soul was his own.

What was the explanation of this mysterious thraldom in which she held him?

Time will show.

Clara, stooping down among the ruins, cleared away the rubbish from a certain place, and said—

"This is a door. Can we open it?"

"I will try."

He in turn stooped down and examined the place.

"If I remove this fallen brickwork I don't think there will be much difficulty—that is, of course, if you have got the key."

"It opens with a spring, when you have cleared the stuff lying upon it. I can manage the rest."

Deville now worked away with a good will, and by

turns using the pick and his hands, cleared away all obstructions in a few minutes.

When he had done Clara leaned forward, and pressed heavily upon a spring which had been hidden from her companion, and protected from injury by a projecting iron ledge of enormous strength.

The door, responsive to the pressure, opened slowly inwards.

"Now follow me just within this archway," she said.

"Yes, madam."

"That is all I require at present."

"Yes, madam."

"You will remain here until I return ?"

"Yes."

"And keep watch."

"And you, madam ?"

"Will go down the subterranean passage."

"Alone ?"

"Yes. I require no assistance."

No more was said on either side.

Edgar Deville kept guard, and the other proceeded silently down the passage.

She knew the way well enough.

It was by the same route by which she had taken her victim to the hiding-place of the jewels.

Passing through several doors, she at length reached the vault.

She entered it in a death-like silence.

Then raised her lantern, and gazed upon the terrible spectacle before her.

A glittering corpse was there, bowed over the iron box.

Diamonds glittered on a brow black and convulsed.

Emeralds glimmered on stained shrunken arms, that looked more like dry bones than human flesh.

Her great eyes, once so beautiful, were now too horrible to look upon.

How long had the miserable creature fought against death, standing there in utter darkness, thus buried alive ?

It required but a glance upon the hideous ghastly countenance, and the emaciated limbs, to see what horrible tortures, mental and physical, the victim had endured.

Carelessly, though, did the hard-hearted woman regard her.

She approached the corpse without a shudder, and began to rob it of its jewels.

"I should not have lent them to her so long," muttered the fiend, "unless I had known that the vault was air-tight, and that they were quite safe. Still there was a certain amount of risk, and I would not have run it, but revenge was so sweet, and I could not resist gratifying my deadly vengeance upon her."

While thus she spoke Clara was busily engaged in collecting together the glittering gems which had proved so fatal to the poor wretch who had coveted them.

They made a large parcel, and it was with great difficulty that she could contrive it so that the silk handkerchief she had brought with her for the purpose should contain them all.

Having, however, got them into it at last, and knotted them up to her satisfaction, she retraced her steps, closing the doors behind her as she went.

She found Edgar Deville leaning against the wall of the passage.

She turned the lantern full upon his face.

"Hullo !" said he, yawning and blinking.

"Were you asleep ?"

"Pretty nearly."

"You call that keeping watch, I suppose ?"

"I kept it as long as I could, but you were such a deuce of a while. I began to think——"

"Well ?"

"That you were buried alive."

A strange smile passed over Clara's face, an awful smile, full of terrible meaning.

"No," she said. "Not yet."

Then, after a pause of a moment, she added—

"Come along. We have no time to waste. We must be going."

He followed her without a word, and she closed the door after him.

"Look," she said. "Can you see it ?"

"See what ?"

"The door we have come out of ?"

Edgar stooped down to examine it.

"I can't see a sign of a door," he replied. "I never should have done if you had not pointed it out in the first instance."

"That will do. Now come away."

*   *   *   *   *   *

A ship, an emigrant vessel, a week after these events was on her way across the Atlantic.

It was night.

The greater part of the crew and passengers were asleep.

Two among the latter, however, might have been seen walking together, and engaged in close conversation.

One was a lady, the other a gentleman.

"Yes, Edgar," the lady said, "the time will soon arrive when I shall be able to reveal to you all the mystery of my life. I will have no secrets from you, for our lives are henceforth bound up one with another. I am rich, as you know. We have money enough to live in ease and plenty all the rest of our lives, and I could be happy if I but thought that you spoke the truth."

"As Heaven is my witness, Clara, I do. With all my heart, I love you."

While the passengers still slept there suddenly arose an awful cry, which echoed fearfully on the still night air.

"Fire ! fire !"

Edgar Deville, rushing from the lower deck, found a dense smoke issuing from the lower hatchway over the hold.

Again the fearful cry arose.

Then the passengers awoke from their sleep, and all was terror and confusion.

During the night the wind had been steadily increasing in violence, and now blew a hurricane.

The sea ran mountains high.

All above was black and starless.

The roaring rushing wind came thick and heavy with the driving brine.

The suffocating smoke grew denser and denser.

The shrieks of the women and children were horrible to listen to.

The whole poop was now blazing, and the flames encircled the mainmast.

The bright light from the burning vessel cast a crimson hue upon the angry waves, which raged and foamed around.

The captain, the first mate, and the other officers, had as soon as possible got the pumps to work, but they were not in very good order, and the flames steadily gained headway.

Although the pumps were worked with unflinching perseverance, the raging element could not be kept under.

The centre part of the deck was all in flames.

The crew and those helping them were driven to the stern of the vessel.

The hatches had to be closed in consequence of the sea washing into them, but those below, terrified by the smoke and heat, rushed on deck, and were driven back shrieking by the flames.

The screams of the agonised women were drowned by the roaring of the storm.

Some men who had been sick below managed to crawl on to the deck, and lay about until the waves washed them overboard.

It became evident now that the ship could not possibly be saved.

The pumps were still kept at work, but all was useless.

The passengers below were already suffocated.

The shrieks and moans of the dying came up to those on deck, but they could do nothing to help them.

No ship hove in sight. No help was within reach.

The flames now spread with fearful rapidity.

The boats were launched, though there was scarcely any hope of their living in such a sea.

The first was immediately swamped. It contained, amongst others, the captain, who had lost all control over himself, and seemed mad with terror.

The second was lowered, but, drifting under the vessel's side, was struck by the screw, and went down almost instantly.

A third boat was launched, but met with as terrible a fate.

Many tied themselves to spars and jumped overboard. The mizenmast fell and the mainmast followed with a crash.

As day broke the last charred remains of the doomed ship sank beneath the waves.

Shortly after the body of a woman, securely fastened to one of the doors of the vessel, was driven among the rocks upon the coast of Ireland.

A fisherman plying his trade was the first to find her. Round her neck, attached by a small chain, was a water-tight packet.

Taking his knife from his pocket, he cut it open, and uttered an exclamation of intense astonishment when his eyes fell on a mass of glittering gems.

While he was looking at them another fisherman joined him.

"See here," said the first.

"Ah!"

"What do you make of them?"

"They can't possibly be real."

"If half of them was real they would be enough to set us up for life."

"Ah, and longer."

"How came she by them, think you?"

"She must have stolen them. No one could possibly come by such a dollop of diamonds as that in any fair way."

"She has been washed up from some vessel I suppose."

"From the vessel we saw burning last night I reckon."

"Is she a foreigner, do you think?"

"I fancy so, by the look of her."

"They must be real, these stones, and if so they are worth thousands."

"If they're real, Jack, I'll tell you one thing."

"What's that?"

"If they are, our fortun's made."

"Yes, but—"

"But what?"

"They're not ours."

"Why not? No one's here to say us nay. No one but her."

"And she's dead."

"Ah, dead enough. If they was hers by right, she's out of the way now, and they belongs to us."

"What shall we do with her?"

"Drop her down again into the sea. Lend a hand."

The ruffians stooped over the woman's prostrate form.

But as they did so she slowly opened her eyes and gazed upon them.

"Great Heavens!" exclaimed one of the men, and, loosing his hold, he turned to fly.

CHAPTER XXX.

ROSE'S PERIL — THE CONSULTATION — HER FATE DISCUSSED — DOOM — INCARNATE FIENDS — FATAL RESOLVE—THE RIVER—"MERCY!"—THE SPLASH.

WITH a startled shriek Rose Mortimer started to her feet.

But the hags surrounding her were so many that it was worse than madness to hope to oppose her feeble strength to their attack.

"Mercy! mercy!" shrieked the unhappy girl.

"Down with her!"

"Kill her!"

"Slay her!"

"Tear her piecemeal!"

"Knock her brains out!"

"Stone her!"

"Burn her for a witch!"

But neither of these suggestions met with any particular notice from the mob.

Every one had a different mode of torture to suggest, and every one considered her own idea the best.

The only good resulting from this diversity of opinion was the slight respite which it afforded Rose.

The unhappy girl, upon her knees and in tears, besought them to have mercy, and declared her innocence of the crime imputed to her.

But still the horrible council went on.

And still poor Rose Mortimer was forced to stay there, to listen while her own condemnation and punishment were discussed.

At each suggestion, punishment the more horrible, cruelties the more refined, were met with the wildest shouts of approval.

One wretch had the inhumanity to propose lopping off her limbs one by one, that her death might be the more awful and lingering.

The reader can therefore readily imagine the horror with which the unhappy girl heard her death discussed by this gang of fiends and she-devils.

Not her death alone, too.

Tortures of the most horrible nature were projected, and as each was greeted by a shout, she had to suffer the menaces and even blows of the more enthusiastic in the bloody business now in contemplation.

At length, after a long harangue of at least twenty minutes' duration, they had come to something approaching a determination.

The poor girl was first to be thrown into the water, to see if she would really sink.

If not, she was, as they had called her before, a witch.

"Good, good!" cried one old hag considerably more hideous than the rest.

"The water, the water!"

"To be sure, my dears," continued the former old harridan. "If she floats, then we can grill her afterwards. If she sinks, why then she'll have been finished off in a style which is much too easy for the likes of her!"

"Bravo, Madge!"

And the infamous old hag was cheered as if she had been a second Boadicea or Queen Elizabeth at Tilbury, after the destruction of the Spanish Armada.

"The water, then!"

"May she swim!" quoth Mistress Madge, in fervent

anticipation of a continuation of the torture feast upon the unhappy victim of their fury.

A wild " Amen !" burst from the strange unearthly-looking throng.

And Rose Mortimer was dragged off in the direction of a river, which she could already see at no great distance.

Arrived upon the banks of the river, Mistress Madge, who had now elected herself executioner of the vengeance of the mob, began to pinion Rose's arms behind her.

" Oh ! if you have any humanity in you," cried the unhappy girl, " if you have a child of your own, if you have ever had one, I beseech you to have mercy !"

" But I haven't !"

And the old hag grinned in a diabolical manner, as if she had uttered a profound witticism.

" Then I conjure you," continued Rose Mortimer, " by the memory of your former life—you were once young, and—"

" Once ?"

" Ay ; therefore—"

" Silence !"

And by way of vengeance for what she deemed an insult to her juvenility and attractions, the old hag gave poor Rose's wrists such a tug with the cords with which she was fastening her that the unhappy victim could not repress a loud wail of agony.

" Music !" cried Mistress Madge, in an ecstacy of delight.

" Look alive, Madge !"

" Ay, ay ; you're spoiling sport," said another.

" She's having it all to herself," said a third.

And the whole of the humane congregation began to yell like a lot of savage hungry wolves at the sight of some delicate morsel in the way of a kid or a young baby.

Even Mistress Madge's tortures could not endure for ever, and at length the operation of fastening the doomed girl was completed.

" Help ! help ! oh, help !" shrieked the unhappy Rose in a frenzy of terror, as the awful moment drew nearer.

" Ha ! ha ! ha !"

" In with her !"

" One, two, three !"

" Heaven have mercy upon me !" cried Rose, almost resigning herself now.

" Now then !"

Two of the women—one of whom was old Mistress Madge—raised the helpless body of the half senseless victim in their arms.

Swung it high in the air.

Cast it far away into the river.

Down, down, it sank with a fatal splash.

The waters closed over it, and in an instant appeared to regain their former tranquillity, as if they were anxious that all traces of the fiend-like cruelty should be cleared away with the execution of the deed of violence.

" Down she goes !" cried Madge.

" Ay, she sinks."

" I can see her still. There, now she's lost."

" What a feed for the fishes !"

This pleasantry created an immense amount of laughter and jocularity, and the gang of wretched women moved off.

One thing they resolved upon, however.

The murdered girl was no witch.

No matter, she had slain Miles Trunnion, and an eye for an eye had been taken.

Poor Rose Mortimer !

CHAPTER XXXI.

THE HAGS DEPART—THE TREE BY THE RIVER—A BOLD SWIMMER—A RESCUE—FAILURE—TO IT AGAIN—THE SWIMMER USED UP.

THE gang of hags cleared off, with shouts of triumph for the fearful vengeance which they had taken upon the helpless girl.

Vengeance taken, and for what ?

Simply because they had discovered the poor girl near the bloody corse of a ruffian miner, who had been slain by a brother villain more rascally and unscrupulous than himself, if possible.

And the momentarily distended waters of that peaceful little rivulet closed over the now inanimate body of our heroine.

The women who had destroyed the innocent girl had barely cleared off when from the branch of a large spreading tree which overhung the water the body of a tall stalwart fellow appeared.

A jacket was cast off and thrown to the ground.

Then a motley-coloured neckcloth.

Then a huge body dived through the air and plunged headfirst into the water.

Apparently this man was an experienced diver, for he cut through the water without the faintest splash.

It was a prodigious dive !

Down, down he went to a very great depth with outstretched hands.

Straight as a die he made the plunge for the sunken body of Rose Mortimer.

A terrible time did he appear to be under water, and had any one been present he must have concluded that the bold diver had perished for his temerity.

But no !

No matter the cause of such bravery, the boldness with which the object was carried deserved success.

Presently there was a faint movement perceptible just below the surface of the water.

Gradually it grew plainer.

Then might be distinctly made out the outlines of two bodies.

One was that of the bold and fearless diver.

The other that of the inanimate girl, which he grasped around the waist with his left arm.

With his disengaged arm he made desperate efforts to swim to the surface.

The weight was great, however, to his well-nigh used up force, and his progress was but slow.

Most painfully did the sturdy fellow labour on the self-allotted task.

Still he would not resign his hold upon the body.

No, sooner would he perish with her, after having with so much pain and exertion dragged her from the river's bed.

And now the right hand of the swimmer appeared above the surface of the water.

Another stroke, and he breathed the fresh air of heaven.

Oh ! what gratitude was expressed on that countenance then.

It was a rough unintellectual face—devoid of wit—but full of cunning on an ordinary occasion.

But the expression it wore rendered it almost sublime.

He breathed painfully, and rested a while by paddling gently about.

And every moment the weight of the rescued girl grew a more fatal burden to her preserver.

Danger stared him in the face.

Still he boldly kept his hold upon the senseless girl.

[FOUND DEAD.]

The river's bank was not more than ten feet off—nay, not so much.

As many strokes would bring him safe to land.

Boldly, then, he struck out with his one disengaged hand for shore.

Little, and fatally slow, was the progress he made. Still he kept to it.

Half a dozen strokes had lessened the distance by one-half, and he grew faint.

It could not be that he was doomed to failure, and worse—to death, after having achieved thus much.

No, no—that would be too cruel, too horrible by far.

His breast heaved up and down, and the agony in the bold swimmer's face was painful to behold.

But two strokes more.

He sank a little.

Now his whole body was nearly immersed.

His head went under once, but still he held the rescued girl aloft.

Then he rose up, with a prodigious exertion, made a wild dash at the bank, and touched it.

The hold was painfully slippery.

His grasp, too, lacked force, and the slimy weeds slipped through his fingers.

"Ah!" cried the desperate swimmer.

One more effort failed, when an idea occurred to him.

He resigned his hold of the bank, and suddenly applied both hands to his insensible burden.

No. 10.

He raised it with a jerk above his head, and cast it rom him on the bank.

The feet were then resting in the water.

The exertion, however, well-nigh proved fatal to the gallant swimmer.

The effort thrust him back into the water, and down he went, touching the bottom once more.

But now he was freed from the weight which had hitherto encumbered him he could exert himself to greater efforts.

A few strokes brought him to the surface.

Then he turned upon his back, and once more drank in a welcome draught of air.

Then he made for the bank.

There was the rescued girl still insensible, to all appearance dead.

"She's a long time without breathing," said the swimmer, staggering to his feet. "Surely she can't be dead. No, I hope—Good God !—I—I—"

And, staggering, he turned a kind of pirouette upon one heel, and fell flat upon his back beside the body of the unhappy Rose Mortimer.

CHAPTER XXXII.

ANOTHER PERSON UPON THE SCENE—ROSE BORNE AWAY — THE MINER'S RESOLVE — A STRANGE HIDING-PLACE — PENRYTH RECOVERS—ROSE DISAPPEARED—THE TRACK—THE BRICK HUT—THE DANGER MINE—"I'LL FOLLOW HER !"

THE swimmer lay upon his back beside the inanimate body of the rescued girl—as senseless and motionless as herself.

Long did he continue in a deathly trance.

The reaction upon the herculean diver was as prodigious as had been his efforts to preserve the drowning girl.

He had lain thus insensible about ten minutes when a third person arrived upon the scene.

It was another of the miners who had witnessed the whole of the dispute between Miles Trunnion and Penryth, and, having heard of the murder of the former by the girl whose possession had been disputed, he had come in pursuit.

It was only after some time had elapsed that he learnt from the gang of murderous old hags who had taken such summary vengeance upon poor Rose Mortimer that this was the scene of their barbarity.

Great was the man's surprise, therefore, when upon reaching the river's bank he discovered not only the girl who had unwittingly caused so much strife and mischief, but also the half-drowned diver who had worked such miracles in her rescue.

As the newcomer approached the body of the man he started back in great alarm.

"Good Heavens !" he ejaculated. "Penryth here, too ?"

The gallant swimmer who had so nearly sacrificed himself to preserve Rose Mortimer's life was none other than her herculean champion who had slain Miles Trunnion.

"So, so !" muttered the man, "I think I can see through all this now. I marvelled much at first that such a deed of violence should have been wrought by that delicate little hand."

The inference which the man drew was, of course, but natural.

So pale, so sad and beautiful did the inanimate body of the half-drowned girl look that the miner was rivetted to the spot.

No freshly-chiselled statue could ever reach that beautiful appearance.

So pale, so sad and melancholy in expression, and the extreme regularity of the features gave the face an angelic look.

"She is lovely !" said the entranced beholder, his eyes still feasting upon her as if she had been some beauteous vision.

"I don't wonder so much that Miles Trunnion and Penryth should hanker after the gal. I'd kill a dozen men myself to get such a gal as that, if she wor alive."

As the fellow glanced from one to the other it was something marvellous to observe the change in his expression.

As he contemplated the insensible miner he looked like a fiend, ready upon a given signal to cut the slight thread which still held him to life.

Had he been aware that the man still breathed there is a great probability that another crime would have been added to that day's fearful work.

Then as he turned towards the motionless form of our heroine his rough brutal features softened into an expression of something almost approaching tenderness.

Suddenly he started back, with a cry of astonishment—

"She moved !"

It was true. The fainting fit was beginning to pass over.

It was one of those inexplicable chances which occur only once in the course of an age.

She had been in the water long enough to have cut short her breath, providing that restoratives had been administered immediately upon her recovery from the water.

Here she had lain with no help at hand for fully twenty minutes.

And yet she breathed—slowly and painfully breathed—but yet life was not extinct.

As soon as the miner had made the discovery that she breathed he at once applied himself to her further recovery.

He was tolerably acquainted with the treatment necessary for bodies after a long immersion in water, and therefore tended not a little to revive the faint animation which was now beginning to make itself apparent.

"If Penryth should happen to wake up, too !" muttered the fellow.

He began to look about him, to provide against such an unpleasant contingency.

"I should finish him, I'm mortal sure," he muttered between his teeth.

Then a better idea occurred to him.

While Rose was yet unable to oppose him he would bear her off to a place of safety.

A hiding-place he knew of.

The thought no sooner occurred to him than he proceeded to put it into execution.

Raising the now breathing but insensible girl in his big brawny arms, he walked hastily from the spot.

Presently he had to climb a dwarf brick wall.

Then to cross a large plain which was covered with carts, trucks, and all kinds of machinery and mining implements.

At length he arrived at his destination.

He paused before a low hut built of brick, and shut in by a rude wooden door, upon which was an inscription almost obliterated by age.

After looking anxiously about, to see if he had been observed, the miner pushed open the door and entered the hut.

As he did so the saturated garments of his insensible burthen caught in a splinter in the woodwork.

Then the door was closed without noise.

All was still.

*   *   *   *   *   *

"Where am I ?"

Then Penryth the miner struck out his arms wildly.

He was just returning to consciousness, and he imagined that he was still in the river, which had so near proved his winding-sheet.

His legs jerked out spasmodically, until, overcome by the exertion, he sank into a light fitful slumber.

From this he presently awakened.

Opening his eyes, he gazed about him in silent wonder.

His thoughts roved wildly upon many things—things which he would fain have forgotten.

But, alas! one dread thing was impressed upon his memory, never to be effaced whilst life and reason held their sway.

The brand of Cain was upon his brow.

He thought upon Miles Trunnion—thought upon him and shuddered.

However much he shuddered, he could not now recall him to life.

Then the bold miner who had risked his life in rescuing Rose Mortimer so shortly before turned upon his face and wept.

Wept like a child.

Still the fatal picture could not be blotted from his memory.

When he grew somewhat calmer his thoughts veered round of a sudden to the object of his suffering and fears, Rose.

What had become of her?

"Hullo!" he cried, in an agony of alarm. "She's gone. Where? Has she fallen into the water? No. Where then? Oh! oh! oh! This would be too awful, after what I've done for her. I—I—I've killed a man, and well-nigh killed myself into the bargain. Oh! Where can she be gone to?"

He staggered to his feet.

His legs and arms were most painfully cramped, from the great exertion he had undergone and the cold and damp he had lain in so long.

"Ah!" he cried of a sudden, his eyes fixed upon the ground by the river's bank. "There's been some-one here whilst I was fainting. Here's the foot-mark. And a man's, too. Her dress has been dragged along the ground, too. And—Hullo! Why, as sure as fate, he's taken her in his arms and carried her off. Here they've gone."

And now for a while he lost the trail.

Patiently he went on, searching closely in every direction.

At length he came to a large patch of moist clay soil, which he examined eagerly.

"Huzzah! huzzah!" he cried. "I have them now. There's his big footmarks. And, then, now for it."

Like a bloodhound Penryth followed the faint track, until he came to another halt, apparently more fatal than the first.

Here he was, in the mining plain, surrounded by the implements of some pit now out of use.

"What can he have crossed here for?" muttered Penryth.

After a long search he came in front of the wooden door of the hut into which Rose Mortimer was borne by the miner.

A piece of her dress was yet clinging to the splintered wood which had caught it upon entering.

At sight of this Penryth turned ghastly pale.

"He's taken her down the Danger Mine!" he muttered. "Then by ——! she's lost to me."

He turned away, but for an instant only.

Then he turned sharply back again, and advanced to the door.

He Entered with a fixed determination, muttering aloud as he went—

"I'll go. I'll follow them to the bottom of the Danger Mine, though it fall in and be the grave of us all."

CHAPTER XXXIII.

ROSE RECOVERS—DARKNESS—"WHERE AM I?"—DEATH—A FEARFUL POSITION—BLIND—THE LAMP—THE MINER—THE DANGER MINE AND THE PIT—GLOOM AGAIN—"COME BACK!"—THE FATAL PIT.

BY slow and painful degrees Rose Mortimer returned to consciousness.

A sensation of stifling closeness was the first the poor girl experienced upon regaining her senses.

A kind of oppression, as in a place imperfectly ventilated.

All was dark and silent as the grave.

Thus went her thoughts to the latter, and she turned faint.

"Is it possible that this can be death?" she asked herself.

This idea, too, was but natural.

The last thing she remembered in her varied career was an action which must surely have terminated her life.

She had been thrown bound and helpless into the river.

Cast into certain death.

In the long trance which had followed her immersion the spirit had fled.

This was a preliminary stage in the after-life which is so enshrouded in mystery.

And yet, while these strange thoughts flitted through her mind, she was conscious that she still retained her earthly form.

While these painful cogitations occupied her attention she moved about and discovered that the surface of the ground was rough and uneven.

Shortly she stumbled, knocking her knees against a stone.

This caused her some momentary pain, and not a little wonder.

The sensation was decidedly mundane and un-pleasant.

The close black darkness of the place was a great puzzle to her.

She was not in the open air.

Two great reasons she had for arriving at this con-clusion—most positively, too.

The impenetrable gloom by which she was sur-rounded.

Had she been beneath the sky, with nothing to intercept the view, she could have distinguished some objects around.

Upon the blackest nights, the moments preceding eclipses or violent storms, the skies at least are visible.

And yet where was she?

The oppression of the atmosphere, the stifling sensation which she experienced, convinced her that she was in some kind of building.

She continued her walk, still more rough and un-even than ever, for some time.

But what could it mean?

She came to no wall—no obstacle to her progress.

Then the idea occurred to her that she might have been proceeding straight through some wide passage.

Even then it must have been of an interminable length.

However, to be more sure, she veered round and continued her walk in the grim dark silence at right angles with her previous route.

Five minutes did she progress, heedless of all obstacles, bumps, or stumbles.

And yet she could find no wall of any kind.

Wonder was now giving way to sensations of some-thing approaching fear.

All was so silent, so fearfully silent.

After looking about her, and straining her eyes

until they were ready to start from her head, she gave way to a flood of bitter tears.

Bravely, right boldly, had she kept up throughout her trials and struggles with poverty—with the brutal father who had rendered her earliest life a misery to her—with the startling and terrible dangers she had undergone throughout the strange drama in her life, in which Count Lerno and the Whartons, father and son, had figured so conspicuously—and yet now that she deemed herself alone and unheeded she gave way to fears and grief.

The solitude and silence of that black black night were infinitely more terrible to her than aught else could have possibly been.

After her tears had had full vent for some few minutes she grew calmer.

Brain and heart were both overcharged with the terrible events which had made up her late existence.

Tears had relieved and solaced the poor girl.

Presently, with renewed hope, she recommenced her wild perambulations.

It was the same as before.

No end—no wall—nothing but space, black and unfathomable.

"This is too terrible !" cried Rose, wringing her hands once more, " too strangely terrible !"

Then she looked around.

Suddenly she gave a wild shriek.

A fearful thought had occurred to her.

"Great mercy !" she cried, " *I am blind !* Oh ! why, why am I thus persecuted ? Why am I thus tortured through a life of penury and want ? Mercy, mercy, I beseech !"

And the unhappy girl sank upon her knees in prayer.

With her beauteous face uplifted in the sombre gloom, her outstretched hands raised above her head, she sued for mercy.

Comforted at length, she arose and gazed around.

"Ah !" she cried, of a sudden, with a wild shriek— a cry which had a thousand answering echoes in the gloom.

But this was a shout of joy.

It would almost seem that Providence had relieved the poor suffering Rose Mortimer immediately after her earnest supplication.

The cause of her extravagant joy was simply that at some considerable distance she perceived what appeared a break in the gloom.

A light, faint and flickering, glistened through the darkness.

Now it moved to the right, now to the left.

Now it bent to the ground, now waved high aloft.

"Thank Heaven !" cried Rose. " Help, help ! help !"

Unhappy girl !

Unfortunate chance ! She little thought what she was doing.

She only thought of succour in her inexplicable prison of night.

She thought also of the glorious eyesight of which she had in her terror imagined herself deprived.

She repeated her cries louder than before.

And now the light appeared to be moving towards her.

Yes. There was no mistaking that now.

It certainly approached.

Larger and more definite it grew every instant.

And now, when it had reached some little distance off, she could see that it proceeded from a dark lantern —such as those known among miners as safety-lamps.

A little later she perceived the hand which grasped it.

"This way—this way !" she cried.

"Oh ! there you are, eh ?" said the answering voice of a man.

Rose could not understand the meaning of his familiar address.

"Here !" she cried.

"I'm coming fast," returned the voice. " Don't be in a hurry. There's a hole down here somewhere."

"A hole !"

"Yes—a pit."

Rose's heart beat quickly at these words.

What a chance it was that she had not fallen down it in her wild perambulations !

Yes," continued the voice, growing louder at each word. " Jerry Treewoof went down it last December twelvemonth—*and there he lies now !*"

This was not exactly a pleasant thing for Rose Mortimer to hear.

It was not in vain, then, she had compared it mentally to a tomb !

And now the man stood beside her.

He held out his hand in the dark, and placed hers in it.

The next instant she repented this.

He clutched her delicate palm with such unnecessary eagerness that the girl was quite startled.

"Why, where did you get to ?" he asked.

"I don't understand you."

"I mean, where did you go. I only put you out of my arms for a minute and went to get a light. When I came back, blessed if you hadn't sheered off."

Rose was bewildered.

She could not at all catch the meaning of these words.

She pressed him to explain.

"Oh ! I see," said the man. " You are quite lost, of course. I didn't think of that awhile, do you see ?"

"Where am I now ?"

"Down the Danger Mine."

"A mine ?"

"Yes, my dear ; but, lor bless your pretty face, it's as safe and as snug as any house we could wish for."

"But how came I here ?"

"I brought you."

"You ?"

"Yes. They chucked you into the river."

"Yes."

"And Penryth the miner fished you out of the water half dead."

"He ? Oh ! how fearful !"

"What's fearful ?"

"That man."

"Why, my dear ?"

"How fearful to have had a murderer's arm around me !"

"Murderer ? Penryth ?"

"Yes. He slew the man."

"Miles Trunnion ?"

"Yes—that was the name that she called him by," replied Rose Mortimer.

"Oh, Master Penryth !" cried the man. " But how prove you that ?"

"I saw the deed."

"Pheugh !"

"But let us not stay here, I beseech you. The darkness frightens me."

"Lor, my dear, I like the darkness myself."

As he spoke he threw his disengaged arm around her shrinking form.

Rose struggled to free herself from his rude embrace, but in vain.

Her feeble strength was as nought.

He drew her to him and enfolded her in both his arms imprinting a loathful kiss upon her face.

"Release me !" replied the indignant girl.

"Lor, my love."

As he spoke the lamp fell from his grasp and was extinguished.

All was dark as before.

"Curse the thing!" growled, the miner releasing Rose Mortimer.

Our heroine sprang off, with a cry of delight.

"Come back!" cried the man.

"Never!"

"You won't? Then by —— I'm after you."

Like a startled fawn Rose sped on in the darkness.

Tripping silently as possible, too, that her pursuer might have no clue.

She could hear him close behind.

Blurting out volleys of oaths he ran on.

Suddenly she could hear that he had slipped and fallen to the ground.

"Ah!" he cried, with a wild yell of agony, "the pit! I'm lost!"

Then all was still once more!

————

CHAPTER XXXIV.

PENRYTH—A FEARFUL STRIFE—HORRORS ACCUMULATE—THE DANGER MINE EARNS ITS TITLE.

FOR some minutes the fearful silence prevailed.

Rose never moved.

She stood upon the spot frozen with horror.

Then, with a shudder, she turned her eyes from the direction in which the sound had proceeded.

Suddenly she fancied that her ear caught the sound of some machinery at work.

The grating of a wheel long out of use.

She looked around her in wonder.

A second light appeared. This time high aloft.

By its stronger rays she could perceive that it proceeded from a large lantern, held by a man who was descending into the mine by the aid of a rope.

As he neared the ground she thought that she recognised in the faint outline a familiar form.

And now he had reached the ground.

Then he held up the lantern, and looked about him in anxious search.

A half-stifled cry rose to the girl's lips as she recognised in the newcomer the man whose hut she had entered to claim refuge for the night—the man whom she had seen a second time under such fearful circumstances — the murderer of Miles Trunnion.

It was Penryth!

"Hullo!" cried the miner. "Where did that cry come from, eh?"

Rose Mortimer was silent.

After listening intently a while for further sounds Penryth advanced in the direction of Rose.

It was a trying moment for the poor girl.

She dared not move, lest she should put him upon her track.

And yet to wait there appeared to be waiting patiently a fate more horrible than death itself.

The miner was now close to her.

She dared not breathe. The faintest sound she felt would be fatal.

On came the miner—perfectly visible to Rose Mortimer, although our heroine was unseen by him.

Waving his arms around him to their full extent just as he arrived by the side of the shrinking girl, he chanced to touch the edge of her dress.

"Ha, ha!" cried the miner, "I have you now, my lass, I think!"

He grabbed at her.

Caught her by the arm.

But his hold was too slight, and she slipped through his fingers, and darted off with a bound.

"Curse the gal!" roared Penryth. "She's as slippery as an eel."

Then, with an oath, he darted after her.

Fear for a while lent poor Rose Mortimer wings, and she contrived for some time to elude him.

Then, growing fatigued with the severe exertions of the day, the suffering she had endured at the hands of the women, and finally the long immersion in the river, she sank upon the ground overcome.

Her only remaining hope now was that in the immense dark space she might by accident elude the vigilance of the miner.

Panting and wearied, she lay upon the cold hard ground.

Resting upon one hand, she followed with feverish eagerness the direction of that will-o'-the-wisp-looking lantern which the miner held.

It grew fainter at one time, and Rose began to hope that he was quite out in his calculation.

Vain hope!

The next minute the light advanced rapidly in the direction which she had taken.

Now it was quite close to her.

"She can't be far off from here," muttered Penryth, as he advanced. "She surely took this way. Confound the baggage, she's as artful as sin!"

He waved round the light once more.

Then stood still, the light resting full upon her pale face.

"Ha, ha!" cried the miner, darting upon her. "So, so, I've got you once more, have I?"

"Oh! have pity!"

"I will."

"I am so exhausted with fatigue and long suffering that I shall die."

"Nonsense, my gal. Why should you die? Who's going to kill you, eh?"

He endeavoured to raise her from the ground, but she resisted him stoutly.

However, her puny strength could avail her nothing against the brutal force of the giant miner.

He took her up in his arms.

"Come on with me, my dear."

"Whither would you take me?" demanded the unhappy girl in tears.

"Only up again, my lass, out to breathe the fresh air. We stifle here."

"Oh! thanks!"

"I thought you'd like that, my lass, eh?" said Penryth coaxingly.

"I should indeed."

"Of course."

"But I can walk."

"No you can't."

"I can, indeed."

"Then you shan't."

Rose Mortimer was silent. To say more she felt would be to incur the further enmity of her brutal captor.

And already she had experienced enough violence.

"What a delicious little morsel it is!" said the miner, hugging her closely.

"Let me go."

"No I shan't," returned Penryth. "I've had enough of that before."

"But I'll not attempt again to—"

"To what? No, of course you won't."

"No, indeed."

"Because I shan't let you."

His caresses now grew alarming, and Rose shrieked for mercy.

"What a little fool it is!" said the miner angrily. "D'ye think I want to eat you, eh?"

"No, but—"

"Then keep quiet, will you?"

But his conduct was not such as to inspire her with confidence, and she screamed in terror.

"Ah! cry away, my gal. No one can hear you here. I suppose that he is gone away, eh?"

"Who ?"

"He as brought you away from the water when I'd fished you out."

"Then it is true ?"

"Of course. You see I know all about it as if I had seen it with my own blessed eyes. He left too many tracks behind him."

"Why did he bring me here ?"

"For the same reason as I am going to take you away."

The brutal miner hugged her in his hideous embrace with such warmth that Rose was filled with alarm.

Now she apprehended the worst of Penryth the miner.

"Ah ! it ain't no use of you to wriggle and wriggle and try to worm yourself out of my arms. You can't do it."

"Beware how you go there," said Rose.

"What do you mean ?"

"That there is a pit somewhere about this part of the mine."

"Oh ! you appear to know everything about it, I think, my gal."

"Because he told me of it."

"He ? Who ?"

"He that brought me here—he who will never move hence."

"What do you mean ?"

"That he has fallen down the pit."

Penryth was not a little startled at this at first.

"However, he very speedily got over any little unpleasant sensations which this intelligence at first occasioned him.

"Ah, well, he won't trouble us much with his company," he said.

"NOT SO FAST, PENRYTH !" said a voice at his elbow.

Penryth and Rose Mortimer turned round horror-stricken.

It was the voice of the man who had brought her down the mine.

"Wat Lynwood ?"

"Yes" said the man. "It is even Wat Lynwood, Penryth."

"Oh ! how glad I am !" said Rose.

"No doubt."

"Indeed I am. I feared that you had fallen down the pit."

The fellow burst into a coarse brutal laugh.

"Of course you did," he said. "I intended that you should. I only stumbled, but I was yards away from the pit when I spoke. It was a lucky thought that occurred to me as I fell down."

"Wherefore ?"

"That you might be taken unawares."

"And a deal of use all your fine manœuvring has been, Wat Lynwood."

"It has truly, Penryth," returned Lynwood, "for you have had all the trouble with the gal, whilst I—"

"Are about as well off as before."

"Nay, better."

"Not much. I've had the trouble and shall reap all the profit."

"That remains to be proved."

Rose began to tremble.

Her old fears had vanished for the moment, but now she was concerned from some fresh cause.

From the angry tone of the two miners she anticipated a quarrel.

She had seen their brutal and unscrupulous ways, and she trembled.

One of them was a murderer.

The other scarcely better.

Neither would hesitate at any act of violence now, she knew, to secure any object.

It was truly a position fraught with horrors to the unhappy ballet-girl.

"Look you here, Master Penryth," said the other miner, after a short pause. "Get you gone, and leave the girl to me, and you will find it all the better for you."

"Oh ?"

"In truth you will."

"Do you menace me ?"

"If you please so to call it."

"And you think you could best me in a tussle for the wench ?"

"Possibly."

"Come and try it."

Rose interposed.

"Stand off, my gal," said Penryth. "Don't be skeared. He won't hurt me."

"No, no," said Lynwood, in the same spirit of sarcasm. "I won't hurt him. I might damage him a little here, but I would only point out at present that I should be much more dangerous in the witness-box than anywhere else."

The light of the lantern flashed at this instant on Penryth's face.

It was ghastly pale.

Then, by a quick transition, of a blood-red hue.

He seemed as if he had lost his voice at the alarming words.

"What do you mean by that, Lynwood ?" he asked in husky tones.

"This—that if you don't let me rest quiet here with the gal—"

"Well ?"

"Why, I'll denounce you."

"Denounce me ?"

"Ay, that's the word."

"For what ?"

"Murder !"

"Murder ?" iterated the miner, in a voice which was now almost inaudible.

"Ay."

"Of whom ?"

"Oh ! you know that well enough. I mean Miles Trunnion."

With a howl more like that of a wild beast than any human cry, Penryth the miner released his hold of Rose Mortimer and sprang forward upon Lynwood.

"Wat Lynwood," he hissed into the other's ear, "you have settled this question in that breath. Either you or I remain behind in the Danger Mine."

"You be it, then."

"I think not."

"Pray, pray be calm," said Rose, in an agony of fright.

"All right, lass. Stand clear."

The two miners grasped each other in a deathlike embrace.

"Now, Wat Lynwood," said Penryth, "let me tell you that you lie in your cussed throat."

"The lie is yours."

"Not so. But, if it were true, the boast you make is idle."

"Idle, forsooth ?"

"Ay. There were no witnesses to the deed," said Penryth the miner.

"'Tis false. The girl herself saw you do it."

"She did ?"

"Ay. Ask her."

"Then, by —— ! she shall have her turn after you are done with."

"After ? Good."

The lantern lay upon the ground.

By its light Rose Mortimer could see the two burly ruffians striving to rob each other of life.

Like two giant gladiators they rocked to and fro.

Neither spoke a word in the earnest eagerness of their hatred.

It was life and death.

They swayed and rolled off together from the spot.

Now Rose had an idea.

If she possessed herself of the lantern she might be enabled to escape whilst the fatal combat proceeded.

In an instant she had pounced upon it, and secreted it beneath her dress.

She then ran some ten or twelve yards from the spot.

The scuffling sound alone now told of the deadly struggle which was taking place.

Occasionally a dull thud told her that one of the brutal combatants had received a fearful blow.

Then, with a shudder, she would increase the distance between herself and the struggling miners.

Turning her back upon the two ruffians, she began to survey the place by the aid of the lantern.

As she raised it it struck against a cord.

Eagerly she looked up.

It was the rope by whose aid Penryth the miner had descended.

Was it not possible for her to escape by it?

She tugged at the rope, pulling as strongly as she could, but it was firm.

She could not see to the top of the rope.

It must be, then, a fearful length.

No matter, it was the only chance which offered itself from death, or a fate even worse, and the attempt should be made.

The first thing she did was to fasten the lantern round her waist.

Then she took the rope in her delicate palms, clutched at the nearest knot, and drew herself up.

There were large knots at every foot or eighteen inches' distance in the rope, which greatly facilitated her progress.

Still the rope swayed about, and she felt uncomfortable.

It was rather fortunate that she could not pierce the gloom beneath, or she must have turned giddy.

Still the sounds of the fatal strife could be plainly heard.

Suddenly she was forced to pause, in spite of herself, to listen—to listen in silent terror.

A desperate blow had been struck by one of the combatants, and the receiver uttered a hollow groan.

Dismally it echoed through the sombre impenetrable labyrinths of the mine.

Fearfully it struck upon the poor fugitive's ear.

Was it the termination of that hideous combat?

Yes, surely.

A wild shout of triumph burst from the lips of one of them—whose, Rose Mortimer was unable to distinguish.

"Where are you, eh?" demanded the victor in a hoarse voice.

Rose was silent.

Even now she could not tell which of the miners claimed the victory.

The wonderful change in his voice told most eloquently that, although chance had decided the fatal conflict in his favour, he had not escaped unscathed.

"Where's the lantern?" demanded the man. "Oh! we've knocked it over, I suppose. Ha-ha! my friend! I don't think that you'll trouble any of us much more now."

Rose shuddered.

"Where's the gal got to?" continued the victorious ruffian. "Where are you? Answer, or I'll precious soon find the means to make you, you Jezebel."

Rose began to recover her senses a little, and her flight was resumed.

Alas! Rose Mortimer, why did your fears overpower you at that critical juncture?

A little more exertion upon your part—a few strides upwards—and you would have been free—at liberty.

But it was not to be.

Now, unhappily, the rope she was ascending began to make a grating noise, similar to that which she had noticed at the descent of Penryth into the mine.

This at once gave the survivor of the combat a clue.

"Ha! ha!" he cried with an oath, "you're got there, have you? Down you come."

Rose, to her terror, felt the rope tugged from below.

She still held firmly, though.

Clung to it with the tenacity of a drowning man.

Then it was swayed backwards and forwards.

She could not hope to preserve her hold much longer now.

She felt that she was giving way!

The rope was slipping through her hands.

Suddenly her attention was attracted by a strange sound.

The whole earth, too, appeared to vibrate.

It was a low rumbling noise, as if from distant thunder!

The earth above began to fall upon her head.

It crumbled, and now huge masses of soil fell about her.

In an instant the whole truth flashed upon her.

The mine was giving way!

She now comprehended the meaning of its too significant title—the "Danger Mine!"

Barely had the thought flitted through her mind—compressing the pent-up terrors of a lifetime into those few brief moments—when there was a terrific crash.

Down came the earth — rolling into the fathomless depths of the fatal mine.

THE DANGER MINE HAD EARNT ITS TITLE!

CHAPTER XXXV.

THE FIRE—GOSSIP—A GLIMPSE AT PREVAILING SENSATION — A NEW PERSONAGE — MERMET THE ARAB—A NECROMANCER'S SEANCES—TWO STRANGE VISITS—THE DRUG — THE CHARM— THE ARAB SERVANT.

THE fire which occurred in Park Lane, at the residence of Count Lerno, completely gutted the house from the basement to the attics.

A heap of charred timber and the blackened brick walls were all that remained to tell of the fatal fire.

How it occurred remained a profound mystery to all.

The strictest investigation was instituted by the authorities.

But with no result.

Not the faintest trace could be obtained of its origin.

Many people in the fashionable quarters were vastly interested in the matter, and their inquiries inspired the diligent officials to greater exertion.

But it baffled all.

The strangest thing of all in connection with the mysterious occurrence was the fatal end of the owner of the mansion, Count Lerno.

So fearfully must he have been burnt, every one remarked.

Not even the remains of his body were ever discovered.

Search the most minute was made over the ruins for the body, but not a trace of it was to be found.

A coat which he had been seen to wear before the occurrence of the fatal fire was discovered near the back entrance to the house.

From this the more inventive deduced the most wonderful reasonings.

Many averred that he had got clear off and disappeared, with a purpose.

But why?

This was also answered by the wiser and better informed.

He had, they did not scruple to assert some very weighty reasons.

The precise nature of these reasons was—like the fire itself—a mystery.

Dark hints and significant shaking of heads were only known upon the subject.

At "White's" Sir Harold King became quite a lion, because he had been rather intimate with the deceased count.

Sir Harold's information appeared to be inexhaustible upon the subject.

The incident of the detected cheat, Captain Roper, was made the most of by every one — and by Sir Harold in particular.

Truth to tell, Sir Harold was just a whit weak-minded, and given to the old-maidish weakness of gossipping.

Like most of the class, he told all he knew to everybody he knew.

Then when his information ran short his invention supplied little ingenious fictions which were really very harmless and amusing, while they gulled the credulous.

Captain Roper had disappeared, too, after the fire.

This looked strange.

At least, it looked so to those who were anxious to solve an impenetrable mystery.

With the disappearance of the detected cheat the world did not hesitate to couple the unexplained fire in Park Lane, in the freest manner.

He had returned to take revenge upon the house in which he had been detected.

To take revenge upon the Count Lerno who had degraded him.

So said the wiseacres.

And yet this was strange.

If the swindling Captain Roper had so panted for vengeance, how was it that he had not sought it upon the author of his undoing?

Wherefore should he have carried his animosity so against Count Lerno, and yet have permitted Sir Harold King to escape?

This was not easily to be argued, and, therefore, probably was never mooted by the overwise.

Count Lerno and the mystery of the Park Lane fire died a natural death.

A few weeks and it was never mentioned in society.

This wonder was succeeded by a new sensation.

Folks grew marvellously pious.

In Kensington the ladies all worked slippers and braces for churchmen.

In Belgravia they came out still stronger.

Altars and candle, spriests in gay robes, and holy confession were now the order of the day in these Protestant (?) churches.

This was not enough.

One bold man—an adroit fellow, who drew upon the attention of the whole world of devotees—donned a serge gown, girded his waist with beads and a cross, walked about in sandals, and shaved his crown.

He called himself Brother Stiggins, and had it all his own way in the clerical line.

There were also a variety of lights in the cloth who created smaller sensation in their circles.

One, who was a bull-headed closely cropped individual, was reported to perform gymnastics in the pulpit in the way of gestures of enthusiasm.

Another, who was semi-dramatic, and of whom the wicked world said wicked things.

Another, who predicted the end of the world.

The latter, we may remark, was slightly out in his calculation, or the globe should now be chaos these ten years.

Then the clergy having had it to themselves too long, the lower orders of the laity became of a sudden inspired.

"Reformed" dustmen doffed their fantails and smocks, donned the clerical choker, and were elevated to the pulpit.

One Dick Steaver became a great magnate.

He "reformed" (i.e.) foreswore his "baccy," abjured his "heavy," washed his face, and did not use bad language), and carried the whole world by storm by his eloquence in preaching.

Then when this had become used up a new sensation awaited the blasé world.

Spiritualism became the leading attraction of the day.

A pair of wonderful brothers created marvels innumerable.

About this time—or, rather, after the sensation was beginning to pall upon the public taste--a strange fellow contrived to establish himself a wonderful reputation as a profound scholar, a wonderful doctor, a compounder of a certain elixir, a specific for every known malady, an astrologer, and, in short, a magician of the greatest skill ever known.

Of course he got greatly laughed at, but everybody visited him—in secret.

It was not only the petticoats who patronised him, it was well known.

Men—wits and scholars—men of high rank and reputation were numbered among his visitors.

He had established himself in a fashionable quarter, too.

Quiet and secluded, but yet in the precise position to be easy of access to the fashionable world, to whom he evidently looked for patronage.

He was an Arab.

His name was Mermet Ben something unpronounceable, but was known to every one as Mermet alone.

As this strange character will have to figure largely in these pages, we propose at once introducing the reader to his abode.

By way of a short introduction, we will be present at a séance.

Mermet was short in statue—a cripple of the most unprepossessing, almost repulsive, appearance which one can possibly conceive.

His head appeared to be monstrous.

A thick shock of grey grissled hair, and a long beard of the same hue, a hideous seared face, ferret eyes, surmounted by a pair of bushy eyebrows, and we have his portrait complete.

He always wore a black velvet skull cap.

Whenever a visitor was ushered into his presence he was ready.

This alone would always have secured him a great deal of respect from the credulous fair sex.

But the general effect of the chamber in which he received company was weird and sepulchral.

It smelt musty, and everything seemed to flavour of æther.

At the back of the room was a small recess separated from the rest of the apartment by a dingy tapestry curtain.

Near the top of this curtain was a small opening, through which the curious visitor could just descern the outlines of sundry crucibles, large bottles, and stuffed monstrosities in reptiles, &c.

Mermet was seated upon a low ottoman smoking a hookah—smelling suspiciously of opium—and which had an endless amount of tube.

There was a low rap at the outer door.

"Enter," said Mermet.

[THE MIDNIGHT EXCURSION.]

A servant, a man of colour, and evidently a country-man of his master, came into the room.

"What is it, Ahmet?"

Ahmet salaamed and then explained.

"A gentleman would have speech with you, sahib."

"Good, admit him."

Then a tall handsome-looking man of four or six and twenty was ushered in.

He had a base dissipated appearance, and the Arab studied him attentively as he advanced.

The visitor bowed and coughed.

Then smiled and looked uncomfortable.

"You are Mermet—Mr. Mermet?" he said after a minute.

"Yes, sir."

"Good. I wish to speak with you."

"Good."

"And in private."

"Good. Ahmet."

"Sahib?"

"Take the sahib's hat and walking cane—place a chair for him—go."

With another salaam, the Arab servant fulfilled these orders and departed.

All was done so quietly, and with so little noise or fuss, that the visitor was divested of his walking gear and seated in a luxurious easy chair in the space of a few seconds, and before he well knew where he was

"Now, sir," said Mermet, laying aside his amber mouthpiece, " I am all attention for your business."

The young man was evidently impressed with all this.

He appeared rather embarrassed.

"Ahem !" he began. " I—I wished to consult you upon a matter—"

"Pardon me," said the Arab calmly. " You do not wish to do anything of the kind."

"Sir ?"

"You have come here to see Mermet the Arab, to gibe and scoff."

"I—sir, I—really—"

"Nay, I read it in your face. This is some wager —some idle boast that you would show me up to the world as an imposter."

The visitor was dumbfounded.

Speechless with astonishment.

"Have I said aright ?" continued the Arab, perfectly collected.

"I confess."

"Enough," said the Arab, waving his hand. " I know what that means. But you might have spared me your ridicule. I court not the world : 'tis the world that runs after me."

The visitor bowed.

"Now you are here, if you would have aught of me, I am at your service. If not, I pray you to leave me to myself."

"I would have something of you, then," said the young man, recovering himself slightly.

"I know you would."

"You know."

"Ay. I read your face as a book ; it needs no necromancer's skill to do that."

"Then what do I desire, pray ?"

"A proof of my skill."

"Granted."

The visitor was even more impressed at these words.

"You would learn that I am a quack, a charlatan."

"Nay."

"Pardon me, you would. Put me to the test. I ask no more."

"I will," said the visitor. " You read men's faces."

"Some men's."

"Can you read men's hearts ?"

"My reply must be again the same—some."

"What is now passing in mine ?"

"The sensations are varied."

"To use your own words, it needed no necromancer's skill to tell that much."

"Right," said the Arab. " But I can give you the outline I believe."

"Do so, then."

"You are wondering now whether I am really a charlatan."

"Nay."

"And mixed with this is a desire to know if I could tell you how to restore your scattered fortunes."

The stranger started.

"Ah !" he exclaimed. " How, in the fiend's name, know you that ?"

"It boots little to know that," returned the Arab with great coolness.

"One word more," said the visitor. " These may be all guesses."

"Doubtless."

"A lucky hit, by which you would secure a reputation for hidden knowledge."

"Granted."

"Your proof, then. If you know so much it would seem but natural that you should know me."

"I do."

The visitor jumped back two or three paces, quite amazed.

"You know me ?"

"Ay."

"And who am I ?"

"A spendthrift."

"Ay, and—"

"Gambler."

"Sir !" began the stranger, indignantly. " You become personal."

"You ask for it."

"Not so. I ask, as a proof of your boasted knowledge and skill—"

"I boast none."

"I ask, I say, if you can tell me who I am—in short, what is my name ?"

The Arab paused.

Bent his gray head, and pursed up his bushy eyebrows.

The visitor watched him with a sarcastic smile upon his lips.

"You are at a loss," he said.

"Not quite."

"Yet you cannot say."

"I can and will."

Here Mermet clapped his hands and his attendant appeared.

A few words were spoken in a foreign tongue, which the visitor could not comprehend, and the attendant brought in a musty-looking volume, filled with strange hieroglyphics.

The Arab studied a page in this attentively for some moments.

Then looked up.

"You have found it ?" said the visitor, with a satirical grin.

"Yes."

"The devil !"

"You are called Sir Harold King."

The amazement expressed upon the baronet's countenance is beyond conception.

He turned pale.

Then red to the roots of his hair.

Then glanced towards the door uncomfortably, evidently wishing himself out of such a strange man's presence.

The Arab sat leaning upon his hands, poring over the contents of his book, and peering occasionally at the electrified baronet from under his beetle brows.

Then, when the visitor's astonishment had had full sway, he looked up.

"Are you satisfied ?" he asked, in a tone implying that he had plenty in reserve if he desired to know more.

"Yes."

"You think now that I am no juggler, no charlatan, quack, or humbug ?"

"Really, I—"

"Enough," said the Arab. " I know the world too well, young man, believe me."

"Well, I confess that when I came here it was to see if I could—"

"Detect me in a cheat," interrupted Mermet. "Now, look here, Sir Harold King, I can, if you like, run you through the whole story of your life. Every little incident could be made known to me even while you wait."

The baronet here interrupted him hastily.

"Nay, I thank you, I have quite enough in what you have already said."

"I thought so," returned the necromancer drily.

The visitor was silent for some minutes.

Then he rose and looked about him, as if doubtful as to the next step to be taken in this mysterious visit.

"You have nothing more to know of me ?" demanded the Arab.

"Nothing."

" Good."

Mermet clapped his hands and the attendant re-appeared.

" Ahmet," said the Arab. " The sahib's hat and cane. He would go."

Ahmet salaamed and withdrew.

" I beg your pardon," said the baronet, as if broaching an unpleasant matter. " But before I go there is a little matter. I believe that I—"

The Arab glanced up inquiringly.

He would not help him at all.

" There should be some little consideration, I believe ?"

" I don't understand."

" A—a fee."

" Oh! payment," said the Arab.

" Well, yes."

" No. I don't barter my knowledge for dross—my learning for coin."

" Pardon me, but in our country everything is bought and sold. Therefore I deemed—"

" Oh! I know well. I am not of this land, but I know well your customs and respect them. But I have no need of wealth. My servant, however, is more worldly in his views. He craves for gold. He is avaricious. If you would indulge the generosity of your nature, give him what you will. You will then gratify me and Ahmet too."

With this the conference terminated, and Sir Harrold King was shown out.

As soon as he was gone the coloured domestic re-entered the room.

" Well, Ahmet," said the Arab necromancer. " And how much did the Englishman leave ?"

" This."

And he placed five sovereigns upon the table.

" Five !" said the Arab in a low tone. " Fool! he's as prodigal as ever with his gold. One would have done as well and given him a great name. Well, well, one thing I see from all this which is useful to know—they haven't yet bled him to death. I must look him up again."

Thus speaking, the Arab swept the gold into a bead-worked bag.

Rising by the aid of his crutches, he lifted the cushion of the ottoman and deposited the bag in a small metal box.

While he was thus engaged another visitor was announced.

He was a tall handsome man of a military appearance.

He bowed stiffly as he entered the room.

The Arab eyed him curiously from beneath his bushy brows.

" Strange," he muttered to himself. " But that face is not unknown to me."

Then he continued aloud.

" You desire to have speech with me ?"

" I do."

" May I ask the nature of your business ?"

" I have heard much of your skill in compounding drugs."

At this point the Arab half rose from his seat.

It would almost appear as if something wonderfully familiar in the visitor's tone had struck him.

Calming himself, however, by an effort (marvellously concealed, by the bye), he resumed his seat, and begged the other to proceed.

" I was about to ask, too, in reference to your drugs, have you any deadly poisons for vermin ?"

" Humph !"

" That do not affect human life ?"

" Yes. I have none other."

As the Arab watched him closely he could trace a faint shade of disappointment stealing over his face.

His object in this being achieved, he hastened to make an amendment to his speech which completely changed its character.

" That is, I keep none but such as those for use."

" You have others ?"

" I have."

" And would dispose of them ?" demanded the visitor eagerly.

" Yes."

" You have them now ?"

" I have, but I only keep them prepared in certain doses for certain maladies."

The visitor eyed him eagerly, as if he would read his very soul.

" No matter," said he. " Let me have such as you have by you. I will pay handsomely if they answer my purpose."

" Who is it you would slay ?"

The visitor turned pale, and looked up half tottering by his seat.

" Slay ?"

" Ay."

" Who ? What do you mean ?"

" I forgot," said the Arab, with his piercing dark eyes fixed upon his visitor. " In my tongue the form of speech would be the same. ' Who would you slay ?' would apply equally to a human slaughter or the killing of reptiles."

" Here it is different," said the visitor, somewhat reasured. " We should rather phrase it ' What would you kill ?' "

" Thank you."

" Well, I would poison a dog."

" A dog ?"

" Ay, a treacherous animal."

There was a brutal intensity of passion in these words, which the Arab mentally noted.

" You think it dangerous ?"

" No."

" Then why would you slay—I beg your pardon—kill it ?"

" Because it has bitten me once."

" And it is rather a revenge—"

The visitor changed colour at the expression.

But Mermet proceeded.

" Upon the poor brute than aught else ?"

" Possibly."

" Then bring me your dog, and I will put him out of your way, so surely and so safely that you may rely upon it that it will never trouble you more."

" No, no, I cannot do that."

" Then I can charm his life away."

" Charm ?"

" Ay, involve it in spells so potent that in an hour he dies."

The visitor burst into a coarse laugh.

" Come, come, my friend," said he. " You do draw it a little too strong. I can stand much, but really, 'pon my soul, that's too much,"

The Arab frowned.

Then he looked up perfectly calm and collected.

" My words sound strange ?"

" Not exactly strange," said the visitor. " I may say ridiculous."

" Silence !"

The visitor looked indignant.

" You rascally old imposter !" he ejaculated. " How dare you presume to address me thus ? I've half a mind to trounce you."

The Arab's long bony hands might be seen to clutch nervously at the cushions of his seat at these words.

But when he spoke his voice betrayed no emotion or anger.

" Silence, I say !" he continued. " Remember that you address one whose age alone should secure the respect of such as you."

"Such as I ?"

"Ay. But be calm. Since you doubt my skill, I shall not condescend to give you explanations, believe me. You refuse to bring the dog to me ?"

"I do."

"Then I shall get him here without your aid."

"You."

"Ay."

"But how ?"

"No matter. Will you give me your dog's name ?"

"No."

"His initials ?"

"Not I."

"No matter, I can procure both."

"How the devil would you manage that ?"

"Shall I show you ?"

"Yes."

"Good. Be seated. It will be a proof of my skill for you."

"Indeed it will."

The same ceremony as before was gone through, and the book filled with hieroglyphics was brought.

Mermet studied it attentively for a while before he looked up.

"This troubles me," he said at length.

"I thought so," said the visitor, with a sneer of triumph.

"Yes, because there are *two* names."

The visitor started to his feet, and an oath burst from his lips.

"Two ?"

"Ay."

"Since you can say that, perhaps you can give them to me."

"Yes."

The gentleman was startled.

"You can give me both names ?"

"Ay. Will you wait ?"

"Willingly."

"Now, will you have the names or the initials simply ?"

"The initials will suffice."

The perusal of the hieroglyphics was resumed.

"I see at first," said the Arab, "an H and—"

The visitor interrupted him with an ejaculation of surprise.

"Go on."

"And then a K."

"By Heavens, it is wonderful."

"Are you satisfied now ?" demanded the Arab triumphantly. "Or do you still doubt ?"

"No. But say, what more do you know upon this matter ?"

"Nothing more than yourself—as yet."

"Then you can learn more ?"

"At your desire."

The visitor rose from the armchair and paced the room greatly agitated.

"And about this dog. You say you can bring him—I mean *it*—here ?"

"I can."

"When ?"

"When you will."

"Now ?"

"I could. But there is a spell to work, which would involve more time than I could well give it."

"When will you, then ?"

"To-morrow."

"The hour ?"

"This."

"Good. I'll be here."

Then as he was turning to depart a thought appeared to strike him, and he turned sharply round.

"By the same rule," said he, "I suppose that you could learn my name or initials."

"If you wish."

"I—no, no—not now. You can do this equally well at any time."

"No. Only in the presence of the person or one closely concerned."

A smile of deep satisfaction stole over his face at these words.

Then he departed.

As soon as he had left the house Mermet summoned his attendant.

"Ahmet," he said, "follow the stranger you have just let out."

"Yes, sahib."

"Dog him as his shadow."

"Good."

"But he must not see you."

"He shall not, sahib. I shall be even by his side and he shall fail to see me."

"Away. Learn his name and abode. Quick, or he will be gone."

The attendant hurried off.

"Ha-ha!" muttered the Arab when he was once more alone. "I wondered much what had taken him from this part. I well knew that he could only live here a schemer. But he seems now in flourishing circumstances. Strange if he can escape detection. I recognised him even as he entered. But these fools have no discernment—no wit. That long beard failed to deceive me. And so after all this time he still cherishes his vengeance. Well, well, he shall serve my purpose, and then— But Sir Harold, too, must be made to give a hand in this business. I think that I can work the two into my purpose."

Thus musing, he sat until Ahmet, the attendant, returned.

"Well ?"

"I have seen him."

"And he went to—"

"A club in St. James's."

"Which ?"

"White's."

"Never !" exclaimed the Arab. "The same club, too. What boldness !"

"And he is called Major Strangeways."

"Good," said the Arab. "Now you will return to the club, and leave this note for Sir Harold King."

"Yes, sahib."

A note was speedily written and sent.

Then another visitor was announced.

But while a third *séance* takes place we must give our attention to some of the other characters in our history.

We left our heroine at a most critical moment, and it is necessary that we should resume her adventures.

CHAPTER XXXVI.

THE FALL OF THE MINE—THE DISCOVERY—EX-CAVATION—THREE BODIES FOUND—ONE LIVES—WHICH ?—THE HOSPITABLE MINER—RE-COVERY—FRESH ALARMS—THE WHARTONS—DEATH—THE WINDING-SHEET—NIGHT—FLIGHT—LIBERTY.

ROSE MORTIMER thought that now her time had come in earnest.

About her fell the crumbling mine on every side.

Twice she was severely knocked by the falling earth.

And twice she thought that she would have been thrown to the ground.

Still she clung with desperation to the rope.

Clung to the last moment.

But yet a more fearful moment that all in this terrible drama awaited her.

The earth upon either side of the cavity to which she had so nearly arrived was giving way bodily.

It was an agonising period for poor Rose Mortimer now.

She expected every instant would be her last.

Every instant might hurl her to the fearful depths below.

The varied terrors which passed through the unhappy girl's mind are utterly impossible to enumerate.

It was a thought so full of terror and anguish that she was about to be hurled to so awful and abrupt a death.

The earth vibrated!

Trembled violently!

Then heaved up, as if some huge monster were sighing heavily beneath the surface.

The whole gave way with a crash!

Down, down she fell.

Senseless she lay and now fell all the earth away.

What can be the fate of Rose Mortimer now?

Can she escape?

*   *   *   *   *   *

The fall of the Danger Mine had created an enormous excitement all over the mining districts.

For miles around the people had hastened to the scene of the catastrophe.

Everybody said that it had certainly been predicted that it would fall any time these three years.

And the crash had come at last.

But most of the fresh arrivals had plenty of sport at first.

The mine had not given way everywhere at once.

Many, in consequence, had the satisfaction of seeing some portion of the earth fall in.

The last part which gave way was the portion surrounding the shaft.

Everybody rejoiced that the mine had been empty at the time of the fall.

Presently, however, it was suggested that it was not empty.

The cap of a man had been discovered by one of the earliest arrivals close to the entrance.

Another had discovered the piece of muslin which had been torn from the dress of Rose Mortimer as she was borne through the doorway by the miner.

As soon as this was made known one of the bystanders made a statement still more startling than anything which had been said.

He averred that he had heard a shriek just before the last portion of the mine fell in.

He could, moreover, swear that it was a woman's voice that uttered it.

The excitement was now intense.

Nobody could understand the meaning of the dreadful suspicions, but still it was readily taken for granted.

A staff of men were wanted to work upon the ruins.

Fifty volunteered for this arduous service at once.

The most hasty preparations were made.

Rude machinery was speedily constructed by the people, enthusiastically in the hope that their efforts might save a human life.

This was scarcely to be hoped.

How was it possible to avert the doom of any unfortunate wretch who might have been down the Danger Mine for any cause?

Hours were spent by these rough people in digging violently—working twice as hard as their own daily avocations demanded of them in the ordinary way.

But no result.

Still they perservered.

Presently many of the people began to murmur.

Some said that the shriek which neighbour so-and-so had heard was all a fable.

But the neighbour now protested more stoutly than ever.

He was certain of what he said.

He had distinctly heard a female shriek.

Moreover, it proceeded as nearly as possible from the shaft or entrance to the mine.

Now they had not much hope, but still they kept to the work.

From the bulk of earth about most were of opinion that there was yet a cavity below.

That there was probably a space sufficiently large to allow one to breathe and move about.

At length there was a startler for the expectant beholders.

One of the diggers gave a cry of astonishment.

Then there was a rush.

All wished to see what was the cause of the excitement.

The digger struck his pick into a hard substance.

Upon examining this he found it to be the boot of a man buried in the *débris*.

Moreover, the boot enclosed a foot, and before many minutes had elapsed a body was dug out of the mine, yet warm. Some one said that it breathed. This was found, however, to be an error.

It was a corpse only recently, it is true, but life was quite extinct.

A litter was very soon constructed, and the body was placed upon it.

In crowds the miners and the startled women and children gathered around the deathly spectacle.

Jostling each other for a front position, the better to observe what would have been to more refined people a repulsive sight.

"I know 'un," cried one."

"Who is it?"

"Penryth."

And Penryth it was—Penryth the ruffian miner—Penryth the murderer of his brother miner Trunnion.

At length he had met his doom.

So fearful a doom.

Death the most horrible, and that, too, to happen when he imagined himself in the moment of victory.

He had succeeded in worsting his adversary in fatal combat—in the fight for the possession of Rose Mortimer.

And justice—retributive and speedy—was done upon him.

The miners continued the digging with a vengeance after this discovery.

Presently one cried out that he had come to an opening.

It was there, as had been supposed.

A large open space was still below.

The earth in falling had lodged upon some large projections, leaving a kind of tunnel beneath.

And now the digging was prosecuted with considerable personal risk.

Still they kept to it,

Presently an opening was formed in the earth large enough to admit the entrance of a man.

One individual volunteered to venture into this dangerous tunnel to search for any one else.

There was no explanation of Penryth's being at the mine, which was so notoriously dangerous, and they therefore judged that he had not been there alone.

Presently the man cried out that he had come across a second body.

In rushed half a dozen of the miners all excitement—heedless of all danger.

Then, in the space of a minute or two, three of them reappeared, carrying a second body.

This was already cold and stiff.

Death had happened some considerable time before.

A cry of horror ran through the assembled multitude as this second body was brought forth.

Then, after a considerable lapse of time, there was a third movement in the mob.

A third body was brought forth !

This was that of a girl !

Rose Mortimer, pale and ghastly, was laid beside the two miners—the two sufferers who had caused her so much anguish.

The women crowded eagerly around, and tendered their assistance.

Presently one cried out that she still breathed.

"See, see, she moves !"

"Let me approach," said a gentleman in a plain black suit, who had that moment arrived upon the scene.

"The doctor. "

"Make way."

"Make way—way for the doctor."

The medical man made his way to the three bodies, and began to examine them.

"Yes," said he, with a casual glance, "she is still alive." Then a cheer burst from those within hearing, and was speedily taken up by the whole assemblage.

"But," said the doctor, "life has not much hold upon her now. She must be very tenderly handled."

"She shall be," cried an enthusiastic woman. "I'll look after her myself, doctor."

"And she must be taken away immediately, or I cannot answer for the consequences."

"Ay, ay."

A hundred hands were ready for the service ere the words were barely spoken by the doctor.

The doctor then made a careful examination of the bodies of the two men.

In a very little time, however, he pronounced it a hopeless case.

Both were past aid.

With much care Rose Mortimer was carried off to the home of one of the more humane of the miners' wives.

*　　*　　*　　*　　*　　*

"Well, my dear, and how do you feel now? Better, I think."

It was the owner of the cottage who spoke to her patient.

Poor Rose Mortimer was returning to consciousness once more.

For a weary time she had hovered upon the verge of the grave.

Nature had asserted its strength, however, and Rose lived.

"Thank you, I'm better," said Rose. "But how came I here ?"

"No matter for that now, my dear."

"That dreadful mine !"

"Hush."

"Why ?"

"The doctor says that the subject is not to be mentioned at present."

"Very well."

"Will you take your medicine now ?"

"If you please."

The good woman took up a small physic bottle, shook it, poured out the requisite dose, and gave it to the patient.

As the bottle stood by the bedside Rose could just perceive that there was a name written upon it—"Margaret Black."

Then the quantity was mentioned, and the frequency of each dose.

"Who is that for ?" demanded Rose, pointing to the bottle.

"You, dear."

"But whose name may that be ?"

"Yours."

"Mine."

"Yes. Margaret Black."

"Margaret Black," repeated Rose. "Where did you learn it ?"

"It was marked upon your linen."

Rose was dumbfounded.

Suddenly the truth flashed upon her.

Margaret Black was the name of the servant whose clothes she had taken as a disguise when escaping from the Whartons.

"You mistake," she said. "My name is not Margaret Black."

The woman looked incredulous.

"All right, my dear," she said. "Don't worry yourself about that. Black or White, it's all one to me."

"But—"

"There, there. I can understand that you should wish to keep your real name a secret on account of the dreadful place you was all found in."

"Not at all. My name is Rose Mortimer I assure you."

"Yes."

She spoke this in a kind of coaxing assenting voice, much in the way that one talks to a maniac.

Rose, seeing that she could not convince her, held her peace.

A day passed thus.

Rose was rapidly improving in health.

Her hardy constitution only appeared to grow more vigorous from the repeated and violent sufferings which she had undergone.

Upon the second day of her stay at the house of the hospitable miner's wife Rose heard a piece of intelligence which created fresh alarms, or rather renewed her old fears.

Mr. Wharton and his son Maurice were arrived at the scene of the disaster.

Moreover, they desired to confer with the fortunate survivor.

Rose was in despair.

Would her troubles never come to a termination ?

Alas! she seemed doomed to fall into the clutches of these unscrupulous men.

She had struggled boldly to avert such a doom, but unavailingly.

She was now, indeed, at her wit's end for means of escape.

It was indeed a dilemma.

She thought it over again and again, but could arrive at no satisfactory means of avoiding seeing the Whartons.

She put it off for two days by feigning to be worse. But this could not last for ever.

As she improved she would have escaped by flight during the night, but her kindly-disposed nurse never quitted her side.

She thought of confiding in the doctor.

But this seemed a very dangerous expedient at best.

How could she hope to convince a man of the world, as he appeared to be, of her innocence of wrong, and of the guilty intentions of the Whartons?

She was there under circumstances highly suspicious.

They had a high repute in the county for their humane dispositions.

No. Some other means must be adopted.

She feigned to grow worse each hour.

Then, suddenly hearing that the Whartons were about to leave the county for some time, and desired an interview, she came to a resolution to aid herself by a bold stroke of acting.

She feigned death.

Still the Whartons came.

They wished to see the body.

This was a trying moment for Rose.

They were shown into the still chamber and allowed to inspect the presumed corpse.

Terror kept the poor girl motionless, and thus aided her project materially.

Neither father nor son betrayed the least surprise at the discovery that the rescued woman from the Danger Mine and Rose Mortimer were one.

They had evidently learnt of the abstraction of Margaret Black's garments, and, coupling it with the account of the rescue of a girl of that name, had arrived pretty nearly at a correct solution of the mystery.

"As I suspected," she heard the elder Wharton say, as he looked at her.

"Yes," said Maurice. "There is no mistake this time, I think."

"Occular proof."

"Well, well," said the father, "she has met with a dreadful end. Had she been able to understand her own interests, as we would have had her, all would have been well."

"And have saved us a deal of unnecessary trouble."

"Ay, indeed."

It was a trying ordeal.

But Rose bore it through with a boldness de-deserving praise.

At length, however, the trial was over.

The Whartons departed.

They were pressed for time, as they were that night starting for London.

But now that this difficulty was got over another remained.

She had to hear her own funeral discussed.

The Whartons had in the most liberal manner provided for the burial, and an undertaker arrived.

This was dreadful.

However, she was now left in tranquillity.

Another day she felt must cause her a relapse.

No. That must not be.

Then she would be irretrievably lost.

Night arrived.

She rose from her couch when all was still, and dressed herself.

Then gently unfastening her window, she climbed over, gained the road, and fled.

Fled she scarcely knew whither.

No matter, so that she quitted that dreadful place.

The sight of everything about her created fresh alarms.

She walked on at a great pace throughout the whole night.

Homeless, friendless, and destitute.

Not a penny did she possess in the world.

Yet she felt light of heart, for she had her liberty.

CHAPTER XXXVII.

MERMET AGAIN—THE TWO VISITORS—THE PERFUMED BOUQUET — THE VISION — THE DOG — THE SPELL — THE WARNING — POISON — A POTENT CHARM—THE PROOF—THE TEST.

BEFORE proceeding further with the adventures of our heroine it is necessary that we should take a glance at the further doings of Mermet, the Arab necromancer.

A day has passed since our last interview with him.

The Arab is holding a second *séance*, which we purpose to relate.

At the same hour as upon the previous day Sir Harold King, the spendthrift baronet, arrived, according to an appointment fixed by letter by Mermet.

"Good day to you, Sir Harold," said the necromancer. "You received my note I see."

"I did."

"And I have to offer my acknowledgements for your courtesy."

"How so?"

"In obeying it."

"Charmed, I assure you."

"Thank you, Sir Harold," said the Arab. "But, believe me, I should never have thought of making such a request unless I had some inducement to offer you."

"Indeed?"

"Ay, and some starting inducement, too, Sir Harold."

"What may be its nature?"

"That you shall learn presently. By the aid of my much-ridiculed charms I have discovered that your life is jeopardised."

"My life?" iterated the baronet, not a little startled.

"Ay."

"By whom?"

"That I know not."

"Not know by whom? Oh, oh! Mr. Mermet, then pray pardon me if I doubt—"

"The correctness of my information?"

"Ay."

"I cannot tell you his name. But I will show him to you."

"When?"

"Shortly. Will you retire this way with me a while? and I will show you."

"Whither?"

Sir Harold King looked rather dubiously in the direction indicated.

"You have no fear, Sir Harold?" said the necromancer, smiling.

The baronet coloured to the roots of his hair before speaking.

"Fear? Oh, no—not the least. I am not more of a coward than most men I believe."

"I know it," said the necromancer, "and can duly appreciate your doubts."

The baronet appeared to be debating within himself for some little time.

Then suddenly he looked towards the Arab, and exclaimed frankly—

"Well, well—I will trust you. I'm sure I don't know why I should doubt. You can mean me no harm."

"Indeed not," said the necromancer, "and that you shall see."

"At least, tell me the name of this enemy I have to dread so much."

"I cannot."

"Why?"

"He has none."

"No name?"

"Not *one*. He has a hundred, two of which, according to my studies, you should well know."

"I? Two?"

"Yes."

The baronet looked more perplexed than ever at this.

"Pardon me," he said. "I know no one who sails under false colours."

"Precisely. You do not know them."

"What mean you?"

"That you have not the discernment to tell friends from foes."

"That's plump!"

"Pardon my words for the good intention."

"Oh! I do."

"I am not skilled in the vain and idle courtesies of life."

"Well, well, my friend," said the baronet, with a light laugh, "I know you are right. I am not over strong aloft — else I should not now be here conjuring in the nineteenth century."

"True," said the necromancer. "But the so-called strong minds frequently overreach themselves."

"How?"

"They are too matter-of-fact—never admit aught that does not come within reach of their comprehension — deny all that bears the slightest appearance of mystery—and lose many truths—"

"Which they are perfectly well unacquainted with."

"Perhaps."

"Well, so it seems to me," said Sir Harold. "I come here for a little hokus-pokus, because it is something new—something a little exciting, and because I'm thoroughly used up. Else I know well that I had better stay away."

"And wherefore?"

Sir Harold King hemm'd and ha'd, but could give no reason for this.

As he was speaking the faint tinkling of a bell reached the Arab.

We say the Arab, because Sir Harold apparently did not observe it.

Mermet looked up and summoned Ahmet the attendant.

"Ahmet."

"Sahib."

"Conduct this gentleman to another apartment."

The servant salaamed both his master and the visitor in great humility.

"Will the sahib follow his humble slave?"

"By all means," said the baronet, "since it must be so."

"I will join you instantly," said the Arab. "I have to see a visitor. I shall be with you as soon as I can dispose of him."

"Good."

Ahmet then led Sir Harold to the next apartment by rather a circuitous route—promenading an unnecessary amount of passage.

Here he ushered him in.

"Do you require anything, sahib?"

"No. I can amuse myself here while old Hokus Pokus gets ready for me."

The servant left.

As Sir Harold looked around him he perceived that the walls were decorated with all kinds of anatomical drawings and scientific diagrams.

The room contained half a dozen globes.

In the centre of the room was an arabasque flower-stand, filled with artificial flowers and leaves, most naturally worked and highly scented.

The flower-stand was in the centre of a small platform, elevated some few inches above the level of the boards.

This was the first object which attracted his attention.

"A neat little contrivance that," he thought. "I wonder if they are real."

Taking a chair, he placed himself beside the flowers and leant over them.

"Delicious!" he said, in raptures of delight. "What beautiful perfume!"

Each flower was differently scented, and it was an intoxicating effect which they all produced together.

Never before had Sir Harold experienced such sensations.

Never had such odours been inhaled.

They seemed to steal upon the senses, bewildering and enrapturing at once.

"Strange," muttered the baronet incoherently. "Strange effect."

The final syllable of the latter word almost died upon his lips ere it was barely uttered.

He remained with his eyes fixed upon the flowers, perfectly still and motionless.

His expression was rather that of a lover gazing upon the face of his mistress than aught else.

Rapturous delight was there clearly delineated, although he neither moved nor spoke.

He appeared insensible to all that was passing around him.

A slight sound like the sliding of a curtain failed to arouse his attention.

There was a fresh stream of light admitted from the further end of the apartment.

A long tapestry curtain was drawn aside, showing the next room.

Still the baronet never moved from the same position.

And yet the opening of the curtain disclosed a sight which of all others would have been the most likely to excite his curiosity and attention.

* * * * * *

The Arab necromancer meanwhile has received another visitor.

This is the gentleman who called upon him the previous day.

Major Strangeways, as Ahmet had ascertained at the club.

"Well, sir astrologer," said the visitor as he entered. "I am here."

"I see."

"And now to the little bit of mummery we were discussing yesterday."

"Mummery?"

"Ay."

"You are not choice in your expressions at appears to me."

"True, I am not."

"Then I would have you a little guarded. Remember that you seek me and my council, not I you."

"Pooh! pooh!"

"And if I am further annoyed by you I shall decline."

"Woa!" said the visitor with a coarse laugh. "Not quite so fast. Do you think I'm going to let you off like that. You are endeavouring to knock up a shine, it strikes me, in order to get out of a fix which you got into by your wonderful promises yesterday."

"What mean you?"

"That you're a humbug."

"Sir!"

"And that I shall expose your devilish humbuggery."

The Arab fixed his eyes quietly upon those of his visitor.

"And the dog?"

These few words, so smoothly uttered, had a striking effect upon the visitor.

He changed colour visibly.

He endeavoured to smile, but met with a lamentable failure.

"I see you are growing to know that I am not the fool and charlatan you would take me for," said the Arab.

"I—I don't understand."

"Truly?"

"No. I really mean no offence in anything I may say."

"And your threats?"

"Threats? Absurd! I offer threats, Mr. Mermet? Preposterous!"

"So I say," quoth the Arab drily.

"But touching the matter of which you spoke yesterday?"

"The dog?"

"Ay."

"You want the drug for him?"

"Ay. Unless—"

"Speak on. Unless I can bring it here, as I said?"

"Yes."

"Then I can. But this can only be done upon one condition."

"Name it."

[THE CRIME.]

"That when I have it here before you you do not speak a word—that you make no noise."

"But why?"

"Because the spell is destroyed with the sound of human voice."

A sneer curled the visitor's lip, but he remained silent.

The Arab clapped his hands, and Ahmet appeared.

Then a conference in some foreign tongue took place, and the attendant left.

Mermet then arose from his seat, and took from an adjacent shelf a small blue phial, from which he poured into a saucer some few drops of a colourless liquid.

Ahmet entered with a lighted taper, which was applied to the liquid.

Then the window curtains were drawn, and the chamber was lighted only by the bright blue flame of the burning spirit.

From above the flame arose a thick grey vapour, which rapidly filled the chamber with an odour which was far from being unpleasant.

Like the fatal opium, it seemed to steal upon the senses.

The visitor could not fail to be impressed with the proceedings.

All was silent.

The only noise he could discover was an occasional

faint rustling of the necromancer's garments as he moved about the apartment hatching his spells and charms.

Faithful to his contract, the visitor neither moved nor spoke.

His eyes remained all the time fixed upon the burning spirit, and the gracefully curling smoke as it wreathed up over the flames.

He seemed to be growing very comfortable.

A blissful sensation stole over him.

He appeared ignorant of all care or sorrow.

Nothing but tranquillity and peaceful happiness.

His eyelids began to droop.

"I wish he'd finish his conjuring," thought the visitor. "I shall be off asleep as soon as it is all ready."

Noiselessly Mermet at this moment appeared upon the other side of the flame.

The reflection of the spirit light upon his hideous face and dark grizzled beard had a most peculiar and weird effect.

The magician's right hand grasped a wand, which he held pointed at the curtain.

Slowly, and as if in obedience to a mentally-uttered command from the Arab, the tapestry withdrew.

Beyond it was discovered a scene which caused the visitor the utmost wonderment.

Seated over a vase of flowers in the centre of the place was Sir Harold King.

A fixed expression was upon his face.

He neither moved nor spoke.

Motionless as a statue he sat.

He appeared to be rather a beautifully executed image in wax than aught else.

The effect upon the visitor was electrifying.

His eyes dilated, and his lower jaw fell as if at the last breath of life.

He essayed to rise, but his limbs were powerless.

"*The dog!*" said the Arab, in a low but impressive tone.

The words sent a shiver through the visitor's frame.

"Stay!" he muttered hoarsely. "I—I—"

As he uttered these words the startling vision was over.

The curtain closed to, shutting out the strange sight.

"You have spoken," said Mermet sternly, "and the charm is dissolved."

The few faint syllables which the visitor had uttered, however, it would appear, had taken what little power of speech remained to him.

His head rested motionless upon his hand.

At first it might have been thought that the effect of the singular illusion which he had just witnessed had caused him to swoon.

But no.

His eyes were wide open.

His face remained immoveable, the expression which it had last worn resting upon his features.

Still he could see nothing.

Hear nothing.

All that passed around him was utterly unheeded.

And yet a second vision was there which would have caused him even more astonishment than the first.

The curtain was again withdrawn, and the figure of Sir Harold King seemed on a sudden inspired with life and animation.

And yet he saw it not.

*   *   *   *   *   *

"I'm at your disposal, sir."

The magician entered the apartment in which Sir Harold King was seated over the flower-stand.

As he spoke the baronet looked up and smiled.

The spell which had seemingly held his faculties enchained was broken.

"What beautiful flowers!" said the baronet rapturously.

"They are pleasing."

"They are most choice."

"And have been frequently admired," said Mermet. "You are at liberty to take them with you, if you will."

"Nay. I could not deprive you of them for worlds."

"Then I will make you a bouquet."

"Make them?"

"Ay. These are all my work."

"Indeed?"

The magician was advanced another step in Sir Harold's esteem.

"Touching the matter of which I spoke to you," said Mermet.

"This hidden foe?"

"Ay."

"Well, well. What would you?"

"Pray you to be upon your guard."

"But at least let me have some clue."

"You shall. I dare not speak a name, but you shall see his image. Behold."

The tapestry glided aside and disclosed the motionless figure of the visitor.

"Strangeways!" ejaculated Sir Harold King.

"Hush!"

And the curtain fell.

"One moment more," said the baronet.

"Too late."

"But how too late."

"You have spoken."

"And—"

"And the spell's dissolved."

Sir Harold looked rather startled.

"So," said he, "this is the man against whom you would warn me?"

"So says my information."

"But this is one of my most intimate friends."

"I know it."

"How?"

"Ay. But since when does he count amongst your friends?"

"Why, in truth, it is only a recent acquaintance-ship—that is, comparatively recent."

"That man's a parvenu," said the magician—"an upstart."

"Why, he had the best of introduction to us I assure you."

"Possibly."

"The Marquis of Stingo is his most intimate friend I hear."

"Possibly."

"And the whole club court his society."

"Possibly."

"But, hang it! how can he be what you say with all these advantages?"

"No matter. You shall see a knave exposed.'

"A knave? Strangeways?"

"Ay."

"But what proof?"

"This is the best that I can offer you. At an early date you will be drinking with your friend—"

"Doubtless. But that happens every day, I should say."

"Good. Well, say to-morrow, when you will see him drinking from one decanter alone. Abstain from touching the other."

"What?" ejaculated the horror-stricken baronet.

"I say, refrain from drinking from any bottle that your best friend will not touch. No matter the pretext, and he'll have one I warrant you, for he's as cunning as the fiend."

"I will," said the baronet, with a resolute air. "I'll do as you say."

"But," said Mermet, "pray observe this—on no account mention to a living soul what I have said—on no account mention it to the assassin himself."

"But tell me at least his motive."

"That you shall learn hereafter."

And with this assurance the baronet was obliged to content himself.

"Let silence and secrecy be your watchwords," said the Arab.

"Trust me."

"And be sure to bring me some of the wine from the poisoned decanter." '

"If what you advance be true, I will."

"Good. But bear in mind that all will be frustrated unless you preserve the strictest silence upon this business."

"I will, believe me," said the baronet. "I think you mean me well."

"*Think!*" interrupted the magician, in a tone of angry surprise.

"I'm sure you do. To-morrow night I will be with you."

"Good."

And with this Sir Harold King departed. .

CHAPTER XXXVIII.

THE FLIGHT—WOES OF THE JOURNEY—EX-
HAUSTION AND SUFFERING—THE ROAD-SIDE
INN—A FRIEND—TRUE CHARITY—A LUCKY
CHANCE—THE DRAMA AGAIN — HOPE—THE
LONELY VILLA—THE GARDEN—THE MASK—
"LET'S FOLLOW!"

To return to Rose Mortimer.

We left her after her flight from the cottage of the hospitable miner's wife, who had deemed her dead.

The whole live-long night did the poor girl pursue her dreary promenade.

At length there was a break in the dull black clouds. They began to grow grey.

"Morning!" murmured Rose in grateful satisfaction. "How beautiful!"

It was not exactly beautiful at the present, however.

Everything goes by comparison, and thus the dull leaden-looking sky which succeeded the grim and sombre hue of night was beautiful to our heroine.

At every fresh piece of light which appeared above she felt her spirits and her courage rise.

She had at length escaped from the terrible bondage.

At length she was free.

Homeless, houseless, and friendless, she still felt that she possessed at least the greatest boon of mankind.

Liberty.

"Thank Heaven!" she murmured fervently. "Had that darkness continued much longer I feel that I should have given myself up to despair."

The morning had now fairly set in.

She found, too, that she had at length left those entertainable mining counties far behind her.

So much had she endured since she beheld the mines that her delight was unbounded to find herself free from the terrible thoughts which their presence conjured up.

At length when she found herself fairly free from the Whartons, and the terrors surrounding that dark and tragic chapter in her career, she began to give a thought to her future movements.

This caused her some alarm.

She had no notion of any line of conduct— no idea even of the name of the place in which she now found herself.

A kind of vague notion possessed her that she must proceed at once to London.

But then ?

No matter. Once in the metropolis she might obtain some kind of employment, although utterly friendless.

Suddenly the thought of the friendly young scene-painter and his good-natured mother occurred to her, and her conscience smote her for her ingratitude.

With such good and sterling friends as these worthy people, how could she be without hope ?

As she contemplated the joyous prospect of again meeting with one she could grasp by the hand and call friend her heart beat quickly.

Instinctively her pace increased as if she would have strode to their sides upon the instant.

It is impossible to say how long Rose had continued this dreary walk, or how many many miles of country she had got over.

At length the courage which had buoyed her up could no longer sustain her.

It was a false strength after all.

Nature began at last to assert her sway, and Rose felt that she was utterly exhausted.

Worn out by toil and travel.

The country in which she now found herself looked more civilised.

Upon every side were signs of the place being inhabited at no great distance.

Up to the present, however, she had not encountered a single dwelling.

Not a house had she passed since she had quitted the mining country.

Presently she arrived at a turn in the road.

Here the sound of some kind of a vehicle struck upon her ear, and on gaining the turn she perceived at no very great distance a waggon laden with hay coming in that direction.

With all speed Rose hastened to meet it.

"What is the name of the next village, pray ?" she asked the waggoner.

"Woa !" said the waggoner, pulling in his horses. "What say, mum ?"

Rose repeated her question.

"The next village is it ?"

"Yes."

"'Taint a village at all."

"Well then, town."

"Ah, that's better," said the waggoner. "It's Springford, that is."

"Springford ?"

"Yes. And who d' ye want ?"

"Nobody in particular, thank you. Is Springford far hence ?"

"'Bout three miles."

Three miles !

This was anything but cheering intelligence for Rose in her present condition.

"Suppose you've left Chubley ?" said the waggoner.

"No."

"Come across country from Waterbeach ?"

"No."

"Then where the deuce have you come from ?" exclaimed the waggoner.

"No—nowhere in particular. Thank you for your information."

"Eh ?"

"Good morning."

And with this our heroine proceeded upon her journey.

Poor Rose now began to foresee an endless list of difficulties which were to spring from her strange position.

She turned round to look after the waggoner when some distance on.

There he stood, stock still, looking after her in great astonishment.

How would she be able to reply to similar questions ?

The time would doubtless arrive when some explanations would be necessary.

A weary weary journey did it now become for Rose Mortimer.

Still she kept up.

At length she saw a house.

The first she had come in sight of since the commencement of that night's troubles.

It was a road-side inn, and not the precise place she would have chosen to sue for charity.

But food she must have or perish.

She was a brave girl, and she gulped down her scruples as best she could, and then boldly advanced.

From the early hour she judged that the business of the day had scarcely began.

The door was open, but there was no one about yet.

No matter. Up to the door walked Rose, advanced to the threshold, and—

Walked off !

No. The pangs of hunger must yet be sharper ere she could beg.

Just facing the door were a few rude wooden benches and rough tables, and upon one of the former Rose sat to rest herself.

Until she sat down she had no conception of the severity of the fatigue which she had undergone.

It was suffering indeed.

Sitting here, she had time to reflect upon the miseries she had passed through.

But, what was far worse, the trials and troubles were yet ahead.

"Oh ! it is hard, cruelly hard, to have such misery to endure !" murmured Rose, a big tear trickling down her careworn pallid cheek. "Why, oh ! why is such a lot of trial and sorrow to be mine ?"

Her grief gave way.

Her heart was overcharged, and she fell to sobbing as if it would burst.

Her head sank upon her hands on the table.

There she sat, insensible to all that was passing around her.

"Lawks !" exclaimed a shrill female voice. "Why me ! if there ain't a woman half dead here !"

Rose raised her head.

Her big bright eyes were now dimmed with the bitter tears she had shed, but her pretty face was still beautiful in its pallor.

"Why she's been a-crying !" said the girl, a stout slapping country wench, whose ruddy cheeks and robust person presented a wonderful contrast to the emaciated girl before her. "What's the matter with you, my girl ?"

Rose could not speak.

"There, then," said the girl, "don't trouble yourself. Have your cry out, and then speak when you've done. You'll choke yourself."

Rose looked into the girl's face earnestly.

There was good nature in every feature, and she would tell her trouble.

"What is it ?" again asked the rustic maiden.

"I am weary," answered Rose, "footsore, and worn out with suffering."

"Poor creature !" said the girl. "Have you had your breakfast yet ?"

Rose shook her head.

"Well, I suppose not. But you don't mean to say you have walked far this morning."

"I have walked all night."

"What ?"

"It is true—too true."

"But you must be half killed."

"I am sick and faint."

"Of course you are—and hungry too, no doubt—ain't you now ?"

"Indeed I need food seriously."

This appeared to shock the well-fed rustic more than all.

"What are you going to eat ?"

A faint flush suffused Rose's palid cheeks at these words.

"I have no money."

"None ?"

She shook her head.

"I am destitute," she said, with a rising sensation at the throat, which almost choked her utterance. "I haven't a penny in the world—no hope of getting one. And, oh ! great Heavens ! this is too fearful !"

And once more did the unhappy Rose fall sobbing over the table.

The country girl grew moist about the eyes at this fresh outbreak.

"What's all this for, my girl ?" she asked in a very thick voice, and with a lamentable failure at an appearance of easiness which she was far from feeling. "Surely it ain't for a meal—else we could easily settle that little matter."

Rose tearfully offered her acknowledgements of the kindness.

"There, there," said the good-natured rustic, interrupting her, "we don't want any thanks. Get into the house, and if you are tired you shall lie upon my bed."

"Heaven bless you," said Rose fervently.

"Amen."

"And if ever it is in my power to repay your kindness, believe me—"

"You will of course."

"And with this she bustled the thoroughly worn-out wanderer into the house.

Fortunately for Rose, the buxom young woman was the mistress of the house—newly married—and had the power to befriend her.

Half dozing with want of rest and the great exertions of the night, Rose sat over the kitchen fire until a bowl of steaming milk and some eggs were brought to her.

This she devoured eagerly, much to the delight of her good benefactress, who stood by to survey the effects of her charity.

Then, the rest of the meal having been discussed, Rose was hurried off to a neat bedchamber to rest.

It was beautifully clean and fresh, and the comforts of such a lodging were most welcome to the weary fugitive.

At first she was even too weary to sleep.

After a while, however, she sunk into a deep slumber.

So heavy and so long was this that it was dusk when she awoke.

The kind treatment she had received by such a hazard completely restored her.

She arose refreshed and strengthened in body and spirits.

Then, dressing herself and making such improvements and amendments in her toilet as she could, she descended.

The hostess was in the bar.

"Well, my dear," said the kind girl, "you've had a long nap of it."

"Yes," said Rose, "thanks to your goodness. But I hope that I have not abused the kindness which you have lavished upon me."

"Nonsense."

"How to express my acknowledgements—how to offer adequate thanks, I'm sure I cannot tell."

"Lor, my dear," exclaimed the hostess, "if you can't tell with all your fine words, how the dickens can I ?"

" No, but—"

" There, there. Suppose we let it drop."

" You are so good."

" Am I. Well, *you* don't know me yet. But I've no time to hear all these flattering things that you've got to tell me. I'm busy."

And with this she darted off to the parlour with two jugs of foaming beer, which she had drawn whilst speaking.

In an instant she was back again.

" Lor ! what rum people these are," she said. " I declare they quite perplexed me."

" Who ?"

" My parlour customers. It's the manager and the head man of the new theatrical company that opens to-morrow night at the Theatre Royal.

Rose pricked up her ears at this.

The Theatre Royal ?" she asked.

" Yes."

" Of this place ?"

" Of the town."

" Is it only just opened ?"

" Just re-opened. The last man that had it failed. In fact, it never did pay; only old Nym managed somehow to make a decent living out of it. He never paid the salaries, though, and some people declare that to be the cause of his success. I can't say."

Rose was not thinking greatly of the hotess's words.

An idea had occurred to her.

A chance here offered itself, and, pay or no pay, she would risk it, if possible.

At any rate she would most probably be enabled to live.

Presently, whilst the youthful landlady was busying herself about, Rose strolled into the parlour.

The entrance was screened off by a dingy green baize curtain, probably put there to keep away draughts, and her appearance was unnoticed by the occupants of the parlour.

As she entered, the manager and his "heavy lead" were engaged in an earnest but agitated conversation, of which we give a brief portion.

" Well, Chowler," said one of them in sonorous bass tones. " Unless she does turn up before rehearsal we must turn *it* up."

" Turn up what ?" demanded the person addressed as Chowler, in a penny-trumpet voice. " Not open with Richard the Third ?"

" No."

" Pooh, pooh. Cut out her part."

" What cut out Lady Anne ?"

" Yes."

" Nonsense, Chowler—might as well leave out Gloster."

" Well," said Chowler, " I have seen that done before now."

" May be, but hark ye, Chowler, I haven't done it, and, what's more, I don't mean to do it. By Saint Paul ! I would sooner cut out ' My horse ! my horse !' "

" And you'd get goosed."

" Never. You don't know me yet, Chowler. I revel in the subtleties of character. I like hidden depths."

" Yes," said Chowler, with a squeaking laugh. " So hidden that very few persons get to the bottom of them."

The heavy man would not appear disconcerted at his sally.

He laughed with Chowler, and heartily. It was a manager's joke !

Suddenly he stopped short, with such an abrupt termination to his boisterous hilarity that its falseness was apparent.

" Well, Chowler," he said seriously. " No matter. Once for all, if Miss Lotty Siddings don't show up at rehearsal I don't go on for Gloster to-morrow night."

The manager was in despair.

He begged, prayed, and threatened by turns, but all in vain.

The heavy lead was inexorable.

" Then what do you propose ?" asked the manager.

" We must open with ' The Stranger.' "

" And Mrs. Haller ?"

" Oh, Miss Wilkins is up in the part."

" That won't do," said the manager. " Wilkins aint bad at a distance. But that glass eye of hers does for everything it touches."

" Then ' George Barnwell.' "

" No. Where's Millwood ?" saith the manager. " If we don't open with Richard III., then we'll do ' The Mountain Gorge ; or, The Hunchback of the Torrent.' "

" What !" exclaimed the heavy lead, aghast. " Cut the legitimate ? "

" Yes."

" My dear Mr. Chowler, you get really absurd."

" Thank you."

" Excuse my little personalities."

" Dear, dear; don't mention it. Quite agreeable."

" But there's one little matter you have overlooked. Where's your boy ?"

" What boy ? "

" Why, Juan, the dumb boy, that Lotty Siddings is down for."

" Oh ! Wilkins must double it."

" No, hang it ! Chowler," exclaimed the other, " she can't double two characters that are on together."

" No, no; of course not. I never thought of that. Then we'll cut it out."

" Cut out the dumb boy. The thing's worse than impossible."

" Well, it is odd, ain't it ? Hang it ! it is a fix. I'll fine Siddings a week's salary when she does turn up."

" Good," said the heavy man. " It can go off the three weeks' arrears."

Chowler coughed a short dry cough.

The allusion was unpleasant.

At this moment Rose advanced into the room to where the theatrical gentlemen were sitting over their beer.

" Hullo !" exclaimed both simultaneously.

" Excuse me," said Rose, " but I have overheard something of what you have said."

" Oh ! "

" Listening."

Rose coloured slightly.

" Unintentionally—yes," she returned. " But as you are in some difficulty, I came to offer my services."

" In what line ? "

" Anything I could do."

" But what have you done before ? "

Rose hesitated.

She scarcely liked to say she had been in the ballet.

" Have you been on the boards ?" asked Chowler.

" Oh, yes. I have danced."

The manager pricked up his ears, and grew interested at once.

" You dance ?"

" Yes, sir."

" Fancy dances ? "

" Some. All ballet practice."

" But hornpipes jigs, tallygorums, and cachucas ? "

" Yes, I can."

" And do you sing ?"

" A little."

The manager and his heavy lead exchanged glances.

Rose watched them earnestly, and saw that their looks were of great satisfaction, and said clearly enough " Here is the girl for our money."

" Have you a quick study ? " demanded the manager.

" Not very; but I will do my best."

" Could you do a dumb boy to-morrow night ? "

" Yes. I think so."

" Good. Then I am all right. You may consider yourself cast for Juan, Miss—Jones ? "

" Rose Mortimer."

" Miss Mortimer," said the manager. " Good. Capital line in a poster."

" Yes," said the heavy man. " But Mortimer's been done so much. I did the midland counties once myself, starring as Leo Mortimer, and drew immense houses."

" I remember. That was Bob Wilkinson's spec I think. Eh ? "

" Yes."

" And he smashed up."

" Ahem ! Yes."

" Well, Miss Mortimer," said Chowler, " we are going to rehearse a farce to-night. Would you like to attend the theatre with us ? "

" I should," replied Rose.

And accordingly they prepared to depart.

Rose hastened to the hostess to inform her of the good fortune which had befallen her.

A brief explanation of the sad plight from which the kindly-disposed woman had rescued her had to suffice for the present, with promises of a lengthy account of the horrors to which she had been subjected at an early date.

It was arranged that Rose should continue to reside there.

The town was at a short distance only, and she could easily reach the theatre.

The only difference now was that our grateful heroine took the footing of a lodger and a customer, instead of a poor houseless wretch suing for bread.

The contrast in her present prospects and in her past career was so great that Rose could scarcely deem it possible that so much good fortune should fall to her lot at once.

Not to dwell too long upon this position of our history, the rehearsal was attended, and Rose had the satisfaction of receiving some small compliments from the manager.

Then, when it was concluded, Mr. Chowler gallantly offered to escort her back to her hotel (as the heavy man designated the public-house).

Rose begged him not to trouble himself, but Mr. Chowler insisted, and she gave way.

Between the town and the road-side house at which Rose Mortimer was to stop there was but one house.

This was a residence of some importance, the property of some of the local gentry, and was a fine building situated on a large piece of ground.

The grounds were noted in that part of the country for their beauty.

Mr. Chowler drew up as they passed, and called Rose's attention to such parts of the garden as they could see from without.

" Why, hullo !" said the manager, " here's the gate open at this hour. There, look in."

Rose looked in as desired, but drew back immediately.

" What is it ?" demanded Chowler.

" Somebody there."

" Is there ? By jingo, so there is—and somebody who doesn't want to be seen."

It was true.

Creeping along the garden with stealthy cat-like strides, they could see the figure of a man.

The faint creaking of the gate evidently caught his ear, for he turned round sharply and looked about him.

" See, see !" whispered Chowler to Rose, " he's got a black mask on ! Here's something queer on. Let's follow !"

CHAPTER XXXIX.

WATCHING—TWO MASKS—THE BEDCHAMBER—THE SEARCH — A FATAL DISCUSSION — THE PILLOW—" HE LIVES !"—THE ASSASSIN—THE KNIFE—HORRORS—NEARLY DISCOVERED.

TREMBLING, and rather pale with the exciting position of her new character of a spy, Rose Mortimer followed Mr. Chowler into the garden.

The man they were watching had not observed them.

This they could easily perceive by the unconcern in his movements after a while.

The whole house was in darkness, with the exception of a faint light which burnt in a side window upon the ground floor.

To this, with stealthily strides, the masked intrude made his way.

The window was guarded by a wooden shutter, which stood just the least bit open, and a faint streak of light shone through it upon the grass plat.

The man advanced and placed his hands upon the shutter.

It creaked, and its rusty hinges sent forth a discordant sound which seemed to grate most harshly upon the man's nerves.

From the distance even they were from him they could perceive that he started and shivered in very apparent alarm.

" He's going to break in," whispered Mr. Chowler, laying a trembling hand upon Rose's arm.

Rose endeavoured to take him from the spot, but he could not stir.

There was a fascination in watching this masked marauder.

What could be his motive for this ?

A minute's patience, and we shall see.

The shutter having been opened to its full extent, the man endeavoured to raise the window.

But it was firm.

It was fastened upon the inside.

This appeared to cause the man some annoyance.

A whispered malediction reached the trembling lookers on.

A second effort to raise the sash proving unsuccessful, he turned away, with an exclamation of disgust, and quitted the spot.

" See, see," whispered Chowler to Rose, " he can't do it, and he's going off."

" Yes."

And Rose felt great satisfaction at this, although she scarcely knew why.

Instinctively she had dreaded to pass the threshold of the garden gate.

But they were wrong.

The masked man was evidently baffled only for the moment.

Not yet defeated.

Quitting the window which was inaccessible, he approached the main entrance.

Here he produced a key from his pocket and opened the door.

A deathly stillness prevailed.

He glanced around him, then entered, noiselessly closing the door.

" He's in !" whispered Mr. Chowler to his companion. " I'm glad he's gone."

" And I, too."

" But why did he attempt to get in by the window when he had the key ?"

" I can't think."

" And yet that was evidently his object."

" Yes."

" I wonder what is taking place in that room there. Let us see."

Rose would have preferred not going.

However, Chowler pressed her to wait and see the mystery out.

To the worthy little manager there was something vastly interesting and exciting in all this.

It was dramatic.

They crept across the lawn to the window which had been the object of the masked man's attack, and peered in.

A glance showed the two watchers why the man had not entered by the front door at first.

The room was the bedchamber of an invalid.

They could see an old man with venerable snow-white hair and beard lying asleep upon a bed.

A peaceful expression was upon his face.

His lips murmured some words, too, which were apparently heard by the masked man who stood by his bedside, but which were quite inaudible to Rose Mortimer and her companion.

Suddenly they perceived a second figure within the room.

It was a woman.

With slow and measured strides she approached the bedside.

Now they perceived that she also wore a short black visor.

Her right hand grasped a dark lantern, which she held above her head.

She surveyed the room around, as if to be the more sure that they were unobserved.

Her close scrutiny seemed to result in a conclusion perfectly satisfactory to herself.

She held the lantern down.

Then turned its rays upon the sleeper.

A nervous twitch agitated his placid countenance for an instant.

Then his expression was serene again.

She beckoned her masked companion to her side.

Then a whispered conversation took place, which apparently interested both parties, to judge by their earnest gestures.

Then they parted.

The masked man resumed his station by the bedside.

The woman moved with a phantom-like gliding motion about the room, opening several drawers and boxes.

At each her expression of disappointment was strongly marked.

Papers in bundles were eagerly searched, but with very little result, as far as Rose Mortimer could judge.

At length, however, a smile of satisfaction showed that the masked woman had found the document of which she was in search.

She eagerly perused it.

Then hastily concealed it.

"She's found something there," whispered the manager to Rose.

"It appears so."

"I wonder what it is."

"Some paper of importance I should say, by her evident satisfaction," replied our heroine, in a whisper.

"A will perhaps."

"But what can they be about to do with the old man?"

"I cannot say."

This was very soon answered.

The old man moved restlessly in his sleep, and now they could see by the movement of his lips that he was muttering something.

The woman pointed to the sleeper and raised her right hand—letting it fall of a sudden with a fatally significant motion.

What could she mean?

Another instant decided this also.

The sleeper moved, turned restlessly upon his side, and then opened his eyes.

As he looked about him dreamily, his glance chanced to light upon the woman, who stood close beside him.

"Is that you, Evelin, my love?" they could now hear him say.

Then the woman made some reply, which they were unable to catch.

From her movements they judged that it was some business of which they were unable to divine the meaning.

Then the expression upon the old man's face changed upon the instant.

Like a summer storm, he was rapidly changed from sunshine to thunder.

He looked unutterable things.

The two watchers were not a little astonished at this, for they could scarcely have deemed his earnest pale face capable of expressing so much intense passion.

Then an animated discussion took place—angry and fierce.

To judge by their gestures, it was something equally unpleasant on both sides.

The attitude of the woman was one of supplication—of earnest entreaty.

That of the old man of stern refusal to her prayers.

At length the woman appeared to be wearied of the discussion.

She put a final question.

The old man replied as before by a positive and angry refusal.

Then her whole face changed colour.

Her expression changed, also, to one the most demonical, the most diabolical that the human countenance can wear.

She hissed out a whispered threat or defiance—evidently the former.

Her eyes flashed fire, and her parted lips showed a set of pearl-white teeth clenched in the deadliest hatred.

She moved a step forward.

Then suddenly snatched up a pillow, pushed back the old man in his bed, and thrust the pillow over his face.

Rose tried to scream.

Her tongue clove to the roof of her mouth—utterance was denied her.

After a minute a sound came from her—but a whisper.

"Great Heavens!" she muttered, with a shudder, which communicated itself to Mr. Chowler, "she is going to smother him!"

"Hush!"

"Oh! Murder! murder!"

But the words died upon her lips.

"Hush!" said Chowler. "We shall come to certain grief if we are not careful."

"Oh, how awful!"

"But silence."

"Oh! See! See!"

Another episode in this tragic business was now taking place.

A few feeble struggles beneath the coverlid of the bed.

A slight rising in the murderous pillow.

Then all was still for a moment.

The man whom they had at first come to watch had all this time been standing in the back part of the apartment, evidently unobserved by the old man.

The woman now beckoned him with the hand which still grasped the lantern.

It was truly a fearful deed.

Murder most horrible.

A trembling old man, apparently an invalid, and one who in the ordinary course of nature could scarcely reckon upon many years of life, to have his time cut short so cruelly !

After passing through so many years of life—through its trials and temptations—hopes, fears, and sorrows—to have one's few short remaining days cut still shorter by the hand of the assassin !

Who could that assassin be ?

This was a question which Rose and the theatrical manager asked themselves in the greatest doubt and horror.

There was a strange resemblance between the woman and her victim.

So marked, so striking, in spite of the opposite sexes, ages, and complexions.

It was his daughter.

This they felt assured of.

While this and similar thoughts were hurrying through the disordered imaginations of the two trembling watchers another phase in this hellish business was about to be enacted.

The masked man, in obedience to the woman's imperious gesture, drew near to the bedside.

A few words were exchanged.

Then both bent their heads to the coverlid of the bed.

"They listen if he breathes," murmured the horrified Chowler to Rose.

"Villany !"

The woman after listening coolly for a while arose.

Then she shook her head with determination.

The pillow was taken off the pale face of the old man, now distorted with the agonies he had undergone.

At this very instant there was a kind of nervous twitching of the lower lip.

"Thank Heaven !" murmured Rose fervently. "He is not dead, then."

"Hush !"

"He lives ! he lives !"

"Hush ! my dear Miss Mortimer," said Chowler. "Be careful, I beg you."

"They cannot hear."

"They might."

"And then ?"

"And then ? Why I wouldn't give an hour's purchase for our two lives, that's all."

"We are safe."

"I doubt it."

"They would not dare—"

"Oh ! Pooh ! pooh !" said Chowler. "You see what they have dared."

"Ay, but—"

"Hush ! What's that ? Oh ! monstrous !"

As they exchanged these few hurried words the old man appeared to recover himself somewhat.

His eyes were fixed upon the woman.

His venerable face now wore one expression only.

It was rather of sorrow than of anger.

To judge from appearances, he was grieved and heartbroken by the scene which had been enacted, rather than hurt by the agonies which he had undergone.

He glanced into the woman's face for the first time during the interview.

Then, for the first time apparently, he observed the mask.

A deep sigh burst from him, and he gazed mournfully upon the masked face.

But the woman was a fiend, a she devil of villany.

No veneration for grey hairs would restrain her hand.

No tie of love or friendship—nay, or blood—could stop her.

The prostrate old man stood in her path, and he must be removed.

She looked upon her wicked companion, and pointed to the old man, but spoke not a word.

A glance conveyed all the fatal meaning which she desired.

The man drew yet nearer to the bed.

Approached the half-murdered victim to their villany.

He raised his arm above the dying man, his hand grasping a long knife.

The agonising apprehension of his doom was a fearful thing to the old man.

His lower jaw fell, his eyes distended, and he could not speak.

The hand fell.

Deep, deep into the old man's breast sank the ponderous blade.

And a sob—a sigh of agony and grief—burst from the slaughtered man.

Then all was still.

*   *   *   *   *   *

For several minutes both the watchers stood motionless, gazing upon the scene of the bloody episode.

Neither could speak a word.

Chowler shivered so violently that his hat slipped over his eyes and tapped the window shutter.

It was ever so light a touch, but they felt that they were discovered.

Chowler, with wonderful presence of mind, dragged Rose aside.

"Hush !"

"What ?"

"Hist—silence on your life !"

The reflection of the lantern now showed at the window.

The woman was alarmed, and probably searching for the cause of the noise which had caught her ready ear.

It was an alarming moment.

Would they be discovered ?

CHAPTER XL.

AFTER THE DEED — THE GARDEN — THE MASK AGAIN—THE LANTERN—THE KNIFE—NARROW ESCAPE — THE LILAC TREE — THE MASK UNMASKED—RETURN—THE WATCHERS WATCHED —CHOWLER'S LOVE—THE WOMAN WHO FOLLOWS —CHOWLER'S RESOLVE.

ROSE's courage left her.

She turned giddy, and must inevitably have fallen had not the supporting arm of the theatrical manager been there to aid her.

Chowler felt that she was tottering, and stretched forward his right hand just in the very nick of time.

"Come away ; let's go," said Rose.

"Gently, my dear Miss Mortimer. Gently, or we shall be discovered."

Both felt unwell.

Chowler's face was ghastly pale.

His hair stuck bold upright.

The deed which they had just witnessed had spoilt his rest.

They moved towards the gate, and paused to look round at the fatal window.

It had a kind of fascination for them which they could not at all understand.

Horror and loathing filled their breasts at what they had seen.

Yet they clung to the scene of the outrage.

"Oh ! how fearful !" said Rose, with a shudder which shook her whole frame.

"Dreadful !" said Chowler, his teeth chattering audibly. "It is too terrible."

"Poor old man !"

She shut her eyes, but in vain.

[THE ABDUCTION.]

The vision was there before them in startling reality.

There was the old man—his long white hair and beard giving such a venerable appearance to his face, and forming such a contrast to the ensanguined stream flowing from the death-blow in his breast.

A tear of sympathy stole down our heroine's face.

Again she pressed Chowler to depart.

"Come then," said he.

Now she suddenly pulled his arm and arrested his progress.

"What is it?"

"Hush! See, see !"

"What?"

"Something moved there."

"Where?"

"Along that path—there, under the shrubs—hist—we are observed."

As she hurriedly whispered these few words the figure of a man emerged from some thick shrubs growing upon the side of the very path upon which they were walking.

Fortunately Rose Mortimer and Chowler were still in the shade.

The man turned round and peered anxiously in their direction.

A cold perspiration seized Chowler as he perceived that the man was masked.

No. 13.

"See," whispered he to Rose in a very hoarse voice, "he's masked !"

"So he is, and it's the same man !"

"By Heaven it is !"

Yes, there was no mistaking the fellow. That slouching gait, that stealthy stride, seemed to express murder most terribly plain.

So it seemed to Rose.

Another little startler awaited the two trembling watchers.

The masked man advanced towards them.

Neither could move nor speak.

They remained as if paralysed for the time—frozen with terror.

From beneath his cloak he now produced a lantern and his right hand grasped a long Spanish knife.

Its blade was draped with blood.

The knife ! the very knife !

With dilated eyes Chowler and Rose Mortimer stood there awaiting every moment the ruffian's approach.

Both anticipated the worst should they be observed.

And nothing appeared more probable now.

Had he advanced to their sides, threatening them with the bloody dagger which had just wrought one fatal deed, neither could have offered the least resistance.

So thoroughly entranced were their faculties and their powers by the fearful crime which they had just witnessed.

On came the mask.

A pair of coal black eyes glistened furiously through the holes in the black visor.

It was a glance never to be effaced from the beholders' memory.

And now only a tree, a lilac, and that not very bushy, separated the assassin from the witnesses of his deed of blood.

The light from his lantern flashed around.

Its rays even rested within a foot of Chowler and Rose.

Nothing could the man discover.

So near was he that they could now even hear him speaking.

"Oh ! it's all quiet enough," he muttered to himself. "It must have been my fancy. I'm growing weak and womanish I suppose."

The searching was resumed.

The nonsuccess was evidently considered as satisfactory at last.

"Confound it !" they heard him mutter as he turned upon his heel. "She's as obstinate as she can be. She no more saw anybody than I did."

He walked up the gravel path and disappeared.

But where?

That it was impossible to say.

His sudden departure had been as singular as had been his appearance.

They had seen him distinctly in the fatal chamber the very minute before.

They had moved in the direction of the front door, by which he entered the house at first, and were, therefore, assured that he had not made his way to that side.

This involved the whole proceeding in a deeper mystery than ever.

Why had he not chosen this entrance at first in preference to either the window or the front door ?

He had returned, too.

There he was once more in the room.

From the distance they could plainly discern the shadows of the two forms about the room.

"There's some damnable piece of villany going on there," said Chowler, "and I should very much like to spoil it."

"Come away," said Rose.

"Ay, we must," quoth Chowler, "or we might get into trouble."

The garden gate was passed.

A sigh of intense relief broke from Rose as they gained the road.

She pressed Chowler to hasten their steps.

"Come, come," she said, "it is growing very late."

"Have no fear," Miss Mortimer," said Chowler valiantly. "But we are turning the wrong way."

It was the truth. Both were so confused by what they had just witnessed that they had turned to the left instead of the right upon emerging from the garden.

Strange to say, too, they had got some forty or fifty yards before the mistake was discovered.

However, they wheeled round and returned.

"Oh !" said Rose, "we shall have to pass that dreadful house !"

They had not advanced two steps when they heard the sound of footsteps a little ahead of them.

"Who's that ?" said Chowler.

The question was immediately answered.

A dark form, whose shadowy outline now began to be familiar to Rose and her companion, stepped forth from the garden which they had only just quitted.

He looked along the road.

Then, perceiving Rose and Chowler advancing, he raised his hand and hastily removed his mask.

Then he came up and confronted them.

Rose trembled very much, but Chowler, to do him justice, was tolerably composed.

"Good night," said the latter.

"Good night," said the man. "Have you seen anybody pass here ?"

"Lately ?"

"Yes—this minute."

"I have—a man. He's only gone by this instant."

"Ah ! Where did he come from ?"

"Well, I can't say. In the same direction as you I think."

"From the—"

"Yes—as near as I can say. But, to speak the truth, I was better engaged at that moment."

The comedian gave his companion a killing leer at this bit of gallantry.

"He went there ?" demanded the assassin in a hurried manner.

"Straight on."

"Was he hurried ?"

"Oh, running."

"Thank you—good night."

And off he started in pursuit.

"May you catch him !" said Chowler with a laugh.

And they once more passed the garden of the house in which they had seen so terrible a tragedy performed.

"What's that ?"

"Nothing," said Chowler. "Fancy, my dear Miss Mortimer. Nothing more."

"I have been so frightened," said Rose, "with all I have seen to-night that I fancy each stirring leaf is a masked murderer."

At each word she uttered in fear Rose clung so sharply to Chowler's arm for protection that he grew quite embarrassed.

Each trifling movement—her unthinking pressure upon his arm, sent his heart flying to his mouth.

Beating, too, as if it were endeavouring to force a way through his waistcoat.

But now unfortunately they felt too secure.

They were, for the critical position in which they had been placed by the force of circumstances, unguarded in their speech.

The full force of this imprudence very shortly made itself apparent.

Behind them at a distance a woman followed with slow and stealthy steps.

As they had passed by the garden of the fatal house she had rushed out and watched them.

Then dogged their steps.

Now they had arrived at the inn where Rose was to rest.

Poor girl! For the first time for many a weary day she felt something like contentment.

A tranquillity which had been a stranger to her heart for so long.

"Good night, Mr. Chowler," said Rose, "and as for what we have seen—"

"Hush," said the manager, looking around him theatrically. "Your finger on your lip—not a word—we shall speak of this to-morrow."

"Very well."

"Don't mention it to anyone.—We might get into trouble about it."

"Very well—"

"To-morrow at ten—rehearsal."

"Yes, sir."

"You'll be punctual?"

"Yes, sir."

"Good. I like to hear that, my dear Miss Mortimer, for we have a sad irregular lot in our company. Now Miss Wilkins is—"

"Indeed," said Rose.

She feared he was about to indulge in a long history, and felt bound to cut him short.

Mr. Chowler lingered long over his good night.

Rose, however, had her thoughts crowded with the horrors they had witnessed, and she got off as soon as possible.

"She's a charming girl!" muttered Chowler as he turned away. "A charming girl!"

Then he walked off.

Not far, however. The sudden shooting at the little manager's heart was so sharp that he was forced to rest a while upon a low boundary stone.

This was by the side of the road and shaded from the moonlight by some tall overhanging trees.

There he sat gazing up at the inn which contained the fair Rose.

Suddenly a figure—a woman—clothed in light coloured garments passed by him.

So close that her dress swept over his boots.

But yet he was unobserved.

Her point, also, seemed to be the house where Rose Mortimer was staying.

She stepped off the footpath into the road and looked up at the house.

A light appeared at one of the windows.

The woman was muttering to herself, but Chowler could not hear what.

Then she turned abruptly away and hurried back in the direction she had come.

"There's something wrong here!" said Chowler. "I shall wait and see it out."

CHAPTER XLI.

CHOWLER'S LOVE — THE WATCH UNDER DIFFICULTIES — THE LANTERN AGAIN — THREE MASKS — THE LADDER—AN ALARM—FLIGHT—THE HEAD AT THE WINDOW — CHOWLER'S RESOLVE — A SHRIEK — THE ABDUCTION — CHOWLER'S FEARS—HIS VISION.

MR. CHOWLER was in love.

It is useless attempting to disguise the fact—the worthy little manager was struck desperately hard.

The object of his passion was Rose Mortimer, his latest acquisition.

Rose Mortimer was attached to his excellent theatrical company.

Mr. Chowler was attached to her.

So poor Chowler not being able to see the pretty face any longer that night—propriety forbidding it, even in the free-and-easy habit of professional life—he resolved to watch her window all night.

The deeds which Chowler and Rose Mortimer had witnessed at the lone house filled them both with horror.

The latter's terrors were to last her through the night to haunt her sleep.

Mr. Chowler was happier.

The effects of what he had seen in that grim and silent garden were half nullified already by the sudden and ardent passion which consumed him.

But then the sudden appearance of the woman who watched Rose Mortimer had brought back all his fears.

He determined to watch.

Ay—to watch, even if his vigil lasted through the night.

After a close scrutiny at the window in which the light had appeared the woman turned and left.

A sigh of relief burst from Mr. Chowler to see her depart.

"Thank goodness that she's gone!" said the worthy manager.

But had she gone?

A doubt crossed his mind, and he grew uncomfortable.

It was possible that she would return.

To be assured of this he must know the object of the woman's presence there at that singular hour.

No, he could not yet look upon danger as being entirely averted, and he was determined to continue his vigil.

He began to look upon it as his duty.

It was pleasant to contemplate it in this light to Chowler.

In fact, as the thought of it being his duty his left waistcoat began to twitter in an alarming fashion.

It was now miserably cold.

The season was not the warmest of the year, and it was unusually cold for the time.

Chowler shivered.

His teeth chattered and his nose grew blue.

But he kept manfully to his self-allotted post for the night.

Was it not a labour of love?

He struck his hands with a fixed determination to the very bottom of his pockets.

His resolution he kept most firmly—for half an hour.

At the expiration of this time the cold which he had with much difficulty endured became alarming.

It was suffering.

He got up, jumped about, cut a double shuffle, and beat himself in the cruellest (cab-driver's) fashion.

Still he felt that the circulation could never be restored.

He turned his face towards the inn which contained all that he loved in life—as he felt at this precise moment.

The light was out.

With the extinguishing of this Mr. Chowler's love seemed to flag.

The sharp east wind which he had endured so long had somewhat cooled his ardour.

"No, I'll have no more of this," thought the manager. "I'm off."

He buttoned up his coat with the very greatest difficulty.

His fingers were frozen.

Numbed and almost without feeling.

"This is a pretty go," he muttered, his teeth chat·

tering like a box of dominoes freshly opened. "What a fool I've been!"

A final glance at the house, another long one at the window, and then Mr. Chowler started off to get warm—and to town.

He had not advanced far along the road when he fancied that he perceived a faint will-o'-the-wisp-looking glimmer of light flickering from a distance.

"What's that?"

With a started look Mr. Chowler arrested his progress.

The light grew plainer.

Then it was advancing towards him.

What could it mean?

Presently the light grew more distinct, and he could see something move.

The light he could now perceive was in the hand of a woman.

And, by all that was wonderful, the same woman again!

"'Tis she!" muttered poor Chowler, turning pale again. "Alone? No!"

Behind the woman came two men.

One of them carried a ladder.

The other held a long cloak.

What could it mean?

But they were rapidly approaching, and Chowler would be observed.

Rousing himself again, the little manager moved back slowly.

He was afraid that, having allowed them to draw so near they might observe him.

He walked back, with his eyes fixed upon the advancing light.

In his progress he came upon a gap in the hedge.

He subsided into it, and stood motionless, never daring to move—scarcely to breathe.

He had barely taken his station here when they passed him.

So close did they brush his hiding-place that the woman's skirts actually touched him.

What could they be after?

A wild suspicion crossed the little manager's mind.

A suspicion which was realised in the space of a few minutes.

They drew up at the inn.

Beneath her window.

Mr. Chowler's heart went faster.

He found that he had suddenly grown much warmer than all his exertions could have made him.

He looked on affrightedly.

Judge, then, if his fears had been so greatly excited by what he saw so far, what must have been his alarm when he saw one of the men place the ladder against the house beneath Rose Mortimer's winow!

The woman held the lantern up to survey the window.

Now he made another discovery. The whole of the party wore masks.

What could it mean?

That he soon saw.

"Go on," whispered the woman holding the lantern. "We will wait here."

"Very well."

"But if she wakes?" said the man.

"The cloak."

"Good."

All was so silent around that Mr. Chowler heard this distinctly.

He was in a great fright.

He had no idea what to do, or how to avert this dire calamity.

"Take the cloak with you."

"Give it to me, then."

The cloak was thrown over his arm, and he began to ascend the ladder.

Poor Chowler was half beside himself with fear and apprehension.

We are bound to say that it was more upon Rose's account than his own.

The men had taken half a dozen steps.

Chowler could no longer endure it.

At all hazards—at any personal risk—he must prevent this.

The man made another step up to the window.

"Thieves!" shouted Chowler.

The man stepped upon the ladder.

"Murder and robbery!" shouted Chowler, much louder.

Down came the man with a run.

"What's that?"

"Hush! We are observed."

"Away!"

To Chowler's inexpressible delight, they did not attempt to search for him.

The two men took the ladder, one at each end, and beat a precipitate retreat.

The woman led the way.

Chowler could not tell in which direction they had disappeared.

Truth to tell, he did not much care either.

Enough for him that they had gone.

For some time he did not dare to venture forth from his hiding-place.

At length he grew bolder.

He peered out.

All was quiet again—that is, the three black masks were gone.

Then a window was opened in the house and a head peeped out.

It was a night-capped head, but Chowler could not say if it was Rose's, never having seen our heroine in that snowy head gear.

"Who's there?"

This decided it.

The voice he well knew did not belong to Rose Mortimer.

"Who's there?" repeated the voice. "Anybody there?"

Chowler longed to reply, but felt that his life would be endangered.

He was by no means assured that the three masks had left the spot, although they were not to be seen just at present.

He allowed the woman at the window—whoever it might be—to call without offering an answer.

The head was withdrawn.

"That's one," said Chowler, "and they won't attempt it again."

Comforting himself with this assurance, he escaped from his hiding-place.

He would greatly have liked to give the inmates of the tavern warning.

No matter—for to-night he had preserved Rose Mortimer.

On the morrow he would put her upon her guard.

With a lingering look at the window, he once more departed.

He hastily retraced his steps along the road.

This time he saw no light as he had seen before.

No will-o'-the-wisp lantern to startle the life out of him.

But the adventures of the night were not yet concluded for him.

He walked along at a brisk pace — but again drew up short.

He turned once more to the house, with a lingering longing look.

Some hidden power—some secret impulse stronger than his resolution—urged him to return to the house.

Something terrible was about to happen—a worthy end to the dark doings of that awful night.

Chowler had a hard struggle with himself.

Back he went.

But he had not advanced many steps when he paused again, irresolute whether to proceed or turn back.

Was he acting foolishly in thus hovering about Rose Mortimer?

Did the something, whatever it was, which urged him on only mean after all a desire to keep within sight of the house which contained the newly-acquired member of his company?

He could not resolve it.

While thus debating the question it was answered in a sudden manner.

There was a smothered shriek.

A loud cry preceded it, and told Mr. Chowler that the second had been stifled while it was upon the utterer's lips.

"Oh!" cried Chowler.

But he could not move a peg.

Near the house he could see some dark forms moving about.

Then one appeared *up high*, and bearing something white in his arms.

It needed no conjuror to divine the meaning of this.

"Oh! what a fearful place!" said Chowler, half aloud. "They've done it at last, in spite of me. Shall I shout out?"

He mentally answered, "No!"

To raise an alarm now that the deed was done would be worse than useless.

It would be dangerous!

If they were such bold and unscrupulous wretches who had borne off Rose Mortimer—who paused at nothing to secure their ends—what would be his fate did he attempt to thwart them?

A life more or less was apparently nothing to the woman.

So Chowler kept his own counsel and returned to the town.

The unhappy manager spent a miserable night.

He slept, it is true, but his rest was disturbed by dreams.

He saw murders enacted every hour.

Men in black visors came and tore off with the Dumb Boy of the Mountain Gorge, who was dressed in white.

Then he went through a ballet of action in dreamland.

The plot of this was the same as that of every ballet of action.

A lover (in which he recognised himself) goes to a house (a road-side inn in this case) to see his mistress.

Then a rival (wearing a black mask this time) appears with a lantern and a ladder.

The ladder is placed against the window and the masked ruffian enters.

Re-appears, bearing the lady (Rose Mortimer), in the whitest of night garments, in his audacious arms.

But there's a sequel to the little manager's *ballet d'action* in dreamland.

The scene changes without any noise, shuffle, or prompter's whistle.

And now Chowler finds himself in the lone house, the scene of the murder.

In a chamber at the back of the house a lady, still in the snowy nightdress, sits bathed in tears.

She raises her head, and Chowler sees that it is not Rose Mortimer.

He forgets the poor creature's woes in his delight, and shouts out joyfully and so loudly that he awakens himself.

But it's a cruel disappointment now!

"Dash it all!" muttered Chowler, starting upright in the bed, "it was so vivid and life-like. I thought that it was all true. I thought that she was saved—

that I had my dumb boy back, and that she—oh, my dear Miss Mortimer! Poor creature! Something must be done to-morrow about her."

CHAPTER XLII.

NEXT DAY — TEN O'CLOCK REHEARSAL — MISS MORTIMER WANTING — NO, SHE COMES — CHOWLER'S DELIGHT — THE REHEARSAL — A STRANGE STORY—THE MASK AND CLOAK—THE OPENING PERFORMANCE—A PRIVATE BOX.

CHOWLER arose unrefreshed by his restless slumbers only in time to attend the full-dress rehearsal which was to take place at the theatre.

Ten o'clock was the hour appointed, and at nine forty-five Chowler yet lingered upon the pillow.

However, he sprang from his bed with a frightened exclamation, fell into his garments, and dashed off to the theatre.

It was five minutes to ten when he walked down the side of the pit.

The company were arriving.

Chowler eagerly scanned the faces of all the ladies upon the stage.

But Rose was not.

Chowler could not be comforted, although he never thought to see her.

"Miss Thingumbob aint come, sir," said the prompter to Chowler. "Miss— I don't know her name. The new singing chambermaid, sir."

"Miss Mortimer?"

"Yes, sir. It don't look the thing for the first rehearsal with us, sir."

Chowler frowned.

"It is not ten yet, is it?"

"No, sir, wants not quite a minute and a half," said the prompter.

"What of that?"

The prompter was subdued upon the instant.

He could not quite understand it, however, for this was one of the few points upon which Mr. Chowler was ordinarily very particular.

Ten o'clock began to strike, and Mr. Chowler to tremble.

He scarcely knew why, but it seemed to jar unpleasantly upon his nerves.

"Three, four—oh! she won't—five—come now —six, seven— Eh? Hullo!"

Rose Mortimer entered, upon the eighth stroke of the hour.

Chowler, who was upon the stage, sprang over the floats into the orchestra to greet her, thereby causing some damage to the green baize of the big drum.

"My dear Miss Mortimer," he cried, with extended hands, "delighted to see you."

"Thank you, sir."

She looked very much frightened about something, and he was dying to question her.

Yet he felt that he dare not speak of last night's doings before the company.

Inquiries would be made, probably, and he would earn the reputation of being a coward.

No. That would never do.

He must smother his curiosity until he could find a convenient opportunity of addressing her in private.

And so the rehearsal proceeded.

"Whistle up, Mr. Sniper," said the manager. "The Swiss chalet on."

The whistle of Mr. Sniper was heard, and up went the curtain again, upon the Swiss chalet—mountains, with frozen peaks in flat — practical bridge across ravine—slanting rocky entrance O.P., etc.

"Now then, chamois hunter," cried Mr. Chowler. "Look alive, please,"

The individual cast for the chamois hunter had been fetched at the last moment from the public-house opposite, and had not time to dress.

He had slipped on a little jacket with an infinitesimal tail, and wore a comical hat all over garters, but his lower members were still garnished with a greasy pair of very loud check trousers.

"I say, now, Glanville Percy," cried Chowler in disgust.

"What now, my trump ?"

"Do you imagine that the make up is good ?"

"Not I."

"Glanville Percy, you're beery."

Mr. Glanville Percy repudiated the slander most scornfully.

"Go on," said Chowler.

Mr. Glanville Percy threw himself into attitude upon a long hunting spear and commenced—

"The sun which sinks in yonder blood-red sky may never rise again."

"Oh ! confound it, Glanville Percy, drop it ; please stick to the text," cried Chowler.

"So I do."

"You don't, sir."

"I do, and I can show you my part, if you choose to doubt my word."

"Then there's a mistake in it."

"Which is yours, ha ! ha ! not mine, ha ! ha !"

"Well, but you should have understood that it was an error."

"I'm not bound to do that."

"You are."

"Why, hang it ! Chowler," said Mr. Glanville Percy, "you only told me a moment ago that I was to stick to the text."

"Now, Glanville Percy, you take refuge in a base subterfuge."

A row ensued, which the company had great difficulty in quelling.

However, the rehearsal at length was got over and Rose Mortimer made a very favourable impression upon all—that is, those who were not too jealous of her to see any merits in her person or performance.

As soon as the rehearsal was over Mr. Chowler begged to speak with Miss Rose Mortimer in " the Treasury."

This was a wretched little shed which served for a variety of purposes.

It was a weakness of Chowler's in the profession to dignify everything with a grand name.

Rose thought that the approaching business was the salary she was to receive.

"Well, my dear Miss Mortimer," said the manager, "I cannot really express my delight at seeing you here this morning."

"You are going to complain of my being late," said Rose.

"No, no."

"I know that it was wrong."

"Not at all."

"But the first morning, and I should have been here in time but for an event—"

"But pardon me. You were in excellent time, Miss Mortimer."

"An event," continued Rose, "which forms a strange and mysterious sequel to the awful doings of which we were both witnesses last night."

Chowler shivered.

"What do you mean ?"

"A blow has been struck at the inn which was intended for me I fear."

"You speak in riddles."

"You remember the hostess, the young and fresh-coloured landlady there ?"

"Yes."

"She has disappeared."

Chowler sprang up.

"What ?"

"Gone—disappeared—leaving but very little trace behind her."

"Then it was she—"

He stopped short.

"What ?" asked Rose.

"Nothing."

Chowler was in a pickle now.

He dared not speak, lest his motives for keeping silent hitherto might look strange.

"But what do you mean, my dear Miss Mortimer, by saying that this blow was intended for yourself ?"

"So it seems to me."

"But why ? How ?"

"She has been carried off."

"Yes, yes."

Rose looked rather astonished at the coolness with which he learnt this.

"Yes, yes," said Chowler, in an unguarded moment. "From her bedroom window."

"Why, how do you know that ?"

"I—oh, no, no, no. Of course I *know* nothing. I merely hazarded a conjecture."

"You are most singularly correct, then," said Rose Mortimer.

"Indeed ?"

"Ay. After you left us last night did you hear a noise ?"

"A cry ?"

"Yes."

"Certainly," said Chowler. " It was I who cried out."

"You ?"

"Yes. I saw some ill-looking villains and the woman whom we had previously seen in the garden bring a ladder to your window."

"Great Heavens !" ejaculated Rose. " It is, then, really as I supposed."

"Well, I couldn't attack the lot, so I gave an alarm."

"And then ?"

"They fled."

"You must have been mistaken."

"How so ?"

"Listen. Just after you had gone last night, and I had got to my room, Mrs. Davis, the landlady, came to my door, and begged me to allow her to leave open a door which communicated from one room to the other. Her husband, who is a cattle dealer, had gone to the nearest market town, and would not be back till morning, and she was rather timid of sleeping alone. I consented. Then, after I had retired, extinguished my light, and begun to doze, I was awakened by Mrs. Davis, who came in a great fright. She had heard a scream outside."

"My scream," said Chowler.

"Yes. I hadn't heard it, but she insisted that a scream had been heard, and she looked out of window, and kept me awake when I was much in need of rest."

"No doubt."

"Well, at length we both got to sleep again, and suddenly I awoke with a start."

"Yes."

"I fancied that *I* had heard a scream this time."

"Yes, yes," said Chowler, with growing excitement and interest.

"So I called out to Mrs. Davis, asking her what was the matter. No reply came. I therefore supposed that she slept, that what I had heard was a dream, and I slept again until morning."

"Yes."

"In the morning Mrs. Davis was missing. She had left her bedroom—not by the door, for it was fastened upon the inside. The window was open, and upon the ground beneath it are the marks of a ladder having been placed against it."

"And are these all the proofs you have of this strange affair?"

"Not quite. A cloak and a black mask were found beside the bed."

"Then we must make it our business to sift the matter."

* * * * * *

It was night.

Night—the day and glory of the theatrical professional world.

The Theatre Royal was full.

This was an unusual occurrence for Chowler in his trips, and was duly appreciated by the worthy little manager.

He darted hither and thither in the greatest glee.

The prompter had the word and "rang up" for the opening farce.

A screamer it was, to play the people in.

Chowler played the comic man of the piece—an outrageous cockney, with impossible h's, and a reversion of the w and v which was never yet met with out of a comic novel or an Irish or American farce.

But in the provinces the farce had been found (in professional slang) "to go no end of a pot."

So Chowler produced it upon every conceivable occasion.

Every joke brought down the house.

When Chowler appeared with his hat crushed, his coat torn, and his hair hanging all over his forehead every one roared with delight.

And Chowler, in his professional pride, forgot everything else.

The terrors of the night which he had passed with Rose Mortimer in the garden of the house, and the misery and the alarming termination to his vigil outside of it were no more thought of.

Chowler eclipsed himself.

At length the farce was over, and down came the curtain to a showers of applause.

Chowler had to make a gracious answer to an unanimous call and amidst thunder of applause.

Then the prompter rang up for the Mountain Gorge.

The audience were now put into admirable humour by Chowler and the farce, and were prepared to like anything and everything.

The opening scene, sunset effect, brought down the house with a run.

Then Miss Mortimer, the dumb boy, made her appearance.

Rose's pretty face and comely person was set off to great advantage by the dress she wore for the part, and she had a greeting that set all the rest of the company dying of envy.

Rose was in excellent spirits now, and played with much animation.

The first scene closed with a dangerous tableaux which stirred up the audience.

Then Rose had to open the second scene with a bit of solo pantomime.

This brought her close to the footlights, and she had time and opportunity to survey the whole of the audience.

But of all the company present she could only see one individual.

In the right hand stage-box a lady and gentleman were conversing in a low tone the whole time of the performance, evidently not in the remotest degree interested with the adventures of the dumb boy.

Once Rose caught the sound of the lady's voice in a little higher tone than that in which she had previously spoken.

Great Heavens! It was a voice she well remembered.

The form, too, she felt she had seen upon some former occasion.

A wild suspicion flitted through her mind, but she hushed it at once.

It was so improbable.

She almost imagined that the lady in the box and the wicked woman who held the lantern over the old man for the perpetration of the assassination in the lone house were one.

"No, no," she thought, "it is impossible. She would never be here if it were she."

Here Rose's thoughts were so abstracted that she quite forgot the dumb boy and the expressive pantomime which she ought to have gone through.

She stood still some few minutes with her eyes riveted upon the box.

The audience, thinking that this was a portion of the play and most naturally acted, began to applaud.

The prompter, however, was in the greatest despair at her strange conduct.

"Miss Mortimer," he whispered at the wing, "Miss Mortimer."

But Rose could not be brought back to her presence of mind with a word.

The prompter was frantic.

Chowler came running up.

"What is it?"

"Our new hand, Miss Mortimer, has made a dead stop."

Chowler caught a glimpse of our heroine just as she had recovered her presence of mind and was continuing the piece.

Chowler could not understand it.

He was all impatience until Miss Mortimer came off the stage.

Then he eagerly questioned her.

"Oh! Mr. Chowler," said Rose, "I have seen that woman, I am sure."

"Who?"

"She whom we saw last night."

Chowler looked frightened.

"The lone house?" he demanded in a hoarse dramatic whisper.

"Yes."

"Where?"

"The O. P. stage-box."

"She? Impossible."

"No; I feel convinced it is she."

"But why?"

"I heard her speak."

"And you recognised her."

"Ay, I'm sure it is she."

Chowler gave another glance at the box.

"Well, we'll test her," he said, "I'm on almost immediately."

"No, no," said Rose, "I would not do anything to arouse their suspicions."

"Nor will I," said Chowler. "Leave it to me. *The play's the thing!* I'll attend to this little matter, and be sure that we are on the right track."

"Very well."

Shortly after this Chowler made his second appearance as a comic Alpine lover.

In this character he had to be an awful coward.

His great fear was a certain brigand, a kind of Mazzaroni-Fra-Diavolo-Marco-Spada individual, who haunted the mountains with a ferocious band of the vilest followers.

In Chowler's part he had to narrate some of the brigand's atrocities, and in another he contrived to introduce, impromptu, a sketch of a little affair which bore a very close resemblance to the adventure of the previous night.

At the outset the lady in the O. P. stage box grew interested.

She clutched her companion by the arm and drew his attention to it.

Then both listened with the most intense interest.

As Chowler warmed, denouncing the villain, he observed that the lady's colour had completely fled from her cheek.

Chowler had retired up the stage, making way for the appearance of the terrible brigand himself, when he noticed that the party in the O. P. box were leaving.

Some one had come to the door of the box, and the lady had left in apparent consternation.

"It is the same," exclaimed Chowler to Rose Mortimer at the wing.

"I was certain of it."

"Would you tell the call boy to come to me, please, Miss Mortimer."

The call boy came, and Mr. Chowler sent him round to the front of the house to see if he could learn who were the occupants of the box.

The boy shortly returned full of news.

It was Lady Bellisle and her cousin, Mr. Spencer Bellisle.

This was not all.

A most alarming tale had just gone round the house.

The Earl of Sloeford, her ladyship's uncle, and an aged invalid, had been found murdered in his bed.

Chowler was amazed.

Rose Mortimer in a perfect state of bewilderment.

She was certainly not fit to go on the stage now.

Chowler questioned the boy eagerly, but that was all he could glean.

How was it that the deed of violence had only then been discovered?

This remained to be seen.

Chowler had better be patient.

There was yet another act to be played in this fearful tragedy in real life.

A drama in which he had played one of the small audience who attended.

The particulars enlightened them upon some points in connection with it.

Some, however, threw a deeper mystery over it for the present.

All in good time.

CHAPTER XLIII.

THE CARD TABLE—HIGH STAKES—THE POISONER DETECTED — THE EVIDENCE DESTROYED — A GOOD SHOT—THE DUEL ON HAMPSTEAD HEATH —THE SWINDLER UNMASKED.

LET us shift the scene from Mr. Chowler's theatre for a little time.

We open in London again.

Our destination is a club in the West End, where a strange scene is about to be enacted by two gentlemen who have appeared several times in these pages.

One is Sir Harold King.

Major Strangeways is the other.

These two gentlemen, who were great cronies, although their acquaintance was only believed to date from the major's introduction to White's, were seated in the card-room at the club playing a quiet little game at *écarte*—just the mildest bit of gambling.

However, one thing was certain.

They might commence with half-crowns, but the game was sure to end in five, ten, twenty pound stakes and higher.

And it was always the loser—Sir Harold King—who proposed to increase the stakes.

Major Strangeways had got a little mountain of Sir Harold King's money beside him, and, strange to say, the baronet to-night was remarkably cool and collected.

Still he kept on.

Major Strangeways urged him to conclude, as the game and the luck were all against him.

But Sir Harold obstinately kept on.

"No, no, Strangeways," he said. "You don't leave me like this."

"But—"

"Nay, you shall not."

"Shall not?"

"No. Do you think you are going to take home all that heap of my losings? Never. I should disgrace my family."

The major laughed uproariously at Sir Harold's pleasantry.

"Well, Sir Harold," said the major reluctantly, "since you will have it so—but really I should say—"

"Tush man, let's have some wine, eh?"

"With all my heart."

"Hochheimer?"

"As you please."

Sir Harold King called for two bottles and glasses.

Meanwhile the play continued.

Sir Harold appeared quite calm, as we have said, the only difference to be observed upon a close study of his movements was the anxious glance he threw towards his companion from time to time.

As he proposed wine he fixed his eyes so intently upon the major that he could not help noticing it, and he looked up.

The baronet turned away his glance and looked at the cards.

"What is it, Sir Harold?" demanded Major Strangeways.

"Nothing, nothing. Merely an old recollection, nothing more."

The major changed colour.

Without appearing to be anxious upon the point, he pressed Sir Harold closely upon the nature of the old recollection.

"I have no particular idea," said the baronet. "Only a kind of vague remembrance that we have met some time before our present acquaintance."

"No," said Major Strangeways. "But I have frequently observed that where one meets a friend to whom one grows speedily attached a similar impression arises. I have noticed the same thing with music. On hearing for the first time an attractive air of a new opera it has frequently seemed quite familiar, in the same way I suppose."

The major appeared so anxious to prove to Sir Harold King that he was mistaken that he rather overreached himself.

When the hock which the former had ordered arrived the major hastened to serve it out.

Now, although Sir Harold King had previously complained of thirst, when the wine came he had his head turned in another direction.

He pretended to grow listless and yawn.

But all the time he had his eyes fixed upon the major over his shoulder.

He saw him take a small blue paper from his pocket, and, closing his palm over it, carelessly but artfully slip the contents of it into the glass from which he —Sir Harold—was to drink.

The baronet started slightly, but beyond this he took no notice.

The major coolly filled the glasses and pushed one to Sir Harold.

"Here's better fortune to you for the next time," said the major, nodding.

"Thank you."

But Sir Harold did not drink.

[DIGGING THE GRAVE.]

He took the glass in his hand and trifled with the brim of it, chatting carelessly.

"Come, Sir Harold," said Major Strangeways. "Your health."

"Thank you."

The baronet replied listlessly, but did not offer to drink.

"You don't drink," said the major.

"What?" exclaimed the baronet, turning upon Major Strangeways sharply.

"I say you don't drink."

"Oh!"

He stared sharply at the major, but he stood his glance quite composedly.

No. 14.

"Nay, true," said the baronet.

He then produced a small phial of a white liquid which he poured into the wine.

"Hullo!" exclaimed Major Strangeways, jumping up. "What's that?"

"Wait."

"What do you mean?"

"You'll see."

Sir Harold King raised the glass and held it up to the light.

The wine in it had turned a bright emerald green.

"Do you see that, Major Strangeways?" asked the baronet.

The major's voice quivered as he replied—

"I don't understand you yet."

"Why, that is surely known to you."

"What?"

"The nature of the liquid."

"I don't see—"

"Pshaw! Major Strangeways," said Sir Harold King. "You don't mean to tell me that you use poisons—"

"Poisons?"

"Without knowing if they are vegetable or animal poisons."

"Nonsense," said the major.

And he endeavoured to laugh, but it resulted in a failure.

The baronet grew serious.

"Come, come, Major Strangeways," said the baronet, "no nonsense. You have tried to murder—"

"Murder?" faltered the baronet.

"Ay, to murder me. Here's the proof of it. I shall take this to the nearest chemist."

"Pooh, pooh!"

"And I shall deliver you over to the care of a constable without further delay."

The major jumped up.

"Come, Sir Harold," said he, growing serious at once. "What do you mean by that assertion?"

"Why, you audacious scoundrel," said Sir Harold, "dare you yet brazen it out in face of these proofs?"

"Which?"

"This."

He held up the glass containing the g een liquid.

"That's none."

"No proof?"

"No."

"It strikes me, major, you'll find it enough proof for a jury."

"Pshaw!" said the major, with scornful coldness, "where are your witnesses?"

His coolness almost dumbfounded the baronet for a while.

"Oh! as for witnesses," he said, "I'll soon settle that."

He jumped up, and, before Major Strangeways could divine his intention, rang the bell violently.

A rush of servants was heard almost immediately.

The major grew pale.

Determination to do something desperate was plainly marked in his face.

A hand was laid upon the door without.

Now then was the time to act, or be lost, and for ever.

Up dashed the major.

With one bound he was upon Sir Harold.

He tore the glass from his hand and threw it to the ground.

This was barely accomplished when the door was opened, and in came two of the servants.

The baronet could not contain his rage and disgust.

"Miscreant!" he ejaculated. "Cheat and traitor, your—"

Passion choked him and he could not iterate.

So he seized hold of the major by the collar, squeezing him so that he was more than half choked.

Then dashed him to the ground.

The major fell all of a heap, considerably shaken, bruised, and half-stunned.

His first care upon gaining his feet was to appeal to the servants who had seen the affront put upon him.

"You see that this man has outraged all the laws of society," said he, "and that he owes me reparation. Sir Harold King," he continued, turning to the baronet, and with bitter emphasis, "you shall suffer for this."

"Good," said the baronet. "I accept what you would propose—although to do justice upon you I should send you to the station-house without a moment's delay."

"In the morning," said Major Strangeways, "a friend of mine will wait upon you."

"Oh! no," said Sir Harold ironically, "not in the morning. I don't lose sight of you now, I can assure you."

"What mean you?"

"This," said Sir Harold. "I am willing to give you the chance of shooting an English gentleman, although I shall be disgraced by opposing myself to your fire. But I shan't give you the chance to get off. I shall disable you, and hand you over to the police."

"Enough, sir."

The major smiled a bitter smile of hate and malice.

"We must have some witnesses to the deed. I don't want to run any risk."

"You shall have witnesses."

Some gentlemen having heard the disturbance in the card-room, came in just at this point in the conversation.

They offered their services, which were at once accepted.

"What is the nature of the quarrel?" was the first question put.

"It is no quarrel," said Sir Harold. "This demon has basely attempted my life."

"Never!"

"Impossible!"

"Just so, gentlemen," quoth the major, with the coolest assurance imaginable. "So would any one say. But the fact is, if you must know, that Sir Harold King and I have been playing écarte for rather foolishly high stakes. I was unusually lucky, and you guess the rest."

"What?" said one of the gentlemen. "Sir Harold lost his temper with his money."

"Exactly."

In vain did Sir Harold protest against this barefaced assertion.

It certainly looked as if he spoke the truth.

The exhibition of choler appeared so much greater upon the baronet's side than that of his adversary.

"Enough, gentlemen," said Sir Harold King, after vainly endeavouring to make himself heard. "This is a plausible scoundrel."

"Come, Sir Harold!"

"Well, hang it! I'll have patience; but I promise you that you will see how he has thrown dust in your eyes by his devilish cunning. Ask for an explanation of that broken glass."

"Oh! that's simple enough," said the major. "I broke it."

"You?"

"Ay."

"He admits it," exclaimed Sir Harold King, all eagerness.

"Yes, I admit it. I broke it because you were about to hurl it at my head, that's all."

Sir Harold was utterly overwhelmed by the coolness of the ruffian major.

He hurried down to the door, followed by the two gentlemen and Major Strangeways.

Here they called a cab.

A hansom drove up.

"No," said Sir Harold. "A four-wheeler. We all go together."

"Why?"

"I cannot spare that man out of my sight until he is in the hands of the police."

"This is nonsense."

"Nonsense or not, I insist upon this point," said Sir Harold.

This settled the discussion, and they had to yield.

"Harley Street," said Sir Harold.

"What for?" demanded one of the gentlemen.

"Home to fetch the tools."

Arrived at the residence of Sir Harold King, in Harley Street, the whole of the party were shown into a long room shut in by two thickly-padded doors.

This Sir Harold called his shooting gallery.

"Shooting gallery?" remarked one of the gentlemen. "Do you practise much, Sir Harold?"

"Yes, every morning."

"Humph!"

The two seconds coughed and looked significantly at the major.

Sir Harold King produced two cases of pistols.

He opened both, and offered them to the major.

"They are loaded," he said.

"Good," returned the major.

He took up the heaviest carelessly, and fired at a target at the end of the gallery.

"A bull's eye, by the Lord Harry!" ejaculated one of the gentlemen.

Sir Harold took up a pistol with his left hand and turned his back to the target, turned sharply round, and fired without even pausing to level.

"Another bull's eye!"

"Splendid firing!"

"This is nothing, gentlemen," said Sir Harold King. "One can't very well miss, you see."

"I might," said one.

"And I, too," said another. "Believe me, gentlemen, this had better not proceed any further."

"Sir," said the baronet sternly, "it must and shall proceed."

"Of course," said the major.

But his tone, in spite of himself, was much less decided than that of his adversary.

The major had counted upon his accurate aim to bring him safely through this business, which looked so ugly at present.

Now, seeing the other was a better shot, it looked awkward.

The weapons were loaded.

Both the cases were taken, *to avoid the trouble of reloading,* as Sir Harold said.

This rather startled the opponent and the two seconds.

He meant it, then, to be a duel *à l'outrance.*

They re-entered the cab and drove off rapidly in the direction of Hampstead Heath.

Here Sir Harold led them to a secluded spot.

It was the very place of all others for an affair of honour.

Quiet and away from all habitations.

"This is rather snug," said one.

"It is," said Sir Harold. "I pinked off Lord Gus Hervey there."

"Indeed?"

"Yes. It is a fortunate bit of ground to me."

The major was very silent and reserved now.

If one could have read his inmost heart then, it would have been seen that he wished himself most heartily through the duel.

He buttoned over his coat—a close-fitting surtout—to the neck.

Not a speck of white was to be seen upon his person.

Nothing which could serve his adversary in the least.

Sir Harold, on the contrary, took no pains with his toilette.

He simply changed his hat for a shooting cap with a long peak to shade the eyes.

During the journey the major had been observed to whisper to his second, and when the proceedings for the encounter were in progress upon the heath the latter objected to the distance chosen.

"I understand," said Sir Harold. "But he over-reaches himself there. I shall not be less steady at another range, and he runs more risk."

"Indeed?"

"Ay, I never miss at sixteen paces."

"Then it seems to me that he stands more chance at other distances."

"No."

"How not?"

"I shall not *miss* at any pace, but at sixteen paces I shoot so true that I could hit when I pleased. As it is, I must risk it."

The confidence in Sir Harold King's tone rather took the party by surprise.

Major Strangeways looked very far from being comfortable now.

The combatants were placed back to back.

It was arranged that they were to fire at twenty paces distance.

They were to walk forward ten paces each way, turn, and fire simultaneously.

The major measured off his ten paces with good military strides.

Then turned sharply, levelled, and fired.

The baronet had not time to fire. He stood still, quite calm.

"Curse it!" muttered the major.

"You fire hastily," said the baronet coolly. "You try all your assassinations too hastily. Your poison was given with a trembling hand, or I should not now live to cry quits with you."

The major turned pale.

A deathly hue overspread his face, so marked that the seconds could not fail to observe it.

His knees appeared to be giving way, and he turned half round.

"He wants to run away," said Sir Harold, laughing. "No, no. He's had two tries at my life to-day, so here goes for the return match."

"Don't turn your back, major," said one of the gentlemen in disgust.

The words appeared to frighten Major Strangeways heartily.

He presented his *full front* immediately.

"Ah! that's stupidly venturesome," said one of the seconds. "It's against all the laws of the duello, and you run double the risk."

The baronet enjoyed his adversary's terror, and he raised his pistol to aim with the cruellest deliberation.

"Good night, major!"

There was a report.

The smoke cleared away, and Major Strangeways was seen still standing, and more upright than before.

"Missed!"

"Missed!" said the other second.

"Missed, by jingo!" exclaimed Sir Harold King, as if in astonishment.

Major Strangeways did not utter a word.

He raised his hand, as if about to address some of them, shook slightly, and fell full length upon the ground.

The seconds hastened to his side.

"By Heavens! he was struck. He's dead!"

It was true.

Major Strangeways was no more. Yet no blood was to be seen.

One of the two tore off his coat and waistcoat.

Something hard encountered the touch beneath the front of his shirt.

What could it mean?

They dragged it open, to search for the wound, and then discovered that the major's breast was protected by a fine steel mail shirt.

This, then, was the secret of the duellist's many successes.

A paper fell from his breast, which Sir Harold picked up and eagerly deciphered.

In the meantime the gentlemen pulled off the steel shirt and searched for the wound.

But all in vain.

There was not the faintest signs of blood.

The mark of the pistol shot was shown by a faint dent in the steel, but it had not penetrated it.

A light blue spot upon the flesh showed that the shot had simply bruised it a little, nothing more.

What, then, caused death ?

Dead he was, it was apparent to an unpractised eye.

"The fellow's an arrant coward," said his second contemptuously. " He's dead through funk."

" What a paltry bully !"

" I told you so," said Sir Harold. " And you would not believe me when I told you of that affair at the club."

" The poison business ?"

" Ay."

" Because you gave no reason for such an extraordinary proceeding."

" But I can now."

" Well ?"

" The paper which has fallen from the rascal shows me that this scamp, who has so imposed upon us all, is an old offender in disguise."

" Never !"

" It's true."

" You know him ?"

" Yes. I trounced the ruffian once before, long, long ago, for palming the king; or something rascally, and this is his revenge."

" But who is he ?"

" Major Strangeways of to day," said Sir Harold, " was Captain Roper the blackleg."

And thus ends the career of this notorious scoundrel and cheat.

CHAPTER XLIV.

MERMET—THE POISON TRAFFIC—THE AGE OF THE BORGIAS REVIVED—A DARK SECRET—THE CANARY—THE VEILED VISITORS—THE WOULD-BE SUICIDE — THE OLD STORY — THE COUNSEL—AHMET'S RETURN.

WE have yet another visit to pay before returning to the fortunes of Rose.

Mermet the Arab magician continues to receive illustrious guests.

The high and mighty, low and humble, alike visit the Eastern necromancer.

Many and curious are the secrets which Mermet now holds.

Many a noble family lies at his mercy.

Many an expectant heir would give the whole wealth to which he aspires, to be free from the power of the Arab, did he know how deeply he was in his clutches.

Amongst the many visitor whom Mermet now received was one whose introductory interview we will attempt to describe.

It was a lady, who observed the strictest secrecy in all her movements.

She arrived incognito, and wore a thick veil throughout the interview.

All this, of course, excited the curiosity of Mermet to the utmost.

When, however, the Arab learnt the nature of the business upon which the mysterious lady had come to consult him he grew so interested in her movements that he determined to discover her name and family, if possible.

As the lady entered the necromancer's chamber she bowed and stared at the attendant Ahmet.

Then she turned towards the Arab.

" You are Mermet ?"

Mermet bowed.

" Can I speak with you ?"

" At your service."

" Alone ?"

" Yes."

" Then dismiss your man," said the lady.

A few words in their tongue were exchanged between master and servant, and the latter left the room.

" Now, my lady."

The visitor started.

Her action was mentally noted by the necromancer.

" My lady," repeated the Arab, "will you please to tell me the service you wish the humblest of your slaves to perform ?"

The lady paused a minute to consider, and then spoke abruptly.

" You deal in poisons ?"

The necromancer was startled by the round manner of putting so dangerous and delicate a proposition.

However, he was a master of deception, and he replied to his visitor as coolly as the question had been put—

" Some poisons."

" And subtle deadly ones, which leave no tell-tale traces ?"

" Even those."

" We must be sure of that."

" You can be."

" I will be. I want no drug of which the victim must take a quart to destroy life, and then turn saffron-coloured."

" My skill does not know such impotent compounds, lady."

" Doubtless."

" Tell me the kind of poison you desire, and you shall be satisfied at once as to its efficacy."

" Have you a drug which would kill by inhaling it ?"

" By smell ?"

" Yes."

" On a bouquet ?"

" Ay, or elsewhere."

" I have."

" You have ?" exclaimed the lady eagerly. " Then that is mine."

" I will show you."

And Mermet hobbled off his perch to a small carved cabinet, from which he took a long narrow-necked phial.

" The liquid within this will kill by the smell alone, and instantly."

" And upon a bouquet?"

" The same."

" Will it destroy colour ?"

" No. It is the more efficacious, of course, the more recently it is applied."

" Good. Oh, it could be applied only at the very last moment—"

The visitor suddenly stopped short and looked anxiously at the Arab, as if she almost feared that her hasty words had put him in possession of her secret.

" You are discreet ?" she asked.

" The nature of our business together should speak for that."

" True."

" Rest assured that you see me now for the first and last time, if you wish it. No one on earth but ourselves need know of your visit here."

" Good."

" And as for the drug, I defy any one on earth to detect its presence, no matter how keen or learned the chemist."

" And of its power you can vouch ?"

" More, I will prove it."

" How ?"

" You shall see."

Mermet called the attendant, who, in obedience to some instructions in their native tongue, brought in a fanciful-looking cage containing a canary.

Mermet opened the door and whistled to the bird, which chirped with delight at the freedom it anticipated it was to enjoy.

Then it hopped out and perched upon the Arab's shoulder.

Mermet fondled the canary a while, and then gave it some sugar, which it pecked from his lips.

"You will pardon an old man's weakness, lady," said the necromancer. "I love my bird, and am sorry to sacrifice it."

The lady looked horrified.

"How sacrifice it?"

"To science," replied the Arab. "But you shall see, as I promised."

He removed the stopper of the bottle, and held it in his left hand, whilst the right was projected for the bird to perch upon.

The canary seemed perfectly accustomed to this exercise, and he hopped upon his master's finger most cheerfully.

"Smell, smell, Dick," said the Arab.

The bird stretched forth his golden neck towards the phial.

Then as its beak encountered the neck of the bottle, it fell from the finger of its master.

"Dead!" ejaculated the lady, in horror-stricken accents. "Dead!"

"Ay."

"Oh, but you might have proved it without killing the bird."

"It would have been difficult."

"Any proof would have sufficed for me, said the lady.

"Indeed?"

"Anything."

"Pardon me, I thought you were rather a sceptic at first."

"No, I come hither only after hearing your great reputation—"

"As a compounder of poisons?"

"No."

"I'm glad of that," said the Arab drily. "Such a reputation is not the most enviable one to have learnt, believe me."

"Can I have that bottle?" asked the lady, preparing to depart.

"Yes."

"And the price?"

The Arab smiled.

"Oh, I can fix no price on such a treasure as that, my lady."

"How so?"

"It is priceless as a work of art."

"Then fear not to name an adequate sum," said the lady.

"Nay, you cannot buy my genius as you buy a dealer's wares. I give you the produce of my skill and years of labour. If you would show me some mark of your kindness, pray exert your liberality upon my servant. He is a worthy fellow, and does me good service."

"This is very strange," said the lady.

"Not at all," said Mermet. "Let me see you again if your object is not achieved by this philtre. I can assist you, doubtless."

The lady was amazed. She offered the greatest and most profuse acknowledgments of the Arab's goodness, but he would not hear of thanks.

Ahmet was called.

"Show the lady out," he said in English.

Then he added a few words in Arabic, which caused the lady to eye them both sharply.

However, as the Arab was pointing to the dead canary, she imagined that the ill-starred little warbler was the subject of their conversation.

She was shown to the door, and hurried off, looking rather anxiously about, as if fearful of having been observed.

Had she suspected that a watch had been set upon her movements she would not have felt quite so easy in her mind.

The secret of the poison is in danger.

Beware, then, of Mermet the Arab!

As soon as the veiled lady had taken her departure Mermet began to chuckle with vicious glee.

"So, so," he muttered, "poisoning thrives mightily. I dreamed that the days of the Borgias and of Brinvilliers had departed, but I find that they only want the opportunity to push them forward into our own age. And a thriving trade I shall drive with it. This woman, whoever she is—and I rely upon Ahmet, the knave! to discover her real name and position—will be a fortune alone, well managed. I am convinced that she is worth the trouble. Well, well, we shall see. How easy it is to gain a name in the world! Ah! who's this? Another visitor, doubtless. It is, and a woman too."

A second veiled lady was here ushered into Mermet's presence.

The necromancer surveyed her from head to foot with a piercing glance.

Beneath her veil might be traced some faint outlines of her face.

It was beautifully formed, pale to ghastliness, and expressionless.

"There's been some grief there," mentally muttered the Arab.

The girl was evidently very much embarrassed to open the interview.

Mermet, seeing this, hastened to her assistance at once.

"Be seated, lady," said he. "Take time to compose yourself, I pray you."

The words of the necromancer appeared to restore her at once.

It would seem that she only then became aware of her abstraction being so visible to everybody.

"What do you wish for?" asked the necromancer after a while.

"I want poison," returned the young girl, almost inaudibly.

"Poison?" iterated the Arab.

"Yes. Something which will send one on a quick journey to the next world with as little pain as possible."

"You must first tell me to what use you would put so fatal a compound."

"I cannot."

"Then I cannot supply you."

"I must seek elsewhere."

"Stay. At least tell me in what quantity you want this poison."

"It is to kill."

"Whom?"

"That cannot be known to you."

"It can and shall," thought Mermet.

But he spoke differently aloud.

"No, I merely wish to know the age of the person to whom it is to be administered."

"Nineteen," faltered the girl.

"Male or female?"

"The latter."

"Good."

"You will give it to me?" demanded the girl eagerly.

"I will."

"Oh! a thousand thousand thanks."

Mermet surveyed the pallid face beneath the veil, and mused thus—

"This is no murdress. She is a young mother, and means self-destruction. I must put her off that, or else I may not count upon her in future. No, no. She shall destroy her child, if it is the babe's existence which troubles her, and then she is my own."

"One moment," said the necromancer. "Before I give you the poison you ask I would confer with you."

"To what end ?"

"Upon a matter of serious importance to you, I believe."

"I don't understand."

"Then I will explain. Be seated."

She sat down.

"I am an astrologer," said Mermet, "and can read the stars."

The girl smiled sadly.

"You laugh," said the Arab. "Wait a little ere you deride me."

"Not deride."

"No matter what you may designate it, you don't credit it."

"I must confess that."

"Then I will give you proofs."

"I don't need them," said the girl. "Let me have the drug and depart."

The girl again demurred, but Mermet overruled her objection.

"I will show you your whole life."

"No, no, no."

"Ah !" said the Arab. "Although you doubt, you appear anxious."

"Not I," said the girl when the first thought which had brought these hasty words was over. "Go on, say what you will, but be as brief as possible, for I am not well enough to listen to you, believe me."

"Give me your hand."

"With a piece of silver to cross it ?" asked the girl, with a sorry smile.

"No, no," said Mermet. "You are in no mood for idle jesting I know."

"True," sighed the girl.

"And I'm in no mood to hear it."

"I beg your pardon."

"It is not necessary."

He took the fair and delicate palm of the girl between his own bony and dark brown hands, and examined it attentively.

An exclamation of disgust and indignation escaped him.

"What's this ?" he said. "Deceit and falsehood here—but not yours, not yours."

This was to re-assure the girl, who was about to utter an indignant repudiation of the aspersion.

"No, no, I see that it is a man's falsehood and deceit."

A deep blush overspread the young girl's face at this.

This confirmed the Arab's suspicions, and he continued—

"I see a broken vow—a pledge of faith and love broken."

The girl trembled.

A sob, which seemed to choke her utterance, burst from her.

"Enough, enough !" she said. "I need hear no more at present."

"Nay, but—"

"No, no. Give me the drug."

"One moment," said Mermet. "It is for your welfare you should hear it."

"How know you ?"

"My art tells me."

The art was consulted again, and Mermet threw out a feeler.

"A child is concerned here."

"A child ?"

There was a faltering in her voice which confirmed his suspicions.

"Ay, a child, and one whose existence will imperil your own."

"What mean you ?"

"You or the child must die."

"*Or the child !*" repeated the girl.

"Ay, or the child. Nay, I find it will be the child."

"Ah ! Oh, mercy, mercy. Never can it be."

The Arab had struck home, and felt wild with triumph.

However, he did not allow it to appear.

"Listen to me," said the Arab. "I read a history here of treachery and confiding innocence—the old old story. A man too base to love, a fond girl too loving to suspect."

As the Arab proceeded he could see by her changing colour how truly he aimed his cruel shafts.

He continued—

"The girl becomes a victim, a mother. To save herself from disgrace, when her friends shall be apprised of her ruin, she seeks to destroy herself."

The girl looked frightened.

"And she leaves her child behind her, the scoff and derision of the whole world."

"Oh, no."

"Nay, but it is true. Who has any consideration for a love child, pray ?"

"True, true."

And the poor girl beat her hands wildly upon her forehead.

"Then I see that there is but one way to avoid this trouble."

"Name it."

"The child."

"What of him ?"

"Must die !"

The girl gave a piercing shriek, which re-echoed through the house.

At the same time it seemed to have caused the necromancer some trouble.

He looked anxiously towards the window, as if expecting that the alarm would have reached the street.

"Restrain yourself," he said, "or I must cease my revelation."

"But, oh ! say not my child," implored the girl in tears.

"And why not ?"

"You are no mother to ask that."

"Pardon me," said the Arab, "but I cannot see why you should fear to take the babe's life any more than your own."

"I should be a murdress."

"Humph !" said the necromancer. "It has an ugly sound."

"Awful."

"Ay. But you would slay yourself—self-murder—suicide—"

"Spare me !"

"And that is as great a crime. The child you would send to rest would be saved a world of sorrows, cares, and troubles—and to what an endless list of these is not the child of shame destined ?"

The girl was frantic.

She threw herself upon her knees before the necromancer.

"Oh, mercy, mercy !" she exclaimed. "I conjure you to advise me for the best."

"I will," returned the Arab, "believe me. Rise and hear me."

"I do. Speak on."

"The child must die."

The girl was about to interrupt him, but he silenced her with a wave of his hand.

"He must die."

"Is there no other way?"

"None."

"Then I will die too."

"Then, to shut out the recollection of your crime, you would add another to the list."

"Have mercy!"

"I can have none if you speak thus," said the necromancer.

"Then I will be patient."

"The child must be removed and buried secretly. Who knows of its existence?"

"None."

"Then your way lies straightforward and simple enough."

"How?"

"I will explain that later. Tell me the age of the child."

"Two weeks."

"So young?"

"Yes."

A long consultation then ensued, in which Mermet advised her how to act, and promised further aid.

At the end of this Ahmet the attendant returned, after a long protracted absence.

"You have seen?" demanded the Arab.

"I have."

"And the name of the lady is—"

"Lady Bellisle!"

———

CHAPTER XLV.

MERMET'S PLANS — THE LAWYER — A JOURNEY BY RAIL—THE GARDEN—DIGGING THE GRAVE —THE TWO WATCHERS — A MOTHER'S WOE — "MERCY!"—THE POLICEMAN—THE SMELLING SALTS — A FATAL STRATAGEM — THE CRYSTAL PHIAL—POISONED—THE RIVER.

MERMET made a mental note of the name and rank of the veiled lady number one, who had purchased the poison of him.

Lady Bellisle.

And a poison too which should kill by the smell alone.

There was surely enough in this to lay her completely in his grasp.

"So much for my Lady Bellisle," muttered the necromancer. "You can be looked after at my leisure. My more immediate attention must be directed to this trembling girl, the young mother who is about to place herself and her fortune—and I doubt not that she has fortune, since she has a family from whom she is so desirous of withholding her shame—to place herself and her fortune, I say, so completely at my command. Poor girl!"—and here the little Arab's face gleamed with a satanic grin—"she little dreams what this day has done for her. However, I must use my power as mercifully as I can. Ho, there, Ahmet."

The attendant entered.

"Did the sahib call?"

"Yes."

The man salaamed.

"You followed that young lady too?"

"Yes, sahib."

"Good. Her name is—"

"Miss Grace Walgrave."

"Where?"

"Grosvenor Square."

The magician started to his feet with an exclamation of astonishment.

"Is it possible?"

"Sahib, I have spoken."

"Good," said the Arab, as if suddenly determined upon some bold step. "Get me my hat and cloak, Ahmet."

"Yes, sahib."

They were brought, and the attendant arrayed his master in them.

"Now my stick."

"Yes."

"Good. Now call a cab."

Mermet got into the cab, directing the driver to conduct him to Furnival's Inn.

Here he sought out a shabby-looking house, and mounted three storeys high.

It was a break-neck staircase, and the Arab ran great risk in hobbling up, from his many physical afflictions.

However, he was a man of determination, and not to be daunted.

He faced the difficulty boldly, and boldly conquered it.

Arrived at the top, the magician tapped with the handle of his stick upon a door on which was painted a name in white letters—

MR. IGNATIUS SCRIBB.

"Come in."

Mermet entered.

Mr. Scribb was a mild respectable-looking gentleman.

He wore a white neckcloth, shaved his cheeks, let his hair grow long, and looked sanctimonious—something in appearance between a Methodist parson and the decayed schoolmaster in the New Road who has seen better days.

"Ah! my dear sir," said Mr. Scribb, popping a quill pen into his mouth, as if to facilitate his speech.

"How d'ye do," said Mermet.

The difference in the necromancer's speech was now remarkable.

He seemed of a sudden to have acquired the more everyday and colloquial English.

"Are you alone?"

"Yes," answered Mr. Scribb. "My clerk is just gone out."

"Very good."

"What can I do for you?"

"A service. This is it. You know Grosvenor Square?"

"Yes."

"And you know the Walgraves' house?"

"No, but that is easily found. I know that it is in the square, that's all."

"Well, you must find it and get me a little information about Miss Grace Walgrave."

"Information?"

"Yes."

"Of what kind?"

"Any kind."

"Yes, but—"

The Arab caught the lawyer's eye and pulled him up short.

"Now, Scribb," said he, "you are not going to worm this or anything else out of me. You're a devilish clever fellow, and as cunning as the whole of the rest of the inn put together, but you can't manage to pump me."

"Sir, I—"

"Enough."

"But I protest."

"I'm satisfied. Let it suffice you, Scribb, that I employ and pay you well. Let us work into each other's hands as well as we can."

"Good."

"Share each other's welfare."

"I ask no more."

"But not their business nor their secrets, if they have any."

"Undoubtedly."

"Now this little matter I came especially upon must be seen to without delay."

"It shall be seen to now."

"And when can I count upon having the result of your researches?"

"I can't say," replied Scribb. "You may count upon them at the earliest. Have you any instructions to attach to them?"

"Only one word. Miss Grace Walgrave must not know of your inquiries."

"Humph!"

"She must be out if possible when you call, if calling be necessary."

"Very good."

"It may make your task more difficult, but you must count the difficulties extra. I shan't grumble, you know."

"You pay like a prince, Mr. ——"

"Mermet."

"Yes, of course, Mr. Mermet."

"Lose no time."

"I go at once."

"Spare no expense."

"None, believe."

"The fastest of cabs. Your fee shall cover that well, I can promise you."

There was significance in the Arab's tone which caused the eyes of Mr. Ignatius Scribb to glisten with greedy anticipation.

Mermet left.

He had perhaps arrived at home an hour—certainly not more than hour—when Mr. Ignatius Scribb was announced.

The lawyer had lost something of his sanctimonious appearance in the brief period which had elapsed.

The white neckcloth was still there, but it sat suspiciously awry.

The coat, that seedy frock, was slightly spattered with mud.

The Arab hobbled to meet him as he entered the room.

"What success?" he demanded eagerly.

"Victoria!" answered the lawyer, slightly elated.

"You have gained the information?"

"Eureka!" cried the lawyer, actually cutting a terpsichorean caper.

"You have gained the information I required of you?"

"I have."

"I thought so, and have been drinking your health upon the strength of your success."

"Pre-cisely."

"Ah! Iggy, my boy, you would be a wonder of a man and a lovely lawyer if you could only cut the bottle."

"Bosh!"

"But what news?"

"Stuff!" said the lawyer, who had not caught the question. "I live to enjoy my life, sir, and I do enjoy life after my own fashion. What would be the use of making myself a fine lawyer if I made myself uncomfortable. Those are my sentiments—"

"After a glass."

"And I glory in 'em."

"Very well. Enough of this. What have you learnt?"

"Much."

"Ah! On what head?"

"That," answered the lawyer, pointing towards his interrogator, with a drunken laugh.

"Fool!"

"Oh, hullo!"

"You're an ass, Scribb."

"And you're—a wizard."

"Now enough of this nonsense. What have you learnt?"

"Of Miss Walgrave?"

"Of course."

"She has left town."

"When?"

"Just now."

"Ah! Say you so? Where has she gone to?"

"Richmond."

"The address—"

"Is here."

"Give it me."

The necromancer snatched the scrap of paper from his hand.

"I say, I say," said Scribb, growing every instant worse, "you aint over polite."

"Silence!" said the Arab. "You are drunk."

"I repudiate the scandalous aspersion of my character," hiccoughed Scribb.

"Here, take this."

He held him a glass of water, with something effervescent in it.

But Mr. Ignatius Scribb did not care much to take liquids then.

"No, thankee, Mr. Mermet. It mightn't do me good perhaps."

"It will sober you."

"To-day perhaps—but I mightn't wake early to-morrow."

He leered significantly at the Arab necromancer at these words.

"What do you mean by that, Iggy?" said Mermet. "Do you think I would injure you?"

"Don't know."

"That I would play traitor with a friend who serves me so well."

"Can't say, I'm sure."

"Be assured, Iggy,' said Mermet, "you are far too useful to me at the present. *I can't say what the future may do.*"

The drunken man looked up startled.

He was more than half sobered by the necromancer's words.

They contained a promise of an unpleasant character to look forward to.

"Go, now, Iggy," said Mermet. "I am busy, and as for my words, think no more of them. I love you too well."

"Oh!"

"I do, in all sincerity."

"In-deed."

"Or, if you will not believe that—"

"'Pon my soul I can't."

"Then think how useful you are to me. How should I prosecute my searches without your aid?"

"Yes, how would you?"

"I should be lost."

"Quite."

"There, there, good night."

"Good night."

And, with a drunken nod, Mr. Ignatius Scribb took his leave.

"My threat to that besotted idiot," mused the necromancer as soon as the lawyer was gone, "is, after all, half joke, whole earnest. If he grows troublesome when in his cups, I must stop him in my own behalf. I'll doctor his grog in my own style, but not at present. So far I was candid with him. He's safe because he's handy just now."

He re-arrayed himself for a journey.

When he had completed his toilet he took a small crystal phial from his little cabinet and secreted it in the breast of his coat.

"There, stop there," said he, addressing the bottle. "Your services may possibly be brought into requisition before the night is over."

The Arab called a cab and drove to the railway station.

[CLARA AND THE RUFFIANS.]

Here he booked for Richmond.

It was an unfortunate chance that he arrived just in time to hear the departing whistle of the engine of the Richmond train.

An hour's delay was occasioned by this little mischance.

Mermet silently gnashed his teeth and said some very wicked things in an undertone.

However, the longest delays must have an end, and off he started at length.

It was night when he got to Richmond.

The moon was up, shining brilliantly, and making the fair country and the noble river almost as light as at noontide.

Mermet started off to walk to his destination.

His locomotion was tediously slow and awkward.

Painful, too, to a degree to the necromancer, and he must have had some powerful motives to induce him to undertake such a journey on foot.

At length he came to a detached villa, some distance from any other habitation.

He looked about him cautiously, to see that there was no one upon the road.

All was silent.

He entered the garden.

The gate creaked alarmingly as he passed through, so he did not stop to shut it after him.

We mention this little incident, as it led to an occurrence in this moonlight trip of the necromancer's upon which we shall touch shortly.

Avoiding the house, for fear that he might be observed, although there was no sign of any living soul being within it, Mermet kept to the extreme right of the gravel walk.

His low stature allowed him to creep along beneath the trees and dwarf shrubs without throwing any telltale shadow.

He skulked down past the back of the house.

Here he found himself in a long garden overlooking the river.

He turned to look round at the house.

The back, like the front, was in darkness.

"I wonder if she is in the house at present," muttered Mermet. "I must and will see her. That must be ascertained, or else my journey will have been without effect."

He turned from the house and walked towards the water.

"The river runs here," said Mermet, half surprised. "Why, then, could the silly girl have paid me a visit with such a resource as this close at hand? Ah! What's that?"

This exclamation was caused by hearing a loud sigh close at hand.

Mermet started and looked around him affrightedly.

He did not dare to stir.

"Ah! She's there!"

Close by the river's bank stood a girl leaning upon a spade stuck into the earth.

"What can she be doing here, I wonder," thought Mermet. "I must see."

He drew closer.

With wary stealthy strides he approached the unsuspecting girl.

And now he could watch her movements closely and unobserved.

His deformed figure was still shielded from view by some overhanging branches of shrubs and trees.

Presently the girl moved.

She raised her hand from the handle of the spade to press her forehead wearily, and to rub her eyes as if they were fevered with weeping.

Another sigh burst from her.

Then she fell to her task again in silence.

The earth was damp at this part of the ground, and it was no slight labour to the unhappy girl to dig it.

Yet she persevered.

Mermet stood in his hiding-place, silently and eagerly watching.

Still the work went on.

The girl had occasionally to pause to wipe the perspiration from her forehead.

Then she would return to it with renewed zest.

At length a hole some three feet deep, and a mound of earth beside it, was the result of her patient toil.

Then she turned towards the long dank grass growing upon the water's edge where it was marshy.

Mermet stretched forward, but could see nothing whatever there.

The girl, however, took a bundle from the grass, where it had lain concealed.

Took it tenderly in her arms.

Looked upon it in such sadness—such distress and woe—that the flintiest-hearted beholder could not fail to be touched by the action.

Then she removed a cloth, which fell over her arm, disclosing the form of a young babe.

Still and peaceful.

Motionless for ever.

Cold and stiff.

"Ah! she speaks now," said Mermet to himself. "I wish I could catch her words."

He leant eagerly forward.

"Farewell, farewell, my pretty one," said the girl, in a low musical tone, full of plaintive sorrow. "I've saved you from a life of misery and woe—but oh! great Heavens! at what a fearful price!"

She pressed her lips to the clay-cold face of the corpse.

Hugged it passionately in her arms and hung her face over it.

"She falls," said Mermet, half aloud.

But no.

She sank upon her knees, with the lifeless babe in her arms, still pressed passionately to her bosom.

Then her bosom heaved heavily and a mighty sob was heard.

But no tears.

Her eyes were ready to burst with fire, but she could not weep now.

She was speaking again.

A low but passionately-earnest tone of supplication.

"Surely there can be no future punishment for my crime," she said, gazing upwards into the starlit heavens. "I have suffered so much here for my fault —so much—so very much."

Suddenly she broke off short.

Covered up the face of the baby corpse and looked around her.

Terror unspeakable was in her beauteous but pale face.

What could it be?

Mermet had not moved, nor scarcely breathed so that one next him could have caught the sound.

But now that the necromancer looked about him he saw the reason of the youthful mother's alarm.

He was not the only person who kept a watch upon her.

Upon the other side of the garden—just peeping from behind a tree—he could see the glistening of a rain-proof hat.

It was a policeman.

Seeing that his presence had been discovered, the constable pushed aside the shrubs and advanced.

"Oh!" cried the girl, with a hasty effort to conceal her ghastly burden. "Who is it? What want you here?"

"What have you there?" said the policeman, slipping up to her.

"Nothing. I—"

"I have watched you," said the man. "I have seen everything, and it is useless denying it."

"Mercy! mercy!" cried the girl.

She prostrated herself before the man, and Mermet could see that he paused irresolutely.

"Will he allow her to escape?" said the necromancer. "No, he cannot—dare not. It is time that I should interpose. This fellow risks everything for me, and all my labours have been in vain."

Mermet the Arab hobbled out from his hiding-place and joined the group.

This was a new alarm.

The unhappy girl now deemed herself lost beyond redemption.

"Hullo!" said the policeman, not a little frightened. "Why, where have you sprung from?"

"I might rather have asked that question of you," replied Mermet.

"Why so?"

"Why so?" iterated the necromancer, affecting an indignant astonishment. "Because I wonder much to see you here at this hour."

"My duty—"

"Doesn't call you into our private grounds."

"No, sir, but—"

"Then why do you presume to spy upon my daughter's movements?"

"Spy, sir? Why, my duty."

"Pshaw!" said the necromancer, again interrupting him, with a contemptuous wave of the hand. "Don't talk so big, please, about such nonsense. If my poor deranged girl chooses to indulge her whims and fancies, that's no business of yours."

"No, sir, but it is the duty of every man, as well as every policeman, to look after anything that looks like—"

He paused.

"Like what?"

"Murder!"

The young mother gave a faint shriek at this word.

It is a terrible word, and must ever raise a twinge of conscience in the guilty one's mind.

"Murder!" said Mermet. "Stuff and nonsense, man. If my daughter chooses to take a fanciful freak into her head and bury her pet dog at night, does it follow that she must be spied upon and overlooked by every paltry impertinent fellow who chooses to pry into what doesn't concern him at all?"

This staggered the man.

However, it could not convince him, for he had witnessed too much.

"It won't do," he said, shaking his head. "*I've seen the body!*"

This settled the matter in the mind of the necromancer.

"You are a cute fellow," said he, "and must be dealt with."

This implied a bribe.

But the policeman still proved himself obnoxious.

"It's no use," he said. "I know my duty too well to be put off it."

"Of course."

"So the young lady must come with me."

With a cry of alarm, the girl sprang to her feet, and with a sudden rush was by the waterside.

Mermet divined her fatal intent upon the instant.

As she darted past him he stretched forth his hand and caught her by her dress.

This checked her wild flight to death until the policeman came up.

"Don't you see that the poor girl is mad?" said the necromancer.

"It certainly does look like madness," returned the policeman.

"It is."

"No matter, I must take her with me."

"Never."

"Ay, and you too."

"That will be dangerous to attempt," said the necromancer sternly.

"Pooh! pooh!"

And the policeman placed his hand upon the Arab's collar.

In an instant the little eyes of Mermet flashed a thousand furies and he shook off the grasp.

Then he placed his hand upon the crystal phial with which he had provided himself before starting.

"What have you got there?" demanded the constable at once.

"Nothing."

"Give it to me."

The Arab pretended to be disinclined to part with the bottle.

However, he held it in such a way that the policeman was able to secure it.

"Well," said Mermet, in a grumbling tone. "It's only a little smelling salts."

"I dare say."

"Oh, give it to me."

"At the station."

"But don't you see, man, that my poor daughter is ready to faint?"

"Then I'll let her smell it."

The Arab sprang forward in a fright at this.

"No, no, no."

"Hullo! why not?"

"Because in her disordered state of mind the head is too weak to bear too strong a dose."

"How can you moderate it?"

"I'll show you," said the necromancer. "You just smell it yourself, and then you'll be satisfied."

The policeman took the stopper out of the bottle with his teeth, his other hand being engaged holding the girl.

Immediately the odour of the contents of the bottle appeared to strike the constable's nostrils, even at the length of his arm, a change came over his countenance.

He did not attempt to raise it to his face.

A suspicion crossed him that something was not altogether right, and he cast the bottle from him.

"Too late!" muttered the Arab necromancer, watching him eagerly.

"Murd—" began the constable.

But the words died on his lips.

His face grew rigid.

A fixed stare was upon his countenance, and his eyes looked glassy.

The last faint glimmering of sense which remained in the unfortunate man was exerted in an endeavour to articulate.

But of no avail.

His lips moved—one faint quiver, but that was all.

His body jerked, as if the stiffening expression in his face had communicated itself to his body.

He swayed to and fro once.

Then fell.

The girl looked up with a wonder-stricken glance.

The necromancer grinned diabolically and hobbled up to the fallen policeman.

He stooped down.

Knelt and placed his hand upon the left breast.

"It's all over," said Mermet. "That's done."

Saying this, he picked up the man by the heels.

Then dragged him towards the water.

It was a tough pull, but the little cripple dragged with a will.

A splash caused the girl to look up.

The policeman had disappeared .

CHAPTER XLVI.

CLARA ST. JOHN—AFTER THE WRECK—THE SLEEP OF DEATH — A FEARFUL AWAKENING — THE JEWELS—TEMPTATION—THE TWO FISHERMEN —MURDER PROPOSED—THE LAST MOMENT— THE SHIPWRECKED MARINER — A STRUGGLE FOR LIFE—THE CRY—THE ALARM—A FRIEND AT HAND.

WE must return to Clara St. John.

So long have we been engaged in the various adventures of our heroine, Rose Mortimer, and Mermet the Arab necromancer that we have quite neglected this important personage in our history.

After the fearful calamities which happened to her and young Edgar Deville, the partner of her flight, her senseless body was washed ashore upon the Irish coast.

Here, as already related in chapter twenty-nine, two fishermen who were plying their trade picked up the body.

A packet fastened to her neck by a small chain was cut open by the fishermen and found, to their infinite surprise, to contain jewels and precious stones of rare value.

The cupidity of the two men, who possibly would have remained honest away from temptation, was excited by the richness of the prize, and a diabolical thought crossed them.

They would keep the treasures !

They had barely shaped their resolve into words ere the woman opened her eyes, and the fishermen turned to fly.

This is the point at which we parted company with Clara St. John.

Now to resume.

With a wearied painful expression the half-drowned woman gazed upwards into the clear blue sky.

Then she turned her head with difficulty aside.

It was a look of wonder more than of anything else which she cast around her now.

She was evidently at a loss to account for her presence there.

She had not yet sufficiently recovered to realise the position in which she now found herself placed.

The rugged beauty of the Irish coast fell upon her gaze like the recollections of some fabled fairyland of which she had read.

She thought that she still slept, and that it was all a dream.

But it was reality—sad and dangerous reality.

Arrived at a few yards from the body of the woman, the two fishermen drew up short to consider what should be their next step.

The jewels lay there in a glittering heap beside their owner.

A tempting pile.

The whole labours of a life could not produce such treasures to the two fishermen.

Every day they risked their lives to gain a bare subsistence for a wife and a numerous family.

And here were treasures — riches untold — lying within their grasp.

One scruple of conscience got over, and they were rich for life.

There was the rub.

How to get over that one scruple ?

How to sacrifice all for a treasure which, priceless as it indeed was, would prove embarrassing to men in their humble walk of life to dispose of ?

And the men paused again, more irresolute than ever.

A serpent was there, whispering evil counsels into their ears, and they listened.

Listened but too greedily, and vicious thoughts arose within them.

"I tell you what, Jack," said one of the men. "It's my opinion she's dead."

"But she moved."

"I don't think so."

The other fisherman regarded his comrade fixedly.

He could scarcely catch his meaning.

He had ever known him honest and true-hearted from a boy.

Was it, then, possible that he contemplated the same black deeds as filled his own evil mind at that moment ?

He was very glad, however, to meet him half-way in an excuse for crime.

"Well," said he, looking in an another direction, "if you was to ask my opinion, I should say as I'm sure she's dead."

"Yes."

"Of course."

And they paused again.

Looked into each other's faces for courage to do a bloody deed.

"Let's go back again," suggested one.

"Come on."

Each would have preferred to see the other take precedence.

But no.

Neither was yet versed sufficiently in crime to be forward in its execution.

Then after a while they started off together, and arrived beside the body.

"I—I think she's dead," began one.

The woman opened her eyes.

"What is this place ?" she asked.

"O lor !"

And the two disappointed fishermen looked puzzled at each other.

They could not even pretend to believe that the woman was dead after having addressed a question to them.

"Where am I ?" continued Clara St. John. "Who are you, and what ? Why don't you speak to me ? I remember something terrible—a ship on fire—a wreck, and—oh ! how horrible !"

Again the woman closed her eyes, as if to shut out the terrible recollections.

Then the two fishermen exchanged a meaning glance.

A glance so full of fatal meaning that the scarcely sensible Clara St. John would have known that now she stood in mortal danger had she but seen it.

But now she lay so still that the fishermen really imagined she had relapsed into a state of utter insensibility once more.

If so their task was easy.

They had merely to secure the prize and make off with it at once.

One pointed to the jewels.

But neither liked the job.

At length one of the fishermen grew bolder and stooped to secure the prize.

"It's no use humming an   ah'ing," he muttered. "Here you are—off we go."

The half swooning woman opened her eyes once more affrightedly.

She was now awake.

"Ah !" she cried. "It's no dream after all. What have you there ?"

"Let go," said the fisherman.

But she stretched forth her hand with an effort and clutched the packet.

The jewels for which she had risked so much.

The prize which had cost her and the companion of her guilty flight so much labour to obtain.

"Put that down," she cried feebly.

"Leave go."

"Would you rob me?"

"It ain't yours," said the fisherman.

"Let it alone," cried Clara. "It is mine, and mine only."

"Where did you get it ?" demanded the fisherman, who was not sufficiently hardened in crime to rob the helpless woman without some explanation, however poor.

It was a chance shot, and told with strongly marked effect.

The guilty means employed to obtain possession of the packet flashed at once through her mind, and a wild idea crossed her that her flight and the abstraction of the jewels had been discovered.

The idea vanished in an instant.

She plainly perceived that they were about to rob her.

Ay, and the treasure would inevitably be lost unless some assistance arrived.

And it was yet such early morning that it was not at all probable.

The part of the coast, too, was so wild in appearance —so far removed from the haunts of civilisation—that Clara despaired.

However, after the toil she had undergone, and the crimes which she had been guilty of to obtain the prize, it should not be snatched from her without a struggle.

Alas ! she was powerless.

Incapable of the smallest exertion to oppose the fishermen.

She was resolved to defend her rights, as she mentally expressed it, but how ?

" If you dare to touch my property," she exclaimed with energy, " you will rue it."

" How do we know as it is yours ?"

" Because you have taken it from me ?"

" We ain't."

" Besides, if you contemplate robbery," she said, " it is useless."

" Of course it is, but we don't."

" You could never get rid of such things."

" Oh ! couldn't we."

" No. Who would take such things in sale from you for a tenth—a hundredth of their value. You would be denounced as robbers at once."

" Don't see it," returned the bolder of the two. " Who could say that they was yours ?"

" I could—I would denounce you."

" You would ?"

" I swear it."

As she said this it occurred to the fishermen that she might say something unpleasant about them whether they committed the robbery or not.

And with this idea came another.

Dead men tell no tales !

Little did Clara St. John dream what was passing in their minds.

Beneath the rock upon which the woman reclined unable to raise herself the sea roared in all its grandeur.

A little push—one slight effort—and all would be over.

The jewels—the mighty prize of such high value—would remain in their possession, undisputed and unquestioned as to right.

Neither spoke.

They could not put the deed of death into words even then.

A glance told all that they thought.

The ideas of both were so much alike upon this subject that they needed no more to understand each other.

The fisherman who had spoken stooped over the prostrate woman and raised her in his arms.

" Ah !" she cried in terror. " What would you do ?"

" You will see."

She gave a shriek.

A wild and piercing cry, which could be heard for miles.

Both the fishermen looked round them alarmed.

But alarm was needless here. Apparently there was nobody stirring yet for a great distance.

" Mercy ! mercy !" cried Clara. " Spare my life at least. Take all."

." Too late."

" You would denounce us."

" Yes."

" No, no, no. I would not. I will swear it. Oh ! spare me."

" You have just sworn the other way, and we don't know what to believe."

He held her over the rock.

But with the tenacity of despair she clung to the ruffian's collar.

He endeavoured to shake off the hold, but to no purpose.

The whole remaining strength in her body seemed thrown into the clutch she held so perseveringly to his collar.

" *Loosen her fingers,*" said the man.

The other came and dragged at her, but it was of no avail.

She tugged at the man, her would-be murderer, as only a dying person can.

" This is no use," said the fisherman. " Catch hold of her as well."

The other fisherman clutched her bodily.

Then swung her over the rock, endeavouring to precipitate her in the dashing waves beneath.

A series of wild and terrible shrieks burst from the unhappy Clara.

Cries which alarmed the men so that they could scarcely preserve their hold upon her.

She made a feeble attempt at struggling to release herself.

Her strength was very speedily exhausted.

And now she lay once more in the arms of the two ruffianly fishermen a dead weight.

Utterly powerless to help herself in the least.

" Now for it !" said one.

" Now then, together."

A fatal swing.

Then—

* * * * * *

A hundred yards from the spot where Clara St. John had been washed ashore a man half naked was struggling to his feet.

A pair of trousers, torn and saturated with the sea water, alone covered his shivering limbs.

His hands and feet were torn with the jagged rocks upon which he had lately clung with desperation.

Clung for his very life.

He had been wrecked upon the previous night, and of all on board deemed himself the only survivor.

He had just recovered consciousness, and was looking about him in the hope of obtaining assistance.

Weary and faint, exhausted by his struggles to reach the land.

And no signs of life for miles. The wild region in which the poor wrecked stranger found himself sent a chill to his very heart.

He had, indeed, suffered. After a battle for life with the roaring sea, which appeared to struggle for his life like some mighty monster, he had succeeded in reaching land.

His enfeebled hold could not, however, procure his immediate salvation.

The sharp jagged rocks cut his hands severely, and he was washed back into the waters.

Thrice did he reach the rocks, and thrice was he thus driven back.

It was a fearful trial for the unfortunate mariner.

At length, when life seemed ebbing from him, with one wild and expiring effort he made fast his hold.

For hours did he rest there half sleeping upon the rocks.

And now it was early morning and the sun was rising gloriously, imparting its genial rays with a glow to his shivering limbs.

" If I make my way inland," thought the man, " I must surely find some assistance. There must be a town or village at some short distance from here. I wonder what part of the coast I am upon."

He meant the English coast.

Making what progress he could, he pushed on inland.

His feet, already cut and bleeding from the disasters of the fatal wreck, were most cruelly punished now.

On, on, he pushed, but no signs of a human habitation.

Suddenly he started and looked about him in hope.

A faint flush suffused his pale cheek. He fancied that a signal had caught his ear.

A cry—and, yes, it was repeated.

This time much louder than before, and he could now tell that it was the cry of a woman, a cry of distress.

It proceeded, too, from the shore. He listened again, and the cries were repeated.

A hundred shrieks in quick succession.

"Some poor creature in trouble," he cried. "I must see what I can do.!'

But he was too feeble to render much assistance.

He crept as fast as possible along the road until he arrived upon the top of a rise, where he could survey the coast for some distance upon either side.

Another shriek as he reached this point gave him the direction of the disaster, whatever it might be.

He could see in the distance the dusky outlines of two forms struggling upon a huge projecting rock.

They held something in their hands.

"Why, great Heavens!" cried the wrecked stranger, "it is a woman—a poor helpless woman—they hold, and they are going to throw her into the water. She clings to them. Ah ! how awful !"

A woman was in danger, and the helpless stranger seemed to gain courage and strength in her behalf which he had been unable to obtain or to exert for himself.

"Hullo ! hi !" he shouted.

He struggled along, shouting to the men.

His cries would appear to have had some good effect.

The men placed the struggling woman upon the rock and turned off.

Before leaving one of them picked up a parcel—of what the shipwrecked stranger could not perceive in the distance—and made off with it.

"They fly ! they fly !" he cried in great glee. "But what's that? Is it not a robbery? I must endeavour to intercept them."

This did not appear to be a difficult matter, for, strangely enough, the two men were advancing right in that direction.

They had not seen him, then.

No. It was true. The two men had only heard the alarm, and had not looked to ascertain in what direction it proceeded.

The shipwrecked stranger could now perceive that they were two big brawny fishermen.

This was an awkward job. What good could he do against two such fellows ?

He jumped behind a low stubbly tree and awaited their arrival.

"Great Heavens !" cried the stranger of a sudden as the men drew nearer, and he saw what the one had picked up from the ground. "Why, it is a packet of jewels he has robbed the woman of. I must see to this."

––––––

CHAPTER XLVII.

A CRITICAL POSITION—A BOLD STROKE—SHARP ENCOUNTER—THE FATAL ROCK—THE FIGHT FOR THE JEWELS—A DOUBLE TRAGEDY—THE DISPUTED PRIZE—WHERE IS IT ?

As the two fishermen arrived at the spot where the shipwrecked stranger was concealed they made a pause.

Strangely enough, just by the dwarf shrubs behind which he lay hidden.

"Why, where could could that cry have come from, Jack ?" said one of them.

"Up this way."

"Then some one has seen us."

"That's sure."

"What's the best game, then ?"

"To bolt."

"Stop a bit, though. The gal said, and with some truth, too, that we should not be able to get rid of these precious jewels without being suspected."

"Ay."

"And we should most certainly get into trouble."

"That we should."

"Then, what do you propose ?"

"I can't say, Jack. What would you like to do, think ?"

"Why," replied the man addressed as Jack, "if you ask me what I should like to do, I should say to drop the gal over the rock."

"And the person or persons who overheard her cries."

"I'd like to drop 'em over, too."

Pleasant this for the shipwrecked stranger to listen to !

However, he was no coward, and in spite of the little chance he ran of rendering much assistance, he determined to risk a little.

He jumped forward from his hiding-place.

Suddenly confronted the men.

Then made a grab at the parcel of jewels and screamed.

"Hell fiends !" cried the man.

But before they could do anything more the man made off with the prize.

The fishermen as soon as they had somewhat recovered made chase.

But the other had a good start before they thought of pursuit.

Whilst they were enveloped in their weighty waterproof clothing, he was scarcely covered.

Their feet were encased in thick heavy boots with stout tops coming high up the thighs.

His were scarcely covered.

Every minute, too, brought him renewed strength and courage, whilst the two fishermen grew more fearful.

He never paused to consider which way he ran, but darted off at a good speed.

As he neared the sea he looked round, and there perceived that the unfortunate woman, whose death he felt confident he had averted by his timely arrival, had risen to her feet, and was advancing in that direction.

He looked around him in wonder.

Apparently he recognised the half-drowned woman as a friend.

As he drew nearer the woman rushed up to meet him.

"Save me, oh ! save me from these fearful men !" she cried in terror.

"Clara !"

"Edgar !"

Such were their mutual exclamations of astonishment at beholding each other.

The shipwrecked stranger was no other than Edgar Deville !

They had now no time for explanations—not a moment for anything but the defence of the treasure which they had undergone so much to obtain.

The two fishermen were drawing near.

They had ventured thus much, and now they felt that there was no retreating.

They were much emboldened, too, by perceiving how utterly helpless the man and woman both were.

Edgar and Clara St. John retreated until they could go no further—until they were once more upon the verge of the rock from which the fisherman would have hurled the woman, but for the timely cry of Edgar Deville.

"Give me back that parcel !" said the man from whom Edgar had snatched it.

But, instead of complying with this demand, he merely placed it upon the ground behind them.

And there they stood, this guilty pair, boldly determined to defend the treasure which they had so sinfully gained.

The unarmed, defenceless, and weak almost at the mercy of the two savage fishermen.

Yet so did they cling to their wealth that they would have sacrificed even life itself to protect it.

The fisherman repeated his command.

"Never!" retorted Edgar Deville. "Never while I have strength to defend it."

"But have you?"

"What?"

"Strength to defend it."

"That shall be seen."

The fisherman who acted as spokesman advanced, and placed his hand upon Edgar's arm.

The young man indignantly shook him off. Then dashed his fist into his face.

This had the effect of bringing matters to a crisis.

The man swore the most fearful oaths to have his life. Then, drawing a knife from his girdle, an ugly looking weapon used in the fisherman's calling, he made a rush at Edgar.

The young man, seeing himself in danger, endeavoured to step aside, but, from the slippery state of the rocks, he missed his footing and fell, half his body hanging over the sea.

With a wild shriek, Clara caught at the falling man and by a sudden and powerful effort succeeded in dragging him back.

All was done so momentarily that the two fishermen had no time to avail themselves of the accident.

To the fellow who had threatened him it proved the source of a disaster.

Wildly rushing on to take vengeance upon him, he stumbled also.

In an instant the other man had pounced upon the disputed treasure which had been left unguarded by Edgar Deville's fall.

But ere he had time to make away with it Clara St. John dashed at him, and with a well-timed push sent him headlong over the rock.

Then she darted upon the prostrate fisherman and pinned him to the ground.

She could not hope to hold him long, but before he could recover himself Edgar was up again and added his strength to hers to secure the fisherman.

"The knife, the knife!" said Clara St. John, pointing to the weapon of the fisherman which had fallen from his grasp. "Pick it up."

Edgar obeyed, just securing the knife in time to oppose its original possessor as he succeeded in shaking off Clara's feeble hold.

"Stab him!" she cried. "Cut him down! Down with him!"

The fisherman was in an unpleasant position at this period.

"Spare me!" he implored.

"Slay him!" cried the remorseless woman. "Down with him!"

Edgar offered to strike, but the guilty wretch before him begged for his life in such abject terms that the young man was touched.

"Get up," he said, "and remember that I spare your life upon condition only that you mention to no one the nature of the accident by which your companion in crime has met his death."

"Hold!" exclaimed Clara, before the fisherman could move from the ground. "Give me the knife."

Edgar Deville appeared reluctant to part with it, however.

Seeing this, the woman snatched it from him ere he could offer to oppose her.

Then, bringing it down with great violence, she buried it up to the hilt in the poor wretch's shoulder.

"Ugh!" groaned the man.

And all was over in the next instant.

Before life was extinct Clara dragged at his now helpless body and pulled it unaided to the edge of the overhanging rock.

The wounded man, with upturned eyes, could now only implore her mercy with a glance.

But it might as well have fallen upon a marble statue.

"An eye for an eye," she said triumphantly, "a tooth for a tooth."

A trifling exertion—for the doomed fisherman was now upon the extreme verge of the rock—and a dull splash.

"Oh, Clara, Clara!" ejaculated Edgar Deville, with a shudder.

"What now?"

"How awful!"

"You're grown childish," said she. "I would do the like again if I had the same provocation."

"But the jewels needed no further defence," urged the young man.

"The jewels?"

"Ay."

"Where are they?"

"I—I can't say. Haven't you got them?"

They searched right and left, but without avail.

They had disappeared.

The truth was that they had been pushed over the rock with the fisherman whom Clara St. John had so remorselessly slain.

CHAPTER XLVIII.

DESPAIR — A FATAL RESOLVE — THE HOMELESS WANDERERS — THE FARM — HOSPITALITY — THE WRECK — TO ENGLAND ONCE MORE — THE COUSINS — RENEWED ACQUAINTANCE — THE EARL OF SLOEFORD — THE SECRET PANEL AND THE WHITE HANDS.

"Lost!"

"Ruined!"

Such were the mutual ejaculations of despair of the two shipwrecked travellers.

Clara St. John and Edgar Deville had undergone so much to obtain the packet of jewels.

A load of guilt had been placed upon them, to bear them down with shame, if not contrition, at some future day, and they had taken life to preserve them.

Two wretched men, whose cupidity had been aroused by the sight of the glittering gewgaws, had perished, not unjustly, for their villainy in attempting to rob them.

Alone, and without a friend on whom to call, theirs was a truly pitiable condition.

To the young man it was the more dreadful.

He had been always nurtured in the lap of luxury and affluence.

Clara St. John, as she was now known, felt it not a little. For wealth and position she had ventured much.

And now, by a cruel stroke of fortune, she was deprived of her ill-gotten wealth at the very last moment.

What was to be done?

Of course they made the most minute search, but the fate of the packet of jewels was not be doubted for an instant.

They had been cast into the water with the body of the fisherman.

Edgar Deville stood upon the edge of the projecting rock and gazed long and wistfully into the foaming waters beneath.

To think that they had such a treasure from his sight, and that he dare not venture to brave its dangers and seek it out!

But no, such a venture would inevitably be certain death.

The thought was maddening. As he stood there, looking into the sea, his cheek grew pale and he bit his nether lip with a fixed determination which there was no misunderstanding.

He had resolved to recover the jewels or perish in the attempt.

Clara St. John saw it and was horror-stricken.

For once her woman's heart, her fears, or whatever sensation she might experience towards the misguided young victim to her wiles, triumphed over her avarice, and she sprang forward ere he could accomplish his fatal purpose.

"Edgar!" she cried, "hold, I entreat.."

"What for, Clara?" said he. "There is no danger in the dive."

"Danger!" echoed the woman. "It is certain death, believe me."

"Nay."

"Edgar, you shall not attempt it!"

Edgar urged no more.

The tone of command which she employed seemed to have great weight with him, and showed plainly enough how thoroughly he was in her power.

Many weary hours they spent there in fruitless search.

Hopeless and sad search. Not the faintest vestige could they discover of their jewels nor of the two unfortunate fishermen.

Faint and exhausted from long suffering, they turned at length from the scene of their disaster.

They had passed several hours upon the rocks, after the fatal end of the two men, in the hunt after the packet, and were now growing faint from hunger.

Clara in particular grew so exhausted that Edgar Deville, whose condition was scarcely less pitiable, had to support her.

And they walked inland.

After a short time they came to a cornfield, where they plucked a few ears and devoured them.

A little further on there was a barn, and beyond it a farmhouse.

As they neared the latter a most savoury odour was emitted, combining the flavours of new milk, eggs, and ham.

They looked wistfully towards the door and at each other, then walked past.

"I can walk no further," said Clara.

"And I'm sick and weary enough, Heaven knows," said Edgar Deville.

"Go to the farmhouse and beg some assistance," said the woman.

"Beg?"

"Some assistance until we can get our property from the wreck."

The flush which had suffused the young man's cheek at the thought of asking charity sobered down, and he volunteered to go to the house.

His appearance amongst the serving men and maids created quite a small sensation.

He explained in as few words as possible that he and a lady who was with him were the sole survivors of the fatal wreck which had taken place off their coast that night.

They were greatly astonished, for no one had dreamed that there had been any.

However, being kindly disposed and hospitable people, they made them welcome and bade them eat— a command which was gratefully received by our two shipwrecked adventurers, as may be well conceived.

They were closely questioned touching the particulars of the fire and the wreck, and contrived to give such an account of the whole proceedings as did not touch upon the untimely end of the two fishermen.

They were clothed and provided with a lodging, which was placed at their service until their property should be recovered from the wreck.

Then the agent for Lloyd's, where the ill-fated vessel was insured, took their business in hand, and in the most kindly way returned them their packages as they were recovered from the wreck.

It was an act quite contrary to all practice.

Something in Clara St. John, however, appeared to fascinate the underwriter's agent, as it did everybody who came in contact with this strange and terrible woman.

They were, however, in the very greatest perplexity still.

If the jewels were not recovered the fugitives were ruined.

Without resources of any kind.

Penniless!

But, on the other hand, if by a fortunate chance they should be recovered, it would undoubtedly excite attention, and probably cause inquiries.

At all events, it would be highly unpleasant to account for their possession.

Some explanation would become an absolute necessity.

"No," she said in a chat with Edgar over their hopes and fears in their guilty career. "There is but one resource for us."

"Name it," said Deville. "For, in truth, Clara, I am weary and heart-sick.'

"We must fly."

"But how?"

"We must endeavour to secure a passage to England by the first vessel."

Edgar was startled.

"Return?" he exclaimed.

"Ay. It is our only resource."

"But what course do you propose to pursue when we are in England?"

"I have thought over that."

"With was result?"

"I have a cousin residing so far removed from London that we should be perfectly screened from all observation."

"But I thought that you had no relations in England."

"None of my father's."

"I see. Then these are maternal cousins?"

"Yes."

"But one word, Clara, ere we decide upon adopting this hastily-formed resolve. How can we hope to escape observation for long with your cousin?"

"Leave that to me."

"But consider the risk."

"Edgar, you grow pusillanimous," said the bold masculine woman testily. "What risk can there possibly be?"

"Every risk."

"What proof?"

"Of our guilt?"

"Ay."

"Our flight is sufficient."

"Pshaw! Since we live in comparative poverty, it is none."

"What other object could prompt us to fly together?"

The sternness in Clara's manner vanished upon the instant, and she looked with such tenderness upon the young man that he melted at once.

"Edgar," she murmured, "they might hint of a strange infatuation."

As the words were spoken Edgar caught her in his arms and stopped her further utterance with burning kisses.

"Enough, Clara!" he exclaimed. "Do as you will. I ask no more."

[AN EXTRAORDINARY SCENE AT A CIRCUS.]

" Dear, dear Edgar."

" Poor or rich, I am yours.   In joy or sorrow, dear Clara, I'm yours."

*   *   *   *   *   *

Time passed on.

The occasion had arrived, and our two adventurers passed over to England.

They landed once more upon Albion's white cliffs, much poorer than they had quitted them, but yet in possession of some slight property.

This was, of course, the result of some swindling deception, but neither Clara St. John nor Mr. Edgar Deville was much troubled with scruples of morality.

They passed along the coast some distance, and spent a little time merrily enough at one of the watering places until their funds began to run low.

Then Clara St. John had to start out in earnest, in quest of the cousin alluded to.

It was a long journey, very long; but she had had the prudence to husband their resources, and so they took their time upon the road.

In these easy stages a fortnight was passed.

At length they arrived at the residence of Clara's cousin, *Lady Bellisle!*

It was a most unfortunate moment, as it appeared, for Clara to have chosen for a visit with her husband, as Edgar was said to be.

A death had recently occurred in the family.

Their uncle, the Earl of Sloeford, had been foully assassinated.

Slain in his bed by the hand of an undiscovered midnight robber.

A robber it was ascertained beyond a doubt, for large sums of money had been abstracted from various parts of the house.

A plate robbery had occurred upon the same night, of such magnitude as to convince any one who could entertain a doubt upon the subject.

Mr. Spencer Bellisle had succeeded to the earldom and estates and a great bulk of the property.

The Earl's favourite niece, Lady Bellisle, had some time previous to his demise disappointed his hopes by having formed an attachment to her cousin, the heir to the title.

It was a wild infatuation, which they deemed could come to no good, for Mr. Spencer Bellisle had returned home, after a protracted sojourn in foreign countries, and a strange reputation had preceded him.

Rumours were given out of certain discreditable transactions with which his name had been connected.

At Spa and Baden-Baden, and other of the great German gambling towns, he had been more than once degraded by reported discoveries of false play.

At least, so it was said.

However, Mr. Spencer Bellisle no sooner became a belted earl than these rumours were heard no more.

The Earl of Sloeford was a most influential man, possessed no end of votes, several livings, and was one of the first of the county magistrates.

As soon as the inquest upon the body of the murdered earl was over, and the funeral obsequies were carried out in all the solemn pomp and grandeur befitting one of the earl's high worldly rank had been got through, it became publicly known that Mr. Spencer Bellisle, the new earl, was betrothed to the Lady Bellisle, his cousin.

Such was the state of affairs when Clara St. John and Mr. Edgar Deville arrived upon the scene of the recent tragedy.

Clara had not been there long when she found good reason to congratulate herself upon the choice of a refuge which she had made.

The murder made her prick up her ears, and at once she was upon the alert.

To this shrewd keen-sighted woman of the world there was a strange significance in the speedy betrothal of the cousins.

Clara, too, soon found means to collect scraps of the infamous reports which had preceded the return of Mr. Spencer Bellisle to his native land.

He was the only person who had, up to the present, benefited by the sudden and awful death of the late earl.

Clara and her avowed husband had not been long at Sloeford House when Lady Bellisle announced her intention of taking a short tour in company with the earl.

It was thought to be rather a singular freak, but people of such high rank were of course above all vulgar suspicion, and so the precious pair of cousins left.

Clara did all that lay in her power to learn the object of their departure, but only succeeded in obtaining reasons which she knew to be false.

A fragment of a conversation which she happened to overhear assured her of this much.

As the words will touch upon a future chapter in some slight degree, we propose to give them.

The Earl of Sloeford and his affianced wife were sitting in the library talking over their projected tour, when Clara came on them by accident in this wise.

Since her residence at Sloeford House she had taken a great fancy to exploring the many secret passages, sliding panels, and other mediæval contrivances with which the mansion abounded.

One day Clara had been examining her own sleeping apartment very narrowly, when, upon raising some faded tapestry which had evidently been upon the walls from very remote ages, she discovered a slight dent in the wall.

At once upon the *qui vive* for adventure and discoveries, she pressed the part eagerly in every direction.

A door, ingeniously concealed in the panel, revolved and opened.

She entered the dark passage upon which it opened, and, not thinking of any risk she might be incurring, proceeded eagerly along.

It was a winding narrow way—so narrow that one person only at a time could proceed along it, and so low that she had to stoop nearly double.

She arrived at the end of this, when suddenly it grew more lofty.

She was able to stand upright and could feel no ceiling.

Another step brought her to a standstill.

"So, so," thought Clara. "There must be a door hereabouts."

She stretched out her hand, but only to encounter the hard wall upon every side.

Many minutes she passed there searching, but vainly, for the door.

Yet she was not to be baffled.

"It must be here," she muttered.

Her conviction inspired her with courage, and she kept to her task.

Minutes grew into an hour, and yet no signs of success.

The closeness of the place, too, was most unpleasant.

The passage was of great length, and there was no ventilation.

Still she persevered in her search, struggling boldly against a close and stifling sensation which appeared to be overpowering her.

By slow degrees—fatally slow—she felt a faintness stealing over her.

So alarming did this presently grow that the bold determined adventuress was forced to pause in her labours to rest her head, throbbing with the difficulty of respiration in the passage, the veins in her forehead swelling to twice their size, and standing out purple, like thick cords, against the cold wall.

Oh! how welcome was the cold to her fevered throbbing brow!

Somewhat revived by this, she was about to rise, when she fancied that her ear caught the faint sound of voices.

"Ah! at last!"

She listened eagerly.

She did not move nor breathe.

But her utmost efforts failed to catch anything more.

She could now distinctly hear the whisperings, but they were too low to allow her to catch even one word distinctly.

It was tantalising.

Teasing to the highest degree.

She renewed her search for the door, which she now felt more convinced than ever was there.

Suddenly her hands were arrested in their progress over the walls.

She heard some voices in angry discussion close at hand.

So loudly was the conversation now carried on that she could almost catch its nature.

Then there was a blow struck, followed by the falling of a body.

Then she could hear a door opened, so near to her that instinctively she glanced up.

But no, not yet.

Another second, and the same sound was repeated.

This time there was no misunderstanding it. *A door was opened close beside her.*

At once anticipating some foul play, and danger in the event of discovery, the adventurous woman threw herself forward upon her face as far as possible from the opening in the panel.

A ray of light was admitted which showed some strange doings.

A bloody corpse was thrust forward.

The form of an old man, a domestic apparently from his apparel, and grasped by two remarkably white hands.

Those hands Clara St. John never forgot.

The left hand, too, was remarkable for one circumstance.

A rich diamond ring of priceless value was upon the little finger.

Not the faintest glimpse could Clara catch of the person owning the white hand and the rich diamond.

The body of the bleeding servant fell upon the prostrate form of Clara.

"Ugh!" she exclaimed, burying her face in her hands. "Horror, horror!"

The warm blood of the body trickled upon her face, causing her a painful sensation.

A feeling of horror never, never to be effaced from her mind until her dying day.

"Great Heavens!" she murmured. "This it too too fearful. Oh! horror!"

―――

CHAPTER XLIX.

THE DARK PASSAGE — THE ASSASSINATION — A TERRIBLE COMPANION—HORRORS ACCUMULATE —THE TALE OF BLOOD—THE SECRET CLOSET—EAVESDROPPING—THE PROJECTED JOURNEY—POISON DISCUSSED — CLARA'S RETURN — THE DEATH CLUTCH—MERCY—THE DYING SERVANT—CLARA'S NEW SCHEME—BUT HOW TO EXECUTE IT?—A PRISONER.

WITH an averted gaze Clara St. John endeavoured to thrust the bleeding corpse of the domestic from her.

The pushing of the body near the hurt which had caused the man's death had a most terrifying effect.

The blood spurted out like a water jet, sprinkling the face and clothes of the shrinking trembling woman.

Clara St. John, as we have shown, was no novice in crime, and yet this caused her the most agonising feelings.

With her eyes closed she rose to her feet, and made for the spot whence the object of terror which she had now to endure so close beside her had been thrust.

She at once, in spite of the terror conjured up, perceived how she had been so thoroughly mistaken with regard to the secret door.

She had directed all her searches straight before her, and the secret door lay to the left.

The secret spring was yet very difficult to discover.

And now her search was continued in the utmost feverish haste.

She would not retrace her steps after all she had ventured without gaining her purpose.

No, let the horror upon horrors here accumulate until they deprived her of her reason, she would yet keep to it until she had obtained some result.

She struggled to repress a sickening sensation which was creeping over her.

Suddenly a faint sound caught her ear.

What was it?

A sigh of agony—a faint but long-drawn wail of suffering.

Clara shivered from head to foot like one palsied.

The bloody object yet breathed.

Could it be this?

But she never paused to see if she could render any assistance.

No thought of sympathy or anything like female weaknesses troubled her.

Another instant, and her fingers touched a projecting knob.

A wild hope possessed her.

It yielded to the touch, and the door which she had seen opened so shortly before, and for such a fatal office, again revolved, like the entrance to the passage from her own sleeping apartment.

It opened into a small closet.

Upon the right was a second door, and this she was just about to pull open, when the sound of voices caught her ear again.

She paused in the act.

Listened eagerly, with her ear touching the door panels.

"It is the earl!"

An expression of triumph, almost of joy, passed over her countenance.

She felt that she was about to learn the secret she had striven for.

Her reward for the horrors which she had endured in that secret passage.

"Alice," she could hear him say in low but perfectly distinct tones. "Alice, one obstacle is now removed from our path. Two only remain to be disposed of, and then we are free."

"True, Spencer," replied a familar voice, which Clara recognised as her cousin's.

"All that remains to secure to us an undisturbed enjoyment of all this for which we have ventured so much."

Clara started.

"Ventured so much," she repeated deliberately, as if to infix it upon her memory the more effectually.

"It is dreadful, Spencer," continued Lady Bellisle, so lowly that the listener with difficulty could distinguish what she said.

"What is?"

"All this."

"Tut, tut, Alice," said the earl, with a sneer. "You are growing scrupulous."

"No, Spencer. Yet I feel a horror of all these crimes, believe me."

"Pah!"

"Spare me your sneers."

"P'shaw, woman!" said the earl. "If you continue to bore me thus eternally with your humbugging pricking of conscience, I shall wish myself heartily rid of the business."

The woman, his destined bride, uttered a cry of sorrow.

"Ah, Spencer, how gladly would I resign all if it were only possible to undo what we have done!"

"Fool!"

"Hush!"

"Your pardon," said the earl, coarsely. "But you put too much upon my patience. We are in for it now and it were worse than useless to retract. It is impossible to undo the past."

"Alas! yes. But I do not feel so sure of our security as you appear to be."

"Pshaw! Wherefore?"

"Do not two eye-witnesses of the—two eye-witnesses yet live?"

"Possibly."

"Nay, it is proved beyond a doubt."

"What then?"

"Why, we are not safe one moment, and then—"

"Nonsense! If they knew all, as you appear to think, why have they not yet spoken?"

"I know not."

"Nor I."

"Unless they wait for a more fitting moment."

"How can they have any choice?"

"That remains to be seen."

"Pshaw! Alice! Your fears blind your reason and your better judgment."

"Perhaps," said Lady Bellisle. "But I feel assured that they will come forward yet when we least expect it."

"By hell! they never shall," ejaculated the earl, with such a voice that the whole place re-echoed with his vehemence. "No, no. If only to silence your silly fears, this night I will start upon my journey. But one thing remains to be told. After then you must not raise up any more spectres to frighten us both into imagining all these horrors. This actress shall perish, and the man too, since it must be so."

"Oh, Spencer, Spencer, beware how you act in this, I beseech you."

"Oh, have no fears for me."

"But Martin."

"Oh! he's gone from this wicked world of suffering," said the Earl of Sloeford.

And he gave a cold horrible grating laugh which jarred upon the ears of the gentle Clara St. John.

She felt that he was alluding to the old servitor whose bleeding corpse was so terribly near to her even then.

"No, no, Alice," resumed the earl. "You must indulge in no more of these gloomy fancies. Your wild notions have already led us into one fearful error from which it required the utmost address to extricate ourselves."

"What mean you?"

"The carrying off of the buxom innkeeper's wife in the night."

"But there is no danger to be apprehended from there now."

"None."

"You will take with you the bottle I got from the old Arab?"

"What you went all the way to London to procure, you mean?"

"Yes."

"I'll take it with me. Yes."

"And remember how to use it."

"Oh! I do. A few drops upon a bouquet will settle the business."

"Yes."

"But are you sure of its efficacy?"

"Beyond all doubt."

"I should prefer to see the effect myself before using it."

"But I tell you that I saw it so wonderfully tested by the old Arab astrologer that not a particle of doubt remains on my mind."

"Poor proof for me."

"It must suffice you."

"Enough."

And thus the conference ended.

Clara could hear no more from her hiding-place at present.

She had heard no opening nor shutting of door, and therefore could not venture to push open the closet door and see where it entered into.

So she turned from the closet, closed the door, and regained the dark passage.

As she was turning off she felt that the edge of her skirt had caught something.

She pulled it, but although it yielded a little, it would not give way.

She stooped down and applied her hand to remove the obstacle.

Judge then her horror and dismay when her hand encountered the clutch of a human being.

A wet hand!

"Oh, how dreadful!" she ejaculated. "How very awful is this!"

The grasp upon her skirt too was such that she could not disengage it.

She took the damp clammy hand in hers and endeavoured to force it open.

But no. Her hand slipped from the ensanguined grasp.

Wet and bedabbled in the life-blood of the poor old servitor.

"Mercy!" gasped a faint voice.

"Ah! he lives then!"

"Save me, in mercy," said the old man feebly.

"What is it?" demanded Clara, stooping down to the wounded man.

"Oh! I am hurt, wounded, grievously stabbed, lady."

"Who has done it?"

"The—the earl!"

The old man's voice was so faint as to be scarcely audible.

"The earl stabbed you?"

"Yes, as he stabbed my dear old master and his uncle."

"The late earl?"

"Ye—es."

"You know this?"

"I saw it."

This interested Clara mightily.

At once she had resolved to render such aid as was possible to the old servant whom Spencer Bellisle and his guilty cousin deemed murdered outright.

"Can you rise?"

"Alas! no."

"Where is your wound?"

"Here, in my side."

Clara took her handkerchief and placed it in the old man's hand.

"Take this," she said. "Hold it firmly to the place. Stop the bleeding if possible."

"Thanks, dear lady."

"I will go for assistance."

"Hush! beware, the earl!"

"There's no fear."

"Silence—I beseech you, silence. He would risk anything to save himself now."

"Fear nothing. I will first get a light, and see if your wound be dangerous."

"Thanks, thanks, dear lady."

"You know me?"

"Is it not Miss Clara?"

"Yes."

"Then Heaven's blessing be upon your dear innocent head."

Clara could not refrain from shuddering at the old man's warm gratitude.

She thought in horror how little she deserved the praises.

"Be comforted, Martin," she said. "I will return in an instant."

"Bless you."

What a singular joy did this guilty woman now feel at the prospect of rendering the poor old man some service!

For the first time for many years she had done an act which was strangely at variance with her ordinary course of life, and the enjoyment, the wholesome healthy enjoyment, she experienced in it was wonderful.

Oh, how different from the feverish triumph experienced in the accomplishment of one of the many crimes with which she stood accounted!

Murmuring words of comfort and consolation to the old man, she gained the end of the narrow passage.

It was pitch dark.

Not the faintest glimmer of light penetrated that gloomy labyrinth of passage in which such bloody work was done.

"The door must have gone to by itself," murmured Clara.

It had.

The door, she was unaware in her eager curiosity, fastened with a spring.

"Dear, dear!" she exclaimed. "This is truly unfortunate at such a moment."

But little did she deem the annoyance it was to cause her yet.

She felt the wall in every direction. Right, left, up, and down.

But no spring could she discover.

At length it began to grow alarming.

After some twenty minutes had been spent thus she could hear the voice of the old servant calling upon her for aid in fainting tones.

"Lady, lady," he cried, "for God's sake do not desert me in this awful place."

"Alas! poor Martin," said Clara, "I cannot find the door. We are both prisoners."

"Then I die. Oh, Heaven have mercy upon—"

"Martin, Martin."

"Too late, Miss Clara!"

CHAPTER L.

ROSE AGAIN—THE WIDOWED HUSBAND—A NIGHT ALARM—ROBBERS—AN ADVENTURE—A SHOOTING MATCH—THE BLACK MASK—A FAMILIAR FOE—DEAD FOR A DUCAT—NO—FLIGHT OF THE WOUNDED MASK—THE LOOK-OUT—A SPECTRE—STARTLING DISCOVERY—AN OLD FRIEND—RE-APPEARANCE.

To return to Rose.

Whilst we have been so occupied with the doings of the other characters in our little drama a variety of changes has occurred in Rose Mortimer's career.

With these we now propose to deal without delay.

The intelligent reader will remember that upon quitting our heroine she had, with Mr. Chowler, the stage manager, made the discovery that the occupants of the stage-box, who appeared so eagerly to scan their forms and faces, were no other than the head of the local gentry—Lady Bellisle and her cousin, the next in succession to the earldom of Sloeford, Mr. Spencer Bellisle.

Upon the occasion of the opening performance of Mr. Chowler's company, with Rose Mortimer, as the Dumb Boy, in a prominent position, it will further be remembered that Lady Bellisle and Mr. Spencer Bellisle had received a strange and startling piece of information whilst in the theatre.

A rumour soon spread about the theatre that the Earl of Sloeford had been found murdered in his bed.

This was for long a most profound mystery to the manager and Rose.

They could not at all comprehend how the fearful deed which they had been witnesses to upon the previous night had only transpired after so long a lapse of time.

It was in everybody's mouth.

But yet Rose Mortimer and the manager, by a mutual understanding, held their peace.

They dreaded some danger, the precise nature of which they would have found it difficult to explain, from the vengeance of the assassins.

The abduction of the landlady of the house at which Rose Mortimer was staying had sufficiently shown them that the guilty parties would hesitate at no crime, however bold and desperate, to hide their guilt from the eyes of the world.

"No, no, my dear Miss Mortimer," said Mr. Chowler, in the course of one of their many conversations upon this head. "We must hold our peace until the fitting moment arrives. Then we will speak and ease our minds."

"As you please," said Rose.

"The strange disappearance of Mrs. Davis has rather alarmed me."

"And me too."

"Yes, it is rather humiliating to own oneself a thorough coward; but these are insidious enemies, who strike in the dark."

"I dread the worst from their enmity," said Rose, with a shudder.

And thus the conference ended.

Two days passed, and yet Mrs. Davis, the landlady, was absent.

Her husband, who had been from home engaged at a neighbouring market town, returned at the expiration of this time.

And now poor Rose was in a greater dilemma than ever.

It was pitiable to hear the young man lamenting for his young wife, so mysteriously disappeared, when Rose Mortimer could by a word have given him such a clue as would perhaps have led to her recovery.

However, one day passed after the young man's return, and not the slightest signs of Mrs. Davis.

Her husband grew frantic.

He tore all over the county, advertising such rewards for the recovery of his wife as would have made him bankrupt to meet.

Rose was now in such great fear from what she had seen of the lengths the audacity of the murderers would lead them that she could not sleep at night.

The consequence was that one night she lay awake listening for voices which always are to be heard by the sleepless in the night, and staring at the window until her eyes ached.

Every instant she expected to see the window pushed open, followed by the appearance of a masked head—a mask to be remembered until her dying day.

"Ah! me," signed Rose wearily as she lay. "What a life of torment and trouble is mine! By the merest string of fortunate and unfortunate accidents I escape one danger only to encounter others more alarming. For I fear that there is more immediate and real injury to be apprehended from these assassins than from the cruelty of the Whurtons."

Her musings stopped abruptly.

She looked about her curiously, as if uncertain of the cause of her fear.

But yet there was cause, and the next instant showed it still more.

She could hear footsteps patrolling the road.

Danger!

But what was the nature of the danger she had yet to learn.

She lay as still in her bed as the shivering caused by her fears would permit.

Presently there was a sound as if the door below was being pushed—a kind of noise that made our heroine imagine that it was about to be forced.

This was an agreeable situation!

Rose sprang from her bed and darted into the passage.

"Mr. Davis! Mr. Davis!" she cried in a frightened whisper.

"Who's there?" cried the watchful husband of poor Mrs. Davis.

"It is I."

"Miss Mortimer?"

"Yes."

"Lor, miss, what is it?"

"Something wrong, I fear, downstairs."

"What do you mean?"

"A noise at the front door."

"Never. Wait, I'll come."

Rose suddenly remembered that she was in rather a loose state of apparel to have an interview with her landlord.

She beat a hasty retreat into the bedchamber and speedily put on a few garments to enable her to proceed unrestrainedly in her movements.

And now Rose fancied that she could hear fresh footsteps without, as if the parties had been reinforced.

She repaired to the passage, and called out her fears to Mr. Davis.

"All right, my dear Miss Mortimer," said the young landlord. "I long for a slap at somebody. I'm after them."

"Be careful," said Rose.

"Oh! I'll be careful."

"I fear that you may come to some harm else."

"Have no fears for me."

"Oh! but you do not know these people."

"Eh?"

Rose bit her lip and was silent.

Another instant, and her indiscreet fears would have given up the secrets which, in common with Chowler, the little theatrical manager, she had contrived to keep so religiously.

She could now hear that the landlord was indeed bestirring himself, and she much feared, by the noise he made in his movements that the party without —who were there, she felt convinced, with some nefarious intent—would be pushed to open violence.

Now she could hear a small table being moved there.

This she knew by the sound to be a toilette table, the property of the lost landady, which stood by the window.

Then he was going to open the window.

Yes, there was no mistake about this, for in the space of two seconds she could hear the lattice unfastened and opened.

Rose Mortimer regained her own apartment and ran up to the window.

Then opened it with as little noise as possible and peeped out.

There was a man there—a figure which she remembered.

The same mask hid his features from view. In his hand he carried some small instrument, which our heroine was unable plainly to distinguish at first.

A keener glance, however, showed that it was a revolver.

As this occurred to her she heard Mr. Davis challenge the masked man from the adjoining window.

"Hullo, there!" he cried. "Who's there?"

But there was no answer.

The mask, even then hoping to escape observation, drew near to the house, and then stepped into the doorway.

Too late.

"Come out of that!" cried the enraged landlord. "Come out, or I'll blow your brains out."

This caused a change in the man's demeanour immediately.

He leant forward, with an upraised hand, pointed at Davis.

"Ah!" shrieked Rose.

This probably preserved the landlord's life.

There was a report of firearms.

The barrel of the masked man's revolver had been discharged, and shivered the next window to atoms!

Then out darted the mask.

Davis had awaited his time, and now no sooner did he get a fair view of the man than he aimed and fired.

His weapon was a fowling-piece, not of a very superior make, and only loaded with duck shot, but it was well aimed and took effect.

Down dropped the mask!

"Brought him to grass!" cried Davis triumphantly.

He sprang from the window and hastily reloaded his fowling-piece.

Then darted downstairs.

Rose was greatly alarmed at all this, as may be naturally supposed, but she could not leave the window until she had seen the termination of the strange drama.

But she repented of the curiosity which prompted her to this.

The wounded man (for wounded he was beyond a doubt) raised himself upon his elbow, and with his disengaged hand pointed directly at Rose Mortimer.

A cry burst from the lips of the startled girl, and she sprang from the window.

A glance had shown her that the hand grasped the pistol still, and that her life was endangered.

Barely had she quitted the window when there was a second report, and a pistol bullet whisked so unpleasantly close to Rose Mortimer's head that she could actually feel the wind of it as it passed.

It lodged in the wall over the doorway.

But the man—this would-be assassin—what had become of him?

As she stood at the further end of her bedroom she could hear that the door below was opened by Mr. Davis, and that he ran out.

This set poor Rose in a greater fright than ever, for she had just learned that the wounded man was not too badly hurt to make himself a very dangerous enemy.

And it was all due to herself, she feared, and to the fatal curiosity which had led her and Chowler to play the spy upon the actions of the highly-born assassins of the Earl of Slocford.

At all risks she must render Mr. Davis what assistance she could.

She ran downstairs to the door.

Mr. Davis and the wounded man had both disappeared.

This was most singular, as the masked ruffian had evidently been hurt in a way which must have seriously impeded his locomotion.

However, this did not cause her much trouble, nor for long.

In the space of a few seconds back came the young landlord, gun in hand, and in hot haste, looking up and down the road.

"Where is he, Mr. Davis?" cried Rose.

"Then you've seen all?"

"Yes. Where did the man go to?"

"Gad! I should like to be told that."

"But had he gone when you got downstairs?"

"I can't possibly say. All I know is that when I ran to the door and pulled at it it was fast from the outside."

"Held?"

"So I thought, but, as it didn't yield in the least, I concluded—rightly, as it turned out—that some sort of fastening had been put to it."

"How?"

"A stick had been passed through the handle of the latch. As the door opens on the inside, this was easy enough."

"How strange!"

"It was. And it resisted a power of strength like you've no idea of. However, I managed to push it through, and when I got out he had flown."

"Strange," said Rose. "I thought he was so badly wounded, too."

"The rascal wasn't alone."

"Are you sure?"

"Certain. I know I lamed him: there's his blood all over the road."

"But he was not quite disabled."

"No, I suppose not, for he fired at me after I had left my room."

"Or rather at me."

"At you? The miscreant!" ejaculated the young landlord. "I wish that I had him once more within range."

At this moment it appeared that his wish was about to be gratified.

At the bend in the road they now perceived a figure emerge from the hedge and make for the house.

In an instant Mr. Davis had popped the gun to his shoulder.

"Now," he exclaimed, with great satisfaction. "When he's in range."

"Stop!" cried Rose. "It's a woman."

Another minute confirmed this.

Rose was not surprised at this, for she well knew what a prominent part a woman had played in the late outrage, and she naturally imagined that this was the same female fiend who had already committed such diabolical crimes.

"She means no good at this hour," said Davis. "I shall fire."

"No, no!" cried Rose.

"Halt!" cried Davis to the woman, as she drew nearer. "Advance another step and I fire!"

"Michael!" said the woman.

Rose and the young landlord started and turned rather sick.

It was Mrs. Davis's voice.

"Who are you?" cried Davis,

"It is me, Michael."

"What, Moggy?"

"Yes."

"Hold hard now."

This appeared a singular greeting for a loving husband of a newly married wife.

The fact of it was that, although not addicted to beliefs that had a supernatural tendency, Mr. Davis could not help being startled by her sudden re-appearance.

The situation, too, was more than usually startling, from the recent adventure with the masked ruffian, whom the young landlord had so dexterously contrived to pepper.

"Michael, Michael!" cried poor Mrs. Davis. "Don't you know me?"

Rose, hearing by the sound of her voice that she was in distress, ran out to meet her.

"Miss Mortimer!" cried the landlady. "Is it really you, dear?"

And as Rose gained her side she fell into her arms in a flood of tears.

"What is it?" demanded Rose.

"Oh! dear, dear!" cried Mrs. Davis. "Oh! I'm so glad to see you again. I thought that I'd lost you for ever."

"Where have you been?"

"I don't know. No I don't. But I've suffered so much."

"Moggy," called Mr. Davis from the door.

"Michael."

"Come, Mr. Davis," said Rose. "Come and assist your wife to the house."

As he now saw that it was really his prodigal wife returned in the flesh (though not so much of it as when she had been carried off), he ran to lend assistance.

An affectionate embrace and another flood of tears —tears of joy—and the husband joyfully led his wife back to the house.

When they were fairly inside, and the door was securely fastened, poor Davis overwhelmed her with questions, so that she was unable to reply to them in detail.

By degrees, however, she recovered herself, and then she gave them the history of what had befallen her.

"All that has occurred to me," she said, "appears like a mystery—a kind of dream. I know not what, but I know that my life has been in danger."

"Oh! Moggy."

"Ah! Michael," she said, with a sad smile, "I never thought to see you again."

"But where is it you have been to?" he again asked, impatiently.

"I know not, I say."

"But—"

"Wait," said Mrs. Davis, "and I will give you the whole tale, and you shall judge for yourself."

───

CHAPTER LI.

MRS. DAVIS'S NARRATIVE—POWERFUL FOES—A SECRET FRIEND — THE TALKING PICTURE — THE MEAL—THE UNSEEN WRITER—"BEWARE!" A KINDLY WARNING—THE TRAP—THE COUCH —HOPES AND FEARS—THE MIDNIGHT VISITOR —A STRANGE PARADE — THE PASSAGES — THE DOOR — THE OLD MAN'S GOODNESS — SAFELY RESTORED.

"ALL I know of this frightful affair," said Mrs. Davis, "is this. One night—I cannot say how long ago, for I have even lost reckoning since I have been away—I was awakened by hearing a noise in the bedroom. I opened my eyes, and there I saw a man in a mask standing by the bedside—"

"Curse him!" muttered Davis.

"I couldn't speak, for I was so dreadfully frightened, until he seized me in his arms, bedclothes and all—

"Curse him!" muttered Davis.

"Then I shrieked out."

"I heard you," said Rose. "But I had just awakened myself, and I did not know what to think of it."

"Then he stifled my cries with something which he threw over my head, and carried me off. There was a ladder at the window.

"I suppose then that I must have fainted, for I can remember nothing more until the next morning, when I found myself in a little room, and the same mask peering over me as I lay upon a couch."

Another spasmodic oath from Davis here interrupted the narrative.

"I was very much frightened, of course, and I begged for mercy, and asked an explanation, promised to reform in future, and all in a breath. I could make nothing of it at all.

"For a long time the masked man remained silent —so quiet that I was frightened even at this. Then after some length of time he put some questions to me, which puzzled me greatly."

"Ah!" said Rose.

"Yes, dear," resumed Mrs. Davis, turning to Rose, "and what's more singular—my trouble appeared to puzzle him as much as his questions did me.

"Well, that day passed over. They were good enough to bring me food, but I didn't like to touch it."

"Why not?"

"You shall hear. After the first day they allowed me the range of two rooms—fine spacious places— which convinced me that I had been borne off to some grand house, though where to will ever remain a mystery to me."

Rose felt that she could have enlightened her had she dared to speak.

"Well," continued Mrs. Davis, "upon the second day the tall man in the mask brought me a sumptuous meal upon a tray. Again, of course, I begged for some explanation of the cruel outrage, but he was silent. Upon my pressing him hardly on the subject he replied, in a voice which will always ring in my ears, 'Let your curiosity be satisfied that it has brought you thus far already. Pushed further, it may lead to such lights as you will find unpleasant!'"

"Ah!" Rose mentally ejaculated. "Then it is as I suspected."

Of this there could be no doubt.

The words clearly implied that they believed she was in the fatal secret which imperilled their safety.

It was galling in the extreme to our heroine that she durst not speak.

"Well," resumed Mrs. Davis. "After this speech, which seemed to contain a deal of hidden meaning and threats, the purport of which I could not understand, he left me, pointing sternly to the meal upon the tray.

"Now this tray, I must tell you, was placed upon a small table near the wall, and just over it hung a picture of some faded beauty of a long long time ago. As I advanced to the table to taste the tempting delicacies with which it was filled—for I was now sinking with hunger—I fancied this picture moved. I was very much frightened at this, for everything seemed to impress me with such horrible sensations; but I drew nearer, and lo! a paper slid from beneath it and fell upon the table.

"I picked it up with a mixture of curiosity and fear, and read these words—

"'*Beware of all food!*'"

"Poison!" exclaimed the landlady's listeners spontaneously.

"So I supposed," said Mrs. Davis, "and I refrained from eating the tempting delicacies. But many and many were the longing glances which I cast towards them. I walked up and down my room lamenting my fate aloud, in the hope of exciting my unseen adviser to render me assistance as well as advice. 'Whoever sends me this warning,' I said, 'pray accept my earnest gratitude, but at the same time I must starve, for I am already sick and faint with hunger.' However, my appeal still remained unheard, until, weary with fatigue, I sank upon a chair in a state of half insensibility.

"When I recovered from this it was to hear a slight noise at my refreshment table. I looked and perceived that an addition had been made to the viands already there, in the form of a small loaf and a piece of a chicken. It had been carefully disjointed and the bones removed."

"I see the object of that," said Rose.

"I did not, but I do now. It was, of course, that no scraps might betray the hand of my strange benefactor.

"With the food was a second note, which is here."

Mrs. Davis took a small blotted paper from her pocket and read—

"'*All may be well if you are careful and keep this from their knowledge. If you betray me, we are both lost, for I am now your only hope. Touch no food whatever. But to gain time and prevent the employment of force, and to destroy all idea that you entertain suspicion of foul play, endeavour to get rid of some of the food and wine. The latter you can empty about in hidden corners. The food you must cut up and sprinkle about. I am here to aid you. Fear nothing and be bold.*'

"I can scarcely say which were my most prominent sensations at reading this—fear or security. It was a mixture of the two I imagine. However, I determined to obey its instructions, and very soon had to commence my counterplot with the masked man. My first care was to assure the picture, for this represented my hidden benefactor or benefactress, that I was all gratitude and obedience, and to be implicitly relied upon. Then I took my bottle of wine and carefully poured about an eighth of it about in small doses. The meat which had been brought up by the masked man I cut about, and threw very small bits in out-of-the-way corners. The next day I found out the real service which my unseen correspondent had rendered me, as I show you. I had just concluded my job when the door handle turned. My last food was yet upon the table. With a bound I was there, and had removed it to a chair upon which I sat down, covering it effectually, as the door opened, and my masked jailor came in."

"Go on," said Mr. Davis, breathless with interest.

"I was in great alarm, of course, and how I contrived to keep it from his piercing gaze I cannot understand. The only thing is, I suppose, that he saw no extra emotion, and imagined it all to spring from the selfsame source. Goodness knows that there was enough to scare away one's wits in being there alone."

"True."

"Poor creature," said Rose.

Mrs. Davis pressed our heroine's hand warmly, and continued—

"As my jailor came in I saw his coal-black eyes, glistening like diamonds with malice and murder, glance eagerly upon the tray through the two holes in the mask.

"My heart beat quickly, but I said nothing.

"'You have eaten?' he said.

"'I have finished,' I replied.

"'*If you have eaten,*' he said, with a satirical smile, '*that says all!*'

"I shivered with this terrible proof of the truth of my unseen benefactor, but held my peace.

"It was evidently a piece of satire, at my expense, which I was not supposed to comprehend. However, I merely bowed my head before him, as he gathered up the things upon the tray. When he had finished he paused by the door and turned round to me, evidently awaiting me to question him again, as I had done upon each previous entrance, as to the cause of my being there.

"However, I would not give him this gratification, if indeed it was any to him, and I fancy that he must have taken a wonderful pleasure in seeing my agony and sufferings, and I had the pleasure in turn of witnessing his disappointment.

"'So, so, madam,' he said, in his harsh grating voice, 'you have grown resigned to your new quarters I am glad to find.'

"'I have,' said I, meekly. 'Why should I not be resigned to them?'

"'Why, indeed?' said he.

"'Am I not treated here in a way that I cannot possibly be at home?'

"He smiled significantly before replying to this observation.

"And we both felt an inward satisfaction, and both with the same cause. But with this difference.—I was supposed to be the deceived, whilst he was actually."

"Capital!" said the husband of the speaker, rubbing his palms, which were moist with eager excitement. "Go on."

"'To be sure you are,' said my jailor, 'and, moreover, in a way that you never will be treated there again.'

[THE LOST ONE.]

"I could not refrain from shuddering at these words, so deliberately uttered, and my pain evidently gave him pleasure to witness.

"'Before you go,' said I, 'there is but one request I have to make.'

"'Name it.'

"'I should like to breathe the fresh air.'

"'Impossible.'

"'But I promise that I will make no effort to escape—not the very least. Only let me walk in the garden, or—'

"Here I broke off short, for the man started and his eyes flashed a thousand fires through the holes in the mask.

"'Garden!' he repeated. 'You have seen that once too often.'

"I was bewildered.

"There was no doubt something significant attached to his words, but I failed to comprehend them.

"He stared at me, and I believe was not a little puzzled by the expression. His words had been apparently uttered with the conviction that I should comprehend the meaning of them, but it was not at all difficult to perceive that I was quite lost.

"'Do you mean to say that you do not catch my meaning?' he asked.

"'I do,' said I.

"'You do not know the garden?'

No. 17.

"'Not I — that I'm aware of. I have scarcely seen a garden but my own for weeks.'

"There was no mistaking the surprise upon his countenance at these words.

"'I think you saw one on Tuesday last,' he said.

"'No. I never stirred from my house upon that day.'

"'Could you swear this?'

"'I could.'

"'That you did not leave your house upon Tuesday at night?'

"'I swear it,' said I solemnly.

"He regarded me sternly in the face, but I was speaking the truth, and I met his glance steadily.

"'Had we known that before,' he muttered. 'But no—impossible.'

"I imagined that he still disbelieved my oath, and again assured him, offering him proof of what I uttered, and thus I made a discovery concerning you, dear."

"Me?" said Rose.

"Yes."

"In what way?"

She faltered as she spoke, and it was plain enough that she well knew how nearly it touched her.

"Go on, my dear," said Davis.

"'I know well,' said I, 'that I was in the whole of Tuesday, for this reason. I had a new lodger come, and a singular thing happened in connection with her which kept me in.' This was of course in allusion to your illness, my dear, and your engagement afterwards in Mr. Chowler's company. He seemed to jump at what I said upon this subject and questioned me closely.

"'Why did you not say all this before?' asked my jailor.

"'Because I was not asked,' I replied.

"'Fool!' he cried. 'But you alone will have to suffer for it.'

"'What do you mean?' I asked.

"'You will know to-morrow.'

"He nodded sternly and left the room.

"As soon as he was gone I took my food (which I had been sitting upon) and eagerly devoured it. Revived a little at this, I sat down to think, but I could arrive at nothing like a decision upon the matter.

"That night before retiring to rest, which I did upon a couch in the room where I had eaten, and in which was the picture which had caused me such satisfaction, I took great care to place enough of the furniture before the door to make a good barricade.

"I addressed my picture again and again that night, but failed to elicit any reply, and at length I fell asleep.

"In the morning I had rather a severe shock. As I rose from the couch and glanced around I perceived some dark object in the corner of the room.

"I drew near to ascertain its nature, and found it to be a monstrous rat, dead.

"Beside it lay a small piece of the meat which I had thrown down to deceive my captor."

"What wretches!" cried Davis.

"Remorseless villains!" said Rose.

"I removed the furniture with which I had barricaded my door during the night, and presently my jailor came in, holding his mask in his hand. As he caught sight of me he seemed as if he would have fallen through the floor. I forgot to mention that he had advanced into the room, and had stooped to the floor to open a trap. I shudder now as I remember that trap. But, glancing up, and perceiving me advancing, he started up, slammed down the trap, and resumed his mask.

"It is clear now to me that he, like you, Michael, almost doubted if I was alive or not. He appeared so thoroughly frightened. But with this all his presence of mind was much to be admired. His very first care was to put on his mask."

"Did you see his face?"

"Yes."

"And would remember it?" eagerly demanded our heroine.

"I'm sure I should."

"Go on, my dear," said the eager Davis again, impatiently.

"I've not much more to add," said his wife. "But what I have is, perhaps, the most important in the story—certainly the most important to me. A day or two passed I know not how. My captor was thoroughly at a loss to account for my obstinacy in not dying. My portrait still continued to supply me with food, and I did not lose all hope.

"One day—I don't know how many after my imprisonment in that dreadful place—I received a note from my invisible friend which caused my heart to leap with joy. This is it."

Here she took another paper from her pocket and read as follows :—

"'Don't sleep to-night. Move the couch in this room over the middle of the room, facing the door. Count three yards from the door and the same from the chimney.'

"I did not understand this at first, but I obeyed it to the letter.

"I soon discovered the benefit of it. I slept, as I told told you, upon the couch, and in the dead of the night I received a terrible explanation of the previous mystery.

"The couch moved!

"'Who's there?' I cried aloud, and I stamped upon the floor.

"This happily had the effect of silencing any one who thought of violence that night.

"But this was growing too horrible. I was dying by slow torments. The next day, when I arose unrefreshed from the couch, I prayed to the picture, and besought it in tears to aid me. My blessings, my eternal blessings, upon the hand which directed the answering solace to my fears. Another note came, which I have not now—I fear I have left it behind me—bidding me to be prepared to leave that night.

"Assistance was at hand, and I was to hope for the best.

"Oh! how my heart leapt with joy and hope! What sensations I experienced are beyond my power to describe. That night, when midnight had sounded, I heard a low grating noise in the room, and I became aware that I was not alone.

"This rather startled me, as I had securely barricaded the door as usual, and I not heard it attempted.

"'Come,' said a voice.

"'Is it the picture?' I demanded, scarcely knowing what to say.

"'It is. Come.'

"'I am ready,' said I, 'and may Heaven reward your goodness.'

"'Hush!'

"And a hand was held out in the darkness, and grasped mine.

"'Come with me fearlessly,' said the voice, in a whisper. 'I have proved how friendly I am towards you, have I not?'

"'You have.'

"'Then as we go along do not breathe a word—no matter what you may see or hear.'

"'Very well,' I said.

"Then he took me in the direction of the picture, and I had to squeeze through a narrow aperture in the wall.

"However, I felt confident that my conductor was true to me, and I proceeded fearlessly.

"We passed through some singular passages in that strange place."

"One word," said Rose. "Where is this house you have been to?"

"I don't know."

"Not know?" said her husband.

"No. You shall hear why I don't. Presently, after treading our way softly through no end of passages, we came to a little door, which my conductor opened with a key. Then oh! what pleasure, what delight! I found myself outside the house, breathing the fresh air of heaven, after such a cruel time."

"Poor Moggy."

"You must have suffered much," said Rose.

"I have," said Mrs. Davis, shaking her head and smiling through her tears. "But then it's all over now."

She gave a hand to her husband and to Rose—who were seated one upon each side of her—kissed them upon the cheek, and then resumed her story.

"When we got outside we crossed a garden, got into a main road, and—"

"You do not know where that is?" demanded Rose incredulously.

"No."

"Strange."

"Well, here a horse awaited us, tied to a hedge by the bridle. My conductor got on the horse and lifted me on behind him. He asked me where I wanted to be taken to.

"I told him, and he said that he would leave me somewhere near, but that he dared not go to the place. I thanked him again and again, and begged him to say how I could repay him for his goodness, and what do you think he replied?"

"Perhaps he wanted a kiss, Moggy," said her husband slyly.

"No—I'd have given him a hundred."

"Gad, would you, though?"

"Ay, Michael, dear. He was a good old man, so like father."

"But what did he answer?"

"That the only return he asked was my silence upon anything I knew which could compromise his superiors."

"Then he was a servant in the house?"

"I suppose so. He took me down to the moor yonder and left me. That's all."

And she began to cry a little more.

CHAPTER LII.

ROSE MEETS WITH AN ADVENTURE — THE AVERTED DANGER — DAVIS SHOWS FIGHT — ROSE'S DEPARTURE—HER NEW FRIENDS—THE CIRCUS—THE BRUTAL ACROBAT—A DISGRACEFUL SCENE — "SHAME!"— BLANCHE BOWERINI —A RIOT.

THE return home of the hostess of the roadside inn soon became known, and was talked about all over the district.

Rose Mortimer, of course, experienced the greatest happiness at this termination of such a fearful business —a business of which she was the innocent cause.

Not only upon her own account—and she was not a little relieved at it naturally—but upon the behalf of the disconsolate husband of the good-natured Mrs. Davis herself.

Inquiries and searches were instituted by Mr. Davis, notwithstanding the promise his wife had given to the old man who had rescued her at such an important epoch.

However, they failed to gain the slightest trace of the perpetrators of the outrage.

Our heroine communicated the whole of Mrs. Davis's narrative to Mr. Chowler, and they held a long consultation upon the point.

"My dear Miss Mortimer," said the little manager, "my opinion is that you are not safe here. You had better make a move."

"What, leave you?"

As Rose said this in a tone of regret—meaning simply the theatrical company, and not Chowler personally— the manager's left waistcoat thumped away in a very lively manner.

"You wouldn't like to leave us?" he demanded very artfully.

"No, no," said Rose. "Indeed I should not."

"That's very kind of you, my dear Miss Mortimer," said Chowler, with a killing glance.

"Not at all."

"Nay, but it is," persisted Chowler, "for after all—"

"All the company have been very kind to me," said our heroine.

"And you will take with you the regrets of all, I'm sure," said Chowler.

"I hope so, if I must leave."

"I believe that to be the only safe course."

"But I've no prospect."

"That delights me, my dear Miss Mortimer," said the manager quickly.

"Sir?"

"Allow me to repeat the obnoxious phrase, Miss Mortimer. It delights me, since it affords me the gratifying opportunity of serving you."

"Oh! indeed," said Rose smiling.

"Yes, by introduction—"

"To another manager?"

"Yes, to an intimate friend of mine—Wippum, the proprietor of Wippum's circus. You've heard of Wippum's circus?"

"No."

"Strange thing! Oh! it's a great affair, I can tell you. Wippum's a great man."

"I've no doubt," said Rose. "But do you think that he can find employment for me in a circus?"

"Not at all, not at all," said Chowler hastily. "I would not have you disgrace your talents so for worlds. But Wippum knows everybody. He's a share with Duncumbe, who has the Theatre Royal, and you'll be put on at once."

That night Rose was returning, after the performance was over, to the roadside inn, when an incident occurred which greatly tended to hasten her movements in the step she meditated.

The reader will remember that from the theatre (which was situated just in the town) she had to walk about a mile to the roadside inn at which she was staying.

On the way she had to pass the fatal garden of Sleeford House.

A shudder went through her frame as she glanced down the garden, and she passed on rather hurriedly.

As soon as she had passed she glanced back over her shoulder from time to time.

There was a fascination in the fatal spot which upon the present occasion did our heroine good service, as we shall see.

As she glanced around for the third time her eye encountered a lurking form creeping along under the shadow of the hedge.

Creeping after her!

Rose was at once upon the *qui vive* for danger, and she darted off at a run.

Presently she looked around, not hearing anything, and to her intense dismay perceived that the lurking individual was running in pursuit.

This she could not understand, as she did not hear the faintest sounds of his flight.

However, she could not hesitate for a second to olve this difficult problem.

Gathering up her skirts well in her hands, she started ff again, and flew along the road at a pace which must have made her pursuer despair.

Not so. He kept to it boldly.

He increased his speed wonderfully, and by rapid degrees lessened the distance which separated them.

Rose looked around presently, hearing the faint plodding of padded feet behind her, and found, to her infinite alarm, that he was close at hand.

With a scream, she started off faster than before.

The pursuer spoke not, but only increased his speed, and appeared to be quite fresh.

The house was approached, she was then in front of it, and, great Heavens ! the door was closed.

Up came the man.

"Help ! help ! oh ! help !" shrieked Rose in terrified accents.

The man came up with a dart, and was beside her.

He held a knife in his hand, and there was a deadly earnestness in his gestures as he advanced.

Rose shrieked with such a will that the house was alarmed upon the instant, and Rose was not a little relieved to hear the window above thrown open.

"Hullo !" shouted Mr. Davis. "Stand off, you blackguard, or, confound you, I'll blow you to atoms !"

He held his famous fowling-piece to his shoulder, and this effectually brought the silent pursuer of Rose Mortimer to a stand at a most critical moment.

The fellow looked as if he could have devoured poor Rose.

But there was the worthy little publican, with the fowling-piece to his shoulder, and looking so formidable that her pursuer was forced to content himself with a look of hatred.

They preserved the striking tableau in all its integrity for a minute perhaps.

Then the door was opened behind Rose by Mrs. Davis, who had, at the instigation of her husband, at once flown to open it.

Seeing his evidently destined prey likely to escape him, the ruffian was about to make a movement in that direction.

However, he thought better of it.

Glancing upward, his eye encountered that of the determined landlord, and he could see at a glance that the latter's fore-finger trembled nervously upon the trigger.

With a howl of disappointment, he turned tail, took to flight, and disappeared.

A shot was fired at his retreating figure by Mr. Davis, but more with the intention of hastening his movements than anything else.

Rose had recourse to the woman's first consolation, tears, after escaping from this danger, which had looked so serious for a while.

"How did this arise ?" demanded Mr. Davis.

But Rose had not the slightest idea.

She had only perceived that she was followed—that her steps were dogged after she had passed Sloeford House.

Where the individual who had caused her such a fright sprang from she had not the remotest conception.

She now touched upon her meditated departure, which was learnt by the good-natured couple with many expressions of serious and earnest regret.

Without entering into too many details (in pursuance of her understanding with Mr. Chowler), she told them that she had enemies who were secretly working her destruction.

The only means of avoiding this was to fly from that part of the country.

She even told them that she believed in all sincerity that the blow which had for a time deprived the road-side inn of its mistress had been a mistake, and was originally intended for herself.

They eagerly pressed her for explanations, but could elicit nothing further from her.

Rose had grown cautious and wary by the varied and numerous dangers which she had passed through thus early in the course of her strangely chequered career, and she would not entrust any one with the fatal secrets of the Sloeford family of which she and the theatrical manager were the sole possessors.

At least so she believed.

Whether they really were the course of our narrative will show.

Regrets and sad partings were exchanged between Rose and her friends.

The good-natured Mrs. Davis and her husband were exceedingly loth to part with their amiable lodger and companion.

At the theatre, too, even her enemies (and she had been long enough amongst them to gain some) were sorry to part with her.

Her good nature, lively habits, and cheerful manners had gained all their hearts, even when they had been resolutely set against her.

And with many little mementoes of the acquaintances she had gathered in her short stay at Mr. Chowler's theatre, and the kind wishes of a speedy re-union upon the part of all the company, she left.

Chowler, as he promised, provided her with several letters of introduction.

The most important of these, in Chowler's opinion, was that addressed to Mr. Wippum, the proprietor of the world-famed circus.

To him, accordingly, Rose Mortimer departed.

They made one great mistake in their manœuvres, however.

This was the publicity given to our heroine's next step.

Of course it went the round of the company, was talked over in the town, and just produced the effect which they were so very desirous of avoiding.

With a heavy heart and a light purse Rose started off.

A day's journey by coach brought our heroine to the town in which Mr. Wippum was staying.

Here her letter of introduction was presented, and Wippum was exceedingly gracious.

He volunteered at once to do all that lay in his power for his friend Chowler's introduction.

That night Rose was introduced to the manager of the local theatre, and forthwith engaged upon terms which could scarcely be considered liberal, even for a provincial theatre.

However, it was a subsistence, and Rose asked for no more.

The house at which she lodged was also the residence of some of the talents of the circus.

There was a family, comprising Signor Bowerini (an artist of unmistakeable cockney origin), his wife (a raw-boned Irish woman), and two girls, supposed to be Mademoiselles Bowerini.

According to a custom in the equestrian profession these two girls assumed the name and were supposed to be daughters of the signor, but were simply his apprentices.

The treatment which these two poor girls received at his hands was something so repulsive that Rose, under whose observation it frequently occurred, was utterly disgusted.

Threats accompanied every command, and something worse even at times.

Rose had not been many days here when she had the misfortune to create a bitter enemy in this cockney Italian acrobat.

The ruffian was not particular about correcting his girls in private, and one day Rose positively discovered him standing over one of the shrinking girls with a whip.

Her blood boiled of course to see a girl treated thus by her inhuman master, and she straightway interfered.

The abuse that Signor Bowerini lavished upon Rose Mortimer showed plainly enough that he was not at all refined, and savoured more of Bilingsgate than Florence, his avowed native place.

However, Rose had passed through too many trying ordeals in which personal violence had played a conspicuous part to quail before the bully.

She bearded the tiger in his lair, and brought off his victim.

It was kindly meant, but proved to be a lamentable mistake.

The poor girl told our heroine in secret that she had even suffered more severely since than before her interference.

One day shortly after this occurrence Rose obtained an interview with the girl. It was the eldest, against whom Signor Bowerini appeared to cherish the greatest spite, and Rose took to her own apartment.

"My poor Blanche," said our heroine, "why do you bear this brutality?"

"Alas! What can I do?"

"Do!" exclaimed Rose. "Why do you stay with a man who treats you thus vilely?"

"I am bound."

"Apprenticed?"

"Yes."

"Then cancel your indentures."

"I would willingly; but he will not."

"But have you tried him?"

"No."

"Then do so. Believe me, he cannot object. He dislikes you so much."

"Ah! You don't know him."

"Possibly."

"Nay, I'm sure you don't," said Blanche Bowerini, earnestly. "If you did, you would quite understand why I should not even dare to broach the subject."

"Dare?" iterated Rose, impatiently. "Have some courage, child.

"Hush!" said the girl with a shudder. "You don't know all that I suffer—all that I have suffered—by attempting to fly from this cruel man."

"Then appeal to a magistrate."

"He would slay me."

"Never fear that," said Rose. "He's a coward at heart, and would not dare to venture far for fear of the authorities."

"If I could only think so!"

"You must. Now listen. Before a month is over my engagement here will have terminated, and I shall move onwards. Then if you like to mix your fortunes with mine, you shall. We shall be some sort of protection for each other."

The girl pressed her hand in silent gratitude.

The tears started to her eyes, and she seized our heroine in her arms and embraced her tenderly.

"Thanks, thanks, my dear Miss Mortimer," she exclaimed. "You are indeed good."

"You must not think of that," said Rose. "Be true to yourself, and your difficulties are at an end."

"I will, I will."

"That's right."

"I must go now," she said, drying away her tears. "It will be an excuse for more cruelty if I am late in the ring."

"I'll come with you," said Rose. "I'm not in the first piece to night, and am not wanted at the theatre until half-past eight."

They had been so much engaged in this conversation of their future prospects that they had not observed the rapid flight of time.

The consequence was that it was a regular rush to the circus for Blanche Bowerini, and a scramble to get dressed (?) for a grand trick act which she had to perform.

Rose Mortimer, like all the professionals in the town, had the free *entrée* into the circus, and she placed herself in the nearest spot to the stable door, through which both artistes and horses had to pass.

This was that she might give a word of encouragement to Blanche Bowerini as she passed.

Such speed had the latter observed in her equestrian toilet that Rose had not been seated more than five minutes when the director of the circle announced in the ring the girl's appearance in these words:—

"Mademoiselle Blanche Bowerini will have the honour of appearing in her celebrated trick act entitled 'The Flight of the Arab's Bride.'"

Why it was thus entitled was not particularly clear.

However, this did not appear greatly to trouble the audience.

The name of the ill-used circus-girl was greeted by all with thunders of applause.

The whole tent shook again with the enthusiastic greetings of the hungry anticipators of a dangerous tour of the brilliant equestrienne.

The time was past for her *entrée*.

And now the audience began to murmur.

"Dear, dear," murmured one person, mentally. "She is late after all."

Not so.

Miss Blanche Bowerini was at the entrance then. Some one amongst the audience had descried the fluttering of her muslin skirts.

The fact was that the poor girl had encountered her brutal lord, who was quarrelling with her.

Words were exchanged, for Blanche, emboldened by the prospect of a release from his tyranny, had dared to retort.

Suddenly a scream was heard.

It was Blanche's voice.

"Ah!" she cried. "Unhand me! You will kill me!"

Then there was a struggle, and the girl tore herself from the signor, and dashed into the ring.

Signor Bowerini had now lost all presence of mind. He flew after her, and, heedless of the presence of the spectators, cut at the shrieking girl savagely with a horsewhip which he grasped.

"Help! help!"

"Bowerini!" cried the ring master.

"Stop that!" called several of the troupe.

But the signor's vicious blood was up, and he heard nothing.

He slashed most mercilessly at the shrieking Blanche.

And now the blood streamed down her face.

"Shame! shame!" cried the spectators.

The cries began with this, but soon grew worse.

Men jumped into the ring and flew to the rescue.

The audience flew from all parts, and Signor Bowerini got very roughly handled.

He struggled and struck out viciously, snarled, and even bit like a rabid dog.

But this was a misfortune for him.

The men caught him, dragging him in every direction, until every bone in his ruffianly body was dislocated.

Rose ran off to poor Blanche's assistance immediately.

This led to some curious and startling incidents in our heroine's career, of which we shall have to speak shortly.

For the present the further movements of Clara St. John claim our attention.

CHAPTER LIII.

CLARA ST. JOHN AGAIN — HER DIFFICULTIES SUBDUED — THE BLEEDING STEWARD — THE NOVEL ANGEL OF MERCY — A NARRATION OF BLOOD—FAMILY SECRETS—THE CONFESSION—CLARA'S DEFIANCE—"COUSIN, BEWARE!"

THE intelligent reader will remember that we parted company with Clara St. John at Sloeford House at a most critical juncture.

Having penetrated the secret passage which she had discovered communicating with her sleeping apartment, she had encountered a host of difficulties, against which it was almost impossible to struggle.

The poor old man was bleeding unto death in the passage.

The door of the panelling had closed, and she had no idea in which direction it was.

She searched around eagerly.

But it was all in vain.

In the meantime the groans of the old man grew fainter and fainter.

At length they were scarcely audible, but by their very indistinctness struck more terribly upon Clara's ear.

He must die.

It was cruelly hard.

For the first time, perhaps, in the course of her life, she felt inclined to do a charitable action, and now adverse fortune so fatally opposed its performance.

"I die, I die!" she could now hear the poor old man murmur in feeble accents. "This is hard indeed. Oh! inhuman monster!"

"I'll come to you," said Clara.

And she began to retrace her steps as rapidly as possible.

"Inhuman dog!" continued the old man. "He has slain me, as he slew my noble lord!"

Clara pricked up her ears at this.

It was something important to learn, and now another motive was added to her desire to preserve the old man's life.

With cautious strides she regained his side.

"I'm here, poor old man," she said, bending over his bleeding form.

"Bless you!"

"How are you now?"

"I don't think there's many minutes' life in me now."

"Say not so."

"Alas! it is too true. Have you the materials to tend my hurt?"

"I cannot find the outlet."

"I can show you—or I could," he added painfully, "if I were not beyond it now. At the end of the passage straight before you, a little above your head to the right, you will feel a round button projecting from the flat wood. Press it."

Ere he could conclude Clara was again upon her feet.

She hastily regained the end of the passage and searched eagerly for the knob.

Yes, he was correct. The knob was there—pressed, and the secret door revolved.

As she regained her own apartment there was a knock at the door.

Another second and she would have been too late.

"Who's there?"

"It is I," answered the voice of Lady Bellisle.

"Oh! come in, pray, my dear cousin," cried Clara warmly.

Her ladyship entered so calmly, with such a serene smile upon her pale face, that Clara was quite startled.

Was it possible that this woman, so young and beautiful, could be connected with the murder of the Earl of Sloeford, her own uncle?

Was it possible, moreover, that she had been so immediately connected with the assassination of the old man who lay weltering in his gore not many yards from that very chamber?

It would indeed seem scarcely possible.

Yet there was no mistaking the voice which Clara had overheard in such earnest conversation with the present Earl of Sloeford.

"My dear Clara," said her ladyship, with the sweetest of smiles, "I thought that you were sleeping."

"Yes," said Clara, with tolerable coolness. "Did you knock more than once?"

"Once. A hundred times—nay, perhaps a dozen times."

"Indeed?"

"Yes. Why, what have you done to your hand, Clara dear?"

Clara looked down, and discovered, to her no trifling confusion, that it was stained with the blood of the dying man.

The poor old man who lay panting for assistance in the secret passage.

The dying victim of the fair girl who stood talking so calmly to his would-be preserver.

"I—I don't know exactly," said Clara.

"It is bleeding."

"Yes. I remember I cut it."

"Remember?" iterated Lady Bellisle. "It would scarcely seem to be so serious as I should take it to be, then?"

"No, no, it is not serious. But for what special business do you come to me, my dear cousin?"

"Only to make a few arrangements for our trip, you know, dear."

"Yes; but can I beg you to put them off for the present?"

"Wherefore?"

"I am unwell."

"Indeed," said Lady Bellisle. "Is it possible, my dear? Can I be of any service?"

"No, I thank you."

"Will you have Doctor Sampson?"

"No, no; it is nothing. It will pass off immediately."

"Can I get you anything?"

"Will you send me some plaster for my hand by the girl?"

"Yes, certainly."

And with this the amiable Lady Bellisle ran off, to her cousin's no small relief.

"What a singular chance!" said Clara. "And so immediately after, too. She must have an iron nerve. She is a wonderful woman, and certainly deserves to succeed, unless I can spoil their fortune, and in truth there seems some appearance of it."

The servant came in with the plaster at this moment.

Clara desired her to bring a bowl of hot water, some lint, and one or two little etceteras.

She carefully closed and fastened her bedroom door, and provided herself with a light.

Then once more she penetrated the passage, which had proved such an eventful spot for her.

As she entered she was rather dismayed at not hearing the murmurs of the wounded man.

However, she lost not a minute in gaining his side.

He was perfectly still.

He lay motionless, pale, and ghastly, and in a perfect pool of his own gore.

It was a spectacle which must have unnerved any woman less determined than Clara St. John.

But now there was a purpose to serve.

And it was not a trifle which could deter her from carrying out an object upon which she had fixed her mind.

Without a moment's delay she proceeded to strip off the old man's coat and waistcoat.

The shirt beneath was saturated with the blood, so much had the sufferer lost.

The only difficulty which this created was to render the precise position of the wound more uncertain.

However, a sponge dipped in the bowl of water which she had provided soon got over this.

Then, with such rough surgery as she was capable of, the old man's wound was dressed.

Yet it remained exceedingly doubtful whether he would ever recover.

Clara could not venture to remove him to her own room for good, lest any of the servants should chance to see him.

She therefore kept the secret panel open as much as possible while she could remain in her chamber.

And with wondrous care and attention the poor old man was nursed slowly but surely towards recovery.

For ten days was she doubtful of achieving her object; but yet, in spite of the patient's age and the severity of his wounds, he struggled through it.

As he approached convalescence he made a long statement of the cause of the outrage which had been inflicted upon him by the Earl of Sloeford and his cousin Lady Bellisle.

This involved some strange and startling proofs of the murder of the late Earl of Sloeford.

It was with an immense satisfaction that Clara St. John took down the wounded man's deposition in writing.

When this was accomplished, however, the old man could not be persuaded to sign.

" No, no," he said. " I have lived in the family for fifty years, before my poor murdered lord's father came from France—before my late lord was brought to this country—and I would not have the last of an honoured race brought to public shame and disgrace."

" But it is not his disgrace we seek," urged Clara.

" Doubtless."

" Then why should you hesitate?"

" Because I would—pardon my brusqueness—learn your motives."

" Those are easily learnt," said Clara.

" Tell me them," said the old man, " and I will do as you wish."

" You know that the late earl was married young?"

" I do."

" And that he had an only child, who was stolen in a most extraordinary manner."

" By gipsies."

" Of course. The crime was laid to their account, but it is certain that gipsies had little ever to do with it."

" Indeed?"

" No. Who it was I am not at liberty to say. But this much I can tell you. The only child of the late earl yet lives, and it is in my power to restore it to its rightful possessions."

" It would be a noble act."

" The day will come when the act will be performed."

" Then I can hesitate no longer."

And with this a document was drawn up and duly signed by the old man.

A smile of triumph lit up the face of Clara St. John.

" Now beware, my good cousin!" she exclaimed, shaking the parchment.

CHAPTER LIV.

GRACE WALGRAVE — A SAD HISTORY — THE OLD STORY — A STRANGE REVELATION — FATAL SEQUEL — THE VISITOR — HIS DEMANDS — THREATS — THE PROMISE — GRACE WALGRAVE'S LONE RAMBLE — FATAL OMENS.

WE shift the scene again.

And now we find ourselves in the drawing-room of one of the largest houses in a fashionable square in the west end of London.

The centre of rank and fashion.

This mansion belongs to one of the oldest families in the United Kingdom — an honourable house of spotless reputation.

But a proverb for the poor is a proverb for the rich.

Every house has its skeleton, and a mansion after all is but a large house.

Walgrave House has its skeleton too, but being in a mansion, it is proportionately large, proportionately grave and awful.

A young and lovely girl walks in silent misery up and down the drawing-room of Walgrave House.

Her cheek is pale.

Her eyes red and dim with weeping.

Her heart is bowed down with grief, the most trying and severe.

Her soul is beat to the very earth with shame.

A load of guilt is upon this creature of nineteen summers.

It is the old story, with some startling addenda.

She has loved not wisely, but too well.

The unhappy but confiding girl has put her trust in one who has proved false to the troth he has plighted.

This is her history, in as few brief words as possible.

Whilst on a visit to a relation of somewhat humbler station than her own, in a rural district, she formed an attachment to a worthless fellow of prepossessing appearance and seductive manners.

The rest is left to the imagination of the reader.

The libertine who gained this fair and gentle creature's affections knew not of her noble birth and high expectations, and, haplessly for both himself and his victim, he fled from the spot as soon as his villainous designs were accomplished.

But retribution has already been taken upon behalf of the too confiding Grace Walgrave.

The libertine has already met a coward and a bully's grave.

This we have already narrated.

By a singular coincidence, the seducer of the nobly-born girl was none other than the detected cheat, the frustrated poisoner, Major Strangeways, alias Captain Roper, of our early narrative.

Had the major but known of the position of his victim, all would have been otherwise.

But 'tis thus ever that the villainous who have but cunning, without wit to back it, overreach themselves.

Major Strangeways did not, of course, imagine for an instant that there was anything very great in the family of the fair Grace, for, wishing to be loved for herself alone, she had carefully suppressed her history from her lover's ears.

Had Major Strangeways but known that the girl was the daughter of a coronet, all would have been different.

Poor artless loving Grace Walgrave! She was not versed in wordly ways.

She was not fit to cope with the villainy that walks abroad, holding aloft its brazen front in the pure face of day.

One false step, one trifling error—yet scarcely an

error, for it grew out of too much love, love misplaced it is true—and Grace Walgrave had fallen.

Fallen beyond redemption.

A child was born to her.

A child of sin.

The living witness of its mother's shame, its viler father's infamy.

How the unhappy mother disposed of her innocent babe we have already had occasion to relate.

The digging of the grave in the garden at night will be remembered.

The violent end of the officer of the law who watched is likewise known.

Thus Grace Walgrave became the partner of one of our leading personages in a course of crime which drove her to phrenzy, whilst it but formed a solitary chapter in the life of her devilish adviser.

He knew, too, that in his hellish cunning he secured her.

She was his, body and soul.

*   *   *   *   *   *

Grace Walgrave paced her drawing-room with short rapid strides.

Her heart is full to bursting.

Her soul is bowed even to the ground with the weight of guilt upon it.

Suddenly a servant knocks.

But Grace Walgrave is too pre-occupied to hear this.

The knock is repeated thrice.

But still Grace Walgrave is so buried in the contemplation of her own hideous torturing reveries that she heeds nothing.

Then a servant enters.

"I beg your pardon, my lady," said the man. "You are wanted."

Grace Walgrave paused suddenly.

Stared at the servant inquiringly, evidently not having heard what he had said the first time.

"A gentleman wants to see you, my lady."

"Oh!"

"Yes. Can I show him in?"

"Yes, yes, yes."

The servant feels uncomfortable and ill at ease in the presence of his mistress, and is perfectly satisfied with the dreamy answer she has given him.

Then the visitor is ushered in.

It proves to be a man of dwarfish stature enveloped in a long cloak and high-crowned felt hat, which shades his unprepossessing countenance.

In a word, Mermet.

The Arab necromancer enters, with a profound bow.

Then he silently turns to the door, carefully closes it, turns the key, but leaves it in the lock, that any eavesdroppers may find their task more difficult.

Then he removes his cloak, places it upon the table, and steps up to the pre-occupied Grace Walgrave.

"My lady."

Grace Walgrave started as if stung by a serpent.

Glanced up for the first time, and perceived that she was no longer alone.

"What is it?" she began, when she perceived who her visitor was.

Then a shriek burst from her.

"What do you want here?" she demanded, in the greatest alarm.

"My dear lady," said Mermet in the purist English, "don't alarm yourself unnecessarily I beseech you."

"What do you want here? Answer me I command you."

"Command?"

"Ay, that was my word."

"Well, since you command, I may tell you that I want money."

"By Heavens! I thought it," exclaimed the girl with a start.

"Which shows a singular precision of judgment," sneered Mermet.

"Silence, dog!"

The Arab winced.

"Madam," said he in a low menacing tone, "I'd have you beware."

"Of what?"

"Of me."

"And for what, forsooth?"

"Simply that I am of a revengeful nature!"

"And what care I for your revenge, man?" she demanded.

"Much."

"'Tis false."

"I hold your life in my hands."

"Take it, fool!" she added, with bitter emphasis. "You cannot see that the greatest boon you could confer upon an unhappy heartbroken wretch would be to be slay her."

"But how?"

"No matter how."

"There is one death you would find objectionable I think."

"Not one."

"Pardon me."

"Not one, by Heaven! Death must at least bring oblivion."

"Is that your faith?"

"Ay. Since the whole fear I have is of my fellow-man. I know well that in the eyes of Heaven I am more sinned against than sinning. I tell you that since that night, which I can allude to no clearer, my eyes are opened."

"Indeed?"

"Ay, indeed."

"To what, pray?"

"To everything. To you, amongst the rest of my unhappy errors."

"Humph! Then since you admit that I am an error, as you call it, you must be at least prepared to pay the piper—excuse the vulgarity—for your mistakes."

"You come to force money from me by threats and extortion."

"These are harsh words."

"Begone, sirrah! I tell you you will get no recompense from me."

"Stay, stay. You forget yourself, my lady. Pray remember, amongst other things, that it is in my power to produce the only effect you dread in this life."

"What is that?"

"Disgrace."

"What mean you?"

"That unless my demands are acceded to before to-morrow morning, your shame shall find itself into print, and shall be circulated most industriously amongst your grand connections before to-morrow night has set in."

This was fearful.

The effects of the wizard's words were so terrifying that the unhappy girl trembled with fear and apprehension.

"No, no!" she muttered. "Impossible. I cannot bear that."

"I thought not," said Mermet, maliciously grinning.

"What do you want?"

"Money."

"How much?"

"Five thousand pounds!"

Miss Grace Walgrave was amazed at the magnitude of the necromancer's demand.

"What?"

[THE LIBERTINE'S DEATH.]

"Five thousand pounds," repeated the Arab, "to begin with."

The poor girl appeared for an instant stunned by the blow which had fallen upon her.

She clasped her hands around her throbing brow.

She stood then in silence, meditating upon the money demanded.

Presently she looked up and spoke.

Her face now looked determined—an expression which caused the necromancer some trifling uneasiness.

"Well?" he demanded, anxiously.

"You shall have it."

Mermet breathed a sigh of the deepest relief.

"Ah! I thought so."

"I will send you a draft to-night."

"It won't do. I must have it now."

"You cannot."

"I will."

In an instant all the innate dignity of Miss Walgrave flew to her rescue.

She drew herself up to her full height, and in a haughty voice bade the Arab begone.

There was a certain something in her tone which caused Mermet to move instinctively towards the door.

"If you will not wait until you hear from me," said Miss Walgrave, "then do your worst. I will meet you no further."

No. 18.

The necromancer bit his nether lip until it started with blood.

But he dared not to press his point further.

He felt that he had now to deal with a desperate woman, and that by pushing her too far it was just possible that he would overreach himself.

"Well, well, my lady," he said. "As your ladyship pleases."

"Of course it is."

"I shall await the money at home."

"I will send to you within an hour."

"A draft for five thousand pounds, and at sight if you please."

"I will say no more."

"But—"

"Begone."

There was a tone of command here which there was no resisting.

The change in the demeanour of the trembling girl was so remarkable that the necromancer was quite startled.

So Mermet the Arab necromancer took his departure.

As soon as he was gone Grace Walgrave's momentary courage gave way.

She had no dignity to support her now.

She seated herself at a writing table and wrote off two long messages.

This done, she addressed them and sent them off by a servant.

Then she repaired to her dressing-room and made some hasty change in her dress and sallied forth.

It was night.

Presently when she had arrived in a dark and deserted street she took something from the bosom of her dress and pressed it passionately to her lips.

It was an infant's shoe.

The sight of this tiny object appeared momentarily to unnerve the poor girl.

She burst into a passionate flood of tears.

"My own sweet babe?" she murmured, as she gazed upwards through her tear-dimmed eyes, "we shall meet again, where I may claim you in life, sweet angel!"

An individual entered the street from the opposite side, and was approaching in her direction.

With a frightened gesture she concealed the infant's shoe and hurried on, panting with the haste she was observing in her progress.

* * * * *

Grace Walgrave has surely some dread purpose in this lonely ramble.

Some dire intent of mischief must now fill her thoughts.

Unhappy girl!

CHAPTER LV.

PLEASANT ANTICIPATIONS—AN ALARMING LETTER —WALGRAVE HOUSE AGAIN—WATERLOO BRIDGE —THE SUICIDE—CAN THEY SAVE HER?—THE BOAT CAPSIZED—A PERILOUS SITUATION.

MERMET the Arab was seated in his chamber of magic and mystery.

A small book lay open before him, in which he was writing hieroglyphic memoranda.

By his eager gestures it would appear that he was greatly interested in his task.

The fact was, that the necromancer was adding up the gains of the past week, and the result as yet appeared highly satisfactory.

"Humph!" he muttered, "it is after all a much more thriving trade than one would suppose. That Walgrave business will swell the amount very nicely.

A dozen such windfalls and I should retire from the business, although I must fain confess that I rather like the sort of life I lead now, since that accursed chance has so misshapen this hideous form. It pleases me to see the fools so gulled—to see how the flimsiest deception takes with these shallow-pated Londoners. Grace Walgrave is booked for five thousand pounds, and I may yet count upon her for at least as much more. Poor creature! it is really most amusing to see how readily she falls into the little pit I have so carelessly dug for her."

As he spoke these words a chuckle of satisfaction rattled in his throat, and he looked quite animated.

There was a knock.

"Enter."

The Arab domestic of the necromancer made his appearance.

"A letter, sahib," he said.

The Arab, his master, took the missive and dismissed the man.

"From whom, I wonder," he said.

He opened the letter and read it through in silence.

As he went on a sudden change came over his countenance.

The expression of satisfaction vanished like magic.

He grew serious and bit his lip until the blood came.

"Confound it!" he muttered. "If this should fail me, I am indeed lost beyond all redemption. I must see to it. It begins to look black, and it seems to me that I was congratulating myself too early upon my success. Let me read."

He went through the letter again.

It ran thus:—

"*Ere you receive this the writer will be beyond your reach. You have too soon declared your real character, and the unhappy and unguarded girl breathes defiance in your teeth. Your deception has met with its just reward. Beware, too, in future, for such damning evidence is left behind of your culpability that it will go hard with you should justice ever lay its avenging hand upon you. And this must come, believe me. Sooner or later the just retribution of Providence will overtake you. You will fall then, and no earthly power, no cunning, can save you!*
"*G. W.*"

It is not to be wondered at that the necromancer was a little bit flustered by this alarming epistle.

The little colour which he had in his cheek deserted it, and it was clear that he was in no trifling embarrasment.

He gradually got to think more calmly over it.

Then he rang the bell, and the ever-ready Ahmet appeared.

"Sahib?" said he.

"My cloak."

"Yes, sahib."

"My hat. Now call me a cab."

"Yes, sahib."

Mermet hobbled down the stairs and got into the cab.

"Walgrave House," said the Arab.

"Yes, sir."

Arrived at the residence of the unhappy Grace Walgrave, Mermet sprang out of the cab with surprising agility.

A peal at the bell and a noisy rat-tat brought a lazy-looking flunkey in a gorgeous livery to the door.

"Miss Grace Walgrave?"

"Gone out," said the menial, as if doing Mermet the greatest personal service.

"Where?"

The servant looked most supremely astonished at the question.

"Don't know," he said, staring rudely.

"How long since?" demanded Mermet, far too occupied to heed the insolent demeanour of the fellow.

"I can't say, my friend," said the flunkey, superciliously.

"Your friend?" iterated Mermet. "Whatever is the idiot talking about?"

This brought John Thomas a little nearer to his natural level.

"Answer my question, you painted jackanapes!" exclaimed the necromancer. "Where has your mistress gone to?"

"I, I can't say, sir. She went out about ten minutes since."

"Not more?"

"No, sir."

"And you don't know if she went right or left? Answer me, fellow. I tell you that I have most important business with her."

John Thomas was now really very much alarmed.

Some great folks, he knew by experience, were very peculiar individuals in appearance.

The necromancer might therefore be even a duke or a marquis. Who could say?

Then upon Mermet further assuring the fellow that he came by appointment, and had instructions in a letter (which he here produced) to ascertain in which direction she had gone and follow with all speed,

"Well, sir," replied the domestic, "I know that Miss Walgrave left in the carriage not more than five minutes since."

"Five minutes?"

"Yes, sir."

"In which direction?"

"Can't say, sir."

"Fool!" exclaimed the Arab, in great wrath. "Can't you say if she went right or left, north or south."

"Yes, sure, she went that way," said the man, now ready to kiss the necromancer's boots, in humility.

Just at this juncture a splendid equipage, high upon the smoothest of springs, came rattling along the square.

"Here is our carriage," said the footman. "Miss Walgrave's back."

"That's fortunate."

The carriage was passing the house when the servant at the door stopped it.

"James."

"Yes," answered the coachman.

"Where did you leave Miss Walgrave?"

"Near Covent Garden."

"Do you know which way she intended going after you left her?" asked Mermet.

"No, sir."

"You quitted her at the market?"

"Close by, sir."

"What do you mean by that?"

"In one of the streets leading into the Strand."

"Ah!"

"Wellington Street, I think, sir."

"And was Miss Walgrave going in the direction of the Strand?"

"Yes, sir."

"Good."

And with no more acknowledgement of the servant's services than this, the little necromancer hobbled off.

He was in the cab again in an instant.

"Waterloo Bridge," he shouted to the driver through the little trap in the roof.

"Yes, sir."

"And double fare if you double your speed."

"Yes, sir."

The cabman whipped up his horse and they flew over the ground in a way which would have brought the jarvey into trouble with the police, had he been noticed by those diligent officials.

A few minutes at this sparkling rate sufficed to bring them to Waterloo Bridge.

As they passed through the toll Mermet tossed a shilling to the toll-keeper, and they drove on without waiting for change.

Mermet stretched over the doors, and drew himself up by the splash-board.

"What was that?"

Something white upon the left parapet of the bridge caught his eye.

He stretched eagerly forward.

Yes. There was a something there which most terribly confirmed some doubts which the Arab had previously entertained.

He saw the white skirts of a woman flutter for an instant upon the stone parapet.

Then disappear.

"Stop! stop!" shouted Mermet.

The cabman pulled up with such suddenness that the horse was thrown almost upon its haunches and Mermet was dashed back upon the seat.

Springing up, however, he jumped from the cab and dashed up to the spot.

His lameness seemed to disappear almost entirely with the necessity for active movements.

He clawed hold of the stone abutment and drew himself up.

Leant eagerly over.

All that he could now see in the dim light was that there was a faint sign beneath of some object having fallen into the water.

The water was but very little agitated, and the only evidences to confirm the necromancer's suspicions were the expanding circles upon the surface.

He rushed back to the cab.

"What's the matter, sir?" demanded the astonished jarvey.

"Woman jumped over the bridge," answered the necromancer.

"Indeed, sir?"

"Yes—back again—drive for your life! We must see what's to be done."

"Yes, sir."

The cab flew back again.

It pulled up short by the steps, and Mermet was out and galloping down before an eye could wink.

"Boat! boat!" he shouted. "Boat ahoy!"

But some little delay was here occasioned, for there were no watermen about at that hour.

Mermet must have despaired now of attaining his object had there not chanced to be two men upon the pier whose attention had been attracted by the falling of the unfortunate suicide.

"Hi!" shouted the Arab. "Hi—a boat ahoy!"

"Hullo!" answered one of the men.

"A boat—come quickly!" shouted Mermet, all excitement. "A woman has thrown herself off the bridge."

"Blessed if I didn't think so," said one of the men.

As he spoke he ran up, and, springing over a handrail, ran to the shore.

Here were two or three boats, and one of them he proceeded to let loose with all possible speed.

Mermet jumped in, and the fellow, shoving off, sprang in after him.

He plied his oars with the skill of an experienced rower, and they ploughed through the muddy waters of the Thames with great rapidity.

"It's more than three minutes ago," said the fellow, throwing in a word or two between each stroke.

"What of that!"

"She's a dead 'un now, for a thousand pounds, your honour."

"Pshaw ! Pull away, and there may yet be a chance of saving her."

"It's a warm job, and I count on your honour's generosity."

"Of course, of course," answered the Arab. Half a crown if we fail—five pounds if you succeed in saving her life."

"Five pounds ?"

"Yes."

"Down ?"

"Yes."

Without another word the boatman bent double, burying his oars deep in the water, and pulled with such a will that the boat appeared to be lifted clean out of the water.

"Stay," said Mermet. "This should be about the spot."

"Yes, sir."

"What's that ?"

"Oh ! that's nothing but a buoy."

"I don't mean that. There's something white—just there."

"I see."

He turned round and pulled sharply to the spot.

They found it to be simply a piece of light silk clinging to the chain of the buoy to which the boatman had at first presumed his fare to be alluding.

"Ah !" cried the necromancer. "This is something like evidence."

"What's that, sir ?"

But Mermet was too much engrossed by his own thoughts to notice what the boatman said to him.

"Yes, yes !" he continued. "This is indeed hers. I have seen her wear such a dress as this. There now is no doubt."

He was here startled into his presence of mind by a remark of the boatman.

"What, sir ! Do you know the young party as jumped overboard ?"

"Oh ! What ? No, no. I was merely passing in a cab over the bridge, and I saw—but no matter for that—see if we can recover the body which has disappeared about here."

"If she fell athwart that chain, sir, she's as good as smashed."

Mermet did not appear at all troubled about the suicide's sufferings.

It was only her death which could spoil her entirely!

"What's that ?"

Both spoke together.

Both had perceived some dark object rise slowly to the surface of the water upon the other side of the buoy.

It was a human head.

"'Tis she !"

"By Heaven it is !"

They spoke in hoarse hasty whispers now.

The presence of death generally awes the most callous.

It was but an instant that the head—that alarming token of the suicide's grave—appeared.

Then it was gone again.

For a second the boatman paused irresolutely.

He was as startled as if he had seen some apparition.

Mermet saw with an eagle glance the fellow's indecision, and hastened to remove it.

"Twenty pounds if she is saved !" he ejaculated.

"I'm after her !" cried the boatman, in the same undertone.

Hastily shipping his oars, he sprang over the boat's side, and disappeared with a plunge beneath the muddy waters.

But now a misfortune occurred to the necromancer. The boat, so suddenly released of its burthen, rocked ominously.

Mermet, rather startled, hastily endeavoured to turn it by jumping to the other side, and his weight, added to the side of the boat when the reaction of the rocking upon that side was already so great, caused it to capsize altogether.

The next instant the necromancer was scrambling in the water, and looked in great danger.

"Help ! help !" he cried. "I drown ! Help ! help !"

And now matters look serious.

Three human souls are struggling in the Thames, and it appears more than doubtful if either will be saved !

We shall see.

———

CHAPTER LVI.

CLARA'S SEARCHES — A NEW DISCOVERY — A FORMER MYSTERY EXPLAINED—THE SUBTERRANEAN PASSAGE — THE DEATH CHAMBER — FAMILY RECORDS — THE TRAIL OF BLOOD — THE SECRET DRAWER—STILL ON THE TRAIL—THE SCREEN—THE RECESS—THE WRITING ON THE WALL—THE ASSASSIN'S NAME—CONCLUSIVE EVIDENCE.

QUITTING Mermet the Arab necromancer for a while at this critical juncture, we must take a further glance at the movements of Clara St. John at Sloeford House.

By slow degrees the old servant recovered.

The hurt he had received was serious, yet by continued care and unremitting attention upon the part of his self-elected nurse, Clara St. John, he proceeded by slow yet none the less sure degrees towards convalescence.

The Earl of Sloeford and his cousin, Lady Bellisle, had departed.

Clara St. John and her new spouse, Edgar Deville, reigned supreme in Sloeford House.

The old steward was kept out of the way, and Clara was not a little surprised at the indifference manifested by the household as to his disappearance.

She took an opportunity, therefore, of questioning one of the servants upon the matter.

Clara was of course far too smart to put a question of this nature plainly to any one. She contrived to lead the servant to it naturally, and then professed ignorance of the person of the old steward even.

"I think that I've missed somebody, Parker," she began.

"Missed, miss? Whom do you mean ?"

"One of the servants."

"Oh ! you mean old Martin, perhaps."

"Ah ! perhaps."

"Oh ! he's gone away. My lady sent him off to Scotland for the benefit of his health. He's been in a very bad way ever since my lord, the late earl, was found murdered in his bed. It seemed to shake him so, and—"

"But I don't really know of whom you speak, Parker," said Clara St. John, with a well-feigned look of wonder.

"Of old Martin the steward."

"Steward? Oh ! no, I mean a gardener—a young man with light hair."

"Oh ! I know, miss. You mean Brock. Red whiskers, ain't he, miss ? Robert calls 'em ' Brockley sprouts '—ha, ha !"

Clara cut the chatterer short.

This conversation, however, led her to entertain a respect for the boldnes with which her two murderous cousins carried out their desperate plots and assassinations—

Here was a startling butchery committed — an old man slain to all intents and purposes but for the timely aid which Clara St. John had arrived by such a singular chance to proffer.

He would inevitably have perished, and who would have been the wiser?

It was a fearful thing to think of.

How many secret crimes may thus have been hushed up from the eyes of justice it is impossible to imagine.

Clara St. John had now fully made up her mind upon a course of action.

She resolved to take elaborate notes—memoranda as authentic as lay in her power to obtain—of the particulars of the tragedy which had so startled all the fashionable world.

The sudden and awful end of the Earl of Sloeford had been freely commented upon by the whole of the metropolitan press.

The local organs were silent upon the strange and mysterious crime.

This is not to be wondered at, for the present earl was the most influential and powerful nobleman in the county.

His lordship was also known to be the greatest patron the local editors possessed, a fact which says much in itself.

However, this very silence was the subject for the commentaries of the busy world.

The scandal-loving people of the Sloeford district declared that it looked as if some one in a high position had locked the editors' mouths with a golden key.

Others did not scruple to aver that Mr. Josiah M'Scribbler, the Scotch editor of the "Sloeford Pitcher In," had been summoned privately to "the house" to receive instructions.

Be this as it may, it showed that, however prolific the gold of the Sloefords was, it could not silence every babbler.

Clara St. John had not established her new note-book upon the great Sloeford mystery a week when an incident occurred which caused her to think that it was now a pretty clear case.

It happened thus.

Since her memorable exploration of the secret passage from her own chamber she had not ceased to ramble about the old house.

The nooks and crevices she found it is impossible to enumerate.

Suffice it to say, therefore, that, amongst other valuable memoranda, she had to jot down the discovery of a subterranean communication with the hall from the garden.

The entrance was concealed by some thickly-grown lilac trees, which served to hide from the visitors to that part of the grounds a spot which was used by the gardeners as a rubbish mound.

This, then, was the spot where Mr. Chowler and Rose Mortimer upon the memorable night of the garden had lost sight of the masked intruder.

It was a dark subterranean passage, as we have said; yet the undaunted woman boldly ventured forward.

Her purpose was so resolutely fixed that no earthly obstacle could deter her.

Springs concealed in out-of-the-way spots no longer could elude the persevering schemer's vigilance.

Not any difficulty, however great, could now put her from the object of her protracted stay in the house of crime.

She pressed her way through the subterranean passage.

Found two exits from it.

One of them led to the hall of Sloeford House.

The other opened into a bedchamber.

In an instant Clara St. John felt that she had achieved by accident what all her policy had failed previously to accomplish.

Since the murder of the late earl this apartment—which had been occupied by the head of the Sloeford family ever since the house was built—had not been opened.

The disposition of the furniture remained the same in every respect, and indeed it was said that the very linen upon the bed remained unchanged.

Clara St. John had noticed this particular in her book, and she eagerly made up to the death couch of the slaughtered nobleman as a preliminary step.

Yes, there was a terrible confirmation of the rumour.

The life-blood of the murdered man still stained the bedclothes.

Clara's satisfaction at this was unbounded.

"This is indeed something," she muttered. "And if I do not discover anything worthy of jotting down, then am I vastly mistaken."

As she spoke even she had commenced the search.

A glance at the drawers and a little carved cabinet, and their disordered condition showed clearly enough that something besides the atrocious murder even had occurred there.

To her it was as clear as noontide that some documents or valuables had been abstracted.

Perhaps valuables, to give a greater colour to the prevalent idea that the assassination was the work of robbers.

Perhaps a document of importance had been abstracted—a will even!

As this idea occurred to her she looked up triumphantly.

"I have it!" she ejaculated. "The will! the will! Fool that I was before! It is clear as possible now that there has been some foul play at work, for the old earl was too much incensed against that scheming woman to leave her a sou. Of that I now feel assured. Be mine the hand to bring such evidence to bear upon this as shall bring both my Lady Bellisle and Mr. Spencer Bellisle under my thumb. The mistress of Sloeford House will yet be Clara St. John!"

The search was continued.

Presently she came upon a whole nest of family documents fastened together by the professional-looking red tape.

These were eagerly opened and scanned by Clara.

The first was a letter of one Edgar Bellisle to a young wife Rosalia.

It ran thus:—

"My dear wife,—The shock has at length arrived, and I am stricken down with grief. The earl has discovered our union, and I have just had an interview with him, in which he has threatened not alone to discard me from my family, his house, and his fortune, but to curse me, Rosalia, if I do not desert you. Rosalia, my own my only love, we must fly from the country to the sunny south, and the storm of my harsh father's anger may spend its fury in the lapse of years. I hasten to impart this to you, my love, that you may lose no time in your preparations for our immediate departure. Forgive me if I distress you, but you must share every secret of my inmost soul, every joy, every sorrow. I fain would spare them you, but I cannot. The only grief I feel about our departure is caused by your own bad health, and the fear that our child may not be a native of its parents' land. To-morrow, dearest Rosalia, I shall be with you.
"EDGAR BELLISLE."

Clara started as she read through this letter, dated many years previously.

"The late earl was married, then," she said musingly. "Not only married, but I suppose had issue by this marriage. I must see into this. My haughty cousin Spencer must look to himself now, for I much fear if his title to the earldom may not be questionable. In any case I shall secure this letter. Information shall be taken upon the matter, and I will consult old Martin when he shall be in a fit condition. He was the friend and confidant of his master, and I doubt not that he shared some portion at least of this secret with him."

The letter was put aside with other scraps which Clara had collected, and the search was once more resumed.

In her rambles over the death chamber the next thing which caught her eye was a deep blood stain upon the right side of the bed.

It had probably passed unnoticed by less interested persons than Clara St. John.

It was in a part of the room farthest from the window, and the bed threw a dark shadow upon the floor, covering the fatal evidences of the assassination.

"The earl must have leant over here after he was struck," said Clara.

She stooped down to examine it closer, and found that the stains proceeded further along.

There was one inference to be drawn from this.

The murdered man had doubtless struggled from his bed after the assassins had left the chamber, and their victim for dead—struggled along, leaving a track of his life-blood as he went.

But for what purpose?

This she determined to discover.

She observed the blood ceased, and collected in larger quantities by the foot of the little carved cabinet.

This, therefore, became the object of her searches at once.

The closest scrutiny at length discovered to her that a bead moulding at the bottom of this cabinet was nothing less than the front of a flat shallow drawer.

The very simplicity of the contrivance foiled all attempts at discovery, which was made in the present case by pure accident.

Clara eagerly opened the drawer.

The first object which caught her eye was a packet tied with a ribbon, which was blood-stained.

It had been put there by the dying earl at his last moments.

Bold as this woman was, courageous and undaunted in her criminal path through life, she could not repress a shudder of horror as she thought of the death throes of the last person who had touched that packet.

As she turned from the drawer, stooping still to the ground, she saw that the train of blood did not even cease there.

She followed it out.

It led to the side of the wall, a narrow recess, the top of which was filled by the portrait of a young and beautiful girl.

This was some eight or ten paces distant from the bedside.

The earl must then have been much stronger than his assassins had imagined when they left him.

Was it not possible that he had had the time to leave some further evidence of the guilt of his murderers?

He had.

The most conclusive.

Evidence the most damning.

Clara paused by the recess and examined it with great eagerness.

But nothing could she discern.

A Chinese folding screen—made on the English fashion—leant against the wall.

Clara had looked all around, and failed to discover anything, when she moved the screen to examine the ingenious work upon it more closely.

Suddenly her eye lighted upon the wall thus laid bare.

An exclamation of horror burst from her in spite of herself.

In large red letters, traced in human gore, and doubtless by the hand of the dying earl, were written these words :—

"SPENCER BELLISLE MY MURDERER !
"EDGAR BELLISLE,
"EARL OF SLOEFORD."

CHAPTER LVII.

MERMET'S ESCAPE — DANGERS—THE RESCUE—THREE HUMAN CORPSES—GRACE WALGRAVE—DEATH — THE WATERMAN—THREATS—A BOLD STROKE FOR SAFETY—MERMET DEFEATED—A RASH SPEECH—THE WATERMAN'S TOMB AND THE SUICIDE'S GRAVE.

WHERE is Mermet the Arab necromancer all this time?

We left him struggling in the water and nearly drowned.

Flying to the rescue of the would-be suicide, he had chanced to upset the boat, and all appeared lost now.

The waterman had seen the body of the drowning girl rise to the surface of the water for the third time, and had boldly jumped in to her rescue.

It was a tough struggle, but at length the hardy waterman had succeeded in dragging the body to the top of the water, and he struck out with something less of fervour than at first.

But arrived near the boat, he was not a little terrified to find it capsized.

The necromancer struggled violently with the keel of the boat, but all he could do was to keep himself above water.

At length he got a better purchase as a wave came rolling along and aided his purpose.

Over went the boat and under went Mermet.

Down, down, till it appeared as if he had reached the bottom.

But he rose again, struggling frantically with the water.

He clutched at the edge of the boat, which had now righted itself, and dragged himself up.

At first he was half blinded by the water, but as he rose above the side of the boat his vision grew clearer, and he saw that a human form hung with equal desperation to the other side.

With catlike agility the half-drowned necromancer scrambled into the boat.

He thought not now of his danger, but, leaning eagerly forward, caught hold of the hand of the drowning man.

The hand was caught immediately in a deadly tight clutch, and a weight hung upon the necromancer, which threatened to drag him over into the water.

"You've—got—the girl?" he gasped, as he struggled violently.

"Ye—es."

A faint and futile effort to nod accompanied these words.

He was well nigh exhausted, and a few seconds more would have rendered his chance of salvation highly doubtful.

But the necromancer had a fortune at stake.

With the most frantic struggles, he at length succeeded in dragging up the half-drowned man.

The form of a woman, suspiciously still, hung upon his left arm.

The face, though pale and saturated with the filthy water of our metropolitan river, was yet plainly beautiful.

It needed no conjuror's eye to recognise upon the first glance the beauteous countenance of Miss Grace Walgrave.

As soon as her body appeared by the boat's side the necromancer relinquished his hold of the waterman and clutched at the body of Grace Walgrave.

Fortunately for the former, he had yet sufficient power to drag himself up as soon as he was relieved from the distressing burthen which had so nearly dragged him to the grave.

"Saved! saved!" said Mermet, triumphantly, as he dragged in the body.

And he fell back powerless.

"Saved!" echoed the waterman, faintly scrambling into the boat.

And he could do no more.

Like Mermet, he sank back exhausted, fainting, and senseless.

There they lay, the three individuals whom we left struggling in the water.

Pale and motionless.

All equally deathlike in appearance.

All as helpless as newly-born babes.

It is a question if any of the three will survive.

It is impossible to see which of the three has the most life.

And this endures for a terribly long time.

So long that an observer, if any had been there, would have thought them dead to all intents and purposes.

But it is not so.

This the reader will judge by his dwelling so long upon this portion of our narrative.

By slow degrees the Arab recovered consciousness.

His immersion in the water had not been so lengthy as that of the two other occupants of the boat.

When he had recovered sufficiently to be aware of what was passing around him he began to turn his attention to the waterman and the rescued Grace Walgrave.

The latter lay still as death.

Was it death?

The former began to show signs of returning animation.

But little interest did the necromancer appear to take in his recovery.

His whole attention was devoted to the girl.

With wonderful perseverance he kept beside her, endeavouring by such scanty means as were at his disposal then to restore her to life.

Whilst thus engaged the waterman recovered himself perfectly and sat up.

But he was quite unnoticed by the Arab, so engrossed was the latter with his attentions to Grace Walgrave.

"That was a narrow squeak!" said the waterman presently.

But Mermet heard him not.

He still kept on in his endeavours to restore animation in the motionless body of the suicide.

The earnestness with which he applied himself to the task so struck the waterman that without more ado he joined in it.

At length their efforts were rewarded with something like success.

The girl heaved a deep-drawn sigh.

"Saved, saved!" murmured the Arab.

"Thank Heaven!"

Both exclamations were equally fervent.

Both were enthusiastic in the efforts they were making.

But with what different objects were both working for the same result!

The waterman was struggling to save the life of a fellow-creature.

The necromancer struggled to save himself five thousand pounds.

Presently the girl opened her eyes.

A second sigh now told the two men that the immediate danger was passed.

"Now to shore," said Mermet.

"All right."

And the watermen turned to pick up the sculls.

They were gone.

In the confusion which prevailed they had not thought of the boat having capsized.

The sculls were then lost, and they were upon the Thames at that late hour, helpless and with no hope of rescue.

This alarming discovery startled both Mermet and the waterman so that neither could utter a word for some considerable time.

In the meanwhile Miss Grace Walgrave was sufficiently recovered to become conscious that she had been rescued from a watery grave.

"Why, why did you not let me rest in peace?" she said bitterly.

"Well that's a pretty question!" said the waterman, utterly disgusted.

"Yes," said Mermet. "The unhappy girl owes us her thanks."

Miss Walgrave no sooner recognised the voice of the Arab than she uttered a piercing shriek.

A shriek which echoed dismally along the black river.

Then she sank back once more.

The Arab muttered something which sounded much like the word "damnation!" and leant eagerly over her.

"She has fainted again," he said.

"That's bad."

"Not dangerously I hope?" said the necromancer eagerly.

"Highly."

"And we have no means of reaching shore?"

"None."

"And no assistance at hand?"

"None; and, as it is so late, I question very much whether it is possible to make ourselves heard."

"Try."

"All right," said the waterman. "Hullo! ho! ahoy there! A boat!"

Mermet still hung over the inanimate body of Grace Walgrave.

She was suspiciously still now.

"*I'm afraid,*" said Mermet, "*that she is very bad still.*"

The waterman leant over the motionless body before speaking again.

"Bad?" he echoed. "As bad as can be, sir."

"What do you mean?"

"Mean? *Why she's dead!*"

"Dead?"

"Dead as a herring!"

*   *   *   *   *   *

It was true.

The sudden shock in her present frail condition had proved too much for her.

Nature had accomplished what suicidal intent had failed to achieve.

The necromancer was in despair.

But, after all, he was a bit of a philosopher in a small way, and he soon perceived the uselessness of grieving over what it was impossible to mend, however hard he tried.

"There goes five thousand pounds!" he muttered between his teeth.

"Eh?" said the waterman.

Mermet was brought to his presence of mind by this remark.

"What do you say?" he demanded of the waterman.

"Why that's what I was a-askin' of you," said the man.

"I was talking to myself."

"And very rum words you was saying, too, my friend, I should say."

"Silence!"

The waterman started at the austerity of the other's tone.

"Hullo! my friend. You're making rather bold it strikes me."

"Hold your tongue, and get back to shore as soon as you can."

"All right. I'm going. We haven't managed to save the poor gal's life, but we've recovered the body, and shall get the society's medal and something handsome if you will say a word for me."

"I shall see."

"And I dare say that I shall get a trifle from her friends, if they can manage to identify her. There's sure to be some papers in her pockets."

"You think so?"

"Most likely."

Mermet at once applied himself to a diligent search in the pocket of the dead girl's dress.

"Hullo!" cried the waterman. "Drop that game, your honour."

"Silence!"

"Silence! silence! Bless'd if you can say anything but 'Silence!'"

"Hold your tongue."

But the man did not like the probability of losing the Humane Society's medal, and the reward which her friends would probably give, supposing the pockets of the deceased had not been tampered with.

"I tell you what, sir," said he to Mermet. "Just keep your hands off the corpse until we get ashore."

The Arab was not at all pleased at being interfered with, and he made a very angry retort to the waterman, which only served to make matters worse, instead of effecting an improvement.

"It's my opinion that you want to rob the body," said the waterman.

"It is?"

"Yes, that it is."

"Then it is an opinion, my friend, best kept to yourself."

"Why so?"

"It is dangerous to make yourself obnoxious to some men."

"Get out!" said the waterman. "What do I care for your threats? I only want you to pay me for the use of my boat and the reward as you promised."

"But you have failed."

"I deny that, guvnor. I saved her life. You killed her."

"Rascal!"

"So you did. Oh! I ain't a-feared of your frowns. She was coming round all right until she saw your ugly face."

Mermet's brow lowered as the waterman spoke this.

Any one who knew the necromancer might have seen by the expression of his countenance that he now meditated mischief.

"Since you have chosen to make yourself unpleasant in your absurd remarks," said the Arab, "you shall pay the penalty of your fault. Thus do I deprive you of all chance of the rewards you speak of."

Then before the man could divine his intention, much less offer to interfere, the necromancer took up the cold wet body of the ill-fated Grace Walgrave and threw it over the side again into the water.

With a dull fatal sounding splash it went to the bottom.

The waterman jumped up with a cry, and leant over the boat's side to save the sinking body.

Too late.

"Since you seem so very anxious about it," said the Arab, "you may go after it."

And with a sudden jerk he launched the waterman after the body.

With a piercing shriek of terror the waterman went down.

Down never to rise again.

"That's off my hands!" said Mermet, with admirable coolness. "And now I can sleep in peace!"

CHAPTER LVIII.

THE SOLITARY BOATMAN—THE MUDBANK—HOME—MERMET'S VICTIMS—ANOTHER TO THE LIST—THE DEBAUCHEE'S THREAT—MERMET'S CUNNING—THE CAB—THE GIRL—FALSE LOVE—A TALE OF TREACHERY AND DECEIT.

AN hour passed.

Dark and gloomy was the silent river at that awful time.

The very witching hour of night—the hour of all others for murder most foul, and crimes such as had been perpetrated.

A few hundred yards up the river—close by the stone terrace of the Houses of Parliament—a little boat, containing a solitary rower, worked its way to the shore by slow and painful degrees.

As it neared the river's bank the reason of its very slow progress was apparent.

The occupant of the boat had only a single oar.

This even he had picked up by chance as he glided along with the tide.

Then he had been obliged to get along as best he could by using the oar upon the stern of the boat.

His dexterity at his work showed him to be better acquainted with boating matters than his appearance might have led one to suppose.

At length the shore was gained, the boat run on to the mud bank, and out sprang Mermet the necromancer.

Mermet himself, bearing a charmed life it would almost appear.

He alone had survived that fearful night.

The scene of horror he had just witnessed must have caused the boldest cheek to blanch, the stoutest heart to quail.

But upon the Arab it had little or no effect whatever.

He sprang ashore, chuckling with glee at his escape.

Upon the other hand he could not fail to feel annoyed at having let the princely prize which he thought to extort from Grace Walgrave slip through his fingers.

"No matter," he muttered, "I must hasten home. I shall be in time to keep the appointment with Miss Lotty Chepstow. Poor Lotty! I should say that Brownbill may look upon his conquest there as achieved."

And muttering thus, the necromancer hastened homewards.

Notwithstanding his great presence of mind, it must be said that the Arab was not a little pleased to find himself once more within his home.

[THE MURDER BY POISON.]

A sigh of relief escaped him as he crossed the threshhold and the Arab attendant came to greet him.

"Has Mr. Brownbill called?" he demanded, before he had entered.

"Yes, sahib."

"Long since?"

"He is here now."

"Ah! In the reception-room?"

"Yes, sahib."

"Good."

The necromancer hurried upstairs, and, having changed his dress, made his way to the reception-room.

As he entered the room a young man rose to greet him.

He was tall and slimly built, rather handsome, pale, and a sensual expression about the mouth told that he knew something of life.

"Good night, Mr. Brownbill," said the necromancer, with a low bow.

The young man returned the salutation with a slight nod only.

"How are you, Mermet?" he said.

"You have called about that matter of which you spoke to me when you were last here?"

"Yes. According to appointment, you know."

"Precisely."

No. 19.

"You told me that you could secure her acquiescence."

"Miss Chepstow's?"

"Yes."

"And so I can, to anything that is upright and honourable—to anything that can bear the light of day."

The young man coloured slightly.

"Humph!" he muttered. "You choose a strange hour for such words."

"What matters the hour?"

"Nothing great, perchance," said Mr. Brownbill. "And yet some people do say that night is the hour for evil deeds. You have been abroad late, too, Mr. Mermet."

He gave such a deep significance to his words that the necromancer coloured deeply beneath his glance.

This speaks for itself.

It must indeed have struck truly home to cause the necromancer to feel uncomfortable in the least degree.

"Babbling old women talk thus," muttered Mermet.

"And not old women alone. However, this is but childish gossip. Can you do as you have told me, or is it merely a fiction?"

"A what?"

"A fiction—or, if you like it better, sir conjuror, a lie."

The necromancer started to his feet in the greatest rage at this.

His hand grasped a small crystal phial, the very one which had stood him in such good stead upon the occasion of his trip to Richmond.

But a great stake was at hand, and he made an effort to put a curb upon his temper.

It was a powerful effort too, for the necromancer was not precisely a philosopher.

On the contrary, he felt an insult as deeply as the most honourable and upright man could do.

"No matter," he muttered, grinding his set teeth ferociously. "I must wait. He shall pay for it—ay, and shortly too."

"Well, my friend," said Mr. Brownbill, "and what does all that whispering mean, eh? Hatching spells and charms, old boy?"

"I am thinking."

"Of what?"

"You."

"And what of me?"

"That youth is as hot-headed now as in the days of yore."

"And age as cunning and as garrulous too," added the visitor.

"No matter. I have no wish to prolong this interview."

"Nor I, 'pon my soul."

"Then say what you wish, and begone at once," said Mermet.

"That's kind. However, I desire no more. I want to know of your boasted skill."

The Arab interrupted him.

"I boast none."

"Well, well, we will not quarrel for a word. Can you tell me—as you in your superstitions fervour or gammon say you can — if Lotty Chepstow is to be mine?"

"Choose your expressions better, or I shall not reply?"

"You don't like the gammon and the superstitious fervour?"

"No, I do not. As for superstition, you must not accuse me of that weakness, since you yourself possess it to a large degree."

"Do I, egad?"

"Else why are you here?"

"The old curmudgeon has me there," thought the visitor. "Well, no matter," he added aloud. "You must make some allowances, Mr. Mermet. Give me the information I desire, if in your power, and I will requite your pains."

"Requite my pains?"

"Ay, as amply as your avarice shall demand of me."

"I have no avarice. I love not gold."

"Bosh! There, there, don't pucker up so. I can't understand a man not liking gold, and that's the fact. I have rather a liking for it, I can tell you. However, I will part with any quantity in moderation to learn what I wish to know."

"Say on, then."

"In a word, shall I succeed?"

"In making this girl yours?"

"Ay."

"This is all I can say upon the matter. You have a greater chance of success this night than ever will present itself again."

"Ah!"

"This is the reason of it. She will not have counsellor at hand to warn her against your villanies."

"Sir!"

It was now the visitor's turn to grow indignant.

The information he got here, however, was so agreeable to him that he soon forgot his indignation.

He rose to depart.

"You are going?" said Mermet.

"Yes."

"Shall my servant call you a cab?"

"No, mine waits."

"Very good."

He rang the bell and Ahmet appeared.

"The gentleman's hat and coat."

"Yes, sahib."

Then he said a few words in a foreign tongue to the man, and, with a bow to the visitor, left the room.

Mermet hurried downstairs before Mr. Brownbill could leave the room, hastily snatched up his cloak and hat from the hall, and left the house.

A cab was waiting close at hand, and Mermet walked quickly up to it.

"You are waiting for a gentleman?" he asked the driver.

"Yes, sir."

"I have to take you. He will not come out."

"There's my back fare, though."

"I'll settle that with you."

"All right, sir."

Mermet got in and called out a direction to the man.

"Double fare if you drive quickly," he said.

"All right, your honour."

And, lashing up his horse, they flew over the stones with the rapidity of a fire engine.

Arrived at the direction given, Mermet got down, remunerated the cabman liberally, and dismissed him.

A gentle rap at the door soon brought a light to one of the windows.

Then the door was opened by a fair comely girl of twenty summers.

She started back, half alarmed at perceiving the Arab, and stopped short as a name rose to her lips.

"Arthur—"

"No," said Mermet. "Not Arthur Brownbill, Miss Chepstow. But I've come upon his behalf."

"From Arthur?"

"Well, not precisely."

The girl looked unspeakably alarmed.

"He is not ill?" she asked nervously.

"No. I left him not long since—that is, to day—quite well. He was then in the company of several persons whose society appeared to keep him in the best of spirits."

"His friends?"

"Well, yes—if you can call them by so cold a name."

"What mean you?"

"I mean that the ladies in whose company I left him appeared something nearer to him than mere friends."

The girl turned pale, and then a blood crimson.

"Do you mean to say that you left Arthur in the company of some vile women?—of—of—oh! I cannot speak the word."

Mermet appeared greatly surprised at this outbreak.

"Not at all," said he, with fiendlike duplicity. "I simply mean that I left him in the company of one lady (amongst others, it is true) who appears to me to possess a very great right to his company, and not alone to his company, but to his affections."

"I do not understand you. Speak more plainly."

"I mean his wife."

"Ah!"

The girl staggered back, clasping her hand to her heart.

"His wife?" she ejaculated. "No, no. By Heaven! I'll not believe it."

"Not believe what?" said Mermet, with a look of great surprise.

"That Arthur can be so false."

"Is it possible, Miss Chepstow, that you were not aware that Arthur Brownbill is a married man?"

"Never, never!" exclaimed the girl, in faltering accents. "It is not possible."

"Not only is it possible," said Mermet, "but it is the fact."

"Give me proofs."

"That is easily done. Do you know his handwriting?"

"Yes."

"It is here."

The necromancer handed her a letter which she hastily read aloud.

"*My dear Louisa,—An important business engagement will call me to Manchester to-night by the mail train. Unfortunately I had not even the time to come and let you know of it personally. I shall return to-morrow, without doubt.*
"*Your affectionate husband,*
"ARTHUR BROWNBILL."

The letter fell from the girl's hand, and she remained for some minutes as if stricken with a sudden paralysis.

Mermet took advantage of the silence to address a few hasty words to her.

"Although I am grieved to see you thus moved, Miss Chepstow," he said, "my sorrow is not unmixed with satisfaction."

"Satisfaction?" iterated the poor creature, with a start.

"Ay, satisfaction. That is the word," said the necromancer.

"Man, man, what do you mean? Why do you come hither at this unearthly hour to tell me this hideous lie?"

"Miss Chepstow!"

"Your pardon; but what proof have I?"

"This letter."

"May be a forgery."

"Then I can give you a further proof if necessary."

"Do so."

"I am here to anticipate the visit of a truant husband."

"You knew, then—"

"That Arthur Brownbill was to come here to see you by appointment? Alas! yes."

"Then what is the purpose of this visit?"

"I come to sue for mercy upon my poor girl's behalf."

"Whom?"

"My daughter—his wife's."

"You, then, are his father-in-law."

"I am."

"And you come to me to supplicate for the happiness of your daughter?"

"I came for that," said Mermet. "But now I am happy to find that you at least were ignorant of the villain's duplicity—devilish duplicity—believe me, I speak the truth—for while feigning a love for you, which can be no pure passion of course, he also pretended to love his wife most passionately."

Miss Chepstow burst into a flood of tears.

"Oh! man! man!" she cried, "why do you so cruelly wrong the hearts that love you so tenderly? Why, why? O Heavens! my heart will burst!"

"Calm yourself, Miss Chepstow," said the necromancer. "This man is unworthy of such tears as these."

"True," said the girl with a proud look. "It is an unworthy weakness, but oh! it is hard to teach the heart to turn from what it has so willingly learnt to love."

"True, but call in pride to your aid, and I'm sure that you will not suffer yourself to be so led away."

After a few minutes her old doubts suddenly returned.

"How am I to know that this is true?" she demanded.

"How?"

"Ay. Your whole story may be a fabrication."

"For what purpose?"

"That I cannot divine—for some cruel deceit perhaps. How learnt you all this?"

She eyed the necromancer sharply as she put this question, but he met her glance unmoved.

"If you would know," he replied, "I may as well inform you that his hopes with you are no secret."

"No secret?" gasped the girl.

"No. I learnt it from a member of his club. He was boasting over his wine with a member that he would make you his."

"Hold!" ejaculated the girl indignantly. "If it is true that I have fallen so low as to become the scandal of a clubroom, then I will at once learn the whole truth. He will be here shortly, I doubt not."

"He will."

"You shall confront him."

"I?"

This was more than the necromancer bargained for.

"Yes, you. If your tale be true—"

"If? It shall prove itself clearly to you in his conduct to you this night."

"Be it so. You seen strangely informed upon the matter, and your air is truthful. Hitherto his conduct has been respect and consideration itself. I do not deem it possible that my heart could so err in its choice."

"Beware of my warning," said Mermet. "And now I must begone."

"You must not leave me," said Miss Chepstow.

"Wherefore?"

She coloured deeply before replying.

"I am alone in the house."

Mermet frowned.

"Is it possible, Miss Chepstow?" he said. "This is something more than ordinary imprudence."

"I deserve it I know, but if you knew all—"

A knock at the street door—a low rap—interrupted her at this moment.

Mermet was a little bit annoyed at this.

However, his ready wit served him once more, and he surmounted the difficulty.

"I shall not confront him," he said, "or his cunning might devise some tale to deceive you yet. Take him off his guard, but fear nothing. I shall be at hand in case of need."

CHAPTER LIX.

THE LOVER'S VISIT — THE MAIDEN'S FEARS — TREACHERY EXPOSED — ACCUSATIONS — THE MASK FALLS—OPEN VIOLENCE—THE RUFFIAN'S ASSAULT—"HELP!"--THE FLIGHT—THE HOUSE-TOP—THE PARAPET—"MY BLOOD BE UPON YOUR HEAD!"—THE DEATH OF THE LIBERTINE.

MERMET hurried downstairs.

As he gained the passage the knocking was repeated.

"I'll open the door myself," he thought, "for after all I've said this girl will never venture to. It is dark, and he will not see me. He is drunk with passion, and will have no eyes nor ears but for her.

The boldness of the freak pleased the Arab, and he proceeded at once to put his project into execution.

But not before the knocking was repeated.

He opened the door and drew back behind it, admitting, as he had anticipated, the lover of the imprudent Lotty Chepstow.

Arthur Brownbill passed in, but, seeing no one there, imagined that his fair one had opened the door and then fled in maidenly diffidence.

He hastily closed the door and hurried on.

Had he been less pre-occupied, he could not have failed to notice the dark form of the Arab there.

As it was, he simply walked on without looking left or right.

He ran upstairs and Mermet slipped from his hiding-place.

"He's gone," muttered the necromancer, "and now for it."

He anticipated a scene, and was already rubbing his hands in glee at the thought.

Little did he care for the anguish he had caused in the breast of the loving and confiding Lotty Chepstow.

His own vile ends were in a fair way of being served, and he cared for no more.

"I wonder what they will be up to," he muttered. "A fit of curiosity is on me, and I must see it out."

Saying which, he drew nearer to the stairs.

Here even he failed to hear anything whatever, and by slow and cautious degrees he mounted the stairs.

Surely never had stairs before creaked so audibly.

Each step he took appeared to ring out an alarm to the whole house.

But he was not to be daunted now.

Muttering curses, not loud, but deep, he crept on.

At the top stair he drew up short.

He could hear voices.

"Now for it," he muttered. "They're at it already. Glorious sport!"

The ardent lover, Arthur Brownbill, with the feverish haste of passion, had pushed his way upstairs.

Miss Chepstow was seated in the apartment where the necromancer had quitted her.

Her eyes were dimmed with tears.

Tears of bitter humiliation.

Tears of outraged affection and maidenly self-esteem, which had flown freely as soon as she had been relieved from the necromancer's presence.

As her lover entered the room a few words murmured through her grief rather startled the expectant and amorous Brownbill.

"Oh, man, man!" she exclaimed, "why do you ever thus trifle with the heart you affect to love? Is there no pure affection in God's own image? It cannot be all deceit."

"Hullo!" thought Mr. Brownbill. "This looks remarkably queer."

He advanced into the room.

It was dark now, for the flickering lamp had expired while Mermet was about to depart, and the unhappy girl was so grief-stricken at the discovery of her lover's perfidy that she had not thought of replenishing it.

"No matter," she muttered, drying her eyes and endeavouring to persuade herself that she was now firm. "No matter. I'll banish him from my heart, from my thoughts—forget that Arthur ever lived there."

The lover's footstep startled her in the middle of her soliloquy.

"Who's there?"

Now Mr. Brownbill was so thoroughly startled by the words which he had chanced to overhear that he felt very little inclined to make himself heard.

"Is that you?" said Miss Chepstow, after a while. "You have not let him in. Oh! sir, spare me, if you can, the pain of seeing him again—dismiss him, if possible."

Mr. Brownbill started back aghast:

"Damnation!" he muttered aloud. "There's a rival in the field I find."

"Who is it?" said Miss Chepstow, this time in rather a tremulous tone.

"'Tis I, madam," said Mr. Brownbill, in an indignant tone. "Perfidious woman!"

"Ah!"

"Lotty, Lotty, I little suspected you of falsehood."

And he pretended to weep.

There was no light to show off his grief-stricken expression of contenance, but he contrived to throw a lachrymose cadence into his voice, which was invariably very effective.

"What do you here?" demanded Miss Chepstow, sternly.

"What?"

"What do you here?"

"I? Why, my dear Lotty."

"Silence! Depart at once. You are discovered, man, I tell you."

"What, what do you mean?"

"This, that your villainies are known to me."

"Lotty, this is madness."

"Leave this house immediately, or, by the heavens above, I will have you ejected with ignominy."

This brought matters to a crisis with an alarming rapidity.

The tone of the roué and debauchee changed in an instant.

He no longer thought it necessary to, assume the tone of injured innocence.

It was clear enough that, wherever she had obtained her information, she had learnt that of him which would render useless all further attempt at deception.

He burst into a coarse laugh.

"Hah! hah! my dear Lotty. You forget one important fact whilst uttering these cruel, not to say unladylike, absurdities."

"What mean you?"

"That you might eject me if you were physically capable, my love, but as for having me ejected, that's a moral impossibility."

"How so?"

"Why the form of speech used implies the presence of other persons in the house."

"Ah!"

"And I happen to know that you are alone here."

"Monster!"

"That *we* are alone!"

"Ruffian!" ejaculated the indignant girl. "The mask has fallen and shown you in your true colours at last."

"That's dramatic, my dear," said the libertine, with admirable *sang-froid*. "Poetical and dramatic both."

"But know, unworthy man," said Miss Chepstow, "that at least you are deceived there—I am not alone."

Mr. Brownbill grew a little uneasy.

"What mean you? Ah! you would deceive me. I *know* you are alone. For your comfort let me assure you that I took all the necessary precautions."

This avowal of such unblushing villainy staggered the blindly confiding girl for a second.

"Oh, inhuman monster!" she exclaimed. "Begone from my sight."

"Nonsense, my dear Lotty. If you must be coy and nonsensical, put your gammon into better language. It is highly unpleasant, I can assure you."

"Brazen ruffian!"

"Come, come, my love," said the cool *roué*. "Give your Arthur a kiss."

He advanced towards her as he spoke, but she sprang to the further end of the apartment like a startled fawn.

"Unmannerly dog!" she ejaculated. "Approach but a step nearer, and I alarm the whole neighbourhood with my cries."

"And gain a nice modest maidenly reputation," said Mr. Brownbill.

"Oh! cunning villain!" said the girl, with withering scorn. "But think not to frighten me with that. Dare to pollute the edge of my dress with your loathsome touch, and, by the heavens above us, I swear that you shall not escape unpunished. Did I become an object for the finger of scorn to point at—for a gapeing crowd to call after—I swear it should be so."

This vehemence completely staggered Mr. Arthur Brownbill.

"This is all very well," he said, "but I am not to be put off with that bosh. As a man of the world, my dear Lotty, I should risk nothing by exposure. The very fact of your letting me into your house at this hour would clear me of any criminal accusation which you might have the insanity to bring against me. You would inevitably sink down to the lowest degradation by such an act of folly, *voila tout*."

At the last word he sprang round the table which separated them.

Then, feinting as she ran off the other side, he dodged and caught her in his embrace.

"Caught!"

"Ah!" shrieked the girl. "Help! oh! help!"

"Foolish girl!" said the libertine. "We are alone here."

"No such thing. I was alone, but am no longer."

"The devil!"

"Help! help!"

"You would deceive me."

"I swear I speak the truth."

"No matter. You are, you must, and shall be mine."

The helpless girl continued to struggle boldly with her assailant.

Her shrieks and cries were heartrending.

But Mermet only listened with renewed interest.

He did not offer to interfere.

"No, no," he said to himself. "This is too good to spoil. I must wait my time, and then—"

With one arm clasped around the maiden's waist, the ruffian held her there with all the strength of maddened passion.

Fainter and fainter grew the virgin's efforts at each struggle.

And yet the heartless man below would not come to her aid.

"Mercy! mercy!" were the last words that Mermet caught.

* * * * * *

There was a loud and prolonged shriek.

A scuffle.

This was followed by a sudden scrambling, and the girl flew wildly up the stairs.

Then there was a second rush, which told Mermet that the libertine was following in pursuit.

Arrived at the top of the house, she turned to face her pursuer.

There was no further escape, unless by flying to the roof.

On came the libertine, and the girl did not hesitate an instant.

She scrambled up the ladder, and endeavoured to pull it up after her, but too late.

Brownbill's foot was upon the ladder ere she could move it.

Up he ran, and dashed across the roof to the terrified maiden.

"Advance another step," she said, "and my blood be upon your head!"

She stood upon the edge of the parapet, ready to precipitate herself into the street below.

"Lotty, Lotty!" cried the ruffian, starting back affrightedly, "what would you do?"

"Stand off!" she cried.

He coaxed and begged her to turn from such madness, but in vain.

Whilst speaking thus to her he continued to draw nearer and nearer at each word.

Then suddenly, with a rush and a grab, he seized her wrist.

"Now I have you, foolish girl!"

The girl swung round with her brutal captor.

The positions were suddenly reversed.

He, the assailant of the maiden's chastity, stood over the parapet.

The outraged girl pushed forward in the very nick of time.

"Great God!" cried the libertine.

He caught at the edge of the parapet.

Too late.

He cut the flesh from his hands, but all in vain.

Down down he fell.

Down to perdition, with all his hot and sinful lusts upon his head.

Thus died the libertine.

Slain by the victim to his infamy and outrage.

CHAPTER LX.

ROSE AND HER FORTUNES—BLANCHE BOWERINI —THEIR WANDERINGS — THE ROAD—THE INN — THE LADY AND HER BLACK ATTENDANT — MISGIVINGS — ALONE IN THEIR POWER — TERRORS.

BUT with these scenes of excitement we fear that we are sadly neglecting the fortunes of our heroine Rose.

After the scandalous outrage by Signor Bowerini in the circus, the unhappy victim to his ferocity managed to elude his vigilance, and escape from his paternal care.

In the circus the people were so thoroughly indignant at what had occurred that they would have torn him piecemeal.

Blanche Bowerini was rescued from the brutal clutches of her tyrant, and he was seized by a dozen indignant hands and borne to the ground.

One young fellow—a stalwart countryman—caught him by the collar of his coat, swung him violently round, and dashed him to the earth.

This treatment he found so to disagree with him that the cowardly ruffian, fearing a repetition of it, thought it better to lie there, shamming insensibility.

An inquiry was held into the outrage, not official, but sufficiently public to do much good in the cause of the girl.

Then this came out.

Signor Bowerini had missed his girl, Blanche, at home at the hour appointed for their departure for the circus, and, upon looking about for her, he had discovered that she was with a young person lodging in the same house, Miss Mortimer.

He had happened to overhear some strange things as he was about to knock at Miss Mortimer's door, which caused him to stop and listen.

She had always proved a refractory daughter and pupil, and he had experienced no end of trouble and difficulty in bringing her up.

She was addicted to falsehood, too, and was, in fine, incurable.

So said the signor.

But, as there are usually two sides to every question, Rose had a word to put in, which seemed to controvert most of what the acrobat had advanced.

"In the first place," said our heroine, "I may show you the falsehood of this man, in the simple fact that Blanche Bowerini is not at all related to him. She is simply his apprentice, and has been treated by him in a way which would bring him within the power of the law, if the poor girl ever had a friend at hand to protect her."

The acrobat scowled upon Rose most viciously.

However, our heroine was speaking now in a good cause, and was not to be intimidated by the tyrant's black looks.

If Rose had only possessed a like degree of courage upon her own behalf, we should not probably have now to prolong the history of her chequered career.

"You can appeal to him," said Rose Mortimer. "He dare not deny what I have advanced. Ask him."

"Is this true, Bowerini?" asked the proprietor of the circus.

"Well, I must say," answered the acrobat, "that the gal's no daughter of mine. But that proves nothing. You all know that in the profession every one takes apprentices."

"True."

"And as for ill-treating her, why that's a flagrant lie."

"I appeal to you all here," said Blanche's advocate boldly. "You are the best witnesses if what I say is truth or not. You have seen how this man has treated his pupil before you all."

"Yes."

"And you can judge," continued our heroine, "if he lets his passion so master him, how she must suffer from his cruelties when he has no need to put a bridle upon his anger."

The argument was convincing.

There was no gainsaying what Rose advanced, and Bowerini could only vent his spleen upon her, thereby strengthening the cause which she was advocating.

The gentlemen forming the committee of inquiry therefore determined that Blanche should at once be removed from Signor Bowerini's protection.

"Wait, wait, wait!" said the brutal acrobat. "You are going a little too far. That girl is apprenticed to me."

"What then ?"

"I refuse to cancel her indentures," replied Bowerini.

"Then the law shall attack you."

"And who will undertake to conduct the prosecution, pray ?"

This was a startler.

The acrobat saw that he had gained a point, and he hastened by every argument in his power to improve upon it.

"Now I warn you, one and all," he said, "that if I am interfered with I shall defend myself and my rights to the last shilling."

This seemed likely to put an end to the discussion.

Bowerini looked around upon the committee of inquiry with a triumphant air.

"Well," said the manager of the circus, "all I have to say in the matter is this, that if you venture to show yourself within any place where I have anything to do with the direction, I shall see that you are immediately kicked out; indeed, I shall take great pleasure in kicking you out myself. As for Miss Blanche, if she likes to accept an engagement independently of you, I am sure that we shall be able to come to terms."

Blanche Bowerini was profuse in her acknowledgments of his kindness and delighted with the arrangement.

Bowerini withdrew, threatening everybody in general, but Blanche in particular.

He was warned by the gentlemen present that her cause would be taken warmly in hand by one and all of them, and that any violence would be resented by violence with such interest that he had better pause ere he put himself in opposition to them.

And so the matter ended for the present.

Bowerini found that he had gained such an unenviable notoriety in the town that he could not stir from his house without being hooted and pelted by the street boys.

After a few days he was forced to leave the town.

One thing resulted from this affair which our heroine could not but contemplate as being woefully unfortunate for her.

The whole affair was detailed at full length in the local newspapers, and was copied into the metropolitan journals.

Rose Mortimer's name figured in it too, and our heroine was in no trifling consternation.

Should any of her enemies discover it, she would in all probability again be subject to their persecution.

This caused her such uneasiness that she determined at once to quit the town and seek an engagement elsewhere under an assumed name.

No sooner had our heroine given notice of her intention than another engagement was offered her in the north, which she unhesitatingly accepted.

Blanche Bowerini was greatly grieved at this, and avowed her intention at once of following Rose Mortimer.

"Wherever you go, dear Rose," said the affectionate girl, "I will accompany you. We will throw our fortunes together if you will still accept me as your sister."

Rose embraced the girl with fervour, sealing the compact without a word.

"But you don't know, my dear Blanche," said our heroine, "that in linking your destiny to my own you may be rushing into dangers more alarming than that from which you have just escaped."

"You frighten me," said Blanche.

"But I am serious."

"How dangers ?"

"I have many enemies."

"You, Rose ?" exclaimed Blanche, as if she deemed it an impossibility. "How can you have created any enemies ?"

"That I will tell you."

She then gave her a hurried sketch of her singular career.

She touched upon her abduction from the theatre by Count Lerno, her captivity by the Whartons, the adventure at the Danger Mine, and finally the murder she had witnessed, and the persecution she had suffered since, and giving her reasons for making a further move now.

"And now, dear Blanche," she said, "you may judge how desperate are the dangers to be apprehended from these fearful people."

"I do indeed. Poor Rose! I should have died I am sure."

"And now what do you think?"

"Upon what?"

"Will you still accompany me?"

"If you will have me."

"Bless you, dear girl," said our heroine warmly. "We shall be a protection to each other. You will serve to lighten my troubles."

"Ah, dear Rose," said the girl, "we have both suffered much, and shall, I hope, see an end to our troubles now."

Rose pointed out to her, whilst now upon the subject, the necessity of preserving silence upon her history, as much of it—and that, too, connected with the incidents which involved the most personal dangers—it was impossible to substantiate.

With many leave-takings, and the best wishes of their brother and sister professionals, the two girls quitted the town, and started upon their new career together.

They were travelling across country by coach, and the town to which they were proceeding was distant two days' journey; so they had to cut it half way at an inn.

The house was rather superior in style to what would have been their choice, from the scanty state of their purses.

However, it was the only house that offered, and they were obliged to accept the accommodation it afforded, and at its own price, resolving to retrench, to make up for the involuntary extravagance, at the end of the journey.

As Rose and Blanche Bowerini entered the hotel a travelling carriage drove up to the door of the inn, from which a lady alighted, accompanied by a coloured woman, evidently her attendant.

Blanche and Rose were seated in the coffee-room, where they had ordered some refreshments to be served previous to retiring for the night.

Now ever since our heroine had confided her strange history to her new sister it had been the constant topic of conversation for them.

Evidently it filled Blanche Bowerini's thoughts.

The horrors which Rose had so briefly touched upon were so startling that Blanche could think of nothing else, and chose it always as a subject for discussion as soon as they were alone.

As they were awaiting the refreshment ordered for their supper she started upon the subject again.

"But dear Rose," she said in an undertone, "you should never be unarmed, with such bold enemies as yours."

"I never am," said Rose.

"Eh! good gracious, dear, you startle me. What a fearful thing!"

"Mr. Chowler, the manager of the theatre I came from, provided me with a small pocket pistol. It also has a spring dagger concealed in it, which flies out, and makes it a very formidable little weapon I can tell you. Here it is."

She was about to produce it, when the lady with her coloured attendant entered the room.

"Tell them to take the luggage to my room," said the lady.

Rose looked up in wonder.

She recognised the voice.

She looked hard at the speaker, and found that her features were familiar to her as well.

But where she had met with them before she was at a loss to divine.

The lady glanced curiously at our heroine, as if she, upon her part, had the same kind of recollection of Rose.

Then, with some excuse, she rose and left the room.

She went straightway to the parlour door and called the landlord, who came out with a run to the service of his illustrious guest.

"Pardon my curiosity," said the lady, with a most amiable smile, "but can you possibly inform me who those two young ladies are?"

"In the coffee-room?"

"Yes."

"No. They have not said anything beyond giving their orders, madam."

"Oh!"

"They are travelling alone."

"Alone?"

"Ay, looks queer, madam."

"Sir!"

"Eh? Oh, no. Perfectly respectable you may feel assured, or they should not stay here, believe me, madam."

"Enough. That is all I wished to know about them."

"Then I'm sure—"

"Thank you."

And, cutting him thus short, the lady returned to the parlour.

Rose glanced up as she entered, and for the third time their eyes met.

This time a mutual gesture of recognition escaped them.

Both would evidently have fain suppressed it, had they then had sufficient command over themselves, but their astonishment was so thoroughly unassumed and natural that it was one involuntary movement.

The instant that Rose Mortimer recognised her, and perceived that she was also recognised, she trembled painfully from head to foot.

So noticeable was this, too, that Blanche Bowerini remarked it.

"What is it, dear?" she asked.

"Nothing," returned Rose, shudderingly, "but pray don't leave."

The tone was so very low that Blanche failed to catch the words.

"What, Rose?"

"Hush! No names!" said Rose, glancing once more to the lady.

Her eyes were still fixed motionless upon our heroine, and the poor girl felt drooping beneath her fascinating basilisk eyes.

"Don't leave me," she murmured once more in a whisper to Blanche.

"Very well, dear."

But she had again misunderstood our heroine.

The tone was so low that she had only caught the last two words.

Imagining that her companion desired, for some purpose or other, to be left with the lady and her black attendant, she rose to her feet and left the room.

Rose, having just spoken upon this matter, did not divine her attention until too late.

She was gone, and Rose was alone with the lady and the black woman.

She jumped up and made for the door.

However, before she could get to it the lady sprang forward and placed herself in her path.

"What would you?" demanded Rose Mortimer, faintly.

"I know you," said the lady.

" I—I'm sure."

" Silence."

She took a small crystal phial from her pocket.

Then, with the cruellest deliberation, a small stiletto was produced.

Rose saw her preparation in terror.

Fear choked her utterance.

She could not breathe a cry for her own salvation.

" Now," said the lady, " which do you prefer ?"

" What mean—" began Rose.

" Not a word. You haven't another minute's life."

" Mercy !"

" Ah ! The dagger or the phial ? Quick."

Rose turned and darted past her.

But it was a vain hope.

The black woman sprang after her, dragged her back, and forced her upon the sofa.

Rose was powerless and at their mercy.

———

CHAPTER LXI.

THE POISON AND THE DAGGER — AN INTERRUPTION — AN OLD FRIEND — A LUCKY ESCAPE — THE LANDLORD'S PROTESTATION—ROSE'S FORBEARANCE — THE LETTERS — MUTUAL UNDERSTANDING — THE OFFERED BRIBE — A NEW DANGER — LADY BELLISLE IN DIFFICULTIES.

ROSE MORTIMER thought that her time had now really come.

Held down in a vice-like grasp by the negro woman and her cruel enemy, in whose path unhappy chance had once more thrown her, matters looked critical for our heroine.

She appeared at this moment nearer the end of her career than she has ever been since we have charged ourselves with the relation of her fortunes.

But she was not to die.

The door was suddenly burst open with a crash.

A loud commotion of voices and a dispute were heard without.

Then in rushed the landlord, followed by two or three men.

" Hullo !" cried the former. " See there, just as I thought."

" Seize her !"

They rushed up to the lady and caught hold of her roughly.

But upon the instant, in spite of the extraordinary scene just enacted, the lady did not appear to lose her composure in the least.

The phial and the dagger both disappeared as if by magic.

And she was there, cold, haughty, and severe as before.

" What mean you by this violence ?" she demanded sternly.

" What do you mean ?" quoth the landlord.

" Sir !"

" Ay, 'taint no use showing off your fine airs upon me, mum," said the landlord. " What's that door locked for ?"

She eyed her questioner with a glance of supreme disdain.

" She won't answer."

" No."

" She can't."

" Then she's guilty."

" Ay. Off with her to the lock-up."

This appeared to have the effect of once more loosening the lady's tongue.

" Unhand me, you ruffians !" she exclaimed.

She spoke with an air of command which appeared so thoroughly natural to her that the men instantly drew away.

The landlord now turned towards our heroine, who stood by the sofa upon which she had been thrust by the black woman, trembling and quaking with fear, and unable to say a word as yet in her own behalf.

" What have ye got to say, miss ?" said the landlord to Rose.

Rose looked up timidly.

So suddenly had the violent and totally unprovoked assault occurred that the poor girl's senses were utterly scared from her for the present.

" I am at a loss to understand what all this means," said the lady.

" So am I," said the landlord.

" Why do you presume to break in upon my privacy thus ?"

" Privacy, privacy, be hanged, madam. You have no right to privacy in the coffee-room."

" Provided it was not agreeable to the rest of the occupants."

" Which it warn't."

" This young lady made no objection," said the other.

" Well, of all the cool affairs ! Why, dash it, 'pon my soul it licks cockfighting."

" Art sure thee wert right, Mickey ?" demanded one of the men.

" Sure. I saw it."

" Saw what ?"

" Why, I was looking in at the parlour window when I see—"

" Nothing, nothing," said Rose.

This was a startler.

Every one looked astonished.

The lady herself looked so thoroughly surprised that it was remarked by all present.

She could not comprehend the motive which prompted our heroine to deny the truth when against her own safety.

However, it very shortly made itself apparent.

" Why !" exclaimed the landlord, " I was a looking through the window there when I saw the old nigger and this other woman seize the young lady and pitch her upon the sofa. Then one holds her down whilst another tries to force something into her mouth."

" Absurd," said the lady.

" I say it's true."

" Nonsense."

Rose said nothing, and the people who had entered in the rush with the landlord began to glance from one to the other, quite perplexed.

" You must have dreamt it, Mickey," said one of the foremost.

" Bah !"

" See, the lady denies it."

" Of course."

" And the young lady herself doesn't say anything about it. You're wrong."

" She doesn't speak, it's true," said the landlord, " and I confess that that looks rum ; but depend upon it they've done something to her to silence her. See how frightened she is."

This was apparent enough to the most ordinary observer.

Rose had not recovered from the terrors which she just undergone.

Yet had she sufficient sense to lay out a line of conduct which was afterwards to lead to some singular results.

These we shall show.

" Well, why don't the young woman speak for herself ?" suggested one.

" Ah, why don't she ?"

Just at this point Blanche Bowerini returned.

She burst through the mob collected at the door, and pushed her way up to Rose.

[A REAL TRAGEDY.]

"What is it, Rose. What has happened?"

Rose shook her head.

"Nothing, dear. Send those people away, if you can," she whispered.

Blanche looked scarcely less astonished than the rest of the people.

However, in the midst of all the confusion which reigned, the prime mover in it preserved a most admirable composure.

"Do you not hear what the young lady says?" she demanded. "Now, good people, if the absurdity of which the landlord speaks were really true, is it likely that she would speak thus?"

"What does it all mean?" asked Blanche.

"I will tell you later," said Rose. "Lead me from room, dear Blanche."

"Come, then."

Supported by the affectionate girl, Rose left the room.

The crowd made way for her as she past, and with her departure the fracas, which had assumed such an ugly appearance at first, was virtually at an end.

The landlord protested as to the truth of what he averred.

The crowd looked incredulous and the lady sneered.

The mob withdrew.

Thus, by a singular chance, as yet unexplained, had the murderous woman and her negro attendant escaped a just punishment for an audacious assault upon a harmless and inoffensive girl in a house of public entertainment.

But our heroine had not yet seen the last of it.

When the lady was once more alone with her negro attendant she paced up and down the room, lost in a deep meditation.

From time to time a few words escaped her and were eagerly picked up by the black woman.

"A singular chance!" she exclaimed. "I cannot at all understand this. A special Providence seems to protect this Rose Mortimer from us. And shall she escape thus? Never, by Heaven! I feel that until she is removed we are not safe. Whilst Rose Mortimer lives and the lost heir of Sloeford still breathes I feel the cord around my neck and see it coiling about Spencer."

Strange thought !

No reflection crossed her guilt-distorted imagination concerning the singularity of her own salvation.

It never appeared to occur to her how singular was the chance which had silenced Rose Mortimer's tongue.

No gratitude to Providence touched the heart of this guilty woman for her undeserved escape when everything was so black against her, had Rose Mortimer chosen to say a word.

The black woman all the time appeared not to consider the extraordinary scene in which she had just enacted so prominent a character by any means an out-of-the-way performance.

On the contrary, she seemed to look upon the interruption only with the greatest vexation.

"My lady," she said, presently.

"What now?" demanded her mistress. "What do you want?"

"I should like to take that old man's life."

"Hush !"

The sentiment thus agreeably uttered did not apparently shock the lady so much as the possibility of it being overheard.

She heard the footstep of the landlord without the coffee-room again.

He knocked this time before entering.

"Come in !"

He walked in, holding a letter humbly in his hand.

"A letter?" said the lady, surprised.

"From the young lady, madam."

"Oh !"

She took it from his hand haughtily.

Then stared him out of countenance rudely, and he retreated in the greatest confusion.

"A letter from her !" she murmured. "What can it mean?"

As she mused thus she broke the seal and opened it.

The first words which caught her eyes caused her to start.

She read it aloud.

"'To LADY BELLISLE.' Oh! she has my name, then !

"'Madam,—Think of my forbearance to-day, and let your unjust cruel enmity pursue me no further. Believe me that your greatest security lies in my silence. I can and do forgive much. Many injuries I allow to pass unrepaid. Then be satisfied. My forgiveness will but avail you here. I cannot now, in spite of myself, carry my mercy into my grave.

"What can the girl mean by that ?"

It was puzzling.

The explanation was to be found in the concluding words.

They ran thus :—

"A sealed account of all that you so dread being known to the world lies in the hands of trusty persons, ready to be opened after a silence of ten days upon my part. I am not, like yourself, revengeful, or you would not have had a second opportunity of offering me violence after the failure of your plans at Sloeford. Be advised by one who wishes you no harm, by one who would fain un-learn what she knows is so deplored by you. In conclusion, be sure that my proofs are so abundant that you could not hope to clear yourself, should I come to an untimely end."

This was startling.

"If the girl speaks the truth, I've had a narrow escape !" she said. "But to resume this extraordinary letter.

"'Be assured of my veracity, and do not deem it a mere safety precaution for myself. Do not either deem me weak or foolish because I thus spared you when by your rashness you had placed yourself at my mercy—when a word would have delivered you over to the hands of justice. I feel an inward monitor which forbids me to harm you, or I might have been less merciful. Spare me your persecution and be prudent.

'ROSE MORTIMER.'

"A strange letter !" said Lady Bellisle, for it was she, as we have seen by the heading of Rose Mortimer's epistle. "Strange ! Perhaps true. If so, then I have had a singularly happy escape again. Let me see."

She walked up and down the room for some considerable time, buried in deep thought.

Presently she seated herself at the table and wrote as follows :—

"Your prudence is commendable. Count upon my protection if you will. Your own precautions ensure you. I appeal to no further sensations than reason and interest. Use caution still, with your defensive weapons, for others might be less prudent than yourself. Think of my offer. Count upon my wealth if pecuniary assistance be desirable."

She put this into an envelope, together with a bank note for a hundred pounds sterling.

She then sealed it and called the landlord.

"Take this to the young lady," she said.

"Any answer ?"

"No."

Rose received the answer and read it carefully through.

"This will never do," she said to herself. "This clearly implies a bribe."

She wrote a few words hastily upon a scrap of paper and enclosed them with the bank note to Lady Bellisle.

As her ladyship opened the envelope, and found it to contain the returned bank note, she could not contain her astonishment.

It was her pet notion that every man and woman had their price.

Could she refuse money ?

The words which our heroine had written in the note ran thus :—

"I return the bank note. I do not desire a bribe to induce me to keep silent. I thus should render myself a partner in an act which my soul abhors. It would render me unhappy by remorse of conscience, and your secret would no longer be safe."

Lady Bellisle tossed her head with a gesture of astonishment.

"So be it," she said. "If she prefers to keep silent without payment, let her do so. I prefer to keep my money."

And she replaced the note in her purse.

As she sat thinking thus an idea suddenly occurred to her which caused her to jump up in something almost approaching alarm.

"And Spencer!" she murmured aloud. "What if he should be pursuing the same task? Doubtless, he is. But if he succeeds, O Heavens! we are lost. I must return at once to Sloeford to see his latest despatch. I scarcely know whether to feel re-assured or alarmed at this day's work."

Then turning to her black attendant, she desired her to give directions to put fresh horses to the carriage.

"Impossible," said the landlord. "I have none fit to leave."

"Ah!" exclaimed Lady Bellisle. "Then the consequences may be fatal."

CHAPTER LXII.

ROSE AND BLANCHE BOWERINI ON THEIR TRA-VELS — THEIR NEW HOME — THE FREAKS OF THE GREEN-ROOM — BEHIND THE SCENES — THE JEALOUS WIFE—A FLIRTATION — SERIOUS CONSEQUENCES — A DRAMA OF REAL LIFE CONCLUDING WITH A TRAGEDY — HAMLET — THE DAGGER.

IN spite of the mutual understanding which might be supposed to exist from henceforth between Lady Bellisle and our heroine, the latter did not yet feel entirely secure upon her ladyship's account.

She passed that night trusting to the "virtues of a lock and key" rather than the honour of Lady Bellisle.

The next morning Rose and her companion, Blanche Bowerini, were up betimes and had recommenced their journey.

Some few hours' travelling brought them to their destination.

The introductions which both brought from the manager of the theatre in the town which they had just quitted smoothed all difficulties which might have stood in their way.

A welcome far more cordial than they could have expected was accorded them by their new companions.

At the outset of their career in their new destination an event of a most unpleasant nature for our heroine occurred.

This we are about to record, as it had a direct influence upon Rose Mortimer's after movements.

The leading member of the dramatic company was an intelligent young actor named Walters.

He was married to a member of the company, a dancer, professionally named Ethel Warner.

He was a light-hearted and not over constant husband.

She was all love and attachment to her husband.

She loved fondly, fiercely, and was fiercely jealous.

It must be admitted that he very frequently gave her cause for jealousy.

It was his delight to watch the rich purple blood mantling her cheek as he would carry on an animated flirtation with one of the prettiest members of the company.

He knew her failing in this respect, and cruelly he worked upon it.

We use the expression "cruelly" advisedly, for though jealousy is a sensation looked upon by all as something to be derided and laughed or sneered at, it is nevertheless an agony the most acute for the sufferer.

Rose Mortimer and Blanche Bowerini had been barely introduced into the company when the husband of the jealous *danseuse* made a violent assault upon the hearts of both the girls.

Rose was invulnerable to such attacks.

Blanche was not far but yet slightly gone when she became aware of the fact of her admirer being married.

However, we must do her the justice to say that no sooner had she made this discovery than she cut her would-be lover particularly short.

Her repulses only served to make the inconstant Walters more pressing in his suit, and he did not take any pains to disguise his ardour from his wife.

Upon the second day after their arrival Rose and Blanche Bowerini were seated in the green-room awaiting the reading of a new piece.

Mr. and Mrs. Walters were present.

The former as attentive as ever to the fair sex and inattentive as usual to his wife.

The latter in unmistakeable agony to witness his flirtations.

"Are you staying long with us, Miss Bowerini?" demanded Walters.

"We are not sure."

"And Miss Mortimer?"

"Nor I either," answered Rose. "It depends on whether the management and the public both are favourable to us."

"The latter ensures the former."

"Not always."

"As a rule."

"Perhaps."

"And the former is sure to be insured."

"Indeed?" said Blanche, laughing.

"Now, really that is extremely good of you, Mr. Walters," said Rose Mortimer, "since you have seen neither of us upon the stage as yet."

"Eh? Oh! that's no matter. It signifies nothing; for talent you have I know."

"How?"

"By reputation."

"Reputation?"

"Ay."

"Of having played for a week in an out-of-the-way provincial theatre?"

"And not only reputation," said the actor, "but with ladies you know that pretty faces and comely persons go for something."

"Yes."

"Then your success is assured, believe me, ladies."

"Thank you."

Rose made this acknowledgment so demurely that its drollery struck all of them, and they laughed heartily.

All this time the unhappy wife sat upon thorns.

At length it grew unbearable for her, and she left the room.

Several members of the company saw the whole manœuvre, and a general titter at the unhappy wife's expense was the consequence.

The poor creature rather needed their pity.

Rose did not yet understand this, or she would have taken immediate steps to avoid a misunderstanding.

As it was, the two girls got a reputation established in the green-room, upon such very slight grounds, for being accomplished flirts.

After the reading of the piece a rehearsal was called.

Then the different members of the company went through their parts, but it was found that Miss Ethel Warner (Mrs. Walters) was not present.

Her husband had to go in quest of her, and in the space of a few seconds returned to announce that he had found his wife in their dressing-room very unwell.

He requested the assistance of some of the ladies present, and appeared to be very much disconcerted.

Several persons went to render what assistance lay in their power, and it was found that the poor creature had sobbed herself into a fit of hysterics.

This passed over after a time, and the husband was all attention to his wife.

He was not actually cruel, but not knowing, or not thinking, of the acute suffering which his wife's jealousy occasioned, he flirted in this way.

Truth to tell, it rather gratified him to see in her fierce passion, suppressed with such inward struggles, with such difficulty, a strong proof of the attachment which she bore him.

A day or two passed, and he had once more resumed his old conduct.

The unhappy victim to the green-eyed monster suffered more than ever.

But an event was about to happen which put an effectual stop to this kind of thing.

Affairs in the domestic drama of the Walters were brought to a crisis in this way.

The actor resumed his violent assault upon Rose Mortimer's heart.

However, our heroine did not give him the slightest encouragement.

She repulsed all his advances with as much firmness as she could under the circumstances, and without making herself objectionably prudish.

One night they were performing Hamlet.

The philosophic Prince of Denmark was represented by Mr. Walters, and our heroine was playing some minor character.

Rose was standing at the O.P. wing when Walters came off the stage and made up to her side at once, and commenced his wonted badinage.

"Your scene next, Miss Mortimer?" he began.

"Yes."

"You mean to take them by storm as usual, I presume?"

"Who?"

"The audience."

"Oh!"

"And everybody, of course."

"Thank you, if you really mean it. If you are only satirical at my expense, I think you might spare me."

"You are cruel, Miss Mortimer," he said, with a languishing glance.

"I cruel?"

"Yes."

"Indeed I don't see it."

"'None so blind—' you know."

"Not all. There is not much opening for taking a house by storm in such a part as the actress."

"True."

"Then you were satirical."

"I?"

"Decidedly."

"Nay."

"Nay, but you must have meant it for satire."

"Not at all. Pray don't misconstrue what I meant, my dear Miss Mortimer."

"Pardon me," interrupted our heroine, rather sharply. "Miss Mortimer is sufficient without any qualification."

"No offence."

"Oh! there's none."

"Ahem!"

He was cut rather short by Rose's sharpness, but not yet beaten off.

He returned to the attack.

"I cannot understand," he began, "that stupid old pump's casting of the piece."

"Indeed?"

"No. Old Quirk is a very bad manager."

"I must beg to differ."

"Nay, but you cannot differ with me until you know my objection."

"I can."

"Indeed?"

"Because I anticipate already the objection you would offer."

"What may it be?"

"Some absurd compliment you are about to pay me I suppose."

"Now who is satirical?"

"Not I."

"Pardon me, you are. But I was about to observe that you are quite out of place as the actress."

"Indeed?"

"Of course."

"I'm sorry that you think so poorly of my abilities as that, Mr. Walters."

The actor gave a mock heroic groan at this wilful misinterpretation of his would-be compliments.

"My dear Miss Mortimer," he began.

"Mr. Walters—"

"I beg your pardon. I mean Miss Mortimer, without the 'my dear.'"

"I wish then you would keep to what you mean, and we should save much time in this aimless discussion."

"Aimless?"

"Ay."

"That is a little bit hard again," said Mr. Walters, making a very wry face. "However, I was only about to remark that I think that if that stupid old pump Quirk had cast Bernard for the actress and you for Ophelia he would have shown much better discrimination and good taste."

"And that is your candid opinion, Mr. Walters?" said Rose.

"Candid."

"Then I must say that I prefer Mr. Quirk's knowledge and discrimination to your own upon such a matter as this."

"Oh!"

"Truly, for it is apparent to any one that I am no more fitted for Ophelia than—than Mr. Quirk himself."

"Oh!"

"Nay, you know it."

"Miss Mortimer, that is little better than to accuse me of falsehood."

"I'm sorry that you should put such a construction upon my words."

"You're sorry?"

"Ay, but I cannot retract."

"But seriously, I think that had you been cast for Gertrude—"

"I should look your mother better than Miss Farnham."

"Eh? oh! no."

He was driven into a corner again.

To say that Rose would have personated the queen well was clearly to pay a bad compliment to her youth.

"No matter, Miss Mortimer," he said, in a fit of desperation. "I must say one thing."

"As many as you like."

"Thank you. I know that if you wouldn't play Ophelia well, as you say (a scandal upon your talents, mark me, which I don't admit), I should work up better in the play scene."

"Wherefore?"

"I know that I could 'lay in your lap, lady,' with real earnestness."

"Indeed," said Rose coldly.

"Yes, truly, for you know that, after all, our Ophelia is but—"

"A charming girl."

"I admit it."

"Handsome."

"Granted."

"And agreeable."

"True again, but I must say that 'here's metal more attractive.'"

Rose Mortimer grew tired of harping upon this continual strain.

She turned impatiently away.

Just then from the other side of the wing against which she leant a figure peered forward.

It was Ethel Warner, with her face flushed almost purple, and her rich full black eyes almost starting from their sockets.

She had, in the violence of her passion, bitten her nether lip so deeply that the blood appeared.

As our heroine encountered the eye of the jealous-mad dancer her own cheek flushed perceptibly.

She had no cause for blushes, but she felt deeply for the unhappy wife of the flimsey Walters.

It was very embarrassing, too, for Rose to feel herself unintentionally the cause of any matrimonial dissensions.

She was as much persecuted by the odious attentions of the fickle actor as his unhappy wife was rendered miserable by them.

"Oh! Mrs. Walters," she faltered.

"Madam!" said the dancer fiercely.

"I don't know if you have heard half the absurdities which your husband has been pouring into my ear—I will not say troubling me with."

"No don't," interrupted the jealous wife, with cutting emphasis.

"Ahem! But believe me—"

"Oh, there's no need for apologies," said the dancer haughtily.

"Not apology of course."

"No, no, these little *flirtations* are admitted behind, you know."

Rose did not like this

"Flirtations?" she said.

"Ay."

"If you can so designate it—but believe me that it was entirely a one-sided flirtation."

"Oh!"

And since your husband is present, and sees that his conduct, which is always embarrassing to me, however he may hide it, is likely to lose me the friendship of his wife, whom I would esteem as a friend, I trust he will spare me in future."

"How spare you?" demanded Mr. Hamlet Walters, elevating his eyebrows.

"As a butt for his raillery and ridicule, whichever it is."

Mrs. Walters turned to our heroine with a look of profound gratitude.

"My dear girl," she said, "I know that you will forgive me, but I have the misfortune to love a man who cares but very little for me."

"Ethel!" said Walters.

"I repeat it," said his wife. "Else he would not seek every opportunity of wringing my poor heart with his cruelty."

"Bosh!" said Mr. Walters.

"He takes a delight in it," said Rose. "You have one fault, Mrs. Walters."

"A fault—not towards him."

"Pardon me."

"Then it is in loving him too much."

"Precisely."

"Then it is one which I cannot mend," she said, with a sigh.

"My dear Ethel," said Walters severely, "you know that if there's one thing more than another which annoys me it is doing the sentimental in the presence of a third person."

His wife looked upon him in such a manner at this heartless and unfeeling speech that he turned away in confusion.

"Oh! man, man!" she exclaimed in an agonised whisper. "Do not push me too far—do not press me to extremities, I beseech you."

"Stuff!"

The dancer's eyes flashed a thousand furies, and she made some short angry reply.

Rose was uncomfortable at being thus thrown into one of the endless domestic squabbles of Walters and his wife, and she quitted the spot.

From the opposite side of the stage she could see by their gestures that an angry altercation was taking place.

Shortly their scene came on.

Rose went through her part as well as she was able after what had occurred.

All the time she was on the stage she could see the dancer's eyes fixed upon her from the wing.

The demon jealousy was yet gnawing at her heart's core.

From the bottom of her heart Rose Mortimer pitied her.

Walters, who was really an intelligent actor, played upon the present occasion in a way which gained him fresh honours, and brought down the curtain with a round of applause.

"Hamlet" was over.

Down rushed the members of the company to their several dressing-rooms.

There was a grand scramble and confusion amongst those who had to appear in the farce after the tragedy.

Rose, amongst the rest, was down below, eagerly preparing for the afterpiece, when a cry was heard above.

This was followed by the falling of a body upon the stage.

The dressing-rooms were underneath the stage, and this could be heard as distinctly as if in the room itself.

Thinking that something unusual had occurred—some accident to the machinery, perhaps—Rose threw a cloak over her half-completed toilet, and hurried out.

The company were flocking out of the rooms up to the stage.

"What is it?" asked Rose.

But every one was putting the same question, and no one could reply.

Rose made her way up with the rest on to the stage.

As she gained the top of the stairs a loud noise and confusion of voices struck upon her ears.

She ran eagerly forward, and saw several persons making for the back of the stage.

She ran with them, and there learnt the cause of the bother.

Stretched upon his back across the stage lay Mr. Hamlet Walters.

Standing over him was his wife.

Her hand grasped an uplifted dagger.

With this she was about to strike her prostrate husband.

CHAPTER LXIII.

DEAD OR ALIVE?—REPROACHES—ALL'S WELL THAT ENDS WELL—ROSE'S LOVER—THE NOTES—REJECTION—TWO BOUQUETS—THE BLACK BEARD—SINGULAR CONDUCT—ETHEL WARNER—THE FLOWERS—SUDDEN ILLNESS—MYSTERY—DEATH OF ETHEL THE BALLET-DANCER.

ROSE ran forward.

There was a general rush and scramble.

One of the girls shrieked out.

But before they could reach the spot the dagger descended.

The blow was struck.

Down went the dagger, borne by the avenging hand of the jealous-mad wife, deep into her husband's breast.

"Ah!" he cried. "Ethel, hold your hand! Oh! I'm slain!"

A cry of horror ran through the crowd.

They pressed forward to raise the woman from the body of her husband.

No sooner had the dagger encountered the actor's breast than his maddened wife repented of the rash deed.

Too late.

She could not stay her hand.

The blow was struck, and Walters the actor—

What of him?

Was he dead?

They raised her at once from the body of her husband.

Now she burst into a passionate flood of tears.

But she did not offer to resist them.

She placidly allowed herself to be taken away.

"Do with me as you will," she said. "I care for nothing now."

"Oh! Mrs. Walters!" said Rose.

The dancer turned fiercely upon Rose Mortimer as she spoke.

"What would you?"

"Nothing," said Rose. "How could you do this fearful deed?"

"Speak not to me," said the dancer. "You are the cause of it."

"I?"

"Yes, you. All the world knows of your doings with him."

"My doings?" iterated Rose.

"Ay, in spite of your hypocritical ways. You have killed him by your intrigues."

Rose said nothing.

She concluded that the severity of the blow which the dancer's brain had received had distracted her.

And she made allowances accordingly.

They pressed her for an explanation, but could glean nothing.

The fact was that Walters had richly earned the treatment he had received.

He had goaded on his jealous wife with such diabolical perseverance that she had been pushed beyond the limits of all human endurance.

At a fatal moment she pushed him violently to the ground.

A dagger which he wore suspended at his waist was fatally handy.

She snatched it as he fell, sprang forward, and struck, as we have seen.

Happily, the blow was not doomed to take the actor's life.

It struck deep, it is true, but it was not in a vital part, and so the maddened actress was spared in deed, if not in thought, the heinous crime of murder.

However, a great public scandal was the result of it, and no less could have been expected.

Ethel Warner was carried off to prison to await the result of the injuries inflicted on her husband.

If he died it would go hard with her.

A few weeks passed over, and he recovered, and his wife was acquitted, with a severe reprimand.

The sympathy was so thoroughly with her that no one of the company who had seen the affair would appear against her for the milder charge of assault which the authorities attempted to establish against her.

But from that day a total change was worked in the actor's career.

His wife had been so shocked by the fearful lengths to which her mad passion had led her that she refused any longer to reside with her husband.

Walters now discovered that he really loved his wife.

As soon as she was again at liberty, and her husband had recovered from his wounds, they both renewed their avocations at the theatre; but Ethel took lodgings at a neighbouring house, and could not be induced to change her mind.

"Ethel, Ethel," said the husband, in a tone of passionate entreaty.

"It is useless to attempt to persuade me," she replied.

"But consider—"

"What?"

"What will the world say?"

"Ah!" said his wife, with a reproachful glance. "You care more for the opinion of the world than for me."

"But, Ethel—"

"I think but of you."

"Pardon me, Ethel," he said angrily. "If you thought but of me, you would not thus wish to separate us."

"Once for all, Walters," said his wife, "it is useless to persuade. My decision is taken and cannot be altered."

"But why, in Heaven's name?"

"Because I fear—"

"But you can trust me now."

"Perhaps."

"You may indeed."

"*But not myself.*"

Her husband started and turned pale at these strange words.

This was the whole secret of her obstinate resistance to his prayer.

She feared, after her fatal ebullition of madness and jealousy, to trust herself any longer.

He pressed her further, but to no avail.

"Ah, Ethel," he said, "I fear that your love for me is dead at last."

She shook her head in sad denial.

"Then why, why do you thus condemn us both to such a miserable existence?"

"I will tell you why," said his wife.

And an answer came which was but very little expected.

"Because in thus going against the dictates of our hearts—in thus outraging our strong affections—we make some atonement in the way of penance for our crimes."

"*Our* crimes?"

"Ay."

"I have none to atone for."

"The sinfulness of my rash act, which so nearly took your life, is as much your own as mine. You goaded me to phrenzy—I madly murdered—"

"This is foolish. No murder was done. Here am I, the murdered man, as strong and lively as a grig after all."

"No matter," said the wife. "It was the intention."

It was useless attempting to reason against such a conclusion.

Walters turned away, and in a sulky fit gave up the discussion.

But presently he would return to it with renewed ardour.

Fresh arguments were brought to bear, but all without result.

The domestic affairs of the Walters family remained thus for some time.

One night during the performance Rose Mortimer noticed that she was the special object of scrutiny through an opera glass from the front.

Her attention was attracted, and she perceived that behind it was a tall handsome man wearing a black beard.

As soon as he discovered that the actress's eyes were upon him he made several familiar signs which rather disgusted her.

He blew her a kiss upon the top of his lavender gloves.

This was done quite with the air of a man who feels sure of a favourable reception.

However, Rose Mortimer looked upon it rather in the light of an impudence than aught else.

She frowned and turned indignantly away.

When the curtain fell the call boy came and brought her a bouquet carefully enveloped in paper.

"What's this?" she asked.

"For you, miss."

"From whom?"

"The dark gentleman in the private box on the right."

In a country theatre, we may here point out, the holder of a private box is always well known from behind.

"You may take it back, Morris," said Rose.

"Take it back?" said the boy.

He was not in the habit of receiving such messages.

"Yes, at once."

"What for, miss?"

"No matter what for. You have only to return it to the gentleman who gave it to you. Say that Miss Mortimer refuses to take it."

"Yes, miss."

"But say this upon your own behalf. Not a word from me, mark you."

And so ended this bit of gallantry.

At least so thought Rose. So she hoped.

But she found very shortly that all was not yet concluded.

Blanche Bowerini and our heroine left the theatre together.

As they passed out of the stage door a man ran up to them and held a pencilled note to Blanche.

"Miss Mortimer?" he said.

"That is I," said Rose.

"Here's a note for you, miss."

"Who from?"

"A gentleman."

Rose thought of the black beard before the fixed opera glass at once.

"Take it back to the gentleman who gave it you," she said.

"Any message?"

"None."

The fellow ran off with the note.

"There's some poor man hit very hard, dear Rose," said Blanche.

"He grows troublesome," said Rose.

"He certainly is pressing."

"Yes, these men of the world believe, or affect to believe, that an actress has never any self-respect—no thought of honour, of virtue, or anything else which is supposed to control the life of every respectable woman."

"That's a harsh way of judging an ardent fellow who sends you a bouquet."

"Believe me, Blanche, it is an insult to the woman who receives it."

At this point in the conversation a gentleman stepped up and confronted them.

He raised his hat with the greatest politeness and saluted Rose.

"Miss Mortimer, I believe," he said.

"Yes, that's my name," said Rose.

"Will you do me the favour to accept my card?" said the gentleman.

"Pardon me, sir," said our heroine, without offering to take the card. "But I do not know you."

"Allow me to introduce myself."

"The time is not exactly convenient," said Rose.

"At least accept my card."

Rose refused.

"What?" said the gentleman. "You refuse my card as well as my bouquet?"

"You will excuse me," said Rose, "but I look upon this rather in the light of an impertinence than anything else."

"Eh?"

"You perceive that your attentions are unpleasant and painful to me."

"I'm sorry—" he began.

"Nay, more," interrupted Rose, "they are insulting."

"Madam, I go," said the gentleman, with a bow. "I am extremely sorry, believe me, that the homage I wished to pay to your exquisite finish in your art should thus be misconstrued."

Rose bowed stiffly.

"At least you cannot prevent my admiration. You cannot keep me from the theatre, and I can admire in silence."

Rose, fearing that he was about to continue a long tirade upon her severity in thus dismissing him, hastily interrupted him.

A second bow cut him short in the beginning of a very flowery appeal.

The two girls pushed on and regained their lodgings unmolested.

But Rose, how little do you dream from what you have escaped!

How little do you imagine the snare which encompassed you!

Did you know who the man really was who thus forced his attentions upon you you would have been able to explain that instinctive shudder which you felt as he approached.

It was a fatal omen.

And Rose happily accepted it.

"You were awfully severe," said Blanche.

"Not too much," said Rose.

"More than I could possibly have been."

"Then Heaven have mercy upon you, my dear Blanche," said Rose, "for the dangers which encompass the life of the ballet-dancer are legion."

The next night, as soon as Rose Mortimer appeared on the stage, a burst of applause greeted her.

She well knew that some hand must be there to stir up the enthusiasm, for country audiences are not as a rule so warm.

In an instant she perceived the opera glass and the black beard.

Ethel Warner chanced to be upon the stage with Rose, and she noticed and remarked it to her in a whisper.

They were playing an extravaganza, and Rose Mortimer was personating a prince, a fascinating youth in pink satin, blue velvet, and spangles.

Ethel Warner was playing the fairy godmother.

A duet which they had to sing brought down the house with a run.

The applause was immense.

The dark beard joined heartily in the applause, more in fact than any one present.

In the midst of it he threw a bouquet to the stage and it fell at Rose Mortimer's feet.

At the same moment a second bouquet was thrown.

Quick as thought Rose picked up the first and presented to the fairy godmother.

The second she reserved for herself.

The black beard's conduct at witnessing this was remarkable.

His gloves, which he had removed to applaud, lay before him.

He took them up in the greatest disgust and dashed them to the ground.

An oath, too, escaped him, which was drowned in the continued applause.

The two actresses ran off.

"What beautiful flowers !" said Ethel Warner.

"Yes."

"This is the bouquet that was thrown to you by the black beard."

"I saw it."

"Ah, you cruel girl! How sweetly these flowers smell! But how peculiar !"

The words were barely uttered when Ethel Warner staggered dizzily against the wing.

Her head fell forward upon her chest.

She sank upon the ground.

They ran to raise her up, and a cry of horror escaped them.

She was dead !

CHAPTER LXIV.

ETHEL WARNER—SUSPICIONS—THE DOCTOR—A GRAVE ACCUSATION — THE SUSPECTED MAN — HIS STRANGE DISAPPEARANCE—THE BOUQUET PRESERVED — LADY BELLISLE — SLOEFORD HOUSE—THE LETTER—ON THE TRACK—FRESH TROUBLES — PURSUIT — BUT WHERE ? — THE RAILWAY—DANGERS.

THE excitement created in the theatre by the sudden demise of the unfortunate Ethel Warner was immense.

It was impossible that such a remarkable occurrence should pass over unnoticed by all.

Our heroine was more grieved than she could possibly express.

In this death, awful and sudden, she saw more than the people generally surrounding the still warm corpse of the ill-fated dancer.

The bouquet excited her suspicions.

At the first idea she thought that she would keep her secret to herself.

But no. Too much, indeed, had already been concealed.

She began to feel the weight of a loaded conscience.

Whilst she kept the secret of murder she felt herself to be almost an accomplice in the foul crimes which her soul abhorred.

At once, therefore, she communicated her suspicions to the manager of the theatre.

To him alone, for she was not yet assured of the truth of her suspicions.

At first the manager was not inclined to believe as Rose Mortimer did in this business.

He did not know the motives which Rose deemed could prompt an enemy to such fearful measures.

He could not believe revenge for having slighted the gallantries of an ensnared lady-killer would have led a man to such a desperate retaliation.

But our heroine was so earnest that he determined at once to see into it.

If there was no truth in it there could be no harm done.

The bouquet would soon decide this.

A doctor chanced to be present.

He had been in the theatre at the time of the catastrophe, and had been called behind the scenes immediately.

"Doctor," said the manager in a whisper to the man of physic, "we have some grave suspicions about this death."

"We ?" said the doctor.

"Ay, that is, I have. They have been uttered to me. I know not if they be worth a second thought. This is for you to decide."

"Explain yourself, Mr. Quirk," replied the Æsculapius.

"We, that is, I presume this lady's death to be the work of poison."

"Ah ?"

"Yes. The flowers."

The doctor darted forward and picked up the fallen bouquet.

Holding his handkerchief to his face, he examined them attentively for several minutes.

All this time Mr. Quirk, the manager, eyed him curiously.

The doctor looked grave.

"It may be true," he said.

"You think so, doctor ?"

"I do, indeed."

"Then it is murder."

"Precisely. But how, why, wherefore, and who is the culprit ?"

"That I scarcely can say."

"Two bouquets were thrown."

"True."

The manager ran from the doctor's side up to Rose Mortimer.

"You know, Miss Mortimer," he said, "that there were two bouquets."

"I do."

"Then from whom did this one come ?"

"The right stage box."

"Are you sure ?"

"Positive."

"How do you know ?"

"Because I purposely kept the one which came from the other side."

"Purposely, you say ?"

"Yes."

"Why ?"

"That this man should not have any further encouragement by my accepting his bouquet."

"I see. The inference you draw is not so unnatural as I at first supposed. You are a much stronger-minded girl—pardon the expression—than I at first imagined."

Without further delay he ran round to the front of the house and made his way with all possible speed to the right hand stage box.

It was empty.

No one had seen its occupant go out.

No one had noticed him there, for he sat very quietly and seemed rather to shun observation.

He ran back to the exit from the theatre and eagerly demanded of the doorkeeper if he had seen the dark gentleman pass out.

"Yes, sir," replied the man.

"Long since ?"

"About ten minutes since."

"Ah! say you so ? Then he must have slipped through our fingers !"

"Who, sir ?"

"Why, the gentleman. Fly off at once and make inquiries, for I am determined that this mystery shall be unravelled."

The man left, and the manager quickly returned to the doctor.

The man of medicine was still engaged attentively scrutinising the fatal bouquet.

"Well ?" he said, without looking up.

"Well, doctor, I think that I have hit upon the culprit."

[THE SWEEP AND HIS VICTIMS.]

"Good."

"But I fear that he's escaped."

"Bad."

"I only fear so."

"Then you must spare no effort to secure him, for it is every man's duty to aid justice in the prosecution of the homicide, if not the perpetrator of the minor crimes of which mankind is guilty."

As he said this Rose Mortimer strolled up.

"For my part," he continued, "I look upon murder as so hideous an offence against the laws of God and man that every other fault—the worst which can be committed—the vilest crimes that guilty man perpetrates—are but as follies in comparison with it.

The person who winks at such a crime, the man who would hesitate to make known his convictions upon such a matter out of fear of any personal embarrassment, deserves to be looked upon as an accomplice in the deed."

This came so near our heroine's late self-accusations that a guilty blush suffused her countenance as she heard it.

"Can we render any assistance, doctor ?" asked the manager.

"You can."

"Command me, then."

"Have you a small box ?"

"Of what description ?"

" A little casket, air-tight, or as nearly so as possible, to contain this bouquet."

" I've nothing exactly answering your description, doctor, but—"

"Stay," interrupted Rose Mortimer anxiously. " I have such a box in my dressing-room. One moment, and I'll fetch it."

She ran off, all eagerness now to render some assistance.

The words coming from the doctor had put her own conduct before her in so reprehensible a light that she was all anxiety to do something to assist the working of justice.

She returned in the space of a few seconds with a small metal-bound box.

It was one she had recently purchased to contain her stage trinkets.

As she rather prized this little casket, the greater was the consolation she felt in making the sacrifice in such a service.

" I shall take the bouquet with me," said the doctor, " and analyse it carefully."

" Do you think there is poison, doctor ?" demanded the manager.

" I don't merely think it. I am convinced of it. It only remains for me to discover what poison it is."

The doctor had only just completed his packing of the bouquet when Mr. Quirk's messenger returned breathlessly.

" Well, Manning," said the manager, " what have you discovered ?"

" Not much."

" That's unfortunate."

" I traced him to the King's Head Hotel, and described him to the landlord."

" Good. Did he recognise the description ?"

" Yes, sir."

" And what is his name ?"

" Smithson."

" Assumed," said the doctor, glancing up from his task.

" No doubt."

" So much the better," said Rose Mortimer. " For if he has disguised his name, and you can prove this, it will be something in the way of evidence against him."

" Yes."

But while the manager thus readily acquiesced, and was even pleased with Rose Mortimer's discernment, the doctor, who saw further, was rather troubled by her reply.

" It strikes me that you are rather quickly grasping at conclusions too," he said.

" Why so ?"

" If this name is an assumed one, it would prove the whole affair to be premeditated, rather than the work of revenge upon Miss Mortimer for having slighted his attentions."

Rose began to feel uncomfortable again.

His reasoning was clear and simple enough.

She felt in fear that she was being gradually drawn back into those fatal incidents which had so embittered her existence during her brief stay at Sloeford.

The manager happily broke in and interrupted this part of the discussion as it began to assume an unpleasant feature for our heroine.

" One moment, doctor," he said. " As the old saying has it, ' First catch your hare.' How about this Mr. Smithson, Manning ?"

" Gone, sir."

" What ?"

" Left the hotel."

" Already ?"

" Yes, sir. Left in a hurry—a letter coming unexpectedly, he said."

The doctor and Mr. Quirk exchanged significant glances.

" It looks strange," said the former.

" Strange ?" echoed the manager. " It looks to me, doctor, a clear case."

*   *   *   *   *

As soon as Lady Bellisle left Rose Mortimer at the inn where so desperate an attempt had been made upon her life she hastened back to Sloeford.

She expected here to see the earl, according to to a previous agreement.

However, the first person she encountered (one of the domestics) informed her that his lordship had only that day departed.

He had left suddenly, after writing a letter to her ladyship, which was here delivered to her.

" And Miss St. John ?" she asked.

" Is within. Shall I tell her you wish to see her, your ladyship ?"

" Yes—yet stay. No. I will see her later."

" She is in her dressing-room."

" Very good."

" Anything further, my lady ?"

" No. Leave me."

As soon as she was alone she eagerly tore open the letter.

" Let me hope," she murmured as her hand nervously tore the letter across, " that he has not departed upon the errand of which he spoke to me. If he has left upon *her* destruction, then there is fresh danger for us."

Whether this was or not the case the contents of the earl's letter will show.

It ran thus :—

" *I have departed upon the important mission of which we had lately so little hope. I have just received a clue which leaves not the slightest doubt upon my mind now of success. Within a week you may reckon upon hearing that the annoyance which you have so keenly felt for some time past has disappeared. Upon another hand means are in operation to secure the man.*"

" Great Heavens !" ejaculated Lady Bellisle. " After all, the worst has come. But what more does he say ?"

" *As soon as anything positive can be determined you may count upon hearing from me. If I do not write shortly you may understand that I have not as yet succeeded in my object. I shall not write oftener than I deem absolutely necessary to quiet your apprehensions, for fear of misadventure with the post.*

" Yours,
" SLOEFORD."

As she concluded she crushed the paper in her hand and thrust it into her pocket.

" I must follow him instantly," she said. " With diligence I may yet overtake him before any steps can be taken in the matter."

She rang the bell, and a domestic made his appearance.

" Did the earl say in which direction he was going ?" she demanded.

" No, my lady."

" Then you know nothing ?"

" Nothing, my lady."

" You may go. Stay. Did the earl leave here on foot ?"

" He drove to Springford in the carriage."

" Ah !"

" And his lordship took the railway from there."

" Where to ?"

" I don't know, my lady."

" Does Thomas know ?"

"He didn't say."

"Go and see."

Thomas, the coachman. came up immediately, in obedience to the summons.

"Where did the earl book to from Springford, Thomas?" asked Lady Bellisle.

"Can't say, my lady."

"How provoking!"

"I can learn at once."

And he was about to withdraw when Lady Bellisle stopped him.

"Stay. Put the horses to."

"Yes, my lady."

"Don't lose an instant."

"No, my lady."

The coachman left the room, and shortly returned to announce that the carriage was ready.

She ran downstairs, and was driven quickly across the country to Springford.

It was about three miles, and her impatience knew no bounds.

It was with much difficulty that she continued to keep her seat.

At length the journey was over, and she was at Springford.

She sprang out of the carriage and ran up to the booking office of the railway station, where she was well known by the clerks and porters about.

"The Earl of Sloeford booked from here yesterday, I believe?"

"Yes, my lady."

"Where to?"

"Hatfield, my lady."

"Thank you."

And she turned away.

But the thought came to her that some explanation was perhaps necessary, and she returned immediately.

"I wished to follow his lordship upon important business," she said, 'and, as he has not left his destination behind, I took this as the only means of finding him."

"Yes, my lady."

"When is the next train?"

"For Hatfield?"

"Yes."

"Half an hour, my lady."

"I shall book by that train, then. Will you get me a ticket?"

"Return?"

"No—single."

Then she called the coachman to her.

"Now, Thomas," she said, "I am going to leave again. I shall telegraph my address to-night, so that my letters may be forwarded to me at once by a special messenger."

"Yes, my lady."

"You can return now."

"Thank you, my lady."

CHAPTER LXV.

LONDON—NIGHT—DARK DEEDS—THE VAULT— THE BODY—THE RESURRECTIONIST—THE VISIT TO THE NECROMANCER—A BARTER FOR FLESH — DOG BITE DOG — THE LONE HOUSE — THE MIDNIGHT JOURNEY—THE CART AND ITS LOAD —ALARM—CHASE—POLICE—MERMET AGAIN— SUPERNATURAL AGENCIES—A COMPACT—"RE-SURRECTION JOE, YOU ARE IN MY POWER!"

WE shift our scene.

Now it is laid in London once again.

It is night—night grim and dark—night in all its terrors.

In a remote part of this large metropolis deeds were being done which would have startled the whole world.

Practices which have been deemed long since dead.

Practices which make the weak heart shudder, the strong revolt.

In a dark and silent vault beneath an untenanted house we open our scene.

The house had long since been out of repair and without a tenant.

The reason of this was that, on account of some heinous crime having been once perpetrated there, it had gained a reputation for being haunted.

The crime alluded to was, however, so remotely connected with the haunted house that not even the oldest inhabitants of the neighbourhood could remember anything concerning it.

Be this as it may, if the house were haunted or entirely free from all spiritual manifestations, it sufficed to gain it the reputation, and to serve the purpose of certain unscrupulous wretches of whom we are about to speak.

In the cellar of the house, a noisesome dark vault, lay a long narrow object wrapt in a white sheet, which but imperfectly hid from the view its contents.

The shuddering yet fascinated eye at once discerns the outline of a human body.

It is a corpse.

A cold clay corpse of one newly dead.

And only a few hours have passed since the cold and inanimate thing before us had life and health, vigour and manhood, and a strong right arm to make the dastard tremble.

A sharp wit, too, to make the scornful draw in their horns before him.

And now the seat of wit is a blank.

The muscles of those once powerful limbs are still in death.

Presently the fearful silence of this grim charnel-house is broken.

A footstep is heard echoing in the street above.

Then, with wonderful distinctness, in the silent night, is heard the lifting of a latch above by a careful hand, a hand evidently using all due caution to prevent the possibility of being overheard.

But the newcomer is heavily laden, and his hand cannot act with the same freedom which it would else use.

Then there is a pause in the newcomer's movements above stairs.

Then a heavy foot is heard descending the stairs, and it approaches the vault containing the dead body.

Now he draws near, and we see a man ferocious in aspect, and employed upon a ghastly office.

A mission which must denote all absence of compunction, all kindly feeling or humanity.

He staggers into the vault beneath the weight of a human body hanging across the right shoulder.

"Pheugh!" he murmurs, panting freely. "This has been a tough job."

Then he prepares to lay his ghastly burthen upon the ground.

"Gently, gently there," he murmurs again. "It wouldn't do to smash you up, my beauty, after all the trouble I've taken to secure you. Gently, gently. All right. Not much damage done. You'll keep the other fellow company. Not over jolly, but you'll be all right. There's no mistake about it— he's a reg'lar beauty; and if Resurrection Joe had only got the office as soon as I did, I shouldn't have stood the ghost of a chance."

As he muttered the word "ghost" he was sorry for having chosen such an expression.

It sounded unpleasant in the present association.

It was easy to see, from the whispered soliloquy which the man indulged in, that he was not exempt from all awe of death.

Or rather we may say that supernatural fears were more excited within him than aught else.

He looked about him a bit, but had too recently left the light to be yet enabled to pierce the gloom of this chamber of death.

He took a metal box from his pocket, containing lucifers, and with nervous despatch struck one and lit up a tallow candle stuck in a stone bottle.

The effect was now even more unpleasant than before.

The flickering rays of the candle shone with a ghastly appearance upon the still stiff bodies lying side by side in cold companionship.

The light reflected, too, upon the soot-begrimed visage of the sweep who had brought the bodies there.

Faint as was the illumination thus afforded, it could be easily seen by the blackened face of the sweep that he had begun to be sadly ill at ease.

There was a nervous twitching about his lips and a furtive glance from time to time towards the bodies which told its own tale.

He shook himself together a bit, as if he would drive all unpleasant thoughts from his mind, and then struck up a whistle.

It was but a faint effort.

Very faint.

He broke down lamentably in the first bar, and shivered from head to foot.

"Bless'd if I can stand it any more !" he said at length, with a burst, still whispered. "I'll go and wake up the old 'un."

Then, with his eyes averted from the ghastly companions of his musings, he left the cellar.

As soon as he got outside he felt considerably relieved.

"They'll be all safe enough there," he mused as he ran along the road. "And now it's over I think it's a good night's work. That fust one is wuth a trifle, but the old 'un is a downright beauty. I don't let him go under my own price for nobody. That I'll take my davy on."

He made his way with all speed to the west end of London.

On his road he called into a barber's shop, where he got shaved and cleansed in spite of the lateness of the hour.

Then, thus refreshened, he hastened towards his destination.

Some ten or fifteen minutes had perhaps elapsed after his departure from the haunted house when a second individual made his appearance there.

He appeared to be as well acquainted with the haunted house as its late occupant, for he made his way directly downstairs to the vaults of death.

Here he rapped upon the door gently.

"Snatchem !" he called.

Then, receiving no reply, he pushed open the door and entered.

"Out ? Well he ain't got it, then. Why, hullo ! what's this?"

This exclamation was caused by his perceiving the second body in the vault.

The presence of the first was already known to him.

"Hullo ! Another stiff 'un, by the holy poker !" he continued, surveying it curiously. "It is the identical feller too. He's been before me. Well I thought as there could be no one else at work on the very same ground there. I know. I'll cart him off. It's easier work than digging him up after all. The trap's outside, and jigger me if I don't do it."

This ruffian, unlike the one who had brought the cadaverous object into the vault, appeared to have no compunctions upon the matter at all.

Long habit had blunted all sense of humanity within him.

He had no respect, no awe for the presence of the grim tyrant who calls alike upon the high-born and the humble.

He stooped down, and taking the last-brought corpse by the shoulders, proceeded to lift it up.

It was very weighty, and caused him a great struggle.

However, he stood by his self-imposed task manfully.

He was resolved to accomplish, and it was not a little that could put him off.

"Come up !" he muttered, groaning under the weight. "You wouldn't have let me tumble you about like this a week ago, I'd swear. Come up."

As he said this he succeeded in raising the corpse upon his back.

Then he marched up the stairs and passed out of the house.

He turned down a lane by the side of the house, where a small spring cart stood awaiting him.

The man tumbled the corpse into the cart. Then he jumped up, and, whipping his horse, started off.

He had not reached the end of the lane when a policeman challenged him.

"Hullo, there ! What are you up to with that cart ?" he cried out.

"Nothing, mate."

"Let me see."

"You be hanged !"

But the constable would not be denied.

He ran up to the horse's head, and, seizing the bridle, forced it back.

"Let go there," said the driver.

"Let me see what you've got there."

"I shan't."

"Then I shall take you off with me to the greenyard," said the policeman.

"Oh, you will ?"

"I shall."

"Now, hark ye, my fine feller, there wants two parties to that bargain."

"Come, come, no fooling."

"Precisely ; so drop it. Let me get past, or I'll settle your hash for you double quick !"

With this he whipped his horse furiously, and the beast sprang forward.

But the constable held the bridle with a firm hand, and forced the bit so sharply back into the horse's mouth that it could not stir.

"If you don't let go that blessed hoss," said the man, "I warn you, my fine feller, I'll give you such a one for your nob as will make you sing out."

"Drop that now."

But, instead of heeding what the policeman said, he slashed at him so savagely with the whip that the man jumped away with a cry of pain.

"Take that !" cried the fellow.

Then, taking advantage of the constable's temporary discomfiture, he whipped his horse up suddenly and sharply.

Off they went at a spanking pace.

The policeman, with an oath, sprang his rattle.

Heads with nightcaps were popped from windows all down the road, but the man in the cart, with its deathly load, got safely away.

It was a rare scramble and a run for it, but the magnitude of the danger lent the robber of death wings, or, rather, additional stings to his whip.

The horse flew madly, snorting with pain.

In the meantime the original possessor of the stolen corpse ran post haste to the house of Mermet, the Arab necromancer.

Here, by a fortunate chance, he found the Arab yet stirring.

"What do you wish of me ?" demanded Mermet, who received his late guest with that stately mystery which so took with his visitors generally.

"A bit of business," replied the bodysnatcher cautiously.

"What is it?"

"I've heer'd as you wanted to buy a few stiff 'uns."

"I don't understand."

"Corpses for experiments, you know, doctor—dead 'uns."

"Oh! bodies."

"That's the hammer."

"Well, and if I do?"

"I've got the percise articles."

"But do you not know that it is a forbidden traffic?"

"Yes."

"And yet you venture openly to propose it to me, a perfect stranger."

"I ain't afeard. You wouldn't split I know. The buyer and seller are both in for it you know, guv'nor."

"Enough," said the necromancer, evidently not relishing the fellow's retort. "What is it you have to sell?"

"A stiff 'un I tell you,"

"A body?"

"Of course."

"Where is it?"

"At home."

"And where is that?"

"Not far."

"When can I see it?"

"Now."

"At this hour?"

"No time like the present, guv'nor, besides which this ain't exackly the sort o' business one likes to do at daylight."

"No, no."

"Will you come and see them now?"

"Yes; but what mean you by 'them?' I thought you had but one."

"Two, doctor. But you can have one or both, as you like, you know."

"All right, and for the removal of them?"

"I can hire a trap."

"Very good."

Without more ado, therefore, the Arab donned his walking apparel and sallied forth with the professor of this infamous traffic in human flesh.

Mermet's impatience to be there could not brook a long delay, and he therefore called a cab, and they drove up to within a short distance of the haunted house.

Then they descended and entered the house with as little noise as possible.

The cellar door was closed.

"That's a rum go," muttered the bodysnatcher, half aloud. "Why, I could have sworn that I left the door open."

He pushed it open and entered the cellar.

Now just as he crossed the threshold the tallow candle which he had left stuck in the stone bottle gave an expiring flicker.

"This way, guv'nor."

"Get a light," said Mermet.

"I ain't got one."

"Here's a match."

"Here's the last one. He ain't been more than three hours in the box."

"Bring it up to the light then."

"Yes, guv'nor."

And the bodysnatcher groped along the black vault in search of its ghostly occupants.

But nothing could be found.

After he had continued his search for some little time the necromancer grew impatient.

"Now then," he said. "What are you after? Be quick, will you?"

"I can't find it, guv'nor."

"Get a light. Here's a match."

"Thank ye, guv'nor."

He struck the lucifer and held it aloft whilst he glanced about the vault.

It was empty.

The Arab was greatly enraged at this.

At first he deemed it to be merely a ruse to get him there and then to extort money from him by some means or other.

But here he was mistaken.

The resurrectionist had no such thought as this.

And fortunate for him it was, for the necromancer carried with him a certain crystal phial more potent than any arm of destruction ever known.

The only pocket pistol which never missed fire.

But so real was the fellow's astonishment that the Arab saw that he had not been wilfully deceived.

It was clear that he had had two bodies to dispose of, which had disappeared by some extraordinary chance.

However, there was no help for it. He must return home at once, baffled in his object, and it was evident enough that Mermet was not a little annoyed by it.

What he wanted with these fearful objects we shall see as we proceed.

Another piece of villany was at work.

And another more rascally than any yet practised by this arch knave.

"I know what it is," said the resurrectionist suddenly, as a thought crossed him. "I know where they be gone to."

"Gone to?"

"Where they've been taken to."

"Do you let others share such matters as these with you?"

"Not others—only one."

"As few confidants as possible will suit my humour. I don't care about having my affairs known to the whole world."

"No, guv'nor," said Snatchem, "but Resurrection Joe and me was pals for a long time, but as we couldn't get on square together I cried off, and—"

"Dissolved partnership."

"Yes."

"And so you think now—"

"As how Joe's been and done an old pal a dirty trick."

"You think that he has taken them, then—that he has robbed you?"

"Yes."

"Well, you must trade with me another time."

"All right, guv'nor."

"If you like to call upon me to-morrow I can put a job in your way."

"In what line?"

"The same."

"Very good, guv'nor."

"A lady is to be buried in a city churchyard."

"City? Pheugh!"

"So much the easier."

"In the city?"

"To be sure. The city is quiet and deserted after evening is past."

And with this the necromancer left and hastily returned home.

As Ahmet, his servant, let him in he told him that another visitor awaited him.

"Ah!" said the necromancer. "They come late to-night."

"He is on important business, sahib, or he should not have waited," said the Arab, with a salaam.

"Where?"

"In the consulting room."

"Good."

Then, leaving his cloak and hat below, he hastily ascended.

This visitor was a trifle more low and ruffianly than Snatchem, the resurrectionist, whom he had just quitted.

"What is your business with me ?" demanded the necromancer.

"I've heard as how you're a doctor, your honour, and—"

"And what ?"

"Make essperiments on dead 'uns, and dissex 'em."

Mermet started.

His reputation in this respect was gaining him an unenviable notoriety.

He thought that he must proceed warily now.

After all it might only be a snare to entrap him into a confession of his strange dealings.

He had been working with considerable boldness of late, and could not hope to continue his proceedings quite out of danger.

"I don't understand you, my man," he said. "You must either speak more plainly or else I cannot converse further with you."

"All right guv'nor. All I want to know is if you'll buy a couple of stiff 'uns of me. I've two lovely ones as ever you set eyes on."

A sudden thought occurred to Mermet here.

It might be Resurrection Joe, the late partner of Snatchem, who had robbed him.

Now Mermet never lost an opportunity for inspiring any one with awe of his great knowledge of occult sciences.

Here was an excellent chance, which was not to be lost.

"I knew of your coming," said the necromancer, looking his visitor steadily in the eyes.

"The devil you did."

"And of your purpose."

"Get on, guv'nor. You are trying to get at a feller, I know."

"What do you mean, fellow ?"

"Why, that it's all bosh."

"Do you think, then, that you can veil your robberies from me as from the man you have robbed ?"

"Eh ?"

"Answer me now—whence did you procure these two bodies ?"

This hit Mr. Resurrection Joe so straight home that he could not face the necromancer any more.

"Why, where do we get 'em from, guv'nor ?" he faltered.

"Ah ! You speak evasively."

"No, I—"

"Silence ! You have stolen these two from a dark vault—you have robbed them from a companion of your works."

"I say, now, guv'nor—"

"Silence !"

"You seem to know all about it."

"I do."

"And where did you get your information from, guv'nor ?"

Mermet replied by pointing his forefinger downwards with silent sternness.

Resurrection Joe trembled from head to foot at this.

"No matter for that," said Mermet. "Do what I bid you, and we can trade together. If you can take charge of one of these bodies to deliver it out of town I can make it worth your while."

"But—"

"Silence !"

"If I refuse ?"

"You cannot."

"Cannot ?"

"Dare not, then, if you like that better."

"Confound your cheek," exclaimed the body-snatcher. "Dare not ?"

"No; for, Resurrection Joe, I know you, and you are in my power !"

CHAPTER LXVI.

LADY BELLISLE — SCHEMES FRUSTRATED — OFF THE SCENT—THE DESPATCH—DANGERS MULTIPLIED — THE FAINTING FIT — THE COUSIN'S LOVE—SUSPICIONS—CLARA ST. JOHN STILL AT WORK—OLD MARTIN — REVELATIONS — LADY BELLISLE'S JOURNEY — STRANGE SCENE IN A MARKET-PLACE — THE WIFE AUCTION — THE END OF THE JOURNEY — THE THEATRE — EXCITEMENT — DEATH OF ROSE MORTIMER — "DEAD! THEN WE ARE LOST !"

BEFORE continuing this portion of our narrative we had better conclude the movements of Lady Bellisle.

The object for which she had taken her sudden departure was one which so nearly touches the interest of our tale that it should not be further delayed.

The life of Rose Mortimer was imperilled.

And thus the safety of Lady Bellisle and her cousin, the new-made earl, was endangered.

Lady Bellisle had the note which the latter had left behind him, and had not failed to construe its fatal meaning aright.

He was upon the track of Rose Mortimer, and had departed with the murderous purpose, which, as we have already seen, had so nearly succeeded.

When Lady Bellisle arrrived at the next station she made inquiries again.

The Earl of Sloeford had booked for London.

This was fatal to her hopes.

From London she well knew that she would lose all clue.

With the most vivid fears and apprehensions for Rose Mortimer's safety, she returned to Sloeford.

A day passed, and there was no letter from the earl.

This was both torture and relief at once to her.

Torture, on account of the silence and the fear that he might be working actively while this continued.

Relief, because she deemed that he would certainly communicate with her as soon as he was near the accomplishment of his cruel purpose.

And she was powerless to act in any way to avert it.

Utterly helpless, whilst he, the partner in her crimes, was blindly hurling them on their doom.

It was maddening to contemplate.

And now Lady Bellisle began to feel some of the pangs of bitter remorse for the crimes which she had so ruthlessly committed.

Crimes of which she had thought nothing at the time.

The second day, however, brought her fears to a climax.

A letter arrived from the earl.

It was dated two days previously, and ran thus :—

"I am now within an ace of the achievement of the object for which you betrayed so much anxiety. Before a day is over I hope to say to you that she is no more."

This was too much for her.

She gave a loud shriek and fainted.

When she recovered her cousin, Clara St. John, was standing over her bathing her temples with eau de Cologne, whilst her waiting-maid was chafing the palms of her hands.

"Are you better, dear ?" said Clara, with a great show of anxiety.

"Yes, much."

She glanced about her eagerly.

"What are you looking for?" demanded Clara, with much feeling.

"Only a letter. Ah! I have it."

She saw it upon the floor as she spoke and she hastily recovered it.

A glance showed her that it was roughly crumpled up.

Then Clara had not read it?

Lady Bellisle was considerably relieved at this, for although she did not at all suspect that her cousin would be guilty of a meanness, yet the risk which they (she and the earl) ran was so great that she felt mistrustful of everything and everybody.

"Has something occurred to disturb you?" demanded Clara St. John.

"Nothing."

"I'm glad of that. I feared that you had received some unpleasant tidings."

Lady Bellisle eyed her sharply, but Clara stood her glance firmly.

"No, dear," she said calmly, "nothing, I suppose, but the late events. They have shaken me sadly. You know I have not your endurance under these trying circumstances."

"She doesn't think that," mused Clara, inwardly. "That's a quiet bit of sarcasm to herself; but she doesn't quite know her cousin yet. The time will come when we may be better acquainted."

Then she added aloud—

"No, dear. You have not. But of course the events which happened before I arrived were naturally more unpleasant to you than to me."

Lady Bellisle turned sharply upon her cousin, at these words.

"Why so?"

"Because you were in the house at the time of the murder I believe."

The shudder which Lady Bellisle struggled vainly to repress was observed and duly noted by Clara St. John.

"No, dear," she replied, with what calmness she could assume. "Not in the house. We did not know of it until the next day."

"Oh?"

"No. I thought you knew all about the unhappy occurrence."

"No, indeed."

"The late earl, my poor uncle, shut himself in his room, and the dreadful truth was not known until the night following the death."

"How did they know then that he had died the night before?"

"The doctors said so."

"Oh!"

It began to look something like a cross-examination, so Lady Bellisle grew sharper in her replies and abruptly changed the topic.

"I have to leave Sloeford again, dear Clara," she said.

"Indeed?"

"Ay, and at once."

"Never."

"I must."

"Shall you be long gone? Pardon my curiosity, but I missed you sadly whilst you have been away."

"No, dear, I shall not be long."

"Thanks."

And, with a fresh embrace, the loving cousins parted.

Clara ran up to her room immediately, and, after shutting herself in against intrusion, she opened the secret panel communicating with the passage in which she had made such important discoveries.

"Come forth, old man," she said.

And old Martin, the steward, leaning upon two sticks, limped out.

Pale and wan with long suffering, yet so far recovered as to be able to walk about, he could scarcely have been recognised for the same old man, robust and stout, as Martin, the late earl's steward and confidential servant.

"Blessings upon you, Miss Clara," he said.

"Martin, a word with you at once."

"A hundred, miss, if you wish it. Your sweet voice is music to my old ears."

"You have too much gratitude for the little service I have rendered you."

"That were impossible."

"Can you tell me if there is any one whom the earl and Lady Bellisle wish dead, any one whom they regard as enemies to be crushed remorselessly from their paths?"

"I should be such a one did they know that I was saved—saved by your goodness."

"Ay, but any one else?"

"Yes, one."

"Who?"

"A girl?"

"Ah!"

"She whom I preserved from their infamous clutches, she for whom I incurred their anger, she for whom I should have died a dog's death, but for your goodness, Miss Clara."

And the poor old man seized Clara St. John's hand in his trembling grasp and smothered it with kisses.

"Do you know her name?" demanded Clara St. John.

"Yes, Davis. Mrs. Davis, of the road-side inn. You know the house, Miss Clara."

"Along the road?"

"Yes."

"But how came this Mrs. Davis to incur her enmity and the earl's too?"

"I know not."

"But how know you that you are correct in your supposition?"

"It is no supposition, Miss Clara," replied old Martin. "I have, alas! two sad proofs of their enmity. This Mrs. Davis one night was brought into the house. How I did not know, but in the course of one of my wanderings through the house I made the discovery that they had got a prisoner. I overheard, too, the most fearful plots on foot for her destruction."

"Never!"

"'Tis true."

"And what did you do?"

"I chose my opportunity, aided her to frustrate an attempt to administer poison, and then in the silent night I helped her to escape."

"But will she not expose them and betray you?"

"Not if she is truthful. I bound her to silence by oath."

"Will she observe it?"

"I know not."

"It is doubtful."

"And yet the risk for them is not very great; for their captive did not know her jailors' name and had no notion of their high rank; and, besides binding her by oath, I was careful to lead her away in the night by such a circuitous route that I am positive, with the confusion and alarm and trouble which prevailed, she did not know in which direction she came away."

"I hope not."

"Eh?"

"For the sake of the honour of the family."

"Ah, Miss Clara," said old Martin, "it wants looking after sadly."

*   *   *   *   *   *

There was no address upon the letter which the Earl of Sloeford had forwarded to his cousin.

This was but another of his endless precautions which, although absolutely necessary, were nevertheless very embarrassing to Lady Bellisle.

The postmark, too, was so badly shown as to be almost illegible.

However, she managed to decipher it.

Then she was off.

Nothing of any very great importance occurred upon her journey.

One little incident only worthy of notice, but which does not in any way affect the progress of our story.

It was this.

As she was crossing one part of the country in a postchaise (for her impatience would admit of nothing but this mode of travelling where there was no railway) she was passing through one of the little mining villages which were scattered here and there when she observed an unusual commotion.

As the postchaise crossed the market place of the village a most astonishing sight met her view.

In the centre of the place a number of rough fellows, miners and colliers, were collected around a pretty and interesting looking woman, young and neatly attired.

One man, a trifle more brutal-looking than the rest, appeared to be the auctioneer, and by his gestures Lady Bellisle judged that he was selling something which appeared of great interest to many bidders around.

The attitude of the girl was puzzling too.

What had she to do with the sale?

Lady Bellisle stopped the chaise, in spite of her impatience to get over the journey, and bade the coachman tell one of the colliers to come to her.

"What may be going on there?" asked her ladyship of the fellow who came up in obedience to the summons, with a bow and scrape.

"A zale, mum," replied the man.

"So I presume. Something interesting, too, from all appearance."

"Ay, mum, it be."

"What may it be to be sold?"

"Why, the gal."

"The what?" exclaimed her ladyship, scarcely crediting the evidence of her ears.

"The gal."

"But you surely don't mean that they are selling a girl by auction there?"

"Yes, I do."

"Good Heavens!"

"'Tain't nought so wery extraordinary. It's Dan Freeman's missus. She wor a bit of a devil."

"And so he retaliates upon her for her sharp tongue by selling her here."

"Ees, mum."

"But surely it can't be allowed."

"Who's to perwent it?"

"Drive on," said Lady Bellisle.

And off she rattled again, not exactly understanding what she had seen and heard nevertheless.

Arrived at the end of this stage, Lady Bellisle instituted further inquiries, and then discovered that the earl had passed on to a neighbouring town.

Not pausing an instant for refreshment, Lady Bellisle started again and reached the town after two hours' hard riding.

It was night.

She happened to pass by the theatre, and the first words which caught her eyes upon a flaming poster were—

ENORMOUS SUCCESS OF

MISS ROSE MORTIMER.

"Here?" ejaculated Lady Bellisle. "Fate has led me to the spot, then. He will perhaps be there."

She paid and entered the theatre, seating herself purposely at the back of the dress circle, to avoid observation.

She had not been seated a second when there was an extraordinary excitement in the theatre.

A piece of alarming intelligence ran from mouth to mouth.

In a state of wild fear and nervous apprehension, Lady Bellisle made inquiries of some persons sitting next her as to the cause of it.

"I can scarcely understand it myself," was the answer received.

"Something has happened."

"Yes. The curtain only came down as you entered. The applause was immense. Rose Mortimer and Ethel Warner were on the stage together and got two bouquets."

"Ah!"

She tried hard, but could not repress this exclamation.

As the lady had got thus far, a gentleman came up to her side.

He had been out to gather the information, and had just returned.

"A painful thing has happened," he said.

Lady Bellisle trembled violently.

"What is it?"

"One of those beautiful girls has dropped down dead."

"Which?"

"I can't learn that. There is so much confusion just now. But I fear that it is poor Rose Mortimer."

"Ah! Poor creature!"

"How dreadful!"

"All is lost," murmured Lady Bellisle. "All—all lost!"

CHAPTER LXVII.

A FEARFUL CRIME—LOTTY CHEPSTOW—DESPAIR—THE MAGICIAN PLOTS AGAIN—THE CARPET BAG—THE LIBERTINE'S DEATH—MERMET THE COMFORTER—THE ARAB'S KNIFE—A MIDNIGHT VISIT—SOHO—THE SLAVE AND HER TYRANT—A JOURNEY.

WE have yet to relate a startling mystery in connection with Lotty Chepstow, the unhappy victim of Mermet the Arab necromancer.

The reader will recall to mind that, incited by the revelation of the necromancer, Lotty Chepstow had slain her libertine lover.

Yes. Arthur Brownbill fell a victim to the indignant girl he would have outraged.

He earnt a dreadful death.

A death of violence, ignominy, and shame.

Hurled in the blush of manhood to eternity, with all his sinful lusts full on him.

It was a fearful thing to contemplate, but pity the youthful debauché no one could.

As Arthur Brownbill fell over the parapet with a fearful cry poor Lotty came to her senses.

She stood transfixed to the spot in fear.

Spell-bound with horror.

The cry which her false lover had given as he fell over sounded in her ears like a hideous death-knell.

"How fearful!" she murmured involuntarily.

"What is fearful?" demanded a low voice at her elbow.

She started, and turned round to see whence the voice proceeded.

There, beside her, stood Mermet the Arab necromancer.

"You here?"

"Ay."

[SELLING A WIFE.]

"Where did you come from?"

"Below."

"And you were in the house?"

"Yes."

"Why did you not come before?"

"I only heard you cry at that moment, or you might have counted upon my assistance."

"Oh! But a minute before, and you might have saved me—"

She paused.

"What?" asked Mermet.

"Nothing—I—"

"I'll tell you what," said the Arab necromance, "I might have spared that ill-fated man's life."

"Ah!"

"I might have spared you the fearful crime of murder."

"Alas!"

"True, I might."

"Then you have heard all?"

"All."

"Oh! man, man, how fearful is all this! Why should the innocent promptings of a guileless heart lead me to a crime which my inmost soul abhors?"

"Come, come," said Mermet. "You must not look upon this matter thus."

"How then?"

"'Tis not murder."

" Not morally."

" No."

" But legally ?"

" Pehaps legally."

" Alas ! I know it."

" But all is not yet lost."

Lotty looked eagerly at the necromancer at these hopeful words.

" Not lost ?"

" No."

" What mean you ?"

" We may succeed in removing all traces and defy unjust justice."

" I fear not."

" Pshaw !"

" Murder will out."

" We shall see."

He handed her down the trap in the roof, and they descended the stairs.

" Now," said Mermet, " what do you think of doing in the matter ?"

" You ask me this ?"

" Ay."

" How can I conjecture?" said Lotty Chepstow. " I may be arraigned for murder, and I must take my chance of it."

" Nay. Let me see first what I can do to assist you."

" Many, many thanks."

" Spare your gratitude until I have been to see what I can do for you."

" Do what you will."

" Have you a carpet bag ?"

" Yes."

" Give it to me."

" For what ?"

" No matter. Give me the carpet bag, and I think that I possess effectual means to rid you of this terror."

Lotty ran eagerly down the stairs to find the carpet bag.

" *Now you are mine, I think,*" murmured the necromancer.

He went down after the girl, who met him by the hall door with a large carpet bag in her hand.

" Give me the bag."

" Take it," she said.

" I shall see you again in the morning."

" Oh !" ejaculated the unhappy girl, in a burst of agony. " May I never see another sun rise !"

" Pshaw !"

" Woe, woe is me !"

" Nonsense," said the Arab. " Keep a stout heart in you. I shall see you to-morrow. All will be well I doubt not, and you cannot reproach yourself with this man's death."

" Not reproach myself ?"

" No."

" Alas ! would it were so !"

" No, it is of his own seeking."

" Man, man," she cried, " you cannot disguise the hideous fact from me."

" What fact ?"

" I am a murderess."

" Ugh ! that's an ugly word," said the necromancer with a shiver. " Pray be more choice in your expressions."

" This hand is stained with blood."

And she wrung her hands piteously and wept aloud.

" You have done no murder," said the Arab. " He fairly earnt the death you gave him. Therefore weep no more."

" No reasoning can absolve a murderer," exclaimed the girl.

" *Such* a murder."

" Not even this."

" Ay, but it can. A maiden's chastity is more than life."

" True." •

" Then why repine ?"

" I should have sacrificed myself, not this perjured lover."

" False reasoning."

" Too true reasoning."

" Self-preservation is the first law of nature—the first of all laws, human and divine."

" You speak thus in kindness, I feel, but I cannot accept your reasoning as absolution for my great crime."

" Because you are blinded by the horrors of this night."

" Perhaps."

" One word, and I must begone."

" Speak."

" Did this man merit death ?"

She hesitated.

" Answer me."

" Not at these hands."

" You quibble with my reasoning," said the necromancer. " If Arthur Brownbill—"

" Hush !" she exclaimed, looking about her affrightedly, as if expecting to see his spectre issue from the ground. " Never let me hear his name mentioned again."

" Well, then, if he merited death, certainly no hand could better execute justice upon the perjured ruffian."

" Alas, alas !"

" You were his executioner by right."

" I ?"

" Yes. Do you not see a retributive justice in this act ?"

" No, I see the frenzy of a maddened girl, an unhappy one who had no other means of salvation."

" Be convinced," said the necromancer. " I must begone now."

" Adieu."

" No, *au revoir.*"

" As you will."

" I go now to destroy all traces of your crime, if you insist on so calling it. To-morrow, early, I shall return."

" As you will."

" Promise me that you will rest quiet until that time."

" Rest ?"

" Yes."

" Never, never again."

" At least, say you will not be influenced to any rash act by what has passed to-night."

" I promise."

" Good, I rely on you."

" You may."

And with a last salutation, the necromancer departed.

He closed the street door noiselessly after him, and tripped lightly down the steps.

He paused to look about him upon the pavement.

The night was pitchy dark, and Mermet could scarcely see a yard before him.

Something of a sudden seemed to catch his ear.

He bent to the ground and listened intently.

Yes. There was a low moan.

A wail of agony of some suffering creature.

And close at hand too.

The necromancer started in the greatest surprise.

Surprise alone, for Mermet was little susceptible to the sufferings of his fellow-creatures, or influenced by them.

" Strange, very strange," he muttered. " He must have more lives than a cat if he has escaped that fall. Let me see."

"Oh, Heavens!" murmured the same voice.

This guided the necromancer to the spot, where he found the hapless libertine, Arthur Brownbill, stretched upon the ground.

Rolling in agony.

Writhing with torture.

Suffering the very torments of the damned.

"Who's there?" said Mermet.

"Oh! help me," exclaimed the sufferer.

"What is it?"

"I am hurt, oh! beyond all surgery, I fear."

"How hurt?"

"Ask me not, but get me assistance, I beseech you," he groaned.

"Nay, tell me where lies your hurt," persisted the necromancer.

"Oh!"

"Have you any limbs broken?"

"All!"

"*All?*"

"Ay, I fell from the housetop. Oh! for death or relief at once!"

"Hush!" said Mermet, as if supremely shocked at these words.

"The worst tortures of hell can be no worse than these."

And the unhappy sufferer writhed painfully in his torments.

"Fetch me a surgeon."

"Wait."

"Oh! fiend!"

"Will you have instant relief?"

"Yes."

"Smell this."

And he produced a phial, which he held beneath the sufferer's nostrils.

The poor maimed wretch glanced up at the necromancer's face doubtfully.

"You would not play me false?" he said.

"I?"

"No, no. Give it to me."

"There."

But whilst he held the phial to the writhing wretch's face Mermet could not help remarking that there was not the slightest sign of blood.

"So much the better," thought the Arab. "It will leave fewer traces."

Then he added aloud to the sufferer—

"How is it that, with all your hurts, you have spilt no blood?"

"I know not. I have broken my thighs, and I fear this arm is fractured as well. Oh, Heaven! it was a fearful fall."

"What?"

"I fell from the housetop."

"The housetop?"

"Ay."

"Great mercies, how did you escape, then?"

"I know not."

"You are easier now?"

"Yes."

"The draught has relieved you?"

"It has; but I feel a singular numbed-like sensation starting over me."

"The effects of the narcotic."

"There is no danger?"

"None."

This poor maimed wretch even clung to life in spite of all his injuries.

Mermet stood over him, eagerly watching the changes which were taking place so rapidly within him.

His face was gradually assuming a stolid settled expression.

Now there were no traces of pain in that counte-nance so lately distorted with agony the most fearful which mortal can endure.

The lower members of his body were rigid.

His arms were motionless and his hands rapidly becoming so.

A few nervous twitches of the fingers, and all was still.

"How are you now?" asked Mermet.

"Better."

"I'm glad of that."

"My thanks for your mercy, but I am dying fast."

"Ah!"

"Yes. Do not trouble yourself. I die from the effects of my own brute passions. Exonerate her from all blame. I have merited the death which I gave myself. 'Tis not her hand which hath wrought it."

"Come, come," said Mermet. "You may yet recover."

"Never."

"Hope always."

"That is kindly said; but no, my time is spent. It is too much mercy to have such kindness in my last moments, when my last act in life was one of cruelty and outrage to the being who loved me most on earth."

Mermet looked uncomfortable at the dying man's thanks.

Reproaches would not have affected him in the least.

But scarcely the most callous of us can be unaffected in such a position.

To have the man you have deceitfully slain—treacherously murdered—when he thinks you aiding him thanking you with his dying breath is rather more than the most unscrupulous could comfortably stand.

"Farewell," said the dying man.

"Ah!"

"I die."

"Nay, you deceive yourself."

"I don't. Remember that my death is of my own seeking."

"Yes, yes."

"Sh—she is entirely exonerated from all share in it."

"Yes."

"Ask her forgive—"

Ere the word could be finished he turned over and expired.

The Arab necromancer gave a sigh of relief.

"That's over," he said coolly. "And now to business."

He then took a knife from beneath his vest and examined it carefully.

Then, apparently satisfied with its keenness, he proceeded to try it upon the still warm corpse of Arthur Brownbill.

But we cannot dwell at much length upon these horrors.

Suffice it therefore for this portion of our narrative to say that the body was mutilated most horribly on the spot.

Limbs were lopped off.

Then the whole was placed with difficulty in the huge carpet bag.

This accomplished, the necromancer looked about him carefully to see that he was not observed.

Satisfied in this particular, he took great pains to destroy all traces of the fearful tragedy which had just been enacted there.

Then, with a strength of which few would have deemed that pigmy stunted body capable, he raised the carpet bag to his shoulders and boldly trudged off with it.

He made his way to a low street in the neighbourhood of Soho Square.

Here he knocked at the door of a house, and had a long time to wait.

At length a nightcapped head was protruded from one of the upper windows.

" Who's there ?"

" Me."

" Lor ! Mr—'"

" Hush," said Mermet. " Don't be a fool, woman. Come down."

" Yes, sir."

" Look sharp."

" Yes, sir."

The head was withdrawn and the window closed again.

" Yes," mused the necromancer half aloud, " she shall do it. I can watch at a convenient distance to see that she works fairly. If not, woe betide her ! At any rate, I am altogether free from blame in this job."

The street door was opened, and the woman owning the nightcapped head made her appearance, but only very scantily clothed.

" What is it, Mr—"

" Silence."

" Lor, sir."

" Are you mad, woman, that you would blab out my name to all the world. Think you I'm proud of your acquaintance ?"

" No offence, sir."

" Go and dress yourself."

" Dress ?"

" Ay."

" I was in bed, sir."

" What then ?"

" It is so late."

" Begone."

" Yes, sir."

And in the most abject humility the woman gallopped off.

" This is the convenience of never missing an opportunity," muttered the magician. " Now that old woman is so thoroughly mine that she dares not say her soul's her own. I shall shift all danger in this night's work from my shoulders to hers. I shall reap all the profit and she the pain. Good. The division of labour is most satisfactory."

By this time the woman appeared, having carefully arranged herself for walking.

" What is it you require of me, sir ?" she asked humbly.

" To come with me."

" Yes, sir."

" You see this bag ?"

" Yes, sir."

" You must carry it."

" Yes, sir."

He handed the bag to the woman, who found great difficulty in lifting it.

" Do you think you can carry it ?"

" Not far."

" Give it to me, then."

" The woman obeyed.

" Follow me close behind," said the necromancer.

" Yes, sir."

And in this way they proceeded through St. Giles's towards the Strand.

But what further befell Mermet the Arab necromancer and his companion we will describe in a new chapter.

CHAPTER LXVIII.

WATERLOO BRIDGE—THE TOLL KEEPER—DANGER —MERMET'S DECISION—TROUBLES AVERTED— THE HANSOM CAB—THE GIRL'S WOES—DESPAIR —THE DEATH COMPACT.

THE Arab, with his weighty carpet bag upon his shoulders, crossed the Strand, turned down by Waterloo Place, and stopped short in Lancaster Place.

He chose the quietest part of the street, which was, for a wonder, quite deserted.

He beckoned to the woman, who was following behind, and she came up with a run to her tyrant master.

" Take the bag now," said the magician.

" Yes, sir."

" Carry it carefully."

" Yes, sir."

" Cross the bridge."

" Yes, sir."

" Half way over watch your opportunity well, and drop the carpet bag over the side."

The woman opened her eyes to their full extent and stared at Mermet.

" You understand ?"

" Yes, sir."

" Away, then, and remember—no matter."

The woman took the bag and trudged off across the bridge.

A little difficulty occurred in passing the toll.

" Hullo !" said the money-taker. " What have you got there ?"

" Nothing."

" Rather a lump of it."

" That can be no business of yours."

" I don't know that."

" Let me pass."

" Wait, wait."

" If you don't think proper to turn the turnstile I shall go round."

" The gate is closed."

" Let me pass, then."

" Now you appear to be so very anxious about it that bless me if I do," exclaimed the money-taker. " So hand over."

And he attempted to take the carpet-bag from her.

Seeing matters arrive at this pitch, Mermet hastened up to the spot.

He popped down a halfpenny upon the iron slab of the turnstile and endeavoured to push through.

" Hold hard !" said the man.

" Come, come."

" Wait a bit."

" Let my bag alone," said the woman.

" What are you about with her bag ?" asked the necromancer, as if only now perceiving that the woman was in trouble.

" She won't show what she has got in it," said the money-taker.

" Why should she ?"

" Why ?"

" Yes, why ?"

" Oh, why—"

" Don't echo me, but reply to my question or let the woman pass."

" She's got something in it that oughtn't to be there I'm sure."

" Oh ! you know it ?"

" Of course."

" Then if you know the contents of her bag, why do you want to see in it now ?"

The man was puzzled for a reply to this.

" Well," he grumbled, " I believe as I was only doing my duty."

"You believe nothing of the kind," said the necromancer. "You think that this is a poor and helpless woman whom you can venture to insult with impunity."

"Sir!"

"Pshaw! No indignation with me. How dare you detain that woman, sir?"

"I never—"

"Don't attempt to exonerate yourself," interrupted Mermet.

"I've nothing to fear."

"Let this woman pass."

"Oh, I can let her pass," grumbled the money-taker.

He touched the turnstile and the woman went through.

"Thank you, sir, for your kindness, I'm sure," she said, dropping a curtsey.

"All right."

"Good night, sir."

"Good night."

The necromancer stopped behind to engage the money-taker in conversation, whilst his messenger got safely over with her load.

"It seems to me that you are an impertinent fellow," quoth Mermet.

"Sir!"

"And I shall report you."

"Lor, sir, I've only done my duty in all this."

"How your duty?"

"Why you see, sir, these women is up to all sorts o' dodges. They pops their children in carpet bags and drops 'em over."

"Oh!" said Mermet dryly.

He shot unpleasantly near the mark this time, and the magician did not at all relish the speech.

"This has been done?" he demanded of the money-taker.

"Often."

"You don't say so."

"Only last Saturday, sir, a woman dropped over a brown paper parcel, which was found to contain the body of a new-born infant."

"Horrible!"

"Yes."

"But still it is not exactly the thing to annoy any passenger who happens to carry a load because such a thing has happened once."

"No, sir, only the out-of-the-way time to be carrying such a load."

"Yes."

Whilst they talked thus Mermet backed the money-taker into his box.

Thus stationed, the latter could only see just before him, whilst Mermet could see right across the bridge.

He perceived the woman struggle along under her load until she arrived in the middle of the bridge, according to instructions.

Then she entered one of the recesses, mounted the seat, and with great difficulty raised the carpet bag to the top of the parapet.

"What was that?"

"What?"

"Didn't you hear something?" asked the money-taker.

"Not I."

"Sounded strange."

"Your fancy."

But Mermet had heard something.

He was waiting for it anxiously, and caught it much more distinctly than the money-taker had done.

It was a dull heavy splash in the water.

The carpet bag was cast over.

The dull muddy Thames was now the unhallowed grave of Arthur Brownbill.

"Well, well," thought the necromancer, "that's all over—well over!"

And nodding to the money-taker he passed on.

"I don't think that that is half right after all," muttered the man.

A hansom cab passed through the gate at this moment.

The toll keeper presented himself at the door to take the passenger's fee, but the latter called through the trap in the roof of the vehicle to the driver.

"Pay the toll, coachman."

"Yes, sir."

And off the cab rattled as only the London hansom can travel.

The money-taker remained stock still staring after it until it had disappeared.

Then he retreated once more into his box.

"I could almost swear to that voice," he said to himself. "It sounded just like that little hunchback. I could see his face. It strikes me very forcibly that there's something queer been up."

* * * * * *

A few days after the events just recorded a great criminal report was in everybody's mouth.

Every one of the metropolitan journals was filled with it.

It was the subject of the most extraordinary discussion.

Speculations upon the matter were made by every one.

A fearful discovery had been made by a waterman upon the river.

A large carpet bag had been found clinging to one of the stone buttresses of Waterloo Bridge.

The waterman had opened it and found it to contain—oh, horror!—a mutilated human body.

It was so cut and hacked about as to be utterly beyond recognition.

The body was taken by the authorities and laid out as well as possible in the dead house.

Many persons had been to see it, but none could decide who the unfortunate being.

Evidence could not be collected.

It defied the utmost efforts of the police, and they got up a story about its being the frolic of some medical students from one of the hospitals.

This tale, absurd as it was, passed muster.

The police, who had so signally failed to trace the fearful crime, escaped censure, and this was all they desired.

A short time, and the crime, which had filled the mouths of all London and the columns of all the newspapers, was heard of no more.

But now to resume.

The day following the tragedy and finish of the ill-fated Arthur Brownbill the necromancer presented himself at Lotty Chepstow's house.

He found the poor girl scarcely more composed than when he had quitted her upon the previous night.

A sleepless night and harrowing thoughts had done their work.

She deemed herself a murderess.

In this horrible word is said enough to account for all her miseries.

"Come, come," said the necromancer soothingly. "You must take heart, my dear young lady. You must shake off this despondency. Reason yourself out of it."

"Impossible."

"Nothing is impossible," said Mermet. "Forget that the word exists."

"Would that I could!"

"Try."

"I cannot."

"And why?"

"Alas! ask me not."

" 'Tis in a cause for which your bitterest enemy could not blame you."

"You are so good."

"Nay, I speak the truth."

"Would I could think so !"

"You may."

"You will see if the law is inclined to look so leniently upon it."

"The law will probably not look upon it at all."

"What mean you ?"

"I have destroyed all traces."

"Ah !"

"I promised, and as I promise, so I ever perform."

"Oh ! you have saved my worthless life," cried the girl in a bitter flood of tears, "and I cannot thank you. But you have preserved my reputation, and so I thank you from the bottom of my heart."

"And you will endeavour to rally now ?"

"I will."

"You promise me ?"

"Yes."

"And if the fit of despair should unhappily come upon you again, you promise to appeal only to me for assistance ?"

"As you will."

"Good."

Lotty Chepstow looked earnestly up into the Arab's face, and then suddenly burst into a fresh flood of tears.

"What now, what now ?" demanded the necromancer soothingly.

"Oh ! I'm so unhappy !" she cried.

"I believe it."

"But oh, how much more than you possibly can conceive !"

"I think not."

"I am indeed, because I am a murderess—because I am also false and perjured to those who have proved themselves my only friends—to those who would serve me kindly and truly."

"What ?"

"Ah ! you may well be surprised."

"Explain yourself."

"I must tell you, but upon condition only that you will not take steps to prevent the accomplishment of my purpose."

"I half guess its intent," said the necromancer, with a sad expression.

"I think not."

"Say, then, what is it ?"

"I have more than half resolved upon—oh ! I dare not speak it now."

"Then I will for you," said Mermet, "for I divine your fatal purpose."

"Ah !"

"Suicide."

The girl hung her head, but said nothing.

"Alas !" said the necromancer. "I thought as much. But have you not reflected that even thus you will just gain that which you so desire to avoid ?"

"What ?"

"Notoriety."

"Ah !"

"Undoubtedly. An inquiry is always held upon any one dying very suddenly."

"And do you think that my fatal secret could transpire ?"

"Yes."

"Nay, nay. Say not so I beseech you !"

"I speak the truth."

"I will drown myself—anything sooner than live with such fearful companionship."

"Which ?"

"My thoughts."

"You take it too severely."

"Ah, sir," said the unhappy girl, "your hand is not stained with another's blood."

"Happily," groaned Mermet.

"No, no ; and therefore you cannot possibly comprehend what a murderer's sensations are."

"And you are resolute upon self-destruction ?"

"Ay."

Mermet looked into her face, and there he read determination—fixed unalterable determination in every line.

And then he mused—

"Now if she kills herself she slips through my fingers, and I gain nothing but my hard work for my pains. No, not so. This must not be. She shall have her way, and yet be mine. I think I have the means of satisfying her upon this head, and yet achieving my own object. A week or so hence her love of life will be full upon her again. It shall be so."

He looked up and spoke.

"Promise me," said he, "at least one thing."

"Name it."

"You think possibly that you owe me some little gratitude ?"

"Nay—"

"I know what you would say. Well then, dear girl, know that I have your interest, your honour, so much at heart that I will even aid you in this strait should your determination continue."

"Till when ?"

"To-morrow."

"And then ?"

"Then, if your purpose still holds good, come to me about this hour."

"Yes."

"And I will give you something which shall produce the effect of apoplexy. Thus an inquiry can be avoided."

Her gratitude for this fresh proof of what she deemed the necromancer's attachment was unbounded. She promised so earnestly to obey his request that he left her quite satisfied.

"To-morrow at this hour," said he.

"Yes."

"You promise ?"

"Faithfully."

"No matter what determination you take ?"

"I do."

"Good, my child, I rely on you."

"You may."

And the Arab left, muttering to himself—

"She's mine, she's mine. To-morrow will see the business closed."

CHAPTER LXIX.

MERMET'S PLOT WORKS BRAVELY—DEATH—THE LAST HOME—THE CHURCHYARD—THE RESURRECTIONISTS AGAIN—THE VAULTS—THE GRAVE —SUCCESS—REPOSE OF THE DEAD DESTROYED —THE ARAB'S HOUSE—MIDNIGHT DOINGS—THE DISSECTING ROOM—FACE TO FACE WITH THE DEAD—WHAT FOLLOWS ?

A DAY passed.

It was about the same hour, when Ahmet, the necromancer's Arab attendant, entered to announce a visitor.

"Show her in," said Mermet.

A veiled lady appeared with the servant upon the threshold.

"Enter, lady," said the necromancer, "and fear nothing. Remove your veil."

She did so.

As Mermet had conjectured, it was none other than Lotty Chepstow, who came there according to the appointment of the previous day.

"You have repented of your rash design?" demanded the Arab.

She shook her head.

"You are still determined upon the same unhappy course?"

"I am."

"Then take this phial."

She eagerly stretched forth her hand and clasped it.

"Now take the contents of this in a glass of water to-night. It is tasteless, and will cause you no pain. All your muscles and pulses will be numbed and deadened, and you will be to all appearance dead in the morning."

"To all appearance?"

"Yes, yes," he added hastily, as if he had made a bit of an error. "'To all appearance,' I say, because you will not actually die till noon."

"Ah!"

"Death is gradual—slow, but none the less sure. It is the only poison by which you certainly avoid all risk of pain."

"You are so good."

"Now begone, dear girl, lest my determination should waiver."

She seized his hand and smothered it with kisses.

Then rushed wildly from the house.

The next morning Mermet passed by the house in which the unhappy girl, Lotty Chepstow, resided.

All the windows were closely covered in.

The blinds were drawn from top to bottom, and the of death was upon the house.

"It takes, it takes!" said the necromancer to himself. "*And now I may look on Lotty Chepstow as mine for life.*"

His for life!

What could he mean!

The progress of our tale will show.

Within a few days there was a funeral from the house.

It was a sad and solemn ceremony.

The remains of the beautiful girl—so young, so fair, to quit this bustling busy scene of life—were borne away and consigned to the tomb.

A loving father and a fond mother saw the earth thrown upon the coffin which contained the departed hope of their declining years, and heavy were their hearts.

They dropped many and many a bitter tear upon the cold earth which contained their darling girl, and then with tottering steps quitted the churchyard.

It was an old city churchyard, and funerals there even at the period of which we write had become a rarity.

A snug little bit of ground—the only remaining portion of the original graveyard, which had been gradually encroached upon by the city authorities as the ground became more valuable.

The earth was smoothed over the grave.

The sexton departed.

And this closes a sad sad chapter in these our veritable chronicles.

But soon it opens again.

Soon we find that we have prematurely put a close to this.

The day is over in the busy city.

Evening has come, and this haunt of commerce, so bustling and noisy during the hours of labour, is now quiet and deserted.

And then the little snug burial ground is the scene of a singular and sacrilegious operation, such as happily seldom occurs in the days.

Two men clamber over the railings.

Stealthy steps bring one of the men to the door of a vault, lying a step below the level of the churchyard.

This door is at the top of a flight of stone steps, which communicate with the vaults and gloomy sepulchres.

It is secured by a padlock affixed to two iron staples in the woodwork.

This offers but little resistance to the man, who is apparently an expert at this kind of operation.

He takes a small instrument from his pocket and inserts it into the lock, prizes it gently, and opens the door.

Now he speaks to his companion, who stands looking on.

"Give me the lantern, Snatchem," he whispers rather loudly.

"Here you are."

Then, taking a dark lantern from the other, he descends the steep steps.

He finds himself in a low arched vault.

On every side are ranges of shelves, all of which have ghostly tenants.

Coffins of old and young—man, woman, and child —are there.

The history of a departed generation.

"Rum pickings here," he mutters, "for some of 'em who have gone before."

But with these deathly objects he does not now trouble himself.

In the centre of the vault is a long plank supported upon tressels, and upon this he finds a mattock and spade, cords and a hammer.

He loads himself and makes his way up the steps again, closing the door after him.

"Why what a long time you've been, Joe," said he whom the other had addressed as Snatchem.

"Why didn't you fetch 'em yourself, then?" demanded Joe, surlily.

"You offered."

"You lie. 'Taint that, it's because you funked the job."

"You lie yourself, for—"

"There, stash it."

The discussion thus unceremoniously concluded, Snatchem proceeded with all speed to disembarrass himself of the implements which he had collected.

"All snug?" asked Joe.

"Yes."

"Boguey been round?"

"Yes, passed once—yawning too—so we're safe enough."

"We are anyhow."

"Why?"

"He can't be round here before a quarter of an hour, and I mean to work this little job in ten minutes."

"All right."

"I'll dig. You take the shovel."

Joe—none other than Resurrection Joe, to whom we have already introduced the reader—took the pick and set to work.

He plied it with such good will upon the newly-made grave that the work went on at a dashing pace.

Everything favoured them, for the grave being so freshly made, the earth had only lain lightly upon the gentle girl as yet.

Ten minutes over, and the job was completed, as Joe had said.

With the cords they had brought up the coffin to earth.

"Hand over the iron," said Joe.

"What iron?"

"The wrenching iron."

"I ain't got it."

"Not got it?"

"No."

"You was to bring it, you know, Snatchem. That was the last arrangement."

"Well, I ain't got it, so it's no use making any bones about it."

"What's to be done, then?"

"I don't know."

"There's only one way."

"What is that?"

"Take the whole concern off."

"What?"

"Box an' all."

"Impossible."

"Why is it more impossible than taking the dead 'un alone? Not more likely to excite attention."

"True."

"And then the box may be wuth something you know, Joe."

"Not much."

"There is silver plates on it."

"Come on, then. Shovel back the earth again."

"I don't think as it matters much."

"Why not?"

"'Cause the box being away, it'll leave a horful 'ole."

"Never mind that. It won't be so much noticed. Pop it in lightly."

"All right."

And in double quick time the earth was shovelled back into the grave.

"Now you be off, Snatchem," said Resurrection Joe, "and bring the cart. I'll wait and keep a sharp look out."

"All right."

"Look lively."

Snatchem ran off, and in the space of a few minutes the rattle of a cart was heard along the deserted street.

The cart pulled up and out jumped Snatchem.

"Here he comes," said Joe.

"Joe!" he whispered through the railings.

"Hullo!"

"Hush!"

"What's up?"

"Some one foxing."

"Where?"

"Come on. I've dodged him. Look alive, and we're all right."

Snatchem pushed open the gate, which creaked in a most alarming manner.

Then he ran lightly across the churchyard up to the coffin.

"Now then."

They raised it at each end and bore it swiftly to the cart.

It was a tough struggle, but time pressed, and they surmounted the difficulty with a dash.

"Now then," said Joe, "whip up the hannimal. Off she goes."

In less than twenty minutes after the desecration of the city churchyard as related Resurrection Joe and Snatchem had driven their cart up to Mermet's residence.

They had provided hemselves with large cloths, and they had so wrapt the coffin in them as to effectually conceal its form.

Snatchem whistled in a peculiar manner, according to arrangement.

Then after a while a window was raised, and Mermet looked out.

He made them a sign of intelligence and disappeared.

In less time than one would have believed it possible for the necromancer to have descended the stairs he was at the street door, *which he opened himself.*

"Success?" he whispered anxiously.

"Yes," replied the bodysnatchers simultaneously.

"Good."

"We've got box an' all, guv'nor."

"Eh?"

"Coffin as well."

"No matter; be quick."

"All right."

They quickly unloaded their cart of its deathly burden, and carried it into the house.

"This way," said Mermet. "Follow me quickly."

"All right, guv'nor."

He led the way upstairs to the first floor, where he opened a door with a key which he took from his pocket.

This disclosed a spacious room, dimly lit by an oil lamp.

All around the chamber were stills, retorts, crucibles, and other analytical and chemical contrivances which are so mysterious to the uninitiated.

At the further extremity of the apartment was a four-post bedstead with dark sombre hangings.

In the centre of the room was a long table, upon which lay several pillows, evidently prepared by the necromancer for a special purpose.

"Place it here," said Mermet.

They obeyed.

"Hullo! Why, the lid is firm!"

"Yes; but that is easily opened."

"Do it, then."

"Can you give me a screwdriver?"

"Yes. But first, one of you must take away your cart. Its presence at my door would possibly excite attention."

"All right," said Snatchem.

And he volunteered to take the cart home without delay.

A screwdriver was brought and the coffin opened.

The white cloth was removed from the face, and disclosed the fair countenance of the hapless girl, Lotty Chepstow!

So calm, so tranquilly happy and serene its expression.

"Scarcely looks like a dead 'un, guv'nor," observed Resurrection Joe.

"Eh? No."

The Arab started from a reverie into which he had fallen.

"You may go now," he said hurriedly. "Away! and be prudent."

"All right, guv'nor."

"Here's for your pains. Away!"

"And Snatchem's?"

"I'll pay him myself."

"Oh, all right, guv'nor."

"Let him call to-morrow early."

"All right, doctor."

"And as you wish for further employment—"

"Which I do, at the price."

"Be prudent."

"I shall, for my own sake."

"You're wise."

The bodysnatcher departed, and Mermet returned to the chamber of death.

For what?

We shall see.

CHAPTER LXX.

EXCITING NEWS—THE JOURNEY—THE HOTEL— A MOB—SMITHSON—LYNCH LAW—OFF THE SCENT—THE RAILWAY—A DARING FEAT—THE WAITING-ROOM—THE FOREIGNER AND THE LAWYER'S CLERK—DISGUISE—ALL LOST— REPROACHES AND RECRIMINATIONS—FRESH PLANS AND RESOLVES—TEN DAYS' SAFETY— MUTUAL ARRANGEMENT—THIRD CONSENTING PARTY—STARTLING DENOUEMENT!

LADY BELLISLE almost made up her mind for the worst which could now befall her.

[THE BODYSNATCHERS.]

The excitement in the theatre became immense after a while.

But little could she glean for some time.

At length she bethought her to go and make inquiries at the stage door.

This she could venture to do in perfect safety.

If Rose Mortimer were indeed dead she had nothing to fear, for no one else could recognise her there.

Accordingly she made her way to the stage door.

"Can you tell me the nature of the accident?" she asked of the doorkeeper.

"Pison," replied the man shortly.

"Poison?"

He nodded.

"One of the actors?"

He shook his head.

"I heard that it was."

"Dancer."

"Ah!" thought Lady Bellisle. "That settles it. She is a dancer, or was originally, I know well, from the inquiries I have made."

She turned from the stage door after thanking the man, and left.

At her wit's end for the next step to take, Lady Bellisle walked dreamily through the town, possessed of a kind of coma from which she could not rouse herself.

Despair at her signal failure after such exertions produced this singular effect.

As she was going along a sudden outburst at the door of an hotel attracted her attention.

She drew near, and joined in the crowd which had hastily collected, and there learnt that it all proceeded from the same matter as that which she had heard so much of.

"Can you tell me what all the noise is about?" she asked.

"The man that poisoned the dancer," replied one of the bystanders.

"What of him?"

"He lives here."

"What do the mob want of him?"

"*To lynch him!*"

This completely staggered Lady Bellisle for an instant.

"Lynch him?" she iterated. "Surely it would never be permitted?"

"Oh, as for that—"

"But the police?"

"What could they do if the mob took the case into their hands?"

"True."

"And for my own part I should not object to see it, although the practice is bad."

Lady Bellisle could not trust herself to reply to such a sentiment.

She was about to turn from the spot when the landlord of the hotel came forward to address the mob.

They had insisted upon forcing an entrance, and the worthy host had only succeeded in keeping them off by a most determined resistance.

"Let us in, let us in," they cried.

"Not if I know it," replied the landlord.

"Down with the poisoner!"

"With all my heart."

"Then let us in."

"But, my good people," said the landlord, "be a little reasonable."

"Down with the poisoner! Give him over to us."

"One moment," said the landlord.

"Give him up."

"Nay, will you hear me speak first?"

"Hear him speak first," said one of the mob. "Let's hear him speak first."

"Thank you," said the landlord. "I will not detain you an instant. In the first place, I don't know whom you mean by the poisoner."

"He that lodged here."

"There are several."

"But a stranger."

"I thought so. You mean Mr. Smithson, of course. Well, then, he left nearly half an hour ago."

A groan went through the crowd.

They began to look savage, and to murmur some very angry things about the landlord.

"Why not say so at once?"

"Why don't you speak?"

"He's got his own reasons for keeping it dark, perhaps," said one.

This suggestion was greeted with a murmur of approval.

"Well," returned the landlord, "the reason of my silence is simple enough."

"He calls it simple," said one.

"Ay, you wouldn't allow me to explain at all before—not even to put in a word."

This only seemed then to occur to the violent crowd, and they began to murmur one amongst another about the justice of what he advanced.

It was a clear case.

The landlord was then voted blameless unanimously.

The mob even grew enthusiastic in his praise, after having accused him wrongfully, and in their enthusiasm so far forgot themselves that for a while the object of their presence there escaped them.

At length one of the more violent against the supposed murderer recalled them to their object by asking in what direction Smithson had gone.

"Towards Whitleigh," said the landlord.

"Long since?"

"Half an hour, I said."

"Then we may yet overtake him," said one. "Who will join me in a hunt?"

"I will."

"And I."

"And I."

A dozen voices assented after this to the amiable proposition.

After hearing this much Lady Bellisle turned from the spot.

It was enough for her.

"Towards Whitleigh," she mused. "Let me see. Whitleigh is east. I doubt not that he has gone due west. This is evidently to put them off the scent, although he had no idea of such a mischance as this discovery."

Without pausing another instant, she ran off to the railway station.

By a most fortunate chance a train was just leaving—an express for the station westward to which she knew that the Earl of Sloeford would proceed if he had the intention of proceeding directly to Sloeford House.

She heard the last bell as she was taking her ticket.

"Quick, quick," she said "'Tis life or death. I must catch this train."

"Too late, ma'am," said the clerk.

"The ticket, quick."

"It's no earthly use."

"The man is mad," she cried.

And, without pausing for the ticket, she dashed on to the platform.

The train was in motion.

"Too late!" cried the guard.

But, heedless of the warning, she ran up and seized one of the doors and wrenched it open.

"Back!"

"Stand clear!"

"Keep that woman back!" cried the guard.

"She'll be dashed to pieces!"

But no. Heedless of all risk, Lady Bellisle had sprang into the carriage.

She was a terrible woman.

Once let her interests be at stake, or those of the man for whom she had so sinned, and nothing upon the earth could stand in her path.

Once started, and settled down to think over her daring jump into the railway carriage, it occurred to her that she might get into some difficulties with the officials.

She had committed a serious offence against one of the railway company's bye-laws.

It was not that she so much feared the consequences of her rashness as the delay which would be occasioned.

So her only hope lay in escaping observation at the station.

How futile this was she very soon discovered.

The ticket collector came round with the guard, and this betrayed her.

"Ticket, ma'am."

"I haven't one," said Lady Bellisle. "Will you take my fare?" and she tendered him a sovereign.

"You haven't a ticket?"

"No."

"Lost it?"

"No, not exactly, I hadn't time to get one you see, and—"

"Oh! that settles it. That's all I wanted to learn.

You are the passenger who got in after the train started, I presume, ma'am?"

"What then?"

"You must leave the train please."

"Such is my intention."

"You are aware that you have committed a serious offence against the bye-laws of the company, and—"

"And what, my good man? I'm pressed for time, or I should never have done it."

"Pardon me, but the offence has increased so much of late that I have the strictest injunctions to—"

"Tut, tut," exclaimed Lady Bellisle, impatiently stamping her little foot, "to what, to extort money? Here."

She handed him a bank note for five pounds and pushed past him.

"Madam, I—"

"Enough."

And she was gone.

What became of the fine thus singularly inflicted and so summarily met we are not in a position to vouch.

This we should certainly say, however, without fear of scandal, that it never found its way into the railway company's exchequer.

"When will the next train for Barford be due?" asked Lady Bellisle.

"Ten minutes," was the reply.

"How long since the last left?"

"Three hours and a quarter."

Then if the Earl of Sloeford had come by that train he must yet be about the station or somewhere at hand.

She strolled about the platform and looked into the first-class waiting room.

It was empty.

She then looked at the next room.

This was half filled with a rough ragged-looking lot of agricultural labourers and farm servants.

Lady Bellisle wore a thick veil, and had not much fear of being recognised by the Sloeford tenantry or servants should any chance to be there.

She therefore entered and peered about at every one.

Now in the whole place there were but two persons who attracted her attention for an instant.

One of these was a meagre-looking man with short iron-grey whiskers covering his cheek bones, short cropped hair of the same hue, and a particularly seedy hat.

He carried a blue legal-looking bag in a cotton-gloved hand.

"That's some country lawyer's clerk," she said mentally. "But the other puzzles me considerably. If it is he the disguise is perfect."

The other was a man of the same height and general build.

A dark swarthy complexion and a bushy black beard of a strictly continental cut gave him the appearance of a Leicester Square refugee.

He glanced up once or twice uneasily beneath a pair of overhanging beetle brows at the lawyer's clerk, who had been endeavouring to engage him in conversation.

As Lady Bellisle drew near the latter made some remark which she could not catch.

Thereupon the foreigner simply shrugged his shoulders with an expressive air of indifference.

Then he rose and sauntered from the room.

There was a certain limp in his gait which seemed familiar to Lady Bellisle.

It was the most trifling matter in the world, but the quick-sighted woman detected it at once.

She waited a few seconds, looked easily about her, and then strolled out after him—very leisurely.

He had entered the first-class waiting room, and was standing at the open window looking down the line, apparently longing for the arrival of the expected train.

Lady Bellisle proceeded very cautiously to work now.

Without appearing to exercise any caution at all, she entered the room without any noise or ostentation.

It was admirably done.

She stared hard at the foreign-looking man with the swarthy skin and the black beard.

"Yes, yes," she murmured, "there is no doubt of it now. Admirably done too."

She walked softly across the room to the foreign-looking man, and placed a gentle hand upon his shoulder.

"Ah—h—h," he gasped.

And when he looked up the change which had taken place in his countenance in that brief moment was positively alarming.

He started as if his shoulder had been touched by a scorpion.

His face was pale as that of a corpse.

His eyes shone with a sudden and unearthly lustre which was terrifying to behold.

"Wha—at charge?" he muttered.

"Spencer."

"You? What a turn you gave me!"

The foreign-looking man was indeed he whom Lady Bellisle had supposed—the object of her rapid journey and the great efforts she had made during the past few days.

In a word, the Earl of Sloeford.

"You look quite scared, Spencer," exclaimed Lady Bellisle.

"Hush!"

"Come, come, be more yourself."

"Ah! you don't know what has occurred."

"Alas!"

"Hush! All is safe if I but get rid of the present difficulty."

"What do you mean?"

"She is gone!"

"Ah! Spencer, there, there lies the horror. Oh! did you know all!"

"Know all?"

"Ay, as I do."

"What do you mean?"

"We are undone!"

The Earl of Sloeford started in undisguised alarm at this.

"Surely you cannot understand me," he said. Rose Mortimer is removed from our path."

"Alas!"

"Alas?" iterated the earl.

"Oh! Spencer, Spencer, we are ruined—undone, lost beyond redemption!"

"Explain yourself."

"Rose Mortimer's death brings about exposure, disgrace, and shame."

"But my incognito is safe."

"'Tis not there that lies the danger."

"Where then?"

"Listen. Rose Mortimer had taken the precaution, with more wit than I gave her credit for, of insuring our forbearance thus:—A written description of—of—" (here Lady Bellisle's voice sank to a still lower whisper) "what we most fear to be known has been prepared by Rose Mortimer, and placed by her in trusty hands, to be opened and made public after a silence of ten days."

"Ah!"

"You see what I mean now."

"I do, I do."

"For the past week I have been running after you from town to town to inform you of this, but all in vain."

"Fate's against us."

And the two guilty cousins began for the first time to despair.

As for the earl, he was the picture of gloom and horror.

His countenance told how fearfully the alarming tidings had acted upon him.

He was powerless to act—lost, destroyed, undone.

Nothing but the woman's guiding hand could now lead him to safety.

Could even her's accomplish this ?

It was doubtful.

"Come, come, Spencer," said Lady Bellisle, after a minute's pause. "This will never do. We are in a great dilemma, and we want action, not despair. Rouse yourself, man."

"Rouse myself ?" iterated the Earl of Sloeford vacantly, "rouse myself ?"

"Ay."

"To what ? For what ?"

"Safety."

"The gallows," said he, with a bitter mocking laugh.

"Hush ! we have yet ten days."

"How ?"

"Did I not tell you that for ten days we are safe ?"

"No."

"Nay, I did. The writing which Rose Mortimer had prepared will not be opened for that time."

"What then ?"

"What then ?" ejaculated Lady Bellisle. "Where is your wit, man ?"

The earl pressed his hand across his brow as if to seek for it.

"I see, I see," he murmured. "For ten days, then, we are safe."

"Of course."

"And then ?"

"Then the blow comes."

"And we are lost."

"Before ten days are over we must be in another land—exiles"

"This is too fearful."

"Not so—exile is better than death, and death it would be."

"Great powers !" exclaimed the unhappy man. "And is it for this after all that we have toiled, sinned, and plotted ? Is it for this that we have done such deeds as would make hell itself gape with horror and cry 'Hold !'"

"Spencer."

"Silence, woman," said the earl. "It is to you I owe you all."

"True," said Lady Bellisle. "It is to me. Ingrate, remember it."

"I do, in bitter humiliation."

"Remember that this hand raised you out of the dust unto—"

"The gallows !"

"Remember, that if you are a belted earl it is this hand which has heaped these honours upon you. Name, title, fortune—all, all you owe to me."

"And what are all these to me with the gallows staring me in the face ?" demanded the earl coarsely.

Lady Bellisle could bear this tone no longer.

She melted into tears.

She could be cold, stern, cruel, even bloody to others, but to him she could but be love while life remained to her.

"Oh ! Spencer, Spencer," she exclaimed, "what are you saying to me ?"

"The truth."

"Ay, but—"

"But what ? Would you have me thank you for placing the noose around my neck ?"

"No, no ; but it is not for you to offer me these reproaches."

"Who then ?"

"Do I not share all with you—even the scaffold, should it come to that ?"

"Pretty consolation that, truly," exclaimed the earl, brutally.

"Oh ! man, man, have you no heart ?"

And she burst into a passionate flood of tears.

But she had the mastery over her feelings sufficiently yet to stay them.

"Come," she said, controlling her emotion, with a powerful effort, "there's no time for idle tears."

"No, indeed."

"Spare me your sarcasm, Spencer," she said, glancing up into his coward face, "for at the worst you fare better than I."

"How so, forsooth ?"

"You can but return to the dust from which this hand raised you, whilst I—I have a fearful fall."

"And you ask me to spare you my sarcasm," exclaimed the earl.

"Tut, tut. This is idle folly. Let us begone."

"Ay."

"*Ay*," said a second voice behind them.

Both the Earl of Sloeford and Lady Bellisle turned round at this.

Behind them stood the man with the blue legal-looking bag.

The bag now was fastened to a coat button by the cord.

His left hand held a glittering pair of steel handcuffs."

His right hand held a small pocket pistol with a brightly burnished barrel.

He nodded coolly.

"Excuse me interrupting this little *tête-à-tête*," he said.

"What do you want ?" demanded Lady Bellisle, sternly.

"Him ?"

"Who ?"

"The gentleman—Smithson, please—thank you."

"What are you about ?"

"About to take this Mr. Smithson into custody, ma'am, for a little job. Only poisoning. *Smithson, I arrest you on a charge of murder. You are my prisoner !*"

CHAPTER LXXI.

THE ASTROLOGER'S LABORATORY—THE CORPSE — MIDNIGHT DEEDS — THE PHILTRE — THE DEAD ALIVE—"MINE FROM THE GRAVE !"—THE MAIDEN'S APPEAL—THE ARAB'S PLOT—DEEDS OF HORROR—THE OATH—THE COMPACT—MAN OR DEVIL ?

RETURN we now for a while to take a brief glance at Mermet.

We left him in his study—alone in the room.

That is, so far alone as one can be in the company of a clay cold corpse.

After the two resurrectionists had left he stood for a long while surveying the white pallid face of the unhappy Lotty Chepstow, for it was the earthly part of this fair girl that they had robbed from the cold grave.

This, after it had been interred only a few short hours.

After gazing for some time in silence at the body a singular expression of gratification escaped him.

"Marvellous !" he said. "Truly marvellous ! Perfection itself !"

Then he placed his ear upon the breast of the

corpse, after the manner of a physician sounding a patient for chest disease.

" Not the faintest," he murmured.

What could he mean ?

This we shall see.

After examining the body thus for some short time he left it.

Then he commenced some odd proceedings with a variety of bottles of every size, colour, and shape.

Drugs, compounds, and philtres of endless kinds were applied to.

This established one fact beyond a doubt, however.

Let the Arab be a quack in his necromancy or not, he certainly had some knowledge of medicines.

It yet remains to be seen to what purpose he could use them.

After some little labour thus he compounded a mixture of some crimson liquids, which he brought to the side of the corpse.

Then he got a glass tube, narrow at one end, a kind of funnel, which he inserted between her tightly clenched teeth.

Then he poured the contents of the glass down it.

Physic for the dead ! Strange proceeding !

He stood still, watching the effect of the potion upon the corpse, and apparently he discovered some difference, although to an ordinary observer it remained precisely the same as before.

" Good, good !" muttered the conjuro-astrologo-physician.

He then procured a basin of warm water, and with a sponge bathed the body incessantly for full twenty minutes.

When he had concluded this strange portion of these out-of-the-way proceedings, he procured a second draught, which was administered to the corpse as before.

The only thing which might have appeared strange or worthy of remark here was that the teeth of the corpse seemed even firmer set than before.

This discovery, however, did not in any way stay the necromancer's energies.

On the contrary, it appeared rather to incite him to fresh vigour in his wild and unearthly project, whatever it might prove to be.

" True as a die," he muttered.

This stage in the proceedings would appear to have been regarded by the operator as most important, for he stood by the side of the corpse for nearly ten minutes, looking upon it in breathless attention.

The first impression would be that he expected the corpse to speak.

Presently he took up one of its hands and examined it.

Then, as if in the greatest triumph, he held it up, with a quiet chuckle.

His action would have given one the notion of a successful trickster exulting before a large audience in the success of a feat of legerdemain.

But this time the certainty was one remarkable fact in connection with the cold still corpse of Lotty Chepstow.

The hands were tightly clenched.

Clenched like the hands of one in a strong fainting fit.

The nails were dug into the palms.

What could this singular phenomenon imply ?

Had the drugs which the necromancer administered to the corpse produced the effect of galvanism upon it ?

Now the Arab simply proceeded to act with the corpse as if it were the ill-fated Lotty Chepstow in life and only fainting.

His first great care was to wrench open her clenched hands.

This accomplished, he patted them tenderly, but with much zeal and perseverance, and then placed a large glass stopper out of a coloured bottle in each, so that the hands could not again clench over them.

Then a bottle of sal volatile was held to the nostrils.

Now, by all that is marvellous, the eyes of the corpse twitch nervously.

Is it merely a delusion, or do they indeed move ?

Vinegar is next resorted to, and the whole face and the temples are bathed copiously with it.

Some three hours have now elapsed since Resurrection Joe and Snatchem brought the body from the cold grave to the necromancer's house.

Still the Arab perseveres with untiring energy in his task.

Does not the reader already divine his object ?

The vinegar seems to have operated more powerfully than all else.

Not so. It is merely the concluding portion of a dangerous and lengthy experiment.

Drugs, potent and marvellous in their efficacy, have been already administered by the Arab, and the vinegar greatly aids their operation.

However, it gets all the credit of the good work, as the completer of a useful invention often derives more credit than its father.

The bosom, fair and white as marble, of the corpse rises.

A heavy deep-drawn sigh comes from the lips.

Then the eyes of the seeming corpse—the corpse no more—open wearily.

It is an enormous effort apparently, and many contrary influences must be at work in her system to produce this curious effect.

A will more powerful than her own would appear to be within her to force them open, whilst some strong opiate keeps them closed.

" EUREKA !" ejaculated the necromancer in extravagant joy.

But Lotty Chepstow's hearing would not appear to be so acute as heretofore.

Although the necromancer had spoken in a loud voice, she took no notice whatever of the sound.

Still she lay, with her eyes—dull and leaden-looking yet—fixed upon vacancy.

The attentions of the Arab never once ceased, never flagged.

He still kept to his task with the same untiring perseverance.

At length his efforts were rewarded with another success.

Lotty Chepstow moved her head towards him and looked into his face.

" At last, at last !" said Mermet.

She sighed again.

" Lotty," said the Arab.

She looked up.

" Lotty, Lotty, how do you feel ? Are you well ? Speak, answer me."

She sighed heavily, and then spoke a few indistinct words.

" Lotty, Lotty, what is it. Speak again."

And he leant down his ear to her lips to catch what she said.

" I am better."

It was so low, so faint, that he could barely catch it even then.

" Better ?"

She looked an affirmative.

" Do you feel cold yet ?"

" Yes."

" Can you move ?"

A pause, during which she evidently essayed to move, but was powerless, and she replied in the negative.

" All in good time," said Mermet.

Now by the change in her countenance it was

evident that she had began to wonder where she had come from.

Clearly she had no idea of the terrible truth.

"Where am I ?" she asked.

"In my house," replied Mermet.

This appeared to afford her poor consolation, however.

Indeed, so much was expressed in her face.

"Do you not remember me, Lotty ?" demanded the necromancer. "Mermet—you know Mermet the Arab, who loves you so well."

"Ah !" And then the light of intelligence shone in her face.

By degrees she remembered all.

Unhappy Lotty !

How gladly would she have accepted oblivion of a portion of her bygone history which had caused her so much uneasiness, so much misery !

"I cannot remember the last few days," she said. "Have I been ill ?"

"You have."

"I thought so."

"Do you not remember the poison ?"

"Ah ! merciful powers protect me ! What do you mean by that ?"

"That you have been dead !"

"Oh ! no, no, no."

"Nay more, you have been—"

Here he pointed mysteriously downwards with his forefinger.

A light of the fearful truth burst in upon the unhappy girl.

"You mean—"

"*The tomb* !"

A wild shriek escaped her.

A wild unearthly cry, that rang alarmingly through the house.

"Hush !"

"Oh ! say not the tomb—the grave !"

"It is true. But why repine now over a fancied horror, and which is past ?"

"Oh ! it is too horrible," said the girl, with a fearful shudder.

"Nay," said the necromancer, "rather look upon it in comfort."

"Comfort ?"

"Ay."

"How comfort ?"

"You have purged away the sin, if ever it rested on you."

"Would I could think so ?"

"You may. Morally you are free from the slightest taint now."

"But legally ?"

The necromancer looked rather dubious upon this head.

In fact, his serious expression was considerably more marked than it need have been.

The girl shuddered.

"Fear nothing whilst you remain with me," said the necromancer.

"But after ?"

"After ?" repeated Mermet. "*There will be no after.*"

"What ?"

"I say there will be no after. You will remain with me."

"What do you mean ?"

"I mean, girl," said the Arab "that you are mine for life. I have plucked you from the grave—taken you a cold clay corpse from the bowels of the earth—and breathed the breath of life into your nostrils. You are *mine*, MINE !"

He spoke so vehemently that the girl was quite startled.

"Oh ! pray don't talk thus to me," she said im-

ploringly. "You fill me with fear. I shiver and turn cold to my very feet."

Fearful of stopping the circulation of the blood at such a critical moment, the Arab immediately modified his tone.

"Nay," he said. "I would not unnecessarily alarm you, but would impress upon you how fully, how justly you are mine."

"Justly yours?"

"Ay, justly mine, because I have given life to your dead form," replied the Arab.

"And then ?"

"I retain every power over you."

"Never. Think you I will submit to it ?"

"*Submit ?*" echoed the necromancer mockingly. "Submit, foolish girl ? Know that the same power which gave you life can take it from you again."

"Ah !"

"Fear nothing. I do not mean to slay you. But this same power can likewise force your submission."

"But you would not ?"

"Right, I would not. You have but to swear truth and loyalty to me and you shall have no cause to complain."

"How if I refuse?"

"Then to what purpose ? You cannot seek the world again."

"Why not ?"

"Lotty Chepstow is dead."

"But my identity may be established."

"True. But to what end, pray ?"

"Restoration to my home—to my friends and kindred."

"Restoration to the gallows. But no, no. You shall not either return to the cold unfeeling world nor to your friends."

"Oh ! be merciful."

"I am. I would not let you suffer the pang of being cast off by those who would not recognise you. If you announce yourself you denounce yourself also. And if gratitude will not force acceptance of the home of freedom and of safety which I offer you, something else shall."

"What ?"

"My power."

The strange sepulchral scene, tone, and associations could not fail to impress the poor girl with awe and superstition.

She could reply no further.

She cowered before the necromancer in fear.

"Come, come," said Mermet, "be happy. I don't wish to make you ill at ease. On the contrary, I would comfort you."

"What do you want of me ?" demanded the girl in a trembling tone.

"Fear not. I shall ask nothing of you that you cannot readily grant."

"Be merciful to me, as you hope for mercy yourself," said Lotty.

This was evidently thrown out as a feeler.

She had her doubts as to whether he was not something superhuman.

He saw this clearly enough, and he did not fail to enlarge upon it.

Her fears were as clearly delineated in the expression she wore as if they had been put into words.

Mermet saw, too, that the accomplishment of his designs with her was the more readily to be arrived at by fostering this belief, and he replied to her appeal in such a tone as did not fail to strength it.

"How should I hope for mercy ?" was his response.

The girl shuddered.

This was a fearful confirmation of her fears.

"What do you wish me to do ?" she asked again, as a final resort.

She was determined to resist coercion of her immortal part to the last breath of life.

"I want you to bind yourself to me for life."

"And after?"

"After? Oh!" returned the Arab, chuckling inwardly at his success, "after is nothing whatever to do with me."

"You mean that?"

"I do."

"Then I must consent—always with a proviso."

"What is that?"

"That I am well treated."

"Have you cause for complaint hitherto?" demanded the magician.

"I know not."

"In rescuing you from the grave?"

"I slept in peace."

"So far—*but what was to come?*"

These words conveyed a hidden knowledge of the secrets of the dreadful future which duly impressed the girl.

"Now," said Mermet after a pause, "tell me how you feel."

"Better."

"Has this coldness gone?"

"Yes."

"Your blood circulates freely?"

"Yes. I feel heavy at the head still, but I am better than before."

"I'm glad of that. Can you rise now?"

She replied to this by sitting up.

And now, for the first time, she perceived the slight covering she had on, and her blushing cheeks told how her maidenly decorum was wounded.

Mermet noticed it too, and remarked upon it.

"You need have no scruples now," said he. "Pruderies are for the world. We can dispense with them. Henceforth you are mine—mine alone. Henceforth you must but think as I think, act as I act, and—"

In bitter shame the maiden drew the fatal winding-sheet around her.

The tearless eyes upturned made a mute appeal to Heaven.

And in this same appeal told her soul's agony.

"Oh! man, man," she exclaimed bitterly, "keep me if you will—slay me; but oh! have mercy upon me!"

"You are mine," was all the reply the necromancer deigned.

"Mercy, if you are a man!"

"Mine."

"Fiend! you have no heart."

CHAPTER LXXII.

STILL ONWARDS—FRESH SCANDAL—A GALLANT PRIEST—THEATRICAL DRESSING-ROOM—THE GREEN-ROOM—THE PET PARSON AND HIS VICTIM—A SCENE IN A CHURCH—MURDER OF THE PET PERSON.

AFTER the fatal occurrence at the theatre our heroine and Blanche Bowerini determined to move onwards.

The fatal associations in connection with it they deemed would always be before them, and they therefore quitted the company and made for an adjacent town.

As in their previous rambles, they did not make a very protracted stay here.

But they came across one or two little incidents, to which we shall refer as we proceed.

The first of these happened immediately upon their arrival.

We shall therefore give it in its order.

One of the most constant visitors to the theatre was a young man who created a deal of excitement amongst the petticoats.

He was the curate of the principal living in the place, a young rake just fresh from Oxford, and whose family had thrust him into the cloth, in the belief that the sacred calling would sober down his vicious propensities.

However, in this they had signally failed.

The young curate carried on such pranks, and was so much run after by the petticoats, that he procured for himself the sobriquet of the "Pet Parson."

At the theatre was one girl who was said to be positively madly in love with this gay clerical Lothario.

She was a minor actress only, of no great talent—indeed of rather humble abilities—and who was said only to retain her position, small as it was, for her pretty face and well-turned ankle.

Now for some time the Pet Parson made a regular dead set at Miss Clitheroe, as she was known to the profession.

Miss Clitheroe, albeit she possessed many ardent admirers, had proved, like the rest of her sex, unable to resist the allurements of the gallant churchman.

And scented cocked-hat billets-doux had passed between them.

Endless promenades had been gone through.

All the celebrated walks denominated by the neighbourhood "ultra-spooney" were used up, and lo! the Pet Parson's passion began to fall off.

He dropped off gradually in his attentions.

Reproaches were coolly met.

Then the gay churchman slighted her altogether.

Now this Kate Clitheroe had a hot temper beneath her fair angelic face.

She had suffered a wrong at the curate's hands, and she resented it fiercely.

Rose Mortimer might have been drawn into this, for the Pet Parson made fierce love to her as soon as she arrived.

But she cut him so dreadfully short that he was sent to the right-about considerably humbled in spirit.

The curate had the *entrée* to the green-room, and he used to carry on the most violent flirtations with most of the ladies who were weak and silly enough to feel flattered by his attentions.

One night in the dressing room the ladies were growing very cruel and sarcastic at Miss Clitheroe's expense concerning the *amours* of herself and the Pet Parson, when she, after tamely submitting to it for a long time, retorted in such a way as to intimate that matters had indeed reached a most serious climax.

In other words, they were shortly to be united in holy wedlock.

One and all of the scandal-loving sisterhood scorned the notion.

"As you please," retorted Miss Clitheroe. "You can have your own way."

"It might be so if you had yours," said one of the actresses spitefully.

"You are a jealous girl," said Miss Clitheroe. "But time will show."

"Time perhaps," said one.

"A very long time," said another.

"Delays are dangerous," quoth a third. "Many a slip 'twixt the cup and the lip, you know."

At length, unable to bear the cruel sneers any longer, Miss Clitheroe rushed out of the dressing-room.

"Poor creature!" said one. "You were really too hard upon her, Miss Evans."

"I severe?"

"Of course. Oh, you poor innocent!" said the others, laughing.

"I appeal to any one if I said anything the least in the world severe."

"Well, perhaps not," said the former speaker. "But, however, it was not your fault if it was not so."

This turned the laugh the other way.

"Now who is severe?" said Miss Evans. "No, no; I didn't say a word to hurt the dear creature's sensibilities. But we all know very well that that Ravenscroft is only making a fool of the girl."

"Girl?"

"Well, young woman. Oh, you shouldn't."

And this little scandalous school laughed and grew merrier.

Rose Mortimer, who was dressing while the foregoing conversation was taking place, had by this time finished and left the room.

She had felt inclined once or twice to remonstrate with them for their tirade against one poor girl; but, not feeling at all assured of being able to render her cause any service, she desisted.

Being dressed now, she made her way into the green-room, to give a look over her part before being called.

At the further end of the room was a large screen drawn round a fire.

To rest and study her part undisturbed Rose Mortimer placed herself here.

This led to a most unpleasant circumstance for our heroine.

She had not been long seated here when two persons entered the room, and, deeming that they were merely some of the company come to await their call, she took no notice of this.

When she found that she was in error she did not like to make known her presence, lest her motives for silence might be misconstrued.

"Oh, Wilfred, Wilfred," exclaimed a female voice, which Rose at once recognised as belonging to Miss Clitheroe, "I have been so insulted."

"What is it, my pet birdie?" demanded another voice, which our heroine also knew to be that of the Pet Parson.

"Those horrid creatures in the dressing-room."

"Horrid creatures? What horrid creatures?"

"Those scandal-making women."

"What, the ladies of the company?"

"Yes."

"Oh, the dears!"

"Listen to me, Wilfred. I am not speaking in jest now. I have been sneered at, gibed, and scoffed at by the whole dressing-room."

"What then, my pet?"

"Upon your account."

"And then?"

"Then, Wilfred?" iterated the astonished girl. "How coldly you speak of it!"

"Well, but what would you have me do?"

"Resent it."

"I resent it?"

"If you love me."

"That's a cruel hypothesis, my birdie," said the Pet Parson. "As for loving you, you are well aware that I cannot exist without you."

"Then you will not wish to see me insulted."

"Wish? No."

"Would not have me insulted, Wilfred?" she said, appealingly.

"Not I: but what can I do? If I hadn't been in orders, and if your offenders had been of my own sex, of course I should have done the needful at fourteen paces. But how I, a reverend divine, am to resent your wrongs upon a set of highly agreeable ladies I am at a loss to conjecture."

"Wilfred," said the girl, "this light ribaldry ill befits you in our present relations."

"What relations?"

"Good Heavens! Wilfred, do not speak thus."

"I will speak any way you please, my angel," said the Pet Parson.

"Nay, Wilfred, did you know really how much my feelings have been hurt by what these cruel women have said, you would sympathise with me I'm sure."

"Indeed?"

"Ay, you would. They even dared to hint that you would play me false."

"Did they, though?"

"Ay, indeed."

"And what did you say?"

"I told them that we were to be one, that—"

"Stop, stop. You told them that?"

"I did, Wilfred, and—"

"And you did me wrong," said the gay Lothario, "to go and blab about my matters to a crowd of gossiping jealous women. You cannot think much of me to talk thus."

"What do you mean, Wilfred?"

"That it would have been time for the world to hear such an absurdity as that you speak of when I informed them myself."

"Eh?"

"And as for you, Miss Clitheroe, I consider your conduct in the matter highly indelicate, to say the very least of it."

Rose trembled with indignation where she was concealed.

Had she not feared that her strange position might have brought her motives into question, she would have boldly advanced as the champion of Miss Clitheroe.

At length Miss Clitheroe found her tongue.

"You say this to me, Wilfred?" she exclaimed, in a tone which told strongly of wonderment and indignation together.

"Whom else could I say it to?"

"After all that has passed between us?"

"Pshaw!"

"Oh! Wilfred, Wilfred!"

"There, there, spare me your nonsense."

"And where are your promises, your vows, and all you have told me?"

"Bosh! Where are my promises?"

"You deny them?"

"Positively."

"Man, man!"

"Now spare your theatricals till your call. Remember we are in the green-room."

"Since you choose to assume this tone," said Miss Clitheroe, "I will meet you with your own weapons. But think not to escape me any the more. Beware of me, for I promise you retribution."

"Oh! you threat?"

"I warn."

"And for what, pray?"

"Hopes deceived—outraged affection. Is it for my ardent love that you would punish me thus?"

"And you me. Did we not share the love?"

"No—on my soul no. 'Twas all my own, or you would not, could not, now speak to me as you do."

"'Twas interest," retorted the Pet Parson, "or you would not—could not feel the slight so much. 'Tis not outraged affection. Hopes deceived I can admit—weighty hopes, eh?"

"You wrong me, man, and well you know it."

"I don't—else why this scene?"

"Scene? Man, would you pretend to ignore the fearful fact that a deceived wronged woman is lost for life—becomes the scoff, the jeer of her own sex, and slighted by yours, unless indeed she descends to the lowest depths of degradation?"

"And I?"

[THE MURDER OF THE PET PARSON.]

"You?"

"Ay, your humble servant."

"Silence!"

"Pshaw! We have shared the pleasure of each other's society."

"And who bears all the opprobrium?"

"Can't say I'm sure."

"You can. You would share it on account of the cloth you wear."

"Oh! you mean to make a fuss?"

"Not I. I know you better. It would not affect you sufficiently."

"I'm glad you think so."

"No, no. You would be disgraced, but you would resume your old position in the laity—become a man of the world in every sense. I should be serving your real tastes I know well."

"Now really, my dear Kate, you are not such a fool as I took you for," replied the amiable parson.

"Beware, sir."

"Thank you."

"You may sneer, you may mock me, but beware I say. You shall yet find that an outraged woman can hate as fiercely as she has loved fondly."

"Thank you again," said the Reverend Wilfred Ravenscroft. "And now, if you have nothing more to say, I'll go."

"Go, and triumph. Glory in your victory," said

the poor girl. " Make the most of it, for I swear that it is short-lived."

" Thank you."

And with the most elaborate politeness the Pet Parson saluted his late lover and left the green-room.

As soon as he was gone Rose could hear a deep sob escape the excited Kate Clitheroe.

Then a fall.

At all risks now our heroine came forward to the girl's assistance.

She lay stretched upon the ground in a strong fit of hysterics.

" Stage waiting for Miss Clitheroe," shouted the call boy.

The stage had to wait.

*   *   *   *   *   *

Upon the following Sunday Rose Mortimer and Blanche Bowerini were at church to hear the Reverend Wilfred Ravenscroft, alias the " Pet Parson," deliver a sermon.

His latest conquest amongst the petticoats was the general theme of conversation, and it was said that he would not venture to appear on the Sunday.

However, Mr. Ravenscroft showed that he was perfectly indifferent about the opinion of his congregation, for he advanced with more than ordinary boldness, and even selected a text which might be supposed to bear in some slight degree upon the late scandal.

A glance of surprise went round the congregation, but of course they could take no further notice of it.

Blanche Bowerini and Rose Mortimer sat side by side.

" Bold !" whispered the former.

Rose nodded.

" The man is utterly without a heart."

" It would seem so."

" And see here who has come in."

It was Kate Clitheroe.

She was pale and grief-stricken.

The last few hours had effected such a change in the poor girl's appearance as to excite the universal commiseration of the congregation.

Singularly enough, she did not appear to court that retirement which one would have imagined.

On the contrary, she placed herself opposite the pulpit, so that the first person the Pet Parson would see upon entering it would be herself.

Until the Reverend Wilfred Ravenscroft appeared in the pulpit he had not observed the unhappy girl.

Then she appeared almost to spring out of the ground, and seemed to have eyes for no one but him.

She sat there staring fixedly upon him as if unconscious that there was a numerous congregation in the church.

" Poor girl !" whispered Rose to her companion.

" Oh ! doesn't she look bad ?"

" She does, indeed."

" And there is a strange expression in her face which I cannot make out."

" It means mischief."

" It looks like it."

And so evidently thought the reverend gentleman, for as he glanced downwards at this very instant his eye lighted upon the upturned face.

He coloured visibly and stammered in his sermon.

" Ah ! villain !" thundered the girl. " You feel the same triumph now ?"

The whole congregation were upon their feet at once.

A dead silence prevailed for an instant.

Then the church was startled more than before by the loud report of a pistol.

The curate was seen to stagger and fall forward.

A cry burst from his lips, and all was over.

Kate Clitheroe rushed madly from the church still grasping the pistol which had murdered a minister of the Gospel in a place of holy worship.

Justice was done.

Kate Clitheroe undone.

The Pet Parson was dead, and his murderer was his victim.

An inquest was held upon the body, and subsequently the unhappy murderess was brought to her trial, at which she was proved to be of unsound mind.

She was, therefore, put under restraint for the term of her natural life.

This tragical episode scarcely proved the proverbial nine days' wonder.

A week, and it was forgotten.

CHAPTER LXXIII.

ROSE AND HER LOVER—THE DRAPER GALLANT—BOUQUETS AGAIN—A PROPOSAL—SLIGHT—THE DRAPER'S VENGEANCE — THE LETTER — THE INSULT—HOW ROSE RETALIATED AND ASTONISHED THE DRAPER.

SHORTLY after the events narrated in the preceding chapter Rose Mortimer found, to her infinite amusement at first, but finally to her extreme annoyance, that she had made another conquest.

This time it was a " knight of the yard measure," i.e., a linendraper of the town, who found himself desperately caught by our fair heroine's charms.

Rose saw him in the pit night after night, casting ardent glances towards her, and full of the very maddest love which ever inspired a mortal draper.

She confided the conquest to Blanche Bowerini, and the two girls had a hearty laugh at the worthy draper's expense.

" He's slow to make himself known," said Rose to Blanche one evening as she was dressing after the last piece.

" Perhaps," said Blanche Bowerini. " But you know the old saying, ' Slow but sure.'"

" And you think that it will answer in his case ?"

" Yes."

" We shall see."

" You are all impatience."

" For what ?"

" Declaration."

" Not all," said Rose, laughing. " Just a little bit anxious, I confess."

" Rose, Rose dear," said the other girl, " I fear you are a terrible flirt."

" Nay, I protest I have not looked at the odious little monster."

" Then how know you that he is always looking at you, dear ?"

" Eh ? Oh—why—"

Blanche Bowerini burst into a fit of laughter, in which her companion joined heartily, after an ineffectual effort to keep a sober countenance.

" Ah ! Rose, Rose dear," said Blanche, " you are playing with the poor man's feelings. But beware ! He might catch you yet."

" You think so ?"

" I think it very likely."

" Why ?"

" Because I really fancy that even now he is not altogether indifferent to you."

" Blanche, my dear, you are a teasing, aggravating, satirical little monster, and I'll soon prove to you what small work I'll make of this draper."

" Very good, dear," said Blanche. " But I don't believe that you'll have the heart to refuse the dear little man anything."

At this period in the conversation Rose had completed her dressing, and they left the place.

As they were passing by the stage door they heard a singular altercation between the doorkeeper and a person whose voice neither of them knew.

However, from the nature of the discussion, both guessed very shrewdly who this individual was.

And the result proved that they were right in their conjecture.

"But you have nothing whatever to do with the matter," said the strange voice above alluded to.

"I beg your pardon, sir," returned the doorkeeper, "I have everything to do with it."

"How can that be?"

"Orders is orders."

"What do you mean by orders? I don't want orders, sir. I pay my money."

"Of course, sir. I don't know nothing about the front of the house. I mean orders concerning the door. And, once for all, I shan't take it in."

"Why not?"

"Because Miss Mortimer expressly forbad any bouquets to be taken in."

"But let her refuse it herself."

"She does," said our heroine, advancing at the moment.

The little man who was presenting the bouquet was thoroughly staggered at this.

He drew back, and made a profound obeisance.

Rose and her companion passed out, making the little gentleman a bow in acknowledgement.

But he was not to be put off like this.

He darted after them, and, taking off his hat by Rose's side, made her another bow, even more gallant than before.

And a truly comical figure he cut there, the bouquet in one hand and his hat in the other.

"Pardon me, Miss Mortimer," he began, with much trepidation in his tone.

"Sir!"

Rose gave this monosyllable with such severe emphasis that the little gentleman was frozen up on the instant.

"Pardon me, Miss Mortimer, but that man—the doorkeeper—has actually refused to accept the bouquet, alleging—"

"That it was my particular order that no bouquet should be taken in upon any account."

"But do you refuse it?" he demanded, with a languishing air.

Blanche felt very much inclined to laugh, and communicated her condition to Rose by a silent pinch on the arm.

"Yes," returned Rose. "I never accept anything from strangers."

"Yes; but a bouquet."

"Bouquets especially. I have painful reasons, which I do not care to explain. Therefore I must beg that you will desist pressing your favours any further."

"As you please, Miss Mortimer," said the little gentleman.

Rose bowed and would have passed on, but he again stayed her.

"One word before I leave you, Miss Mortimer."

"Pray be brief, sir."

"Would you give me five minutes' conversation?"

"Sir, the hour and the singularity of your request cannot surely have been considered before being made."

"No time like the present."

"Such are not my sentiments," said Rose. "I wish you a very good night."

And she passed on, cutting the little man still smaller.

"That's a terrible blow to him," said Blanche.

"It is, and I hope it has put a stop to his impertinence."

"Oh, that's rather hard."

"Not at all. Whilst he confined it to casting stupid glances from the pit it could only be laughed at, but when he comes to inflict personal annoyance on one it ought to be stopped in a summary manner. I hope that that has effected the desired object."

* * * * * *

The next morning betimes the landlady of the lodging-house at which Rose and Blanche Bowerini were staying came to announce that a gentleman wished to see Miss Mortimer.

"Did he send his name?" asked our heroine.

"No, miss. He is a short gentleman."

"I expected no one."

She made some little improvement in her toilet, and descended to the parlour, where was seated the persevering little draper who had failed to induce her acceptance of the bouquet upon the previous night.

Rose was annoyed at this, and would have retreated at once; but, being in the room, she would not do this, lest the impudent little rascal might draw his own inferences.

However, her reception of him was still icier than it had been upon the previous night.

She bowed stiffly.

"May I ask what is your business with me, sir?" she demanded.

"Oh, you recognise me, I perceive," he said with a ghastly smile. "Well, you see, Miss Mortimer, the fact is—the fact is that it is rather an embarrassing matter which—in fact—pray excuse a little agitation."

"A little?"

"Eh? Oh, yes—a little of course. You mean to say that there is a great deal to excuse. Of course—good joke—ha! ha!"

But not a smile did it elicit from our heroine, great as the joke was, but, on the contrary, she appeared a trifle graver than before.

"Excuse my abruptness, sir," said Rose, "but I'm rather pressed for time, and I have not the honour of—"

"Of my acquaintance. Precisely—of course not—oblige me."

And with a wonderfully shoppy gesture he jerked out a card.

Rose took it and read it off as follows:—

Mr. HARRY FANE,

LINENDRAPER, HABERDASHER, AND SILK MERCER.

Millinery in all its Branches. The latest Paris fashions.

"Yes, yes, miss—that's all—excuse me—a business card, you see."

But Rose was inexorable.

She had another opening for a quiet little bit of satire, and she would not miss it.

"*An immense assortment of Paris kid gloves (best makers).*"

"Miss Mortimer—"

"N.B.—"

"That is all. I wish to remark—"

"*Three doors up the High Street, and no connection with the next door.*"

"Merely my business card, as I remarked before, Miss Mortimer."

"Yes, you did. And what may you have to say to me now? You will pardon my abruptness, as I remarked before, I think; but I'm rather occupied just now."

" I come, then, in short, to be brief, since you wish me to be so—"

" I do."

" Then to introduce my humble self to your notice."

" It would have been done in better taste—much better taste, believe me—by a third party."

" Of course."

" Introductions are unpleasant except in the usual form, and so you will pardon me, I know, if I put an end at once to the present interview without further ceremony."

Mr. Harry Fane's confusion at this was really painful to behold.

" One word more, Miss Mortimer," said he. " I came here to speak of a very serious matter."

" Indeed ?"

" Yes. I merely came to say that—" and he made a tremendous effort to appear calm, but failed miserably—"that you have made an impression upon me, Miss Mortimer, which no other wom—I mean lady—that is, in short, I am in very tolerable circumstances, and I should be happy if you—"

And Mr. Harry Fane was cut up sadly.

Surely there never was so eccentric a declaration made as this.

The vanity and egotism displayed in this confused address were such as utterly to disgust our heroine.

She rose to her feet and moved towards the door.

" Mr. Fane," she said, " I am sure that when you reflect upon what you have said to me you will think that, to put it in the mildest form, the words were an impertinence."

" Miss Mor—"

" Enough. I wish you good day."

And she quitted the room.

" I tell you what," he shouted as she left the room, " you shall repent this insolent treatment. At any rate, I have honoured you, Miss Mortimer, a ballet-girl, by what I've offered, and, hang it ! you shall yet have your pride humbled."

Rose little thought how vindictive the little draper could prove.

* * * * * *

The next day Rose Mortimer was late at rehearsal.

When she arrived there was a grand stir in the green-room.

Everybody in the company exchanged glances of a peculiar meaning, and our heroine perceived at once that something had occurred concerning herself.

She asked several persons what it meant, but no one would reply.

At length, in despair, she applied to Mr. Snaffles, the prompter.

" Occurred, Miss Mortimer?" said he. " Nothing that I am aware of. Here is a letter for you, by the bye."

And he offered her the missive, which was open.

" It was delivered like that, Miss Mortimer," said the prompter, anticipating her looks, " or, rather, not like that, for I found it here opened, and, not knowing what is was, or to whom it was addressed, I—"

" Read it."

" Yes."

" And not you alone," said Rose, glancing around her.

Now she thought that she began to comprehend the meaning of all the strange glances which had puzzled her so at first.

She opened the letter and read as follows :—

" *My Dear Rose,—Touching the proposition I made you, you have yet to consider. I cannot possibly allow you more than two hundred a year pin-money, whatever you may urge. Further persua-*sion, *as I have already told you, is useless. In every respect you will be treated as my wife, although you cannot be admitted into my family circle ; but this will be no great grievance, as you shall find. It is no use attempting to gain this point, because the opinion of the world is more to me than your love—the love which you so freely offer.*"

This clearly enough indicated that she had made arrangements with some one to become his mistress, but that the price for the sale of herself had been the matter of dispute.

It was an overwhelming blow.

Rose had been always most strict in her demeanour.

She knew too well to what slurs the moral character of the actress is liable, and she had acted in such a way hitherto that she had procured for herself the title of " the prude."

She was at no loss to divine from whom this artful and villainous composition had emanated.

Unfortunately, there was no signature to it, or she would have taken immediate legal steps to retaliate upon the slanderer.

However, she at once narrated the whole of the draper's proposals to her, and the way in which she had retorted to the vain little rascal's addresses.

The whole of the company were supremely shocked at his impudence.

It reflected discredit upon their order.

Now, although they were one and all a scandal-loving lot, they did not choose that their scandals should go further than themselves.

A speedy and signal retaliation upon the draper was resolved upon.

However, before they could put their plans into execution Rose had avenged herself in the following manner.

It was a bold and dangerous exploit, but was a glorious success, and touched Mr. Harry Fane in a quarter which was his tenderest point—his pocket.

The circus at which Blanche Bowerini was engaged was close to the theatre, and Rose Mortimer had been in the habit of taking a little equestrian exercise in the morning when Blanche went to practice.

It happened that a party of them had been out for a canter one morning, when they chanced to pass up the High Street.

Mr. Harry Fane's shop was the centre of attraction for the whole group since the disgraceful affair of which we have just written.

" If I were you, Miss Mortimer," said one of the ladies, " I would ride into his shop and spoil some of his stock for him."

" I would indeed for the smallest consideration under the sun."

" I fear Miss Mortimer," said one of the gentlemen, " that you would find the feat rather beyond your courage."

" Nay."

" I think you would."

" Not I."

" I should wager—"

" Stay," said Rose. " What would you wager that I don't fly in through the window as it now stands ?"

" I'll bet you a hundred pounds to your sixty that you don't accomplish it."

" You shall see."

And, drawing back, she prepared for a spring.

" Now then, forward !"

And off dashed the horse towards the shop.

There was a cry of alarm, but Rose did not pause.

She put her head low down to the horse's ear, and whispered some words which appeared to inspire him with renewed courage.

The horse sprang into the air, dashed forward, and in the flashing of an eye had bounded through the shop window, carrying glass and everything with him.

The wonder and alarm of the shopkeepers was something startling.

There was a crash, a cry, and a rush.

But all in vain.

The mischief was done, and Mr. Harry Fane was certainly some pounds the poorer by the transaction.

CHAPTER LXXIV.

MERMET—DOUBTS—DISTRUSTS — LOTTY ACCUSES THE ARAB—PROOFS—THE SKELETON'S FEAST—FURTHER PLOTS — THE LABORATORY — OVER-REACHED—FEARFUL DENOUEMENT.

LOTTY CHEPSTOW was Mermet's—his own body and soul, for she had no possibility of delivering herself from the clutches of the cunning little Arab.

She deemed herself the murderess of Arthur Brownbill, the ill-fated libertine who could not prize the jewel he had won, but would fain have destroyed it.

She deemed herself in the clutches of the necromancer and irredeemably lost.

All the proceedings in his house she watched in secret awe and wonder.

There was a mystery—a quiet fear-inspiring manner in all his movements, which set poor Lotty upon the rack.

However, one day the necromancer was caught napping, and then Lotty Chepstow grew suspicious.

One of the easily gulled public—a gentleman of high station in society, who could not restrain his curiosity, but who would not for worlds have had it known that he had visited the necromancer, came to see Mermet in the strictest incognito.

Now Mermet was shrewd-sighted enough to see which way the wind blew, or, in other words, he at once perceived the gentleman's weakness, and he set to work to attack him in this way.

He egged him on with one or two chance shots to come again upon the morrow to hear and see some astonishing wonder.

The gentleman agreed and left the house, and a messenger was immediately despatched to dodge his steps until he should be safely housed.

Now Lotty chanced to be present then, and also upon the following day, when the gentleman paid his second visit.

The revelation of his name, supposed to be conjured up from the hidden knowledge of astrology and other occult sciences which the necromancer possessed, caused much wonder and awe upon the part of the stranger, but were quite without effect upon Lotty Chepstow.

She saw through the humbug of it, and boldly accused Mermet of tricking the stranger.

The annoyance and vexation of the Arab at this are indescribable.

He denied the accusation with startling vehemence.

But she would not be silenced.

"It is useless now," she said with firmness. "You cannot further deceive me."

"Deceive you?"

"Ay, for I *know*. Let me remain in doubt, and I will not question a word, but I have proofs too convincing at present."

"Silly girl!"

"Not only that do I see," continued Lotty, "but I find something else of a more serious and personal nature."

"Name it."

"I find that I have been most egregiously deceived in allowing my weak girlish mind to be led away by your shallow tales and artifices."

"What mean you?"

"The knowledge you pretend to about the hidden sciences."

"Foolish girl! But that I would not have you longer in doubt I would not deign to speak another convincing word. As it is, I merely bid you put me to the test. Give me some cunning test, as if I were a base impostor—as if I were other than the Mermet who has saved you from an early grave—who has drawn you from the very womb of the earth, where your friends and family had lain you."

"Would that you had never disturbed me!"

"Ungrateful girl!"

"Nay, not ungrateful."

"What, then, do you call her who reproaches one for having saved her life?"

"I fear that I am reserved for a worse fate yet—that I am doomed to a living death."

"Lotty Chepstow, I lose all patience with you. You accuse me of deception."

"And with reason."

Mermet broke out into a torrent of angry and passionate invectives at this, which quite frightened Lotty Chepstow.

He stopped short.

His passion was at an end of a sudden.

It was as a sudden calm following upon a violent gale at sea.

"One word more, Lotty," he said. "You would have proof of my truth and sincerity?"

"Nay, I—"

"No hesitation. You shall have it. I will furnish you with proof so conclusive that no trace of doubt shall live in your mind."

"Nay, sir. I—"

"Tut, tut! Tell me what nature of proof you would have, and I—"

"Enough. Since you insist, I wish to ask you a question rather to comfort my own mind than to put you to a test. Did Arthur Brownbill really die?"

"Yes."

"By my hand?"

"You shall have proof of it."

"What proof?"

"The best—ocular proof."

Lotty Chepstow started back as if stung by a reptile.

"Ocular proof?" she iterated. "Surely you do not mean to say that you have anything to offer me as *ocular* proof?"

"You shall judge for yourself."

"No, no, no!"

"Nay, but you shall."

And then, as she resisted, he caught her by the wrist and dragged her off in spite of her struggles.

The girl was forced thus to follow him up the stairs, where he dragged her into a room darkened by long tapestry hangings before the windows.

Upon the right of the entrance was a small sliding window, which Mermet silently pointed to.

"There!"

"What?" demanded the girl, still trembling in anticipation.

"Look through there, and you will see."

"Tell me what."

"You asked me if Arthur Brownbill really fell by your hand."

The girl shuddered, and buried her face in her hands.

"Look!"

She rose and moved mechanically towards the window and peered through.

"There, you now see what Arthur Brownbill is—what he has thus speedily become."

Lotty looked on in unaffected horror, for what she saw was the most terrible and fear-inspiring.

In the centre of a sumptuously furnished chamber was a table well spread with the choicest viands, and seated there, apparently partaking of the banquet, was A HUMAN SKELETON.

Lotty looked on fascinated for a while.

She then turned with a cry from the place and fell upon the floor.

*   *   *   *   *

Mermet raised the swooning girl from the ground, and bore her off to her chamber.

"That was an excellent idea of mine," said the Arab to himself, "and I never dreamt of succeeding so well. As soon as she recovers I will prepare another little surprise for her, that shall put the clincher upon her doubts. She shall see her dear Arthur next in the flesh as well as the bone. Ha, ha, ha!"

And down stairs he hobbled, chuckling with fiendish glee.

He made straightway for his laboratory, where he commenced a variety of experiments such as it was his wont to indulge in.

Surely now some experiment of the deepest interest was about to be performed.

He had barely commenced making up his furnace ere a peal at the bell startled him.

"Ahmet," he called to his attendant, "admit no one, remember."

"Yes, sahib."

But unfortunately the attendant could not prevent the entrance of the visitor.

It chanced to be a lady, thickly veiled, and who appeared to be in such urgency that nothing whatever could stay her entrance.

"Where is your master?" she said. "I must see him immediately."

"He cannot be seen to-night. He is engaged in his studies, lady."

"Where?"

"In the laboratory," answered the attendant, pointing downstairs.

"Enough," said the lady, and she hurried past the attendant, and pushed her way into the laboratory.

Mermet was at work still.

Holding a glass crucible, he was poring over its seething contents, and his little sharp eyes glistened with wonderful interest through the glass mask he wore.

"Is it possible," said the visitor to herself as she entered, "that he can have given up all his former life for this?"

Mermet started up from his task and put down the crucible in a hurry.

"How now, Ahmet?" he exclaimed. "What did I say? I wished to see no one."

"Not even me?" said the lady.

The Arab started and looked up affrightedly, for the voice was evidently known to him.

"Who are you?" he demanded.

"One who knows you well. One who deemed you long since dead. One who recognises beneath that now crooked form, and that seared and blotched face, the traces of the man she once loved—the man who betrayed her trust—who turned her from a woman into a devil—who made her to thirst only for vengeance, and to lose all human sensations in crime and bloodshed."

Mermet was quite staggered by this outburst.

"Woman, who are you?" he demanded in a hoarse tone of voice.

"Would you know me? Then, deformed misshapen Lerno, behold!"

The woman raised her veil, disclosing the well-remembered features of Clara St. John.

"Clara!" gasped the magician.

"Ay, Count Lerno—Clara your wife—the wife of the galley slave."

"Hush!" said Lerno, for this deformed misshapen little object, so full of craft, of cunning, and deceit, was indeed none other than Count Lerno, so long supposed dead—killed in the fire at Park Lane.

"Woman, woman, what would you?" said Lerno, for so must we now call him. "Are you not satisfied with the mischief you have already caused. See, see the miserable wreck you have made of me."

"No, no, I am not satisfied. I shall not be satisfied, either, until I have had my vengeance in full."

"Woman, woman!"

"Silence, monster! You are hideous now, but even less hideous than your mind."

"What would you?"

"Your life. Your heart's blood. I have found that fire will not destroy you. Then I shall try the knife. Thus do I deliver up all the hatred in my heart for you."

She sprang forward, and with a knife unexpectedly produced she stabbed Count Lerno, alias Mermet the Arab magician, to the heart.

Lerno gasped painfully, and let the crucible fall from his grasp into the furnace.

There was a sudden puff, then an explosion, and up went the laboratory, shivering the house into a thousand fragments.

At length the measure of Count Lerno's crimes was full.

Thus he died the death of a dog.

But what of Clara?

CHAPTER LXXV.

A FIRST-CLASS CARRIAGE—FREEDOM AND FLIGHT OF THE ASSASSINS—THE VESSEL—THE END OF LADY BELLISLE—REVELATIONS — THE ARTIST AND THE DEATH-BED—ROSE AGAIN—TWO MESSENGERS—SUMMONED AWAY—BEGINNING OF THE END.

WE left the Earl of Sloeford, the reader will remember, at a country railway station, where, under the assumed name of Smithson, and in the company of his cousin, Lady Bellisle, he was arrested on the charge of murder.

The earl made no attempt at resistance, but quietly suffered the handcuffs to be placed upon his wrists. At a moment when the constable's eyes were averted for an instant, however, the earl took the opportunity of casting a meaning glance towards Lady Bellisle, who immediately perceived that it was an intimation to be prepared for any emergency.

The constable, thinking that he now had his prisoner secure, very readily acquiesced in a desire expressed by him that they should proceed in a private first-class carriage. The earl also asked, as a favour, that his wife, Mrs. Smithson (Lady Bellisle), might accompany them, and to this also the constable consented.

As the train passed through a tunnel there was a silent struggle in a first-class carriage, and a man's life was lost.

It was a long time ere the fate of the constable became known; but at length a train passing over his body chanced to drag it into the light.

How or at whose hands the unhappy man met with such a fearful fate remains a mystery to the present day.

*   *   *   *   *   *

The Earl of Sloeford and his cousin could now no longer endure each other's society.

The guilty love which had bound them together had ceased to exist.

As soon as they had fallen into crime they had grown weary of each other.

The gloss of innocence was no longer there to impart that *couleur de rose* which is the very life of love.

Still they must fly together.

They could no longer remain in the land against whose laws they had so fearfully offended.

They returned to the Hall and packed up some things for travelling, secured all the valuables they could lay hands upon, and started post haste for the nearest seaport.

To cross the Channel was an impossibility, it was said, and they found no boatman who would care to venture the journey, as the weather was rather rough.

However, the well-lined purse of the Earl of Sloeford smoothed away all difficulties, and a small craft was chartered to carry the fugitive earl and his paramour away from the land of their birth.

It was a rough night, and there was no moon up, and the sailors who accepted the heavy bribe which the earl gave them told his lordship to prepare for heavy weather.

They did not seem to think much of risking their own lives, however.

The earl and Lady Bellisle were standing by the low bulwarks at the head of the vessel whilst the three men who had ventured forth to risk their lives for gold were busily occupied astern.

"Farewell, my country," said the earl, sadly, as he gazed upon the fast receding white cliffs of his native soil. "Farewell! I see you for the last time. Had it not been for you I might have been saved from the path of crime into which I have been led by that base intriguing woman."

"Spencer, Spencer!" cried his unhappy lover at his side, "what mean you by these accusations? Know you not—"

"That I am ruined through you? Yes."

"Nay—that you would have been made through me—that for you, ingrate, I have sacrificed everything."

"What, forsooth, constitutes everything?"

"Did I not raise you from the dust? Answer me that."

"What do you mean, woman?"

"That you were but a man of straw, an insolvent thing, not worth the slightest credit, when I—oh! I could dash out my brains when I think of it—fell in with you. Where could my woman's wit have been? But I'll be revenged upon myself for my fooling."

"Do so," said the earl, with a mocking laugh. "But how?"

"I'll expose myself to all interested. I will reinstate the daughter of Rosalia Hargreaves in her rights. I know that she lives. She is in the charge of Seymour yet, and can be found. At any rate, I can take this vengeance against myself—against you."

The brow of the earl grew clouded with passion.

"At your peril you will breathe one word!" he said.

"How, sir? You dare to threaten me? Man, I can blow this air-built castle to pieces as easily as I have made it—nay, more, I will."

The earl glanced over his shoulder towards the three men and perceived that they were busily engaged in the management of the vessel.

Then he raised his hand, and—

"What was that, Joe?" asked one of the sailors of his mate.

"Sounded like a cry."

They went forward, but found their male passenger sitting quietly enough upon a coil of rope half asleep!

"What noise was that, sir?" asked one of the sailors.

"What noise? Didn't hear any. Where's the lady, my wife? Tell her that I want her to come here."

"She's not here, sir. It must be—"

"What?" interrupted the earl, with a start of fear and surprise. "What do you mean? Tell me. Say, what is it?"

"I know not, sir. She has, perhaps, fallen over board."

"It is not possible."

But whether possible or not, one fact is assured.

Only one passenger landed on the coast of France, and this was the man.

About three weeks after that an Englishman got one of his lungs shot away at Baden-Baden by a pot-bellied German, who had detected him in the act of cheating at cards.

He gave a name which the authorities felt convinced must be assumed, as it did not at all correspond with the initials marked on his linen.

The only thing which he left behind was a packet of manuscript, which he directed to Rosalia Hargreaves, care of one Seymour, in London.

Now we must follow the transmission of this packet, as some wonderful things depend upon it.

When the packet arrived in London at the house of this Seymour he was found to be dying.

He was at last succumbing to the ravages which alcohol had made on him for the last fifteen years.

By his bedside was a young man of rather eccentric appearance and habits, good-looking, thoroughly good-hearted, and exhibiting the utmost patience with the dying man, who was excessively fretful and impatient.

"Ah, Jack," said the dying man, "I shall never look upon her sweet sunny face again. You—you, Jack, must implore her forgiveness, or I feel that I shall not rest in my grave. You know not how much she has to forgive."

"Oh, sir," interrupted the artist—for such he was— "you must have forgotten her sweet nature if you let this trouble you further. You should know better than any one how forgiving she is."

"True, true, Jack," said the dying man. "But you know not all she has to forgive. It was I who drove her to the stage. I would have driven her to worse, but she was too pure—too pure. I cannot tell you more, lest you, too, Jack Halliday should turn against me; and I would not lose the friendship of the man who has kept the wolf from my door for this long time, nor have you hate me as the last breath leaves my worn-out carcase. Give me the packet again."

The young man handed him the packet.

"Ah!" he said, reading off the direction with difficulty, for his eyes were fast dimming in death, "this is the first time I have been called *Seymour* for many a long day, *and it will be the last time too!*"

"Nay, my old friend—"

"Hush! Remember what I've said. Don't speak with levity at this moment. Do not attempt to persuade me that I'm not dying. You do not think it, and if you did you can have no reason for the thought. How can you tell what is passing within me here? How can you know the death-clutch that I feel stealing upon me inch by inch? Slowly it comes—now quicker —remember the packet—forgiveness you know—"

All was over.

* * * * * *

The night following the morning of our heroine's equestrian exploit at the linendraper's shop she was entering the theatre when a young man looking rather weary and travel-stained ran up just in time to catch her as she was passing through the door.

"Rose, Rose—Miss Mortimer," he called.

Our heroine turned round sharply to see who it was who was thus familiar with her name.

"Miss Mortimer," said the young man, "do you not know me? Is it possible that you have so soon forgotten an old acquaintance?"

"What! Mr. Halliday?" ejaculated Rose. "Is it possible? Oh, how glad I am to see you! How are you? You are surely not coming to the theatre? Are you engaged?"

"No—"

"How well you look!" continued Rose. "You are growing quite stout. Shake hands again."

"I'm so pleased that you are glad to see me," said the poor artist, "for I've had rare work to find you, I can tell you."

"I dare say."

"But you must forgive all this joy, this exuberant delight, my dear Rose—Miss Mortimer—I beg your pardon—"

"No, no; call me Rose if you will. I should prefer it."

"Then I will. I bear some unpleasant tidings of your father."

"What of him?" asked Rose, her expression changing on the instant. "Does he still seek to control my actions? I would not have you think me an undutiful child, Mr. Halliday, but I have borne so much that he has forfeited all authority over me, believe me."

"Be re-assured, Rose. It is not that. Your father is—is grievously ill."

"Not dead?"

The artist nodded.

Rose raised her handkerchief to her face and wiped away a solitary tear, and then she was as calm and collected as ever.

"I am glad of it," she said. "I have long ceased to love my father, and it was painful in the extreme to see him rushing on to his ruin day by day."

"He charged me dying to implore your forgiveness."

"Oh, he had it unasked," said Rose. "I cherish no animosity to any one living, much less to a dead father."

"He gave me also this packet to deliver to you."

"Thank you. Some letter I suppose. Well, I will read it at a more convenient opportunity."

These words had barely passed her lips when a mounted messenger galloped up to the stage door with a letter in his hand.

He sprang from the saddle and ran up to the door calling out, "Miss Mortimer."

"For me?" said Rose. "Who does this come from, pray?"

"Miss Clara St. John, Sloeford House, Sloeford, miss. No time to be lost. My lady is dying fast. Doctor says can't survive the night."

Rose hastily tore open the letter, and to her surprise read as follows:—

"*Follow the bearer of the present immediately, without loss of time, if you would know all that can affect your future, all that is of vital import to you. Lose not an instant, for my breath is almost spent, and I would fain do an act of restitution ere I die to atone for the multitude of sins with which I am loaded.*

"CLARA ST. JOHN."

Rose, having read it through, handed it to Jack Halliday for his advice.

At the same time she gave him a hurried sketch of what had taken place at Sloeford House—the tragedy of which she had been an eye-witness.

"Now, tell me pray," she said, "after what has occurred, do you not rather believe this to be a ruse—some fresh scheme to get me into their power?"

"Possibly, and yet I would advise you to go."

"Yes. Something seems to urge me to go at once, although I apprehend danger."

"I will accompany you. Therefore fear nothing. But do you know this Clara St. John?"

"Yes, slightly. I know that she was in some way connected with that infamous Count Lerno."

"Lerno? How strangely your enemies are all mixed up!"

CHAPTER LXXVI.

FINIS.

WHEN Rose arrived at Sloeford House she was immediately ushered into the presence of the dying Clara St. John.

The bold unscrupulous woman of the world was now not even the shadow of her former self.

The injuries which she had received in wreaking her final vengeance upon Count Lerno had slain her.

Horribly mutilated, she lay in the last fearful agonies of death.

Rose hastened to her death-bed with her friend Jack Halliday.

"Rose Mortimer," said Clara St. John, "the feeble life yet remaining within me is fast departing; but I have that to say which would not let me rest in my grave did I not disclose it. The Earl of Sloeford, who now owns this title and noble property, is but a base impostor, an assassin."

"Alas! I know—"

"You know it?" interrupted Clara St. John in the greatest astonishment.

"Ay. I witnessed the murder myself from the garden. But I should not mention it were you not in your last moments, and it cannot injure the usurper."

"Cannot? Nay, it must," said the dying woman, with startling energy. "Your duty to God and man, to dead and living alike, demands that you should pursue this Spencer Bellisle with the deadliest vengeance. Else you are no true girl — no true daughter."

"What mean you?" demanded our heroine.

"Mean that you cannot, must not allow to escape unpunished the man whom *you saw murder your own father!*"

Rose Mortimer felt that she was trembling violently.

Controlling her emotions with a powerful effort, she begged the dying woman to explain the meaning of her singular exhortation.

"You do not understand me," said Clara. "It is but natural, for my words must sound wild and strange to you. But know, then, that Reginald Bellisle, Earl of Sloeford, was your father—that you are his only child, and heiress to his vast domains."

Rose started back affrightedly.

She began to imagine that the injuries received by the dying woman had turned her brain.

"You mistake," she said. "It is true that my father is dead, but only recently. I have here a packet which was delivered to me even as your messenger arrived."

"Ah! Seymour dead?" exclaimed Clara. "Then perhaps the proof may be wanting too. Break your packet, and let us know the contents of it."

Rose did as Clara directed, and found the outer wrapper to be a letter from Thomas Seymour, alias Mortimer, in which he renounced all claim to be the father of Rose Mortimer, and stated the circumstances by which she had passed into his possession when a very young child.

He begged in earnest terms her forgiveness for the cruel treatment received at his hands, as he was dying then, and hoped that he in some little way compen-

[ROSE ASTONISHES THE DRAPERS.]

sated for this by handing her with his expiring effort the enclosed packet.

"Open—open it," said Clara, "for I feel certain that we shall find more important matters yet in it. Open it."

"Read it, Mr. Halliday," said Rose, handing the enclosure to the artist.

Jack Halliday opened the packet and read aloud the following:—

"I, SPENCER BELLISLE, EARL OF SLOEFORD, being now upon my bed of death, do confess myself guilty of the crime of murdering my uncle, Edgar Bellisle, the late earl, and suppressing the proofs of his marriage with Rosalia Hargreaves, by which marriage he had issue one daughter, who was for some years lost to me, owing to the disappearance of Thomas Seymour, the man in whose hands I placed her. I have since traced her out, and have received conclusive proofs that this daughter is the actress, Rose Mortimer, whom I have so mercilessly pursued. But the all-seeing Providence has frustrated my sinful purposes, and Rose, my cousin, lives in spite of the hand that would have destroyed her. I deemed that I had really slain her—all in my eagerness to render my sinfully gotten position the more secure. Then I learnt from my cousin that the death of Rose Mortimer would be ruin to us, as her know-

ledge of the foul murder would transpire shortly after her death, and, thinking that all was lost, we fled the country. My cousin and partner in crime died by my hand on the voyage, and this has been the canker gnawing at my heartstrings ever since. I feel as if this were the only crime which could not be forgiven.

" It was only upon the last day that I discovered that the actress who fell by my poison-bouquet, procured of Mermet, the Arab necromancer, in London, was not Rose Mortimer ; but until I had received fresh intelligence from home I did not dare to return. Deprived of my dead cousin's aid and counsel, I was lost, and thus was her retribution worked upon me. Now I die a disgraceful death—but one whose justice I can but admit. I cannot ask the forgiveness of my cousin Rose for having slain her father. I can scarcely look for forgiveness anywhere."

Here was despair. Utterly lost—beyond all hope—had Spencer Bellisle, Earl of Sloeford, died in a foreign land.

"This is retribution," exclaimed Clara St. John. "With this I doubt not you will easily establish your right. If not, I have one witness who can do all that is necessary."

Old Martin the steward was called, and immediately upon seeing our heroine he seized her hands and embraced them with respectful fervour.

"Ah, my dear young lady," said the old steward, "I knew your mother—beautiful and good as an angel. There is no questioning your parentage there to look upon you."

"Look upon her," said Clara. "She, too, nearly fell a victim to their bloody vengeance."

"But for you, Miss Clara," said old Martin—"but for you. Ah! my dear mistress, this is a sad parting."

"Do not weep for me, Martin," said Clara. "I hope that my sins will be forgiven me for the little good which I have wrought. I feel that my breath is fast failing me. One word more, Rose, ere I die. I have much to ask your forgiveness for."

"Ask it not," said our heroine, kissing the dying woman's forehead. "You have it. I have nothing to forgive."

"Nay, but you have, even more than you know of. It was I who put you in that deadly danger with the Whartons. It was I who kept Edgar Deville from the knowledge of his property, that Cecil Wharton might enjoy Edgar's possession. But I am rightly punished for that. I took Edgar away from them that he might be defrauded of his rights—and now, how I have loved him ! Now I would have re-instated him in his possessions, for we have suffered poverty together, and yet I dared not speak, lest I might sacrifice his love. Keep this from him if you can. I would have him love my memory if he could."

"Where is he now ?"

"Away upon a fishing excursion. He has been absent two days, and knows not of what has happened. Explain all, that I may be spared his hate. Ah !" And Clara St. John was no more.

"Come, miss—my lady," said Jack Halliday, "let us leave. If you will allow me I will put all this into a lawyer's hands, and you shall be troubled no further."

They left the death-chamber—Rose, much affected, leaning upon the artist's arm.

As they gained the ante-room Rose pressed his arm tenderly and looked up in his face.

The artist blushed up to the roots of his hair, and his heart fluttered like that of a maiden of sixteen upon receiving a declaration.

Still he kept his eyes averted.

"Mr. Halliday," said Rose in a low voice.

"My lady."

"Hush ! Do not call me that. If you assume this sternness you make me think that by this accession to wealth, which I do not want, I lose the only friend I have in the world. Call me Rose."

"But pray consider—"

"I desire it."

"If you desire it, then—Rose. And you make me so happy."

Then followed a silence of some minutes' duration. Rose was having a grand mental discussion.

"Mr. Halliday," at length said Rose, " or Jack, if I may."

The artist looked up all over gratitude.

You will not think me unmaidenly if—"

"If what ? Oh! speak. You cannot think how I suffer."

"If I ask you frankly, Do you love me ?"

The artist was speechless.

"Will you take me for your wife ? I ask interestedly," she continued, smiling, "for I want a helpmate in all these difficulties."

"Oh! Rose, Rose, you make me the happiest man alive," said the artist. "For I could never have asked your love—I deemed that wealth had placed an insuperable barrier between us."

"Ah! Jack, Jack," she said, "you are not like me. I can sacrifice my womanly dignity even for you. Your pride is stronger than your love."

*   *   *   *   *   *

Two days passed over, and Edgar Deville returned from his fishing excursion to Sloeford House.

Of course he was immensely astonished to find the mansion in the hands of strangers.

But surprise gave way to grief—genuine unfeigned sorrow—when he was apprised of the death of Clara St. John, and he gave himself up for a time to unmitigated woe.

Indeed, Edgar Deville displayed far more affliction than any one would have deemed him capable of.

Rose introduced herself to him, and acquainted him with the circumstances of Clara's death, and then she broached the subject of the estates and rich property of which he had been defrauded up to the present by the machinations of Mr. Wharton and his son Cecil.

To Rose's surprise Edgar coolly informed her that he knew well that he was the heir to the property, but that he had purposely abstained from putting forward his claim, as he had a particular reason to fear that the Whartons were not alone concerned in the conspiracy.

Then, upon Rose pressing him for an explanation, he said that he had long suspected that Clara had been party to it, but that, as he had been very much attached to her, he would not let her know that he had become aware of anything which could let her lose caste in his eyes.

However, now that there was no further need of concealment he was determined to take proceedings against the Whartons.

Accordingly he put the whole affair into the hands of an eminent firm of solicitors, engaged the first counsel of the day, and a very strong case was prepared silently for the Whartons.

At length all was prepared, and an action for conspiracy was brought against them, falling upon them like a thunderbolt.

In the meantime, whilst the evidence was being gone into with wonderful elaboration with the solicitors, Rose and Edgar Deville came to some mutual explanations which cleared up more than one startling mystery.

It was to Edgar Deville's no small surprise that he learnt from our heroine that the man whom she had so long supposed to be her father was no other than

Hugh Mortimer, who had shared his captivity at Count Lerno's house with the coiner's gang.

"Ah! my lady," he said, "you can form no idea of what I have suffered upon that unhappy man's account."

"Indeed?" said Rose. "Surely he never injured you?"

"Well, it is not his fault if he didn't," returned Deville. "But I was not alluding to the injuries he inflicted upon me, but rather to the injuries I saw inflicted upon him. You may remember Count Lerno?"

"Alas! I do."

"He was the chief of a gang of coiners, and upon one occasion held Hugh Mortimer and myself prisoners. Mortimer robbed them, and was caught attempting to escape, so they coolly doomed him to death."

"But it must have been merely a threat to produce some result, for he lived until lately," said Rose.

"Yes, he did, thanks to one of the most miraculous escapes that man ever yet knew. They certainly condemned him to death, and carried out their sentence upon him, as they thought. But yet he contrived to escape them, by what means I never could ascertain."

* * * * * *

The day appointed for the trial of the Whartons at length arrived.

They were there bold enough, and had, in spite of the short notice, prepared an elaborate defence. They had a crack man, too, for their leading counsel, and a deal of surprise was manifested everywhere at their boldness.

However, it was destined to a fall.

The defence, prepared with such scrupulous care and minuteness, was never gone into, for from the moment that Lady Losalia Bellisle (as our heroine must now be called) made her appearance the case was virtually at an end.

It so stunned the guilty father and son to see there the girl whom they thought dead that their efforts were quite paralysed.

Mr. Wharton was observed to take something from his pocket and raise it to his mouth.

However, none heeded the gesture until Cecil Wharton uttered a cry of alarm.

"My father has poisoned himself," he cried. And even as the word was spoken Mr. Wharton fell forward, upsetting the documents prepared for the defence with so much care and precaution.

They raised him up and found him a corpse.

This put an end to the trial for the present.

It was resumed later, and the whole weight of it was boldly supported by Cecil Wharton, who defended himself with much audacity and boldness; but the conspiracy to defraud Edgar Deville, his cousin, out of his property was clearly established.

To Edgar Deville Rose related all that had occurred to her whilst she was on his estate assuming his title —an innocent abettor in the fraud of the Whartons. Amongst other matters she related the incidents of the mine accident, her illness and kind treatment by the miner's wife, and her pretended death and escape.

She also sent the good woman a handsome present in remembrance of the kindness she had received at her hands.

A few days after Rose had been installed at Sloeford House she took a drive out, accompanied by her betrothed—Jack Halliday—and old Martin the steward.

The carriage drew up before the roadside inn at which our heroine had first stopped, weary and footsore, to beg for food and drink.

Mrs. Davis came running out all in a fluster at having a carriage stop at her humble house.

"Why, Davis!" cried she. "Here's Miss Mortimer come back. My dear girl, how are you?"

It was apparent that the good landlady did not guess the truth, by the way in which she seized Rose and warmly embraced her.

Rose explained how matters stood as briefly as possible.

Then she left, having Mrs. Davis's promise that she would call at Sloeford House at a very early date.

About a fortnight after this Rose was one morning sitting alone, when a servant announced that a clergyman wished to speak with her upon most important business.

Rose could not understand what this important business might be, but desired that the reverend gentleman might be shown into the room.

Judge, then, her surprise upon recognising an old acquaintance in this individual.

However, at a glance, it was clear that the recognition was not mutual.

"I come, my lady," he said as he entered, "as collector for a missionary fund. We have several good names upon our books. Lord Liverwing has put his name down for fifty pounds. The object of this mission is to provide the natives of the Sandwich Islands with spiritual advisers—"

"Might I inquire your name?" interrupted our heroine.

"The Reverend Abel Booth."

"I thought so."

"You know me, then, my lady?"

"We have met before. My especial recollection of you is from a circumstance which you would no doubt be well pleased to forget."

"Indeed?" said Abel Booth, with a long face.

Rose rang the bell, and desired a servant to send Mr. Halliday to her.

As the latter entered the room he recognised the hypocritical shepherd in an instant.

"Why, you impudent old scoundrel!" he said, bearing in mind the assault upon Rose when he had rescued her from Abel Booth's clutches, "how dare you show your villanous face here? You shall repent this, mark me!"

Booth was all amazement.

Time and ardent liquors had somewhat dimmed his vision, and he did not so quickly recognise them as they did him.

"Sir," said he indignantly, "I come from a charitable company for a holy work."

"Then you'll get your ardour in the holy work damped before you leave Sloeford."

Without more ado Mr. Halliday, called up two men-servants, and ordered the shepherd to be kicked out.

The men obeyed their orders to the letter, and Mr. Abel Booth got severely damaged. Not content with this, they carried him off to the horsepond, and drew him through and through, only releasing him when it appeared that respiration had ceased.

* * * * * *

The wedding of our heroine was fixed at an early date by Jack Halliday, in whose hands Lady Rosalia Bellisle had vested the right of choice which is usually the prerogative of the opposite sex.

Then for several weeks Blanche Bowerini was busily occupied with her companion—to whom she was just as dear as ever—in preparing the wedding *trousseau*.

One day they were out in the carriage with the good-natured Mrs. Davis, who was now a constant visitor at Sloeford House, when an incident occurred which led to some serious results, which we will briefly relate.

As they were seated in a mercer's shop a man of a particularly brutal aspect passing the door paused to peer in curiously at them.

Blanche Bowerini, chancing to look up at the owner of the shadow darkening the doorway, uttered a scream, and the man passed hurriedly on.

"Look, Rose, look," she cried.

"What is it?"

"Signor Bowerini. He has seen me. I saw him looking in. What can he want?"

"No matter. He cannot harm you now."

"No, no. I know. But it has made me tremble so. I seem to dread that man as much as ever.

That night, when all the household were wrapped in slumber, Lady Rosalia was rudely startled from her sleep by a loud shriek.

A succession of piercing screams caused her to spring from her bed, hastily throw on a loose wrapper, and run from the room.

The cries were repeated, and Rose was not a little surprised and alarmed to find that they proceeded from the direction of Blanche's chamber.

She ran along the passage, and speedily found that not she alone had been aroused by the cries.

The artist, from the opposite side, dashed up to the spot as Rose appeared in sight.

"What is it?" cried he.

"I don't know. Burst open the door."

Jack Halliday raised his foot, and with one well-directed kick sent the door flying in.

There a fearful sight met their view.

Blanche was struggling upon the ground with a burly ruffian, whose face was blackened to disguise him.

But, in spite of this, our heroine recognised the form upon the instant as that of Signor Bowerini.

The artist sprang forward and jumped upon the midnight intruder.

With one blow upon the face he sent him staggering back.

A second stretched him full length upon the ground, and sent a bloodstained knife spinning from his hand.

Rose ran up to poor Blanche, who was bleeding copiously from an ugly looking gash in the shoulder.

"Dear Blanche, are you badly hurt?"

"I doubt not," said Blanche faintly. "I'm glad you came as you did."

And she fainted.

"Oh! Blanche, Blanche!" cried rose in agony. "He has killed her!"

That's some satisfaction, then," said the ruffian.

By this time the servants had been aroused, and came running there in dozens.

"Secure him," said our heroine. "Bind him securely. He must be carried at once to prison."

"I don't mind that, my dear," said the ruffian scornfully.

"Bowerini," said Rose, "if that poor girl is hurt badly—if anything should happen to her—you shall hang for it as sure as there is a sky above us."

He was borne away, and then they began to institute an inquiry as to how he had contrived to effect an entrance into the house.

One of the servants soon discovered that the window of Blanche's room was open, and this explained all.

He had clambered up the ivy and broken open the window.

A surgeon was sent for without delay, and the wound upon being examined was found to be but slight.

It was only a flesh wound in the shoulder, and a little sponging and strapping settled the matter.

But Bowerini was fairly caught now, and it was not likely that he would find it an easy matter to escape from the clutches of avenging justice.

He was brought to trial, and found guilty of wounding with intent to murder Blanche. Many ugly circumstances came out in connection with his past career, and it went hard with him.

He was audacious and insolent to the court upon the trial, and penal servitude for life was the result of it.

He was sent to one of the penal settlements, and was never heard of again in England, for good or evil.

*   *   *   *   *   *

A fortnight passed, and Sloeford House was all excitement.

From top to bottom of the house was one grand movement.

Early in the morning a grand equipage drove up to the house, and who should alight but Edgar Deville, arrayed in an unmistakeably Hymeneal livery?

He had come to give the bride away.

And presently the party drove off to the village church, the whole of the route being thronged with the tenants of the Sloeford estate, who had turned out to do honour to their landlady and their future landlord.

In the course of a very little while the artist quitted the church smiling all over his intelligent face, and bearing upon his arm, all blushes and smiles, Lady Rosalia Halliday.

And thus ends, we trust to the satisfaction of all, the history of Rose Mortimer.

THE END.

www.ingramcontent.com/pod-product-compliance
Lightning Source LLC
Chambersburg PA
CBHW080840250626

47161CB00009B/3138